The Holcroft Covenant
The Rhinemann Exchange

Robert Ludlum

Diamond Books,
An Imprint of HarperCollins*Publishers*,
77–85 Fulham Palace Road
Hammersmith, London W6 8JB

This Diamond Books Omnibus
edition first published 1993
9 8 7 6 5 4 3 2 1

The Holcroft Covenant © Robert Ludlum 1978
The Rhinemann Exchange © Robert Ludlum 1974

ISBN 1 85813 258 4 (UK)
ISBN Diamond Books 0261 66162 0 (international edition)

Phototypeset in Ehrhardt by Intype, London

Printed in Great Britain by Mackays of Chatham Ltd

The Author asserts the moral right to
be identified as the author of this work

Contents

By the same author

The Scarlatti Inheritance
The Osterman Weekend
The Matlock Paper
The Gemini Contenders
The Chancellor Manuscript
The Bourne Identity
The Matarese Circle
The Road to Gandolfo
The Parsifal Mosaic
The Aquitaine Progression
The Bourne Supremacy
The Icarus Agenda
Trevayne
The Bourne Ultimatum
The Road to Omaha
The Scorpio Illusion

The Holcroft Covenant

For Michael and Laura
A lovely, talented, wonderful couple

Prologue

MARCH 1945

The hull of the submarine was lashed to the huge pilings, a behemoth strapped in silhouette, the sweeping lines of its bow arcing into the light of the North Sea dawn.

The base was on the island of Scharhörn in the Heligoland Bight, several miles from the German mainland and the mouth of the Elbe River. It was a refuelling station never detected by Allied Intelligence, and in the cause of security little known among the strategists of the German High Command itself. The undersea marauders came and went in darkness, emerging and submerging within several hundred feet of the moorings. They were Neptune's assassins, come home to rest or going forth to press their attacks.

On this particular dawn, however, the submarine lashed to the dock was doing neither. For it, the war was over. Its assignment was intrinsic to the origins of another war.

Two men stood in the well of the conning tower, one in the uniform of a commanding officer of the German Navy, the other a tall civilian in a long dark overcoat, the collar turned up to ward off the North Sea winds, yet hatless, as if to defy the North Sea winter. Both looked down at the long line of passengers who slowly made their way towards the gangplank at midships. As each passenger reached the plank, the name was checked off against a list, and then he or she was led – or carried – aboard a submarine.

A few walked by themselves, but they were the exceptions. They were the oldest, some having reached their twelfth or thirteenth birthdays.

The rest were children. Infants in the arms of stern-faced army nurses, who surrendered their charges to a unit of naval doctors at the plank; pre-schoolers, and early graders clutching identical travelling kits and each other's hands, peering up at the strange black vessel that was to be their home for weeks to come.

"Incredible," said the officer.

"Simply incredible."

"It's the beginning," replied the man in the overcoat. "Word comes from everywhere. From the ports and the mountain passes, from the remaining airfields all over the Reich. They go out by the thousands. To every part of the world. And people are waiting for them. Everywhere."

"An extraordinary accomplishment," said the officer, shaking his head in awe.

"This is only one part of the strategy. The entire operation is extraordinary."

"It's an honour to have you here, Herr Clausen."

"I wanted to be. This is the last shipment." The tall civilian kept his eyes on the dock below. "The Third Reich is dying. These are its rebirth. These are the *Fourth* Reich. Unencumbered by mediocrity and corruption. These are the *Sonnenkinder*. All over the world."

"The children . . ."

"The Children of the Damned," said the tall man, interrupting. "They are the Children of the Damned, as millions will be. But none will be like these. And these will be everywhere."

1

"Attention! Le train de sept heures pour Zürich partira Sortie Douze!"

The tall American in the dark blue raincoat glanced up at the cavernous dome of the Geneva railway station, trying to locate the unseen speakers. The expression on his sharp, angular face was quizzical; the announcement was in French, a language he spoke poorly and understood less. Nevertheless, he was able to distinguish the word Zürich; it was his signal. He brushed aside the light brown hair that fell with irritating regularity over his forehead and started for the north end of the station.

The crowds were heavy. Bodies rushed past the American in all directions, hurrying to the gates to begin their journeys to scores of different destinations. None seemed to pay attention to the harsh announcements that echoed throughout the upper chambers in a continuous metallic monotone. The travellers in Geneva's *Eisenbahn* knew where they were going. It was the end of the week; the new mountain snows had fallen and the air outside was crisp and chilling. There were places to go, schedules to keep, and people to see; time wasted was time stolen. Everyone hurried.

The American hurried, too, for he also had a schedule to keep and a person to see. He had learned before the announcement that the train for Zürich would leave from Track Twelve. According to the plan, he was to walk down the ramp to the platform, count seven cars from the rear, and board the first entrance. Inside, he was to count again, this time five compartments, and knock twice on the fifth door. If everything was in order, he would be admitted by a director of the Grande Banque de Genève, signifying the culmination of twelve weeks of preparations. Preparations that included purposely obscured cablegrams, transatlantic calls made and received on telephones the Swiss banker had determined were sterile, and a total commitment to secrecy.

The American did not know what the director of the Grand Banque de Genève had to say to him, but he thought he knew why the precautions were deemed necessary. His name was Noel Holcroft, but Holcroft was not his name at birth. He was born in Berlin in the summer of 1939, and the name on the hospital registry was Clausen. His father was Heinrich Clausen, master strategist of the Third Reich, the financial magician who put together the coalition of disparate economic forces that ensured the supremacy of Adolf Hitler.

Heinrich Clausen won the country but lost a wife. Althene Clausen was an American; more to the point, she was a headstrong woman with her own

13

standards of ethics and morality. She had deduced that the National Socialists possessed neither; they were a collection of paranoids, led by a maniac, and supported by financiers interested solely in profits.

Althene Clausen gave her husband an ultimatum on a warm afternoon in August: withdraw. Stand against the paranoids and the maniac before it is too late. In disbelief, the Nazi listened and laughed and dismissed his wife's ultimatum as the foolish ravings of a new mother. Or perhaps the warped judgement of a woman brought up in a weak, discredited system that would soon march to the step of the New Order.

That night the new mother packed herself and the new child and took one of the last planes to London, the first leg on her journey back to New York. A week later the *Blitzkrieg* was executed against Poland; the Thousand Year Reich had begun its own journey, one that would last some nine hundred days from the first sound of gunfire.

Holcroft walked through the gate, down the ramp, and on to the long concrete platform. *Four, five, six, seven* . . . the seventh car had a small blue circle stencilled beneath the window to the left of the open door. It was the symbol of accommodations superior to those in first-class, enlarged compartments properly outfitted for conferences in transit or clandestine meetings of a more personal nature. Privacy was guaranteed; once moving, the doors at either end of the car were manned by armed railway guards.

Holcroft entered and turned left into the corridor. He walked past successive closed doors until he reached the fifth. He knocked twice.

"Herr Holcroft?" The voice behind the wood panel was firm but quiet, and although the two words were meant as a question, the voice was not questioning. It made a statement.

"Herr Manfredi?" said Noel in reply, suddenly aware that an eye was peering at him through the pinpoint viewer in the centre of the door. It was an eerie feeling, diminished by the comic effect. He smiled to himself and wondered if Herr Manfredi would look like the sinister Conrad Veidt in one of those 1930s English films.

There were two clicks of a lock, followed by the sound of a sliding bolt. The door swung back and the image of Conrad Veidt vanished. Ernst Manfredi was a short, rotund man in his middle to late sixties. He was completely bald, with a pleasant, gentle face; but the wide blue eyes, magnified beyond the metal-framed glasses, were cold. Very light blue and very cold.

"Come in, Herr Holcroft," said Manfredi, smiling. Then his expression changed abruptly; the smile disappeared. "Do forgive me. I should say *Mister* Holcroft. The *Herr* may be offensive to you. My apologies."

"None necessary," replied Noel, stepping into the well-appointed compartment. There was a table, two chairs, no bed in evidence. The walls were wood-panelled; dark red velvet curtains covered the windows, muffling the sounds of the figures rushing by outside. On the table was a small lamp with a fringed shade.

"We have about twenty-five minutes before departure," the banker said. "It

14

should be adequate. And don't be concerned, we'll be given ample warning. The train won't start until you've disembarked. You'll not have to travel to Zürich."

"I've never been there."

"I trust that will be changed," said the banker enigmatically, gesturing for Holcroft to sit opposite him at the table.

"I wouldn't count on it." Noel sat down, unbuttoning his raincoat but not removing it.

"I'm sorry, that was presumptuous of me." Manfredi took his seat and leaned back in the chair. "I must apologize once again. I'll need your identification. Your passport, please. And your international driver's licence. Also, whatever documents you have on your person that describe physical markings, vaccinations, that sort of thing."

Holcroft felt a rush of anger. The inconvenience to his life aside, he disliked the banker's patronizing attitude. "Why should I? You know who I am. You wouldn't have opened the door if you didn't. You probably have more photographs, more information on me, than the State Department."

"Indulge an old man, sir," said the banker, shrugging in self-deprecation, his charm on display. "It will be made clear to you."

Reluctantly, Noel reached into his jacket pocket and withdrew the leather case that contained his passport, health certificate, international licence, and two AIA letters that stated his qualifications as an architect. He handed the case to Manfredi. "It's all there. Help yourself."

With seemingly greater reluctance, the banker opened the case. "I feel as though I'm prying, but I think . . ."

"You should," interrupted Holcroft. "I didn't ask for this meeting. Frankly, it comes at a very inconvenient time. I want to get back to New York as soon as possible."

"Yes. Yes, I understand," said the Swiss quietly, perusing the documents. "Tell me, what was the first architectural commission you undertook outside the United States?"

Noel suppressed his irritation. He had come this far; there was no point in refusing to answer. "Mexico," he replied. "For the Alvarez hotel chain, north of Puerto Vallarta."

"The second?"

"Costa Rica. For the government. A postal complex in 1973."

"What was the gross income of your firm in New York last year? Without adjustments."

"None of your damned business."

"I assure you, we know."

Holcroft shook his head in angry resignation. "A hundred and seventy-three thousand dollars and change."

"Considering office rental, salaries, equipment, and expenses, that's not an altogether impressive figure, is it?" asked Manfredi, his eyes still on the papers in his hands.

"It's my own company and the staff is small. I have no partners, no wife, no heavy debts. It could be worse."

"It could be better," said the banker, looking up at Holcroft. "Especially for one so talented."

"It could be better."

"Yes, I thought as much," continued the Swiss, putting the various papers back in the leather case and handing it to Noel. He leaned forward. "Do you know who your father was?"

"I know who my father *is*. Legally, he's Richard Holcroft of New York, my mother's husband. He's very much alive."

"And retired," completed Manfredi. "A fellow banker, but hardly a banker in the Swiss tradition."

"He was respected. *Is* respected."

"For his family's money or for his professional acumen?"

"Both, I'd say. I love him. If you have reservations, keep them to yourself."

"You're very loyal; that's a quality I admire. Holcroft came along when your mother — an incredible woman, incidentally — was most despondent. But we split definitions. Holcroft is once removed. I referred to your natural father."

"Obviously."

"Thirty years ago, Heinrich Clausen made certain arrangements. He travelled frequently between Berlin, Zürich, and Geneva, beyond official scrutiny, of course. A document was prepared that we as . . ." Manfredi paused and smiled, " . . . as biased neutrals could not oppose. Attached to the document is a letter, written by Clausen in April of 1945. It is addressed to you. His son." The banker reached for a thick manila envelope on the table.

"Just a minute," said Noel. "Did those certain arrangements concern money?"

"Yes."

"I'm not interested. Give it to charity. He owed it."

"You may not feel that way when you've heard the amount."

"What is it?"

"Seven hundred and eighty million dollars."

16

2

Holcroft stared at the banker in disbelief; the blood drained from his head. Outside, the sounds of the huge station were a cacophony of muted, disconsonant chords, barely penetrating the thick walls of the car.

"Don't try to absorb it all at once," said Manfredi, placing the letter to one side. "There are conditions, none of them, incidentally, offensive. At least, none we're aware of."

"Conditions? . . .", Holcroft knew he could hardly be heard; he tried to find his voice. "What conditions?"

"They're spelled out very clearly. These vast sums are to be channelled into a great good for people everywhere. And, of course, there are certain benefits to yourself personally."

"What do you mean there's nothing offensive that you're . . . 'aware of'?"

The banker's magnified eyes blinked behind his glasses; he looked away briefly, his expression troubled. He reached into his brown leather briefcase which lay at the corner of the table and pulled out a long, thin envelope with curious markings on the back side; they were a series of four circles and appeared to be four dark coins affixed to the border of the flap.

Manfredi held the envelope across the table under the light. The dark circles were not coins but, instead, waxed seals. All were intact.

"Following the instructions given to us thirty years ago, this envelope – unlike your father's letter here – was not to be opened by directors in Geneva. It is separate from the document we prepared, and to the best of our knowledge Clausen was never aware of it. His own words to you would tend to confirm that. It was brought to us within hours after the courier delivered your father's letter, which was to be our final communication from Berlin."

"What is it?"

"We don't know. We were told it was written by several men aware of your father's activities. Who believed in his cause with great fervour; who considered him in many ways a true martyr of Germany. We were instructed to give it to you with the seals unbroken. You were to read it before you saw your father's letter." Manfredi turned the envelope over. There was writing on the front side. The words were in German and written by hand. "You are to sign below to so state that you received it in the proper condition."

Noel took the envelope and read the words he could not understand:

Der Brief ist mit ungebrochenem Siegel empfangen worden. Neuaufbau oder Tod.

"What does it say?"

"That you've examined the seals and are satisfied."

"How can I be sure?"

Young man, you're talking to a director of the Grande Banque de Genève." The Swiss did not raise his voice but the rebuke was clear. "You have my word. And, in any event, what difference does it make?"

None, reasoned Holcroft, yet the obvious question bothered him. "If I sign the envelope, what do you do with it?"

Manfredi was silent for several moments, as if deciding whether or not to answer. He removed his glasses, took a silk handkerchief from his breast pocket, and cleaned them. Finally he replied. "That is privileged information . . ."

"So's my signature," interrupted Noel. "Privileged, that is."

"Let me finish," protested the banker, putting back his glasses. "I was about to say it was privileged information that can't possibly be relevant any longer. Not after so many years. The envelope is to be sent to a post office box in Sesimbra, Portugal. It is south of Lisbon on the Cape of Espichel."

"Why isn't it relevant?"

Manfredi held up the palms of his hands. "The post office box no longer exists. The envelope will find its way to a dead-letter office and eventually be returned to us."

"You're sure?"

"I believe it, yes."

Noel reached into his pocket for his pen, turning the envelope over to look once again at the waxed seals. They had not been tampered with; and, thought Holcroft, what difference *did* it make? He placed the envelope in front of him and signed his name.

Manfredi held up his hand. "You understand, whatever is contained in that envelope can have no bearing on our participation in the document prepared by the Grand Banque de Genève. We were neither consulted, nor were we apprised of the contents."

"You sound worried. I thought you said it didn't make any difference. It was too long ago."

"Fanatics always worry me, Mr Holcroft. Time and consequence cannot alter that judgement. It's a banker's caution."

Noel began cracking the wax; it had hardened over the years and took considerable force before it fell away. He tore the flap open, removed the single page, and unfolded it.

The paper was brittle with age; the white had turned to a pale brownish yellow. The writing was in English, the letters printed in an odd block lettering that was Germanic in style. The ink was faded but legible. Holcroft looked at the bottom of the page for a signature. There was none. He started reading.

From this moment on the son of Heinrich Clausen is to be tested. There are those who may learn of the work in Geneva and who will try to stop him, whose only purpose in life will be to kill him, thus destroying the dream conceived by the giant that was his father.

This must not happen, for we were betrayed — all of us — and the world must know what we really were, not what the betrayers showed us to be, for those were the portraits of traitors. Not us. And particularly not Heinrich Clausen.

We are the survivors of Wolfsschanze. We seek the cleansing of our names, the restoration of the honour that was stolen from us.

Therefore the men of Wolfsschanze will protect the son for as long as the son pursues the father's dream and returns our honour to us. But should the son abandon the dream, betray the father, and withhold our honour, he will have no life. He will witness the anguish of loved ones, of family, children, friends. No one will be spared.

None must interfere. Give us our honour. It is our right and we demand it.

Noel shoved the chair back and stood up. *"What the hell is this?"*

"I've no idea," replied Manfredi quietly, his voice calm but his large, cold blue eyes conveying his alarm. "I told you we were not apprised . . ."

"Well, *get* apprised!" shouted Holcroft. "Read it! Who *were* the clowns? Certifiable *lunatics?*"

The banker began reading. Without looking up he answered softly. "First cousins to lunatics. Men who'd lost hope."

"What's Wolfsschanze? What does it mean?"

"It was the name of Hitler's staff headquarters in East Prussia, where the attempt to assassinate him took place. It was a conspiracy of the generals: von Stauffenberg, Kluge, Hoepner — they were all implicated. All shot. Rommel took his own life."

Holcroft stared at the paper in Manfredi's hands. "You mean it was written thirty years ago by people like that?"

The banker nodded, his eyes narrowed in astonishment. "Yes, but it's not the language one might have expected of them. This is nothing short of a threat; it's unreasonable. Those men were not unreasonable. On the other hand, the times *were* unreasonable. Decent men, brave men, were stretched beyond the parameters of sanity. They were living through a hell none of us can picture today."

"Decent men?" asked Noel incredulously.

"Have you any idea what it meant to be a part of the Wolfsschanze conspiracy? A bloodbath followed, thousands massacred everywhere, the vast majority never having heard of Wolfsschanze. It was yet another final solution, an excuse to still all dissent throughout Germany. What began as an act to rid the world of a madman ended in a holocaust all its own. The survivors of Wolfsschanze saw that happen."

"Those survivors," replied Holcroft, "followed that madman for a long time."

"You must understand. And you will. These were desperate men. They were caught in a trap, and for them it was cataclysmic. A world they had helped create was revealed not to be the world they envisaged. Horrors they never dreamed of were uncovered, yet they couldn't avoid their responsibility for them. They were appalled at what they saw but couldn't deny the roles they played."

"The well-intentioned Nazi," said Noel. "I've never heard of that elusive breed."

"One would have to go back in history, to the economic disasters, to the Versailles Treaty, the Pact of Locarno, the Bolshevik encroachments – to a dozen different forces – to understand."

"I understand what I just read," Holcroft said. "Your poor misunderstood storm troopers didn't hesitate to threaten someone they couldn't know! 'He will have no life . . . no one spared . . . family, friends, children.' That spells out murder. Don't talk to me about well-intentioned killers."

"They're the words of old, sick, desperate men. They have no meaning now. It was their way of expressing their own anguish, of seeking atonement. They're gone. Leave them in peace. Read your father's letter . . ."

"He's *not* my father!" interrupted Noel.

"Read Heinrich Clausen's letter. Things will be clearer. Read it. We have several items to discuss and there isn't much time."

A man in a brown tweed overcoat and dark Tyrolean hat stood by a pillar across from the seventh car. At first glance, there was nothing particularly distinguishing about him, except perhaps his eyebrows. They were thick, a mixture of black and light grey hair that produced the effect of salt-and-pepper archways in the upper regions of a forgettable face.

At first glance. Yet if one looked closer one could see the blunted but not unrefined features of a very determined man. In spite of the pockets of wind that blew in gusts through the platform, he did not blink. His concentration on the seventh car was absolute.

The American who came out of that doorway, thought the man by the pillar, would be a much different person from the American who went in. During the past few minutes his life had been changed in ways few men in this world would ever experience. Yet it was only the beginning; the journey he was about to embark on was beyond anything of which the modern world could conceive. So it was important to observe his initial reaction. More than important. Vital.

"Attention! Le train de sept heures . . ."

The final announcement came over the speakers. Simultaneously, a train from Lausanne was arriving on the adjacent track. In moments the platform would be jammed with tourists flocking to Charing Cross for a brief fling in London, thought the man by the pillar.

The train from Lausanne came to a stop. The vacationers disgorged; the platform was again packed with bodies.

The figure of the tall American was suddenly in the vestibule of car seven. He was blocked at the doorway by the porter carrying someone's luggage. It was an irritating moment that might have provoked an argument under normal circumstances. But the circumstances were not normal for the American known as Holcroft. This American born in Berlin with the name of Clausen. He expressed no annoyance; his face was set, unresponsive to the moment, his eyes aware of the physical confusion but not concerned with it. There was an air of detachment about him; he was in the grips of lingering astonishment. It was emphasized by the way he clutched the thick manila envelope between his arm and his chest, his hand curved around the edge, his fingers pressed into the paper with such force they formed a fist.

It was the cause of his consternation, this document prepared a lifetime ago. It was the miracle *they* had waited for, lived for – the man by the pillar and those who had gone before him. Over thirty years of anticipation. And now it had surfaced at last!

The journey had begun.

Holcroft entered the flow of human traffic towards the ramp that led up to the gate. Although jostled by those around him, he was oblivious to the crowds, his eyes absently directed ahead. At nothing.

Suddenly, the man by the pillar was alarmed. Years of training had taught him to look for the unexpected, the infinitesimal break in a normal pattern. He saw that break now. Two men, their faces unlike any around them, joyless, without curiosity or expectation, filled only with hostile intent.

They were surging through the crowds, one man slightly ahead of the other. Their eyes were on the American; they were after him! The man in front had his right hand in his pocket. The man behind had his left hand concealed across his chest, beneath his unbuttoned overcoat. The hidden hands gripped weapons! The man by the pillar was convinced of that.

He sprang away from the concrete column and crashed his way into the crowd. There were no seconds to be lost! The two men were gaining on Holcroft. They were after the envelope! It was the only possible explanation. And if that were the case, it meant that word of the miracle had leaked out of Geneva! The document inside that envelope was priceless, beyond value. The American's life was of such inconsequence beside it that no thought would be expended taking that life. The men closing in on Holcroft would kill him for the envelope *mindlessly*, as if removing a disagreeable insect from a bar of gold. And *that* was mindless! What they did not know was that without the son of Heinrich Clausen the miracle would not happen!

They were within yards of him now! The man with the black-and-white eyebrows lunged forward through the mass of tourists like a possessed animal. He crashed into people and luggage, throwing aside everything and everyone in his path. When he was within feet of the killer with his hand concealed under his overcoat, he thrust his own hand into his pocket, clutching the gun inside, and screamed directly at the assailant:

"Such nach Clausen's Sohn! Nach der Genfer Urkunde!"

The killer was partially up the ramp, separated from the American by only

21

a few people. He heard the words roared at him by a stranger and spun around, his eyes wide in shock.

The crowd pressed forward rapidly up the ramp, skirting the two obvious antagonists. Attacker and protector were in their own miniature arena, facing one another. The observer squeezed the trigger of the gun in his pocket, then squeezed it again. The spits could barely be heard as the fabric exploded. Two bullets entered the body of Holcroft's would-be assailant, one in the lower stomach, the other far above, in the neck. The first caused the man to convulse forward, the second snapped his head back, the throat torn open.

Blood burst from the neck with such force that it splattered surrounding faces, and the clothes and suitcases belonging to those faces. It cascaded downwards, forming small pools and rivulets on the ramp. Screams of horror and revulsion filled the walkway.

The observer-protector felt a hand gripping his shoulder, digging into his flesh. He spun; the second attacker was on him, but there was no gun in his hand. Instead, the blade of a hunting knife came towards him.

The man was an amateur, thought the observer, as his reactions – instincts born of years of training – came instantly into play. He stepped sideways quickly – a bullfighter avoiding the horns – and clamped his left hand above his assailant's wrist. He pulled his right hand from his pocket and gripped the fingers wrapped around the knife. He snapped the wrist downwards, vicing the fingers around the handle, tearing the cartilage of the attacker's hand, forcing the blade inwards. He plunged it into the soft flesh of the stomach and ripped the sharp steel diagonally up into the rib cage, severing the arteries of the heart. The man's face contorted; a terrible scream was begun, cut off by death.

The pandemonium had escalated into uncontrollable chaos; the screaming increased. The profusion of blood in the centre of the rushing, colliding bodies fuelled the hysteria. The observer-protector knew precisely what to do. He threw up his hands in frightened consternation, in sudden, total revulsion at the sight of the blood on his own clothes, and joined the hysterical crowds racing away like a herd of terrified cattle from the concrete killing ground.

He rushed up the ramp past the American whose life he had just saved.

Holcroft heard the screaming. It penetrated the numbing mists he felt engulfed in; clouds of vapour that swirled around him, obscuring his vision, inhibiting all thought.

He tried to turn towards the commotion, but the hysterical crowd prevented him from doing so. He was swept farther up the ramp, and pummelled into the three-foot-high cement wall that served as a railing. He gripped the stone and looked back, unable to see clearly what had happened, but clearly enough to see a man below arch backwards, blood erupting from his throat. He saw a second man lunging forward, his mouth stretched in agony, and then Noel could see no more, the onslaught of bodies sweeping him once again up the concrete ramp.

A man rushed by, crashing into his shoulder. Holcroft turned in time to see frightened eyes beneath a pair of thick, black-and-white brows.

An act of violence had taken place. An attempted robbery had turned into an assault, into a killing, perhaps. Peaceful Geneva was no more immune than the wild streets of New York at night, or the impoverished alleyways of Marrakesh.

But Noel could not dwell on such things; he could not be involved. He had other things to think about. The mists of numbness returned. Through them he vaguely understood that his life would never be the same again.

He gripped the envelope in his hand and joined the screaming mass racing up the ramp to the gate.

3

The huge aircraft passed over Cape Breton Island and dipped gently to the left, descending into its new altitude and heading. The route was now south-west towards Halifax and Boston, then into New York.

Holcroft had spent most of the time in the upstairs lounge, at a single chair in the right rear corner, his black attaché case against the bulkhead.

It was easier to concentrate there; no straying eyes of an adjacent passenger could fall on the papers he read and re-read over and over again.

He had begun with the letter from Heinrich Clausen, that unknown but all-pervading presence. It was an incredible document in itself. The information contained in it was of such an alarming nature that Manfredi had expressed the collective wish of the Grande Banque directors that it be destroyed. For it detailed in general terms the sources of millions banked in Geneva three decades ago. Although the majority of these sources were untouchable in any contemporary legal sense – thieves and murderers stealing the national funds of a government headed by thieves and murderers – other sources were not so immune to modern scrutiny. Throughout the war Germany had plundered. It had raped internally and externally. The dissenters within had been stripped, the conquered without stolen from unmercifully. Should the memories of those thefts be dredged up, the international courts in The Hague could tie up the funds for years in protracted litigation.

"Destroy the letter," Manfredi had said in Geneva. "It's only necessary that you understand why he did what he did. Not the methods; they are a complication without any conceivable resolution. But there are those who may try to stop you. Other thieves would move in; we're dealing in hundreds of millions."

Noel re-read the letter for roughly the twentieth time. Each time he did so, he tried to picture the man who wrote it. His natural father. He had no idea what Heinrich Clausen looked like; his mother had destroyed all photographs, all communications, all references whatsoever that pertained to a man she loathed with all her being.

Berlin, 20 April 1945

My Son

I write this as the armies of the Reich collapse on all fronts. Berlin will soon fall, a city of raging fires and death everywhere. So be it. I shall waste no moments on what was, or what might have been. On concepts betrayed, and the triumph of evil over good through the treachery of morally bankrupt leaders. Recriminations born in hell are too suspect, the authorship too easily attributed to the devil.

24

Instead, I shall permit my actions to speak for me. In them, you may find some semblance of pride. That is my prayer.

Amends must be made. That is the credo I have come to recognize. I and my two dearest friends and closest associates who are identified in the attached document. Amends for the destruction we have wrought, for betrayals so heinous the world will never forget. Or forgive. It is in the interest of partial forgiveness that we have done what we have done.

Five years ago your mother made a decision I could not comprehend, so blind were my loyalties to the New Order. Two winters ago – in February 1943 – the words she spoke in rage, words I arrogantly dismissed as lies fed her by those who despised the Fatherland, were revealed to be the truth. We who laboured in the rarefied circles of finance and policy had been deceived. For two years it was clear that Germany was going down to defeat. We pretended otherwise, but in our hearts we knew it was so. Others knew it, too. And they became careless. The horrors surfaced, the deceptions were clear.

Twenty-five months ago I conceived of a plan and enlisted the support of my dear friends in the *Finanzministerium*. Their support was willingly given. Our objective was to divert extraordinary sums of money into neutral Switzerland, funds that could be used one day to give aid and succour to those thousands upon thousands whose lives were shattered by unspeakable atrocities committed in Germany's name by animals who knew nothing of German honour.

We know about the camps. The names will haunt history. Belsen, Dachau, Auschwitz.

We have been told about the mass executions, of the sight of helpless men, women, and children lined up in front of trenches dug by their own hands, and then slaughtered.

We have learned of the ovens – oh, God in heaven – ovens for human flesh! Of the showers that sprayed not cleansing water, but lethal gas. Of intolerable, obscene experiments carried out on conscious human beings by insane practitioners of a medical science unknown to man. We bleed at the images, and our eyes burst, but our tears can do nothing. Our minds, however, are not so helpless. We can plan.

Amends must be made.

We cannot restore life, we cannot bring back what was so brutally, viciously taken. But we can seek out all those who survived, and the children of those both surviving and slaughtered, and do what we can. They must be sought out all over the world and shown that we have not forgotten. We are ashamed and we wish to help. In any way that we can. It is to this end that we have done what we have done.

I do not for a moment believe that our actions can expiate our sins, those crimes we were unknowingly a part of. Yet we do what we can – I do what I can – haunted with every breath by your mother's perceptions. Why, oh eternal God, did I not listen to that great and good woman?

To return to the plan.

Using the American dollar as the equivalent currency of exchange, our goal was ten million monthly, a figure that might appear excessive, but not when one considers the capital flow through the economic maze of the *Finanzministerium* at the height of the war. We exceeded our goal.

Using the *Finanzministerium*, we appropriated funds from hundreds of sources within the Reich and to a great extent beyond, throughout Germany's ever-expanding borders. Taxes were diverted, enormous expenditures made from the Ministry of Armaments for non-existent purchases, Wehrmacht payrolls re-routed, and monies sent to occupation territories constantly intercepted, lost. Funds from expropriated estates and the great fortunes, factories, and individually held companies, did not find their way into the

Reich's economy but, instead, into our accounts. Sales of art objects from scores of museums throughout the conquered lands were converted to our cause. It was a master plan carried out masterfully. Whatever risks we took and terrors we faced – and they were daily occurrences – were inconsequential compared to the meaning of our credo: Amends must be made.

Yet no plan can be termed a success unless the objective is secured permanently. A military strategy that captures a port only to lose it to an invasion from the sea a day later is no strategy at all. One must consider all possible assaults, all interferences that could negate the strategy. One must project, as thoroughly as projection allows, the changes mandated by time, and protect the objective thus far attained. In essence, one must *use* time to the strategy's advantage. We have endeavoured to do this through the conditions put forth in the attached document.

Would to the Almighty that we could give aid to the victims and their survivors sooner than our projections allow, but to do so would rivet attention on the sums we have appropriated. Then *all* could be lost. A generation must pass for the strategy to succeed. Even then there is a risk, but time will have diminished it.

The air raid sirens keep up their incessant wailing. Speaking of time, there is very little left now. For myself and my two associates, we wait only for confirmation that this letter has reached Zürich through an underground courier. Upon receipt of the news, we have our own pact. Our pact with death, each by his own hand.

Answer my prayer. Help us atone. Amends must be made.

This is our covenant, my son. My only son, whom I have never known but to whom I have brought such sorrow. Abide by it, honour it, for it is an honourable thing I ask you to do.

Your father,
Heinrich Clausen

Holcroft put the letter face down on the table and glanced out the window at the blue sky above the clouds. Far in the distance was the jet stream of another aircraft; he followed the streak of vapour until he could see the tiny silver gleam of the fuselage.

He thought about the letter. Again. The writing was arch, the words from another era, melodramatic. It did not weaken the letter; rather, it gave it a certain strength of conviction. Clausen's sincerity was unquestioned, his emotions genuine.

What was only partially communicated, however, was the brilliance of the plan itself. Brilliant in its simplicity, extraordinary in its use of time and the laws of finance to achieve both execution and protection. For the three men understood that sums of the magnitude they had stolen could not be sunk in a lake or buried in vaults. The hundreds of millions had to exist in the financial marketplace, not subject to discontinued currency or brokers who would have to convert and sell elusive assets.

Hard money had to be deposited, the responsibility for its security given to one of the world's most revered institutions, the Grande Banque de Genève. Such an institution would not – could not – permit abuses where liquidity was concerned; it was an international economic rock. All the conditions of its contract with its depositors would be observed. Everything was to be legal in the eyes of Swiss law. Covert – as was the custom of the trade – but

26

ironbound with respect to existing legalities, and thus current with the times. The intent of the contract – the document – could not be corrupted; the objectives would be followed to the letter.

To permit corruption or malfeasance was unthinkable. Thirty years . . . *fifty* years . . . in terms of the financial calendar was very little time indeed.

Noel reached down and opened his attaché case. He slipped the pages of the letter into a compartment and pulled out the document from the Grande Banque de Genève. It was encased in a leather cover, folded in the manner of a Last Will and Testament, which it was. He leaned back in the chair and unfastened the clasp that allowed the cover to unfold, revealing the first page of the document.

His "covenant", Holcroft reflected.

He skimmed over the words and the paragraphs, now so familiar to him, flipping the pages as he did so, concentrating on the salient points.

The identities of Clausen's two associates in the massive theft were Erich Kessler and Wilhelm von Tiebolt. The names were vital not for the two men themselves, but because the oldest child of each had to be reached. It was the first condition of the document. Although the designated proprietor of the numbered account was one Noel C. Holcroft, *American*, it was to be released only upon the signatures of all three oldest children. And only then if each child satisfied the directors of the Staats-Banque that he or she accepted the conditions and objectives set forth by the original proprietors with respect to the allocation of the funds.

However, if these offspring did not satisfy the Swiss directors or were judged to be incompetent, their brothers and sisters were to be studied and further judgements made. If all the children were considered incapable of the responsibility, the millions would wait for another generation, when further sealed instructions would be opened by executors and issue yet unborn. The resolve was devastating . . . *another* generation.

The legitimate son of Heinrich Clausen is now known as Noel Holcroft, a child, living with his mother and stepfather in America. At the specific date chosen by the directors of the Grande Banque de Genève – to be not less than thirty years, nor more than thirty-five – said legitimate son of Heinrich Clausen is to be contacted and his responsibilities made known to him. He is to reach his co-inheritors and activate the account under the conditions set forth. He shall be the conduit through which the funds are to be dispensed to the victims of the Holocaust, their families and surviving issue . . . .

The three Germans gave their reasons for the selection of Clausen's son as the conduit. The child had entered into a family of wealth and consequence . . . an *American* family above suspicion. All traces of his mother's first marriage and flight from Germany had been obscured by the devoted Richard Holcroft. It was understood that in the pursuit of this obscurity a death certificate had been issued in London for an infant male named Clausen, dated 17 February 1942, and a subsequent birth certificate filed in New York City for the male child Holcroft. The additional years would further obscure events to the point of obliteration. The infant male Clausen had already become the child Holcroft. He would become the man Holcroft, with no visible relationship to his origins. Yet those origins could not be denied, and, therefore, he was the perfect choice, satisfying both the demands and the objectives of the document.

An international agency was to be established in Zürich, its funds held confidential in perpetuity. Should a spokesman be required, it was to be the American Holcroft, for the others could never be mentioned by name. Ever. They were the children of Nazis, and their exposure would inevitably raise demands that the account be examined, its various sources be revealed. And if the account *was* examined, its sources even hinted at, forgotten confiscations and appropriations would be remembered. The international courts would be swamped with litigations.

But if the spokesman and co-ordinator was a man without the Nazi stain, there would be no cause for alarm, no examinations, no demands for exhumation or litigation. He would act in concert with the others, each possessing one vote in all decisions, but he alone would be visible. The children of Erich Kessler and Wilhelm von Tiebolt were to remain anonymous.

Noel wondered what the "children" of Kessler and von Tiebolt were like. He would find out soon.

The final conditions of the document were no less startling than anything that preceded them. All the monies were to be allocated within *six months* of the release of the account. Such an imposition would demand a total commitment from each of the offspring, and that was precisely what the depositors demanded: total commitment to their cause. Lives would be interrupted, sacrifices required. The commitment had to be paid for. Therefore, at the end of the six-month period and the successful allocation of the funds to the victims of the Holocaust, the Zürich agency was to be disbanded and each descendant was to receive the sum of two million dollars.

Six months. Two million dollars.

Two million.

Noel considered what that meant to him personally and professionally. It was freedom. Manfredi had said in Geneva that he was talented. He *was* talented, but frequently that talent was obscured in the final product. Far too often during the past eight years since he had formed his own company, he'd had to accept assignments he would have preferred not taking, compromised designs when the architect in him dictated otherwise, refused jobs he wanted very much to do because financial pressures prohibited time spent on lesser commissions. He was turning into a cynic.

Nothing was permanent; planned obsolescence went hand in hand with depreciation and amortization. No one knew it better than an architect who once had a conscience. Perhaps he would find his conscience again. With freedom. With the two million.

Holcroft was startled by the progression of his thoughts. He had made up his mind, something he had not intended to do until he'd thought things through. Everything. Yet he was reclaiming a misplaced conscience with money he had convinced himself he was capable of rejecting.

What *were* they like, these oldest children of Erich Kessler and Wilhelm von Tiebolt? Not like him, obviously. One was a woman, to begin with, the other a scholar. But beyond the differences of sex and profession, they had been a part of something he had never known. They'd been there; they'd seen it. Neither had been too young not to remember. They had lived in that strange, demonic world that was the Third Reich. He would have so many questions to ask.

Questions to ask. *Questions?*

He had made his decision. He had told Manfredi that he needed time – a few days at least before he reached it.

"Do you really have a choice?" the Swiss banker had asked.

"Very much so," Noel had replied. "I'm not for sale, regardless of conditions. And I'm not frightened by threats made by maniacs thirty years ago."

"Nor should you be. Discuss it with your mother."

"*What?*" Holcroft was stunned. "I thought you said . . ."

"Complete secrecy? Yes, but your mother is the single exception."

"Why? I'd think she'd be the last . . ."

"She's the first. And only. She'll honour the confidence."

Manfredi had been right. If his answer was *yes*, he would by necessity suspend his firm's activities and begin his travels to make contact with the offspring of Kessler and von Tiebolt. His mother's curiosity would be aroused; she was not a woman to let her curiosity lie dormant. She would make inquiries and if by any chance – however remote – she unearthed information about the millions in Geneva and Heinrich Clausen's role in the massive theft, her reaction would be violent. Her memories of the paranoids and gangsters of the Third Reich were indelibly printed on her mind. If she made public damaging disclosures, the funds would be tied up in the international courts for years.

"Suppose she isn't persuaded?"

"You must be convincing. The letter is convincing, and we'll step in, if need be. Regardless, it's better to know her position at the outset."

What would that position be? wondered Noel. Althene was not your run-of-the-mill mother as run-of-the-mill mothers were understood by this particular son. She did not fit into the mould of the wealthy Manhattan matron. The trappings were there – or had been. The horses, the boats, the weekends in Aspen and the Hamptons, but not the frantic chase for ever-expanding acceptance and social control.

She'd done it all before. She'd lived in the turbulence that was the European thirties, a young, carefree American whose family had something left over after the crash and were more comfortable away from its less fortunate peers. She had known the Court of St James as well as the expatriate salons of Paris . . . and the dashing new inheritors of Germany. And out of those years had come a serenity shaped by love, exhaustion, loathing, and rage.

Althene was a special person, as much a friend as a mother, that friendship deep and without the need for constant reaffirmation. In point of fact, thought Holcroft, she was more friend than mother; she was never entirely comfortable in the latter role.

"I've made too many mistakes, my dear," she said to him once, laughing, "to assume an authority based on biology."

Now he would ask her to face the memory of a man she had spent a great deal of her life trying to forget. Would she be frightened? That wasn't likely. Would she doubt the objectives set forth in the document given him by Ernst Manfredi? How could she after reading the letter from Heinrich Clausen? Whatever her memories, his mother was a woman of intellect and perception. All men were subject to change, to remorse. She would have to accept that regardless of how distasteful it might be to her in this particular case.

It was the weekend; tomorrow was Sunday. His mother and stepfather spent the weekends at their house in the country, in Bedford Hills. In the morning he would drive up and have that talk.

And on Monday he would take the first steps on a trip that would lead him back to Switzerland. To an as yet unknown agency in Zürich. On Monday the hunt would begin.

Noel recalled his exchange with Manfredi. They were among the last words spoken before Holcroft left the train.

"The Kesslers had two sons. The oldest, Erich — named for the father — is a professor of history at the University of Berlin. The younger brother, Hans, is a doctor in Munich. From what we know, both are highly regarded in their respective communities. They're very close. Once Erich is told of the situation, he may insist on his brother's inclusion."

"Is that permitted?"

"There's nothing in the document that prohibits it. However, the stipend remains the same and each family has but one vote in all decisions."

"What about the von Tiebolts?"

"Another story, I'm afraid. They may be a problem for you. After the war the records show that the mother and two children fled to Rio de Janeiro. Five or six years ago they disappeared. Literally. The police have no information. No address, no business associations, no listings in the other major cities. And that's unusual; the mother became quite successful for a time. No one seems to know what happened, or if people do, they're not willing to say."

"You said two children. Who are they?"

"Actually, there are three children. The youngest, a daughter, Helden, was born after the war in Brazil, conceived obviously during the last days of the Reich. The oldest is another daughter, Gretchen. The middle child is Johann, the son."

"You say they disappeared?"

"Perhaps it's too dramatic a term. We're bankers, not investigators. Our inquiries were not that extensive, and Brazil's a very large country. Your inquiries must be exhaustive. The offspring of each man must be found and examined. It's the first condition of the document; without compliance, the account will not be released."

Holcroft folded the document and put it back in his attaché case. As he did so, his fingers touched the edge of the single sheet of paper with the odd block-lettering written by the survivors of Wolfsschanze thirty years ago. Manfredi was right, they were sick old men trying to play their last desperate roles in a drama of the future they barely understood. If they had understood, they would have appealed to the "son of Heinrich Clausen". Pleaded with him, not threatened him. The threat was the enigma. Why was it made? For what purpose? Again, perhaps, Manfredi was right. The strange paper had no meaning now. There were other things to think about.

Holcroft caught the eye of the stewardess chatting with two men at a table across the way and gestured for another scotch. She smiled pleasantly, nodded, and indicated that the drink would be there in moments. He returned to his thoughts.

The inevitable doubts surfaced. Was he prepared to commit what amounted to a year of his life to a project so immense that his own qualifications had to be examined before the children of Kessler and von Tiebolt were examined – if, indeed, he could find the latter? Manfredi's words came back to him. *Do you really have a choice?* The answer to that question was both yes and no. The two million, which signified his own freedom, was a temptation difficult to reject, but he could reject it. His dissatisfactions were real, but professionally things were going well. His reputation was spreading, his skills acknowledged by a growing number of clients who in turn told potential clients. What would happen if he suddenly stopped? What would be the effect should he abruptly withdraw from a dozen commissions for which he was competing? These too were questions to be considered deeply; he was not ruled by money alone.

Yet as his mind wandered, Noel understood the uselessness of his thoughts. Compared to his . . . covenant . . . the questions were inconsequential. Whatever his personal circumstances, the dissemination of millions to the survivors of an inhumanity unprecedented in history was long overdue; it was an obligation impossible to dismiss. A voice had cried out to him through the years, the voice of a man in agony who was the father he had never known. For reasons he was incapable of explaining to himself, he could not be deaf to that voice; he could not walk away from that man in agony. He would drive to Bedford Hills in the morning and see his mother.

Holcroft looked up, wondering where the stewardess was with his drink. She was at the dimly lit counter that served as the bar in the 747's lounge. The two men from the table had accompanied her; they were joined by a third. A fourth man sat quietly in a rear seat reading a newspaper. The two men with the stewardess had been drinking heavily, while the third, in his search for cama- raderie, pretended to be less sober than he was. The stewardess saw Noel looking at her and arched her eyebrows in mock desperation. She had poured his scotch, but one of the drunks had spilled his drink; she was wiping it up with a cloth. The drunk's companion suddenly lurched backwards against the rim of a chair, his balance lost. The stewardess dashed around the counter to help the fallen passenger; his friend laughed, steadying himself on an adjacent chair. The third man reached for a drink on the bar. The fourth man looked up in disgust, crackling his paper, the sound conveying his disapproval. Noel returned to the window not caring to be a part of the minor confusion.

Several minutes later the stewardess approached his table. "I'm sorry, Mr Holcroft. Boys will be boys, more so on the Atlantic run, I think. That was scotch on the rocks, wasn't it?"

"Yes. Thanks." Noel took the glass from the attractive girl and saw the look in her eyes. It seemed to say *thank you for not coming on like those crashing bores*. Under different circumstances he might have pursued a conversation, but not now. Now he had other things to think about. In his mind he was listing the things he would do on Monday. Closing his office was not difficult in terms of personnel; he had a small staff: a secretary and two draughtsmen he could easily place with friends – probably at higher salaries. What would be difficult was the explanation. Why in heaven's name would Holcroft, Incorporated, New York, close up shop just when its designs were being considered for projects that could triple its staff and quadruple its gross income? The explanation had to be both reasonable and not subject to scrutiny.

Suddenly, without warning, a passenger on the other side of the cabin sprang from his seat, a hoarse, wild cry of pain coming from his throat. He arched his back spastically, as if gasping for air, then clutched first his stomach, then his chest. He crashed into the wooden divider that held magazines and airline schedules and twisted maniacally, his eyes wide, the veins in his neck purple, as if bursting. He lurched forward and fell sprawling to the deck of the cabin.

It was the third man who had joined the two drunks at the bar with the stewardess.

The next moments were chaotic. The stewardess rushed to the fallen man, observed him closely, and followed procedure. She instructed the three other passengers in the cabin to remain in their seats, placed a cushion beneath the man's head, and returned to the counter and the intercom on the wall. In seconds a male flight attendant rushed up the circular staircase; the British Airways captain emerged from the flight deck. They conferred with the stewardess over the unconscious body. The male attendant walked rapidly to the staircase, descended, and returned within a few moments with a clipboard. It was obviously a passenger list.

The captain stood up and addressed the others in the lounge. "Will you all please return to your seats below. There's a doctor on board. He's being summoned. Thank you very much."

As Holcroft sidestepped his way down the staircase, a stewardess carrying a blanket climbed quickly past him. Then he heard the captain issue an order over the intercom. "Radio Kennedy for emergency equipment. Medical. Male passenger, name of Thornton. Heart seizure, I believe."

The doctor knelt by the prone figure stretched out on the rear seat of the lounge and asked for a flashlight. The first officer hurried to the flight deck and returned with one. The doctor rolled back the eyelids of the man named Thornton, then turned and motioned for the captain to join him; he had something to say. The captain bent over; the doctor spoke quietly.

"He's dead. It's difficult to say without equipment, without tissue and blood analysis, but I don't think this man had a heart attack. I think he was poisoned. Strychnine would be my guess."

The small grey-walled room that was a customs inspector's office was suddenly quiet. Behind the inspector's desk set a homicide detective from New York's Port Authority police, a British Airways clipboard in front of him. The inspector stood rigidly embarrassed to one side. In two chairs against the wall sat the captain of the 747 and the stewardess assigned to its first-class lounge. By the door was a uniformed police officer. The detective stared at the customs inspector in disbelief.

"Are you telling me that two people got off that plane, walked through sealed-off corridors into the sealed-off, guarded customs area and *vanished?*"

"I can't explain it," said the inspector, shaking his head despondently. "It's never happened."

The detective turned to the stewardess. "You're convinced they were drunk, Miss?"

"Not now, perhaps," replied the girl. "I've got to have second thoughts. They drank a *great* deal, I'm certain of it; they couldn't have faked that. I served them. They appeared quite sloshed. Harmless but sloshed."

"Could they have poured their drinks out somewhere? Without drinking them, I mean."

"Where?" asked the stewardess.

"I don't know. Hollow ashtrays, the seat cushions. What's on the floor?"

"Carpeting," answered the pilot.

The detective addressed the police officer by the door. "Get forensic on your radio. Have them check the carpet, the seat cushions, ashtrays. Left side of the roped-off area facing front. Dampness is enough. Let me know."

"Yes, sir." The officer left quickly, closing the door behind him.

"Of course," ventured the captain, "alcoholic tolerances vary."

"Not the amounts the young lady described," the detective said.

"For God's sake, why is it important?" said the captain. "Obviously they're the men you want. They've vanished, as you put it. That took some planning, I daresay."

"Everything's important," explained the detective. "Methods can be matched with previous crimes. We're looking for anything. Crazy people. Rich, crazy people who jet around the world looking for thrills. Signs of psychosis, getting kicks while on a high – alcohol or narcotics, it doesn't matter. As far as we can determine, the two men in question didn't even know this Thornton; your stewardess here said they introduced themselves. Why did they kill him? And accepting the fact that they did, why so brutally? It *was* strychnine, Captain, and take my word for it, it's a rough way to go."

The telephone rang. The customs inspector answered it, listened briefly, and handed it to the Port Authority detective. "It's the State Department. For you."

"State? This is Lieutenant Miles, NYPA police. Have you got the information I requested?"

"We've got it, but you won't like it . . ."

"Wait a minute," broke in Miles, as the door opened and the uniformed officer reappeared. "What have you got?"

"The seat cushions and the carpet on the left side of the lounge are soaked."

"Then they were cold sober," said the detective in a monotone. He nodded and returned to the telephone. "Go ahead, State. What won't I like?"

"Those passports in question were declared void more than ten years ago. They belonged to two men from Flint, Michigan. Neighbours, actually; worked for the same company in Detroit. In June of 1966 they both went on a business trip to Europe and never came back."

"Why were the passports voided?"

"They disappeared from their hotel rooms. Three days later their bodies were found in the river. They'd been shot."

"*Jesus!* What river? Where?"

"The Isar. They were in Munich, Germany."

One by one the irate passengers of Flight 591 passed through the door of the quarantined room. Their names, addresses, and telephone numbers were checked off against the 747's list by a representative of British Airways. Next to the representative was a member of the Port Authority police making his own marks on a duplicate list. The quarantine had lasted nearly four hours.

Outside the room the passengers were directed down a hallway into a large cargo area, where they retrieved their inspected luggage, and headed for the doors of the main terminal. One passenger, however, made no move to leave the cargo area. Instead, this man, who carried no luggage, but had a raincoat over his arm, walked directly to a door with thick, stencilled printing on the panel:

US Customs. Control Center
Authorized Personnel Only

Showing identification, he stepped inside.

A grey-haired man in the uniform of a high-ranking customs official stood by a steel-framed window smoking a cigarette. At the intrusion, he turned. "I've been waiting for you," he said. "There was nothing I could do while you were quarantined."

"I had the ID card ready in case you weren't here," replied the passenger, putting the identification back into his jacket pocket.

"Keep it ready. You may still need it; the police are all over the place. What do you want to do?"

"Get out to that aircraft."

"You think they're there?"

"Yes. Somewhere. It's the only explanation."

The two men left the room and walked rapidly across the cargo area, past the numerous conveyor belts, to a steel doorway marked *No Admittance*. Using a key, the customs official opened it and preceded the younger man with the raincoat through the door. They were inside a long cinder-block tunnel that led to the field. Forty seconds later they reached another steel door, this one guarded by two men, one from US Customs, the other from the Port Authority police. The grey-haired official was recognized by the former.

"Hello, Captain. Hell of a night, isn't it?"

"It's only begun, I'm afraid," said the official. "We may be involved after all." He looked at the policeman. "This man's Federal," he continued, angling his head at his companion. "I'm taking him to the 591 aircraft. There may be a narcotics connection."

The police officer seemed confused. Apparently his orders were to allow no one through the door. The customs guard interceded.

"Hey, come on. This man runs all of Kennedy Airport."

The policeman shrugged and opened the door.

Outside a steady rain fell from the black night sky as pockets of mist rolled in from Jamaica Bay. The man with the customs official put on his raincoat. His movements were swift; in the hand beneath the coat held over his arm had been a gun. It was now in his belt, the raincoat button at his waist unfastened.

The 747 glistened under floodlights, rain streaking down its fuselage. Police and maintenance crews were everywhere, distinguished from each other by the contrasting black and orange of their slickers.

"I'll build your cover with the police inside," said the customs official, gesturing at the metal steps that swept up from the back of a truck to a door in the fuselage. "Good hunting."

The man in the raincoat nodded, not really listening. His eyes were scanning the area. The 747 was the focal point; thirty yards from it in all directions were stanchions connected by ropes, policemen at mid-points between them. The man in the raincoat was inside the enclosure; he could move freely. He turned right at the end of the parallel ropes and proceeded towards the rear of the aircraft. He nodded to the police officers at their posts, slapping his identification open casually to those whose looks were questioning. He kept peering through the rain into the faces of those entering and leaving the plane.

Three-quarters around the plane, he heard the angry shout of a maintenance crewman.

"What the fuck are you *doing?* Get that winch secure!"

The target of the outburst was another crewman, standing on the platform of a fuel truck. This crewman had no rain slicker on; his white overalls were drenched. In the driver's seat of the truck sat another crewman, also without rain apparel.

That was *it*, thought the man in the raincoat. The killers had worn overalls beneath their suits. But they had not taken into consideration the possibility of rain. Except for that mistake, the escape had been brilliantly planned.

The man in the raincoat walked over to the fuel truck, his hand on his gun concealed beneath his raincoat. Through the rain he stared at the figure beyond the window in the driver's seat; the second man was above him, to his right on the platform, turned away. The face behind the window stared back in disbelief, and instantly lurched for the opposite side of the seat. But the man in the raincoat was too quick. He opened the door, pulled out his revolver, and fired, the gunshot muted by a silencer. The man in the seat fell into the dashboard, blood streaming out of his forehead.

At the sound of the report, the second man spun around on the steel platform of the truck and looked below.

"*You!* In the *lounge!* With the newspaper!"

"Get inside the truck," commanded the man in the raincoat, his words clear through the pounding rain, his gun concealed behind the door panel.

The figure on the platform hesitated. The man with the gun looked around. The surrounding police were preoccupied with their discomfort in the downpour, half blinded by the floodlights. None was observing the deadly scene. The man in the raincoat grabbed the white cloth of the killer's overalls and yanked him into the frame of the open door of the fuel truck.

"You failed. Heinrich Clausen's son still lives," he said calmly. Then he fired a second shot. The killer fell back into the seat.

The man in the raincoat closed the door and put his gun back into his belt. He walked casually away, directly underneath the fuselage towards the roped-off alleyway that led to the tunnel. He could see the customs official emerging from the 747's door, walking rapidly down the steps. They met and together headed for the door of the tunnel.

"What happened?" asked the official.

"My hunting was good. Theirs wasn't. The question is, what do we do about Holcroft?"

"That's not our concern. It's the Tinamou's. The Tinamou must be informed."

The man in the raincoat smiled to himself, knowing his smile could not be seen in the downpour.

4

Holcroft got out of the taxi in front of his apartment on East Seventy-Third Street. He was exhausted, the strain of the last three days heightened by the tragedy on board the flight. He was sorry for the poor bastard who'd had the heart attack, but furious at the Port Authority police who treated the incident as if it were something else. Good Lord! *Quarantined* for damned near four hours!

The doorman greeted him. "A short trip this time, Mr Holcroft. But you got a lot of mail. Oh, and a message."

"A message?"

"Yes, sir," said the doorman, handing him a business card. "This gentleman came in asking for you last night. He was very agitated, you know what I mean?"

"Not exactly." Noel took the card and read the name. *Peter Baldwin, Esq.* It meant nothing to him. *Wellington Security Systems, Ltd, The Strand, London, W1A.* There was a telephone number underneath. Holcroft had never heard of the British company. He turned the card over; on the back was scribbled *St Regis Hotel. Rm 411.*

"He insisted that I ring your apartment in case you'd got back and I hadn't seen you come in. I told him that was crazy."

"He could have telephoned me himself," said Noel walking towards the lift. "I'm in the book."

"He told me he tried, but your phone was out of order." The lift door closed on the man's last words. Holcroft read the name again as the lift climbed to the fifth floor. *Peter Baldwin, Esq.* Who was he? And since when was his phone out of order?

He opened his apartment door, and reached for the light switch on the wall. Two table lamps went on simultaneously; Noel dropped his suitcase and stared in disbelief at the room.

Nothing was the same as it was three days ago! *Nothing.* Every piece of furniture, every chair, every table, every vase and ashtray were moved into another position. His couch had been in the centre of the room; it was now in the far right corner. Each sketch and painting on the walls had been shifted around, none where they had been before! The stereo was no longer on the shelf, instead it was neatly arranged on a table. His bar, always at the rear of the living room, was now at the left of the door. His drawing board, usually by the window, was now by itself ten feet in front of him, the stool somewhere else – God knew where. It was the strangest sensation he had ever experienced. Everything familiar, yet not familiar at all. Reality distorted, out of focus.

He stood in the open doorway. Images of the room as it had been kept reappearing in front of his eyes, only to be replaced by what was in front of him now.

"What *happened?*" He heard his own words, unsure they were his at first.

He ran to the couch; the telephone was always by the couch, on a table at the right end of the couch. But the couch had been moved; of course there was no telephone by the couch now! He spun around towards the centre of the room. Where was the table? It was not there; an armchair was where the table should be. The telephone was not there, either! *Where* was the telephone? Where was the table? Where the *hell* was the *telephone?*

It was by the window. There was his *kitchen* table by the *living-room window*, and the telephone was on top of it. The telephone *wires* had been taken out from under the wall-to-wall carpeting and moved to the window. It was crazy! Who would take the trouble to lift tacked down carpeting and move *telephone* wires?

He raced to the table, picked up the phone, and pressed the intercom button that connected him to the switchboard in the lobby. He stabbed the signal button repeatedly; there was no answer. He kept his finger on it; finally, the harried voice of Jack the doorman answered.

"All right, all right. This is the lobby . . ."

"Jack, it's Mr Holcroft. Who came up to my apartment while I was away?"

"Who came what, sir?"

"Up to my *apartment!*"

"Were you robbed, Mr Holcroft?"

"I don't know yet. I just know that everything's been moved around. Who was here?"

"Nobody, I mean nobody *I* know of. And the other guy didn't say anything. I'm relieved at four in the morning by Ed, and he's off at noon. Louie takes over then."

"Can you call them?"

"Hell, I can call the police!"

The word was jarring. Police meant questions and Noel was not sure he wanted to give any answers. *Where was he? Where had he gone? Whom did he see?*

"No, don't call the police. Not yet. Not until I see if anything's missing. It might be someone's idea of a joke. I'll call you back."

"I'll call the other guys."

Holcroft hung up. He sat on the wide windowsill and appraised the room. *Everything.* Not a single piece of furniture was where it had been before!

He was holding something in his left hand: the business card. *Peter Baldwin, Esq.*

" . . . *he was very agitated, you know what I mean? . . . he insisted I ring your apartment . . . your phone was out of order . . .*"

St Regis Hotel. Rm 411.

Noel picked up the phone and dialled. He knew the number well; he lunched frequently at the King Cole Grill.

"Yes? Baldwin here." The voice was British, the greeting abrupt.

"This is Noel Holcroft, Mr Baldwin. You tried to reach me."

"Thank heavens! Where are you?"

"Home. In my apartment. I just got back."

"Back? From where?"

"I'm not sure that's any of your business."

"For God's sake, I've travelled over three thousand miles to see you! It's dreadfully important. Now where *were* you?"

The Englishman's breathing was audible over the phone; the man's intensity seemed somehow related to fear. "I'm flattered you came all that distance to see me, but it still doesn't give you the right to ask personal questions . . ."

"I have *every* right!" broke in Baldwin. "I spent twenty years with MI6, and we have a great deal to talk about! You have no idea what you're doing. No one does but me."

"You *what? We* what?"

"Let me put it this way. Cancel Geneva. *Cancel* it, Mr Holcroft, until we've talked!"

"Geneva? . . ." Noel felt suddenly sick to his stomach. How would this Englishman know about Geneva? How *could* he know?

A light flickered outside the window; someone in an apartment directly across the courtyard was lighting a cigarette. Despite his agitation, Holcroft's eyes were drawn to it.

"There's someone at the door," Baldwin said. "Stay on the phone. I'll get rid of whoever it is and be right back."

Noel could hear Baldwin put the telephone down, then the sound of a door opening and indistinguishable voices. Across the courtyard, in the window, a match was struck again, illuminating the long blonde hair of a woman behind a sheer curtain.

Holcroft realized there was silence on the line; he could hear no voices now. Moments went by; the Englishman did not return.

"Baldwin? Baldwin, where are you? *Baldwin!*"

For a third time a match flared in the window across the way. Noel stared at it; it seemed unnecessary. He could see the glow of a cigarette in the blonde woman's mouth. And then he saw what was in her other hand, silhouetted behind the sheer curtain: a telephone. She was holding a telephone to her ear and looking over at his window, looking, he was sure, at him.

"*Baldwin?* Where the hell *are* you?"

There was a click; the line went dead.

"*Baldwin.*"

The woman in the window slowly lowered the telephone, paused for a moment, and walked away out of sight.

Holcroft stared at the window, then at the telephone in his hand. He waited until he got the active line, then redialled the St Regis.

"I'm sorry, sir, Room 411's telephone seems to be out of order. We'll send someone up right away. May I have your number and we'll give it to Mr Baldwin."

. . . your phone was out of order. . .

Something was happening that Noel did not understand. He only knew that he would not leave his name or number with the operator at the St Regis. He hung up and looked again at the window across the courtyard. Whatever light there had been was gone. The window was dark; he could see only the white of the curtain.

He pushed himself away from the windowsill, and wandered aimlessly about the room, around familiar possessions in unfamiliar locations. He was not sure what to do; he supposed he should see if anything was missing. Nothing seemed to be, but it was difficult to tell.

The telephone buzzed; the intercom from the lobby switchboard. He answered it.

"It's Jack, Mr Holcroft. I just spoke to Ed and Louie. Neither of 'em know anything about anyone going up to your place. They're honest guys. They wouldn't screw around. None of us would."

"Thanks, Jack. I believe you."

"You want me to call the police?"

"No." Noel tried to sound casual. "I have an idea someone at the office was playing a joke. A couple of the fellows have keys."

"I didn't see anybody. Neither did Ed or . . ."

"It's okay, Jack," interrupted Holcroft. "Forget it. The night I left we had a party. One or two stayed over." It was all Noel could think of to say.

Suddenly, it occurred to him that he had not looked in his bedroom. He went there now, his hand reaching for the light switch on the wall.

He expected it but it was still a shock. The disorientation was now somehow complete.

Again, each piece of furniture had been moved to a different position. The bed was the first thing that struck his eye; it was oddly frightening. No part of it touched the wall. Instead, it was in the centre of the room, isolated. His bureau stood in front of a window; a small writing desk was dwarfed against the expanse of the right wall. As minutes ago, when first he'd seen the living room, the images of what his bedroom looked like three days ago kept flashing before him, replaced by the strangeness of what he now observed.

Then he saw it and gasped. Hanging down from the ceiling, strapped together with dull black tape, was his second telephone, the extension cord snaking up the wall and across the ceiling to the hook that held it.

It was spinning slowly.

The pain shifted from his stomach to his chest; his eyes were transfixed on the sight, on the suspended instrument revolving slowly in midair. He was afraid to look beyond, but he knew he had to; he had to understand.

And when he did, his breath came back to him. The phone was in the direct path of his bathroom door and the door was open. He saw the curtains billowing in the window above the basin. The steady stream of cold wind was making the telephone spin.

He walked quickly into the bathroom to shut the window. As he was about to pull the curtains he saw a brief flash of illumination outside; a match had been struck in another window across the courtyard, the flare startling in the darkness. He looked out.

There was the woman again! The blonde-haired woman, her upper body silhouetted beyond another set of sheer curtains. He stared at the figure, mesmerized by it.

She turned as she had turned before, and walked away as she had walked away minutes ago. Out of sight. And the dim light in the window went out.

What *was* happening? What did it mean? Things were being orchestrated to frighten him. But by whom and for what purpose? And what had happened to *Peter Baldwin, Esq.*, he of the intense voice and the command to cancel Geneva? Was Baldwin a part of the terror or was he a victim of it?

Victim . . . *victim?* It was an odd word to use, he considered. Why should there be any victims? And what did Baldwin mean when he said he had "spent twenty years with MI6"?

MI6? branch of British Intelligence. If he remembered correctly, MI5 was the section that dealt with domestic matters; 6 concerned itself with problems outside the country. The English CIA, as it were.

Good God! Did the British know about the Geneva document? Was British Intelligence aware of the massive theft of thirty years ago? On the surface, it would appear so . . . yet that was not what Peter Baldwin implied.

You don't know what you're doing. No one does but me.

And then there was silence, and the line went dead.

Holcroft walked out of the bathroom and paused beneath the suspended telephone; it was barely moving now, but it had not stopped. It was an ugly sight, made macabre by the profusion of dull, black tape that held the instrument. As if the phone had been mummified, never to be used again.

He continued towards the bedroom door, then instinctively stopped and turned. Something had caught his eye, something he had not noticed before. The centre drawer of the small writing desk was open. He looked closer. Inside the drawer was a sheet of paper.

His breathing stopped as be stared at the page below.

It couldn't *be*. It was *insane*. The single sheet of paper was brownish-yellow. With *age*. It seemed identical to the page of paper that had been kept in a vault in Geneva for thirty years. The letter filled with threats written by fanatics who revered a martyr named Heinrich Clausen. The writing was the same; the odd Germanic printing of English words, the ink that was faded but still legible.

And what was legible was astonishing. For it had been written over thirty years ago.

Noel Clausen-Holcroft

Nothing is as it was for you. Nothing can ever be the same . . .

Before he read further, Noel picked up an edge of the page. It crumpled under his touch.

Oh, God! It *was* written thirty years ago!

And that fact made the remainder of the message frightening.

The past was preparation, the future is committed to the memory of a man and his dream. His was an act of daring and brilliance in a world gone mad. Nothing must stand in the way of that dream's fulfilment.

We are the survivors of Wolfsschanze. Those of us who live will dedicate our lives and bodies to the protection of that man's dream. It will be fulfilled, for it is all that is left. An act of mercy that will show the world that we were betrayed, that we were not as the world believed us to be.

We, the men of Wolfsschanze, know what the best of us were. As Heinrich Clausen knew.

It is now up to you, Noel Clausen-Holcroft, to complete what your father began. You are the way. Your father wished it so.

Many will try to stop you. To throw open the floodgates and destroy the dream. But the men of Wolfsschanze do survive. You have our word that all those who interfere will be stopped themselves.

Any who stand in your way, who try to dissuade you, who try to deceive you with lies, will be eliminated.

As you and yours will be should you hesitate. Or fail.

This is our oath to you.

Noel grabbed the paper out of the drawer; it fell apart in his hand. He let the fragments fall to the floor.

"*Goddamned maniacs!*" He slammed the drawer shut and ran out of the bedroom. Where was the telephone? Where the *hell* was the goddamned *telephone?* By the window, that was it; it was on the *kitchen* table by the fucking *window!*

"*Maniacs!*" he screamed again at no one. But not really at no one; at a man in Geneva who had been on a train bound for Zürich. Maniacs may have written that page of garbage thirty years ago, but now, thirty years later, other maniacs had delivered it! They had broken into his home, invaded his privacy, touched his belongings . . . God knows what else, he thought, thinking of *Peter Baldwin, Esq.* A man who had travelled thousands of miles to see him, and talk to him . . . silence, a click, a dead telephone line.

He looked at his watch. It was almost 1.00 in the morning. What was it in Zürich? 6.00? 7.00? The banks in Switzerland opened at 8.00. The Grande Banque de Genève had a branch in Zürich; Manfredi would be there.

The window. He was standing in front of the window where he had stood only minutes ago, waiting for Baldwin to come back on the phone. The *window.* Across the courtyard in the opposite apartment. The three brief flares of a match . . . the blonde-haired woman in the window!

Holcroft put his hand in his pocket to make sure he had his keys. He did.

He ran to the door, let himself out, raced for the lift, and pushed the button. The indicator showed that the car was on the tenth floor; the arrow did not move.

Goddamn it!

He ran to the staircase and started down, taking the steps two at a time. He reached the ground floor and dashed out into the lobby.

"*Jesus*, Mr Holcroft!" Jack stared at him. "You scared the shit out of me!"

"Do you know the doorman in the next building?" shouted Noel.

"Which one?"

"*Christ! That* one!" Holcroft gestured to the right.

"That's 380. Yeah, sure."

"Come on with me!"

"Hey, wait a minute, Mr Holcroft. I can't leave here."

"We'll only be a minute. There's twenty dollars in it for you."

"Only a minute"

The doorman at 380 greeted them, understanding quickly that he was to give accurate information to Jack's friend.

"I'm sorry, sir, but there's no one in that apartment. Hasn't been for almost three weeks. But I'm afraid it's been rented; the new tenants will be coming in . . ."

"There *is* someone there!" said Noel, trying to control himself. "A blonde-haired woman. I've *got* to find out who she is."

"A blonde-haired woman? Kind of medium height, sort of good looking, smokes a lot?"

"Yes, that's the one! Who is she?"

"You live in your place long, mister?"

"What?"

"I mean, have you been there a long time?"

"What's that got to do with anything?"

"I think maybe you've been drinking . . ."

"What the hell are you talking about? Who is *that woman?*"

"Not *is*, mister. *Was*. The blonde woman you're talking about was Mrs Palatyne. She died a month ago."

Noel sat in the chair in front of the window, staring across the courtyard. Someone was trying to drive him crazy. But why? It did not make sense! Fanatics . . . maniacs from thirty years ago had sprung across three decades, commanding younger, unknown troops thirty years later. Again, *why?*

He had called the St Regis. Room 411's telephone was working, but there was no answer now. And a woman he had seen clearly did not exist. But she did exist! And she was a part of it; he *knew* it.

He got out of the chair, walked to the strangely placed bar, and poured himself a drink. He looked at his watch; it was 1.50. He had ten minutes to wait before the overseas operator would call him back; the bank could be reached at 2.00 A.M., New York time. He carried his glass back to the chair in front of the window. On the way, he passed his FM radio. It was not where it usually was, of course; that was why he noticed it. He turned it on. He liked music; it soothed him.

But there were words, not music, that he heard. The rat-tat-tatting beneath an announcer's voice indicated one of those "all-news" stations. The dial had been changed. He should have known. *Nothing is as it was for you* . . .

Something being said on the radio caught his attention. He turned quickly in the chair, part of his drink spilling on to his trousers.

" . . . police have cordoned off the hotel's entrances. Our reporter, Richard Dunlop, is on the scene, calling in from our mobile unit. Come in, Richard. What have you learned?"

There was a burst of static followed by the voice of an excited newscaster.

"The man's name was Peter Baldwin, John. He was an Englishman. Arrived yesterday, or at least that's when he registered at the St Regis; the police are contacting the airlines for further information. As far as can be determined he was over here on vacation. There was no listing of a company on the hotel registry card."

"When did they discover the body?"

"About half an hour ago. A maintenance man went up to the room to check the telephone and found Mr Baldwin sprawled out on the bed. The rumours here are wild and you don't know what to believe, but the thing that's stressed is the method of killing. Apparently it was vicious, brutal. Baldwin was garrotted, they said. A wire pulled through his throat, severing most of his head off. An hysterical maid from the fourth floor was heard screaming to the police that the room was drenched with . . ."

"Was robbery the motive?" interrupted the anchorman.

"We haven't been able to establish that. The police aren't talking. I gather they're waiting for someone from the British consulate to arrive."

"Thank you, Richard Dunlop. We'll stay in touch . . . That was Richard Dunlop at the St Regis Hotel on Fifty-Fifth Street in Manhattan. To repeat, a brutal murder took place at one of New York's most fashionable hotels this morning. An Englishman named Peter Baldwin . . . ."

Holcroft shot out of the chair to the radio, turning it off. He stood above it, breathing rapidly. He did not want to admit to himself that he had heard what he had just heard. It was not anything he had really considered; it was simply not possible.

But it was possible. It was real; it had happened. It was death. The maniacs from thirty years ago were not caricatures, not figures from some melodrama. They were vicious killers. And they were deadly serious.

Peter Baldwin, Esq., had told him to cancel Geneva. Baldwin had interfered with the dream, with the covenant. And now he was dead, brutally killed with a wire through his throat.

With difficulty, Noel walked back to the chair and sat down. He raised his glass to his lips and drank several long swallows of whisky; the scotch did nothing for him. The pounding in his chest accelerated.

A flare of a match! Across the courtyard, in the window! There she was! Silhouetted beyond the sheer curtains in a wash of dim light stood the blonde-haired woman. She was staring across the way, staring at *him!* He got out of the chair, drawn hypnotically to the window, his face inches from the panes of glass. The woman nodded her head; she was slowly *nodding her head!* She was telling him something. She was telling him that what he perceived was the truth!

... *The blonde woman you're talking about was Mrs Palatyne. She died a month ago.*

A dead woman stood silhouetted in a window across the darkness and was sending him a terrible message. Oh" Christ, he was going *insane!*

The telephone rang; the bell terrified him. He held his breath and lunged at the phone; he could not let it ring again. It did awful things to the silence.

"Mr Holcroft, this is the overseas operator. I have your call to Zürich ..."

Noel listened in disbelief at the sombre, accented voice from Switzerland. The man on the line was the manager of the Zürich branch of the Grande Banque de Genève. *A directeur*, he said twice, emphasizing his position.

"We mourn profoundly, Mr Holcroft. We knew Herr Manfredi was not well, but we had no idea his illness had progressed so."

"What are you talking about? What happened?"

"A terminal disease affects individuals differently. Our colleague was a vital man, an energetic man, and when such men cannot function in their normal fashions, it often leads to despondency and great depression."

"What *happened?*"

"It was suicide, Mr Holcroft. Herr Manfredi could not tolerate his inca-pacities."

"*Suicide?*"

"There's no point in speaking other than the truth. Ernst threw himself out of his hotel window. It was mercifully quick. At ten o'clock, the Grande Banque will suspend all business for one minute of mourning and reflection."

"Oh, my *God* ... "

"However," concluded the voice in Zürich, "all of Herr Manfredi's accounts to which he gave his personal attention will be assumed by equally capable hands. We fully expect ..."

Noel hung up the phone, cutting off the man's words. *Accounts ... will be assumed by equally capable hands.* Business as usual; a man was killed but the affairs of Swiss finance were not to be interrupted. And he *was* killed.

Ernst Manfredi did not throw *himself* out of a hotel in Zürich. He was *thrown* out. Murdered by the men of Wolfsschanze.

For God's sake, *why?* Then Holcroft remembered. Manfredi had dismissed the men of Wolfsschanze. He had told Noel the macabre threats were meaningless, the anguish of sick old men seeking atonement.

. . . I'm not frightened by threats made by maniacs thirty years ago . . .

. . . Nor should you be . . .

That was Manfredi's error. He had undoubtedly told his associates, the other directors of the Grande Banque, about the strange letter that had been delivered with the wax seals unbroken. Perhaps he had laughed to them at the men of Wolfsschanze.

The match! The flare of light! Across the courtyard the woman in the window nodded! Again – as if reading his thoughts – she was confirming the truth. A dead woman was telling him he was right!

She turned and walked away; all light went out in the window.

"Come back! Come *back!*" Holcroft screamed, his hands on the panes of glass. "Who *are* you?"

The telephone beneath him buzzed. Noel stared at it, as if it were a terrible thing in an unfamiliar place; it was both. Trembling, he picked it up.

"Mr Holcroft, it's Jack. I *think* I may know what the hell happened up at your place. I mean, I didn't think about it before, but it kinda hit me a few minutes ago."

"What was it?"

"A couple of nights ago these two guys came in. Locksmiths. Mr Silverstein on your floor was having his lock changed. Louie told me about it, so I knew it was okay. Then I began to think. Why did they come at night? I mean, what with overtime and everything, why didn't they come in the daytime? So I just called Louie at home. He said they came *yesterday.* So who the hell were those other guys?"

"Do you remember anything about them?"

"You're damned right I do! One of them in particular. You could pick him out in a crowd at the Garden! He had . . ."

There was a loud, sharp report over the line.

A *gunshot!*

It was followed by a crash. The telephone in the lobby had been dropped!

Noel slammed down the receiver and ran to the door, yanking it open with such force that it crashed into a framed sketch on the wall, smashing the glass. There was no time to consider the lift. He raced down the stairs, his mind a blank, afraid to think, concentrating only on speed and balance, hoping to God he would not trip on the steps. He reached the landing and bolted through the lobby door.

He stared in shock. The worst had happened. Jack the doorman was arched back over the chair, blood pouring out of his neck. He had been shot in the throat.

He had interfered. He had been about to identify one of the men of Wolfsschanze and he had been killed for it.

Baldwin, Manfredi . . . an innocent doorman. Dead.

. . . all those who interfere will be stopped . . . any who stand in our way, who

try to dissuade you, who try to deceive you . . . will be eliminated.
    . . . as you and yours will be should you hesitate. Or fail.
    Manfredi had asked him if he really had a choice. He did not any longer.
He was surrounded by death.

5

Althene Holcroft sat behind the desk in her study and glared at the words of the letter she held in her hand. Her chiselled, angular features – the high cheekbones, the aquiline nose, the wide-set eyes beneath arched, defined brows – were taut, as rigid as her posture in the chair. Her thin, aristocratic lips were tight, her breathing steady, but each breath was too controlled, too deep for normalcy. She read Heinrich Clausen's letter as one studying a statistical report that contradicted information previously held to be incontrovertible.

Across the room, Noel stood by a curving bay window that looked out on the rolling lawn and gardens behind the Bedford Hills house. A number of shrubs were covered with burlap; the air was cold, and the morning frost produced intermittent patches of light grey on the green grass.

Holcroft turned from the scent outside and looked at his mother, trying desperately to conceal his fear, to control the intermittent trembling that came upon him when he thought about last night. He could not allow the terror he felt to be seen by her. He wondered what thoughts were going through her head, what memories were triggered by the sight of the handwritten words in blue ink put down by a man she had once loved, then grew to despise. Whatever she was thinking it would remain private until she chose to speak. Althene communicated only that which she cared to convey deliberately.

She seemed to sense his gaze and raised her eyes to his, but only briefly. She returned to the letter, allowing a briefer moment to brush away a stray lock that had fallen from the grey hair that framed her face. Noel wandered aimlessly towards the desk, glancing at the bookcases and photographs on the wall. The room reflected the owner, he mused. Graceful, even elegant, but withal there was a pervading sense of activity. The photographs showed men and women on horses at the hunt, in sailboats in rough weather, on skis in mountain snow. There was no denying it: there was an undercurrent of masculinity in this very feminine room. It was his mother's study, her sanctuary where she repaired for private moments of consideration. But it could have belonged to a man.

He sat down in the leather chair in front of the desk and lit a cigarette with a gold Colibri, a parting gift from a young lady who had moved out of his apartment a month ago. His hand trembled again; he gripped the lighter as tightly as he could.

"That's a dreadful habit," said Althene, her eyes remaining on the letter. "I thought you were going to give it up."

"I have. A number of times."

"Mark Twain said that. At least be original."

Holcroft shifted his position in the chair, feeling awkward. "You've read it several times now. What do you think?"

"I don't *know* what to think," said Althene, placing the letter on the desk in front of her. "He wrote it; it's his handwriting, his way of expressing himself. Arrogant even in remorse."

"You agree it's remorse then?"

"It would appear so. On the surface, at any rate. I'd want to know a great deal more. I have a number of questions about this extraordinary financial undertaking. It's beyond anything conceivable."

"Questions lead to other questions, mother. The men in Geneva don't want that."

"Does it matter what they want? As I understand you, although you're being elliptical, they're asking you to give up a minimum of six months of your life and probably a good deal longer."

Again, Noel felt awkward. He had decided not to show her the document from the Grande Banque. If she was adamant about seeing it, he could always produce it. If she was not, it was better that way; the less she knew the better. He had to keep her from the men of Wolfsschanze. He had not the slightest doubt Althene would interfere.

"I'm not holding back any of the essentials," he said.

"I didn't say you were. I said you were elliptical. You refer to a man in Geneva you won't identify; you speak of conditions you only half describe, the oldest children of two families you won't name. You're leaving out a great deal."

"For your own good."

"That's condescending and, considering this letter, very insulting."

"I didn't mean to be either." Holcroft leaned forward. "No one wants that bank account even remotely connected with you. You've read that letter; you know what's involved. Thousands and thousands of people, hundreds of millions of dollars. There's no way to tell who might hold *you* responsible. You were the wife who told him the truth; you left him because he refused to accept it. When he finally realized that what you said *was* true – he did what he did. There may be men still alive who would kill you for that. I won't let you be put in that position."

"I see." Althene drew out the phrase, then repeated it as she rose from her chair and walked slowly across the room to the bay window. "I see . . . Are you sure that's the concern the men in Geneva expressed?"

"They – he – implied it, yes."

"I suspect it was not the only concern."

"No."

"Shall I speculate on another?"

Noel stiffened. It was not that he underestimated his mother's perceptions – he rarely did that – but, as always, he was annoyed when she verbalized them before he had the chance to state them himself.

"I think it's obvious," he said.

"Do you?" Althene turned from the window and looked at him.

"It's in the letter. If the sources of that account were made public there'd be legal problems. Claims would be made against it in the international courts."

"Yes." His mother looked away. "It's obvious, then. I'm amazed you were allowed to tell me anything."

Noel leaned back in the chair apprehensively, disturbed at Althene's words. "Why? Would you really do something?"

"It's a temptation," she answered, still gazing outside. "I don't think one ever loses the desire to strike back, to lash out at someone or something that's caused great pain. Even if that hurt changed your life for the better. God knows mine – ours – was changed. From a hell to a level of happiness I'd given up looking for."

"Dad?" asked Noel.

Althene turned. "Yes. He risked more than you'll ever know protecting us. I'd been the fool of the world and he accepted the fool – and the fool's child. He gave us more than love; he gave us our lives again. He asked only love in return."

"You've given him that."

"I'll give it till I die. Richard Holcroft is the man I once thought Clausen was. I was so wrong, so terribly wrong . . . The fact that Heinrich has been dead these many years doesn't seem to matter; the loathing won't go away. I do want to strike back."

Noel kept his voice calm. He had to lead his mother away from her thoughts; the survivors of Wolfsschanze would not let her live. "You'd be striking back at the man you remember, not the man who wrote that letter. Maybe what you saw in him at first was really there. At the end, it came back to him."

"That would be comforting, wouldn't it?"

"I think it's true. The man who wrote that letter wasn't lying. He was in pain."

"He deserved pain, he caused so much; he was the most ruthless man I ever met. But on the surface, so different, so filled with purpose. And – oh, *God* – what that purpose turned out to be!"

"He changed, mother," interrupted Holcroft. "You were a part of that change. At the end of his life he wanted only to help undo what he'd done. He says it: 'Amends must be made.' Think what he did – what the three of them did – to bring that about."

"I can't dismiss it, I know that. Any more than I can dismiss the words. I can almost hear him say them, but it's a very young man talking. A young man filled with purpose, a very young, wild girl at his side." Althene paused; then she spoke again clearly. "Why did you show me the letter? Why did you bring it all back?"

"Because I've decided to go ahead. That means closing the office, travelling around a lot, eventually working out of Switzerland for a number of months. As the man in Geneva said, you wouldn't have accepted all that without asking

50

a lot of questions. He was afraid you'd learn something damaging and do something rash."

"At *your* expense?" asked Althene.

"I guess so. He thought it was a possibility. He said those memories of yours were strong. 'Indelibly printed' were his words."

"Indelibly," agreed Althene.

"His point was that there were no legal solutions; that it was better to use the money the way it was intended to be used. To make those amends."

"It's possible he was right. If it can be done. God knows it's overdue. Whatever Heinrich touched, very little of value and truth was the result." Althene paused, her face suddenly strained. "You were the one exception. Perhaps this is the other."

Noel got out of the chair and went to his mother. He took her by the shoulders and drew her to him. "That man in Geneva said you were incredible. You are."

Althene pulled back. "He said that? 'Incredible'?"

"Yes."

"Ernst Manfredi," she whispered.

"You *know* him?" asked Holcroft.

"It's a name that goes back many years. He's still alive then."

Noel did not answer her question. "How did you know it was he?"

"A summer afternoon in Berlin. He was there. He helped us get out. You and I. He got us on the plane, gave me money. Dear *God* . . ." Althene disengaged herself from her son's arms and walked across the room towards the desk. "He called me 'incredible' then, that afternoon. He said they would hunt me, find me. Find us. He said he would do what he could. He told me what to do, what to say. An unimpressive little Swiss banker was a giant that afternoon. My God, after all these years . . ."

Noel watched his mother, his astonishment complete. "Why didn't he say anything? Why didn't he *tell* me?"

Althene turned, facing her son but not looking at him. She was staring beyond him, seeing things he could not see. "I think he wanted me to find out for myself. This way. He was not a man to call in old debts indiscriminately." She sighed. "I won't pretend the questions are put to rest. I promise nothing. If I decide to take any action, I'll give you ample warning. But for the time being I won't interfere."

"That's kind of open-ended, isn't it?"

"It's the best you'll get. Those memories are, indeed, indelibly printed."

"But for now you'll do nothing?"

"You have my word. It's not lightly given, nor will it be lightly taken back."

"What would change it?"

"If you disappeared, for one thing."

"I'll stay in touch."

Althene Holcroft watched her son walk out of the room. The sharp, chiselled features of her aristocratic face – so tense, so rigid only moments ago – were relaxed. Her thin lips formed a smile; her wide eyes were reflective, in them a look of quiet satisfaction and strength.

She reached for the telephone on her desk, pressed the single button *O*, and seconds later spoke.

"Overseas operator, please, I'd like to place a call to Geneva, Switzerland."

He needed a professionally acceptable reason to close up Holcroft, Incorporated. Questions of substance could not be asked. The survivors of Wolfsschanze were killers for whom questions were easily construed as interference. He had to disappear legitimately, but one did *not* disappear legitimately; one found plausible explanations that gave the appearance of legitimacy.

The *appearance* of legitimacy.

Sam Buonoventura.

Not that Sam wasn't legitimate; he was. He was one of the best construction engineers in the business, but Sam had followed the sun so long he had blind spots. He was a fifty-year-old professional drifter, a City College graduate from Tremont Avenue in the Bronx who had found a life of instant gratification in the warm climates.

A brief tour of duty in the Army's Corps of Engineers had convinced Buonoventura that there was a sweeter, more generous world beyond the borders of the United States than within them, preferably south of the Keys. All one had to be was good – good in a job that was part of a larger job in which a great deal of money was invested. And during the fifties and sixties, the construction explosion in Latin America and the Caribbean was such that it might have been created for someone like Sam. He built a reputation among corporations and governments as the building tyrant who got things done in the field.

Once having studied blueprints, labour pools, and budgets, if Sam told his employers that a hotel or an airport or a dam would be operational within a given period of time, he was rarely in error beyond four per cent. He was also an architect's dream, which meant that he did not consider himself an architect.

Noel had worked with Buonoventura on two jobs outside the country, the first in Costa Rica, where if it had not been for Sam, Holcroft would have lost his life. The engineer had insisted that the well-groomed, courteous architect from the classy side of Manhattan learn to use a handgun, not just a hunting rifle from Abercrombie & Fitch. They were building a postal complex in the back country and it was a far cry from the cocktail lounges of the Plaza or the Waldorf or San Jose. The architect had thought the weekend exercise ridiculous but courtesy demanded compliance. Courtesy and Buonoventura's booming voice.

By the end of the following week, however, the architect was profoundly grateful. Thieves had come down from the hills to steal construction explosives. Two men had raced through the camp at night; they'd crashed into Noel's shack as he slept. When they realized the explosives were not there one man had run outside, shouting instructions to his colleagues.

"*Asesinar al Americano!*"

But the *Americano* understood the language. He reached for his gun – the handgun provided by Sam Buonoventura – and shot his would-be killer.

Sam had only one comment: "Goddamn. According to some societies, I'm supposed to take care of you for the rest of your life."

Noel reached Buonoventura through a shipping company in Miami. He was in the Dutch Antilles, in the town of Willemstad on the island of Curaçao. Noel called him there.

"How the hell *are* you, Noley?" Sam yelled. "Christ, it must be four, five years! How's your pistol arm?"

"Haven't used it since the *colinas*, and never expect to use it again. How are things with you?"

"These mothers got money to burn down here, so I'm lighting a few matches. You looking for work?"

"No. A favour."

"Name it."

"I'm going to be out of the country for a number of months on private business. I want a reason for not being in New York, for not being available. A reason that people won't question. I've got an idea, Sam, and wondered if you could help me make it work."

"If we're both thinking the same thing, sure I can."

They were thinking the same thing. It was not out of the ordinary for long-range projects in faraway places to employ consulting architects, men whose names would not appear on schematics or blueprints but whose skills would be used. The practice was generally confined to those areas where the hiring of native talent was a question of local pride. The native talent lacked sufficient training and experience. Investors covered their risks by employing highly skilled outside professionals who corrected and amended the work of the locals, seeing the projects through to completion.

"Have you got any suggestions?" Noel asked.

"Hell, yes. Take your pick of half a dozen underdeveloped countries. Africa, South America, even some of the islands here in the Antilles and the Grenadines. The internationals are moving in like spiders, but the locals are sensitive. The consulting jobs are kept separate and quiet; graft is soaring."

"I don't want a job, Sam. I want a cover. Some place I can name, someone I can mention who'll back me up."

"Why not me? I'll be buried in this motherlode for most of the year. Maybe more. I've got two marinas and a full-scale yacht club to go to when the hotel's finished. I'm your man, Noley."

"That's what I was hoping."

"That's what I figured. I'll give you the particulars and you let me know where I can reach you in case any of your high-society friends want to throw a tea dance for you."

Holcroft placed his two draughtsmen and his secretary in new jobs by Wednesday. As he suspected, it was not difficult; they were good people. He made fourteen telephone calls to project development executives at companies where his designs were under consideration, astonished to learn that of the fourteen he was the leading contender in eight. Eight! If all came through, the fees would have totalled more than he had earned during the past five years.

But not two million dollars; he kept that in the back of his mind. And if it was not in the back of his mind, the survivors of Wolfsschanze were.

The telephone answering service was given specific instructions. Holcroft, Incorporated was unavailable at the time for architectural projects. The company was involved in an overseas commission of considerable magnitude. If the caller would leave his name and number . . .

For those who pressed for further information, a post office box in Curaçao, Netherlands Antilles, under the name of Samuel Buonoventura, Limited, was listed. And in the last extremity, for the few who insisted on a telephone number, Sam's was to be given.

Noel had agreed to phone Buonoventura once a week; he would do the same with the answering service.

By Friday morning, he had the feeling that he had severed life lines he was not sure should be completely cut so. He was taking himself out of a garden he had cultivated to walk into an unfamiliar forest.

Nothing is as it was for you. Nothing can ever be the same.

Suppose he could not find the von Tiebolt children? Suppose they were dead? They had disappeared five years ago in Rio de Janeiro; what made him think he could make them reappear? And if he could not, would the survivors of Wolfsschanze strike? He was afraid.

But fear itself did not cover everything, thought Holcroft as he walked to the corner of Seventy-Third Street on Third Avenue. There were ways to handle fear. He could take the Geneva document to the authorities, to the State Department, and tell them what he knew of Peter Baldwin and Ernst Manfredi and a doorman named Jack. He could expose the massive theft of thirty years ago and grateful thousands over the world would see to it that he was protected.

That was the sanest thing to do, but somehow sanity and self-protection were not so important. Not now. There was a man in agony thirty years ago. And that man was his rationale.

He hailed a cab, struck by an odd thought, one he knew was in the deep recesses of his imagination. It was the something-else that drove him into the unfamiliar forest.

He was assuming a guilt that was not his. He was taking on the sins of Heinrich Clausen.

Amends must be made.

"630 Fifth Avenue, please," he said to the driver as he climbed into the cab. It was the address of the Brazilian Consulate.

The hunt had begun.

6

"Let me understand you, Mr Holcroft," said the ageing attaché, leaning back in his chair. "You say you wish to locate a family that you won't identify. You tell me this family immigrated to Brazil some time in the forties, and according to the most recent information dropped from sight several years ago. Is this correct?"

Noel saw the bemused expression on the attaché's face and understood. It was a foolish game perhaps, but Holcroft did not know any other one to play. He was not going to give anyone the chance to further complicate a search that had enough disadvantages at the start. He smiled pleasantly.

"I didn't quite say that. I asked how such a family might be found, given those circumstances. I didn't say I was the one looking."

"Then it's a hypothetical question? Are you a journalist?"

Holcroft considered the medium-level diplomat's question. How simple it would be to say yes; what a convenient explanation for the questions *he* would ask later. On the other hand, he'd be flying to Rio de Janeiro in a few days. There were immigration cards to be filled out, and a visa, perhaps; he did not know. A false answer now might become a problem later.

"No, an architect."

The attaché's eyes betrayed his surprise. "Then you'll visit Brasilia, of course. It's a masterpiece."

"I'd like to very much."

"You speak Portuguese?"

"A bit of Spanish. I've worked in Mexico. And in Costa Rica."

"But we're straying," said the attaché, leaning forward in his chair. "I asked you if you were a journalist and you hesitated. You were tempted to say you were because it was expedient. Frankly, that tells me you are, indeed, the one looking for this family that has dropped from sight. Now, why not tell me the rest?"

If he was going to consider lying in his search through this unfamiliar forest, thought Noel, he'd better learn to analyse his minor answers first. Lesson one: preparation.

"There isn't that much to tell," he said awkwardly. "I'm taking a trip to your country and I promised a friend I'd look up these people he knew a long time ago." It was a variation on the truth and not a bad one, thought Holcroft. Perhaps that was why he was able to offer it convincingly. Lesson two: base the lie on an aspect of truth.

"Yet your . . . *friend* has tried to locate them and was unable to do so."

"He tried from thousands of miles away. It's not the same."

"I daresay it isn't. So, because of this distance, and your friend's concern that there could be complications, shall we say, you'd prefer not to identify the family by name."

"That's it."

"No, it isn't. It would be far too simple a matter for an attorney to cable a confidential inquiry-of-record to a reciprocating law firm in Rio de Janeiro. It's done all the time. The family your friend wants to find is nowhere in evidence, so your *friend* wants you to trace them." The attaché smiled and shrugged as though having delivered a basic lecture in arithmetic.

Noel watched the Brazilian with growing irritation. Lesson three: don't be led into a trap by pat conclusions casually stated. "You know something?" he said. "You're a very disagreeable fellow."

"I'm sorry you think so," replied the attaché sincerely. "I want to be of help. That's my function here. I've spoken to you this way for a reason. You're not the first man, God knows, nor will you be the last, to look for people who came to my country 'some time in the forties'. I'm sure I don't have to amplify that statement. The vast majority of those people were Germans, many bringing to Brazil great sums of money transferred by compromised neutrals. What I'm trying to say is simply put: be careful. Such people as you speak of do not disappear without cause."

"What do you mean?"

"They have to, Mr Holcroft. *Had* to. The Nuremberg Tribunals and the Israeli hunters aside, many possessed funds – in some cases, fortunes – that were stolen from conquered peoples, from their institutions, often from their governments. Those funds could be reclaimed."

Noel tensed the muscles of his stomach. There *was* a connection – abstract, even misleading under the circumstances, but it was there. The von Tiebolts were part of a theft so massive and complex it was beyond accounting procedures. But it could not be the reason they had vanished. Lesson four: be prepared for unexpected coincidences, regardless of how strained; be ready to conceal reactions.

"I don't think the family could be involved in anything like that," he said.

"But, of course, you're not sure, since you know so little."

"Let's say I'm sure. Now, all I want to know is how I go about finding them – or finding out what happened to them."

"I mentioned attorneys."

"No attorneys. I'm an architect, remember? Lawyers are natural enemies; they take up most of our time." Holcroft smiled. "Whatever a lawyer can do, I can do faster by myself. I do speak Spanish. I'll get by in Portuguese."

"I see." The attaché paused while he reached for a box of thin cigars on his desk. He opened it and held it out for Holcroft, who shook his head. "Are you sure? It's Havana."

"I'm sure. I'm also pressed for time."

"Yes, I know." The attaché reached for a silver table lighter on the desk, snapped it, and inhaled deeply; the tip of the cigar glowed. He raised his eyes abruptly to Noel. "I can't convince you to tell me the name of this family?"

"Oh, for Christ's sake . . ." Holcroft got up. He'd had enough; he'd find other sources.

"*Please*," said the Brazilian, "sit down, please. Just a minute or two longer. The time's not wasted, I assure you."

Noel saw the urgency in the attaché's eyes. He sat down. "What is it?"

"*La comunidad alemana*. I use the Spanish you speak so well."

"The German community? There's a German community in Rio, is that what you mean?"

"Yes, but it's not solely geographical. There's an outlying district, the German *barrio*, if you will, but I'm not referring to it. I'm speaking of what we call the *lado de abajo alemán*. Can you understand that?"

"The 'underside' . . . What's underneath, below the German surface."

"Precisely. Below the surface. What makes them what they are; what makes them do what they do. It's important that you understand."

"I think I do. I think you explained it. Most were Nazis getting out of the Nuremberg net, bringing in money that wasn't theirs; hiding, concealing identities. Naturally, such people would tend to stick together."

"Naturally. But you'd think after so many years there'd be greater assimilation."

"Why? You work here in New York. Go down to the Lower East Side, or the south Village, or up to the Bronx. Enclaves of Italians, Poles, Jews. They've been here for decades. You're talking about twenty-five, thirty years. That's not much."

"There are similarities, of course, but it's not the same, believe me. The people you speak of in New York associate openly; they wear their heritages on their sleeves. It's not like that in Brazil. The German community pretends to be assimilated, but it isn't. In commerce, yes, but in very little else. There's a pervading sense of fear and anger. Too many have been hunted for too long; a thousand identities are concealed daily from everyone but themselves. They have their own hierarchy. Three or four families control the community, their estates dot our countryside. Of course they call them Swiss or Bavarian." Once more the attaché paused. "Do you begin to grasp what I'm saying? The consul general will not say it; my government will not permit it. But I'm far down the ladder. It's left to me. *Do* you understand?"

Noel was bewildered. "Frankly, no. Nothing you've said surprises me. At Nuremberg they called it 'crimes against humanity'. That kind of thing leads to a lot of guilt, and guilt breeds fear. Of course such people in a country that isn't their own would stay close to each other."

"Guilt *does* breed fear. And fear in turn leads to suspicion. Finally, suspicion gives birth to violence. That's what you must understand. A stranger coming to Rio looking for Germans who have disappeared is undertaking a potentially dangerous search. The *lado de abajo alemán*. They protect each other." The attaché picked up his cigar. "Give us the name, Mr Holcroft. Let *us* look for these people."

Noel watched the Brazilian inhale his precious Havana. He was not sure why, but he felt suddenly uneasy. *Don't be led into a trap by pat conclusions casually stated.*

"I can't. I think you're exaggerating, and obviously you won't help me." He stood up.

"Very well," said the Brazilian. "I'll tell you what you would find out for yourself. When you get to Rio de Janeiro, go to the Ministry of Immigration. If you have names and approximate dates, perhaps they can help you."

"Thanks very much," said Noel, turning towards the door.

The Brazilian walked rapidly out of the office into a large anteroom that served as a reception area. A young man sitting in an armchair quickly got to his feet at the sight of his superior.

"You may have your office back now."

"Thank you, Excellency."

The older man continued across the room, past a receptionist, to a pair of double doors. On the left panel was the Great Seal of the *República Federal do Brasil*; on the right was a plaque with gold printing that read: *Cônsul-Geral*.

The consul general went inside to another, smaller anteroom that was his secretary's office. He spoke to the girl and walked directly to the door of his own office.

"Get me the embassy. The ambassador, please. If he's not there, locate him. Inform him that it's a confidential matter; he'll know whether he can talk or not."

Brazil's highest-ranking diplomat in America's major city closed the door, strode to his desk, and sat down. He picked up a sheaf of papers stapled together. The first several pages were xeroxes of newspaper stories, accounts of the killing on British Airways Flight 591 from London to New York, and the subsequent discovery of the two murders on the ground. The last two pages were copies of that aircraft's passenger manifest. The diplomat scanned the names: *Holcroft, Noel. Dep. Geneva. BE 577. O. Lon. BA 591. X. NYC.* He stared at the information as if somehow relieved that it was still there.

His telephone hummed; he picked it up. "Yes?"

"The ambassador is on the line, sir."

"Thank you." The consul general heard an echo in his ear that meant the scrambler was in operation. "Mr Ambassador?"

"Yes, Geraldo. What's so urgent and confidential?"

"A few minutes ago a man came up here asking how he might go about locating a family in Rio he had not been able to reach through the usual channels. His name is Holcroft. Noel Holcroft, an architect from New York City."

"It means nothing to me," said the ambassador. "Should it?"

"Only if you've recently read the list of passengers on the British Airways plane from London last Saturday."

"Flight 591?" The ambassador spoke sharply.

"Yes. He left that morning from Geneva on British European, and transferred at Heathrow to 591."

"And now he wants to locate people in Rio? Who are they?"

"He refused to say. I was the 'attaché' he spoke to, naturally."

"Naturally. Tell me everything. I'll cable London. Do you think it's possible . . ." The ambassador paused.

"Yes," interrupted the consul general softly. "I think it's very possible he's looking for the von Tiebolts."

"Tell me everything," repeated the man in Washington. "The British believe those killings were the work of the Tinamou."

Noel felt a sense of déjà-vu as he looked around the lounge of the Braniff 747. The colours were more vivid, the uniforms of the aircraft's personnel more fashionably cut. Otherwise, the plane seemed identical to British Airways Flight 591. The difference was in attitude. This was the *Rio Run*, that carefree holiday that was to begin in the sky and continue on the beaches of the Gold Coast.

It was no holiday for him thought Holcroft, no holiday at all. The only climax awaiting him was one of discovery. The whereabouts or the non-whereabouts of the family von Tiebolt.

They'd been in the air something over five hours. He had picked his way through a dismissible meal, slept through an even more dismissible film, and finally decided to go up to the lounge.

He had put off going upstairs. The memory of seven days ago was still uncomfortable. The unbelievable had happened in front of his eyes; a man had been killed not four feet from where he'd been sitting. At one point he could have reached over and *touched* the writhing figure; death had been inches away, unnatural death, chemical death, murder.

Strychnine. A colourless crystalline alkaloid that caused paroxysms of unendurable pain. Why had it happened? Who was responsible and for what reason? The accounts were specific, the theories speculative.

Two men had been physically close to the victim in the lounge of Flight 591 from London. Either one could have administered the poison by way of the victim's drink; it was presumed one had. But again, why? According to the Port Authority police, there was no evidence that the two men had ever known Thornton. And the two men themselves – the suspected killers – had met *their* deaths by gunshot in a fuel truck on the ground. They had disappeared from the aircraft, from the sealed-off customs area, from the quarantined room, and themselves been murdered. Why? By whom?

No one had any answers. Only questions. And then even the questions stopped. The story faded from the newspapers and the broadcasts as dramatically as it had appeared, as though a black-out had been called. Again, why? Again, who was responsible?

"That was scotch on the rocks, wasn't it, Mr Holcroft?"

The déjà-vu was complete. The words were the same but spoken by another. The stewardess above him, placing the glass on the round formica table, was attractive – as the stewardess on Flight 591 had been attractive. The look in her eyes had that same quality of directness he remembered from the girl on British Airways. The words, even to the use of his name, were uttered in a similar tone, only the accent varied. It was all *too* much alike. Or was his mind – his eyes, his ears, his senses – too preoccupied with the memory of seven days ago?

He thanked the stewardess, almost afraid to look at her, thinking that any second he would hear a scream beside him and watch a man in uncontrollable agony lunge out of his seat.

Then Noel realized something else, and it discomforted him further. He was sitting in the same seat he had occupied during those terrifying moments on Flight 591. In a lounge identically constructed to that lounge a week ago. It was not really unusual; he preferred the location and often sat there, but now it seemed macabre. His lines of sight were the same, the lighting no different now than it was then.

That was scotch on the rocks, wasn't it, Mr Holcroft?

An outstretched hand, a pretty face, a glass.

Images, sounds.

Sounds. Raucous, drunken laughter. A man with too much alcohol in him, losing his balance, falling backwards over the rim of the chair. His companion reeling in delight at the sight of his unsteady' friend. A third man – the man who would be dead in moments – trying too hard to be a part of the revelry. Anxious to please, wanting to join. An attractive stewardess pouring whisky, smiling, wiping the bar on which two drinks had been reduced to one because one had been spilled, rushing around the counter to help a drunken passenger. The third anxious man, embarrassed perhaps, still wanting to play with the big boys, reaching . . .

A *glass. The* glass! The single, remaining glass on the bar.

The third man had reached for that glass!

It was scotch on the rocks. The drink intended for the passenger sitting across the lounge at the small formica table. Oh, my *God!* thought Holcroft, the images racing back and forth in sequence in his mind's eye. The drink on the bar – the drink a stranger named Thornton had taken – was meant for *him!*

The strychnine was meant for *him!* The twisting, horrible convulsions of agony were to be *his!* The terrible death assigned to *him!*

He looked down at the glass in front of him on the table; his fingers were around it.

That was scotch on the rocks, wasn't it? . . .

He pushed the drink aside. Suddenly he could no longer stay at that table, remain in that lounge. He had to get away; he had to force the images out of his mind. They were too clear, too real, too horrible.

He rose from the chair and walked rapidly, unsteadily, towards the staircase. The sounds of drunken laughter weaved in and out between an unrelenting scream of torment that was the screech of sudden death. No one else could hear those sounds, but they pounded in his head.

He lurched down the curving staircase to the deck below. The light was dim; several passengers were reading under the beams of tiny spotlights, but most were asleep.

Noel was bewildered. The hammering in his ears would not stop, the images would not go away. He felt the need to vomit, to expunge the fear that had settled into his stomach. Where was the toilet? In the galley . . . behind the galley? Beyond the curtain, that was it. Or was it? He did not know, so he parted the curtain.

Suddenly, his eyes were drawn down to his right, to the front seat of the 747's second section. A man had stirred in his sleep. A heavy-set man whose face he had seen before. He did not recall where, but he was sure of it! A face creased in panic, racing by, close to his. What was it about the face? Something had made a brief but strong impression. What *was* it?

The eyebrows, that was it! Thick eyebrows, the coiled, matted hair an odd mixture of black and white. Salt-and-pepper eyebrows; *where* was it? He could not remember, and because he could not, he felt the blood rushing to his head. The pounding grew louder; his temples throbbed.

Suddenly, the man with the thick coiled eyebrows woke up, somehow aware that he was being stared at. Their eyes locked; recognition was absolute.

And there was violence in that recognition. But of *What? When? Where?*

Holcroft nodded awkwardly, unable to think. The pain in his stomach was knifelike, the sounds in his head were now cracks of thunder. For a moment he forgot where he was; then he remembered and the images returned. The sights and sounds of a killing that but for an accident would have claimed his life.

He had to get back to his seat. He had to control himself; stop the pain and the thunder and the pounding in his chest. He turned and walked quickly beyond the curtain, past the galley, up the aisle to his seat.

He sat down in the semi-darkness, grateful there was no one beside him. He pressed his head into the rim of the chair and closed his eyes, trying with all his concentration to rid his mind of the terrible sight of a grotesque face, screaming away the last few seconds of life. But he could not.

That face became *his* face.

Then the features blurred, as if the flesh were melting, only to be formed again. The face that now came into focus was no one he recognized. A strange, angular face, parts of which seemed familiar, but not as a whole.

Involuntarily, he gasped. He had never seen that face but suddenly he knew it. Instinctively. It was the face of Heinrich Clausen. A man in agony thirty years ago. The unknown father with whom he had his covenant.

Holcroft opened his eyes, stung by the perspiration that had rolled down his face. There was another truth and he was not sure he wanted to recognize it. The two men who had tried to kill him with strychnine had themselves been murdered. They had interfered.

The men of Wolfsschanze had been aboard that plane.

7

The clerk behind the desk of the Porto Alegre Hotel pulled Holcroft's reservation from the file. A small yellow message-envelope was stapled to the back of the card. The clerk tore it off and handed it to Noel.

"This came for you shortly past seven o'clock this evening, *senhor*."

Holcroft knew no one in Rio de Janeiro, and had told no one in New York where he was going. He ripped open the flap and drew out the message. It was from Sam Buonoventura. He was to return the overseas call as soon as possible, regardless of the hour.

Holcroft looked at his watch; it was nearly midnight. He signed the register and spoke as casually as he could, his mind on Sam.

"I have to telephone Curaçao. Will there be any trouble at this hour?"

The clerk seemed mildly offended. "Certainly not with our *operadores*, *senhor*. I cannot speak for Curaçao."

The origins of the difficulty notwithstanding, it was not until 1.15 in the morning that he heard Buonoventura's rasping voice over the line.

"I think you've got a problem, Noley."

"I've got more than one. What is it?"

"Your answering service gave my number to this cop in New York, a Lieutenant Miles; he's a detective. He was hot as hell. Said you were supposed to inform the police if you left town, to say nothing about leaving the country."

Christ, he had forgotten! And now he understood just how vital those instructions were. The strychnine was meant for him! Had the police reached the same conclusion?

"What did you tell him, Sam?"

"Got hot myself. It's the only way to handle angry cops. I told him you were off in the out-islands doing a survey for a possible installation Washington was interested in. A little bit north, we're not too far from the Zone; it could mean anything. Nobody talks."

"Did he accept that?"

"Hard to tell. He wants you to call him. I bought you time, though I said you radioed in this afternoon and I didn't expect to hear from you for three or four days, and I couldn't make contact. That's when he yelled like a cut bull."

"Did he buy it?"

"What else could he do? He thinks we're all fucking—a stupid down here, and I agreed with him. He gave me two numbers for you. Got a pencil?"

"Go ahead."

Holcroft wrote down the numbers – a Port Authority police telephone and Miles's home – thanked Buonoventura, and said he'd be in touch next week.

Noel had unpacked during the interminable wait for the Curaçao connection. He sat down in a cane-backed chair in front of the window and looked out at the night-white beach and the dark waters beyond, reflecting the bright half-moon. Below, on that isolated section of the street bordering the ocean walkway, were the curving, black-and-white parallel lines that signified the Copacabana, the golden coast of Guanabara. There was an emptiness about the scene that had nothing to do with its being deserted. It was too perfect, too pretty. He would never have designed it that way; there was an absence of character. He focused his eyes on the window panes. There was nothing to do now but think and rest and hope he could sleep. Sleep had been difficult for the past week; it would be more difficult now. Because he knew now what he had not known before: someone had tried to kill him.

The knowledge produced an odd sensation. He could not believe that there was someone who wanted him dead. Yet someone had to have made the decision, had to have issued the order. Why? What had he done? Was it Geneva? His covenant?

We're dealing in millions. Those were not only the dead Manfredi's words, they were his warning. It was the only possible explanation. The information had got out, but there was no way to know how far it had spread, or who was affected by it, who infuriated. Or the identity of the unknown person – or persons – who wanted to stop the release of the Geneva account, consigning it to the litigation of the international courts.

Manfredi was right: the only moral solution was found in carrying out the intent of the document drawn up by three extraordinary men in the midst of the devastation their own monster had created. *Amends must be made.* It was the credo Heinrich Clausen believed in; it *was* honourable, it was right. In their misguided way, the men of Wolfsschanze understood.

Noel poured himself a drink, walked over to the bed and sat down on the edge, staring at the telephone. Next to it were the two numbers written on a hotel message pad, given to him by Sam Buonoventura. They were his links to Lieutenant Miles, Port Authority police. But Holcroft could not bring himself to call. He had begun the hunt; he had taken the first step in his search for the family of Wilhelm von Tiebolt. Step, hell! It was a giant leap of 4,000 air miles; he would not turn back.

There was so much to do. Noel wondered whether he was capable of doing it, whether he was capable of making his way through the unfamiliar forest.

He felt his eyelids grow heavy. Sleep was coming and he was grateful for it. He put down the glass and kicked off his shoes, not bothering with the rest of his clothes. He fell back on the bed and for several seconds stared at the white ceiling. He felt so alone, yet knew he wasn't. There was a man in agony thirty years ago, crying out to him. He thought about that man until sleep came.

Holcroft followed the translator into the dimly lit, windowless cubicle. Their conversation had been brief; Noel sought specific information. The name was von Tiebolt, the family German nationals. A mother and two children – a daughter and a son – had immigrated to Brazil on or about 15 June 1945, a third child, another daughter, had been born several months later, probably in Rio de Janeiro. The records had to contain *some* information. Even if a false name was used, a simple cross-check of the weeks involved – two or three either way – would certainly unearth a pregnant woman with two children coming into the country. If there were more than one, it was his problem to trace them. At least a name, or names, would surface.

No, it was not an official inquiry. There were no criminal charges, no seeking of revenge for crimes going back thirty years. On the contrary, it was a *benigno buscar* – a benign search.

Noel knew that an explanation would be asked of him, and he remembered one of the lessons learned at the consulate in New York, *Base the lie on an aspect of truth*. The family von Tiebolt had relations in the United States, went the lie. People who had immigrated to America in the twenties and thirties. Very few were left, and there was a large sum of money involved. Surely, the officials at the *Ministério da Imigração* would want to help find the inheritors. It was entirely possible that the von Tiebolts would be grateful . . . and he, as the intermediary, would certainly make known their co-operation.

Ledgers were brought out. Hundreds of photostats from another era were studied. Faded, soiled copies of documents, so many of which were obviously false papers purchased in Berne and Zürich and Lisbon. Passports.

But there were no documents relating to the von Tiebolts, no description of a lone pregnant woman with two children entering Rio de Janeiro during the months of June or July in 1945. At least, none resembling the wife of Wilhelm von Tiebolt. There were pregnant women, even pregnant women with children, but none with children that could have been von Tiebolt's. According to Manfredi, the daughter, Gretchen, was twelve or thirteen years old, the son Johann, ten. *Every one* of the women entering Brazil during those weeks was either accompanied by a husband – or a false husband – and where there were children, none, not *one*, was over seven years of age.

This in itself was not only unusual, it struck Holcroft as being mathematically impossible. He stared at the pages of faded ink, at the often illegible entries made by harried immigration officials thirty-odd years ago.

Something was wrong; his architect's eye was troubled. He had the feeling he was studying blueprints that had not been finished, filled with minute alterations; tidy lines erased and changed, but very delicately so as not to disturb the larger design.

Erased and changed. *Chemically* erased, *delicately* changed. That was what bothered him! The birth dates! Page after page of miniature figures, digits subtly altered! A *3* became an *8*, a *1* a *9*, a *2* a *40*, the curve retained, a line drawn down, a zero added. Page after page in the ledgers for the weeks of June and July of 1945. The birth dates of all the children entering Brazil had been changed so that none was born prior to 1938!

It was a painstakingly clever ruse, one that had to be thought out carefully, deliberately. Stop the hunt at the source. But do it in a way that appeared above suspicion. Small numbers faithfully – if hastily – recorded by unknown immigration personnel over thirty years ago. Recorded from documents, the majority of which had been long since destroyed, for most were false. There was no way to substantiate, to confirm or deny the accuracies. Time and conspiracies had made that impossible. Of course, there was no one resembling the von Tiebolts! *Good Lord*, what a deception!

Noel pulled out his lighter; its flame would provide more light on a page where his eye told him there were numerous, minute alterations.

"*Senhor!* That is forbidden!" The harsh command was delivered in a loud voice by the translator. "Those old pages catch fire easily. We cannot take such risks."

Holcroft understood. It explained the inadequate light, the windowless cubicle. "I'll bet you can't," he said, extinguishing his lighter. "And I suppose these ledgers can't be removed from this room."

"No, *senhor*."

"And, of course, there are no extra lamps around, and you don't have a flashlight. Isn't that right?"

"*Senhor*," interrupted the translator, his tone now courteous, even deferential. "We have spent nearly three hours with you. We've tried to co-operate fully, but as I'm sure you're aware, we have other duties to perform. So, if you've finished . . ."

"I think you made sure of that before I started," broke in Holcroft. "Yes, I'm finished. Here."

He walked in the bright afternoon sunlight, trying to make sense out of things, the soft ocean breezes caressing his face, calming his anger and his frustration. He strolled on the white boardwalk overlooking the immaculate sand of Guanabara Bay. Every now and then he stopped and leaned against the railing, watching the grown-up children at their games. The beautiful people, sunning and stunning. Grace and arrogance coexisted with artifice. Money was everywhere. But again, where was the character? It was somehow absent on the Copacabana this afternoon.

He passed that section of the beach that fronted his hotel and glanced up at the windows, trying to locate his room. For a moment he thought he had found it, then realized he was wrong. He could see two figures behind the glass, but the maids had straightened his room that morning.

He returned to the railing and lit a cigarette. The lighter made him think about the thirty-year-old ledgers so painstakingly doctored. Had they been altered just for him? Or had there been others over the years looking for the von Tiebolts? Regardless of the answer, he had to find another source. Or other sources.

La comunidad alemana. Holcroft recalled the words of the attaché in New York. He remembered the man saying there were three or four families who were the arbiters of the German community. It followed that such men had to know the most carefully guarded secrets. *Identities are concealed every day . . . A stranger coming to Rio looking for Germans who have disappeared is undertaking a potentially dangerous search . . . the "lado de abajo alemán". They protect each other.*

There was a way to eliminate the danger, Noel thought. It was found in the explanation he had given the translator at the Ministry of Immigration. He travelled a great deal, so it was plausible that someone somewhere had approached him, knowing he was flying to Brazil, and asked him to locate the von Tiebolts. It had to be a person who dealt in legitimate confidentiality, a lawyer or a banker. Someone whose own reputation was above reproach. Who might that someone be? Without analysing it deeply, Holcroft knew that whoever he decided upon would be the key to his explanation.

An idea for a candidate struck him, the risks apparent, the irony not lost. Richard Holcroft, the only father he had ever known. Stockbroker, banker, naval officer . . . father.

Noel looked at his watch. It was ten minutes past five – past three in New York. Mid-afternoon on a Monday. He did not believe in omens, but he had just come upon one. Every Monday afternoon Richard Holcroft went to the New York Athletic Club. Noel could have him paged, talk to him alone – ask for help. Help that was to be rendered confidentially, for confidentiality was not only the essence of the cover, it was the basis of his protection. Someone, *anyone*, had contacted Richard Holcroft – man of stature – and asked him to locate a family named von Tiebolt in Brazil. Knowing his son was going to Rio, he quite logically in turn asked his son to make inquiries. It was a confidential matter; it would not be discussed. No one could turn away the curious with greater authority than Dick Holcroft.

But Althene was not to be told. That was the hardest part of the request. Dick adored her; there were no secrets between them. But his father – damn it, *step*father – would not refuse him if the request was based in genuine need. He never had.

He crossed the smooth marble floor of the hotel lobby towards the bank of lifts, oblivious to sights and sounds, his concentration on what he would say to his *step*father. As a result, he was startled when an obese American tourist tapped his shoulder.

"They calling you, Mac?" The man pointed towards the front desk.

Behind the counter the clerk was looking at Noel. In his hand was the familiar yellow message-envelope; he gave it to a bellhop, who started across the lobby.

The single name on the slip of paper was unknown to him. *Cararra.* There was a telephone number below, but no message. Holcroft was bewildered. The lack of a message was unusual; it was not the Latin way of doing things. Senhor Cararra could phone again; he had to reach New York. He had to build another cover.

Yet in his room, Holcroft read the name again: *Cararra.* His curiosity was aroused. Who was this Cararra that he expected to be called back on the basis of a name alone, a name the man knew meant nothing to Holcroft. In South American terms it was discourteous to the point of being insulting. His stepfather could wait a few minutes while he found out. He dialled the number.

Cararra was not a man, she was a woman, and from the sound of her low, strained voice she was a frightened woman. Her English was passable but not good; it did not matter. Her message was as clear as the fear she conveyed.

"I cannot talk now, *senhor*. Do not call this number again. It is most not necessary."

"You left it with the operator. What did you expect me to do?"

"It was a . . . *èrro*."

"*Yerro*? Mistake?"

"Yes. A mistake. I will call you. *We* will call."

"What about? Who are you?"

"*Mais tarde!*" The voice descended to a harsh whisper and was abruptly gone with the click of the line.

Mais tarde . . . mais tarde. Later. The woman would call him again. Holcroft felt a sudden hollowness in his stomach, as sudden as the abrupt disappearance of the frightened whisper. He could not recall when he had heard a woman's voice so filled with fear.

That she was somehow connected with the missing von Tiebolts was the first thought that came to his mind. But in what way? And how in God's name would she know about *him?* The feeling of dread came over him again . . . and the image of the horrible face contorted in death 30,000 feet in the air. He was being observed; strangers were watching him.

The whine of the telephone receiver interrupted his thoughts; he had forgotten to hang up. Instead, he depressed the button, released it, and made the call to New York. He needed his protection quickly; he knew that now.

He stood by the window, staring out at the beach front, waiting for the operator to call him back. There was a flash of light from the street below. The chrome of a car grille had caught the rays of the sun and reflected them skywards. The car had passed that section of the boardwalk where he had been standing only minutes ago. Standing and absently glancing up at the hotel windows, trying to spot his room.

The *window* . . . The angle of *sight*. Noel moved closer to the panes and studied the diagonal line from the spot below – where he had been standing – to where he stood now. His architect's eye was a practised eye; angles did not deceive him. Too, the windows were not that close to one another, befitting the separation of rooms in an ocean-front hotel on the Copacabana. He had looked up at *this* window, thinking it was not his room because he saw figures inside, behind the glass. But it *was* his room. And there *had* been people inside.

He walked to his closet and stood looking at his clothes. He trusted his memory for detail as much as he trusted his eye for angular lines. He pictured the closet where he had changed clothes that morning. He had fallen asleep in the suit he had worn from New York. His light tan slacks had been on the far right, almost against the closet wall. It was habit: trousers on the right, jackets on the left. The slacks were still on the right, but not against the wall. Instead, they were several inches towards the centre. His dark blue blazer was *in* the centre, *not* on the left side.

His clothes had been searched.

He crossed to the bed and his open attaché case. It was his office when he travelled; he knew every millimetre of space, every compartment, the position of every item in every slot. He did not have to look long.

His attaché case had been searched as well.

The telephone rang, the sound an intrusion on his fears. He picked it up and heard the voice of the Athletic Club's operator, but he knew he could not now ask for Richard Holcroft; he could not involve him. Things were suddenly too complicated. He had to think them through.

"New York Athletic Club. Hello? Hello? . . . Hello, Rio operator? There's no one on the line, Rio. Hello? New York Athletic Club . . ."

Noel replaced the receiver. He had been about to do something *crazy*. His room had been searched! In his need for a cover in Rio de Janeiro, he had been about to lead someone directly to the one person closest to his mother, once the wife of Heinrich Clausen. What had he been *thinking* of?

And then he realized that nothing was wasted. Instead, another lesson had been learned. *Carry out the lie logically, then re-examine it, and use the most credible part.* If he could invent a reason for such a man as Richard Holcroft to conceal the identity of those seeking the von Tiebolts, he could invent the man himself.

Noel was breathing hard. He had almost committed a terrible error, but he was beginning to know what to look for in the unfamiliar forest. The paths were lined with traps; he had to keep his guard up and move cautiously. He could not permit himself a mistake like the one he had nearly made. He had come very close to risking the life of the father that was, for one he had never known.

Very little of value or truth ever came from anything he touched. His mother's words, and like Manfredi's meant as a warning. But his mother – unlike Manfredi – was wrong. Heinrich Clausen was as much a victim as he was a villain of his time. The anguished letter he had written while Berlin was falling confirmed it, and what he had done confirmed it. Somehow his son would prove it.

La comunidad alemana. Three, four families in the German community, the

70

arbiters who made irreversible decisions. One of them would be his source. And he knew exactly where to look.

The old, heavy-set man with thick jowls and steel-grey hair cut short in the fashion of a Junker looked up from the huge dining-room table at the intruder. He ate alone, no places set for family or guests. It seemed strange, for as the door was opened by the intruder, the voices of other people could be heard; there were family and guests in the large house, but they were not at that table.

"We have additional information on Clausen's son, Herr Graff," said the intruder, approaching the old man's chair. "You know about the Curaçao communication. Two other calls were made this afternoon. One to the woman, Cararra, and the second to a men's club in New York."

"The Cararras will do their job well," said Graff, his fork suspended, the puffed flesh around his eyes creased.

"What's this club in New York?"

"A place called the New York Athletic Club. It is . . ."

"I know what it is. A wealthy membership. Who was he calling?"

"The call was placed to the location, not to a person. Our people in New York are trying to find out."

The old man put down his fork. He spoke softly, insultingly. "Our people in New York are slow, and so are you."

"I beg your pardon!"

"Undoubtedly among the members will be found the name of Holcroft. If so, Clausen's son has broken his word; he's told Holcroft about Geneva. That is dangerous. Richard Holcroft is an old man, but he is not feeble. We always knew that if he lived long enough, he might be a stumbling block." Graff shifted his large head and looked at the intruder. "The envelope arrived in Sesimbra; there is no excuse. The events of the other night had to be clear to the son. Cable the Tinamou. I don't trust his associate here in Rio. Use the eagle code and tell him what I believe. Our people in New York will have another task. The elimination of a meddling old man. Richard Holcroft must be taken out. The Tinamou will demand it."

8

Noel knew what he was looking for: a bookstore that was more than a place to buy books. In every resort city there was always one major shop that catered to the reading requirements of a specific nationality. In this case, its name was *A Livraria Alemã*. The German Bookshop. According to the desk clerk, it carried all the latest German periodicals and Lufthansa flew in newspapers daily. That was the information Holcroft sought. Such a store would have accounts; someone there would know the established German families in Rio. If he could get just one or two names ... It was a place to start.

The store was less than ten minutes from the hotel. "I'm an American architect," he said to the clerk, who was halfway up a ladder, rearranging books on the top shelf. "I'm down here checking out the Bavarian influence on large residential homes. Do you have any material on the subject?"

"I didn't know it was a subject," replied the man in fluent English. "There's a certain amount of Alpine design, chalet-style building, but I wouldn't call it Bavarian."

Lesson six, or was it seven? Even if the lie is based on an aspect of truth, make sure the person you use it on knows less than you do.

"Alpine, Swiss, Bavarian. They're pretty much the same thing."

"Really? I thought there were considerable differences."

Lesson eight or nine. Don't argue. Remember the objective.

"Look, to tell you the truth, a rich couple in New York are paying my way here to bring back sketches. They were in Rio last summer. They rode around and spotted some great homes. They described them as Bavarian."

"Those would be in the northwest countryside. There are several marvellous houses out there. The Eisenstat residence, for example, but then I think they're Jewish; there's an odd mixture of Moorish, if you can believe it. And, of course, there's the Graff mansion. That's almost too much, but it's really spectacular. To be expected, I imagine. Graff's a millionaire many times over."

"What's the name again? Graff?"

"Maurice Graff. He's an importer, but then, aren't they all?"

"Who?"

"Oh come now, don't be naive. If he wasn't a general, or a mucky-muck in the High Command, I'll piss port wine."

"You're English."

"I'm English."

"But you work in a German bookstore."

"*Ich spreche sehr gut Deutsch.*"

"Couldn't they find a German?"

"I suppose there are advantages hiring someone like myself," said the Englishman cryptically.

It was Noel's turn to feign surprise. "Really?"

"Yes," replied the clerk, scaling another rung on the ladder. "No one asks me questions."

The clerk watched the American leave and stepped quickly down from the ladder, sliding it across the shelf track with a shove of his hand. It was a gesture of accomplishment of minor triumph. He walked so rapidly down the book-lined aisle and left into an intersecting stack that he collided with a customer examining a volume of Goethe.

"*Verzeihung,*" said the clerk under his breath, not at all concerned.

"*Schwesterchen,*" said the man with the thick black-and-white eyebrows.

At the reference to his lack of masculinity, the clerk turned, "You!"

"The friends of Tinamou are never far away," replied the man.

"You followed him?" asked the clerk.

"He never knew. Make your call."

The Englishman continued on his way to the door of an office at the rear of the store. He went inside, picked up the telephone, and dialled. It was answered by the aide of the most powerful man in Rio.

"Senhor Graff's residence. Good afternoon."

"Our man at the hotel deserves a large tip," said the clerk. "He was right. I insist on talking to Herr Graff. I did precisely as we agreed, and I did it superbly. I've no doubt he'll be calling. Now, Herr Graff, please."

"I'll pass along your message, butterfly," said the aide.

"You'll do no such thing! I have other news I'll tell only to him."

"What does it concern? I don't have to tell you he's a busy man."

"Shall we say a countryman of mine? Do I make myself clear?"

"We know he's in Rio; he's already made contact. You'll have to do better than that."

"He's still here. In the store. He may be waiting to talk to me."

The aide spoke to someone near by. The words, however, were distinct. "It's the actor, *Mein Herr.* He insists on speaking to you. Everything went as scheduled during the past hour, but there seems to be a complication. His countryman is in the bookshop."

The phone passed hands. "What is it?" asked Maurice Graff.

"I wanted you to know that everything went exactly as we anticipated . . ."

"Yes, yes, I understand that," interrupted Graff. "You do excellent work. Now, what's this about the *Englander?* He's there?"

"He followed the American. He was no more than ten feet from him. He's still here and I expect he'll want me to tell him what's happening. Should I?"

"No," replied Graff. "We're perfectly capable of running things here without interference. Say to him that we're concerned he'll be recognized; that we suggest he remain out of sight. Tell him I do not approve of his methods. You may say you heard it from me personally."

"*Thank* you, Herr Graff! It will be a pleasure."

"Yes, I know it will."

Graff handed the telephone to his aide. "The Tinamou must not let this happen," he said, quietly. "It starts again."

"What, *Mein Herr?*"

"All over again," continued the old man. "The interference, the silent observations, one upon the other. Authority becomes divided, everyone's suspect."

"I don't understand."

"Of course you don't. You weren't there." Graff leaned back in his chair. "Send a second cable to the Tinamou. Tell him that we request he order his wolf back to the Mediterranean. He's taking too many risks. We object and cannot be responsible under the circumstances."

It took several phone calls and the passage of twenty-four hours but finally the word that Graff would see him came shortly past two o'clock the next afternoon. Holcroft leased a car at the hotel and drove northwest out of the city. He stopped frequently, studying the tourist map provided by the rental agency, but finally found the house and swung through the iron gates into the ascending drive that led to the house on top of the hill.

The road levelled off into a large parking area of white concrete, bordered by green shrubbery that was broken up by flagstone paths leading through groves of fruit trees on either side.

The clerk at the bookstore was right. The Graff estate was spectacular. The view was magnificent; plains near by, mountains in the distance, and far to the east the hazy blue of the Atlantic. The house itself was three stories high. A series of balconies rose on both sides of the central entrance: a set of massive double doors – oiled mahogany, hinged with large, pitted triangles of black iron. The effect *was* Alpine; as if a geometric design of many Swiss chalets were welded into one and set down on a tropical mountain.

Noel parked the car to the right of the front steps and got out. There were two other cars in the parking area, a white Mercedes limousine and a low-slung, red Maserati. The Graff family travelled well. Holcroft gripped his attaché case and camera and started up the marble steps.

"I'm flattered our minor architectural efforts are appreciated," said Graff. "It's natural, I suppose, for transplanted people to create a touch of their

homeland in new surroundings. My family came from the *Schwarzwald* . . .
The memories are never far away."

"I appreciate your having me out here, sir." Noel put the five hastily drawn sketches back into his attaché case and closed it. "I speak for my client as well, of course."

"You have everything you need?"

"A roll of film and five elevation sketches are more than I had hoped for. Incidentally, the gentleman who showed me around will tell you the photographs were limited to the exterior structural detail."

"I don't understand you."

"I wouldn't want you to think I was taking pictures of your private grounds."

Maurice Graff laughed softly. "My residence is very well protected, Mr Holcroft. Besides, it never crossed my mind that you were examining the premises for purposes of theft. Sit down, please."

"Thank you." Noel sat opposite the old man. "These days some people might be suspicious."

"Well, I won't mislead you. I did call the Porto Alegre Hotel to see if you were registered. You were. You are a man named Holcroft from New York whose reservation was made by a reputable travel agency that obviously knows you, and you use credit cards cleared by computers. You entered Brazil with a valid passport. What more did I need? The times are technically too complicated for a man to pretend to be someone he's not, wouldn't you agree?"

"Yes, I guess I would," replied Noel, thinking that it was the moment perhaps to shift to the real purpose of his visit. He was about to speak, but Graff continued, as if filling an awkward silence.

"How long will you be in Rio?" he asked.

"Only a few more days. I have the name of your architect, and naturally I'll consult him when he's free to see me."

"I'll have my secretary telephone; there'll be no delay. I have no idea how such financial arrangements are made – or, indeed, if there are any – but I'm quite sure he'd let you have copies of the plans if they would be helpful to you."

Noel smiled, the professional in him aroused. "It's a question of selective adaptation, Mr Graff. My calling him would be as much a matter of courtesy as anything else. I might ask where certain materials were purchased, or how specific stress problems were solved, but that'd be it. I wouldn't ask for the plans and I think he'd be reluctant to say yes if I did."

"There would be *no* reluctance," said Graff, his bearing and intensity an arrogant reflection of a military past.

. . . *If he wasn't a general, or a mucky-muck in the High Command, I'll piss port wine* . . .

"It's not important, sir. I've got what I came for."

"I see." Graff shifted his heavy frame in the chair. It was the movement of a weary old man towards the end of a long afternoon. Yet the eyes were not weary; they were strangely alert. "An hour's conference would be sufficient then?"

"Easily."

"I'll arrange it."

"You're very kind."

"Then you can return to New York."

"Yes." It was the moment to mention the von Tiebolts. Now. "Actually, there's one other thing I should do while I'm here in Rio. It's not terribly important, but I said I'd try. I'm not sure where to begin. The police, I imagine."

"That sounds ominous. A crime?"

"Quite the contrary. I meant whichever department of the police it is that could help locate some people. They're not in the telephone directory. I even checked unlisted numbers; they done have one."

"Are you sure they're in Rio?"

"They were when last heard from. And I gather the other cities in Brazil were checked out, again through the telephone companies."

"You intrigue me, Mr Holcroft. Is it so important these people be found? What did they do? But then you said there was no crime."

"None. I know very little. A friend of mine in New York, an attorney, knew I was coming here and asked me to do what I could to locate this family. Apparently it was left some money by relatives in the Midwest."

"An inheritance?"

"Yes."

"Then perhaps legal counsel here in Rio . . ."

"My friend sent what he termed inquiries-of-record to several law firms down here," said Noel, remembering the words of the attaché in New York. "There weren't any satisfactory responses."

"How did he explain that?"

"He didn't. He was just annoyed. I guess the money wasn't enough for three attorneys to get involved."

"Three attorneys?"

"Yes," replied Noel, astonished at himself. He was filling a gap instinctively, without *thinking*. "There's the lawyer in Chicago – or St Louis – my friend's firm in New York, and the one down here in Rio. I don't imagine what's confidential to an outsider is confidential between attorneys. Perhaps splitting a fee three ways wasn't worth the trouble."

"But your friend is a man of conscience." Graff arched his brows in appreciation. Or something else, Holcroft thought.

"I'd like to think so."

"Perhaps I can help. I have friends."

Holcroft shook his head. "I couldn't ask you. You've done enough for me this afternoon. And, as I said, it's not that important."

"Naturally," said Graff, shrugging, "I wouldn't care to intrude in confidential matters." The German looked over at the windows, squinting. The sun was setting above the western mountains; shafts of orange light streamed through the glass, adding a rich hue to the dark wood of the study.

"The name of the family is von Tiebolt," said Noel, watching the old man's face. But whatever he expected to find, nothing could have prepared him for what he saw.

Old Graff's eyes snapped open, their glance shooting over at Holcroft, filled with loathing. "You are a *pig*," said the German, his voice so low it could barely be heard. "This was a trick, a devious ruse to come into my house! To come to me!"

"You're wrong, Mr Graff. You can call my client in New York . . ."

"*Pig!* . . .", the old man screamed. "The von Tiebolts! *Verrater!* Below filth! Cowards! *Verfaulte Menschen! Schlangen!* How *dare* you?"

Noel watched, mesmerized and helpless. Graff's face was discoloured with rage; the veins in his neck were on the surface of his flesh, his eyes red and furious, his hands trembling, gripping the arms of the chair.

"I don't understand," said Holcroft, getting to his feet.

"You understand . . . you *garbage!* You're looking for the von Tiebolts! You want to give them life again!"

"They're *dead?*"

"Would to the Almighty they *were!*"

"Graff, listen to me. If you know something . . ."

"*Get out of my house!*" The old man struggled up from the chair and screamed at the closed door of the study. "Werner! *Kommen Sie her!*"

Graff's aide burst through the door. "*Mein Herr? Was ist? . . .*"

"Take this imposter away! Get him out of my house!"

The aide looked at Holcroft. "This way. *Quickly!*"

Noel reached down for his attaché case, and walked swiftly towards the door. He stopped and turned to look once more at the enraged Graff. The old German stood like a bloated, grotesque manikin, yet he could not control his trembling.

"Get out! You are *contemptible!*"

The searing accusation shattered Noel's self-control. It was not he who was contemptible; it was the figure of arrogance in front of him, this swollen image of indulgence and brutality. This monster who betrayed, then destroyed a man in agony thirty years ago . . . and thousands like him. This *Nazi.*

"You're in no position to call me names."

"We'll see who's in what position. Get *out!*"

"I'll get out, General, or whatever the hell you are. I can't get out fast enough, because now I understand. You don't know me from the last corpse you bastards burned, but I mention one name and you can't stand it. You're torn apart because you know — and I know — that von Tiebolt saw through you thirty years ago. When the bodies piled up. He saw what you *really* were."

"We did not conceal what we were. The world knew. There was no deception on our part."

Holcroft stopped and swallowed involuntarily. In his burst of anger, he had to justify a man who had cried out to him from the grave; he had to strike back at this symbol of once-awesome might and decay that had stolen a father from him. He could not help himself.

"Get this clear," said Noel. "I'm going to find the von Tiebolts, and you're not going to stop me. Don't think you can. Don't think you've got me marked. You haven't. I've got *you* marked. For exactly what you are. You wear your Iron Cross a little too obviously."

Graff had regained control. "Find the von Tiebolts by all means. We'll be there!"

"I'll find them. And when I do, if anything happens to them, I'll know who did it. I'll brand you for what you are. You sit up here in this castle and bark your orders. You're still pretending. You were finished years ago – before the war was over – and men like von Tiebolt knew it. They understood, but you never did. You never will."

"Get *out!*"

Werner's hands grabbed Noel from behind. An arm plunged over his right shoulder and down across his chest. He was yanked briefly off his feet and pulled backwards out of the room. He swung his attaché case and felt the impact on the large, weaving body of the man dragging him through the door. He rammed his left elbow into the stomach of that unseen body and kicked viciously, jabbing his heel into his attacker's shin bone. The response was immediate; the man sagged; the grip across Noel's chest was momentarily lessened. It was enough.

Holcroft shot his left hand up, grabbing the cloth of the extended arm, and pulled forward with all his strength. He angled his body to the right, his right shoulder jammed into the chest that rose behind him. His assailant stumbled. Noel rammed a last shoulder block into the elevated chest, throwing his attacker into an antique chair against the wall. Man and delicate wood met in a crushing impact; the frame of the chair collapsed under the weight of the body. Werner was stunned, his wide eyes blinking, his focus temporarily lost.

Through the open door Holcroft could see Graff start for the telephone on his desk. Werner tried to get up.

"*Don't*," said Holcroft. He walked across the large hallway towards the front entrance. On the opposite side of the foyer several men and women stood in an open archway. None made a move towards him; none even raised his voice. The German mentality was consistent, thought Noel, not unhappy with the realization. These minions were awaiting orders.

"Do as I've instructed," said Graff into the telephone, his voice calm, with no trace of the fury he had exhibited only minutes ago. "Wait until he's halfway down the hill, then throw the switch. It's vital that the American thinks he's escaped." He hung up and turned to Werner. "Are you hurt?"

"No, *Mein Herr.*"

"Holcroft's angry," mused Graff. "He's filled with himself, exhilarated, consumed with purpose. That's good. Now he must be frightened, made to tremble at the unexpected, at the sheer brutality of the moment. Tell the guard to wait five minutes and then take up pursuit. He must do his job well."

"He has his orders; he's an expert marksman."

"Good." The former general of the Wehrmacht walked slowly to the window and squinted into the final rays of the sun. "Soft words, lover's words . . . and then sharp, hysterical rebukes. The embrace, and the knife. One must follow the other in rapid succession until Holcroft has no judgement left. Until he can no longer distinguish between ally and enemy, knowing only that he must press forward. Finally, when he breaks, we'll be there and he'll be ours."

9

Noel slammed the huge door behind him and walked down the marble steps to the car. He swung it in reverse so that his bonnet faced the downhill drive out of the Graff estate, pressed the accelerator, and headed for the exit.

Several things occurred to him. The first was that the afternoon sun had descended behind the western mountains, creating pockets of shadows on the ground. Daylight was disappearing; he needed his headlights. Another concern was that Graff's reaction to the mention of the von Tiebolts had to mean two things: the von Tiebolts were alive and they were a threat. But a threat to what? To whom? And where were they?

A third was more of a feeling than a specific thought. It was his reaction to the physical encounter he had just experienced. Throughout his life he had taken whatever size and strength he possessed as a matter of course. Because he was large and relatively well co-ordinated, he never felt the need to seek physical challenge except in competition against himself, in bettering a tennis game or besting a ski slope. As a result, he avoided fights, they struck him as unnecessary.

It was this general attitude that had made him laugh when his stepfather had insisted he join him at the club for a series of lessons in self-defence. The city was turning into a jungle; Holcroft's son was going to learn how to protect himself.

He took the course, and promptly forgot everything he had learned when it was over. If he had actually absorbed *anything*, he had done it subconsciously.

He *had* absorbed something, reflected Noel, pleased with himself. He remembered the glazed look in Werner's eyes.

The last thought which crossed his mind as he turned into the downhill drive was also vague. Something was wrong with the front seat of the car. The furious activity of the last minutes had blurred his usually acute eye for such things, but something about the chequered cloth of the seat cover bothered him.

Terrible sounds interrupted his concentration: the barking of dogs suddenly, the menacing faces of enormous long-haired black shepherds lunged at the windows on both sides of the car. The dark eyes glistened with hatred and frustration; the fur-lined, saliva-soaked jaws snapped open and shut, emitting the shrill, vicious sounds of animals reaching a quarry but unable to sink their teeth into flesh. It was a pack of attack dogs – five, six, seven – at all windows now, their paws scratching against the glass. An animal leaped up on the bonnet, its face and teeth against the windscreen.

Beyond the dog, at the base of the hill, Holcroft saw the huge gate beginning to move, the movement magnified in the beams of his headlights. It was starting the slow arc that would end with its closing! He pressed the accelerator against the floor, gripped the wheel until his arms were in pain, and drove at full speed, swerving to his left through the stone pillars, missing the steel gate by inches. The dog on the hood flew off to the right in midair, yelping in shock.

The pack on the hill had pulled up behind the gate in the darkening twilight. The explanation had to be that a high-frequency whistle – beyond human ears – had caused them to stop. Perspiring, Noel held the pedal against the floorboard and sped down the road.

He came to a fork in the countryside. Did he take the right or the left? He could not recall; he reached for his map on the seat.

That was what had bothered him! The map was no longer there. He took the left fork, reaching below the seat to see if the map had fallen to the floor. It had not. It had been removed from the car!

He arrived at an intersection; it was not familiar, or if it was the darkness obscured any familiarity. He turned right out of instinct, knowing he had to keep going. He kept the car at high speed, looking for anything that he could relate to the drive out from Rio. But the darkness was full now; he saw nothing he remembered. The road made a wide, sweeping curve to the right and then there was a sharp, steep incline of a hill. He recalled no curve, remembered no hill. He was lost.

The top of the hill flattened out for approximately a hundred yards. On his left was a lookout, bordered by a parking area enclosed by a chest-high wall fronting the cliff. Along the wall were rows of telescopes with round casings, the type activated by coins. Holcroft pulled over and stopped the car. There were no other cars but maybe one would come. Perhaps if he looked around he could get his bearings. He got out and walked to the wall.

Far below in the distance were the lights of the city. Between the cliff and the lights, however, there was only darkness . . . no, not total darkness; there was a winding thread of light. A road? Noel was next to one of the telescopes. He inserted a coin and peered through the sight, focusing on the weaving thread of light he presumed was a road. It was.

The lights were spaced far apart; they were street-lamps welcome, but out of place in a path cut out of the Brazilian forests. If he could reach the beginning of that road . . . the telescope would move no further to his right. Goddamn it! Where did the road begin? It *had* to be . . .

Behind him he heard the sound of an engine racing up the hill he had just climbed. Thank God! He would stop the car if he had to stand in the middle of the road to do it. He ran from the wall across the concrete towards the tarred pavement.

He reached the edge and froze. The car lunging over the final incline into the lookout area was a white Mercedes limousine. The same car that stood gleaming in the afternoon sun on top of another hill. Graff's car!

It stopped abruptly, tyres screeching. The door opened and a man got out. In the reflecting spill of the headlights he was recognizable: Werner!

He reached into his belt. Holcroft stood paralysed. The man raised a gun, aiming at him. It was unbelievable! It could not be happening!

The first gunshot was thunderous; it shook the silence like a sudden cracking of the earth. A second followed. The road several feet away from Noel exploded in a spray of rock and dust. Whatever instincts remained beyond his paralysis, his *disbelief*, commanded him to run, to save himself. He was doing to die! He was about to be killed in a deserted tourist lookout above the city of Rio de Janeiro!

His legs were weak, he forced himself to race towards the rented car. His feet *ached*; it was the strangest sensation he had ever felt. Two more gunshots filled the night; there were two more explosions of tar and concrete.

He reached the car and fell below the door panel for protection. He reached up for the handle.

Another gunshot, this one louder, the vibration deafening. Accompanying the detonation was another kind of explosion. The car's rear window had been blown out.

There was nothing else to do! Holcroft pulled the door open and leaped inside. In panic he turned the ignition key. The engine roared; his foot pressed the accelerator against the floor. He jammed the gearshift into drive; the car bolted forward in the darkness. He spun the wheel; the car swerved, narrowly missing impact with the wall. His instincts ordered him to switch on the headlights. In a blur he saw the downhill road, and in desperation he aimed for it.

The descent was filled with curves. He took them at high speed, sliding, skidding, barely able to hold the car in control, his arms aching. His hands were wet with sweat; they kept slipping. Any second now he fully believed he would crash; any moment now he would die in a final explosion.

He would never remember how long it took, or precisely how he found the winding road with the intermittent streetlights, but at last it was there. A flat surface heading left, heading *east*, the road into the city.

He was in dense countryside; tall trees and thick forests bordered the asphalt, looming up like the sides of an immense canyon.

Two cars approached from the opposite direction; he wanted to cry with relief at the sight of them. He was approaching the outskirts of the city. He was into the suburbs! The streetlights were close together now, and suddenly there were other cars everywhere, turning, blocking, passing. He never knew he could be so grateful to see traffic.

He came to a red traffic light. He was again grateful for its reality and the brief rest it brought him. He reached into his shirt pocket for his cigarettes. *God*, he wanted a cigarette!

A car pulled alongside him on his left and he stared once more in disbelief. A man beside the driver – a man he had never seen before in his life – had rolled down his window and was raising a pistol. On the barrel was a perforated cylinder, a silencer. The unknown man was aiming the gun at him!

Holcroft recoiled, ducking his head, spinning his neck, yanking the gearshift, plunging the accelerator to the floor. He heard the terrible spit and the crash of glass behind him. The rented car sprang forward into the intersection. Horns blew crazily; he swerved in front of an approaching car, turning at the last second to avoid a collision.

The cigarette had fallen from his lips, burning a hole in the seat.

He sped into the city.

The telephone was moist and glistening with sweat in Noel's hand. "Are you *listening* to me?" he shouted.

"Mr Holcroft, calm down, *please*." The voice of the attaché at the American Embassy was disbelieving. "We'll do everything we can. I have the salient facts and we'll pursue a diplomatic inquiry as rapidly as possible. However, it *is* past seven o'clock; it'll be difficult reaching people at this hour."

"Difficult to *reach* people? Maybe you didn't *hear* me. I was damn near killed! Take a look at that car. The windows were blown out!"

"We're sending a man over to your hotel to take possession of the vehicle," said the attaché matter-of-factly.

"I've got the keys. Have him come up to my room and get them."

"Yes, we'll do that. Stay where you are and we'll call you back."

The attaché hung up. *Christ!* The man sounded as if he had just heard from an irritating relative and was anxious to get off the phone so he could go to dinner!

Noel was frightened beyond any fear he had ever known. It gripped him and panicked him and made breathing difficult. Yet in spite of that sickening, all-pervasive fear, something was happening to him that he did not understand. A minute part of his mind was angry and he felt that anger growing. He did not want it to grow; he was afraid of it, but he could not stop it. Men had attacked him and he wanted to strike back.

He had wanted to strike back at Graff, too. He had wanted to call him by his rightful name: monster, liar, corruptor . . . *Nazi*.

Amends must be made!

A man in agony had cried out to him through the years . . . was *still* crying out to him. Those cries were louder now, clearer, and more heartbreaking with each new barrier. He could not turn his back, he could not run. The face that had melted in his mind's eye and formed again into that unknown but unmistakable image of his father was in too much pain.

What *was* happening to him?

The telephone rang. He spun around as if it were an alarm, signifying another attack. He gripped his wrist to steady the trembling and walked quickly to the bedside table.

"Senhor Holcroft?"

It was not the attaché at the American Embassy. The accent was Latin.

"What is it?"

"I must speak with you. It is very important that I speak with you right away."

"Who's this?"

"My name is Cararra. I am in the lobby of your hotel."

"*Cararra?* Someone named Cararra called me yesterday. A woman."

"My sister. We are together now. We must both speak with you now. May we come up to your room?"

"*No.* I'm not seeing anyone!" The sounds of the gunshots, the terrible muted spit, the explosions of concrete and glass – they were all still too sharp in his mind. He would not be an isolated target again.

"*Senhor,* you *must!*"

"I *won't!* Leave me alone or I'll call the police."

"They can't help you. We can. We wish to help you. You seek information about the von Tiebolts. We have information."

Noel's breathing stopped. His eyes strayed to the mouthpiece of the telephone. It was a trap. The man on the phone was trying to trap him. Yet, if that were so, why did he announce the trap?

"Who sent you here? Who told you to call me? Was it Graff?"

"Maurice Graff does not talk to people like us. My sister and I, we are beneath his contempt."

You are contemptible! Graff held most of the world in contempt, thought Holcroft. He breathed again and tried to speak calmly. "I asked you who sent you to me. How do you know I'm interested in the von Tiebolts?"

"We have friends at Immigration. Clerks for the most part, not important people. But they listen, they observe. You will understand when we speak." The Brazilian's words suddenly accelerated, the phrases tumbled awkwardly. Too awkwardly to be studied or rehearsed. "*Please, senhor.* See us. We have information and it is information you should *have.* We want to help. By helping you, we help ourselves."

Noel's brain raced. The lobby of the Porto Alegre was always crowded and there was a certain truth in the bromide that there was safety in numbers. If Cararra and his sister really knew something about the von Tiebolts, he had to see them. But not alone. He spoke slowly.

"Stay by the reception desk, at least ten feet in front of it, with both hands out of your pockets. Have your sister on your left, her right hand on your arm. I'll be down in a little while, but not in the lift and you won't see me first. I'll see you."

He hung up, astonished at himself. Lessons *were* being learned. They were basic, no doubt, to those abnormal men who dealt in a clandestine world, but new to him. Cararra would not have his hand gripped around a gun in his pocket; his sister – or whoever she was – would not be able to reach into a purse without his seeing it. They would have their attention on the doorways, not the lifts, which of course he would use. And he would know who they were.

He walked out of the lift in a crowd of tourists. He stood briefly with them, as if one of the party, and looked at the man and woman by the front desk. As instructed, Cararra's hands were at his sides, his sister's right hand linked to her brother's arm, as if she were afraid to be set adrift. And he *was* her brother; there was a distinct similarity in their features. Cararra was in his early thirties, perhaps; his sister several years younger. Both dark – skin, hair, eyes. Neither looked at all imposing; their clothes were neat but inexpensive. They were out of place among the furs and evening gowns of the hotel's guests, aware of their awkward status, their faces embarrassed, their eyes frightened. Harmless, thought Holcroft, then realized he was making too fast a judgement.

They sat in a back booth of the dimly lit cocktail lounge, the Cararras across the table from Noel. Before they'd gone inside, Holcroft had remembered that the embassy was supposed to call him back. He told the desk that if the call came, he was to be given it in the lounge. But only the embassy, no one else; he was out to any other callers.

"Tell me first how you learned I was looking for the von Tiebolts," said Noel after their drinks arrived.

"I told you. A clerk at Immigration. The word was passed discreetly last Friday among the sections that an American would be coming in asking about a German family named von Tiebolt. Whoever took the request was to call in another, a man from the *policia de administraçao*. That's the secret police."

"I know what it is. He called himself a 'translator'. I want to know why *you* were told."

"The von Tiebolts – Johann, Gretchen, even Helden – were our friends. Very close friends."

"Where are they?"

Cararra exchanged a brief look with his sister. The girl spoke.

"Why do you look for them?" she asked.

"I made that clear at Immigration. It's nothing out of the ordinary. They were left some money by relatives in the United States."

Brother and sister again looked at each other, and again the sister spoke. "Is it a large amount of money?"

"I don't know," replied Holcroft. "It's a confidential matter. I'm merely a go-between."

"A what?" Again the brother.

"*Um intermediaro*," answered Noel, looking at the woman. "Why were you so frightened on the telephone yesterday? You left your number and when I called you back you told me I shouldn't have. Why?"

"I made a . . . mistake. My brother said it was a bad mistake. My name, the telephone number, it was wrong to leave them."

"It would anger the Germans," explained Cararra. "If they were watching you, intercepting your messages, they would see that we called you. It would be dangerous to us. But my sister was filled with anxiety."

"If they're watching me now they know you're here."

"We talked it over," continued the woman. "We made our decision; we must take the risk."

"What risk?"

"The Germans despise us. Among other things, we are Portuguese Jews," said Cararra.

"That's ridiculous. What's that got to do with anything?"

"I said we were close to the von Tiebolts. Perhaps I should clarify. Johann was my dearest friend; he and my sister were to be married. The Germans would not permit it."

"Who could stop them?"

"Any number of men. With a bullet in the back of Johann's head."

"Good *Christ*, that's crazy!" But it was not crazy and Holcroft knew it. He had been a target high in the hills; gunshots still rang in his ears. As the sight of a huge, ugly pistol in a car window was in front of his eyes.

"For certain Germans it would be the final insult," said Cararra. "There are those who say the von Tiebolts were traitors to Germany. These people still fight the war three decades later. Great injustices were done to the von Tiebolts here in Brazil. They deserve whatever can be done for them. Their lives were made most difficult for causes that should have died years ago."

"And you figured I could do something for them? What made you think that?"

"Because powerful men wanted to stop you; the Germans have a great deal of influence. Therefore you, too, were a powerful man, someone the Graffs in Brazil wanted to keep from the von Tiebolts. To us that meant you intended no harm to our friends, and if no harm you meant well. A powerful American who could help them."

"You say the, Graffs in Brazil'. That's Maurice Graff, isn't it? Who is he? What is he?"

"The worst of the Nazis. He should have been hanged at Nuremberg."

"You know Graff?" asked the woman, her eyes on Holcroft.

"I went out to see him. I used a client in New York as an excuse, said he wanted me to look over Graff's house. I'm an architect. At one point, I mentioned the von Tiebolts and Graff went out of his mind. He began screaming and ordered me out. When I drove down the hill a pack of attack dogs came after the car. Later, Graff's guard followed me. He tried to kill me. In traffic, the same thing happened again. Another man shot at me from a car window."

"Mother of God!" Cararra's lips parted in shock.

"We should not be seen with him," said the woman, gripping her brother's arm. Then she stopped, studying Noel closely. "If he's telling the truth."

Holcroft understood. If he was to learn anything from the Cararras, they had to be convinced he was exactly who he said he was. "I'm telling the truth, I promise you. I've also told it to the American Embassy. They're sending someone over to take the car as evidence."

The Cararras looked at each other, then both turned to Holcroft. His statement was the proof they needed; it was in their eyes.

"We believe you," said the sister. "We must hurry."

"The von Tiebolts are alive?"

"Yes," said the brother. "The Nazis think they are somewhere in the southern mountains, around the Santa Catarina colonies. They're old German settlements; the von Tiebolts could change their names and melt in easily."

"But they're not there."

"No . . ." Cararra seemed to hesitate, unsure of himself.

"Tell me where they are," pressed Noel.

"Is it a good thing you bring to them?" asked the girl, concern in her voice.

"Far better than anything you can imagine," replied Holcroft. "*Tell* me."

Once again the brother and sister exchanged glances. Their decision was made. Cararra spoke. "They are in England. As you know, the mother is dead . . ."

"I didn't know," said Noel. "I don't know anything."

"They go by the name of Tennyson. Johann is known as John Tennyson; he is a journalist for a newspaper, *The Guardian*. Gretchen, the oldest, is married to a British naval officer. We don't know where she lives but her husband's name is Beaumont; he is a commander in the Royal Navy. Of Helden, the youngest daughter, we know nothing. She was always a little distant, a bit headstrong."

"Helden? It's an odd name."

"It fits her," said Cararra's sister softly.

"The story is that her birth certificate was filled out by a doctor who did not speak German, who did not understand the mother. According to Senhora von Tiebolt, she gave the child's name as Helga, but the hospital staff was rushed. They wrote down Helden. In those days, one did not argue with what was written on papers. The name stayed with her."

"Tennyson, Beaumont . . ." Holcroft repeated the names. "England? How did they get out of Brazil and over to England without Graff finding out? You say the Germans have influence; passports were needed, transportation had to be arranged. How did they do it?"

"Johann . . . John," corrected Cararra. "He's a remarkable man, a brilliant man."

"*Um homem formoso*," added his sister, her strained features softening with the words. "I love him very much. After five years we still love each other."

"Then you've heard from him? From them?"

"Every now and then," said Cararra. "Visitors from England get in touch with us. Never anything written on paper."

Noel stared at this man. "What kind of a world do you live in?" he asked incredulously.

"One where your own life can be taken," answered Cararra.

It was true, thought Noel as a knot of pain formed in his stomach. A war that was lost thirty years ago was still being fought by those who had lost it.

It had to be stopped. Geneva would do that. It was part of his covenant. It had to be.

"Mr Holcroft?" The greeting was tentative, the stranger standing by the table not sure he had the right party.

"Yes, I'm Holcroft," said Noel warily.

"Anderson, American Embassy, sir. May I speak with you?"

The Cararras rose as one from the table and sidestepped out of the booth. The embassy man stepped back as Cararra approached Holcroft.

"If it is a large sum of money," Cararra whispered, "John . . . will help us. We will get out, and he and my sister will be together again. *Adeos, senhor.*"

"*Anda com Deus.*" The woman whispered also, reaching out to touch Noel's arm.

Without looking at the man from the embassy, brother and sister walked rapidly out of the lounge.

Holcroft sat beside Anderson in the embassy car. They had less than an hour to get to the airport; if the ride took any longer he would miss the Avianca flight to Lisbon, where he could transfer to a British Airways plane for London.

Anderson had agreed – reluctantly, petulantly – to drive him.

"If it'll get you out of Rio," Anderson had drawled, "I'll go like a greased pig in a slaughterhouse and pay the speeding tickets from my *per diem.* You're trouble."

Noel grimaced. "You don't believe a word I've said, do you?"

"Goddamn it, Holcroft, do I have to tell you again? There's no car at the hotel, no window's blown out. There's no record of you even renting a car!"

"It was there! I rented it! I saw Graff!"

"You *called* him. You didn't *see* him. To repeat, he says he got a call from you – something about looking at his house – but you never showed up."

"That's a lie. I was there! After I left, two men tried to kill me. One of them I saw . . . hell, I *fought* with . . . inside his place!"

"You're juiced, man."

"Graff's a fucking Nazi! After thirty years, he's *still* a Nazi, and you people treat him like he's some kind of statesman."

"You're damn right," said Anderson. "Graff's very special material. He's protected."

"I wouldn't brag about it."

"You've got it all backward, Holcroft. Graff was at a place called Wolfsschanze in Germany in July of 1944. He's one of the men who tried to kill Hitler."

10

There was no sunlight outside his hotel window now; no one playing on the white sands of the Copacabana. Instead, the London streets were mottled with drizzle, and gusts of wind swept between the buildings and through the alleys. Pedestrians rushed from doorways to bus queues, tube stations, pubs. It was that hour in London when Englishmen felt sprung from the coils of daylight drudgery; making a living was not living. In Noel's experience no other city in the world took such pleasure at the end of the workday. There was a sense of controlled exhilaration in the streets, even with the rain and the wind.

He turned from the window and went to the bureau and his silver flask. It had taken nearly fifteen hours of flying to reach London and now that he was here he was not sure how to proceed. He had tried to think on the planes, but the events in Rio de Janeiro were so stunning and the information gathered so contradictory that he felt lost in a maze. His unfamiliar forest was too dense. And he had just begun.

Graff, a survivor of *Wolfsschanze?* One of the *men of Wolfsschanze?* It wasn't possible. The men of Wolfsschanze were committed to Geneva, to the fulfilment of Heinrich Clausen's dream, and the von Tiebolts were an intrinsic part of that dream. Graff wanted to destroy the von Tiebolts, as he had ordered the death of Heinrich Clausen's son on a deserted lookout above Rio and from a car window in a city street at night. He was no part of Wolfsschanze. He could not be.

The Cararras. They were complicated, too. What in heaven's name prevented them from leaving Brazil? It was not as though the airports or the piers were closed to them. He believed what they had told him, but there were too many elementary questions that needed answers. No matter how he tried to suppress the idea, there was something contrived about the Cararras. What *was* it?

Noel poured himself a drink and picked up the telephone. He had a name and a place of work. *John Tennyson. The Guardian.* Newspaper offices did not close down at the end of the day. He would know in minutes if the initial information given him by the Cararras was true. If there was a John Tennyson writing for *The Guardian*, then Johann von Tiebolt had been found.

If so, the next step according to the Geneva document was for John Tennyson to take him to his sister, Gretchen Beaumont, wife of Commander Beaumont, Royal Navy. She was the person he had to see; she was the *oldest surviving issue of Wilhelm von Tiebolt.* The key.

"I'm terribly sorry, Mr Holcroft," said the polite voice at *The Guardian's* reporters' desk, "but I'm afraid we can't give out the addresses or telephone numbers of our journalists."

"But John Tennyson does work for you." It was not a question; the man had already stated that Tennyson was not in the London office. Holcroft merely wanted a direct confirmation.

"Mr Tennyson is one of our people on the Continent."

"How can I get a message to him? Immediately, it's urgent."

The man at *The Guardian* desk seemed to hesitate. That would be difficult, I think. Mr Tennyson moves around a great deal."

"Come on, I can go downstairs, buy your paper, and see where his copy's filed from."

"Yes, of course. Only Mr Tennyson does not use a byline. Not in daily dispatches; only in major retrospectives . . ."

"How do *you* get in touch with him when you need him?" broke in Holcroft, convinced that the man was stalling.

Again there was the hesitation, a clearing of the throat. *Why? "Well* . . . there's a message pool. It could take several days."

"I don't *have* several days. I've got to reach him right away." The subsequent silence was maddening. The man at *The Guardian* had no intention of offering a solution. Noel tried another tack. "Listen, I probably shouldn't say this . . . it's a confidential matter . . . but there's money involved. Mr Tennyson and his family were left a sum of money."

"I wasn't aware that he was married."

"I mean *his* family. He and his two sisters. Do you know them? Do you know if they live in London? The oldest is – "

"I know nothing of Mr Tennyson's personal life, sir. I suggest you get in touch with a solicitor." Then, without warning, he hung up.

Bewildered, Holcroft replaced the phone. Why was there such a deliberate lack of co-operation? He had identified himself, given the name of his hotel, and for several moments the man at *The Guardian* seemed to listen, as if he might offer help. But no offers came, and suddenly the man had ended their conversation. It was all very strange.

The telephone rang; he was further bewildered. No one knew he was at this hotel. On the Immigration card he'd filled out on the plane he had purposely listed the Dorchester as his London residence, not the Belgravia Arms where he was staying. He did not want anyone – especially anyone from Rio de Janeiro – to be able to trace his whereabouts. He picked up the receiver, trying to suppress the pain in his stomach.

"Yes?"

"Mr Holcroft, this is the front desk, sir. We just wanted to make certain everything was satisfactory."

"Sure. Everything's fine."

"Well, not exactly fine," said the desk clerk.

"I beg your pardon?"

"We've just learned that your courtesy basket was not delivered in time.

We're dreadfully sorry. Will you be in your room for a while, sir?"

For God's sake, thought Noel. Millions upon millions were being held in Geneva and a desk clerk was concerned about a basket of fruit. "Yes, I'll be here."

"Very good, sir. The steward will be there shortly."

Holcroft replaced the phone, the pain in his stomach subsiding. His eyes fell on the telephone directory on the bottom shelf of the bedside table. He picked it up and turned the pages to the letter *T.*

There was an inch and a half of *Tennysons*, about fifteen names, no *John* but three Js. He'd start with those. He lifted up the phone and made the first call.

"Hello, John?"

The man on the line was Julian. The other two Js were women. There was a Helen Tennyson, not *Helden*. He dialled the number. An operator told him the phone was disconnected.

He turned the pages back to the letter B. There were six Beaumonts in London, none indicating any rank or affiliation with the Royal Navy. But there was nothing to lose; he picked up the phone and started dialling.

Before he finished the fourth call, there was a knock at the door; his basket of English courtesy had arrived. He swore at the interruption, put the phone down, and walked to the door, reaching into his pocket for some change.

Two men stood outside, neither in stewards' uniform, both in overcoats, each with hat in hand. The taller of the two was in his fifties, straight grey hair above a weathered face; the younger man was about Noel's age, with clear blue eyes, curly reddish hair, and a small scar on his forehead.

"Yes?"

"Mr Holcroft?"

"Yes."

"Noel Holcroft, United States citizen, passport number F-two-zero-four-seven-eight?"

"I'm Noel Holcroft. I've never memorized my passport number."

"May we come in, please?"

"I'm not sure. Who are you?"

Both men held black identification cases in their hands; they opened them unobtrusively. "British Military Intelligence, Five-branch," the older man said.

"Why do you want to see me?"

"Official business, sir. May we step inside?"

Noel nodded uncertainly, the pain returning to his stomach. Peter Baldwin, the man who had ordered him to *cancel Geneva*, had been with MI6. And Baldwin had been killed by the men of Wolfsschanze because he had interfered. Did these two British agents know the truth about Baldwin? Did they know Baldwin had *called* him? Oh, *God*, telephone numbers could be traced through hotel switchboards! They *had* to know! . . . Then Holcroft remembered: Baldwin had *not* called him; he had come to his apartment. Noel had called *him*.

You don't know what you're doing. I'm the only one who does.

If Baldwin was to be believed, he had said nothing to anyone. If so, where was the connection? Why was British Intelligence interested in an American named Holcroft? How did it know where to find him? *How?*

The two Englishmen entered. The younger, red-haired man walked to the bathroom, looked inside, then turned and went to the window. His older associate stood by the desk, his eyes scanning the walls, the floor, and the open closet.

"All right, you're inside," Noel said. "What is it?"

"The Tinamou, Mr Holcroft," said the grey-haired man.

"The what?"

"I repeat. The Tinamou."

"What the hell is that?"

"According to the OED, the Tinamou is a ground-dwelling bird whose protective colouring makes him indistinguishable from his background; whose short bursts of flight take him swiftly from one location to another."

"That's very enlightening, but I haven't the vaguest idea what you're talking about."

"We think you do," said the younger man.

"You're wrong. I've never heard of a bird like that, and don't know any reason why I should. Obviously you're referring to something else, but I don't make the connection."

"Obviously," interrupted the agent by the desk, "we're not referring to a bird. The Tinamou is a man; the name is quite applicable, however."

"It means nothing to me. Why should it?"

"May I give you some advice?" The older man spoke crisply, with an edge to his voice.

"Sure. I probably won't understand it anyway."

"You'd do far better co-operating with us than not. It's possible you're being used, but frankly we doubt it. However, if you help us now, we're prepared to assume that you *were* being used. I believe that's eminently fair."

"I was right," said Holcroft. "I don't understand you."

"Then let me clear up the details and perhaps you will. You've been making inquiries about John Tennyson, born Johann von Tiebolt, emigrant to the UK roughly six years ago. He is currently employed as a multilingual correspondent for *The Guardian*."

"The man at *The Guardian* desk," interrupted Noel. "He called you – or had someone call. That's why he stalled, why he went on the way he did, then cut me off. And that goddamned fruit; it was to make sure I didn't go out. What *is* this?"

"May we ask why you're trying to find John Tennyson?"

"No."

"You've stated, both here and in Rio de Janeiro, that a sum of money is involved . . ."

"*Rio de!* . . . Jesus!"

"That you're an 'intermediary'," continued the Englishman. That was the term you used."

"It's a confidential matter."

"We think it's an international one."

"Good God, why?"

"Because you're trying to deliver a sum of money. If the ground rules are followed, it amounts to three-quarters of the full payment."

"For what?"

"For an assassination."

"Assassination?"

"Yes. In the data banks of half the civilized world, the Tinamou has a single description. Assassin. Master assassin, to be precise. And we have every reason to believe that Johann von Tiebolt alias John Tennyson, is the Tinamou."

Noel was stunned. His mind raced furiously. An *assassin!* Good *God!* Was that what Peter Baldwin had been trying to tell him? That one of the Geneva inheritors was an assassin!

No one knows but me. Baldwin's words.

If they were true, under no condition could he reveal his real reason for wanting to find John Tennyson. Geneva would explode in controversy, the massive account frozen, thrown into the international courts, his covenant destroyed. He could not allow that to happen; he knew it now.

Yet on the other hand, it was equally vital that his reasons for seeking Tennyson be above suspicion, beyond any relationship to – or cognizance of – the Tinamou.

The Tinamou! An assassin! It was potentially the most damaging news possible. If there was any truth in what MI5 believed, the bankers in Geneva would suspend all discussions, close the vaults, and wait for another generation. Yet their actions would be for appearance, not for reality. If Tennyson *was* this Tinamou, he could be exposed, caught, severed from all association with the Geneva account, and the covenant would remain intact. Amends *would* be made, the men of Wolfsschanze assuaged, the killing stopped. According to the conditions of the document, the elder *sister* was the key, she was the oldest surviving child, not the brother.

An assassin! Oh, *God.*

First things first. Holcroft knew he had to dispel the convictions of the two men in his room. He walked unsteadily to a chair, sat down and leaned forward.

"Listen to me," he said, his voice weak in astonishment. "I've told you the truth. I don't know anything about any Tinamou, any assassin. My business is with the von Tiebolt *family*, not a particular member of the family. I was trying to find Tennyson because I was told he was von Tiebolt and worked at *The Guardian.* That's all there is to it."

"If so," said the red-haired man, "perhaps you'll explain the nature of your business."

Base the lie on an aspect of truth.

"I'll tell you what I can, which isn't a great deal. Some of it I pieced together myself from what I learned in Rio. It *is* confidential, and it *does* concern money." Noel took a deep breath, and reached for his cigarettes. "The von Tiebolts were left an inheritance – don't ask me by whom because I don't know and the lawyer won't say."

"What's the name of this lawyer?" asked the grey-haired man.

"I'd have to get his permission to tell you," answered Holcroft, lighting his cigarette, wondering who in New York he could call from an untraceable pay phone in London.

"We may ask you to do that," said the older agent. "Go on, please."

"I found out in Rio that the von Tiebolts were despised by the German community there. I have an idea – and it's only an idea – that somewhere along the line they opposed the Nazis in Germany, and someone, perhaps an anti-Nazi German – or Germans – left them the money."

"In America?" asked the red-haired man.

Noel sensed the trap and was prepared for it. *Be consistent.* "Obviously, whoever left the von Tiebolts money has been living there for a long time. If he – or they – came to the United States after the war, that presumes they had a clean bill of health. On the other hand, they could be relatives who came to the States years ago. I honestly don't know."

"Why were you chosen as the intermediary? You're not a lawyer."

"No, but the lawyer's a friend of mine," replied Holcroft. "He knows I travel a lot, knew I was going to Brazil for a client . . . I'm an architect. He asked me to call around, gave me some names, including Rio's immigration people."

Keep it simple, avoid complication.

"That was asking quite a bit of you, wasn't it?" The red-haired agent's disbelief was in his question.

"Not really. He's done me favours; I can do him one." Noel drew on his cigarette. "This is crazy. What started out as a simple . . . well, it's just crazy."

"You were told Johann von Tiebolt was John Tennyson and that he worked in London – or was based in London," said the older intelligence man, his hands in his overcoat pockets, looking down at Noel. "So, as a favour, you decided to make the trip from Brazil to the UK to find him. As a *favour* . . . Yes, Mr Holcroft, I'd say it was crazy."

Noel glared up at the grey-haired man. He remembered Sam Buonoventura's words. *I got hot myself . . . It's the only way to handle angry cops.*

"Now just a minute! I didn't make a special trip from Rio to London for the von Tiebolts. I'm on my way to Amsterdam. If you check my office in New York, you'll find out that I'm doing some work in Curaçao. For your benefit, it's Dutch, and I'm going to Amsterdam for design conferences."

The look in the older man's eyes seemed to soften. "I see," he said quietly. "It's quite possible we drew the wrong conclusions, but I think you'll agree the surface facts led us to them. We may owe you an apology."

Pleased with himself, Noel suppressed the urge to smile. He had adhered to the lessons, handled the lie with his guard up.

"It's okay," he replied. "But now I'm curious. This Tinamou. How do you know it's von Tiebolt?"

"We're not certain," replied the grey-haired agent. "We were hoping you'd provide that certainty. I think we were wrong about that."

"You certainly were. But why Tennyson? I guess I should tell the lawyer in New York . . ."

"No," interrupted the Englishman. "Don't do that. You must not discuss this with anyone."

"It's a little late for that, isn't it?" Holcroft said, gambling. "The 'matter' *has* been discussed. I'm under no obligation to you, but I do have an obligation to that lawyer. He's a friend."

Both MI5 men looked at each other, their mutual concern in the exchange.

"Beyond an obligation to a friend," the Englishman continued, "I suggest that you have a far greater responsibility. One that can be substantiated by your own government. This is a highly classified, intensely sensitive investigation. The Tinamou is an international killer. His victims include some of the world's most distinguished men."

"And you believe he's Tennyson?"

"The evidence is circumstantial, but very, very strong."

"Still not conclusive."

"Not conclusive."

"A few minutes ago you sounded positive."

"A few minutes ago we tried to trap you. It's merely a technique."

"It's damned offensive."

"It's damned effective," said the red-haired man.

"What's the circumstantial evidence against Tennyson?"

"Will you hold it in the strictest confidence?" asked the older agent. "That request can be transmitted by the highest law enforcement officials in your country, if you wish."

Holcroft paused. "All right, I won't call New York, I won't say anything. But I want information."

"We don't bargain." The younger man spoke offensively, cut off by a look from his associate.

"It's not a question of a bargain," said Noel. "I said I'd reach *a* member of the family and I think I should. Where can I contact Tennyson's sisters? One's married to a commander in the navy named Beaumont. The lawyer in New York knows that; he'll try to find her, if I don't. It might as well be me."

"Far better that it's you," agreed the grey-haired man. "We're convinced that neither woman is aware of her brother's activities. As near as we can determine the family is estranged from one another. How seriously, we don't know, but there's been little or no communication. Frankly, your showing up is a complication we'd rather not be saddled with. We don't want alarms raised; a controlled situation is infinitely preferable."

"There won't be any alarms," said Noel. "I'll deliver my message and go about my business."

"To Amsterdam?"

"To Amsterdam."

"Yes, of course. The older sister is married to Commander Anthony Beaumont; she's his second wife. They live near Portsmouth, several miles north of the naval base, in a suburb of Portsea. He's in the telephone directory. The younger girl recently moved to Paris. She's a translator for Gallimard Publishers, but she's not at the addresses listed with the company. We don't know where she lives."

Holcroft rose from the chair and walked between the two men to the desk. He picked up the hotel pen and wrote on a page of stationery.

"Anthony Beaumont, Portsmouth. Gallimard Publishers . . . How do you spell Gallimard?"

The red-haired agent told him.

Noel finished writing. "I'll make the calls in the morning and send a note to New York," he said, wondering to himself how long it would take to drive to Portsmouth. "I'll tell the lawyer I reached the sisters but was unable to contact the brother. Is that all right?"

"We couldn't persuade you to drop the entire matter?"

"No. I'd have to say why I dropped it and you don't want that."

"Very well. It's the best we can hope for then."

"Now, tell me why you think John Tennyson is this Tinamou. You owe me that."

The older man paused. "Perhaps we do," he said. "I reemphasize the classified nature of the information."

"Who would I tell it to? I'm not in your line of work."

"All right," said the grey-haired man. "As you say, we owe it to you. But you should know that the fact that you've been told gives us a certain insight. Very few people have been."

Holcroft stiffened; it wasn't difficult to convey his anger. "And I don't imagine too many have had men like you knock on their doors and been accused of paying off assassins. If this were New York, I'd haul you into court. You *do* owe me."

"Very well. A pattern was uncovered, at first too obvious to warrant examination until we studied the man. For several years, Tennyson consistently appeared in or near areas where assassinations took place. It was uncanny. He actually reported the events for *The Guardian*, filing his stories from the scene. A year or so ago, for example, he covered the killing of that American in Beirut, the embassy fellow who was, of course, CIA. Three days before he'd been in Brussels, suddenly he was in Teheran. We began to study him and what we learned was astonishing. We believe he's the Tinamou. He's utterly brilliant and, quite possibly, utterly mad."

"What did you find out?"

"For starters, you know about his father. One of the early Nazis, a butcher, of the worst sort . . ."

"Are you sure about that?" Noel asked the question too rapidly. "What I mean is, it doesn't necessarily follow . . ."

"No, I suppose it doesn't," completed the grey-haired agent. "But what does follow is, to say the least, unusual. Tennyson is a manic over-achiever. He completed two university degrees in Brazil by the time most students had barely matriculated. He mastered five languages, speaks them fluently. He was an extremely successful businessman in South America, amassing a great deal of money. These are hardly the credentials of a newspaper correspondent."

"People change, interests change. This *is* circumstantial. Pretty damned weak, too."

"The circumstances of his employment, however, lend strength to the conjecture," said the older man. "No one at *The Guardian* remembers when or how he was employed. His name simply appeared on the payroll computers one day, a week before his first copy was filed from Antwerp. No one had ever heard of him."

"Someone had to hire him."

"Yes, someone did. The man whose signature appeared on the interview and employment records was killed in a most unusual accident that took five lives on an underground train."

"A subway in London . . ." Holcroft paused. "I remember reading about that."

"A trainman's error they called it, but that's not good enough," added the red-haired man. "That man had eighteen years' experience. It was bloody well murder. Courtesy of the Tinamou."

"You can't be sure," said Holcroft. "An error's an error. What were some of the other . . . coincidences? Where the killings took place."

"I mentioned Beirut. There was Paris, too. A bomb went off under the French Minister of Labour's car in the rue de Bac, killing him instantly. Tennyson was in Paris; he'd been in Frankfurt the day before. Seven months ago, during the riots in Madrid, a government official was shot from a window four storeys above the crowds. Tennyson was in Madrid; he'd flown in from Lisbon only hours before. There are others; they go on."

"Did you ever bring him in and question him?"

"Twice. Not as a suspect obviously, but as an expert on the scene. Tennyson is the personification of arrogance. He claimed to have analysed the areas of social and political unrest, and followed his instincts, knowing that violence and assassination were certain to erupt in those places. He had the cheek to lecture us; said we should learn to anticipate and not so often be caught unawares."

"Could he be telling the truth?"

"If you mean that as an insult, it's noted. In light of this evening, perhaps we deserve it."

"Sorry. But when you consider his accomplishments, you've got to consider the possibility. Where's Tennyson now?"

"He disappeared four days ago in Bahrain. Our operatives are watching for him from Singapore to Athens."

The two MI5 men walked into the empty lift. The red-haired agent turned to his colleague.

"What do you make of him?" he asked.

"I don't know," was the soft-spoken reply. "We've given him enough to send him racing about; perhaps we'll learn something. He's far too much of an amateur to be a legitimate contact. Those paying for a killing would be fools to send the money with Holcroft. The Tinamou would reject it if they did."

"But he was lying."

"Quite so. Quite poorly."

"Then he's being used."

"Quite possibly. But for what?"

11

According to the car rental agency, Portmouth was roughly seventy miles from London, the roads clearly marked, the traffic not likely to be heavy. It was five past six. He could be in Portsea before 9.00, thought Noel, if he settled for a quick sandwich instead of dinner.

He had intended to wait until morning, but a telephone call made to confirm the accuracy of the MI5 information dictated otherwise. He reached Gretchen Beaumont, and what she told him convinced him to move quickly.

Her husband, the commander, was on sea duty in the Mediteranean; tomorrow at noon she was going on "winter holiday" to the south of France where she and the commander would spend a weekend together. If Mr Holcroft wished to see her about family matters, it would have to be tonight.

He told her he would get there as soon as possible, thinking as he hung up that she had one of the strangest voices he had ever heard. It was not the odd mixture of German and Portuguese in her accent, for that made sense; it was in the floating, hesitant quality of her speech. Hesitant or vacuous, it was difficult to tell. The commander's wife made it clear – if haltingly so – that in spite of the fact that the matters to be discussed were confidential, a naval aide would be in an adjoining room. Her concerns gave rise to an image of a middle-aged, self-indulgent *hausfrau* with an over-inflated opinion of her looks.

Sixty miles south of London, he realized that he was making better time than he had thought possible. There was little traffic and the sign on the road, reflected in the headlights, read:

Portsea – 15 M.

It was barely ten past eight. He could slow down and try to collect his thoughts. Gretchen Beaumont's directions had been clear; he'd have no trouble finding the residence.

For a vacuous-sounding woman, Gretchen Beaumont had been very specific when it came to giving instructions. It was somehow contradictory in light of the way she spoke, as if sharp lines of reality had suddenly, abruptly shot through clouds of mist.

It told him nothing. He was the intruder, the stranger who telephoned and spoke of a vitally important matter he would not define – could not define except in person.

How *would* he define it? How could he explain to the middle-aged wife of a British naval officer that she was the key that could unlock a vault containing 780 million dollars?

He was getting nervous; it was no way to be convincing. Above all, he had to be convincing; he could not appear afraid or unsure or artificial. And then it occurred to him that he could tell her the truth – as Heinrich Clausen saw the truth. It was the best lever he had; it was the ultimate conviction.

Oh, *God!* Please make her *understand!*

He made the two left turns off the highway and drove rapidly through the peaceful, tree-lined suburban area for the prescribed mile and a half. He found the house easily, parked in front, and got out of the car.

He opened the gate and walked up the path to the door. There was no bell; instead there was a brass knocker and so he tapped it gently. The house was designed simply. Wide windows in the living room, small ones on the opposite bedroom side, the façade old brick above a stone foundation – solid, built to last, certainly not ostentatious and probably not expensive. He had designed such houses, usually as second homes on the shore for couples still unsure they could afford them. It was the ideal residence for a military man on a military budget. Neat, trim, and manageable.

Gretchen Beaumont opened the door herself. Whatever image she had evoked on the telephone vanished at the sight of her; it disappeared in a rush of amazement, with the impact of a blow to his stomach. Simply put, the woman in the doorway was one of the most beautiful he had ever seen in his life. The fact that she was a woman was almost secondary. She was like a statue, a sculptor's ideal, refined over and over again in clay before chisel was put to stone. She was of medium height with long blonde hair that framed a face of finely boned, perfectly proportioned features. Too perfect, too much in the sculptor's mind . . . too cold. Yet the coldness was lessened by her large, wide eyes; they were light blue and inquisitive, neither friendly nor unfriendly.

"Mr Holcroft?" she asked in that echoing, dreamlike voice that gave evidence of Germany and Brazil.

"Yes, Mrs Beaumont. Thank you so much for seeing me. I apologize for the inconvenience."

"Come in, please."

She stepped back to admit him. In the doorway he had concentrated on her face, on the extraordinary beauty that was in no way diminished by the years; it was impossible now not to notice the body, emphasized by her translucent dress. The body, too, was extraordinary, but in a different way from the face. There was no coldness, only heat. The sheer dress clung to her skin, the absence of a brassiere apparent, accentuated by a flared collar, unbuttoned to the midpoint between her large breasts. On either side, in the centre of the swelling flesh, he could see her nipples clearly, pressing against the soft fabric as if aroused.

When she moved, the slow, fluid motion of her thighs and stomach and pelvis combined into the rhythm of a sensual dance. She did not walk, she glided, an extraordinary body screaming for observation as a prelude to invasion and satisfaction.

Yet the face was cold and the eyes distant; inquisitive but distant. And Noel was perplexed.

"You've had a long trip," she said, indicating a couch against the far wall. "Sit down, please. May I offer you a drink?"

"I'd appreciate it."

"What would you care for?" She held her place in front of him, momentarily blocking his short path to the couch, her light blue eyes looking intently into his. Her breasts were revealed clearly – so close – beneath the sheer fabric. The nipples were taut, rising with each breath, again in that unmistakable rhythm of a sexual dance.

"Scotch, if you have it," he said.

"In England that's whisky, isn't it?" she asked, walking towards a bar against the wall.

"It's whiskey," he said, sinking into the soft pillows of the couch, trying to concentrate on Gretchen's face. It was difficult for him, and he knew she was trying to make it difficult. The commander's wife did not have to provoke a sexual reaction; she did not have to dress for the part. But dress for it she had, and provoke she did. Why?

She brought over his scotch. He reached for it, touching her hand as he did so, noting that she did not withdraw from the contact, but instead briefly pressed his curved fingers with her own. She then did a very strange thing; she sat down on a leather hassock only feet away and looked up at him.

"Won't you join me?" he asked.

"I don't drink."

"Then perhaps you'd prefer that I don't."

She laughed throatily. "I have no moral objections whatsoever. It would hardly become an officer's wife. I'm simply not capable of drinking or of smoking, actually. Both go directly to my head."

He looked at her over the rim of the glass. Her eyes remained eerily on his, unblinking, steady, still distant, making him wish she'd look away.

"You said on the phone that one of your husband's aides would be in an adjoining room. Would you like us to meet?"

"He wasn't able to be here."

"Oh? I'm sorry."

"Are you?"

It was *crazy*. The woman was behaving like a courtesan unsure of her standing, or a high-priced whore evaluating a new client's wallet. She leaned forward on the hassock, picking at an imaginary piece of lint on the throw rug beneath his feet. The gesture was foolish, the effect too obvious. The top of her dress parted, exposing her breasts. She could not have been unaware of what she was doing. He had to respond; she expected it. But he would not respond in the way she anticipated. A father had cried out to him; nothing could interfere. Even an unlikely whore.

101

An unlikely whore who was the key to Geneva.

"Mrs Beaumont," he said, placing his glass awkwardly on the small table next to the couch, "you're a very gracious woman and I'd like nothing better than to sit here for hours and have a few drinks, but we've got to talk. I asked to see you because I have extraordinary news for you. It concerns the two of us."

"The two of *us?*" said Gretchen, emphasizing the pronoun. "By all means talk, Mr Holcroft. I've never met you before; I don't know you. How can this news concern the two of us?"

"Our fathers knew each other years ago."

At the mention of the word "father" the woman stiffened. "I have no father."

"You had, so did I," he said. "In Germany over thirty years ago. Your name's von Tiebolt. You're the oldest child of Wilhelm von Tiebolt."

Gretchen took a deep breath and looked away. "I don't think I want to listen further."

"I know how you feel," replied Noel. "I had the same reaction myself. But you're wrong. *I* was wrong."

"Wrong?" she asked, brushing away the long blonde hair that swung across her cheek with the swift turn of her head. "You're presumptuous. Perhaps you didn't live the way we lived. Please don't tell me I'm wrong. You're in no position to do that."

"Just let me tell you what I've learned. When I'm finished, you can make your own decision. Your knowing is the important thing. And your support, of course."

"Support of what? Knowing what?"

Noel felt oddly moved, as if what he was about to say were the most important words of his life. With a normal person the truth would be sufficient, but Gretchen Beaumont was not a normal person; her scars were showing. It would take more than truth; it would take enormous conviction.

"Two weeks ago I flew to Geneva to meet a banker named Manfredi . . ."

He told her it all, leaving out nothing save the men of Wolfsschanze. He told it simply, even eloquently, hearing the conviction in his own voice, feeling the profound commitment in his mind, the stirrings of pain in his chest.

He gave her the figures: *seven hundred and eighty million* for the survivors of the Holocaust, and the descendants of those survivors still in need. Everywhere. *Two million* for each of the surviving oldest children to be used as they saw fit. Six months – possibly longer – of a collective commitment.

Finally, he told her of the pact in death the three fathers made, taking their lives only after every detail in Geneva was confirmed and iron-bound.

When he had finished, he felt the sweat rolling down his forehead. "It's up to us now," he said. "And a man in Berlin, Kessler's son. The three of us have to finish what they started."

"It all sounds so incredible," she said quietly. "But I really don't see why it should concern me."

He was stunned at her calm, at her complete equanimity. She had listened to him in silence for nearly half an hour, heard revelations that had to be shattering to her, yet she displayed no reaction whatsoever. *Nothing*. "Haven't you understood a *word* I've said?"

"I understand that you're very upset," said Gretchen Beaumont in her soft, echoing voice. "But I've been very upset for most of my life, Mr Holcroft. I've been that way because of Wilhelm von Tiebolt. He is nothing to me."

"He *knew* that, can't you see? He tried to make up for it."

"With money?"

"More than money."

Gretchen leaned forward and slowly reached out to touch his forehead. Her fingers extended, she wiped away the beads of perspiration. Noel remained still, unable to break the contact between their eyes.

"Did you know that I was Commander Beaumont's second wife?" she said.

"Yes, I heard that."

"The divorce was a difficult time for him. And for me, of course, but more so for him. But it passed for him; it will not pass for me."

"What do you mean?"

"I'm the intruder. The foreigner. A breaker of marriages. He has his work, he goes to sea; I live among those who don't. The life of a naval officer's wife is a lonely one in usual circumstances. It can become quite difficult when the circumstances are not usual, when one is ostracized."

"You must have known there'd be a degree of that."

"Of course."

"Well, if you knew it? . . ." He left the question suspended, not grasping the point.

"Why did I marry Commander Beaumont? Is that what you mean to ask?"

He did not want to ask *anything!* thought Holcroft. He was not interested in the intimate details of Gretchen Beaumont's life. Geneva was all that mattered, the covenant everything. But he needed her co-operation; there was nothing without it.

"I assume the reasons were emotional; that's generally why people get married. I only meant that you might have taken steps to lessen the tension. You could live farther away from the naval base, have different friends." He was rambling, awkwardly, a little desperately. He only wanted to break through her maddening reserve.

"My question's more interesting. Why did I marry Beaumont?" Her voice floated again; it rose quietly in the air. "You're right, it's emotional. Quite basic."

She touched his forehead once more, her dress parting once more as she leaned forward, her lovely naked breasts exposed again. Noel was tired and aroused and angry. He *had* to make her understand that her private concerns were meaningless beside Geneva! To do that she had to like him; yet he could not touch her.

"Naturally it's basic," he said. "You love him."

"I loathe him."

What was she trying to say? Her hand was now inches from his face, her fingers a blur at the corner of his eyes – a blur because their eyes were locked; he dared not shift them. And he dared not touch her.

"Then why did you marry him? Why do you stay with him?"

"I told you. It's basic. Commander Beaumont has a little money; he's a highly respected officer in the service of his government, a dull, uninteresting man more at home on a ship than anywhere else. All this adds up to a very quiet, very secure niche. I am in a comfortable cocoon."

There was the lever! Geneva provided it. "Two million dollars could build a very secure cocoon, Mrs Beaumont. A far better shelter than you have here."

"Perhaps. But I would have to leave this one in order to built it. I'd have to go outside."

"Only for a while."

"And what would happen?" she continued, as if he had not interrupted. "Outside? Where I'd have to say yes or no. I don't want to think about that; it would be so difficult. You know, Mr Holcroft, I've been unhappy most of my life, but I don't look for sympathy."

She was infuriating! He felt like slapping her. "I'd like to return to the situation in Geneva," he said.

She settled back into the hassock, crossing her legs. The sheer dress rose above her knees, the soft flesh of her thigh revealed. The pose was seductive; her words were not.

"But I have returned to it," she said. "Perhaps awkwardly, but I'm trying to explain. As a child I came out of Berlin. Always running, until my mother and my brother and I found a sanctuary in Brazil that proved to be a hell for us. I've floated through life these past years. I've followed – instincts, opportunities, men – but I've followed. I haven't led. I've made as few decisions as possible."

"I don't understand."

"If you have business that concerns my family, you'll have to talk to my brother Johann. He makes the decisions. He brought us out of South America after my mother died. He is the von Tiebolt you must reach."

Noel suppressed his desire to yell at her. Instead, he exhaled silently, a sense of weariness and frustration sweeping over him. Johann von Tiebolt was the one member of the family he had to avoid, but he could not tell Gretchen Beaumont why. "Where is he?" he asked rhetorically.

"I don't know. He works for *The Guardian* newspaper in Europe."

"Where in Europe?"

"Again, I have no idea. He moves around a great deal."

A ground-dwelling bird . . . indistinguishable from his background; whose short bursts of flight take him swiftly from one location to another.

"I was told he was last seen in Bahrain."

"Then you know more than I do."

"You have a sister."

"Helden. In Paris. Somewhere."

All the children will be examined . . . decisions made.

Johann had been examined and a judgement made – rightly or wrongly – that disqualified him from Geneva. He was a complication they could not afford; he would draw attention where none could be permitted. And this strange, beautiful woman on the hassock – even if she felt differently – would be rejected by Geneva as incompetent. It was as simple as that.

Paris. Helden von Tiebolt.

Noel reached for his cigarettes, his thoughts now on an unknown woman who worked as a translator for a publishing house in Paris. He was only vaguely aware of the movement in front of him, so complete was his concentration. Then he noticed and he stared at Gretchen Beaumont as he had when he first saw her in the doorway. Speechless.

The commander's wife had risen from the hassock and had unfastened the buttons of her dress to the waist. Slowly she parted the folds of silk. Her breasts were released; they sprang out at him, the nipples taut, stretched, swollen with tension. She raised her skirt with both hands, bunching it above her thighs, and stood directly in front of him. He was aware of the fragrance that seemed to emanate from her entire body. It was a delicate perfume with a sensuousness that was as provoking as the sight of her exposed flesh. She sat down beside him, her dress now above her waist, her body trembling. She moaned and reached for the back of his neck, drawing his face to hers, his lips to hers. Her mouth opened as she received his mouth; she sucked, breathing rapidly, her warm breath mixed with the juices that came from her throat. She put her hand on his trousers and groped for his penis . . . hard, soft, hard. *Harder.* She became suddenly uncontrollable; her moans were feverish. She pressed into him. Everywhere.

Her parted lips slid off his mouth and she whispered. "Tomorrow I go to the Mediterranean. To a man I loathe. Don't say anything. Just give me tonight. Give me *tonight!*"

She moved away slightly, her mouth glistening, her eyes so wide they seemed manic. Slowly, she rose above him, her white skin everywhere. The trembling subsided. She slid a naked leg over his and got to her feet. She pulled his face into her waist and reached for his hand. He stood up, embracing her. She held his hand in hers, and together they walked towards the door of the bedroom. As they went inside, he heard the words, spoken in that eerie, echoing monotone.

"Johann said a man would come one day and talk of a strange arrangement. I was to be nice to him and remember everything he said."

12

Holcroft awoke with a start, for several seconds not sure where he was; then he remembered. Gretchen Beaumont had led him into the bedroom with the incredible statement. He had tried to press her, tried to learn what else her brother said, but she was in no state to answer clearly. She was in a frenzy, needing the sex desperately; she could concentrate on nothing else.

They had made love maniacally, she the aggressor, writhing on the bed at fever pitch, beneath him, above him, beside him. She'd been insatiable; no amount of exploration and penetration could gratify her. At one point she had screamed, clasping her legs around his waist, her fingers digging into his shoulders long after he was capable of response. And then his exhaustion had caught up with him. He'd fallen into a deep but troubled sleep.

Now he was awake and he did not know what had interrupted that sleep. There'd been a noise, not loud, but sharp and penetrating, but he did not know what it was or where it came from.

Suddenly, he realized he was alone in the bed. He raised his head. The room was dark, the door closed, a dim line of light at the bottom.

"Gretchen? . . ." There was no reply; no one else was in the room.

He threw the covers off and got out of the bed, steadying his weakened legs, feeling drained, disorientated. He lurched for the door and yanked it open. Beyond, in the small living room a single table lamp was on, its light casting shadows against the walls and the floor.

There was the noise again! A metallic sound that echoed throughout the house, but it did not come from inside the house. He ran to a living-room window and peered through the glass. Under the spill of a street-lamp he could see the figure of a man standing by the bonnet of his rented car, a flashlight in his hand.

Before he knew what was happening, he heard a muffled voice from somewhere else outside, and the beam of light shot up at the window. At him. Instinctively, he pulled his hand up to shield his eyes. The light went out and he saw the man race towards a car parked diagonally across the street. He had not noticed that car, his concentration so complete on his own and on the unknown man with the flashlight. Now he tried to focus on this car; there was a figure in the front seat. He could not distinguish anything but the outline of the head and shoulders.

The running man reached the door on the street side, pulled it open, and climbed in behind the wheel. The engine roared; the car shot forward, then skidded into a U-turn before it sped away.

Briefly, in the wash of light from the street-lamp, Noel saw the person in the seat next to the driver. For less than a second the face in the window was no more than twenty yards away, racing by.

It was Gretchen Beaumont. Her eyes stared ahead through the windscreen, her head nodding as if she were talking rapidly.

Several lights went on in various houses across from the Beaumont residence. The roar of the engine and the screeching of the tyres had been a sudden, unwelcomed intrusion on the peaceful street of Portsea. Concerned faces appeared in the windows, peering outside.

Holcroft stepped back. He was naked, and he realized that a naked man seen in Commander Beaumont's living room in the middle of the night while Commander Beaumont was away was not to anyone's advantage, least of all his own.

Where had she gone? What was she doing? What was the sound he had heard?

There was no time to think about such things; he had to get away from the Beaumont house. He turned from the window and ran back to the bedroom, adjusting his eyes to the dim light, trying to find a light switch or a lamp. He remembered that in the frenzy of their lovemaking, Gretchen had swung her hand above his head into the shade of the bedside light, sending it to the floor. He knelt down and found it. It was on its side, the bulb protected by the linen shade surrounding it. He snapped it on. Light filled the room, its spill washing up from the floor. There were elongated shadows and patches of darkness, but he could see his clothes. They were draped over an armchair, his socks and shorts by the bed.

He stood up and dressed as rapidly as he could; where was his jacket? He looked about, remembering vaguely that Gretchen had slipped it off his arms and dropped it near the door. Yes, there it was. He walked across the room towards it, glancing briefly at his reflection in the large mirror above the bureau.

He froze, his eyes riveted on a photograph in a silver frame on the bureau. It was of a man in naval uniform.

The *face*. He had seen it before. Not long ago, weeks . . . *days*, perhaps. He was not sure from where, but he was certain he *knew that face. He* walked to the bureau and studied the photograph. There was something about the face that triggered a memory.

It was the eyebrows! They were odd, different; they stood out as an entity in themselves . . . like an incongruous cornice above an undefined tapestry. They were heavy, a thick profusion of black-and-white hair interwoven into a mass of . . . salt and pepper. *Salt-and-pepper-eyebrows.* Eyes that blinked open suddenly, sleep interrupted; eyes that stared up at him. He remembered!

The plane to Rio de Janeiro! He had stumbled out of the lounge of the 747 and down the winding staircase with fear. The realization had been made clear to him: an ampoule of strychnine given to another a week before had been meant for *him.* His terror had been such that he knew he would vomit; he had to find the lavatory. He had parted the curtains and seen the face that was now the photograph in his hands. The same face, the same thick black-and-white eyebrows.

And something else. The face at that moment on the plane to Brazil prodded another memory – a memory of violence. But it was clouded, obscure; there was no definition. A blurred racing figure was all he recalled.

Noel turned the silver frame over and clawed at the surface until he loosened the backing. He slid it out of the groove and removed the photograph. He saw minute indentations on the glossy surface; he turned it over. There was writing. He held it up to catch the light, and for a moment stopped breathing. The words were in German.

Neuaurbau oder Tod

Like the face in the picture, he'd seen them before! But they were meaningless to him; German words that meant nothing . . . yet he had seen them!

Bewildered, he folded the photograph and stuffed it into his trouser pocket.

He opened a closet door, shoved the silver frame between folded clothes on the shelf, picked up his jacket, and went into the living room. He knew he should get out of the house as fast as he could, but his curiosity about the man in the photograph consumed him. He had to know *something* about him.

There were two doors in the near and far walls of the living room. One was open and led to the kitchen; the other was closed. He opened it and walked into the commander's study. He turned on a light; photographs of ships and men were everywhere, along with citations and military decorations. Commander Beaumont was a career officer of no mean standing. A bitter divorce followed by a questionable marriage may have created messy personal problems for the man, but the Royal Navy obviously overlooked them in the officer. The latest citation was only six weeks old, for outstanding leadership in coastal patrols off the Balearic Islands during a week of gale-force seas.

A cursory look at the papers on the desk and in the drawers added nothing. Two bank books showed accounts in four figures, neither over three thousand pounds; a letter from his former wife's solicitor demanded property in Scotland; there were assorted copies of ship's logs and sailing schedules.

Holcroft wanted to stay in that room a while longer, to look more thoroughly for clues to the strange man with the odd eyebrows, but he knew he dared not. He had already tested the situation beyond reason; he had to get out.

He left the house and looked across the way, up to the windows that only minutes ago had been filled with lights and curious faces. There were no lights now, no faces; sleep had returned to Portsea. He walked rapidly down the path and swung the gate open, annoyed that the hinges squeaked. He opened the door of the rented car, and quickly got behind the wheel. He turned the key in the ignition.

Nothing. He turned it again. And again and again. Nothing! Absolutely nothing!

He released the bonnet and raced to the front of the car, not worried about the noise; worried about something far more serious. There was no reason for the rented car's battery to be worn down, but even if it were, there would still be a faint click in the ignition. The light of the street-lamp spread over the exposed engine, showing him what he was afraid he might find.

The wires were cut, severed at their source with a surgeon's precision. No amount of simple splicing would start the car; it would have to be towed away.

And if it had to be towed away, whoever was responsible knew that an American would be without means of travel in an unfamiliar area in the middle of the night. If there were taxis in this outlying suburb it was doubtful they'd be available at that hour; it was past 3.00. Whoever immobilized the car wanted him to remain where he was; it had to follow that others would come after him. He had to run. As far and as fast as he could . . . reach the highway . . . hitch a ride north out of the area.

He closed the bonnet. The sharp, metallic noise echoed throughout the street. He was grateful it had done so before.

He started up the block towards the traffic light; it was not operating now. Crossing the intersection, he began walking faster, then broke into a run. He tried to pace himself; there was a mile and a half before he reached the highway. He was sweating and he could feel the knot in his stomach forming again.

He saw the lights before he heard the furious pitch of the engine. Up ahead, directly ahead on the straight road, the glare of headlights came out of the darkness, drawing closer so rapidly that the car had to be travelling at tremendous speed.

Noel saw an opening to his right, a space between a line of waist-high privet hedge, an entrance to another path to another doorway. He dived through it and rolled into the dirt beneath the shrubbery, wondering if he'd been seen. It was suddenly very important to him not to be involved with Gretchen Beaumont. She was a dismissible enigma, an unhappy, highly erotic . . . beautiful woman. But in herself a threat to Geneva, as was her brother.

The approaching car raced by. He had not been seen. Then the sound of the roaring motor was replaced by the screeching of tyres. Holcroft crawled halfway through the break in the hedge, his face turned to his left, his eyes focused on the block behind him.

The car had stopped directly in front of Beaumont's house. Two men leaped from it and raced up the path. Noel could hear the squeaking of the gate hinges. There was no point in remaining where he was; it was the moment to run. Now he heard the tapping of the door knocker a hundred yards away.

He moved to his right on his hands and knees along the pavement by a privet hedge, until he was in the shadows between the streetlamps. He got to his feet and ran.

He kept running straight ahead up the dark, tree-lined street, block after block, corner after corner, hoping to God he would recognize the first turn to the highway when he came to it. He swore at cigarettes as his breath became shorter and turned into pain-filled gasps; sweat poured down his face and the pounding in his chest became intolerable. The rapid cracks of his own footsteps on the pavement frightened him. It was the sound of a man running in panic in the middle of the night, and that man in panic was himself.

Footsteps. *Racing* footsteps. They were his but *more* than his! Behind him, steady, heavy, gaining on him. There was someone running after him! Someone running in silence, not calling his name, not shouting, not demanding that he stop! . . . Or was his hearing playing tricks on him? The hammering in his chest vibrated throughout his entire body; were his footsteps echoing in his ears? He dared not turn, *could* not turn. He was going too fast – into light, into shadow.

He came to the end of yet another block, to another corner, and turned right, knowing it was not the first of the turns that would take him to the highway, but turning anyway. He had to know if his hearing was true, if there was someone, something, behind him. He raced into the street.

The footsteps *were* there, the rhythm different, not his own, closer, ever closer, shortening the distance between them. He could stand it no longer, nor could he run any faster. He twisted his waist, trying to look over his shoulder.

It was there; *he* was there! The figure of a man silhouetted in the light of a streetlamp on the corner. A stocky man, running in silence, shortening the gap, only yards away.

His legs aching, Noel hammered his feet on the surface in a final burst of speed. He turned again, his panic complete.

And his legs gave out, tangled in the chaos and the terror of the chase. He plunged headlong into the street, his face scraping the asphalt, his extended hands ice-like and stinging. He twisted over on to his back, instinctively raising his feet to ward off his assailant – the silent, racing figure that shot out of the darkness and was suddenly over him.

Everything was a blur, only the thrashing outlines of arms and legs silhouetted in the darkness penetrated his sweat-filled eyes. And then he was pinned. An enormous weight was crushing his chest, a forearm – like a heavy iron bar – was across his throat, choking off all sound.

The last thing he saw was a hand raised high, a dark claw in the night sky, a curved hand that held an object in it. And then there wasn't anything. Only a huge chasm filled with wind. He was falling towards unseen depths in darkness.

He felt the cold first. It made him shiver. Then the dampness; it was every-where. He opened his eyes to distorted images of grass and dirt. He was surrounded by wet grass and mounds of cold earth. He rolled over, grateful to see the night sky; it was lighter to his left, darker at his right.

His head ached, his face stung, his hands were in pain. Slowly he raised himself and looked around. He was in a field, a long flat stretch of ground that appeared to be a pasture. In the distance he could see the faint outlines of a wire fence – barbed wire strung between thick posts ten or fifteen yards apart. It *was* a pasture.

He smelled cheap whisky or rancid wine.

His clothes were drenched with it, his shirt sopping wet, sending the awful fumes into his nostrils. His *clothes* . . . his wallet, his money! He rose unsteadily to his feet and checked his pockets, both hands stinging as he plunged them into the moist cloth.

His wallet, his money clip with the bills in it, his watch . . . all were there. He had not been robbed, only beaten unconscious and taken away from the area where the Beaumonts lived. It was crazy!

He felt his head. A bump had formed, but the skin was not broken. He had been hit with some kind of padded blackjack or pipe. He took several awkward steps; he could move and that was all that mattered. And he could see more clearly now; it would be morning soon.

Beyond the fence there was a slight rise in the ground, forming a ridge that extended as far as he could see in both directions. Along the ridge he saw highway lights. He started across the field towards the fence and the ridge and the highway, hoping to convince a driver to give him a ride. As he climbed over the fence, a thought suddenly occurred to him. He checked his pockets again.

The photograph was gone!

A milk truck stopped and he climbed in, watching the smile of the driver fade abruptly as the stench filled the cab. Noel tried to make light of it: a predicament brought on by an innocent American having been taken in by some very sharp British sailors in Portsmouth – *base the lie on an aspect of truth* – but the driver found nothing amusing. Holcroft got out at the first town.

It was an English village, the Tudor architecture of the square marred by a profusion of delivery trucks in front of a coffee house.

"There's a telephone inside," said the milkman. "And a gents room, too. A wash would do you no harm."

Noel walked into the sight and sounds of the early morning lorry-drivers, the smell of hot coffee somehow reassuring. The world went on; deliveries were made and small comforts accepted without particular notice. He found the washroom, and did what he could to minimize the effects of the night. Then he sat in a booth next to the pay telephone on the wall and had black coffee, waiting for an angry driver to conclude an argument with an obviously angrier dispatcher on the other end of the line. When the call was finished, Noel got out of the booth and went to the phone, Gretchen Beaumont's telephone number in his hand. There was nothing else to do but try to find out what had happened, try to reason with her, if, indeed, she had returned.

He dialled.

"Beaumont residence." A male voice was on the line.

"Mrs Beaumont, please."

"May I ask who's calling?"

"A friend of the commander. I heard Mrs Beaumont was leaving today to join him. I'd like her to take a message to him."

"Who is this, please?"

Noel replaced the receiver. He did not know who had answered the phone, he knew only that he needed help. Professional help. It was possibly dangerous for Geneva to seek it, but it was necessary. He would be cautious – very cautious – and learn what he could.

He rummaged through his jacket pockets for the card given him by the MI5 man at the Belgravia Arms. There was only a name, Harold Payton-Jones, and a telephone number. The clock on the coffee house wall read ten minutes to seven; Noel wondered if anyone would answer the phone. He placed the call to London.

"Yes?" There was only the single word of greeting.

"This is Holcroft."

"Oh, yes. We wondered if you'd ring up."

Noel recognized the voice. It was the grey-haired intelligence agent from the hotel. "What are you talking about?"

"You've had a difficult night," the voice said.

"You *expected* me to call! You were there. You were watching!"

Payton-Jones did not respond directly. "The rented car's at a garage in Aldershot. It should be repaired by noon. The name's easily remembered; it's Boots. Boots Garage, Aldershot. There'll be no charge, no bill, no receipt."

"Wait a minute! What the hell is this? You had me followed! You had no right to do that."

"I'd say it was a damned good thing we did."

"You were in that car at three o'clock this morning! You went into Beaumont's house!"

"I'm afraid we weren't and we didn't." The MI5 man paused briefly. "And if you believe that, then you didn't get a very good look at them, did you?"

"No. Who were they?"

"I wish we knew. Our man got there closer to five."

"Who ran after me? Who bashed my head in and left me in that goddamned field?"

Again the agent paused. "We don't know anything about that. We only knew you had left. In a hurry, obviously, your car immobilized."

"It was a set-up! I was the pigeon!"

"Quite so. I'd advise you to be more cautious. It's both tasteless and dangerous to take advantage of the wife of a commander in the Royal Navy while her husband's at sea."

"Bullshit! The commander's no more at sea than I am! He's got something to do with the von Tiebolts."

"Most assuredly," replied Payton-Jones. "He married the oldest daughter. But he's been in the Mediterranean for the past three months."

"No! I *saw* him on an aircraft two weeks ago! Listen to me, there was a photograph in the bedroom. I took it. It was him! And something else. There was writing on the back. In German."

"What did it say?"

"I don't know. I don't speak German. But it's goddamned unusual, don't you think?" Holcroft stopped. He had not meant to go this far. In his anger, he had lost his control. *Goddamn it!*

"What's unusual?" asked the agent. "German is Mrs Beaumont's native tongue; the family's spoken it for years. An endearing phrase, words of devotion to or from her new husband? Not unusual at all."

"I guess you're right," said Noel, backing off. Then he realized he had retreated too quickly. The MI5 man was suspicious; Noel could sense it in his next words.

"On second thought, perhaps you should bring the photograph to us."

"I can't. I don't have it."

"I thought you said you took it."

"I don't have it now. I . . . I just don't have it."

"Where are you, Holcroft? I think you should drop in and see us."

Without consciously making the decision, Noel pressed down the lever, severing the connection. The act preceded the thought, but once done he understood clearly why he did it. He could not ally himself with MI5; he could not solidify any relationship whatsoever. On the contrary, he had to get as far away from British Intelligence as was possible. There could be no association at *all*. MI5 had *followed* him. After they had told him they would leave him alone, they had gone back on their word.

The survivors of Wolfsschanze had spelled it out. *There are those who may learn of the work in Geneva . . . who will try to stop you, deceive you . . . kill you.*

Holcroft doubted that the British would kill him, but they *were* trying to stop him. If they succeeded, it was as good as killing him. The men of Wolfsschanze did not hesitate. *Peter Baldwin, Esq. Ernst Manfredi. Jack.* All dead.

The men of Wolfsschanze would kill him if he failed. And that was the terrible irony. He did *not want* to fail. Why couldn't they understand that? Perhaps more than the survivors of Wolfsschanze, he wanted to see Heinrich Clausen's wish realized.

He thought of Gretchen Beaumont, follower of instincts, opportunities, and men. And of her brother the arrogant, brilliant multilingual newspaperman who was suspected of being an assassin. Neither would be remotely acceptable to Geneva.

There was one child left. Helden von Tiebolt – now Helden Tennyson – currently living in Paris. Address unknown. But he had a name. Gallimard.

Paris.

He had to get to Paris. He had to elude MI5.

13

There was a man in London, a stage designer who'd had a brief vogue among the wealthy on both sides of the Atlantic as a decorator. Noel suspected that Willie Ellis was more often hired for his outrageous personality and his talents as a raconteur than for any intrinsic abilities as an interior decorator. He had worked with Willie on four occasions, for the truth of the matter was that Noel liked Willie immensely. The mad Englishman was not all artifice and elegance. Underneath, in quiet moments, there was a thinking, talented man of the theatre who knew more about the history of design than anyone Holcroft had ever met. He could be fascinating.

When he was not outrageous.

They had kept in touch over the years and whenever Noel was in London there was always time for Willie. He had not thought there would be this trip; that was changed now. He needed Willie. He got the number from London information and dialled.

"Noel, my friend, you're out of your mind! No one's up but those stinking birds and street-cleaners."

"I'm in trouble, Willie. I need help."

Ellis knew the small village where Holcroft was calling from and promised to be there as soon as he could, which he estimated to be something close to an hour. He arrived thirty minutes late, cursing the idiots on the road. Noel climbed into the car.

"You're an absolute mess and you smell like a barmaid's armpit. Keep the window open and tell me what the hell happened."

Holcroft kept the explanation simple, giving no names and obscuring the facts. "I have to get to Paris and there are people who want to stop me. I can't tell you much more than that except to say that I haven't done anything wrong, anything illegal."

"The first is always relative, isn't it? And the second is generally subject to interpretation and a good barrister. Shall I presume a lovely girl and an irate husband?"

"That's fine."

"That keeps me clean. What stops you from going to the airport and taking the next plane to Paris?"

"My clothes, briefcase and passport are at my hotel in London. If I go there to get them the people who want to stop me will find me."

"From the looks of you, they're quite serious, aren't they?"

"Yes. That's about it, Willie."

"The solution's obvious," said Ellis. "I'll get your things and check you out. You're a wayward colonial I found in a Soho gutter. Who's to argue with my preferences?"

"There may be a problem with the front desk."

"I can't imagine why. My money's coin of the realm, and you'll give me a note; they can match signatures. We're nowhere near as paranoid as our cousins across the sea."

"I hope you're right, but I've got an idea the clerks have been reached by the people who want to find me. They may insist on knowing where I am before they let you have my things."

"Then I'll tell them," said Willie, smiling. "I'll leave them a forwarding address and a telephone number where your presence can be confirmed."

"What?"

"Leave it to me. By the way, there's some cologne in the glove compartment. For Christ's sake, use it."

Ellis made arrangements for the whisky-soaked clothes to be picked up by the cleaners and returned by mid-afternoon, then left the Chelsea flat for the Belgravia Arms Hotel.

Holcroft showered, shaved, put the soiled clothes in a hamper outside the door, and called the car rental agency. He reasoned that if he went for the car in Aldershot, MI5 would be there. And when he drove away, the British would not be far behind.

The rental agency was not amused, but neither did it have a choice. If it wanted its automobile back, it would have to pick it up itself. Noel was sorry, but there was an emergency; the bill could be sent to his office in New York.

He had to get out of England with as little notice as possible. Undoubtedly, MI5 would have the airports and the Channel boats watched. Perhaps the solution was to be found in a last-minute ticket on a crowded plane to Paris. With any luck, he'd reach Orly Airport before MI5 knew he had left England. The shuttles to Paris were frequent, the customs procedures lax. Or he could buy two tickets, one to Amsterdam, one to Paris . . . go through the KLM gates, then on some pretext come back outside and rush to the Paris departure where Willie held his luggage.

What was he *thinking of*? Ruses, evasions, deceptions. He was a followed man, his stalkers unreasonable men who wanted him for the wrong reasons. He was a criminal without a crime, a man who could not tell the truth because in that truth was the destruction of his covenant.

He began to perspire again, and the pain returned to his stomach. He felt weak and disorientated. He lay down on Willie's couch in Willie's bathrobe and closed his eyes. The image of melting flesh came back into focus. The face emerged, he heard the cry clearly, and he fell asleep, the plaintive sound in his ears.

He awoke suddenly, aware that someone was above him, looking down at him. Alarmed, he whipped over on his back, then sighed in relief at the sight of Willie standing by the couch.

"You've had some rest and it shows. You look better and God knows you smell better."

"Did you get my things?"

"Yes, and you were right. They were anxious to know where you were. When I paid the bill, the manager came out and behaved like a rep company version of Scotland Yard. He's mollified, if confused. He's also got a telephone number where you're currently in residence."

"In residence?"

"Yes. I'm afraid your reputation hasn't been vastly improved, unless you've had a change of heart. The number's for a hospital in Knightsbridge that doesn't get a penny from National Health. It specializes in venereal diseases. I know a doctor there quite well."

"You're too much," said Noel, standing. "Where are my things?"

"In the guest room. I thought you'd want to change."

"Thanks." Holcroft started towards the door.

"Do you know a man named Buonoventura?" Ellis asked.

Noel stopped. He had sent Sam a three-word cablegram from the airport in Lisbon. *Belgravia Arms, London.* "Yes. Did he call?"

"Several times. Quite frantically, I gather. The hotel switchboard said the call came from Curaçao."

"I know the number," said Holcroft. "I have to get in touch with him. I'll put the call on my credit card."

It was five minutes before he heard Sam's voice, and less than five seconds before he realized it was not fair to ask the construction engineer to lie any longer.

"Miles isn't fooling around any more, Noley. He told me he's getting a court order for your return to New York. He's going to serve it on the owners down here, figuring they're American. He knows they can't force you to go back, but he says they'll know you're wanted. It's a little rough, Noley, because you're not on any payroll."

"Did he say why?"

"Only that he thinks you have information they need."

If he could get to Paris, Noel thought, he wanted Buonoventura to be able to reach him, but he did not want to burden him with an address. "Listen, Sam. I'm leaving for Paris later today. There's an American Express office on the Champs Elysées, near the Avenue Georges Cinq. If anything comes up, cable me there."

"What'll I tell Miles if he calls again? I don't want to get my ass burned."

"Say you reached me and told me he was trying to find me. Tell him I said I'd get in touch with him as soon as I could. That's all you know." Noel paused. "Also tell him I had to get to Europe. Don't volunteer, but if he presses, let him know about the American Express office. I can phone messages."

"There's something else," said Sam awkwardly. "Your mother called, too. I felt like a goddamned idiot lying to her; you shouldn't lie to your mother, Noley."

Holcroft smiled. A lifetime of deviousness had not taken the basic Italian out of Sam. "When did she call?"

"Night before last. She sounds like a real lady. I told her I expected to hear from you yesterday; that's when I started phoning."

"I'll call her when I get to Paris," said Noel. "Anything else?"

"Isn't that enough?"

"Plenty. I'll be in touch in a few days, but you know where to cable me."

"Yeah, but if your mother calls I'm going to let her know, too."

"No sweat. And thanks, Sam. I owe you."

He hung up, noticing that Willie Ellis had gone into the kitchen where he had turned on the radio. Among other attributes, Willie was a gentleman. Noel sat by the phone for several moments, trying to figure things out. His mother's call was not surprising. He had not spoken to her since that Sunday morning in Bedford Hills nearly two weeks ago.

Miles was something else again. Holcroft did not think of the detective as a person; he knew no face or voice. But Miles had arrived at certain conclusions, he was certain of that. And those conclusions tied him to three deaths connected with British Airways Flight 591 from London to New York. Miles was not letting go; if he persisted he could create a problem Noel was not sure he could handle. The detective could ask for international police cooperation. And if he did, attention would be drawn to the activities of a United States citizen who had walked away from a homicide investigation.

Geneva would not tolerate that attention; the covenant would be destroyed. Miles had to be contained. But *how?*

His unfamiliar forest was lined with traps; every protective instinct he possessed told him to turn back. Geneva needed a man infinitely more cunning and experienced than he. Yet he could not turn back. The survivors of Wolfsschanze would not permit it. And deep in his own consciousness he knew he did not want to. There was the face that came into focus in the darkness. He had to find his father, and in the finding show the world a man in agony who was brave enough and perceptive enough to know that amends must be made. And brilliant enough to make that credo live.

Noel walked to the kitchen door. Ellis was at the sink washing teacups.

"I'll pick up my clothes in a couple of weeks, Willie. Let's go to the airport."

Ellis turned, concern in his eyes. "I can save you time," he said, reaching for china mug on a shelf. "You'll need some French money until you can convert. I keep a jar full for my bimonthly travels to the fleshpots. Take what you need."

"Thanks." Holcroft took the mug, looking at Willie's exposed arms beneath rolled-up sleeves. They were as powerful and muscular as any two arms he'd

117

ever seen. It struck Noel that Willie could break a man in half.

The madness started at Heathrow and gathered momentum at Orly.

In London he bought a ticket on KLM to Amsterdam, on the theory that the story he gave MI5 had been checked out and considered plausible. He suspected it had been both, for he saw a bewildered man in a raincoat watch him in astonishment as he raced out of the KLM departure gates back to Air France. There Willie was waiting for him with a ticket on a crowded plane to Paris.

Immigration at Orly was cursory but slow. As he stood in line Noel had time to study the faces in the crowds in the customs area, and beyond the swinging doors that led to the terminal proper. Beyond those doors he could see two men; there was something about them that caught his attention. Perhaps it was their sombre faces, their intensity. They were talking quietly, their heads immobile, as they watched the passengers walk out of customs. One held a piece of paper in his hand; it was small, shiny. A photograph. And Noel knew it was a photograph of *him*.

These were not the men of Wolfsschanze. The men of Wolfsschanze knew him by sight; and the men of Wolfsschanze were never seen. MI5 had reached its counterparts in Paris. They were waiting for him.

"*Monsieur.*" The customs clerk stamped Holcroft's passport routinely. Noel picked up his luggage and started towards the exit, feeling the panic of a man about to walk into an unavoidable trap.

As the doors parted, he saw the two men turn away to avoid being noticed. *They* turned away; they did not want *him* to see *them*. They were not going to approach him; they were going to . . . follow him.

The realization gave painful birth an an unclear strategy. Painful because it was so alien to him, unclear because he was not sure of the procedures. He only knew that he had to go from point *A* to point B and back again to *A*, losing his pursuers somewhere in the vicinity of B.

Up ahead in the crowded terminal he saw the sign.

Lignes Aériennes Intérieures.

France's domestic airline that shuttled about the country with splendid irregularity. The cities were listed in three columns. *Rouen, Le Havre, Caen . . . Orléans, Le Mans, Tours . . . Dijon, Lyons, Marseilles.*

Noel walked rapidly past the two men, as if oblivious to all but his own concerns. He hurried to the Intèrieures counter. There were four people ahead of him.

His turn came. He inquired about flights south. To the Mediterranean. To Marseilles. He wanted a choice of several times.

There was a flight that landed at five cities in a southwest arc from Orly to the Mediterranean, the clerk told him. The stops were le Mans, Nantes, Bordeaux, Toulouse, and Marseilles.

Le Mans. The flight time to LA Mans was forty minutes. Estimated driving time, three . . . three and a half hours. It was now twenty minutes to four.

"I'll take that one," Noel said. "It gets me to Marseilles at just the right time."

"Pardon, *monsieur*, but there are more direct flights."

"I'm being met at the airport. No point in being early."

"As you wish, *monsieur*. I will see what is available. The flight leaves in twelve minutes."

Five minutes later Holcroft stood by the departure gate, the *Herald-Tribune* opened in front of him. He looked over the top of the page. One of the two sombre-faced British was talking with the young lady who had sold him his ticket.

Fifteen minutes later the plane was airborne. Twice Noel wandered up the aisle to the lavatory, looking at the passengers in the cabin. Neither of the two men was on the aircraft; no one else seemed remotely interested in him.

At Le Mans he waited until the departing passengers got off the plane. He counted; there were seven of them. Their replacements began coming on board.

He grabbed his suitcase from the luggage rack, walked quickly to the exit door and down the metal steps to the ground. He went inside the terminal and stood by the window.

No one came out of the plane; no one was following him.

His watch read seventeen minutes to five. He wondered if there was still time to reach Helden von Tiebolt. Again he had the essence of what he needed – a name and a place of work. He walked to the nearest telephone, thankful for Willie's jar of franc notes and coins.

In his elementary French, he spoke to the operator. "*S'il vous plait, le numero de Gallimard a Paris . . .*"

She was there. Mademoiselle Tennyson did not have a telephone at her desk, but if the caller would hold on, someone would get her on a line. The woman at the Gallimard switchboard spoke better English than most Texans.

Helden von Tiebolt's voice had that same odd mixture of Portuguese and German as her sister's, but it was not nearly so pronounced. There was too a trace of the echo Noel remembered so vividly in Gretchen's speech, but not the halting, once-removed quality. Helden von Tiebolt – Mademoiselle Tennyson – knew what she wanted to say and said it.

"Why should I meet you? I don't know you, Mr Holcroft."

"It's urgent. Please, believe me."

"There's been an excess of urgencies in my life. I'm rather tired of them."

"There's been nothing like this."

"How did you find me?"

"People . . . people you don't know in England told me where you worked. But they said you didn't live at the address listed with your employer, so I had to call you here."

"They were so interested they inquired where I lived?"

"Yes. It's part of what I have to tell you."

"Why were they interested in me?"

"I'll tell you when I see you. I *have* to tell you."

"Tell me now."

"Not on the phone."

There was a pause. When the girl spoke, her words were clipped, precise . . . afraid. "Why exactly do you wish to see me? What can there be that's so urgent between us?"

"It concerns your family. *Both* our families. I've seen your sister. I've tried to locate your brother . . . "

"I've spoken to neither in over a year," interrupted Helden Tennyson. "I can't help you."

"What we have to talk about goes back over *thirty* years."

"No!"

"There's money involved. A great deal of money."

"I live adequately. My needs are . . ."

"Not only for *you*," pressed Noel, cutting her off. "For thousands. Everywhere."

Again there was the pause. When she spoke, she spoke softly. "Does this concern events . . . people going back to the war?"

"Yes." *Was he getting through to her at last?*

"We'll meet," said Helden.

"Can we arrange it so we . . . we . . ." He was not sure how to phrase it without frightening her.

"So we won't be seen by those watching for us? Yes."

"How?"

"I've had experience. Do exactly as I say. Where are you?"

"At the Le Mans airport. I'll rent a car and drive up to Paris. It'll take me two or three hours."

"Leave the car in a garage and take a taxi to Montmartre. To the Sacre Coeur Cathedral. Go inside to the far end of the church, to the chapel of Louis IX. Light a candle and place it first in one holder, then change your mind and place it in another. You'll be met by a man who will take you outside, up to the square, to a table at one of the street cafés. You'll be given instructions."

"We don't have to be *that* elaborate. Can't we just meet at a bar? Or a restaurant?"

"It's not for your protection, Mr Holcroft, but mine. If you're not who you imply you are, if you're not *alone*, I won't see you. I'll leave Paris tonight and you'll never find me."

14

The solid granite splendour of Sacre Coeur rose in the night sky line like a haunting song of stone. Beyond the enormous bronze doors, an infinite cavern was shrouded in semi-darkness, flickering candles playing a symphony of shadows on the walls.

From near the altar, he could hear the strains of the *Te deum laudamus*. A visiting choir of monks stood in isolated solemnity, singing quietly.

Noel entered the dimly lit circle beyond the apse that housed the chapels of the kings. He adjusted his eyes to the dancing shadows and walked along the balustrades that flanked the entrances to the small enclosures. The rows of scattered candles provided just enough light for him to read the inscription. Louis IX. Louis the Pious, Louis the Just, Son of Aquitaine, Ruler of France, Arbiter of Christendom.

Pious. Just . . . Arbiter.

Was Helden trying to tell him something?

He inserted a coin in the prayer box, removed a thin, tapered candle from its receptacle, and held it to the flame of another near by. Following instructions, he placed it in another several rows away.

A hand touched his arm, fingers gripped his elbow, and a voice whispered into his ear from the shadows behind him.

"Turn around slowly, *monsieur*. Keep your hands at your side."

Holcroft did as he was told. The man stood not much over five feet six or seven, with a high forehead and thinning dark hair. He was in his early thirties, Noel guessed, and pleasant looking, the face pale, even soft. If there was anything particularly noticeable about him, it was his clothes; the dim light could not conceal the fact that they were expensive.

An aura of elegance emanated from the man, heightened by the mild fragrance of cologne. But the man acted neither elegantly nor softly. Before Noel knew what was happening, the man's hands were jabbed into both sides of his chest, and strong fingers spanned the cloth in rapid movements, descending to his belt and the pockets of his trousers.

Holcroft jerked backwards.

"I said, be still!" the man whispered.

In the candlelight, by the chapel of Louis IX, in the Cathedral of Sacré Coeur on the top of Montmartre, Noel was checked for a weapon.

"Follow me," said the man. "I will walk up the street to the square; stay quite far behind. I will join two friends at an outside table at one of the street cafés, probably Bohème. Walk around the square; take your time, look at the artists' work, do not hurry. Then come to the table and sit with us. Greet us as if we are familiar *faces*, not necessarily friends. Do you understand?"

"I understand."

If this was the way to reach Helden von Tiebolt, so be it. Noel stayed a discreet distance behind the man, the fashionably cut overcoat not hard to follow among the less elegant clothes of the tourists.

They reached the crowded square. The man stood for a moment, lighting a cigarette, then proceeded across the street to a table beyond the pavement, behind a planter filled with shrubbery. As he had said, there were two people at the table. One was a man dressed in a ragged field jacket, the other a woman in a black raincoat, a white scarf around her neck. The scarf was in contrast to her very dark, straight hair, as dark as the black raincoat. She wore tortoise-shell glasses, framed intrusions on a pale face with no discernible make-up. Noel wondered if the plain-looking woman was Helden von Tiebolt. If she was, there was little resemblance to her sister.

He started his sojourn around the square, pretending interest in the art works on display everywhere. There was little of merit, nor was there meant to be. This was the tourist marketplace, the bazaar where the bizarre was for sale.

Nothing had changed in Montmartre, thought Holcroft, as he threaded his way around the last turn towards the café.

He walked by the planter and nodded at the two men and the woman seated at the table beyond. They nodded back; he proceeded to the entrance, walked in, and returned *to the familiar faces, not necessarily friends*. He sat down in the empty chair; it was beside the dark-haired woman with the tortoise-shell glasses.

"I'm Noel Holcroft," he said to no one in particular.

"We know," answered the man in the field jacket, his eyes on the crowds in the square.

Noel turned to the woman. "Are you Helden von . . . Excuse me, Helden Tennyson?"

"No, I've never met her," replied the woman. "But I will take you to her."

The man in the expensive overcoat turned to Holcroft. "You alone?"

"Of course. Can we get started? Helden . . . Tennyson . . . said I'd be given instructions. I'd like to see her, talk for a while, and then find a hotel. I haven't had any sleep during the past few days." He started to get up from the table.

"Sit down!" The woman spoke sharply.

He sat, more out of curiosity than from the command. And then he had the sudden feeling that these three people were not testing him, they were frightened. The elegantly dressed man was biting the knuckle of his index finger; staring at something in the middle of the square. His companion in the field jacket had his hand on his friend's arm, his gaze levelled in the identical direction. They were looking at someone; someone who disturbed them profoundly.

Holcroft tried to follow their line of sight, tried to peer between the criss-crossing figures that filled the street in front of the café.

He stopped breathing. Across the street were the two men he thought he had eluded at Le Mans. It didn't make sense! No one had followed him off the plane.

"It's *them*," he said.

The elegantly dressed man turned his head swiftly; the man in the field jacket was slower, his expression disbelieving; the dark-haired woman studied him closely.

"Who?" she asked

"Those two men over there, near the entrance to the restaurant. One's in a light topcoat, the other's carrying a raincoat over his arm."

"Who are they?"

"They were at Orly this afternoon; they were waiting for me. I flew to Le Mans to get away from them. I'm almost sure they're British agents. But how did they know I was *here?* They weren't on the plane. No one followed me, I'd *swear* to it!"

The three exchanged glances; they believed him and Holcroft knew why. He had picked out the two Englishmen himself, volunteered the information before being confronted with it.

"If they're British, what do they want with you?" asked the man in the field jacket.

"That's between Helden von Tiebolt and myself."

"But you think they *are* British?" pressed the man in the jacket.

"Yes."

"I hope you're right."

The man in the overcoat leaned forward. "What do you mean you flew to Le Mans? What happened?"

"I thought I could throw them off. I was convinced I *had*. I bought a ticket to Marseilles. I made it clear to the girl at the counter that I had to get to Marseilles, and then picked a flight that had stops. The first was Le Mans and I got off. I saw them *questioning* her. I never said anything *about* Le Mans!"

"Don't excite yourself," said the man in the field jacket. "It only draws attention."

"If you think they haven't spotted me, you're crazy! But how did they *do* it?"

"It's not so difficult," said the woman.

"You rented a car?" asked the elegantly dressed man.

"Of course. I had to drive back to Paris."

"At the airport?"

"Naturally."

"And naturally you asked for a map. Or at least directions, no doubt mentioning Paris. I mean, you were not driving to Marseilles."

"Certainly, but lots of people do that."

"Not so many, not at an airport that has flights to Paris. And none with your name. I can't believe you have false papers."

Holcroft was beginning to understand. "They checked," he said.

"One person on a telephone for but a few minutes," said the man in the field jacket. "Less, if you were reported having left the plane at Le Mans."

"The French would not miss the opportunity of selling an empty seat," added the man in the elegant coat. "Do you see now? There are not so many places that rent cars at airports. The make, the colour, the licence would be given. The rest is simple."

"Why simple? Out of all Paris to find *one car*?"

"Not *in* Paris, *monsieur*. On the road *to* Paris. There is but one main highway; it is the most likely to be used by a foreigner. You were picked up outside Paris."

Noel's astonishment was joined by a sense of depression. His ineptness was too apparent. "I'm sorry. I'm really sorry."

"You did nothing intentionally," said the elegant man, his concentration back on the Englishmen who were now seated in the first booth of the restaurant in the middle of the square. He touched the arm of the man in the field jacket. "They've sat down."

"I see."

"What are we going to do?" asked Holcroft.

"It's being done," answered the dark-haired woman. "Do exactly what we tell you to do."

"*Now*," said the man in the expensive coat.

"Get up!" ordered the woman. "Walk with me out into the street and turn right. Quickly!" Bewildered, Holcroft rose from his chair and left the café, the woman's fingers clasped around his arm. They stepped off the kerb.

"To the right!" she repeated.

He turned to his right.

"Faster!" she said.

He heard a crash of glass behind them, then angry shouts. He turned and looked back. The two Englishmen had left the booth, colliding with a waiter. All three were covered with wine.

"Turn right again!" commanded the woman. "Into the doorway!"

He did as he was told, shouldering his way past a crowd of people in the entrance of yet another café. Once inside, the woman stopped him; he whirled around instinctively and watched the scene in the square.

The Englishmen were trying to disengage themselves from the furious waiter. The man in the topcoat was throwing money on the table. His companion had made better progress; he was under the trellis looking frantically to his left – in the direction Holcroft and the girl had taken.

Noel heard shouts; he stared in disbelief at the source. Not twenty feet from where the agents stood was a dark-haired woman in a shiny black raincoat with thick, tortoise-shell glasses, and a white scarf around her neck. She stood yelling at someone loudly enough to draw the attention to everyone around her.

Including the Englishmen.

She stopped abruptly and began running up the crowded street towards the south end of Montmartre. The British agents took up the chase, away from the doorway in which Holcroft stood. Their progress was unexpectedly slowed by a number of young people in jeans and jackets who seemed purposely to be blocking the Englishmen. Furious shouts erupted; then he could hear shrill whistles of the *gendarmes*.

Montmartre became pandemonium.

"Come! *Now!*" The dark-haired woman – the one at his side – grabbed Noel's arm again, and again propelled him into the street. "Turn left!" she ordered, pushing him through the crowds. "Back where we were."

They approached the table behind the planter box. Only the man in the expensive overcoat remained; he stood up as they drew near.

"There may be others," he said. "We don't know. Hurry!"

Holcroft and the woman continued running. They reached a side street no wider than a large alley; it was lined with small shops on both sides, the dimly lit store-fronts providing the only light in the block.

"This way!" said the woman, now holding Noel's hand, running beside him. "The car's on the right. The first one by the corner!"

It was a Citroën; it looked powerful but nondescript. There were layers of dirt on the body, the wheels were filthy and caked with mud. Even the windows had a film of dust on them.

"Get in front! Drive," commanded the woman, handing him a key. "I'll stay in the back seat."

Holcroft climbed in, trying to orient himself. He started the engine. The vibrations caused the chassis to tremble. It was an outsized motor, designed for a heavier car, guaranteeing enormous speed for a lighter one.

"Go straight towards the bottom of the hill!" said the woman behind him. "I'll tell you where to turn."

The next forty-five minutes were blurred into a series of plunges and sudden turns. The woman issued directions at the last second, forcing Noel to turn the wheel violently to obey. They sped into a highway north of Paris from a twisting entrance road that caused the Citroën to lurch sideways, careering off the mound of grass that was the centre island. Holcroft held the wheel with all his strength, first straightening the car and then weaving between two nearly parallel cars up ahead.

"Faster!" screamed the dark-haired woman in the back seat. "Can't you go *faster?*"

"Jesus! We're over ninety-five!"

"Keep looking in your mirrors! I'll watch the side roads! And go faster!"

They drove for ten minutes in silence, the wind and the steady, high-pitched hum of the tyres maddening. It was all maddening, thought Noel as he shifted his eyes from the windscreen to the rear-view mirror to the side-view mirror caked with dirt outside the window. What were they *doing?* They were out of Paris; who were they running from *now?* There was no time to think; the woman was screaming again.

"The next exit, that's the one!"

He barely had time to brake and turn the car into the exit. He screeched to a halt at the stop sign.

"Keep going! To the left!"

The split seconds of immobility were the only pause in the madness. It began again: the accelerated speed over the dark country roads, the sudden turns, the commands barked harshly in his ear.

The moonlight that had washed over the splendour of Sacre Coeur now revealed stretches of rock-hewn farmland. Barns and silos loomed in irregular silhouettes; small houses with thatched roofs appeared and disappeared.

"There's the road!" yelled the woman.

It was a dirt road angling off the tarred surface over which they travelled; the trees would have concealed it if one did not know where or when to look. Noel slowed the Citroën and turned in. The whole car shook, but the voice behind him did not permit more cautious driving.

"Hurry! We have to get over the hill so our lights won't be seen."

The hill was steep, the road too narrow for more than one vehicle. Holcroft pressed the accelerator; the Citroën lurched up the primitive road. They reached the crest of the hill, Noel gripping the steering wheel as if it were uncontrollable. The descent was rapid; the road curved to the left and flattened out. They were level again.

"No more than a quarter of a mile now," said the woman.

Holcroft was exhausted, the palms of his hands soaked. They were in the loneliest, darkest place he could imagine. In a dense forest, on a road unlisted on any map.

Then he saw it. A small thatched house on a flat plot of ground dug out of the forest. There was a dim light on inside.

"Stop here," was the command, but it was not rendered in the harsh voice that had hammered into his ears for nearly an hour.

Noel stopped the car directly in front of the path that led to the house. He took several deep breaths and wiped the sweat from his face, closing his eyes briefly, wishing the pain would leave his head.

"Please turn around, Mr Holcroft," said the woman, no stridency in her tone.

He did so. And he stared through the shadows at the woman in the back seat. Gone was the shining black hair and the thick-rimmed glasses. The white scarf was still there but now it was partially covered by long blonde hair that cascaded over her shoulders, framing a face – a very lovely face – he had seen before. Not *this* face but one like it; delicate features modelled lovingly in clay before a chisel was put to stone. This face was not cold and the eyes were not distant. There was vulnerability and involvement. She spoke quietly, returning his stare through the shadows.

"I am Helden von Tiebolt and I have a gun in my hand. Now, what do you want of me?"

15

He looked down and saw a tiny reflection of light off the barrel of the automatic. The gun was pointed at his head, the bore only inches away, her fingers curved around the trigger.

"The first thing I want," he said, "is for you to put that thing away."

"I'm afraid I can't do that."

"You're the last person on earth I'd want to see hurt. You've got nothing to fear from me."

"Your words are reassuring, but I've heard such words before. They weren't always true."

"Mine are." He looked into her eyes through the dim light, holding his gaze steady. The tenseness of her expression diminished. "Where are we?" Noel asked. "Was all that craziness necessary? The riot in Montmartre, racing around the country like maniacs. What are you running from?"

"I might ask the same question of you. You're running, too. You flew to Le Mans."

"I wanted to avoid some people. But I'm not afraid of them."

"I also avoid people, and I *am* afraid of them."

"Who?" The spectre of the Tinamou intruded on Noel's thoughts; he tried to push it away.

"You may or may not be told, depending upon what you have to say to me."

"Fair enough. Right now you're the most important person in my life. That may change when I meet your brother, but right now, it's you."

"I can't imagine why. We've never met. You said you wanted to see me over matters that could be traced back to the war."

"Traced back to your father, would be more specific."

"I never knew my father."

"Both our fathers. Neither of us knew them."

He told her, as he had told her sister, with all the conviction he could summon. But he did not mention the men of Wolfsschanze; she was frightened enough. And he heard his words again, as if echoes from last night in Portsea. It *was* only last night, and the woman he spoke to now was like the woman then – but only in appearance. Gretchen Beaumont had listened in silence, Helden did not. She interrupted him quietly, continuously, asking questions he should have asked himself.

"Did this Manfredi show you proof of his identity?"

"He didn't have to; he had the papers from the bank. They were legitimate."

"What are the names of the directors?"

"The directors?"

"Of the Grande Banque de Genève. The overseers of this extraordinary document."

"I don't know."

"You should be told."

"I'll ask."

"Who will handle the legal aspects of this agency in Zurich?"

"The bank's attorneys, I imagine."

"You imagine? It's six months of your life. I'd think it would be."

"*Our* lives."

"We'll see. I'm not the oldest child of Wilhelm von Tiebolt."

"I told you when I called you from Le Mans," said Holcroft, "that I've met your sister."

"And?" asked Helden.

"I think you know. She's not capable. The directors in Geneva won't accept her."

"There's my brother Johann. He's next in age."

"I know that. I want to talk about him."

"Not now. Later."

"What do you mean?"

"I mentioned on the phone that there had been an excess of urgencies in my life. There has also been an excess of lies. I'm an expert in that area; I know a liar when I hear his words. You don't lie."

"Thank you for that." Noel was relieved; they had a basis for talking. It was his first concrete step. In a way, in spite of everything, he felt exhilarated. She lowered the gun to her lap.

"Now we must go inside. There's a man who wants to speak to you."

Holcroft's exhilaration crashed with her words. He could not share Geneva with anyone but a member of the von Tiebolt family. "No," he said, shaking his head. "I'm not talking to anyone. What I've discussed with you is between us. No one else."

"Give him a chance. He must know that you don't mean to hurt me. Or hurt others. He must be convinced that you are not part of something else."

"Part of what?"

"He'll explain."

"He'll ask questions."

"Say only what you wish to say."

"No! You don't understand. I can't say *anything* about Geneva and neither can you. I've tried to explain . . ."

He stopped. Helden raised the automatic. "The gun is still in my hand. Get out of the car."

He preceded her up the short path to the door of the house. Except for the dim light in the windows, it was dark. The surrounding trees filtered the moonlight to such a degree that only muted rays came through the branches.

Noel felt her hand reaching around his waist, the barrel of the gun in the small of his back.

"Here's a key. Open the door. It's difficult for him to move around."

Inside, the small room was like any other one might imagine in such a house deep in the French countryside, with one exception: two walls were lined with books. Everything else was simple to the point of primitiveness – sturdy furniture of no discernible design, a heavy old-fashioned desk, several unlit lamps with plain shades, a wood floor, and thick, plastered walls. The books were somehow contradictory, out of place.

In the far corner of the room sat an emaciated man in a wheelchair. He was between a floor lamp and a short table, the light over his left shoulder, a book on his lap. His hair was white and thin, combed carefully over his head. Holcroft guessed he was well into his seventies. In spite of his gaunt appearance, the face was strong, the eyes behind the steel-rimmed spectacles alert. He was dressed in a cardigan sweater buttoned to the throat, and a pair of corduroy trousers.

"Good evening, *Herr Oberst*," said Helden. "I hope we didn't keep you waiting too long."

"Good evening, Helden," replied the old man, putting the book to one side. "You're here and obviously safe. That's all that matters."

Noel watched, mesmerized, as the gaunt figure put his hands on the arms of the wheelchair and rose slowly to a standing position. He was extremely tall, over six feet two or three. He continued speaking in an accent obviously German and just as obviously aristocratic.

"You're the young man who telephoned Miss Tennyson," he said, not asking a question. "I'm known simply as *Oberst* – colonel – which was not my rank, but I'm afraid it will have to do."

"This is Noel Holcroft. He's an American and he is the man. Helden took a step to her left, revealing the gun in her hand. "He's here against his will. He didn't want to talk to you."

"How do you do, Mr Holcroft?" The colonel nodded, offering no hand. "May I ask why you're reluctant to speak to an old man?"

"I don't know who you are," replied Noel as calmly as he could. "Further, the matters I've discussed with Miss . . . Tennyson . . . are confidential."

"Does she agree?"

"Ask her." Holcroft held his breath. In seconds he would know how convincing he had been.

"They are," said Helden, "if they're true. I *think* they're true."

"I see. But you must be convinced, and I'm the devil's advocate without a brief." The old man lowered himself back into the wheelchair.

"What does that mean?" asked Noel.

"You won't discuss these confidential matters, yet I must ask questions, the answers to which could allay our anxieties. You see, Mr Holcroft, you have no reason to be afraid of me. On the contrary, we may have a great deal to fear from you."

"Why? I don't know you; you don't know me. Whatever it is you're involved with has nothing to do with me."

"We must *all* be convinced of that," said the old man. "Over the telephone you spoke to Helden of urgency, of a great deal of money, of concerns that go back over thirty years."

"I'm sorry she told you that," interrupted Noel. "Even that's too much."

"She said very little else," continued the colonel. "Only that you saw her sister, and that you're interested in her brother."

"I'll say it again. It's confidential."

"And finally," said the old man, as if Holcroft had not spoken, "that you wish to meet secretly. At least, you implied as much."

"For my own reasons," said Noel. "They're none of your business."

"Aren't they?"

"No."

"Let me summarize briefly then." The colonel pressed the fingers of his hands together, his eyes on Holcroft. "There's urgency, a great sum of money, matters traced back three decades, interest in the offspring of a ranking member of the Third Reich's High Command, and – most important, perhaps – a clandestine meeting. Doesn't all this suggest something?"

Noel refused to be drawn into speculation. "I have no idea what it suggests to you."

"Then I'll be specific. A trap."

"A *trap?*"

"Who are you, Mr Holcroft? A disciple of *Odessa*? Or a soldier of the *Rache*, perhaps?"

"The *Odessa*? . . . Or the . . . what?" asked Holcroft.

"The *Rache*," replied the old man sharply, pronouncing the word with phonetic emphasis.

"The '*Rah-kah*'? . . ." Noel returned the cripple's penetrating stare. "I don't know what you're talking about."

Oberst glanced at Helden, then pulled his eyes back to Holcroft. "You've heard of neither?"

"I've heard of the *Odessa*. I don't know anything about the . . . '*Rah-kah*' . . . or whatever you call it."

"Recruiters and killers. Yet both recruit. Both kill. The *Odessa* and the *Rache. The* pursuers of children."

"Pursuers of children?" Noel shook his head. "You'll have to be clearer, because I haven't the vaguest idea what you're saying."

Again, the old man looked at Helden. What passed between them Holcroft could not decipher, but *Oberst* turned back to him, the hard eyes boring in as if studying a practised liar, watching for signs of deception – or recognition. "I'll put it plainly to you," he said. "Are you one of those who seek out the children of Nazis? Who pursue them wherever they can be found, killing them for revenge – for crimes they never committed – making *examples* of the innocent? Or forcing them to join you? Threatening them with documents portraying their parents as monsters, promising to expose them as offspring of psychopaths and murderers if they refuse to be recruited – destroying what lives they have for the insanity of your cause? These are the people who seek the children, Mr Holcroft. Are you one of them?"

Noel closed his eyes in relief. "I can't tell you how wrong you are. I won't tell you any more than that, but you're so wrong it's incredible."

"We have to be sure."

"You can be. I'm not involved in things like that. I've never heard of those kind of things before. People like that are sick."

"Yes, they're sick," agreed *Oberst*. "Don't mistake me. The Wiesenthals of this world search out the real monsters, the unpunished criminals who still laugh at Nuremberg, and we can't object; that's another war. But the persecution of the children must stop."

Noel turned to Helden. "Is this what you're running from? After all these years they're still after you?"

The old man answered. "Acts of violence take place every day. Everywhere."

"Then why doesn't anyone know about it?" demanded Holcroft. "Why aren't there stories in the newspapers? Why are these things kept quiet?"

"Would . . . 'anyone', as you put it . . . really care?" asked the colonel. "For the children of Nazis?"

"For God's sake, they were *kids*." Again Noel looked at Helden. "Is what I saw tonight part of this? You have to *protect* each other? Is it so widespread?"

"We're called the 'children of hell'," answered Helden. "Damned for what we are and damned for what we're not."

"I don't *understand* it," protested Holcroft.

"It's not vital that you do," the colonel said. "It's only important that we be convinced you're from neither army. Are you satisfied, Helden?"

"Yes."

"There's nothing more you wish me to know?"

The woman shook her head. "I'm satisfied," she repeated.

"Then so am I." The colonel extended his hand to Noel. "Thank you for coming. As Helden will explain, my existence is not widely known nor do we want it to be. We would appreciate your confidence."

Holcroft took the hand, surprised at the old man's firm grip. "If I can count on yours."

"You have my word."

"Then you have mine," Noel said.

They drove in silence, headlights knifing the darkness. Holcroft was behind the wheel, Helden in the front seat beside him, directing him by nodding wearily, pointing to the turns as they approached succeeding roads. There was no screaming now, no harsh commands barked at the last second. Noel had the distinct impression that Helden was as exhausted from the events of the night as was he. But the night was not over; they had to talk.

"Was all that necessary?" he asked. "Was it so important for him to see me?"

"Very much so. He had to be convinced you weren't part of the *Odessa*. Or the *Rache*."

"What exactly are they. He spoke as if I should know, but I don't. I didn't really understand him."

"They're two extremist organizations, sworn enemies of each other. Both fanatic, both after us."

"Us?"

"The children of Party leaders. Wherever we are; wherever we've scattered to."

"Why?"

"The *Odessa* seeks to revive the Nazi Party. The disciples of *Odessa* are everywhere."

"*Seriously?* They're for real?"

"Very real. And very serious. The *Odessa's* recruiting methods range from blackmail to physical force. They're gangsters."

"And this . . . '*Rah-kah*'?"

"*Rache*. The German word for vengeance. In the beginning it was a society formed by the survivors of the concentration camps. They hunted the sadists and the killers, those thousands who were never brought to trial."

"It's a Jewish organization, then?"

"There are Jews in the *Rache*, yes, but now they're a minority. The Israelis formed their own groups and operated out of Tel Aviv and Haifa. The *Rache* is primarily Communist; many believe it was taken over by the KGB. Others think Third World revolutionaries gravitated to it. The 'vengeance' they spoke of in the beginning has become something else. The *Rache* is a haven for terrorists."

"But why are they after *you?*"

Helden looked at him through the shadows. "Like everyone else, we have our share of revolutionaries. They're drawn to the *Rache*; it represents the opposite of what they're running from. For most of us, however, it's no better than the Party at its worst. And for us, the *Rache* reserves its harsher tactics. We're the scapegoats, the fascists they're stamping out. They use our names – often our corpses – to tell people Nazis still live. Not unlike the *Odessa*, it's frequently recruit or kill."

"It's *insane*," said Noel.

"Insane," agreed Helden. "But very real. We say nothing; we're not anxious to call attention to ourselves. Besides, who would care? We're Nazi children."

"The *Odessa*, the *Rache* . . . No one I know knows anything about them."

"No one you know has any reason to."

"Who's *Oberst?*"

"A great man who must remain in hiding for the rest of his life because he had a conscience."

"What do you mean?"

"He was a member of the High Command and saw the horrors. He knew it was futile to object; others had and they were killed. Instead, he remained and used his rank to countermand order after order, saving God knows how many lives."

"There's nothing dishonourable in that."

"He did it the only way he could. Quietly, within the bureaucracy of command, without notice. When it was over, the Allies convicted him because of his stature in the Reich; he spent eighteen years in prison. When what he did finally came out, thousands of Germans despised him. They called him a traitor. What was left of the Officer Corps put a price on his head."

Noel remembered Helden's words inside the house. "Damned for what he was and damned for what he wasnt."

"Yes," she answered, pointing suddenly to a turn in the road she'd nearly missed.

"In his own way," said Noel, turning the wheel, "*Oberst* is like the three men who wrote the Geneva document. Didn't it occur to you?"

"It occurred to me."

"You must have been tempted to tell him."

"Not really. You asked me not to."

He looked at her; she was looking straight ahead through the windscreen. Her face was tired and drawn, her skin pale, accentuating the dark hollows beneath her eyes. She seemed alone, and that aloneness was not to be intruded upon lightly. But the night was *not* over. They had things to say to each other; decisions had to be made.

For Noel was beginning to think that this youngest child of Wilhelm von Tiebolt would be the one selected to represent the von Tiebolt family in Geneva. Neither of the older two would be acceptable to the directors of the Grande Banque.

"Can we go some place where it's quiet? I think a meal and a few drinks would do us both good."

"There's a small inn about four or five miles from here. It's out of the way; no one will see us."

As they swung off the road, Noel's eyes were drawn to the rear-view mirror. Headlights shone in the glass. It was an odd turn off the Paris highway, odd in the sense that there were no signs; an unmarked exit. The fact that a driver behind them had a reason to take this particular exit at this particular time seemed too coincidental for comfort. Holcroft was about to say something when a strange thing happened.

The lights in the mirror went out. They simply were not there any longer.

The inn had once been a farmhouse, part of the grazing field now a gravelled parking lot bordered by a post-and-rail fence. The small dining room was through an archway off the bar. Two other couples were inside, both distinctly Parisian, and just as obviously having discreet dinners with companions they could not see in Paris. Eyes shot up at the newcomers, no signs of welcome in the glances. A fireplace filled with flaming logs was at the far end of the room. It was a good place to talk.

They were shown to a table to the left of the fire. Two brandies were ordered and delivered.

"It's nice here," said Noel. "How did you find it?"

"It's on the way to the colonel's. My friends and I often stop here to talk among ourselves."

"Do you mind if I ask you some questions?"

"Go ahead."

"When did you leave England?"

"About three months ago. When the job was offered."

"Were you the Helen Tennyson in the London directory?"

"Yes. In English, the name Helden seems to require an explanation, and I was tired of having to give one. It's not the same in Paris. The French don't have much curiosity about names; there's not such a rigidity attached to them."

"But you don't call yourself von Tiebolt." Holcroft saw the flash of resentment on her face.

"No."

"Why Tennyson? Why does your brother call himself John Tennyson?"

"I think that's rather obvious. Von Tiebolt is extremely German. When we left Brazil for England it seemed a reasonable change."

"Just a change? Nothing else?"

"No." Helden sipped her brandy and looked at the fire. "Nothing else."

Noel watched her; the lie was in her voice. She was not a good liar. She was hiding something, but to call her on it now would only provoke her. He let the lie pass. "What do you know about your father?"

She turned back to him. "Very little. My mother loved him, and from what she said he was a better man than his years in the Third Reich might indicate. But then, you've confirmed that, haven't you? At the end, he was a profoundly moral man."

"Tell me about your mother."

"She was a survivor. She fled Germany with nothing but a few pieces of jewellery, two children, and a baby inside her. She had no training, no skills, no profession, but she could work, and she was . . . convincing. She started selling in dress shops, cultivated customers, used her flair for clothes – and she had that – as the basis for her own business. Several businesses, actually. Our home in Rio de Janeiro was quite comfortable."

"Your sister told me it was . . . a sanctuary that turned into a kind of hell."

"My sister is given to melodramatics. It wasn't so bad. If we were looked down upon, there was a certain basis for it."

"What was that."

"My mother was terribly attractive . . ."

"So are her daughters," interrupted Noel.

"I imagine we are," said Helden matter-of-factly. "It's never concerned me. I haven't had to use it – whatever attractiveness I may have. But my mother did."

"In Rio?"

"Yes. She was kept by several men . . . We were kept, actually. There were two or three divorces, but she wouldn't marry the husbands involved. She broke up marriages, extracting money and business interests as she did. When she died we were quite well off. The German community considered her a pariah. And, by extension, her children."

"She sounds fascinating," said Holcroft smiling. "How did she die?"

"She was killed. Shot through the head while she was driving one night."

The smile faded abruptly. Images returned: a deserted lookout high above the city of Rio; the sounds of gunfire and the explosions of cement; the shattering of glass . . . *Glass*. A car window blown out with the spit of silenced gunshot; a heavy black pistol levelled at his head . . .

Then the words came back to him, spoken in the booth of a cocktail lounge. Words Holcroft had believed were ridiculous, the products of unreasonable fear.

The Cararras, brother and sister. Dearest friend and fiancée of Johann von Tiebolt.

He and my sister were to be married. The Germans would not permit it.

Who could stop them?

Any number of men. With a bullet in the back of Johann's head.

The Cararras. Dear friends and supplicants for the ostracized von Tiebolts. It suddenly struck Noel that if Helden knew how the Cararras had helped him, she might be more co-operative. The Cararras had risked their lives to send him to the von Tiebolts. She would have to respond to that confidence with her own.

"I think I should tell you," he said. "In Rio it was the Cararras who contacted me. They told me where to start looking for you. They were the ones who told me your new name was Tennyson."

"Who?"

"Your friends, the Cararras. Your brother's fiancée."

"The Cararras? In Rio de Janeiro?"

"Yes."

"I've never heard of them. I don't know any Cararras."

16

The tactic blew up in his face with the impact of a backfired rifle. Suddenly Helden was wary of him, apprehensive of saying anything further about her family.

Who were the Cararras?

Why had they told him things that were not true?

Who sent them to him? Her brother had no fiancée, or any best friend that she could recall.

Who *were* the *Cararras?*

He could not lie; it would make matters worse. He could only speculate as truthfully as possible. For reasons known only to them, the Cararras had created a relationship that did not exist; still Noel was convinced they were *not* the von Tiebolts' enemies. They had reached him for the purpose of *helping* the two sisters and the brother who had been driven from Brazil. There were those in Rio – Graff, for one – who would pay a great deal of money to locate the von Tiebolts. The Cararras, who had much to gain and very little to lose, had not told him.

"They wanted to help," he said. "They weren't lying about that. They said you'd been persecuted; they did want to help you."

"It's possible," said Helden. "Rio is filled with people who're still fighting the war, still hunting for those they call traitors. One is never sure who's a friend and who's an enemy. Not among the Germans."

"Did you know a Maurice Graff?"

"I knew who he was, of course. Everyone did. I never met him."

"I did," Noel said. "*He* called the von Tiebolts traitors.

"I'm sure he did. We were pariahs, but not in the nationalistic sense."

"What sense, then?"

The girl looked away again, lifting the brandy glass to her lips. "Other things."

"Your mother?"

"Yes," replied Helden. "It was my mother. I told you, the German community despised her."

Again Holcroft had the feeling she was telling him only part of the truth. He would not pursue it now. If he gained her confidence, she would tell him later. She *had* to tell him; whatever it was might have an effect on Geneva. Everything affected Geneva now.

"You said your mother broke up marriages," he said. "Your sister used almost the same words about herself. She said she was shunned by the officers and their wives in Portsmouth."

"If you're looking for a pattern, I won't dissuade you. My sister is quite a bit older than I. She was closer to my mother, watched her progress, saw the advantages that came mother's way. It wasn't as if she were oblivious to such things. She knew the horror of Berlin after the war. At the age of thirteen she slept with soldiers for food. American soldiers, Mr Holcroft."

It was all he had to know about Gretchen Beaumont. The picture was complete. A whore, for whatever reasons, at fourteen. A whore – for whatever other reasons – at forty-five-plus. The bank's directors in Geneva would rule her out. The Swiss would not make a moral judgement; such judgements were not within their purview. They would base the rejection on grounds of instability and incompetence. She would not be permitted to function as an executor.

But Noel knew there were stronger grounds. They were found in the man Gretchen Beaumont said she loathed, but lived with. A man with odd, heavy eyebrows who had followed him to Brazil.

"What about her husband?"

"I barely know him."

She looked away again at the fire. She was frightened; she *was* hiding something. Her words were too studiously nonchalant. Whatever it was she would not talk about had something to do with Beaumont. There was no point in evading the subject any longer. Truth between them had to be a two-way matter; the sooner she learned that, the better for both of them.

"Do you know anything about him? Where he came from? What he does in the navy?"

"No, nothing. He's a commander on a ship, that's all I know."

"I think he's more than that, and I think you know it. Please don't lie to me."

At first her eyes flashed with anger, then just as rapidly the anger subsided. "That's a strange thing to say. Why would I lie to you?"

"I wish I knew. You say you barely know him, but you seem scared to death. *Please.*"

"What are you driving at?"

"If you know something, tell me. If you've heard about the document in Geneva, tell me what you've heard."

"I know nothing. I've heard nothing."

"I saw Beaumont two weeks ago on a plane to Rio. The same plane I took from New York. He was following me."

He could see fear clearly in Helden's eyes. "I think you're wrong," she said.

"I'm not. I saw his photograph in your sister's house. His house. It was the same man. I stole that photograph and it was stolen from me. After someone beat the *hell* out of me for it."

"Good *Lord* . . . You were beaten for his *photograph?*"

"Nothing else was missing. Not my wallet or my money or my watch. Just his picture. There was writing on the back of it."

"What did it say?"

"I don't know. It was in German and I can't read German."

"Can you remember any of the words?"

"One, I think. The last word. T-O-D. *Tod*."

"*'Ohne dich sterbe ich'*. Could that be it?"

"Could be. I don't know. What does it mean?"

"'Without you I die.' It's the sort of thing my sister would think of. I told you, she's melodramatic." She was lying again; he *knew* it!

"An endearment?"

"Yes."

"That's what the British said, and I didn't believe them, either. Beaumont was on that plane. That picture was taken from me because there was some kind of message on it. For Christ's sake, what's going *on?*"

"I don't know!"

"But you know *something*." Noel tried to control himself. Their voices were low, almost whispers, but their argument carried over to the other diners. Holcroft reached across the table and covered her hand. "I'm asking you again. You know something. Tell me."

He could feel a slight tremble in her hand. "What I know is so confusing it would be meaningless. It's more what I sense than what I know, really." She took her hand from his. "A number of years ago Anthony Beaumont was a naval attaché in Rio de Janeiro. I didn't know him well, but I remember him coming to the house quite often. He was married at the time but interested in my sister – a diversion I suppose you might call it. My mother encouraged it. He was a high-ranking naval officer; favours could be had. But my sister argued violently with my mother. She despised Beaumont and would have nothing to do with him. Yet only a few years later we moved to England and she married him. I've never understood."

Noel leaned forward, relieved. "It may not be as difficult to understand as you think. She told me she married him for the security he could give her."

"And you believed her?"

"Yes." Holcroft did not care to delve into the evening with Gretchen Beaumont, but he could allude to the obvious. "Her behaviour would seem to confirm what she said."

"Then I can't believe you met my sister."

"She was your sister. You look alike; both beautiful."

"If that's what you think, then it's my turn to ask you a question. Given that beauty, do you really think she would settle for a naval officer's salary and the restricted life of a naval officer's wife? I can't. I never have."

"What do you think then?"

"I think she was forced to marry Anthony Beaumont."

Noel leaned back in the chair. She had told him the truth as she saw it. And if she was right, the connection was in Rio de Janeiro. With her mother, perhaps; with whatever caused her mother to become a pariah. With her mother's murder.

"How could Beaumont force her to marry him? And why?"

"I've asked myself both questions a hundred times. I don't know."

"Have you asked her?"

"She refuses to talk to me."

"What happened to your mother in Rio?"

"I told you. She manipulated men for money. The Germans despised her, called her immoral. Looking back, it's hard to refute."

"Was that why she was shot?"

"I guess so. No one really knows; the killer was never found."

"But it could be the answer to the first question, couldn't it? Isn't it possible that Beaumont knew something about your mother that was so damaging he could blackmail your sister?"

Helden turned her palms up in front of her. "What could possibly *be* so damaging? Accepting everything that was said about my mother as being true, why would it have any effect on Gretchen?"

"That would depend on what it was."

"There's nothing conceivable. She's in England now. She's her own person, thousands of miles away. Why should she be concerned?"

"I've no idea." Then Noel remembered. "You used the words 'children of hell'. Damned for what you were, and damned for what you weren't. Couldn't that apply to your sister as well?"

"Beaumont isn't interested in such things. It's an entirely different matter."

"Is it? You don't know that. It's your opinion he forced her to marry him. If it isn't something like that, what is it?"

Helden looked away, deep in thought now, not in a lie. "Something much more recent."

"The document in Geneva?" he asked, Manfredi's warning repeated in his ears, the spectre of Wolfsschanze in his mind. *We're dealing in hundreds of millions. There's been nothing like it in history. Many will try to stop you.*

"How did Gretchen react when you told her about Geneva?" asked Helden.

"As if it didn't matter."

"Well? . . ."

"It could have been a diversion. She was too casual – just as you were too casual when I mentioned Beaumont a few minutes ago. She could have expected it and steeled herself."

"You're guessing."

It was the moment, thought Noel. It would be in her eyes; the rest of the truth she would not talk about. Did it come down to Johann von Tiebolt?

"Not really guessing. Your sister said that her brother told her 'a man would come one day and talk of a strange arrangement'. Those were her words."

Whatever he was looking for – it was not there. There was *something*, but nothing he could relate to. She looked at him as if she herself were trying to understand. Yet there was a fundamental innocence in her look and that was what *he* could not understand.

"'A man would come one day.' It doesn't make sense," she said.

"Tell me about your brother."

She did not answer for several moments. Instead, her eyes strayed to the red tablecloth, her lips parted in astonishment. Then, as if she were coming out of a trance, she said, "Johann? What's there to say?"

"Your sister told me he got the three of you out of Brazil. Was it difficult?"

"There were problems. We had no passports and there were men who tried to stop us from obtaining them."

"You were immigrants. At least, your mother, brother, and sister were. They had to have papers."

"Whatever papers there were in those days were burned as soon as they served their purpose."

"Who wanted to stop you from leaving Brazil?"

"Men who despised us, despised Johann. Who wanted to bring him to trial."

"For what?"

"After mother was killed, Johann took over her business interests. She never allowed him to do much when she was alive. Many people thought he was ruthless, even dishonest. He was accused of misrepresenting profits, withholding taxes. I don't think any of it was true; he was simply faster and brighter than anyone else."

"I see," said Noel, recalling MI5's evaluation of overachiever. "How did he avoid the courts and get you out?"

"Money. And all-night meetings in strange places with men he never identified. He came home one morning and told Gretchen and me to pack just enough things for a short overnight trip. We drove to the airport and were flown in a small plane to Recife where a man met us. We were given passports; the name on them was Tennyson. The next thing Gretchen and I knew we were on a plane for London."

Holcroft watched her closely. There was no hint of a lie. "To start a new life under the name of Tennyson," he said.

"Yes. Completely new. We'd left everything behind us." She smiled. "I sometimes think with very little time to spare."

"He's quite a man. Why haven't you stayed in touch? You obviously don't hate him."

Helden frowned, as if she were unsure of her own answer. "Hate him? No. I resent him, perhaps, but I don't hate him. Like most brilliant men, he thinks he should take charge of everything. He wanted to run my life and I couldn't accept that."

"Why is he a newspaperman? From all I've learned about him, he could probably own one."

"He probably will one day, if that's what he wants. Knowing Johann, I suspect it's because he thought that writing for a well-known newspaper would give him a certain prominence. Especially in the political field where he's very good. He was right."

"Was he?"

140

"Certainly. In a matter of two or three years, he's considered one of the finest correspondents in Europe."

Now, thought Noel. MI5 meant nothing to him; Geneva was everything. He leaned forward.

"He's considered something else, too . . . I said in Montmartre that I would tell you – and *only* you – why the British questioned me. It's your brother. They think I'm trying to reach him for reasons that have nothing to do with Geneva."

"What reasons?"

Holcroft kept her eyes engaged. "Have you ever heard of a man they call the Tinamou?"

"The assassin? Certainly. Who hasn't?"

There was nothing in her eyes. Nothing but vague bewilderment. Absolutely *nothing*. "I, for one," said Noel. "I've read about killers for hire and assassination conspiracies, but I've never heard of the Tinamou."

"You're an American. His deeds are more detailed in the European press than in yours. But what's he got to do with my brother?"

"British Intelligence thinks he may *be* the Tinamou."

The expression of Helden's face was arrested in shock. So complete was her astonishment that her eyes were suddenly devoid of life . . . as noncommittal as a blind man's eyes. Her lips trembled as the words came. They were barely audible.

"You can't be *serious*."

"I assure you, I am. What's more to the point, the British are."

"It's outrageous. Beyond anything I've ever heard! On what basis can they possibly *reach* such a conclusion?"

Noel repeated the salient points analysed by MI5.

"My *God*," said Helden, when he had finished. "He covers all of Europe as well as the Middle East! Certainly the English could check with his editors. He doesn't *choose* the places they send him. It's preposterous!"

"Newspapermen who write interesting copy, who file stories that sell papers, are given a very free hand when it comes to the places they cover. That's the case with your brother. It's almost as though he knew he'd gain that prominence you spoke of; knew that in a few short years he'd be given a flexible schedule."

"You can't *believe* this."

"I don't know what to believe," said Holcroft. "I only know that your brother could jeopardize the situation in Geneva. The mere fact that he's under suspicion by MI5 could be enough to frighten the bankers. They don't want that kind of scrutiny where the Clausen account is concerned!"

"But it's unjustified!"

"Are you sure?"

Helden's eyes were angry. "Yes, I'm sure. Johann may be a number of things, but he's no killer. The viciousness starts again: the Nazi child is hounded."

Noel remembered the first statement made by the grey-haired MI5 man: *For starters, you know about the father* . . . Was it possible Helden was right? Did MI5's suspicions come from memories and hostilities that went back thirty years to a brutal enemy? *Tennyson is the personification of arrogance* . . . It was possible.

"Is Johann political?"

"Very, but not in the usual sense. He doesn't stand for any particular ideology. Instead, he's highly critical of them all. He attacks their weaknesses and he's vicious about hypocrisy. That's why a lot of people in government can't stand him. But he's no assassin!"

If Helden was right, Noel thought, Johann von Tiebolt could be an enormous asset to Geneva, or more specifically to the agency that was to be established in Zurich. A multilingual journalist whose judgements were listened to, who had experience in finance . . . such a man was eminently qualified to dispense millions throughout the world. Certainly more qualified than he was.

If the shadow of the Tinamou could be removed from Johann von Tiebolt, there was no reason for the directors of the Grande Banque de Genève to ever learn of MI5's interest in John Tennyson. The second child of Wilhelm von Tiebolt would be instantly acceptable to the bankers. He might not be the most personable man alive, but Geneva was not a personality contest. He could be an extraordinary asset. But first the Tinamou's shadow *had* to be removed, British Intelligence's suspicions laid to rest.

Then Holcroft smiled. *A man would come one day and talk of a strange arrangement* . . . Johann von Tiebolt – John Tennyson – was waiting for him!

"What's funny?" said Helden, watching him.

"I have to meet him," answered Noel, ignoring the question. "Can you arrange it?"

"I imagine so. It'll take a few days. I don't know where he is. What will you say to him?"

"The truth; maybe he'll reciprocate. I've got a damned good idea he knows about Geneva."

"There's a telephone number he gave me to call if I ever needed him. I've never used it."

"Use it now. Please."

She nodded. Noel understood that there were questions left unanswered. Specifically, a man named Beaumont, and an event in Rio de Janeiro that Helden would not discuss. Whatever that event was, it had to be connected to the naval officer. And it was possible that Helden knew nothing about that connection.

Perhaps John Tennyson did. He certainly knew a lot more than he told either sister.

"Does your brother get along with Beaumont?" asked Holcroft.

"He despises him. He refused to come to Gretchen's wedding."

What *was* it? wondered Noel. Who was the enigma that was Anthony

Beaumont? *Despised, loathed* ... yet so much a part of the von Tiebolt puzzle.

17

Outside the small inn, in the far corner of the parking area, a dark sedan waited in the shadow of a tall oak tree. In the front seat were two men, one in the uniform of the British Navy, the other in a charcoal grey business suit, his black overcoat opened, the edge of a brown leather holster visible beneath his unbuttoned jacket.

The naval officer was behind the wheel. His blunt features were tense. The eyebrows of black-and-white hair arched minutely every now and then, as if prodded by a nervous tic.

The man beside him was in his late thirties. He was slender but he was not thin; his was the tautness that comes with discipline and training. The breadth of his shoulders, the long muscular neck, and the convex line of a chest that stretched his tailored shirt, were evidence of a body honed to physical precision and strength. Each feature of his face was refined, the whole co-ordinated with itself. The result was striking, yet cold, as if the face were chiselled out of granite. The eyes were light blue, almost rectangular, their gaze steady and non-committal; they were the eyes of a confident animal, quick to respond, the response unpredictable. The sculptured head was covered by a glistening crown of blond hair that reflected the light of the distant parking-lot lamps; above this face, it had the appearance of pale yellow ice. The man's name was Johann von Tiebolt, for the past five years known as John Tennyson.

"Are you satisfied?" asked the naval officer, obviously apprehensive. "There's no one."

"There *was* someone," replied the blond man. "Considering the precautions taken since Montmartre, it's not entirely surprising there's no one now. Helden and the other children are quite effective."

"They run from idiots," said Beaumont. "The *Rache* is filled with Marxist subhumans."

"When the time comes, the *Rache* will serve its purpose. Our purpose. But it's not the *Rache* I'm concerned with. I want to know who tried to kill him." Tennyson turned in the shadows, his cold eyes glaring. He slammed his hand on top of the leather dashboard. *"Who tried to kill Clausen's son?"*

"I *swear* to you, I've told you everything we know! Everything we've learned. It was *not* a mistake on our part."

"It was a mistake because it nearly happened," replied Tennyson, his voice quiet again.

"It was Manfredi; it *had* to be Manfredi," continued Beaumont. "He broke the seals and restored them. He read the message from Wolfsschanze and pieced it together. He said as much; he meant as much. It's the only explanation, Johann . . ."

"My name is John. Remember that."

"Sorry. It is the only explanation. We don't know what Manfredi said to Holcroft on that train in Geneva. It's possible he tried to convince him to walk away. And when Holcroft refused, he sent out the orders for his execution. They failed in the station because of me. I think you should remember that."

"You won't let me forget it," interrupted Tennyson. "You may be right, but for the wrong reasons. Manfredi pieced nothing together but his own interests. Even in Switzerland, the removal of assets totalling 780 million dollars is a painful exercise."

"Just as the promise of two million is an irresistible temptation to Holcroft, perhaps."

"Two million he banks only in his mind. But his death will come at *our* hands, no one else's."

"Manfredi acted alone, believe that. His executioners have no one to take orders from now. Since the hotel room in Zürich, there've been no further attempts."

"That's a statement Holcroft would find impossible to accept . . . There they *are*." Tennyson sat forward. Through the windscreen, across the parking area, he could see Noel and Helden coming out of the door. "Do the colonel's children meet here frequently?"

"Yes," answered Beaumont. "I learned of it from an *Odessa* agent who followed them one night."

The blond man coughed. "*Odessa! Caricatures!*"

"They're persistent."

"And they, too, will be useful," said Tennyson, watching Noel and Helden get into the car. "As before, they'll be the lowest footsoldiers, fed to the enemy's cannon. First seen, first sacrificed. The perfect diversion for more serious matters."

Holcroft backed the car out of its slot, then drove through the entrance posts on to the country road.

Beaumont turned on the ignition. "I'll stay a fair distance behind. He won't spot me."

"No, don't bother," said Tennyson. "I'm satisfied. Take me to the airport. You've made the arrangements?"

"Yes. You'll be flown on a Mirage to Athens. The Greeks will get you back to Bahrain. It's all military transport, US courier status, Security Council immunity. The pilot on the Mirage has your papers."

"Well done, Tony."

The naval officer smiled, proud of the compliment. He pressed the accelerator; the sedan roared out of the parking lot into the darkness of the country road. "What will you do in Bahrain?"

"Make my presence known by filing a story on an oil field negotiation. A prince of Bahrain has been most cooperative. He had no choice. He made an arrangement with the Tinamou. The poor man lives in terror that the news will get out."

"You're extraordinary."

"And you're a devoted man. You always have been."

"After Bahrain, what?"

The blond man leaned back in the seat and closed his eyes. "Back to Athens and on to Berlin."

"Berlin?"

"Yes. Things are progressing well. Holcroft will go there next. Kessler's waiting for him."

There was a sudden burst of static from a radio speaker beneath the dashboard. It was followed by four short, high-pitched hums. Tennyson opened his eyes; the four hums were repeated.

"There are telephone booths on the highway. Get me to one. Quickly!"

The Englishman pressed the accelerator to the floor; the sedan sped down the road, reaching seventy miles an hour in a matter of seconds. They came to an intersection. "If I'm not mistaken, there's a petrol station around here."

"Hurry!"

"I'm sure of it," said Beaumont, and there it was; at the side of the road, dark, no light in the windows. "Damn, it's closed!"

"What did you expect?" asked Tennyson.

"The phone's inside . . ."

"Stop the car."

Beaumont obeyed. The blond man got out and walked to the door of the station. He took out his pistol and broke the glass with the handle.

A dog leaped up at him, barking and growling, fangs bared, jaws snapping. It was an old, nondescript animal, stationed more for effect than for any physical protection. Tennyson reached into his pocket, pulled out a perforated cylinder and spun it into the barrel of his pistol. He raised the gun and fired through the shattered glass into the dog's head. The animal fell backwards. Tennyson smashed the remaining glass by the latch above the doorknob.

He let himself in, adjusted his eyes to the light and stepped over the dead animal to a telephone. He reached an operator and gave her the Paris number that would connect him to a man who would, in turn, transfer his call to a telephone in England.

Twenty minutes later he heard the breathless echoing voice. "I'm sorry to disturb you, Johann, but we have an emergency."

"What is it?"

"A photograph was taken. I've very concerned."

"What photograph?"

"A picture of my husband."

"Who took it?"

"The American."

"Which means he recognized him. Graff was right, your devoted husband can't be trusted. His enthusiasm outweighs his discretion. I wonder where Holcroft saw him?"

"On the plane, perhaps. Or through the doorman's description. It doesn't matter. Kill him."

"Yes, of course." The blond man paused, then spoke thoughtfully. "You have the bank books?"

"Yes."

"Deposit ten thousand pounds. Let the transfer be traced through Prague."

"KGB? Very good, Johann."

"The British will suffer another defection. Friendly diplomats will argue among themselves, each accusing the other of a lack of candour."

"*Very* good."

"I'll be in Berlin next week. Reach me there."

"So soon Berlin?"

"Yes. Kessler's waiting. *Wiederaufleben oder Tod.*"

"*Oder Tod*, my brother."

Tennyson hung up and stared through the night light at the dead animal on the floor. He had no more feeling for the clump of lifeless fur than for what he was about to do. Feelings were kept for more important things, not animals and misfits – regardless of how devoted either might be.

Beaumont was a fool, a judgement contained in a dossier sent from Scotland to Brazil years ago. But he had a fool's energy and a fool's sense of surface accomplishment. He had actually become an outstanding naval officer. This son of a *Reichsoberführer* had climbed the ladder of Her Majesty's Royal Navy to the point where he was given vital responsibility. Too much for his intellect; that intellect needed to be directed. In time, they had projected that Beaumont might become a power within the Admiralty, an expert consulted by the Foreign Office. It was an optimum situation; extraordinary advantages could be handed to them through Beaumont. He had remained a *Sonnenkind*; he was permitted to live.

But no more. With the theft of a photograph, Beaumont was finished, for in that theft was the threat of scrutiny. There could be no scrutiny whatsoever; they were too close and there was still too much to accomplish. If Holcroft gave the photograph to the wrong people in Switzerland, told them of Beaumont's presence in New York or Rio, military authorities might be alerted. Why was this outstanding officer so interested in the Geneva document? The question could not arise. This son of the *Reichsoberführer* had to be removed. In a way, it was a pity. The commander would be missed; at times he'd been invaluable.

Gretchen knew that value. Gretchen was Beaumont's teacher, his guide . . . his intellect. She was enormously proud of her work, and now she called for Beaumont's death. So be it. They'd find another to take his place.

They were everywhere, thought Johann von Tiebolt as he walked to the door. Everywhere. *Die Sonnenkinder.* The Children of the Sun, never to be confused with the damned. The damned were wandering refuse, entitled to nothing.

Die Sonnenkinder. Everywhere. In all countries, in all governments, in armies and navies, in industry and trade unions, commanding intelligence branches and the police. All quietly waiting. Grown-up children of the New Order. *Thousands*. Sent out by ship and plane and submarine to all points of the civilized world. So *far* above the average – confirmed every day by their progress everywhere.

They were the proof that the concept of racial superiority was undeniable. Their strain was pure, their excellence unquestioned. And the purest of all, the most excellent of all, was the Tinamou.

Von Tiebolt opened the door and stepped outside. Beaumont had driven the sedan fifty yards down the country road, away from the station, headlights extinguished. The commander went by the book; his training was apparent in everything he did – except when his enthusiasm overrode his discretion. That enthusiasm would now cost him his life.

Tennyson walked slowly towards the sedan. He wondered how it all had begun for Anthony Beaumont. The son of the *Reichsoberführer* had been sent to a family in Scotland; beyond that Tennyson had never inquired. He had been told of Beaumont's tenacity, his stubbornness, his singleness of purpose, but not how he had been sent out of Germany. It was not necessary to know. There'd been thousands; all records were destroyed.

Thousands. Selected genetically, the parents studied, families traced back several generations for organic and psychological frailties. Only the purest were sent out, and everywhere these children were watched closely, guided, trained, indoctrinated – but told nothing until they grew up. And even then, not all. Those who failed to live up to their birthright, who showed weakness or gave evidence of being compromised, were never told, only weeded out.

Those that remained were the true inheritors of the Third Reich. They were in positions of trust and authority everywhere. Waiting . . . waiting for the signal from Switzerland, prepared to put the millions to immediate use.

Millions funnelled judiciously, *politically*. One by one, nations would fall in line, shaped internally by the *Sonnenkinder* who would have at their disposal extraordinary sums to match and consolidate their influence. Ten million here, forty million there, one hundred million where it was necessary.

In the so-called free world the election processes would be bought, the electorates having fewer and fewer choices, only echoes. It was nothing new; successful experiments had already taken place. Chile had cost less than twenty-seven million, Panama no more than six. In America, Senate and congressional seats were to be had for a few hundred thousand. But when the signal came from Switzerland, the millions would be dispensed scientifically, the art of demographics employed. Until the Western world marched to identical drums everywhere, led by the grown-up children of the Reich. *Die Sonnenkinder.*

The Eastern bloc would be next, the Soviet Union and its satellites succumbing to the blandishments of their own emerging bourgeoisie. Marx had never understood: there could be no such thing as a classless society. The human condition would not permit it. Three-year plans and five-year plans meant only continuing austerity; the citizens of socialist programmes were tired of it. But when the signal came, promises would be made and people's collectives everywhere would suddenly realize there was a better way. Because suddenly extraordinary funds would be available; austerity could be replaced by the simple replacing of loyalties. *Die Sonnenkinder.*

The Fourth Reich would be born, not confined to the borders of one or two countries, but all over the world. The Children of the Sun would be the rightful masters of the globe. *Die Sonnenkinder.*

Some might say it was preposterous, inconceivable. It was not; it was happening. Everywhere.

But mistakes were made, thought Tennyson, as he approached the sedan. They were inevitable, and just as inevitable was the fact that they had to be corrected. Beaumont was a mistake. Tennyson put the pistol back in his holster; it would not stay there long.

He walked around the car to the driver's window; it was rolled down, the commander's face turned in concern. "What was it? Is anything wrong?"

"Nothing that can't be fixed. Move over, I'll drive. You can direct me."

"Where to?"

"They said there's a lake somewhere in the vicinity, not more than eight or ten kilometres away. It was difficult to hear; it was a bad connection."

"Only lake near here is just east of Saint-Gratien. It's nearer twelve to fifteen."

"That must be the one. There are forests?"

"Profuse."

"That's the one," Tennyson said, getting into the car as Beaumont moved over on the seat. "I know the headlight codes. You tell me where to go, I'll concentrate on the lamps."

"Seems odd."

"Not odd. Complicated. They may pick us up along the way. I'll know what to look for. Quickly, now. Which direction do we go?"

"Turn around to begin with. Head back to that dreadful road, then turn left."

"Very well." Tennyson started the engine.

"What is it?" Beaumont asked. "It must be a bloody emergency. I've heard a four-dash signal only once before, and *that* was our man at Entebbe."

"He wasn't our man, Tony. He was our puppet."

"Yes, of course. The *Rache* terrorist. Still, he was our *connection*, if you know what I mean."

"Yes I know. Turn here? Left?"

"That's it. Well, for God's sake *tell me!* What the devil's going on?"

Tennyson steadied the car and accelerated. "Actually, it may concern you. We're not sure, but it's a possibility."

"*Me?*"

"Yes. Did Holcroft ever spot you? See you more than once? Be aware that you were following him?"

"*Spot me?* Never, never, *never!* I *swear* it."

"In Geneva? Think."

"Certainly not."

"In New York?"

"I was never within a mile of him! Impossible."

"On the plane to Rio de Janeiro?"

Beaumont paused. "No . . . He came through a curtain; he was quite drunk, I think. But he took no notice, no notice at all. I saw him; he didn't see me."

That was it, thought Tennyson. This devoted child of the Reich believed what he had to believe. There was no point in discussing the matter any further.

"Then it's all a mistake, Tony. A wasted half-hour. I talked to your wife, my dear sister. She said you were much too discreet for such a thing to have happened."

"She was right. She's *always* right, as you well know. Remarkable girl. Regardless of what you may think, ours was not purely a marriage of convenience."

"I know that, Tony. It makes me very happy."

"Take the next right. It goes north towards the lake."

It was cold in the forest, colder by the water. They parked at the end of a dirt road and walked up the narrow path to the edge of the lake. Tennyson carried a flashlight he had taken from the glove compartment of the sedan. In Beaumont's hand was a narrow shovel; they had decided to build a small pit fire to ward off the chill.

"Will we be here that long?" Beaumont asked.

"It's possible. There are other matters to discuss and I'd like your advice. This is the east shore of the lake?"

"Oh, yes. A good rendezvous. No one here this time of year."

"When are you due back to your ship?"

"Have you forgotten? I'm spending the weekend with Gretchen."

"Monday, then?"

"Or Tuesday. My exec's a good chap. He simply assumes I'm prowling around on business. Never questions if I'm a day or so late."

"Why should he? He's one of us."

"Yes, but there are patrol schedules to be observed. Can't muck them up."

"Of course not. Dig here, Tony. Let's have the fire not too near the water. I'll go back and watch for the signals."

"Good."

"Make the hole fairly deep. We wouldn't want the flames too obvious."

"Righto."

Fire. Water. Earth. Burned clothing, charred flesh, smashed and scattered bridgework. John Tennyson walked back over the path and waited. Several minutes later he removed his pistol from the holster and took out a long-bladed hunting knife from his overcoat pocket. The knife, like the shovel, had been in the trunk of the sedan. They were emergency tools and always there.

A mistake had been revealed. It would be rectified by the Tinamou.

18

Holcroft sipped coffee and stood in front of the window, looking out at the cold, bright Paris morning. It was the second morning since he had seen Helden, and she was no nearer reaching her brother than she was the night before last.

"He'll call me, I know he will," she had told him over the phone minutes ago.

"Suppose I go out for a while?" he had asked.

"Don't worry. I'll reach you."

Don't worry. It was an odd remark for her to make, considering where he was and how he got there – *they* got there.

It had been an extension of the madness. They had left the country inn and driven back to Montmartre, where a man had come out of a doorway and relieved them of the Citroën; they had walked through the crowded streets past two pavement café's where successive nods meant they could return to Noel's rented car.

From Montmartre she had directed him across Paris, over the Seine and into Saint-Germain des Prés, where they had stopped at one hotel; he had registered and paid for the night. It was a diversion; he did not go to his room. Instead, they had proceeded to a second hotel on the rue Chevalle, where a soft-drink sign provided him with a name for the registry.

N. Fresca.

She had left him in the lobby, telling him she would call him when she had news of her brother.

"Explain something," he had asked. "Why are we doing all this? What difference does it make where I stay or whether or not I use my own name?"

"You've been seen with me."

Helden. Strange name, strange woman. An odd mixture of vulnerability and strength. Whatever pain she had endured over the years, she refused to turn into self-pity. She recognized her heritage, understood that the children of Nazis were hounded by the *Odessa* and the *Rache* and they had to live with it: damned for what they were and damned for what they were not.

Geneva could help these children, *would* help them. Noel had settled that for himself. He would find a way. Herr Oberst was right: the world cared little for these people – but the persecution had to stop. Holcroft identified with them easily. But for the courage of an extraordinary mother, he could be one of them.

Odessa, Rache ... Wolfsschanze. What drove such men? What rages made them what they were? The world had never found the answers, and perhaps it never would.

But there were other, more immediate concerns, thought Noel, going to the table and pouring himself more coffee. Questions that affected Geneva. Who was the elusive Anthony Beaumont; what did he stand for? What really happened to the von Tiebolts in Brazil? How much did Johann von Tiebolt know about the covenant?

A man will come one day and talk of a strange arrangement . . .

Helden. Strange name, strange girl. Filled with complications and contradictions. He was drawn to her, not solely because she was beautiful but because he had never met anyone like her.

The Rache. The Odessa . . . Wolfsschanze. All fanatics. Adversaries in a bloodbath that had no meaning now. It was over, *had* been over for thirty years. It was dead history, finished.

Yet it was *not* over. The war itself had been revived. By Geneva!

There will be men who will try to stop you, deceive you, kill you . . .

The *Odessa.* The *Rache. These* were Geneva's enemies! Fanatics and terrorists who would do anything to destroy the covenant. Anyone else would have exposed the account by appealing to the international courts; neither the *Odessa* nor the *Rache* could do that. Helden was wrong – at least, partially wrong. Whatever interest both had in the children of Party leaders was suspended to fight the cause of Geneva! To stop *him*. They had learned about the account in Switzerland – somehow, somewhere – and were committed to blocking it. If to succeed meant killing him, it was not a decision of consequence; he was expendable.

It was explained the strychnine on the plane – a horrible death that was meant for him. The terror tactics of the *Rache.* It clarified the events in Rio de Janeiro – gunshots at a deserted lookout and a shattered car window in the night traffic. Maurice Graff and the psychopathic followers of Brazil's *Odessa.* They knew – they *all* knew – about Geneva!

And if they did, they also knew about the von Tiebolts. That would explain what had happened in Brazil. It was never the *mother*, it was Johann von Tiebolt. He was running from Graff's *Odessa*; the protective brother saving what was left of the family, spiriting himself and his two sisters out of Rio.

To live and fulfil the covenant in Geneva.

A man will come one day and talk of a strange arrangement . . . And in that "strange arrangement' was the money and the power to destroy the *Odessa* – and the *Rache* – for certainly these were legitimate objectives of the covenant.

Noel understood now clearly. He and John Tennyson and a man named Kessler in Berlin would control Geneva; they would direct the agency in Zürich. They would rip out the *Odessa* wherever it was; they would crush the

Rache. Among the amends that had to be made was the stilling of fanatics.

He wanted so much to call Helden, to tell her what he believed was true: that soon she could stop running – they could *all* stop running – stop hiding, stop living in fear. He wanted to tell her that. And he wanted to see her again.

But he had given his word not to call her at Gallimard, not to try to reach her for any reason whatsoever. It was maddening; *she* was maddening, yet he could not break his word. She had to trust him, trust what he said to her. That was suddenly very important to him.

The telephone. He had to call the American Express office on the Champs Elysées. He had told Sam Buonoventura that he would check for messages there.

It was a simple matter to get messages by telephone; he had done so before. No one had to know where he was. He put down his coffee and went to the phone, suddenly remembering that he had a second call to make. His mother. It was too early to call her in New York; he'd reach her later in the day.

"I'm sorry, *monsieur*," said the clerk at the American Express office. "You must sign for the cables in person. I'm very sorry."

"Cables!" Noel replaced the phone, annoyed but not angry. Getting out of the hotel room would be good for him, take his mind off the anticipated call from Helden; the waiting *was* maddening.

He walked along the rue Chevalle, a cold wind whipping his face. A taxi took him across the river into the Champs Elysées. The air and the bright sunlight were invigorating; he rolled the window down, feeling the effects of both. For the first time in days he felt confident; he knew where he was going now. Geneva was closer, the blurred lines between enemies and friends more defined. And there was something else, too. He wanted to share his thoughts, and he knew precisely with whom he wanted to share them.

Whatever was waiting for him at the American Express office seemed inconsequential. There was nothing he could not handle in New York or London. His concerns were now in Paris. He and John Tennyson would meet and talk and draw up plans, the first of which would be to go to Berlin and find Erich Kessler. They knew who their enemies were; it was a question of eluding them. Helden's network could help.

As he got out of the taxi, he looked over at the tinted glass window of the American Express office, struck by a thought. Was the refusal to read him his messages over the phone a trap? A means of getting him to show himself? Or locating him for further surveillance? If so, it was a little obvious and, no doubt, a tactic of British Intelligence.

Noel smiled. He knew exactly what to say if the British picked him up: John Tennyson was no more an assassin than he was, and probably far less so than numerous personnel in MI5.

He might even go a step further and suggest that the Royal Navy take a good, long look one of its more decorated officers. All the evidence pointed to the probability that Commander Anthony Beaumont was a member of the *Odessa*, recruited in Brazil by a man named Graff.

He felt he was falling through space, plunging downwards, unable to catch his breath. His stomach was hollow and pain shot through his lower chest. He was gripped by combined feelings of grief, and fear ... and anger. The cablegram read

Your father died four days ago stop Unable to contact you stop Please respond by telephone Bedford Hills

Mother

There was a second cable from Lieutenant David Miles, New York Police Department.

The recent death of Richard Holcroft makes it imperative you contact me immediately. Professionally I recommend you speak to me before reaching anyone else.

There were the same two telephone numbers Buonoventura had given him in Rio de Janeiro, and six – six – follow-up inquiries listed by day and hour since the original message had been received at the American Express office. Miles had checked twice a day to see if his message had been picked up.

Noel walked to the Champs Elysées, trying to collect his thoughts, trying to control his grief.

The only father he had ever known. *Dad, Pop ... my father*, Richard Holcroft. Always said with affection, with love. And always with warmth and humour, for Richard Holcroft was a man of many graces, not the least of which was an ability to laugh at himself. He had guided his son – stepson – no, *goddamn it*, his *son!* Guided but never interfered, except when interference was the only alternative.

Oh, God, he was *dead!*

What caused the sharp bolts of pain – pain he understood was part of the fear and the anger – was implied in Miles's cable. Was he somehow responsible for Richard Holcroft's death? Oh, *Christ!* Was that death related to a vial of strychnine poured into a drink thirty thousand feet over the Atlantic? Was it woven into the fabric of *Geneva?*

Had he somehow sacrificed the father he had known all his life for one he never knew?

He reached the corner of the Avenue Georges Cinq. Across the broad intersection, teeming with traffic, he saw a sign above awnings that stretched the length of the pavement café. *Fouquet's*. It was all familiar to him. To his left was the Hôtel Georges Cinq. He had stayed there briefly a year ago, courtesy of an extremely wealthy hotelman who had delusions, later proven just that, of duplicating its exterior in Kansas City.

Holcroft had struck up a friendship with the assistant manager. If the man was still there, perhaps he'd let him use a telephone. If telephone calls *were* traced back to the Georges Cinq, it would be a simple matter to learn about them. And a simpler matter to leave misleading information regarding his whereabouts.

Anticipate.

"But, of course, it's my pleasure, Noel. It's so good to see you again. I am chagrined you do not stay with us, but at these prices I don't blame you. Here, use my office."

"I'll charge the calls to my credit card, of course."

"I'm not worried, my friend. Later, an *apéritif*, perhaps?"

"I'd like that," said Noel.

It was 10.45, Paris time. Quarter to six in New York. If Miles was as anxious as his message implied, the hour was insignificant. He picked up the phone and placed the call.

Noel looked at Miles's message again.

The recent death of Richard Holcroft . . . Professionally, I recommend you speak to me before reaching anyone else.

Professionally, I recommend you speak to me before reaching anyone else. The recommendation had an ominous sound; the *anyone else* had to mean his mother.

He put the paper down on the desk and reached into his pocket for Althene's cablegram.

Your father died four days ago . . . unable to contact you . . .

The guilt he felt at not having been with her nearly matched the guilt and the fear and the anger that consumed him when he considered the possibility that he was responsible for the death. Possibility? He *knew* it, he *felt* it.

He wondered – painfully – if Miles had reached Althene. And if he had, what had he said to her?

The telephone rang.

"Is this Noel Holcroft?"

"Yes. I'm sorry you had trouble reaching me . . ."

"I won't waste time going into that," interrupted Miles, "except to say you've violated federal laws."

"*Wait* a minute," broke in Noel, angrily. "What am I guilty of? You found me. I'm not hiding."

"*Finding* you after trying to locate you for damn near a week is called flagrantly ignoring and disregarding the law. You were not to leave the city of New York without telling us."

"There were pressing personal matters. I left word. You haven't got a case."

"Then let's try obstruction of justice."

"What?"

"You were in the lounge of that British 747 and you and I both know what happened. Or, should I say, what *didn't* happen?"

"What are you talking about?"

"That drink was meant for you, not Thornton."

Holcroft knew it was coming, but his knowing it did not lessen the impact. Still, he was not about to agree without a protest. "That's the craziest goddamn thing I've ever heard of," he said.

"Come on! You're a bright, upstanding citizen from a bright, upstanding family, but your behaviour for the past five days has been stupid and less than candid."

"You're insulting me, but you're not saying anything. You mentioned in your message . . ."

"We'll get to that," interrupted the detective. "I want you to know where you stand. You see, I want you to cooperate, not fight."

"Go ahead."

"We traced you to Rio. We spoke to . . ."

"You *what?*" Had Sam turned on him?

"It wasn't hard. Incidentally, your friend Buonoventura doesn't know. His cover for you didn't wash. He said you were in a boat out of Curaçao, but Dutch immigration didn't have you in the territory. We got a list of the overseas telephone numbers he called and checked the airlines. You were on Braniff out of New York and you stayed at a Porto Alegre Hotel in Rio."

The amateur could not match the professionals. "Sam said you called a couple of times."

"Sure did," agreed Miles. "You left Rio and we wanted to find out where you went; we knew he'd get in touch with you. Didn't you get my message at the hotel in London?"

"No."

"I'll take your word. Messages get lost."

But that message had not been lost, thought Noel. It had been stolen by the men of Wolfsschanze. "I know where I stand now. Get to the point."

"You don't *quite* know," Miles replied. "We talked to the embassy in Rio, to a man named Anderson. He said you told him quite a story. How you were trapped, chased, shot at. He said he didn't believe a word of it; considered you a troublemaker and was glad to get you out of Brazil."

"I know. He drove me to the airport."

"Do you want to tell me about it?" asked the detective.

Noel stared at the wall. It would be so easy to unburden himself, to seek official protection. "No, there's nothing you can do. It's been resolved."

"Has it?"

"Yes."

Neither spoke for several seconds. "All right, Mr Holcroft. I hope you change your mind, because I think I can help you. I think you *need* help." Miles paused. "I now make a formal request for your return to the city of

New York. You are considered a prime witness in a homicide and intrinsic to our jurisdictional interrogations."

"Sorry. Not now."

"I didn't think you would. So let me try informally. It concerns your father."

The terrible news was coming, and he could not help himself. He said the words quietly. "He was killed, wasn't he?"

"I didn't hear that. You see, if I did, I'd have to go to my superior and report it. Say you said it without provocation. You drew a conclusion that couldn't possibly be based on anything I said to you. I'd have to request extradition."

"Get off it, Miles! Your telephone message wasn't subtle! '*The recent death*', et cetera; '*professionally speaking, I recommend*', et cetera! What the hell am I supposed to think?"

Again, there was a pause in New York. "Okay. It's checkmate. You've got a case."

"He was murdered, wasn't he?"

"We think so."

"What have you said to my mother?"

"Nothing. And that answers my next question. You haven't talked to her yet."

"Obviously. Tell me what happened."

"Your father was in what can best be described as a very unusual accident. He died an hour later in the hospital as a result of the injuries."

"What was the accident?"

"An old man from the Bronx lost control of his car near the Plaza Hotel. The car went wild, jumped the kerb, and plunged into a crowd of people on the pavement. Three were killed instantly. Your father was thrown against the wall. Actually, he was pinned, almost crushed."

"You're saying the car aimed for him!"

"Hard to tell. There was mass confusion, of course."

"Then what *are* you saying?"

Miles hesitated. "That the car aimed for him."

"Who was the driver?"

"A seventy-two-year-old retired accountant with an inflamed heart, a pace-maker, no family at all, and a licence that expired several years ago. The 'pacer' was shorted in the accident; the man died on the way to the hospital."

"What was his connection to my father?"

"So far, no definite answers. But I've got a theory. Do you want to hear it?"

"Of course!"

"Will you come back to New York?"

"Don't press me. What's your theory?"

"I think the old guy was recruited. I think there was someone else in that car, probably in the back seat, holding a gun to his head. During the confusion, he smashed the pacer and got away. I think it was an execution made to look like a freak accident in which more than the target got killed."

Noel held his breath. There had been another "freak accident". An underground train in London had gone out of control, killing five people. And among those killed was the only man who could shed light on John Tennyson's employment at *The Guardian*.

It was bloody well murder . . .

The thought of a connection was appalling. "Aren't you reaching, Miles?" Holcroft asked.

"I said it was a theory, but not without some support. When I saw the name Holcroft on the accident report, I did a little digging. The old man from the Bronx has an interesting history. He came to this country in "47, supposedly a penniless Jewish immigrant, a victim of Dachau. Only he wasn't penniless, as half a dozen bank books show, and his apartment is a fortress. Besides which, he made thirteen trips to Germany and back since he got here."

Beads of perspiration broke out on Noel's forehead. "What are you trying to say?"

"I don't think that old guy was ever near Dachau. Or if he was, he was part of the management. No one hardly knew him in his apartment building; no one ever saw him in a synagogue. I think he was a Nazi."

Holcroft swallowed. "How does that connect him to my father?"

"Through you. I'm not sure how yet, but through you."

"Through me?" Noel felt the acceleration of his heartbeat.

"Yes. In Rio, you told Anderson that someone named Graff was a Nazi and tried to kill you. Anderson said you were crazy on both points, but I don't. I believe you."

"I was mad as hell. I didn't *mean* to tie one into the other. It was a misunderstanding . . ." Noel sought desperately to find the words. "Graff's paranoid, a hot-tempered German – so I called him a Nazi – that's all. He thought I was making sketches, taking pictures of his grounds."

"I said I *believed* you, Holcroft," broke in the detective. "And I've got my reasons."

"What are they?" Noel knew he could barely be heard: he was suddenly afraid. His father's death was a warning. The *Rache*. The *Odessa*. Whichever, it was another *warning*. His mother had to be protected!

Miles was talking, but Holcroft could not hear the detective; his mind raced in panic. Miles had to be stopped! He could not be allowed near Geneva.

"Those men on the plane who tried to kill you were German," Miles explained. "They used passports taken off two Americans killed in Munich five years ago, but they were German; the dental work gave them away. They were shot at Kennedy Airport, their bodies were found in a fuel truck. The bullets that killed them came from a German Heckler and Koch nine-millimetre pistol. The silencer was made in Munich. Guess where that little old man travelled when he went to Germany – at least on the six trips we were able to trace?"

"Munich," whispered Noel.

"That's right. Munich. Where it all began and where it's still going on. A bunch of Nazis are fighting among each other thirty years after that goddamn war is over, and you're right in the middle of it. I want to know *why*."

Noel felt drained, swept by exhaustion and fear. "Leave it alone. There's nothing you can do."

"There's something I might be able to *prevent*, goddamn it! Another *murder*."

"Can't you understand?" said Holcroft in pain. "I can say it because he *was* my father. Nothing can be resolved in New York. It can only be resolved over here. Give me time; for the love of God, give me *time*. I'll get back to you."

"How long?"

"A month."

"Too much. Cut it in half. You've got two weeks."

"Miles, *please* . . ."

There was a click on the line, the connection in New York was severed.

Noel held the telephone in his hand and looked at it. It was heavy and grotesque, a terrible thing. He recalled the sight of the phone in his apartment – bound with ugly black tape, suspended from the ceiling, spinning slowly.

Nothing is as it was for you. Nothing can ever be the same . . . The men of Wolfsschanze did not lie. They killed but they did not lie. Others killed, but they did not speak the truth. The *Rache*. The *Odessa*. They killed with lies, with deceit, with traps, without cause. Not the men of Wolfsschanze.

What was he *thinking* of? What moral absolute made killing with truth more acceptable than killing with deceit? *Two weeks*. Oh, God, it wasn't possible!

But it *had* to be possible. In two weeks he had to be in a position to stop Miles from going further. He could do that with the resources in Geneva. A philanthropic agency with assets of seven hundred and eighty million dollars would be listened to – quietly, in confidence. Once the account was freed, arrangements could be made, understandings reached, cooperation given and received. The *Odessa* would be exposed, the *Rache* destroyed.

All this would happen – and it would *only* happen – when three acceptable offspring presented themselves to the bank in Geneva. Three people willing, able, and in agreement to suspend all other interests and devote themselves to the covenant. It *would* happen, Noel was convinced of that, but until then he had to protect his mother. He had to reach Althene and convince her that for the next few weeks she had to disappear.

What could he say to her? She'd never obey him. She'd never *listen* to him if she believed for an instant her husband had been murdered. What in God's name could he *say* to her?

"Allo? Allo, *monsieur?*" The voice of the operator floated out from the telephone. "Your call to New York . . ."

Holcroft hung up so quickly he jarred the instrument's bell. He would not give the operator the number in Bedford Hills; he could not talk to his mother.

Not now. In an hour or so, not now. He had to think. There was so much to think about, so much to do, so little time.

He was going mad.

19

"He'll go mad," said the blond-haired man into the telephone at Athen's Hellinikon Airport. "He must have heard the news by now. It will be a strain that may tear him apart; he won't know what to do. Tell our man in Paris to stay close to him for the next twenty-four hours. He must not return to America."

"He won't," said Gretchen Beaumont, thousands of miles away.

"You can't be sure. The psychological stresses are building properly. Our subject's in a delicate frame of mind. However, he can be guided. He's waiting for me; he sees me now as his answer to so many things, but the string must be drawn tighter. I want him to go to Berlin first. For a day or two. To Kessler."

"Shall we use his mother? We could plant the idea with her."

"No. Under no circumstances must she be touched. It would be far too dangerous."

"Then how will you suggest Berlin?" asked Gretchen Beaumont in England.

"I won't," answered John Tennyson in Athens. "I will convince our sister to lead him to that conclusion. She's trying to reach me, of course."

"Be careful with her, Johann."

"I will."

Holcroft walked along the concrete banks of the Seine, unaware of the biting winds that came off the river. An hour ago he had been filled with confidence; now he felt lost. He only knew that he had to keep moving, clear his head, make decisions.

He had to re-evaluate some things, too. An hour ago the one man he believed he could count on was Helden's brother. That judgement was suspect now. A runaway car on a New York street that took the life of the only father he had ever known was too similar to an unexplained disaster in the London Underground.

The man was killed in a most unusual accident that took five lives . . . MI5.

An execution . . . a freak accident in which more than the target got killed . . . David Miles, NYPD.

The meeting with Tennyson was suddenly *not* the answer to everything; the shadow of the Tinamou had appeared again. *A man would come one day and talk of a strange arrangement.* Tennyson was waiting for him, but perhaps he was waiting for the wrong reasons. Perhaps he had sold out their covenant for a higher price.

If he had, he was as responsible for Richard Holcroft's death as surely as if his foot had been on the accelerator and his hands on the wheel. Should that be the case, Tennyson would not leave the meeting alive. The son would kill for the father; he owed Richard Holcroft that.

Noel stopped and put his hands on the concrete wall, astonished at himself . . . at his thoughts. He was actually projecting himself into the role of a killer! His covenant was extracting a cost more terrible than anything he had considered.

He would confront Tennyson with the facts as they had been given to him. He would watch the son of Wilhelm von Tiebolt closely. The truth or the lie; it would be in Tennyson's words, in his eyes. Holcroft hoped to God he would know which.

One step at a time. His mind was clearing; each move had to be considered carefully, yet that caution could not slow him down.

First things first, and first there was the indisputable fact that he could no longer move freely, carelessly. The most deadly warning of all had been given him: the killing of a loved one. He accepted that warning in fear and in rage. The fear would make him careful, the rage would give him a degree of courage. It *had* to; he was depending on it.

Next was his mother. What could he say that she would accept without being suspicious? Whatever it was, she had to believe him. If she thought for an instant that her husband's death was the work of men spawned by the Third Reich, she would raise her voice in fury. And her first cry would be her last. What *could* he say to her that would sound plausible?

He started walking again, absentmindedly, his eyes unfocused. As a result, he collided with a short man strolling in the opposite direction.

"Excuse me. *Pardon, monsieur*," Noel said.

The Frenchman had been glancing at a newspaper; he shrugged and smiled pleasantly. *"Rien."*

Noel stopped. The Frenchman reminded him of someone. The round face, the spectacles, the pleasant face.

Ernst Manfredi.

We're dealing in hundreds of millions, Manfredi had warned. His mother had respected Manfredi, owed the Swiss banker a great debt. Perhaps he could speak to Althene through Ernst Manfredi, invent an explanation given him by the banker. Why not? The words would not be contradicted; Manfredi was dead.

It was Manfredi who was concerned for his old friend, Althene Clausen. *He* was frightened for her. He was afraid that during the coming weeks while the extraordinary account in Geneva was being released, Clausen's name would surface. There would be those who remembered a headstrong young woman who left her husband in revulsion, whose words became the basis for Heinrich Clausen's moral conversion. A conversion that resulted in the theft of *hundreds of millions*. Dormant hostilities might be aroused, revenge sought against that woman.

It was *Manfredi's* fear that she had to respect. The old banker knew more than either of them, and if he had thought it best that she disappear for a while, until the impact of the account's release was diminished, she should take his advice. A sick old man about to end his life did not draw frivolous conclusions.

The explanation made sense; it was consistent with their conversation in Bedford Hills three weeks ago. His mother would see that consistency. She would listen to the "words" of Ernst Manfredi.

Instinctively, Noel glanced over his shoulder to see if anyone was following him. The action would soon become a habit, he reflected. Fear made him careful . . . the rage he felt gave him a certain strength; he wanted very much to see an enemy. He was getting used to his unfamiliar forest.

He walked back towards the hotel. He had rushed out of the Georges Cinq in panic and bewilderment, avoiding the assistant manager, needing the cold air of the streets to clear his head. He would go back now. He would accept an *apéritif* and ask to make another transatlantic call. To his mother.

He walked faster, stopping twice abruptly, turning quickly; was there anyone there?

It was possible. A dark green Fiat had slowed down a block behind. *Good.*

He crossed the street rapidly, went into the front entrance of a pavement café, and emerged seconds later from an exit that led out to the Avenue Georges Cinq. He walked up the block, stopping at a news-stand for a paper.

He could see the green Fiat careening around the corner near the café. It stopped abruptly. The driver parked at the kerb and lowered his head. *Good.* It was suddenly made clear to Noel what he would do after the *apéritif* and the call to Althene.

He would see Helden. He needed a gun.

Von Tiebolt stared at the mouthpiece of the pay phone in the Athens airport, his lips parted in shock.

"*What did you say?*" he asked.

"It's true, Johann," said Helden in Paris. "British Intelligence thinks you may be the Tinamou."

"How *extraordinary.*" The astonished blond man drew out the word. "And outrageous!"

"That's what I said to Holcroft. I told him you were being hounded for the things you write . . . and because of who you are. What *we* are."

"Yes, I imagine so." Von Tiebolt could not concentrate on his sister's reasoning; he gripped the receiver in anger. An error had been made somewhere; steps had to be taken immediately to correct it. What led MI5 to *him?* Every track had been covered! But then he could produce the Tinamou at will; it was his final strategy. No one was more trusted or beholden than the suspect who produced the killer. This was the ultimate tactic of his creation. He might have to employ it sooner than he thought.

"Johann, are you there?"

"Yes, sorry."

"You *must* meet Holcroft as soon as possible."

"Of course. I'll be in Paris in four or five days . . ."

"Not until then?" interrupted Helden. "He's very anxious."

"It's quite impossible."

"There's so much more to tell you . . ." *An account in Geneva, an agency in Zürich to dispense hundreds of millions. The American son of Heinrich Clausen. Erich Kessler in Berlin. The von Tiebolts in Rio.* Finally, haltingly, she repeated the words uttered by their sister. *A man will come one day and talk of a strange arrangement.* "Did you say that?"

"Yes. There's a great deal you've never been told. I didn't know when or how it would happen, only that it would. I spoke to Gretchen earlier. This Holcroft saw her the other night. I'm afraid she wasn't much help to him. We have a commitment as profound and as moving as anything in recent history. Amends must be made . . ."

"That's what Holcroft said," broke in Helden.

"I'm sure he did."

"He's frightened. He tries not to show it, but he is."

"He should be. It's an enormous responsibility. I have to learn what he knows in order to help."

"Then come to Paris now."

"I can't. It's only a few days."

"I'm worried. If Noel's what he says he is, and I see no reason to doubt him . . ."

"'Noel?'" asked the brother with mild surprise.

"I like him, Johann."

"Go on."

"If he's the one that's to bring the three of you together, nothing can happen in Geneva without him."

"So?"

"Others know that. I think they know about the account in Switzerland. Terrible things have happened. They've tried to stop him."

"Who?"

"My guess would be the *Rache*. Or the *Odessa*."

"That's doubtful," said John Tennyson. "Neither is capable of keeping such extraordinary news quiet. Take a newspaperman's word for it."

"The *Rache* kills, so does the *Odessa*. Someone tried to kill Noel."

Tennyson smiled to himself; errors may have been made, but the primary strategy was working. Holcroft was being pounded on all sides. When everything came together in Geneva, he'd be exhausted, completely malleable. "We must be very cautious then. Teach him the things you know, Helden. As much as you can. The tricks we've all learned from one another."

165

"He's seen some of those tricks," said the girl, a soft, compassionate laugh in her voice. "He hates using them."

"Better than dead." The blond man paused. The transition had to be casual. "Gretchen mentioned a photograph, a picture of Beaumont. She thinks Holcroft took it."

"He did. He's convinced he saw Beaumont on the plane from New York to Rio. He thinks he was following him. It's part of what he'll tell you."

So it *was* the plane, thought Tennyson. The American was more observant than Beaumont had wanted to believe – because he had not wanted to believe it. Beaumont's disappearance would be explained in a matter of days, but it would be difficult to explain the photograph in Holcroft's possession if he showed it to the wrong people in Switzerland. The fanatic commander may have left too obvious a trail, from Rio to the Admiralty. They had to get the photograph back. "I don't know how to answer that, Helden. I never liked Beaumont. I never trusted him. But he's been in the Mediterranean for months. I don't see how he could have left his ship and turn up on a plane out of New York. Holcroft's wrong." Tennyson paused again. "However, I think . . . Noel . . . should bring the photograph with him when we meet. He shouldn't be carrying it around. Nor should he talk about Beaumont, tell him that. It could lead people to Gretchen. To us. Yes, I think it would be a good idea if he brought the photograph with him."

"He can't do that. It was stolen from him."

The blond man froze. It was *impossible*. None of *them* had taken the photograph! No *Sonnenkind*. He'd be the first to know. Someone *else*? He lowered his voice. "What do you mean, stolen from him?"

"Just that. A man chased him, beat him unconscious, and took the picture. Nothing else, just the photograph."

"*What* man?"

"He didn't know. It was night; he couldn't see. He woke up in a field miles away from Portsmouth."

"He was attacked in *Portsmouth?*"

"About a mile from Gretchen's house, as I gather."

Something *was* wrong. Terribly wrong. "Are you sure Holcroft wasn't lying?"

"Why should he?"

"What *exactly* did he tell you?"

"That he was chased by a man in a black sweater. The man hit him with a blunt weapon and took the photograph out of his pocket when he was unconscious. Just the photograph. Not his money or anything else."

"I see." But he did *not* see! And it was the unseen that disturbed him. He could not convey his fears to Helden; as always, he had to appear in total control. Yet he had to search out this unseen, unknown disturbance. "Helden, I'd like you to do something . . . for all of us. Do you think you could arrange to take a day off from work?"

"I imagine so. Why?"

"I think we should try and find out who it is that has so much interest in Holcroft. Perhaps you might suggest a drive in the country, to Fontainebleau or Barbizon."

"But why?"

"I have a friend in Paris. He often does odd jobs for me. I'll ask him to follow you, very discreetly, of course. Perhaps we'll learn who else takes the trip."

"One of our people could do it."

"No, I don't think so. Don't involve your friends. *Herr Oberst* should not be a part of this."

"All right. We'll start out around ten in the morning. From his hotel. Les Douzaines Heures, rue Chevalle. How will I know the man?"

"You won't. He'll pick you up. Say nothing to Holcroft; it would upset him needlessly."

"Very well. You'll call me when you get to Paris?"

"The minute I arrive, *meine Schwester.*"

"*Danke, mein Bruder.*"

Tennyson replaced the phone. There was a last call to make before he boarded the plane to Berlin. Not to Gretchen now; he did not want to speak to her. If Beaumont's actions proved to be as disastrous as they appeared, if in his recklessness he had impeded the cause of Wolfsschanze, then all the strings that led to him and through him to Geneva would have to be severed. It was not an easy decision to make. He loved Gretchen as few men on earth loved their sisters; in a way that the world disapproved because it did not understand. She took care of his needs, satiated his hungers so that there were never any outside complications. His mind was free to concentrate on his extraordinary mission in life. But that, too, might have to end. Gretchen his sister, his lover, might have to die.

Tactics changed with sudden necessities. Perhaps the death of Anthony Beaumont would not be the result of a KGB bribe in Prague, with diplomats arguing over candour and defections. Perhaps a family tragedy might have to be substituted. A tragedy that took place while husband and wife were on holiday. He picked up the phone, inserted the Greek coin, and dialled the operator. He would speak with a *Sonnenkind* in London.

Holcroft listened to Althene's last words, stunned at her equilibrium, astonished that it had been so easy. The funeral had been yesterday.

"You do what you must, Noel. A good man died needlessly, foolishly, and that's the obscenity. But it's over; there's nothing either of us can do."

"There's something you can do for me."

"What's that?"

He told her of Manfredi's death – as the Swiss believed it happened. An old man racked with pain, preferring a quick end to prolonged suffering and infirmity. "The last thing he did as a banker was to meet me in Geneva."

Althene was silent for a moment, reflecting on a friend who once meant a great deal to her. "It was like him to fulfil an agreement as important as the one he brought to you. He wouldn't leave it to others."

"There was something else; it concerned you. He said you'd understand." Holcroft held the telephone firmly and spoke as convincingly as he could. He expressed Manfredi's "concern" about those who might remember a headstrong woman many believed responsible for the conversion of Heinrich Clausen, and his decision to betray the Reich. How it was entirely possible that there remained even now fanatics who might still seek revenge. Manfredi's old friend, Althene Clausen, should not risk being a target; she should go away for a while, where no one could find her if Clausen's name surfaced. "Can you understand, mother?"

"Yes," answered Althene. "Because he said it to me once before, several hundred years ago. He said they would look for us then, too. He was right; he's right now. The world is filled with lunatics."

"Where will you go?"

"I'm not sure. Take a trip perhaps. It's a very good time for it, isn't it? People are so embarrassingly solicitous about death."

"I'd rather you went some place where you were out of sight. Just for a few weeks."

"It's easy to be out of sight. I have a certain expertise in that. For two years after we left Berlin, you and I kept moving. Until Pearl Harbor, actually. The Bund's activities were too varied for comfort in those days; it took its orders from the Wilhelmstrasse. We were out of sight."

"I didn't know that," said Holcroft, moved.

"There's a great deal . . . No matter. Richard put an end to it all. He made us stop running, stop hiding. I'll let you know where I am."

"How?"

His mother paused. "Your friend in Curaçao, Mr Buonoventura. He was positively reverential. I'll let him know."

Holcroft smiled. "All right. I'll call Sam."

"I never did tell you about those days, did I? Before Richard came into our lives. I really must; you might be interested."

"I'd be very interested. Manfredi was right. You're incredible."

"No, dear. Merely a survivor."

As always, they said rapid goodbyes; they were friends. Noel walked out of the assistant manager's office. He started across the Georges Cinq lobby towards the bar where his friend was waiting with *apéritifs*, then decided to take a short detour. He crossed to the huge window to the left of the entrance and peered out between the folds of the red velvet drapes. The green Fiat was still down the street.

Noel continued across the lobby towards the bar. He would spend a quarter of an hour in pleasant conversation with the assistant manager, during which he would impart some very specific, if erroneous, information and ask a favour or two.

168

And then there was Helden. If she did not call him by five o'clock, he would telephone her at Gallimard.

"Four or five *days?*" exploded Holcroft into the phone. "I don't want to wait four or five days. I'll meet him anywhere! I can't waste time."

"He said he wouldn't be in Paris until then and suggested you go on to Berlin in the meantime. It would only take you a day or so."

"He knew about *Kessler?*"

"Perhaps not by name, but he knew about Berlin."

"Where was he?"

"At the airport in Athens."

Noel remembered. *He disappeared four days ago in Bahrain. Our operatives are watching for him from Singapore to Athens.* British Intelligence would have its confrontation with John Tennyson soon if it had not taken place already. "What did he say about the British?"

"He was serious, as I knew he would be. It's not unlike Johann to write an article that would embarrass the Foreign Office. He was outraged."

"I trust he won't. The last thing any of us want is a newspaper story. Can you call him back? Can *I* call him? He could fly in tonight. I could pick him up at Orly."

"I'm afraid not. He was catching a plane. There's only a number in Brussels; it's where he picks up his messages. It took him nearly two days to get mine."

"Goddamn it!"

"You're overwrought."

"I'm in a hurry."

"Noel . . ." Helden began haltingly. "I don't have to work tomorrow. Could we meet? Perhaps go for a drive. I'd like to talk."

Holcroft was startled. He wanted to see *her.* "Why wait until tomorrow? Let's have dinner."

"I can't. I have a meeting tonight. I'll be at your hotel at ten o'clock tomorrow morning. In the afternoon you could fly to Berlin."

"Are you meeting your friends?"

"Yes."

"Helden, do something for me. I never thought I'd ask this of anyone, but I want a gun. I don't know how to go about getting one, what the laws are."

"I understand. I'll bring it. Until morning."

"See you tomorrow." Holcroft hung up and looked at his open attaché case on the hotel chair. He could see the cover of the Geneva document. It reminded him of the threat from the men of Wolfsschanze. *Nothing* is *as it was for you* . . . He knew now how completely true that was. He had borrowed a gun in Costa Rica. He had killed a man who was about to kill him, and he never wanted to see a gun in his hand again, for as long as he lived. That, too, was changed. Everything was changed, because a man he never knew had cried out to him from the grave.

20

"Do you like mountain trout?" asked Helden, as she handed him the automatic in the front seat of his rented car.

"Trout's fine," he said, laughing.

"What's funny?"

"I don't know. You hand me a gun, which isn't the most normal thing for a person to do, and at the same time you ask me what I'd like for lunch."

"One has nothing to do with the other. I think it might be a good idea if you took your mind off your problems for a few hours."

"I thought you wanted to talk about them."

"I do. I also wanted to know you better. When we met the other night, you asked all the questions."

"Before I asked those questions, you did all the yelling."

Helden laughed. "I'm sorry about that. It was hectic, wasn't it?"

"It was crazy. You have a nice laugh. I didn't know you laughed."

"I do quite frequently. At least twice a month, regular as clockwork."

Holcroft glanced at her. "I shouldn't have said that. I don't imagine you find much to laugh at."

She returned his look; a smile was on her lips. "More than you think, perhaps. And I wasn't offended. I'm sure you think me rather solemn." There was a gamin quality about her Noel had not noticed before. "Do you ever think about them?" she asked.

"Who?"

"Those fathers you and I never knew. What they did was so incredible, such an act of daring."

"Not just one act. Hundreds . . . thousands of them. Each different, each complicated, going on for months. Three years of manipulations."

"They must have lived in terror."

"I'm sure they did."

"What drove them?"

"Just what . . . Just what Heinrich Clausen wrote in his letter to me. They were shocked beyond anything we can imagine when they learned about the 'rehabilitation' camps. Auschwitz, Belsen; it blew their minds."

Helden touched his arm. "You call him Heinrich Clausen. You can't say 'father', can you?"

"I *had* a father." Noel stopped. It was not the moment to talk about Richard Holcroft; he had to control himself. "He's dead. He was killed five days ago in New York."

"Oh, *God* . . ." Helden stared at him; he could feel the intensity of her concern. "Killed? Because of Geneva?" she asked.

"I don't know."

"But you think so."

"Yes." He gripped the wheel and was silent. A shell was forming, and it was an awful thing.

"I'm sorry, Noel. I don't know what else to say. I wish I could comfort you somehow, but I don't know how."

He looked at her, at her lovely face, and the clear brown eyes filled with concern. "With all your problems, just saying that is enough. You're a nice person, Helden. I haven't met too many people like you."

"I could say the same . . . nice person."

"We've both said it. Now, what about that trout? If we're going to take a few hours off, why not tell me where we're going?"

"To Barbizon. There's a lovely restaurant in the centre of the town. Have you ever been to Barbizon?"

"Several times," said Noel, his eyes suddenly on the small, rectangular mirror outside the window.

There was a dark green Fiat behind them. He had no idea whether it was the same car that had waited for him yesterday on the Avenue Georges Cinq, but he intended to find out – without alarming Helden. He slowed down; the Fiat did not pass. Instead, it veered into the right lane, allowing another car to come between them.

"Is something wrong?" asked Helden.

Holcroft pressed and depressed the accelerator. The car lurched slightly at the slower speed. "No, not really. I had trouble with this damn thing yesterday. It needs a carburetter adjustment, I think. Every now and then there's an airlock. It passes if you nurse it."

"You sound very efficient."

"I'm a fair mechanic. You don't take jobs in Mexico and points south unless you are." He stepped on the pedal and held it down; the car sped forward.

He could see the green Fiat in the rear-view mirror now. It swerved to the left, passing the intervening car, then returned to the right lane behind them. The question was answered. They were being followed.

His fear was making him cautious. Yet behind the fear was anger and it was infusing him with a kind of strength; he could suppress his fear, exchange it for a purpose. Whoever was in that Fiat was indirectly involved with Richard Holcroft's death; he was certain of it. And he was going to trap that man.

"There. Everything's fine now," he said to Helden. "The airlock's passed. Lunch in Barbizon sounds like a hell of a good idea. Let's see if I remember the way."

He did not. On purpose. He took several wrong turns, covering his mistakes with laughter, insisting the whole French countryside had been changed around. It became a silly game with a deadly serious objective: he had to see the face of the man in the Fiat. In Paris, that face had been obscured behind a windscreen and a cloud of cigarette smoke; he had to be able to recognize it in a crowd.

The Fiat's driver, however, was no amateur. He may have been bewildered by Noel's aimless turns and shifting speeds, but he gave no indication of it, staying a discreet distance behind them, never allowing the gap between them to become too close. There was a disabled car on a narrow road south of Corbeil-Essonnes; it was as good an excuse as any to stop. Holcroft pulled alongside to see if he could help; the driver of the Fiat had no choice. He drove swiftly past the two parked cars. Noel looked up. The man was fair-complexioned, his hair light brown; and there was something else. There were splotches or pockmarks on the man's cheek.

He would know that face again. That was all that mattered.

The driver of the disabled car thanked Holcroft, indicating that help was on the way.

Noel nodded and started up again, wondering if he'd see the green Fiat soon. Would it be in a side road waiting for him, or would it simply emerge from nowhere and appear in the rear-view mirror? What did a man following another man do under the circumstances?

"That was a very nice thing to do," said Helden.

"We ugly Americans do nice things every once in a while. I'll get back on the highway."

If the green Fiat was in a side road, he did not see it. It was simply there in his mirror on the highway. They got off at the Seine-et-Marne exit and drove into Barbizon. The green Fiat stayed far behind, but it was there.

Their lunch was a strange mixture of ease and awkwardness. Brief starts and abrupt stops; short conversations begun, suddenly suspended at midpoint, the purpose unremembered. Yet the ease was in their being together, physically close to one another. Holcroft thought she felt it as surely as he did.

The sense of closeness was confirmed for Noel by something Helden did without obviously thinking about it. She touched him repeatedly. She would reach over briefly and touch his sleeve, or, more briefly, his hand. She would touch him for emphasis, or because she was asking a question, but she touched him as if it were the most natural thing in the world for her to do. And it was natural for him to accept her touch. He returned it frequently.

"Your brother didn't discuss Beaumont?" he asked.

"Yes, he did. He was very angry. Everything about Beaumont angers him. He thinks you were wrong about seeing him on the plane, though. He wanted you to bring the photograph. I told him you didn't have it. He was furious."

"About the photograph?"

"Yes. He said it might be dangerous. It could lead 'people', he said, to Gretchen, to you. To Geneva."

"I think the answer's simpler. The Royal Navy's no different from any other military organization. The officers protect each other."

"My promiscuous sister, you mean?"

Holcroft nodded; he really did not want to discuss Gretchen Beaumont, not with Helden. "Something like that."

She touched his fingers. "It's all right, Noel. I don't sit in judgement where my sister's concerned." Then she took away her hand, embarrassed. "What I mean is, I have no right . . . No, I don't mean that, either. I mean where you're concerned, I have no right . . ."

"I think we both know what you mean," interrupted Holcroft, covering her hand with his. "Feel free to have a right. I think I like it."

"You make me feel foolish."

"Do I? It's the last thing I want to make you feel." He pulled back his hand, and followed her glance out of the window. She was looking at the small stone pond on the terrace, but his attention did not remain where hers did. His gaze rose to several groups of tourists strolling in the Barbizon street beyond the gates of the restaurant. The man with the light brown hair and pockmarked complexion was standing motionless on the far pavement. A cigarette was in mouth, what appeared to be an artist's brochure in his hands. But the man was not looking at the brochure. His head was raised slightly, his eyes angled over at the entrance of the restaurant.

It was time to make his move, thought Noel. His rage was rekindled; he wanted that man.

"I've got an idea," he said as casually as he could. "I saw a poster by the door that – in my schoolboy French – I think said *Fêtes d'Hiver*. Some place called Montereau- something-or-other. Isn't that a kind of carnival?"

"The *fête* is, not the village. It's about seven or eight miles south of here, I think."

"What is it: the carnival, I mean."

"*Fêtes d'Hiver?* They're quite common and usually run by the local churches. As a rule, they're associated with a saint's day. It's like a flea market."

"Let's go."

"Really?"

"Why not? It might be fun. I'll buy you a present."

Helden looked at him quizzically. "All right," she said.

The bright afternoon sunlight bounced off the side-view mirror in harsh reflections, causing Holcroft to squint and blink repeatedly, trying to rid the blind-spots from his eyes. The dark green Fiat appeared now and then. It was far behind them, but never out of sight for very long.

He parked the car behind the inevitable church, which was the focal point of the small town. Together he and Helden walked around the rectory to the front and into the crowds.

The village square was typically French, the cobblestone streets spreading

174

out like irregular spokes from an imperfect wheel, old buildings and winding lanes everywhere. Stalls were set up in no discernible order, their awnings in various stages of disrepair, crafts and foodstuffs of all descriptions piled on counters. Shiny dishes and a profusion of oilcloth caught the rays of sun; shafts of light shot through the crowd.

The first impression Noel had was that this *fête* was not aimed at the tourist trade. Foreigners belonged to the spring and summer months.

The man with the pockmarked face was standing in front of a stall halfway across the square. He was munching on a piece of pastry, his eyes darting in Holcroft's direction. The man did not know he had been spotted, Noel was certain of that. He was far too casual, too intent on eating. He had his targets under surveillance; all was well. Holcroft turned to Helden at his side.

"I see the present I want to get you!" he shouted.

"Don't be silly . . ."

"Wait here! I'll be back in a few minutes."

"I'll be over there," she pointed to her right, "at the pewter display."

"Fine. See you soon."

Noel began edging his way through the crowd. If he could weave enough, make sufficiently quick movements, he could reach the outskirts of the crowd without the light-haired man seeing him. Once on the cobblestone pavement beyond the crowd, he could inch his way around to within yards of the pastry stall.

He reached the cobblestone pavement; the man had not seen him get there. He had ordered another piece of pastry and was eating it absentmindedly, rising on the balls of his feet, peering anxiously over the heads of the crowd. Abruptly, he seemed to relax and settle back, his attention only half on his targets. He had spotted Helden; apparently he was convinced that if he could see her, her companion was not far away.

Noel feigned a suddenly lame ankle and limped around the border of the crowd, his new injury allowing him to bend over in pain. There was no way the man could see him now.

He was directly behind the pastry stall, no more than ten yards from it. He watched the light-haired man closely. There was something primitive about him as he stood there motionless, eating deliberately, every now and then stretching to make sure his quarry was still in sight. It struck Holcroft that he watching a predator. He could not see the predator's eyes but he somehow knew they were cold and alert. These thoughts made him angry, raising images in his mind of such a man seated behind a driver, a gun perhaps at the driver's head, waiting for Richard Holcroft to emerge on a New York pavement. It was the sense of ice-cold, deadly manipulation that suddenly enraged him.

Noel lunged into the crowd, his right hand gripping the automatic in his pocket, his left extended in front of him, his fingers taut. When he touched him, it would be a grip the light-haired man would never forget.

Suddenly he was blocked. *Blocked!* As he parted the shoulders of a man and a woman in front of him, a third figure met him head on, cross-checking him with his body, his face turned away. He was being stopped deliberately!

"Get out of my way! Goddamn it, let go of me!"

Only feet beyond, he could see that his shouts, or his English, or both, had alarmed the light-haired man, who spun in place, dropping his pastry. His eyes were wild, his face flushed. He spun again and forced his way through the crowd, away from Noel.

"*Get out of* . . ." Holcroft could feel it before he saw it. Something had sliced through his jacket, ripping the lining above his left pocket. He whipped his head down, his eyes unbelieving. A knife had been plunged into his side; had he not twisted his body, it would have stabbed him!

He grabbed the wrist holding the knife, pushing it away, afraid to let go, crashing his shoulder up into the chest of the man who held it. Still the man kept his face from being seen! Who *was* he? There was no time to think or wonder; *get the terrible knife away!*

Noel screamed. He bent over, his enemy's wrist viced in both his hands, the blade thrusting about in the crowded space, his whole body writhing, twisting, rolling into those surrounding him. He yanked the fist with the blade extended from it upwards, then smashed it down with his full weight, falling to the street as he did so. The blade fell away, clattering on the stone.

Something crashed into his neck. Suddenly dazed, he still knew what it was; he had been hit with an iron pipe. He lay curled up in terror and confusion, but he could not stay down! Instinct made him lurch up; fear made him hold his place, waiting for an attack, prepared to fend it off. And rage made him seek out his attackers.

They were gone. The body that belonged to the unseen face was gone. The knife on the ground was gone! And all around him people backed away, staring at him as if he were deranged.

My God! he thought, with a terrible awareness. If they would kill him, they would kill Helden! If the light-haired man with the pockmarked face was protected by killers, and those killers knew without a doubt that he had spotted their charge, they would assume that Helden had spotted him, too. They would go after her! They would kill *her* because she was part of *his trap!*

He broke his way through the circle of onlookers, and dodged a hundred angry arms and hands in the direction he instinctively remembered she'd indicated only minutes before. A stall that was selling some kind of pitchers, or plates or . . . pitchers, plates, *pewter.* That was it! A stall with pewter. Where was it? Over there? No, *there.* Was it there?

It was, but she was not. She was nowhere to be seen. He ran up to the counter of the stall and shouted.

"A woman! A blonde woman was here!"

"*Pardon? Je ne parle pas* . . ."

"*Une femme . . . Aux cheveux blondes! Elle était ici!*"

The vendor shrugged and continued polishing a small bowl.

"*Où est-elle?*" shouted Holcroft.

"*Vous êtes fou! Fou!*" yelled the stallkeeper. "*Voleur! Gendarmes!*"

176

"*Non! S'il vous plait! Une femme aux . . .*"

"Ah," broke in the vendor, "*Une blonde. Dans cette direction.*" He gestured to his left.

Holcroft pushed himself away from the stall and raced into crowds again. He pulled at overcoats and jackets, crashing a path for himself. Oh, Christ, he had *killed* her! His eyes searched everywhere, every corridor, every pair of eyes, every thatch of hair. She was nowhere.

"*Helden!*"

Suddenly, a fist hammered into his right kidney, and an arm shot over his shoulder, locking itself around his neck, choking the air out of his throat. He slammed his right elbow into the body of his assailant, now behind him, now dragging him backwards through the crowd. Gasping for air, he jammed his left elbow into the hard, twisting figure holding him, then his right again. He had caught his attacker in the rib cage; the lock around his throat loosened for an instant, and that instant was enough. He spun to his left, his fingers digging into the forearm around his neck, and pulled downwards, throwing his assailant over his hip. Both men fell to the ground.

Noel saw the face! Beneath the unruly crop of red hair was the small scar on the forehead, and beneath it the angry blue eyes. The man was the younger of the two MI5 agents who had questioned him in his London hotel. Noel's rage was complete; the madness based on a terrible error had gone unchecked. British Intelligence had intruded and that intrusion might well have cost Helden her life.

But *why?* Why here in an obscure French village? He had no answers. He knew only that this man whose throat he now clutched was his enemy, as dangerous to him as the *Rache* or the *Odessa.*

"Get *up!*" Holcroft pulled at the man and struggled to his feet. His mistake was in momentarily releasing the agent. Without warning, a paralysing blow hammered into his stomach. His eyes spun out of focus and for several moments he was only aware of being yanked through a sea of astonished faces. Suddenly he was slammed against the wall of a building; he could *hear* the impact of his head on the hard surface."

"You goddamn fool! What the devil do you think you're doing? You were nearly killed back there!"

The MI5 man did not scream, but he might well have, so intense was his tone. Noel focused his eyes; the agent had him pinned. The man's forearm was again pressed against his throat.

"You son of a bitch!" He could barely whisper the words. "You're the ones who tried to kill me . . ."

"You're a certifiable lunatic, Holcroft. The Tinamou wouldn't *touch* you. I've got to get you out of here."

"The *Tinamou?* Here?"

"Let's go!"

"*No!* Where's Helden?"

"Certainly not with us! Do you think we're crazy?"

177

Noel stared at the man; he was telling the truth. It was all *insane*. "Then someone's taken her! She's gone!"

"If she's gone, she went willingly," said the agent. "We tried to warn you. Leave it alone!"

"No, you're wrong! There was a man – with pockmarks on his face . . ."

"The Fiat?"

"*Yes! Him.* He was following us. I went after him and his men caught me. They tried to kill me!"

"Come with me," ordered the agent, grabbing Holcroft's arm and propelling him down the pavement.

They reached a dark, narrow alleyway between two buildings. No rays of sunlight penetrated; everything was in shadows. The alley was lined with rubbish bins filled with refuse. And beyond the third rubbish bin on the right Noel could see a pair of legs. The rest of the figure was hidden by the receptacle.

The agent pushed Noel into the alley; it was only necessary to take four or five steps before the upper part of the body was clearly seen.

On first glance, the man with the pockmarked face appeared to be drunk. In his hand he clutched a bottle of red wine; it had spilled into the crotch of his trousers. But it was a different red from the stain that had spread over his chest.

The man had been shot.

"There's your killer," said the agent. "Now will you listen to us? Go back to New York. Tell us what you know and leave it alone."

Noel's mind churned; mists of confusion enveloped him. There was violent death in the skies, death in New York, death in Rio, death here in a small French village. The *Rache*, the *Odessa*, the survivors of *Wolfsschanze* . . .

Nothing is as it was for you . . .

He turned to the MI5 man, his voice no more than a whisper. "Don't you understand? *I can't* . . ."

There was a sudden skirmish at the end of the alleyway. Two figures raced by, one propelling the other. Commands were shouted – guttural, harsh, the words not distinguishable, but the violence clear. Cries for help were cut short by the sound of flesh against flesh, vicious slaps repeated again and again. And then the blurred figures were gone, but Holcroft could hear the scream.

"Noel! *Noel!* . . ."

It was Helden! Holcroft found his mind again and knew what he had to do. With all his strength he slammed his shoulder into the side of the agent, sending him crashing over the rubbish bin that concealed the dead body of the man with the pockmarked face.

He ran out of the alley.

21

The screams continued, how far away he could not tell, the crowds in the village square were so boisterous. Music had broken out from a number of concertinas and cornets. Pockets of space were formed for couples, skipping, twirling, turning in countryside dances. The *Fêtes d'Hiver* was now a carnival.

"*Noel! Noel . . .*"

Up the curving street to the left of the square; the cries came from that direction! Holcroft ran wildly, colliding with a pair of lovers embracing against a wall. *There.*

"*Noel!*"

He was on a side street lined with three-storey buildings. He raced down it, hearing the scream again, but no words, no name, only a scream cut short by the impact of a blow that produced a cry of pain.

Oh, *God*, he had to find . . .

A *door!* A door was partially open; it was the entrance to the fourth building on the right. The scream had come from there!

He ran to it, remembering as he drew near that he had a gun in his pocket. He reached in and pulled it out, thinking insanely as he held it that he had never really looked at the weapon. He did so now, and for an instant he stopped and stared at it, feeling sick.

He knew little about handguns, but he knew this one. It was a Budischowsky TP-70 Autoloading Pistol, the same type of gun Sam Buonoventura had lent him in Costa Rica. The coincidence gave him no confidence. It only made him sick. This was not his world.

He checked the safety catch and pulled the door open, staying out of sight. Inside was a long, narrow, dimly lit corridor. On the left wall, spaced perhaps twelve feet from each other, were two doors. From what he remembered of this type of structure he had to presume that there were identically spaced doors on the right wall; he could not see them from where he stood.

He darted into the entrance, the gun held steady in front of him. There *were* the two doors on the right wall. Four doors. Behind one of them Helden was a captive. But which one? He walked to the first door on the left and put his ear to it.

There was a stratching sound, erratic, unfamiliar. He had no idea what it was. Cloth, fabric . . . the tearing of cloth? He put his hand on the knob and twisted it; the door swung free and he opened it, his weapon in firing position.

Across the dark room was an old woman on her knees, scrubbing the floor.

She was in profile, her gaunt features sagging, her arm working in circles on the soft wood. She was so old she neither saw him nor heard him. He closed the door.

A black ribbon tied in the form of a bow was nailed to the door on the right. A death had taken place behind that door; a family was in mourning. A *death* behind *that door*. The thought was too unnerving; he listened.

This was it! A struggle was going on. Heavy breathing, movement, tension; inside that room there was desperation. Helden was behind that door!

Noel stepped back, his automatic levelled, his right foot raised. He took a deep breath, and as if it were a battering ram he drove his foot into the wood to the left of the knob. The force of the blow sent the door crashing inward.

Inside, on a filthy bed, were two naked teenagers, a dark-haired boy on top of a fat, fair-skinned girl, the girl's legs spread up towards the ceiling, the boy lying between them, both hands on her breasts. At the sound of the crash and the sight of the stranger, the girl screamed. The boy spun off her, rolling on to the floor, his mouth open in shock.

The crash! The sound of the crash was an alarm. Holcroft ran into the corridor and raced to the next door on the left. There was no time to be concerned about anything but finding Helden. He slammed his shoulder into the door, twisting the knob awkwardly with his left hand, his right gripping the handle of the gun. There was no need for force; the door gave way.

Noel stood in the doorframe, for an instant feeling ashamed. Against the wall by a window was a blind man. He was an old man, trembling at the unseen, unknown violence that had invaded his dark privacy.

"*Sacré nom de Dieu . . .*" he whispered, holding his hands in front of him.

The sound of racing footsteps came from the hallway, footsteps that grew louder – the sound of a man not simply running, but running frantically, leather slipping against wood. Holcroft turned quickly, in time to see the figure of the MI5 agent rush past. There was a crash of glass from somewhere outside. Noel lurched out of the blind man's room, looking to the left where the crash had come from; there was sunlight streaming through an open door at the end of the corridor. Its panes of glass had been painted black; he had not seen it in the dim light.

How did the agent know a door was there? Why had he kicked it open and raced outside? Did the MI5 man think *he* had gone out that way? Instinct told him the agent would not give him that much credit; he was an amateur, a lunatic. No, he was after *someone else*.

It could only be Helden! But Helden was behind the door across from the blind man's room: it was the only place left. It *had* to be. The agent was wrong!

Holcroft kicked the door in front of him; the lock broke, the door swung open, and he rushed inside.

It was empty, had been empty a very long time. Layers of dust were everywhere . . . and there were no footprints. No one had been inside that room for weeks.

The MI5 man had been right. The amateur had not known something that the professional had not perceived.

Noel ran out of the empty room, down the dark corridor, through the shattered door and out into a courtyard. On the left was a heavy wooden doorway that led back to the side street. It was open, and Holcroft raced through it. He could hear sounds of the carnival from the square, but they were not the only sounds. Far down the deserted street to his right he could hear a scream, cut off now as it had been cut off before. He ran in the direction of the scream, in Helden's direction, but he could see no one.

"Get *back!*" The command came from a recessed doorway.

There was a gunshot; above him stone shattered and he could hear the sickening whine of a ricochetting bullet.

Noel threw himself to the ground, on to the hard, irregular surface of the cobblestones. As he broke his fall, his finger touched the trigger of his gun. It fired, the explosion next to his face. In panic, he rolled over and over towards the recessed doorway. Hands grabbed him, pulling his body into the shadows. The man from British Intelligence, the young man with the scar on his forehead, yanked him back against the stone entranceway.

"I repeat! You're a fool! I should kill you myself and save them the trouble." The agent was crouched against the wall; he inched his face to the edge.

"I don't *believe* you," said Noel, "I don't believe *any* of this. Where is she?"

"The bastard's holding her across the way, about twenty yards down. My guess is he's got a radio and has contacted a car."

"They're going to *kill* her!"

"Not now they won't. I don't know why, but that's not what they have in mind. Perhaps because she's his sister."

"Get off that! It's *wrong*, it's crazy! I told her; she reached him. He's no more this Tinamou than you are. And he is mad as hell."

The MI5 agent stared at Holcroft. His look was that of a man studying the ravings of a psychopath, equal parts curiosity, revulsion, and astonishment. "He *what? You* what?"

"Your heard me."

"My *God* . . . Whoever you are, whatever you're involved with, you're not remotely connected with any of this."

"I told you that in London," said Noel, struggling to sit up, trying to find his breath again. "Did you think I was lying?"

"We knew you were lying, we just didn't know why. We thought you were being used by men wanting to reach von Tiebolt."

"For what?"

"Make a blind contact, neither side exposing itself. It was a fair cover: money in America, left for the family."

"But for *what?*"

"Later! You want the girl, I want the bastard who's got her. Listen to me." The agent gestured at the automatic in Noel's hand. "Do you know how to use that?"

"I once had to use a gun like it. I'm no expert."

"You don't have to be, you'll have a large target. If I'm right they've got a car cruising the area."

"Don't you?"

"No, I'm alone. Now listen to me. If a car drives up, it'll have to stop. The second it does I'm going to dash over to that doorway across the street. As I'm running, cover me by shooting directly at the car. Aim for the windscreen. Hit the tyres, the radiator. I don't care what, but try to get the windscreen. Shoot it up, immobilize the damn car, if you can, and pray to God that the locals stay away at that fucking wingding in the square."

"Suppose they don't, suppose someone? . . ."

"Try not to hit him, you ass!" broke in the Englishman. "And keep your fire to the right side of the car. *Your* right. Expose yourself as little as possible."

"The *right* side of the car?"

"Yes, unless you want to hit the girl, which, frankly, I don't give a piss about, but I want *him*. Of course, if I'm wrong, none of this applies and we'll have to think of something else."

The agent's face was pressed against the stone. He inched it forward, peering down the street. The unfamiliar forest belonged to such men, not well-intentioned architects. "You weren't wrong back in that old building," Noel said. "You knew there was another way out."

"A second exit. No one worth his pecker would allow himself to be trapped inside."

Once more the professional was right. Noel could hear the screeching of tyres; a car careened around an unseen corner and drew rapidly closer. The agent stood up, gesturing for Noel to follow. He looked around the edge of the entranceway, his forearm angled across his chest, his pistol in his hand.

There was a second screech of tyres; the car came to a stop. The agent shouted at Holcroft as he leaped from the doorway, firing his pistol twice at the car, and raced across the street.

"*Now!*"

It was a brief nightmare, made intensely real by the shattering sounds and the frantic movement. Noel was actually *doing* it. He could see the automatic in front of him, at the end of *his* arm, being held in *his* hand. He could feel the vibrations that travelled through his body each time he squeezed the trigger. *The right side of the car. Your right. Unless* . . . he tried desperately to be accurate. Amazed, he saw the windscreen crack and shatter; he heard bullets enter the door; he heard – oh *God*, he *heard* – the screams of a human being . . . and then he saw that human being fall out of the door and on to the cobblestones beside the car. It was the driver; his arms were extended in front of him; blood poured out of his head and he did not move.

Across the street he could see the MI5 man come out of a doorway, crouching, his pistol out in front of him. Then he heard the command:

"Release her! You can't get out!"

"*Nie und nimmer!*"

"Then she can go with you! I don't give a piss! . . . Spin to your right, miss! *Now!*"

Two explosions took place, one on top of the other; a woman's scream echoed throughout the street. Noel's thoughts went wildly out of focus. He raced across the pavement, afraid to think, afraid to see what he might see, find what he dared not find for his own sanity.

Helden was on her knees, trembling, her breathing a series of uncontrollable sobs. She stared at the dead man, splayed out on the pavement to her left. But she was *alive*; that was all he cared about. He ran to her and fell down beside her, pulling her shivering head on to his chest.

"Him . . . *Him!*" Helden whispered, pushing Noel away. "Quickly."

"What?" Noel followed her look.

The MI5 agent was trying to crawl; his mouth opened and closed – he was trying to speak and no sound emerged. And over the front of his shirt was a spreading stain of red.

A small crowd had gathered at the entrance to the square. Three or four men stepped forward tentatively.

"Get him," said Helden. "Get him quickly."

She was capable of thinking and he was not; she was able to make a decision and he was immobile. "What are we going to do? Where are we going to go?" was all he could say, not even sure the words were his.

"These streets, the alleys. They connect. We have to get him away."

"Why?"

Helden's eyes bore into his. "He saved my life. He saved yours. *Quickly!*"

He could only do as he was ordered; he could not think for himself. He got to his feet and ran to the agent, bending over him, their faces inches apart. He saw the angry blue eyes that floated in their sockets, the mouth that struggled to say something but could not.

The man was dying.

Noel lifted the agent to his feet; the Englishman could not stand, and so Noel picked him up, astonished at his own strength. He turned and saw Helden lurching towards the car at the kerb; the motor was still running. He carried the agent over to the shot-up car.

"I'll drive," Helden said. "Put him in the back seat."

"The windscreen! You can't see!"

"You can't carry him very far."

The next minutes were as unreal to Holcroft as the sight of the gun still in his hand. Helden made a swift U-turn, careening over the pavement, swerving out to the middle of the street. Sitting beside her, the dying agent in the back seat, Noel realized something in spite of the panic. He realized it calmly, almost dispassionately: he was beginning to adjust to this terrible new world. His resistance was wearing down, confirmed by the fact that he *had* acted; he had *not* run away. People had tried to kill him. They had tried to kill the girl beside him. Perhaps that was enough.

"Can you find the church?" he asked, now amazed at his own control.

She looked at him briefly. "I think so. Why?"

"We can't drive this car even if you could see. We have to find ours." He gestured through the cracked glass of the windscreen; steam was billowing up from the hood. "The radiator was punctured. Find the church."

She did, mostly by instinct, driving up the narrow streets and alleys which connected the irregular spokes that spread out from the village square. The last few blocks were frightening. People were running beside the car, shouting excitedly. For several moments Noel thought it was the shattered windscreen, rife with bullet-holes, that drew the villagers' attention; it was not. Figures rushed by towards the hub of the square; the word had spread.

Des gens tués!

Helden swung into the street that passed the church rectory and fronted the entrance to the parking lot. She turned in and drove up beside the rented car. Holcroft looked in the rear seat. The MI5 man was angled back in the corner, still breathing, his eyes on Noel. He moved his hand, as if to draw Noel closer.

"We're switching cars," said Holcroft, "we'll get you to a doctor."

"Listen . . . to me first," whispered the Englishman. His eyes strayed to Helden. "Tell him."

"Listen to him, Noel," she said.

"What is it?"

"Payton-Jones. You have the number?"

Holcroft remembered. The name on the card given him by the middle-aged, grey-haired intelligence agent in London was Harold Payton-Jones. He nodded. "Yes."

"Call him . . ." The MI5 man coughed. "Tell him what happened . . . everything."

"You can tell him yourself," said Noel.

"You're a piss ant. Tell Payton-Jones there's a complication we don't know about. The man we thought was sent by the Tinamou, von Tiebolt's man . . . "

"My brother's *not* the Tinamou," cried Helden.

The agent looked at her through half-closed lids. "Maybe you're right, miss. I didn't think so before, but you may be. I only know that the man who followed you in the Fiat works for von Tiebolt."

"He followed us to protect us! To find out who was after Noel."

Holcroft spun in the seat and stared at Helden. "You knew about him?"

"Yes," she replied. "Our lunch today was Johann's idea."

"Thanks a lot."

"*Please.* You don't understand these things. My brother does. I do."

"Helden, I tried to trap that man! He was killed!"

"What? Oh, my *God* . . ."

"That's the complication," whispered the agent. "If von Tiebolt's not the Tinamou, what is he? Why was his man shot? Those two men, why did they try to take *her*, kill *you?* Who were they? This car . . . trace it." The Englishman gasped; Noel reached over the seat but the agent waved him away. "Just listen. Find out who they were, who owns this car. They're the complication."

The MI5 man was barely able to keep his eyes open now; his whisper could hardly be heard. It was obvious that he would die in moments. Noel leaned over the seat.

"Would the complication have anything to do with a man named Peter Baldwin?"

It was as though an electric shock had jolted the dying man. His eyelids sprang open, the pupils beneath came briefly back from death. "*Baldwin?* . . ." The whisper echoed and was eerily plaintive. "What . . . do you know about Baldwin?"

"He called me in New York," said Holcroft. "He told me not to do what I was doing, not to get involved. He said he knew things that no one else knew. He was killed an hour later."

"He was telling the *truth!* Baldwin was telling the truth!" The agent's lips began to tremble; a trickle of blood emerged from the corner of his mouth. "We never believed him; he was trading off *nothing*; we were sure he was *lying* . . ."

"Lying about what?"

The MI5 man stared first at Noel, then with effort shifted his gaze to Helden. "There isn't time . . ." He struggled pathetically to look again at Holcroft. "You're clean. You must be . . . you wouldn't have said what you just said. I'm going to trust you, both of you. Reach Payton-Jones . . . as fast as you can. Tell him to go back to the Baldwin file. *Code Wolfsschanze* . . . It's Wolfsschanze."

The agent's head fell forward. He was dead.

22

They sped north on the Paris highway as the late afternoon sun washed the countryside with rays of orange and cold yellow. The winter sun was the same everywhere; it was a constant, and Holcroft was grateful for it.

Code Wolfsschanze. It's Wolfsschanze.

Peter Baldwin had known about Geneva. He had tried to tell MI5 but the doubters in British Intelligence had not believed him.

He was trading off nothing!

What was he trading *for?* What was the bargain he sought? Who *was* Peter Baldwin?

Who *had been* Peter Baldwin?

Who was von Tiebolt – Tennyson?

If von Tiebolt's not the Tinamou, what is he? Why was his man shot? Why did they try to take her, kill you?

Why?

At least one problem was put to rest. John Tennyson was *not* the Tinamou. Whatever else the son of Wilhelm von Tiebolt was – and it might well be dangerous to Geneva – he was not the assassin. But then, who was he? What had he done to become involved with killers? Why were men after him – and, by extension, his sister?

The questions kept Noel's mind from dwelling on the last hours. He could not think about them; he would explode if he did. Three men killed – one by him. Killed by gunfire in the back street of a remote French village during a carnival. Madness.

"What do you think Wolfsschanze means?" asked Helden.

"I know what it means," he said.

She turned, surprised.

He told her. Everything he knew about the survivors of Wolfsschanze. There was no point in concealing facts now. When he had finished, she was silent. He wondered if he had pushed her too far. Into a conflict she wanted no part of. She had said to him only a few days ago that if he did not do as she instructed him to, if he was not who he said he was, she would leave Paris and he would never find her. Would she do that now? Was the threat of Wolfsschanze the final burden she could not accept?

"Are you afraid?" he asked.

"That's a foolish question."

"I think you know what I mean."

"Yes." She leaned her head back on the seat. "You want to know if I'll run away."

"I guess that's it. Will you?"

She did not reply for several moments, nor did he press her. When she spoke there was the echoing sadness in her voice – so like her sister's and yet so different. "I can't run away any more than you can. Morality and fear aside, it's simply not practical, is it? They'd find us. They'd kill us."

"That's pretty final."

"It's realistic. Besides, I'm tired of running. I have no energy left for it. The *Rache*, the *Odessa*, now Wolfsschanze. Three hunters who stalk each other as well as us. It's got to end. *Herr Oberst* is right about that."

"I came to the same conclusion yesterday afternoon. It occurred to me that except for my mother, I'd be running with you."

"Heinrich Clausen's son," said Helden reflectively.

"And someone else's." He turned her look. "Do we agree? We don't get in touch with this Payton-Jones?"

"We agree."

"MI5'll look for us. They have no choice. They had a man on us; they'll find out he was killed. There'll be questions."

"Which we can't answer. We were followed, we did not follow."

"I wonder who they were? The two men."

"The *Rache*, I would think. It's their style."

"Or the *Odessa*."

"Possibly. But the German spoken by the one who took me was odd. The dialect wasn't recognizable. It wasn't from Munich, and certainly not from Berlin. It was strange."

"How do you mean?"

"It was very guttural, but still soft, if that makes sense."

"Not too much. Then you think they were from the *Rache?*"

"Does it matter? We've got to protect ourselves from both. Nothing's changed. At least, not for me." She reached over and touched his arm. "I'm sorry for you, though."

"Why?"

"Because now you're running with us. You're one of the children now. *Verwünschte Kinder*. The damned. And you've had no training."

"It seems to me I'm getting it in a hurry."

She withdrew her hand. "You should go to Berlin."

"I know. We've got to move quickly. Kessler has to be reached and brought in; he's the last of the . . .' Holcroft paused, " . . . the issue."

She smiled sadly at the word. "There's you and my brother; you're both knowledgeable, both ready to move. Kessler must be made ready, too . . . *Zürich* is the issue. And the solution to so much."

Noel glanced at her. It did not take much perception to know what she was thinking. Zurich meant resources beyond imagination; surely a part of them would be used to curb, if not eliminate, the fanatics of the *Odessa* and the *Rache*. Holcroft knew that she knew he had witnessed their horrors for himself; a one-third vote was hers for the asking. Her brother would agree.

"We'll make Zurich work," he said. "You can stop running soon. We can all stop."

She looked at him pensively. Then she moved over on the seat next to him and put her hand through his arm and held it. She laid her head on his shoulder, her long blonde hair falling over his jacket.

"I called for you and you came to me," she said in her odd, floating voice. "We nearly died this afternoon. A man gave his life for us."

"He was a professional," replied Noel. "Our lives may have been incidental to him. He was after information, after a man he thought could give it to him."

"I know that. I've seen such men before, such professionals. But at the last, he was decent; many aren't. They sacrifice others too easily in the name of professionalism."

"What do you mean?"

"You're not trained; you would have done as he told you. You could have been used for bait, to draw fire. It would have been easier for him to let you take the bullets, and then me. I wasn't important to him. In the confusion he might have saved his own life and got his man. But he saved us."

Aim for the right side of the car. Your right. Expose yourself as little as possible . . . Release her! Spin to your right, miss. Now!

"Where shall we go in Paris?"

"Not Paris," said Helden. "Argenteuil. There's a small hotel on the river. It's lovely."

Noel raised his hand from the wheel and let it fall on the hair that cascaded down his jacket. "You're lovely," he said.

"I'm frightened. The fear has to go away."

"Argenteuil?" he mused. "A small hotel in Argenteuil. You seem to know a lot of places for someone who's been in France for only a few months."

"You have to know where they don't ask questions. You're taught quickly, you learn quickly. Take the Billancourt exit. Please hurry."

Their room overlooked the Seine, with a small balcony beyond the glass doors directly above the river. They stood for a few minutes in the night air, his arm around her, looking down at the dark waters. Neither spoke; comfort was in their touch.

There was a knock on the door. Helden tensed; he smiled and reassured her.

"Relax. While you were washing I ordered a bottle of brandy."

She returned his smile and breathed again. "You should really let me do that. Your French is quite impossible."

"I can say 'Remy Martin'," he said, releasing her. "Where I went to school it was the first thing we learned." He went towards the door.

Holcroft took the tray from the waiter, and stood for a moment watching Helden. She had closed the doors to the balcony and was staring out of the windows at the night sky. She was a private woman, a lonely woman, and she was reaching out to him. He understood that.

He wished he understood other things. She was beautiful; it was the simple fact and needed no elaboration. Nor could she be unaware of that beauty. She was highly intelligent, again an attribute so obvious no further comment was necessary. And beyond that intelligence she was familiar with the ways of her shadow world. She was street-smart in a larger sense ... an international sense; she moved swiftly, decisively: there had to have been dozens of times when she had used sex to get an advantage, but he suspected it was used in cold calculation – buyer beware, there is nothing but a body for you to take, my thoughts are mine, you'll share none of them.

She turned from the glass doors; her eyes were soft, her expression warm and yet still distant, still observing. "You look like an impatient *maitre d'* waiting to escort me to my table."

"Right this way, *mademoiselle*," said Noel, carrying the tray to the small bureau across the room and placing it on top. "Would the lady care for a table by the water?" He moved a small chaise in front of the glass doors and faced her, smiling and bowing. "If the lady would care to be seated, brandy will be served, and the fireworks will begin. The torchbearers on the boats await only your presence."

"But where will you sit, my attractive *garçon?*"

"At your feet, lady." He leaned over and kissed her, holding her shoulders, wondering if she would withdraw or push him away.

Whatever he expected, he was not prepared for what happened. Her lips were soft and moist, parted as if swollen, moving against his, inviting him into her mouth. She reached up with both her hands and cupped his face, her fingers gently caressing his cheeks, his eyelids, his temples. Still her lips kept moving, revolving in desperate circles, pulling him into her. They stood together. He could feel her breasts pressed against his shirt, her legs against his, pushing into him, matching strength for strength, arousing him.

Then a strange thing happened. She began to tremble; her fingers crept around his neck and dug into his flesh, holding him fiercely as if she were afraid he might move away. He could hear the sobs that came from her throat, feel the convulsions that gripped her. He moved his hands to her waist and gently pulled his face from hers, forcing her to look at him.

She was crying. She stared at him for a moment; pain was in her eyes, a hurt so deeply searing Noel felt he was an intruder watching a private agony she did not want him to see.

"What is it? What's the matter?"

"Make the fear go away," she whispered plaintively. She reached for the buttons on her blouse and undid them, exposing the swell of her breasts. "I can't be alone. Please, make it go *away.*"

He pulled her to him, cradling her head against his chest, her hair beneath his face soft and lovely, as she was soft and lovely.

"You're not alone, Helden. Neither am I."

They were naked beneath the covers, his arm around her, her head on his chest. With his free hand, he kept lifting the strands of her long blonde hair, letting them fall back into place, covering her face.

"I can't see when you do that," she said, laughing.

"You look like a sheep dog."

"Are you my shepherd?"

"I have a staff."

"That's dreadful. You have a dirty mouth." She reached up with her index finger and tapped his lips. He caught her finger between his teeth and growled. "You can't frighten me," she whispered, raising her face above his, depressing his tongue playfully. "You're a cowardly lion. You make noises but you won't bite."

He took her hand. "Cowardly lion? *The Wizard of Oz?*"

"Of course," she answered. "I loved *The Wizard of Oz.* I saw it dozens and dozens of times in Rio. It's where I began to learn English. I wanted so to be called Dorothy. I even named my little dog Toto."

"It's hard to think of you as a little girl."

"I was, you know. I didn't spring full-flower . . ." She stopped and laughed. She had raised herself above him; her breasts were in front of his face. His hand instinctively reached for the left nipple. She moaned and covered his hand, holding it where it was as she lowered herself back down on his chest. "Anyway, I *was* a little girl. There were times when I was very happy."

"When?"

"When I was alone. I always had a room to myself, mother made sure of that. It was always in the back of the house or the apartment, or if we were in a hotel it was separate, away from my brother and sister. Mother said I was the youngest and should not be disturbed by the hours they kept."

"I imagine that could get pretty lonely . . ."

"Oh, *no!* Because I was *never* alone. My friends were in my mind, and they would sit in chairs and on my bed and we'd talk. We would talk for hours, telling each other our secrets."

"What about school? Didn't you have flesh-and-blood friends?"

Helden was silent for a moment. "A few, not many. As I look back, I can't blame them. We were all children. We did as our parents told us to do. Those of us who had a parent left."

"What did the parents tell them?"

"That I was a von Tiebolt. The little girl with the strange first name. My mother was . . . well, my mother. I think they thought my stigma was contagious."

She may have been branded with a stigma, thought Noel, but her mother was not the cause of it. Maurice Graff's *Odessa* had more important things on its mind. Millions upon millions siphoned off their beloved Reich to be used by traitors such as von Tiebolt for a massive apology.

"Things got better when you grew up, didn't they?"

"Better? Certainly. You adjust, you mature, you understand attitudes you didn't as a child."

"More friends?"

"Closer ones, perhaps, not necessarily more. I was a poor mixer. I was used to being by myself; I understood why I was not included in parties and dinners. At least, not in the so-called respectable households. The years curtailed my mother's social activities, shall we say, but not her business interests. She was a shark; we were avoided by our own kind. And of course the Germans were never really accepted by the rest of Rio, not during those years."

"Why not? The war was over."

"But not the embarrassments. The Germans were a constant source of embarrassment then. Illegal monies, war criminals, Israeli hunters . . . it went on for years."

"You're such a beautiful woman, it's difficult to think of you . . . let's say, isolated."

Helden raised herself and looked at him. She smiled, and with her right hand pushed her hair back, holding it at the base of her neck. "I was very stern-looking, my darling. Hair straight, wrapped in a bun, large glasses and dresses always a size too large. You wouldn't have looked at me twice . . . Don't you believe me?"

"I wasn't thinking about that."

"What then?"

"You just called me 'my darling'."

She held his eyes. "Yes, I did, didn't I? It seemed quite natural. Do you mind?"

He reached for her, his answer his touch.

She sat back on the chaise, her slip serving as a negligee, sipping brandy. Noel was on the floor beside her, leaning against the small couch, his shorts and open shirt taking the place of a bathrobe. They held hands and watched the shimmering lights of the boats on the water.

He turned his head and looked at her. "Feeling better?"

"Much better, my darling. You're a very gentle man. I haven't known many in my life."

"Spare me."

"Oh, I don't mean that. For your information, I'm known among *Herr Oberst's* ranks as *Fräulein Eiszapfen*."

"What's that?"

"Icicle. Mademoiselle Icicle. At work, they're convinced I'm a lesbian."

"Send them to me."

"I'd rather not."

"I'll tell them you're a faggot in drag who uses whips and bicycle chains. They'll run at the sight of you."

"That's very sweet." She kissed him. "You're warm and gentle and you laugh easily. I'm terribly fond of you, Noel Holcroft, and I'm not sure that's such a good thing."

"Why?"

"Because we'll say goodbye and I'll think of you."

Noel reached up and held the hand that still touched his face; he was suddenly alarmed. "We just said hello. Why goodbye?"

"You have things to do. I have things to do."

"We both have Zurich."

"*You* have Zurich. I have my life in Paris."

"They're not mutually exclusive."

"You don't know that, my darling. You don't know anything about me. Where I live, how I live."

"I know about a little girl who had a room to herself and saw *The Wizard of Oz* dozens of times."

"Think kindly of her. She will of you. Always."

Holcroft took her hand from his face. "What the hell are you trying to say? Thanks for a lovely evening, now goodbye?"

"No, my darling. Not like that. Not now."

"Then what *are* you saying?"

"I'm not sure. Perhaps I'm just thinking out loud . . . we have days, weeks, if you wish them."

"I wish them."

"But promise me you'll never try to find where I live, never try to reach me. I'll find you."

"You're married!"

Helden laughed. "No."

"Then living with someone."

"Yes, but not in the way you think."

Noel watched her closely. "What am I supposed to say to that?"

"Say that you'll promise."

"Let me understand you. Outside where you work, there's no place I can reach you. I can't know where you live or how to get in touch with you."

"I'll leave the number of a friend. In an emergency she'll reach me."

"I thought I was a friend."

"You are. But in a different way. Please don't be angry. It's for your own protection."

Holcroft remembered three nights ago. In the midst of her own anxieties, Helden had been worried about him, worried that he had been seen by the wrong people. "You said in the car that Zurich was the solution to so much. Is it the answer for you? Could Zurich change the way you live?"

She hesitated. "It's possible. There's so much to do . . ."

"And so little time," completed Holcroft. He touched her cheek, forcing her to look at him. "But before the money's released, there's the bank in Geneva and specific conditions that have to be met."

"I understand. You've explained them and I'm sure Johann knows about them."

"I'm not so sure. He's laid himself open to a lot of speculation that could knock him out of the box."

"Knock him where?"

"Disqualify him. Frighten the men in Geneva; make them close the vaults. We'll get to him in a minute. I want to talk about Beaumont. I think I know what he is, but I need your help to confirm it."

"How can I help?"

"When Beaumont was in Rio, did he have any connection with Maurice Graff?"

"I have no idea."

"Can we find out? Are there people in Rio who would know?"

"Not that I know of."

"Goddamn it, we've got to learn. Learn everything we can about him."

Helden frowned. "That will be difficult."

"Why?"

"Three years ago, when Gretchen said she was going to marry Beaumont, I was shocked, I told you that. I was working at the time for a small research firm off Leicester Square – you know, one of those dreadful places that you send five pounds to and they get you all the information you want on a subject. Or a person. They're horribly superficial, but they do know how to use sources." Helden paused.

"You checked on Beaumont?" asked Noel.

"I tried to. I didn't know what I was looking for, but I tried. I went back to his university records, got all the available information about his naval career – everything was filled with approvals and recommendations, as well as awards and advancements. Why I can't tell you – except that there seemed to me to be an inconsistency – I went further back to find out what I could about his family in Scotland."

"What was the inconsistency?"

"Well, according to the naval records, his parents were quite ordinary. I got the impression they were rather poor. Owners of a greengrocery or a florist shop in a town called Dunheath, south of Aberdeen on the North Sea. Yet when he was at the university – Cambridge – he was a regular student."

"Regular? . . . What should he have been?"

"On a scholarship, I would think. There was need and he was qualified, yet there were no applications for a scholarship. It seemed odd."

"So you went back to the family in Scotland. What did you learn?"

"That's the point. Next to nothing. It was as if they had disappeared. There was no address, no way to reach them. I sent off several inquiries to the town clerk and the Post Office – obvious places people never think of. The Beaumonts were apparently an English family who simply arrived in Scotland one day shortly after the war, stayed for a few years, then left the country."

"Could they have died?"

"Not according to the records. The navy always keeps them up to date in case of injury or loss of life. They were still listed as living in Dunheath, but they had gone. The Post Office had no information at all."

It was Holcroft's turn to frown. "That sounds crazy."

"There's something more." Helden pushed herself up against the curve of the chaise. "At Gretchen's wedding, there was an officer from Beaumont's ship. His second-in-command, I think. The man was a year or two younger than Beaumont, and obviously his subordinate, but there was a give-and-take between them that went beyond friendship, beyond that of officer-to-officer."

"What do you mean, 'give-and-take'?"

"It was as if they were always thinking exactly alike. One would start a sentence, the other might finish it. One would turn in a particular direction, the other would comment on what the first was looking at. Do you know what I mean? Haven't you seen people like that? Men like that?"

"Sure. Brothers who are close, or lovers. And often military men who've served a long time together. What did you do?"

"I checked on that man. I used the same sources, sent out the same inquiries that I had with Beaumont. What came back was extraordinary. They *were* alike; only the names were different. Their academic and military records are almost identical, superior in every way. They both came from obscure towns, their parents undistinguished and certainly not well off. Yet each had gone to a major university without financial aid. And each had become an officer without any prior indication that he was seeking a military career."

"What about the family of Beaumont's friend? Were you able to locate them?"

"No. They were listed as living in a mining town in Wales, but they weren't. They hadn't been there in years, and no one had any information about them."

What Helden had learned was consistent with Noel's theory that Anthony Beaumont was an *Odessa* agent. What was important now was to take Beaumont – and any "associates" – out of the picture. They could not be allowed to further interfere with Geneva. Perhaps he and Helden were wrong, perhaps they should reach Payton-Jones and let Beaumont become his problem. But there were side issues to consider, among which was the danger of British Intelligence reopening the Peter Baldwin file, going back to *Code Wolfsschanze*.

"What you've told me fits in with what I've been thinking," Noel said. "Let's go back to your brother. I have an idea what happened in Rio. Will you talk about it now?"

Helden's eyes widened. "I don't know what you mean."

"Your brother learned something in Rio, didn't he? He found out about Graff and the Brazilian *Odessa*. That was why he was hounded, why he had to get out. It wasn't your mother, or his business dealings, or anything like that. It was Graff and the *Odessa*."

Helden slowly let out her breath. "I never heard that, believe me."

"Then what was it? Tell me, Helden."

Her eyes pleaded with him. "Please, Noel. I owe you so much, don't make me pay like this. What happened to Johann in Rio has nothing to do with you. Or with Geneva."

"You don't know that. *I* don't know that. I just know that you have to tell me. I have to be prepared. There's so much I don't understand." He gripped her hand. "Listen to me. This afternoon I broke into a blind man's room. I smashed the door in; the sound was awful – sudden and loud. He was an old man and, of course, he couldn't see me. He couldn't see the fear in my own eyes. His hands shook and he whispered a prayer in French . . ."

"For a moment I wanted to go to that man and hold his hands and tell him I knew how he felt. You see, he *didn't* see the fear in my eyes. I'm frightened, Helden. I'm not the sort of person who crashes into people's rooms, and shoots guns, and gets shot at. I can't turn back, but I'm scared. So, you've got to help me."

"I want to, you know that."

"Then tell me what happened in Rio. What happened to your brother?"

"It's simply not important," she said.

"*Everything's* important." Noel stood up and got his jacket. He showed her the torn lining. "Look at this! Someone in that crowd this afternoon tried to put a knife in me. I don't know about you, but that's never happened to me before; it's just not something I know anything about. It petrifies me . . . and it makes me goddamned angry. And five days ago in New York, the man I grew up with – the only man I ever called my father – walked out and was killed by an 'out-of-control' car that *aimed* for him and crushed him against a building! His death was a warning. For me! So don't talk to me about the *Rache*, or the *Odessa*, or the men of Wolfsschanze. I'm beginning to learn all about those sick sons of bitches, and I want every last one of them put away! With the money in Zürich, we can do that. Without it, no one'll listen to us. It's an economic fact of life; you don't dismiss people who have 780 million dollars. You *listen* to people like that." Holcroft let the jacket fall to the floor. "The only way we'll get to Zürich is to satisfy the bank in Geneva, and the only way to reach Geneva is to use our heads. There's no one really on our side; there's just us. The von Tiebolts, the Kesslers . . . and one Clausen. Now, *what happened in Rio?*"

Helden looked down at the torn jacket, then back at Noel.

"Johann killed someone."

"Who?"

"I don't know – I really don't. But it was someone important."

23

Holcroft listened to her, watching for false notes. There were none. She was telling him what she knew, and it was not a great deal.

"About six weeks before we left Brazil," Helden explained, "I drove home one night after a seminar at the university; we lived out in the countryside then. There was a dark coloured limousine, one of those expensive cars, in front, so I parked behind it. As I walked up to the porch I heard yelling from inside. There was a terrible fight and I couldn't imagine who it was; I didn't recognize the one screaming. He kept yelling things like: 'killer', 'murderer', 'it was you' . . . things like that. I ran inside and found Johann standing in the hallway in front of the man. He saw me and told the man to be still. The man tried to strike Johann, but my brother's very powerful; he held the man's arms and pushed him out the door. The last words the man screamed were to the effect that others also knew; that they would see Johann hanged as a murderer, and if that didn't happen, they'd kill themselves. He fell on the steps, still screaming, then he ran to the limousine and Johann went after him. He said something to him through the window; the man spat in my brother's face and drove off."

"Did you ask your brother about it?"

"Naturally. But Johann wouldn't discuss it other than to say the man was mad. He had lost a great deal of money in a business venture and had gone crazy."

"You didn't believe him?"

"I wanted to, but then the meetings began. Johann would be out all hours, away for days; he behaved quite abnormally. Then only weeks later we flew to Recife with a new name and a new country. Whoever was killed was very rich, very powerful. He had to be to have friends like that."

"You have no idea who the man was inside your house that night?"

"No. I'd seen him before, but I couldn't remember where, and Johann wouldn't tell me. He ordered me never to bring up the matter again. There were facts I should not be told."

"You accepted that?"

"Yes. Try to understand. We were children of Nazis and we knew what that meant. It was often best not to ask questions."

"But you had to know what was going on."

"Oh, we were taught, make no mistake about it," said Helden. "We trained to elude the Israelis; they could force information from us. We learned to spot a recruiter from the *Odessa*, a maniac from the *Rache*; how to get away, how to use a hundred different tricks to throw them off."

Noel shook his head in amazement. "Your everyday training for the high school glee club. It's crazy."

"That's a word you could use three weeks ago," she said, reaching for his hand. "Not now. Not after today."

"What do you mean?"

"In the car I said I felt sorry for you because you had no training."

"And I said I thought I was getting it in a hurry."

"But so little and so late. Johann told me to teach you what I could. I want you to listen to me, Noel. Try to remember everything I tell you."

"What?" Holcroft felt the strength of her grip and saw the concern in her eyes.

"You're going to Berlin. I want you back."

With those words she began. There were moments when Noel thought he might smile – or worse, laugh – but her intensity kept him in check; she was deadly serious.

And that afternoon three men had been killed: They might easily have been the fourth and the fifth victims. And so he listened and tried to remember. Everything.

"There's no time to get false papers; they take days. You have money; buy an extra seat on the plane. Stay alert and don't let anyone sit next to you, don't get hemmed in. And don't eat or drink anything you didn't bring with you."

"That's a suggestion I won't forget."

"You might. It's so easy to ask for coffee or even a glass of water. Don't."

"I won't. What happens when I get to Berlin?"

"To any city," she corrected. "Find a small hotel in a crowded district where the main business is pornography, where there's prostitution, narcotics. Front desks never ask for identification in those areas. I know someone who'll give us the name of a hotel in Berlin."

Her words poured forth, describing tactics, defining methods, telling him how to invent his own variations.

False names were to be used, rooms switched daily, hotels changed twice a week. Phone calls were to be placed from public booths, never from hotel rooms, never from residences. A minimum of three changes of outer clothing, including hats and caps and dissimilar glasses, were to be carried; shoes were to have rubber soles. These were best for running with a minimum of sound, for stopping and starting quickly, and walking silently. When and if questioned, he was to lie indignantly, but not arrogantly and never in a loud tone of voice. That kind of anger triggered hostility and hostility meant delay and further questions. While flying from airport to airport, a gun was to be dismantled, its barrel separated from the handle, the firing pin removed. These procedures generally satisfied the European customs clerks; inoperable weapons did not concern them, contraband did. But if they objected, let them confiscate the gun; another could be purchased. If they let the weapon through, reassemble it immediately in the toilet of a men's room.

The street ... he knew something about the streets and crowds, he told Helden. One never knew enough, she replied, telling him to walk as close to the kerb as possible, ready to dash out among the traffic at any sign of hostility or surveillance.

"Remember," she said, "you're the amateur, they're the professionals. Use that position, turn your liability into an asset. The amateur does the unexpected, not because he's clever or experienced, but because he doesn't know any better. Do the unexpected rapidly, obviously, as if confused. Then stop and wait. A confrontation is often the last thing surveillance wants. But it he does want it, you might as well know it. Shoot. You should have a silencer; we'll get you one in the morning. I know where."

He turned, stunned, unable to speak. She saw the astonishment in his eyes. "I'm sorry," she said, leaning forward, smiling sadly and kissing him.

They talked through most of the night, the teacher and the pupil, lover and lover. Helden was obsessed; she would invent situations and then demand that he tell her what he would do in the hypothetical circumstances.

"You're on a train, walking through a narrow corridor; you're carrying important papers. A man comes towards you from the opposite direction; you know him, he's the enemy. There are people behind you; you can't go back. What do you do?"

"Does the man – the enemy – want to hurt me?"

"You don't know. What do you do? Quickly!"

"Keep going, I guess. Alert, expecting the worst."

"No, my darling! The *papers*. You've got to protect them! You trip; you fall to the floor!"

"Why?"

"You'll draw attention to yourself; people will help you up. The enemy won't make his move in that situation. You create your own diversion."

"With *myself*," said Noel, seeing the point.

"Exactly."

It went on – and on – and on, until the teacher and the pupil were exhausted. They made quiet love and held each other in the comfort of their warmth, the world outside a faraway thing. Finally, Helden fell asleep, her head on his chest, her hair covering her face.

He lay awake for a while, his arm across her shoulders, and wondered how a girl who'd been entranced by *The Wizard of Oz* grew up to become so skilled a practitioner in arts of deception and escape.

They awoke too late for Helden to go to work.

"It's just as well," she said, reaching for the phone. "We have shopping to do. My boss will accept a second day of illness. I think she's in love with me."

"I think I am too," said Noel, letting his fingers trace the curve of her neck. "Where do you live?"

She looked at him, smiling as she gave the number to the operator. Then she covered the mouthpiece. "You'll not extract vital information by appealing to my baser instincts. I'm trained, remember?" She smiled again.

"I'm serious. Where do you *live?*"

The smile disappeared. "I can't tell you." She removed her hand from the telephone and spoke rapidly in French to the Gallimard switchboard.

An hour later they drove into Paris, stopping first at his hotel to pick up his things, then on to a district profuse with second-hand clothing stores. The teacher once more asserted her authority; she chose the garments with a practised eye. The clothes she selected for the pupil were nondescript, difficult to spot in a crowd.

A Mackinaw jacket and a brown topcoat were added to his raincoat. A battered country walking hat, a dark fedora – its crown battered – and a black cap whose visor fell free of the snap, were bought. All were well used.

Except the shoes; they were new. One pair with thick crêpe soles, a second, less informal, whose leather soles were the base for a layer of rubber attached by a shoemaker down the street.

The shoe-repair shop was four blocks away from a shabby store-front. Helden went in alone, instructing him to remain outside. She emerged ten minutes later with a perforated cylinder, the silencer for his automatic.

He was being outfitted with uniforms and the proper weapon, thought Holcroft. He was being processed and sent into combat after the shortest period of basic training one could imagine. He had seen the enemy. Alive and following him . . . and then dead in the streets and alleyways of Barbizon. Where was the enemy now?

Helden was confident they had lost him for a while. She thought the enemy might pick him up at the airport, but once in Berlin, he could lose that enemy again.

He *had* to. She wanted him back; she would be waiting. They stopped at a small café for lunch and wine. Helden made a final phone call and returned to the booth with the name of a hotel in Berlin. It was in the Hurenviertel, that section of the city where sex was an open commodity.

She held his hand, her face next to his; in minutes he would go out on the street alone and hail a taxi for Orly Airport.

"Be careful, my darling."

"I will."

"Remember the things I've told you. They may help."

"I'll remember."

"The hardest thing to accept is that it's all real. You'll find yourself wondering, why me? Why this? Don't think about it, just accept it."

Nothing is as it was for you. Nothing can ever be the same.

"I have. I've also found you."

She glanced away, then turned back to him. "When you get to Berlin, near the hotel, pick up a whore in the street. It's a good protective device. Keep her with you until you make contact with Kessler."

The Air France 707 made its final approach to Tempelhof Airport. Noel sat on the right side of the plane, in the third seat on the aisle, the space next to him unoccupied.

You have money; buy an extra seat . . . and don't let anyone sit next to you, don't get hemmed in.

The ways of survival spoken by a survivor, thought Holcroft. And then he remembered that his mother had called herself a survivor. Althene had taken a certain pride in the term, her voice 4,000 miles away over the telephone.

She had told him she was taking a trip. It was her way of going into hiding for several weeks, the methods of evasion and concealment learned over thirty years ago. God, she *was* incredible! Noel wondered where she would go, what she would do. He would call Sam Buonoventura in Curaçao, in a few days. Sam might have heard from her by then.

The customs inspection at Tempelhof was swift. Holcroft walked into the terminal, found the men's room, and reassembled his gun.

As instructed, he took a taxi to the Tiergarten park. Inside the cab, he opened his suitcase, changed into the worn brown topcoat and the battered walking hat. The cab stopped; he paid the fare, got out, and walked into the park, sidestepping strollers, until he found an empty bench and sat down. He scanned the crowds; no one stopped or hesitated. He got up quickly and headed for an exit. There was a taxi stand near by; he stood in line, glancing around unobtrusively to see if he could spot the enemy. It was difficult now to single out anything or anyone specifically; the late afternoon shadows were becoming longer and darker.

His turn came. He gave the driver the names of two intersecting streets. The intersection was three blocks north and four blocks west of the hotel. The driver grinned and spoke in thickly accented but perfectly understandable English.

"You wish a little fun? I have friends, *Herr Amerikaner*. No risk of the French sickness."

"You've got me wrong. I'm doing sociological research."

"*Wie?*"

"I'm meeting my wife."

They drove in silence across Berlin. With each turn they made, Noel watched for a car somewhere behind them that made the same turn. A few did, but none for any length of time. He recalled Helden's words.

"They often use radios. Such a simple thing as a change of coat or the wearing of a hat will throw them off. Those receiving instructions will look for a man in a jacket and no hat, but he is not there."

Were there unseen men watching for a specific taxi and a specific passenger wearing specific clothing? He would never know; he knew only that no one appeared to be following him now.

During the twenty-odd minutes it took to reach the intersection, night had come. The streets were lined with gaudy neon signs, and suggestive posters. Young fair-haired cowboys co-existed with whores in slit skirts and low-cut blouses. It was another sort of carnival, thought Holcroft, as he walked south for the prescribed three blocks towards the corner where he would turn left.

He saw a whore in a doorway, applying lipstick to her generous mouth. She was in that indeterminate age bracket so defiantly obscured by whores and chic suburban housewives – somewhere between thirty-five and forty-eight, and losing the fight. Her hair was jet black, framing her pallid white skin, her eyes deep, hollowed with shadows. Beyond, in the next block, he could see the shabby hotel's marquee, one letter shorted out in its neon sign.

He approached her, not entirely sure what to say. The unfamiliar language aside, he had never been with a whore.

He cleared his throat. "Good evening, *Fräulein*. Can you speak English?"

The woman returned his look, coolly at first, appraising his cloth topcoat. Then her eyes dropped to the suitcase in his right hand, his attaché case in his left. She parted her lips and smiled; the teeth were yellow. "*Ja, mein Amerikaner* friend. I speak good. I show you a good time."

"I'd like that. How much?"

"Twenty-five Deutschmarks."

"I'd say the negotiations are concluded. Will you come with me?" Holcroft took his money clip from his pocket, peeling off three bills, and handing them to the woman. "Thirty Deutschmarks. Let's go to that hotel down the street."

"*Wohin?*"

Noel gestured at the hotel in the next block. "There," he said.

"*Gut*," agreed the woman, taking his arm.

The room was like any room in a cheap hotel in a large city. If there was a single positive feature it was to be found in the naked light bulb in the ceiling. It was so dim it obscured the stained, broken furniture.

"*Dreissig Minuten*," announced the whore, removing her coat and draping it over a chair with a certain militaristic *élan*. "You have one half-hour, no more. I am, as you Americans say, a businessman. My time is valuable."

"I'm sure it is," said Holcroft. "Take a rest or read something. We'll leave in fifteen or twenty minutes. You'll stay with me and help me make a phone call." He opened the attaché case and found the paper with the information on Erich Kessler. There was a chair against the wall; he sat down and started to read in the dim light.

"*Telephonieren?*" asked the whore. "You pay thirty Deutschmarks for me to do nothing for you but help you with a *Telephonieren?*"

"That's right."

"That's *verrückt!*"

"I don't speak German. I may have trouble reaching the person I've got to call."

"Why do we wait here then? There is a telephone on the corner."

"For appearances, I guess."

The whore smiled. "I am your *Entschuldigung.*"

"What?"

"You take me up to a room, no one asks questions."

"I wouldn't say that," replied Noel uneasily.

"It's not my business, *Amerikaner.*" She came over to his chair. "But as long as we're here . . . why not have a little fun? You paid. I'm not so bad."

Holcroft returned her smile. "You're not so bad at all. But no thanks. I've got a lot on my mind."

"Then you do your work," said the whore.

Noel read the information given to him by Ernst Manfredi a lifetime ago in Geneva.

Erich Kessler, Professor of History, Free University of Berlin. Dahlen district. Speaks fluent English. Contacts: University telephone – 731–426. Residence – 824–114. Brother named Hans, a doctor. Lives in Munich . . .

There followed a brief summary of Kessler's academic career, the degrees obtained, the honours conferred. They were overwhelming. The professor was a learned man, and often learned men were sceptics. How would Kessler react to the call from an unknown American who travelled to Berlin without prior communication to see him about a matter he would not discuss over the telephone?

It was nearly 6.30, time to find out the answer. And to change clothes. He got up, went to his suitcase, and took out the Mackinaw jacket and the visored cap. "Let's go," Noel said.

The whore stood by the phone booth while Holcroft dialled. He wanted her near by in case someone other than Kessler answered, someone who did not speak English.

The line was busy. He pressed the hook down and indicated as much to the woman outside; she nodded in agreement and smiled. Noel remained still, looking through the glass panels at the gaudy, brightly coloured neon carnival that was the Hurenviertel. All around he could hear the sounds of the German language – emphatic conversations as couples and roving packs of pleasure-seekers passed the telephone booth. Shouts of urgency and drunkenness came from the street where pedestrians and traffic met in sudden combat; metallic appeals blared from competing loudspeakers over storefronts luring customers off the pavements. All German.

He wondered. If his mother had been anyone else but Althene, would he be one of those outside the glass booth right now? Not where he was right *now*, but somewhere in Berlin, or Bremerhaven, or Munich? Noel Clausen. German. Speaking the language that was so foreign to him as Noel Holcroft. Or would he be living as Johann von Tiebolt, with a different name, brought up thousands of miles away from home, still running from a legacy for which he was not responsible, training others – brothers and sisters, perhaps – to survive in a world that loathed them?

What *would* his life had been like? It was an eerie feeling. Fascinating, repulsive . . . and compulsive. As if he were going back in time, through the layers of his personal mist, and found a fork in a fog-bound road he might have taken but did not. That fork was re-examined now; where would it have led?

Helden? Would he have known her in that other life? He knew her now. And he was very aware that he wanted to get back to her as soon as he could; he wanted to see her again, and hold her again, and tell her that . . . .*things* . . . were going to be all right. He wanted to see her laugh and have a life where three changes of outer clothing and guns with silencers were not intrinsic to survival. Where the *Rache* and the *Odessa* were no longer threats to sanity and existence.

Kessler. Geneva. An agency in Zürich.

A man answered, the voice deep and soft.

"Mr Kessler? Dr Kessler?"

"I shan't cure any diseases, sir," came the pleasant reply in English, "but the title is correct, if abused. What can I do for you?"

"My name is Holcroft. Noel Holcroft. I'm from New York. I'm an architect."

"Holcroft? I have a number of American friends and, of course, university people with whom I correspond, but I don't recognize the name."

"No reason for you to; you don't know me. However, I've come to Berlin to see you. There's a confidential matter to discuss that concerns the two of us."

"Confidential?"

"Let's say, a family matter."

"*Hans?* Did something happen to Hans?"

"No . . ."

"I have no other family, Mr Holcroft."

"It goes back a number of years. I'm afraid I can't say any more over the telephone. Please, trust me; it's urgent. Could you possibly meet me tonight?"

"Tonight?" Kessler paused. "Did you arrive in Berlin today?"

"Late this afternoon."

"And you want to see me tonight . . . This matter must, indeed, be urgent. I have to return to my office for an hour or so this evening. Would nine o'clock be satisfactory?"

"Yes," said Noel, relieved. "Very satisfactory. Any place you say."

"I'd asked you to my house, but I'm afraid I have guests. There's a ratskeller on the Kurfurstendamm. It's often crowded but they have quiet booths in the back and the manager knows me."

"It sounds perfect."

Kessler gave him the name and address. "Ask for my table."

"I will. And thanks very much."

"You're quite welcome. I should warn you, I keep telling the manager that the food is grand. It isn't really, but he's such a pleasant fellow and good to the students. See you at nine o'clock."

"I'll be there. Thanks again." Holcroft put the phone back in its cradle, swept by a sudden feeling of confidence. If the man matched the voice over the telephone, Erich Kessler was intelligent, humorous, immensely likeable. What a relief!

Noel hung up and smiled at the whore. "Thanks," he said, giving her an additional ten marks.

"*Auf wiedersehen.*" The whore turned and walked off. Holcroft watched her for a moment, but his attention was suddenly drawn to a man in a black leather jacket halfway down the short block. He stood in front of a bookstore, but he was not interested in the pornography displayed in the window. Instead, he was staring directly at Noel. As their eyes met, the man turned away.

Was he one of the enemy? A fanatic from the *Rache?* A maniac of the *Odessa?* Or perhaps someone assigned to him from the ranks of Wolfsschanze? He had to find out.

A confrontation is often the last thing surveillance wants. But If he does want it, you might as well know it . . .

Helden's words; part of the instructions she had given him. He would try to remember the tactics; he would use them now. He felt the bulges in the cloth of his Mackinaw; weapon and silencer were there. He pulled the visor of his cap free of its snap, gripped the handle of his attaché case, and walked away from the man in the black leather jacket.

He hurried down the street, staying close to the kerb, prepared to race out into the traffic. He reached the corner and turned right, walking swiftly into a crowd of spectators watching two life-sized plastic manikins performing the sex act on a black bearskin rug. Holcroft was jostled; his attaché case was crushed against his leg, then pulled, as if being yanked aside by a victim of its sharp corners . . . Yanked, pulled – *taken*; his attaché case could be taken, the papers inside read by those who should never read them. He had not been totally stupid; he had removed Heinrich Clausen's letter and the more informative sections from the Geneva document. No figures, no sources, only the bank's letterhead and the names – meaningless legal gibberish to an ordinary thief, but something else entirely to the extraordinary one.

Helden had warned him about carrying even these, but he had countered with the possibility that the unknown Erich Kessler might think him a madman and he needed at least fragments to substantiate his incredible story.

But now – if he *was* being followed – he had to leave the case in a place where it would not be stolen. Where? Certainly not at the hotel. A locker in a train station, or a bus depot. Unacceptable, because both were accessible; such places would be child's play for the experienced thief. Off his person would be child's play.

Besides, he needed those papers – those fragments – for Erich Kessler. Kessler. The ratskeller. *The manager there knows me. Ask for my table.*

The ratskeller on the Kurfurstendamm. Going there now would serve two purposes: on the way, he could see if he was actually being followed; once there, he could either stay or leave his case with the manager.

He pushed his way into the street, looking for an empty taxi, glancing behind him for signs of surveillance – for a man in a black leather jacket. There was a cab in the middle of the block. He ran towards it.

As he entered he spun around quickly. And he saw the man in the black leather jacket. He was not walking now. Instead, he was in the saddle of a small motorbike, propelling it along the kerb with his left foot. There were a number of other bikes in the street, cruising in and out between the traffic.

The man in the black leather jacket stopped pushing his machine, turned away, and pretended to be talking to someone on the pavement. The pretence was too obvious; there was no one responding to his conversation. Noel climbed in the cab and gave the name and address of the ratskeller. They drove off.

So did the man in the black leather jacket. Noel watched him through the rear window. Like the man in the green Fiat in Paris, this Berliner was an expert. He stayed several car-lengths behind the taxi, swerving quickly at odd moments to make sure the object of his surveillance was still there.

It was pointless to keep watching. Holcroft settled back in the seat and tried to figure out his next moves.

A confrontation is often the last thing surveillance wants . . . if he does . . . you might as well know it.

Did he want to know it? Was he prepared for confrontation? The answers were not easy. He was not someone who cared to test his courage deliberately. But in the forefront of his imagination was the sight of Richard Holcroft crushed into a building on a pavement in New York.

Fear was the caution; rage was the strength. The single answer was clear. He wanted the man in the black leather jacket. And he would get him.

24

He paid the driver and got out of the cab, making sure he could be seen by the man on the motorbike, who had stopped down the block.

Noel walked casually across the pavement to the ratskeller and went inside. He stood on a platformed staircase and studied the restaurant. The ceilings were high, the dining area on a lower floor. The place was half full. The wooden tables were places in ranks throughout the central area. Everything was heavy, massive.

He saw the booths Kessler had described. They were along the rear wall and the sides: tables flanked by high-backed seats. Running across the fronts of the booths were brass rods holding red-checked curtains. Each booth could be isolated from its surroundings by drawing a curtain across the table, but with the curtains open one could sit at almost any booth and observe whoever came through the door on top of the staircase.

Holcroft descended the stairs to a lectern at the bottom and spoke to a heavy-set man behind it. "Pardon me, do you speak English?"

The man looked up from the reservation book in front of him. "Is there a restaurateur in Berlin who doesn't, sir?"

Noel smiled. "Good. I'm looking for the manager."

"You've found him. What can I do for you? Do you wish a table?"

"I think one's been reserved. The name's Kessler."

The manager's eyes showed immediate recognition. "Oh, yes. He called not fifteen minutes ago. But the reservation was for nine o'clock. It's only . . ."

"I know," interrupted Holcroft. "I'm early. You see, I've got a favour to ask." He held up the attaché case. "I brought this for Professor Kessler. Some historical papers lent him by the university in America where I teach. I have to meet some people for an hour or so, and wondered if I could leave it here."

"Of course," said the manager. He held out his hand for the case.

"You understand, these are valuable. Not in terms of money, just academically."

"I'll lock them in my office."

"Thank you very much."

"*Ist nichts.* Your name, sir?"

"Holcroft."

"Thank you, Herr Holcroft. Your table will be ready at nine o'clock." The manager bowed, turned, and carried the attaché case towards a closed door under the staircase.

Noel stood for a moment considering what to do next. No one had entered since he had arrived. That meant the man in the leather jacket was outside, waiting for him. It was time to bait the trap, time to corner that man.

He started up the staircase, suddenly struck by a thought that made him sick. He had just done the most stupid thing he could think of! He had led the man in the black leather jacket directly to the spot where he was making contact with Erich Kessler. And to compound that enormous mistake, he had given his own name to the manager.

Kessler and *Holcroft. Holcroft* and *Kessler.* They were tied together. He had revealed an unknown third of Geneva! Revealed it as clearly as if he had taken out a newspaper ad.

It was no longer a question of whether he was capable of setting the trap, he *had to* do it. He had to immobilize the man in the black leather jacket.

He pushed open the door and walked on to the pavement. The Kurfürstendamm was lit up. The air was cold, and in the sky above the moon was circled by a rim of mist. He started walking to his right, his hands in his pockets to ward off the chill. He passed the motorbike at the kerb, and continued to the corner. Ahead, perhaps three blocks away on the left side of the Kurfürstendamm, he could see the outlines of the enormous Kaiser Wilhelm Church, floodlights illuminating the tower. He would use the church as his landmark.

He continued walking along the pavement, slower than most of the strollers around him, stopping frequently in front of store windows. He checked his watch at regular intervals, hoping to give the impression that the minutes were important, that perhaps he was pacing himself to reach a rendezvous at a specific time to make contact with a specific person.

Directly opposite the Kaiser Wilhelm Church, he stood for a while at the kerb under the glare of a streetlight. He glanced to his left. Thirty yards away the man in the black leather jacket turned around, his back to Holcroft, watching the flow of traffic.

He was there; that was all that mattered.

Noel started up again, his walk faster now. He came to another corner and looked up at the street sign. *Schonberg Strasse.* It angled off the Kurfürstendamm, lined with shops on both sides. The pavements seemed more crowded, the strollers less hurried than those on the Kurfürstendamm.

He waited for a break in the traffic and crossed the street. He turned right on the pavement, staying close to the kerb, excusing himself past the strollers. He reached the end of the block, crossed over into the next, and slowed his walk. He began stopping as he had stopped on the Kurfürstendamm to gaze into the shop windows – and checking his watch with growing concentration. He kept going from doorway to doorway, window to window.

He saw the man in the leather jacket twice.

Noel proceeding into the third block. No more than fifty feet from the corner there was a narrow alley, a thoroughfare between the Schonberg Strasse and a parallel street about a hundred yards away. The alley was dark and dotted along its sides with shadowed doorways. The darkness and the length were uninviting, obvious deterrents for pedestrians during the evening hours.

But this alley, at this time, was the trapping ground, an unlit stretch of concrete and brick into which he'd lead the man who followed him.

He continued walking down the block, past the alley towards the corner, his pace quickening with every stride, Helden's words heard in his ears.

The amateur does the unexpected, not because he's clever or experienced, but because he doesn't know any better . . . Do the unexpected rapidly, obviously, as if confused . . .

He reached the end of the block and stopped abruptly under a streetlight. As if startled, he looked around, pivoting on the pavement, a man who was undecided but knew a decision must be made. He stared back towards the alleyway and suddenly broke into a run, colliding with pedestrians entering the alley – a man in panic.

He ran until the darkness was nearly full, until he was at the midpoint of the alley, shadows upon shadows, the lights at either end distant. There was a delivery entrance of some sort – a wide metal door. He lunged towards it, spinning into the corner, his back pressed against steel and brick. He put his hand into his jacket pocket and gripped the handle of the automatic. The silencer was not attached; it was not necessary. He had no intention whatsoever of firing the weapon. It was to be only a visible threat and, at first, not even that.

The wait was not long. He could hear racing footsteps and thought as he heard them that the enemy, too, knew about rubber-soled shoes.

The man ran by; then, as if sensing a trick, slowed down, looking about in the shadows. Noel stepped out of his hidden corner, his hand in his jacket pocket.

"I've been waiting for you. Stay right where you are." He spoke intensely, frightened at his own words. "I've got a gun in my hand. I don't *want* to use it but I will if you try to run."

"You did not hesitate two days ago in France," said the man in a thick accent, his calm unnerving. "Why should I expect you to stop now? You're a pig. You can kill me, but we will stop you."

"Who are you?"

"Does it matter? Just know that we will stop you."

"You're with the *Rache*, aren't you?"

In spite of the darkness, Noel could see an expression of contempt on the man's face. "The *Rache?*" he said. "Terrorists, revolutionaries. Butchers. I'm no part of the *Rache!*"

"The *Odessa* then."

"You'd like that, wouldn't you?"

"What do you mean?"

"You'll use the *Odessa* when the time comes. It can be blamed for so much. You can kill so easily in its name. I suppose the irony is that we'd kill the *Odessa* as quickly as you would. But you're the ones we want; we know

208

the difference between clowns and monsters. Believe me, we'll stop you."

"You're not making sense! You're not part of Wolfsschanze; you couldn't be!"

The man lowered his voice. "But we are all part of Wolfsschanze, aren't we? In one way or another," he said, a challenge in his eyes. "I say it again. You can kill me but another will take my place. Kill him, another his. We *will* stop you. So shoot, Herr Clausen. Or should I say son of Reichsführer Heinrich Clausen.

"What the hell are you talking about? I don't want to kill you. I don't want to kill anybody!"

"You killed in France."

"If I killed a man, it was because he tried to kill me."

"*Aber natürlich, Herr* Clausen."

"Stop calling me that."

"Why? It's your name, isn't it?"

"No! My name's Holcroft."

"Of course," said the man. "That was part of the plan. The respected American with no discernible ties to his past. And if anyone traced them, it would be too late."

"Too late for what? Who *are* you? Who sent you?"

"There's no way you can force that from me. We're not part of your plan."

"What plan?" he asked, hoping to learn something, *anything*."

"Geneva."

"What about Geneva? It's a city in Switzerland."

"We know everything and it's finished. You won't stop the eagles. Not this time. We'll stop *you!*"

"*Eagles? What* eagles? Who's *we?*"

"Never. Pull the trigger. I won't tell you. You won't trace *us*."

Noel was sweating, yet the winter night was cold. Nothing this enemy said made sense. It was possible that an enormous error had been made. The man in front of him was prepared to die, but he was not a fanatic; there was too much intelligence behind the eyes.

"You say you're not with the *Rache*, not with the *Odessa*. For God's sake, why do you want to stop Geneva? Wolfsschanze doesn't want to stop it, you must know that!"

"Not *your* Wolfsschanze. But we can put that fortune to great use."

"*No!* If you interfere, there won't be anything. You'll never get the money."

"We both know that doesn't have to be."

"You're wrong! It'll go back into the ground for another thirty years."

The unknown enemy drew himself up in the shadows. "That's the flaw, isn't it? You put it so well: 'back into the ground'. But if I may be permitted, there'll be no scorched earth then."

"No what?"

"No scorched earth." The man stepped backwards. "We've talked enough. You had your chance, you have it still. You can kill me, but it will do you no good. We have the photograph. We're beginning to understand."

"The *photograph?* In Portsmouth? *You?*"

"A most respected commander in the Royal Navy. It was interesting that you should take it."

"For Christ's sake! Who *are* you?"

"One who fights you."

"I told you . . ."

"I know," said the German. "I should not say that. In point of fact I shall say nothing further. I will turn around and walk out of this alleyway. Shoot, if you must. I'm prepared. We're all prepared."

The man turned slowly and began walking. It was more than Noel could stand.

"Stop!" he yelled.

The man spun around. "We have nothing further to say."

"Yes, we *do.* We're going to stay here all night, if we have to! You're going to tell me who you are and where you came from and what the hell you know about Geneva and Beaumont and . . ."

It was as far as he got. The man's hand shot out, his fingers clasping Noel's right wrist, twisting it inwards and downwards as his right knee hammered up into Holcroft's groin. Noel doubled forward in agony, but he would not let go of the gun. He shoved his shoulder into the man's mid-section, trying to push him away, the pain from his testicles spreading up into his stomach and chest. The man brought his fist crashing down into the base of Holcroft's skull, causing shockwaves through his ribs and spine. But not the gun! The man could not have the gun! Noel gripped it as if it were the last steel clamp on a lifeboat. He lurched up, springing with what strength he had left in his legs, wrenching the automatic away from the man's grip.

There was an explosion; it echoed through the alley. The man's arm fell away and he staggered backwards, grabbing his shoulder. He had been wounded, but he did not collapse. Instead, he braced himself against the wall and spoke through gasps of breath.

"We'll stop you. And we'll do it our way. We'll take Geneva!"

With those words he propelled himself down the alley, clawing at the wall for support. Holcroft turned; there were figures clustered about the alley's entrance on the Schonberg Strasse. He could hear police whistles and see the coruscating beams of flashlights. The Berlin police were moving in.

He was caught.

But he could *not* be caught! There was Kessler; there was Geneva. He could not be detained now!

Helden's words came back to him. *Lie indignantly.. with confidence . . . invent your own variations.*

Noel shoved the automatic in his pocket and started towards the Schonberg Strasse, towards the cautiously approaching flashlights and the two uniformed men who held them.

"I'm an American!" he yelled in a frightened voice. "Does anyone speak English?"

A man from the crowd shouted, "I do! What happened?"

"I was walking through here and someone tried to rob me! He had a gun but I didn't know it! I shoved him and it went off . . ."

The Berliner translated quickly for the police.

"Where did he go?" asked the man.

"I think he's still there. In one of the doorways. I've got to sit down . . ."

The Berliner touched Holcroft's shoulder. "Come." He began leading Noel out through the crowd towards the kerb.

"Thanks very much," said Noel. "I'd just like to get some air, calm down, you know what I mean?"

"*Ja*. A terrible experience."

"I think they've got him," added Holcroft suddenly, looking back towards the police and the crowd.

The Berliner turned; Noel stepped off the kerb into the street. He started walking, slowly at first, then found a break in the traffic and crossed to the other side. There he turned and ran as fast as he could through the crowds towards the Kurfürstendamm.

He had done it, thought Holcroft, as he sat coatless and hatless, shivering on a deserted bench within sight of the Kaiser Wilhelm Church. He had absorbed the lessons and put them to use; he had invented his own variations and eluded the trap he had set for another, but which had sprung back, ensnaring himself. Beyond this he had immobilized the man in the black leather jacket. That man would be detained, if only to find a doctor.

Above all, he had learned that Helden was wrong. And the dead Manfredi – who would not say the names – had been wrong. It was not the *Odessa*, not the *Rache*, who were Geneva's most powerful enemies. It was someone else, someone infinitely more knowledgeable and more deadly. An enigma that counted among its adherents men who would die calmly, with intelligence in their eyes and reasonable speech on their tongues.

The race to Geneva was against three violent forces wanting to destroy the covenant, but one was far more ingenious than the other two. The man in the black leather jacket had spoken of the *Rache* and the *Odessa* in terms so disparaging they could not have sprung from envy or fear. He had dismissed them as incompetent *butchers* and *clowns*, of which he wanted no part. For he was part of something else, something far superior.

Holcroft looked at his watch. He had been sitting in the cold for nearly an hour, the ache in his groin still sickening, the base of his skull throbbing still with pain. He had stuffed the Mackinaw coat and the black visored cap into a refuse bin several blocks away. They would have been too easy to spot if the Berlin police had an alarm out for him.

It was time to go now; there were no signs of the police, no signs of anyone interested in him. The cold air had done nothing for his pain, but it had helped clear his head, and until that had happened he dared not move. He could move now; he had to. It was almost 9.00. It was time to meet Erich Kessler, the third key to Geneva.

25

The ratskeller was now crowded, as he had expected it would be. The manager greeted him pleasantly, but his eyes betrayed his thoughts: something had happened to this American within the last hour. Noel was embarrassed; he wondered if his face was scratched, or streaked with dirt.

"I'd like to wash. I had a nasty fall."

"Certainly. Over there, sir." The manager pointed to the men's room. "Professor Kessler's arrived. He's waiting for you. I gave him your briefcase."

"Thanks again," said Holcroft, turning towards the door of the washroom.

He looked at his face in the mirror. There were no stains, no dirt, no blood. But there was something in his eyes; a look associated with pain and shock and exhaustion. And fear. That's what the manager had seen.

He ran the water in the basin until it was lukewarm, doused his face and combed his hair, and wished he could take that look out of his eyes. Then he returned to the manager, who led him to a booth at the rear of the hall, furthest from the room's activity. The red-checked curtain was drawn across the table.

"*Herr Professor?*"

The curtain was pulled aside, revealing a man in his mid-forties with a large girth and a full face framed by a short beard and thick brown hair combed straight back over his head. It was a gentle face, the deep-set eyes alive, tinged with anticipation, even humour.

"Mr Holcroft?"

"Dr Kessler?"

"Sit down, sit down." Kessler made a brief attempt to rise as he held out his hand; the contact between his stomach and the table prevented it. He laughed and looked at the ratskeller's manager. "*Next* week! *Ja, Rudi?* Our diets."

"*Ach, natürlich, Professor.*"

"This is my new friend from America. Mr Holcroft."

"Yes, we met earlier."

"Of course you did. You gave me his briefcase." Kessler patted Noel's attaché case next to him on the seat. "I'm drinking scotch. Join me, Mr Holcroft?"

"Scotch'll be fine. Just ice."

The manager nodded hand left. Noel settled back in the seat. Kessler exuded a kind of weary warmth; it was an expression of tolerance from an intellect constantly exposed to lesser minds, but too kind to dwell on comparisons. Holcroft had known several men like that. Among them were his finest teachers. He was comfortable with Erich Kessler; it was a good way to begin.

"Thanks so much for seeing me. I've got a lot to tell you."

"Catch your breath first," said Kessler. "Have a drink. Calm down."

"What?"

"You've had a difficult time. It's written all over your face."

"It's that obvious?"

"I'd say you were that distraught, Mr Holcroft."

"It's Noel, please. We should get to know each other."

"A pleasant prospect, I'm sure. My name is Erich. It's a chilly night outside. Too cold to go without an overcoat. Yet you obviously arrived without one. There's no checkroom here."

"I *was* wearing one. I had to get rid of it. I'll explain."

"You don't have to."

"I'm afraid I do. I wish I didn't, but it's part of my story."

"I see. Ah, here's your scotch."

A waiter deposited the glass in front of Holcroft, then stepped back and drew the red-checked curtain across the booth.

"As I said, it's part of the story." Noel drank.

"Take your time. There's no hurry."

"You said you had guests at your house."

"*A* guest. A friend of my brother's from Munich. He's a delightful fellow, but long-winded. A trait not unknown among doctors. You've rescued me for the evening."

"Won't your wife be upset?"

"I'm not married. I was, but I'm afraid university life was rather confining for her."

"I'm sorry."

"She's not. She married an acrobat. Can you imagine? From the academic groves to the rarefied heights of alternating trapezes. We're still good friends."

"I think it would be difficult not to be friendly with you."

"Oh, I'm a terror in the lecture rooms. A veritable lion."

"Who roars but can't bring himself to bite," said Noel.

"I beg your pardon?"

"Nothing. I was remembering a conversation I had last night. With someone else."

"Feeling better?"

"That's funny."

"What is?"

"That's what I said last night."

"With this someone else?" Kessler smiled again. "Your face seems more relaxed."

"If it was any more relaxed, it'd be draped over the table."

"Perhaps some food?"

"Not yet. I'd like to start; there's a great deal to tell you and you're going to have a lot of questions."

"Then I shall listen carefully. Oh, I forgot. Your briefcase." The German reached beside him and lifted the attaché case on top of the table.

Holcroft unlocked the case, but did not open it. "There are papers in here you'll want to study. They're not complete, but they'll serve as confirmation for some of the things I tell you."

"Confirmation? Are the things you say you must tell me so difficult to accept?"

"They may be," said Noel. He felt sorry for this good-natured scholar. The peaceful world he lived in was about to collapse around him. "What I'm going to say to you may interrupt your life, as it has mine. I don't think that can be avoided. At least I couldn't avoid it, because I couldn't walk away from it. Part of the reason was selfish; there's a great deal of money involved that will come to me personally – as it will come to you. The kind of money that will give us a freedom I don't think either of us has ever thought about. But there are other factors that are much more important than either you or me. I know that's true because if it wasn't, I'd have run away by now. But I won't run. I'm going to do what I've been asked to do because it's *right*. And because there are people I hate who want to stop me. They killed someone I loved very much. They tried to kill another." Holcroft stopped suddenly; he had not meant to go this far. The fear and the rage were coming together. He had lost control; he was talking too much. "I'm sorry. I could be reading a lot of things into all this that don't belong. I don't mean to frighten you."

Kessler put his hand on Noel's arm. "Frightening me isn't a concern. You're overwrought and exhausted, my friend. Apparently terrible things have happened to you."

Holcroft drank several swallows of whisky, trying to numb the pain in his groin and his neck. "I won't lie. They have. But I didn't want to start this way. It wasn't very smart."

Kessler removed his hand from Noel's arm. "Let me say something. I've known you less than five minutes and I don't think being smart is relevant. You're obviously a highly intelligent man – a very honest one, too – and you've been under a great strain. Why not simply start at the beginning without worrying how it affects me?"

"Okay." Holcroft put his arms on the table, his hands around the glass of whisky. "I'll begin by asking you if you've ever heard the names von Tiebolt and . . . Clausen."

Kessler stared at Noel for a moment. "Yes," he said. "They go back many years – to when I was a child – but of course I've heard them. Clausen and von Tiebolt. They were friends of my father's. I was very young, around ten or eleven. They came to our house frequently, if I recall, at the end of the war. I *do* remember Clausen; at least I think I do. He was a tall man and quite magnetic."

"What do you mean, 'magnetic'?"

"I'm not sure how to say it. Imposing, I imagine. There was his height, of course. He looked magnificent in his uniform."

"Tell me about him."

"There's not much I can remember."

"Anything you can. *Please.*"

"Again, I'm not sure how to put it. Clausen dominated a room without making any effort to do so. When he spoke everyone listened, yet I don't recall him ever raising his voice. He seemed to be a kind man, concerned for others, but extremely strong-willed. I thought once – that he was someone who had lived with much pain."

A man in agony had cried out to him. "What kind of pain?"

"I've no idea; it was only a child's impression. You would have to have seen his eyes to understand. No matter whom he looked at, young or old, important or not, he gave that person his full concentration. I do remember that; it was not a common trait in those days. In a way, I picture Clausen more clearly than I do my own father, and certainly more than von Tiebolt. Why are you interested in him?"

"He was my father."

Kessler's mouth opened in astonishment. "You?" he whispered. "Clausen's *son?*"

Noel nodded. "My natural father, not the father I knew."

"Then your mother was . . ." Kessler stopped.

"Althene Clausen. Did you ever hear anyone speak of her?"

"Never by name, and never in Clausen's presence. Ever. She was spoken of in whispers. The woman who left the great man, the American enemy who fled the Fatherland with their . . . *You.* You were the child she took from him!"

"Took with her, *kept* from him, is the way she puts it."

"She's still alive?"

"Very much so."

"It's all so *incredible.*" Kessler shook his head. "After all these years, a man I remember so vividly."

"More clearly than your own father."

"An exaggeration, perhaps, but minor. Heinrich Clausen was not a man who disappears from one's memory. He was extraordinary."

"They were all extraordinary."

"Who?"

"The three of them. Clausen, von Tiebolt, and Kessler. Tell me, do you know how your father died?"

"He killed himself. It was not unusual then. When the Reich collapsed, a lot of people did. For most of them it was easier that way."

"For some it was the only way."

"Nuremberg?"

"No, Geneva. To protect Geneva."

"I don't understand you."

"You will." Holcroft opened his attaché case, took out the pages he had clipped together, and gave them to Kessler. "There's a bank in Geneva that has an account that can be released for specific purposes only by the consent of three people. This account has funds totalling 780 million dollars . . ."

As he had done twice before, Noel told the story of the massive theft of over thirty years ago. But with Kessler, he told it all. He did not, as he had done with Gretchen, withhold specific facts; nor did he tell the story in stages, as he had with Helden. He left out nothing.

" . . . Monies were intercepted from the occupied countries, from the sales of art objects and the looting of museums. Wehrmacht payrolls were rerouted, millions stolen from the Ministry of Armaments and the – I can't remember the name, it's in the letter – but from the industrial complex. Everything was banked in Switzerland, in Geneva, with the help of a man named Manfredi."

"Manfredi? I remember the name."

"It's not surprising," said Holcroft. "Although I don't imagine he was mentioned too frequently. Where did you hear it?"

"I don't know. After the war, I think."

"From your mother?"

"I don't think so. She died in July of '45 and was in the hospital for most of the time. From someone else . . . I don't know."

"Where did you live? With your father and mother dead."

"My brother and I moved in with our uncle, my mother's brother. It was lucky for us. He was an older man and never had much use for the Nazis. He found favour with the occupation forces. But, please, go on."

Noel did. He detailed the conditions of competence required by the directors of the Staats-Banque de Genève, which led him into the dismissal of Gretchen Beaumont. He told Kessler of the von Tiebolts' clouded migration to Rio, the birth of Helden, the killing of their mother, and their eventual flight from Brazil.

"They took the name of Tennyson and have been living in England for the past five years. Johann von Tiebolt is known as John Tennyson. He's a reporter for *The Guardian*. Gretchen married Beaumont and Helden moved several months ago to Paris. I haven't met the brother, but I've become friends with Helden. She's a remarkable girl."

"Is she the 'someone else' you were with last night?"

"Yes," replied Holcroft. "I want to tell you about her, what she's gone through, what she's going through now. She and thousands like her are part of the story."

"I think I may know," said Kessler. "*Verwünschte Kinder.*"

"The 'Children of the Damned'," said Noel. "She used the expression."

"It's a term they gave themselves. Thousands of young people – not so young now – who fled the country because they convinced themselves they couldn't live with the guilt of Nazi Germany. They rejected everything

German, sought new identities, new life-styles. They're very much like those hordes of young Americans who left the United States for Canada and Sweden in protest against the Vietnam War. Can you understand?"

"Not really," said Holcroft. "But then I'm not built that way. I'm not going to take on a guilt that isn't mine."

Kessler looked into Noel's eyes. "I submit you may have. You say you won't run from this covenant of yours, yet terrible things have happened to you."

Holcroft considered the scholar's words. "There may be some truth in that, but the circumstances are different. I didn't *leave* anything. I guess I was selected."

"Not part of the damned?" asked Kessler, "but part of the chosen?"

"Privileged, anyway."

The scholar nodded. "There's a word for that, too. Perhaps you've heard of it. *Sonnenkinder*."

"*Sonnenkinder*?" Noel frowned. "If I remember, it was in one of those courses I didn't exactly shine in. Anthropology, maybe."

"Or philosophy," suggested Kessler. "It's a philosophical concept developed by Thomas J. Perry in England in the 1920s, and before him Bachofen in Switzerland and Bachofen's disciples in Munich. The theory being that the *Sonnenkinder* – the Children of the Sun – have been with us throughout the ages. They're the shapers of history, the most brilliant among us, rulers of epochs . . . the privileged."

Holcroft nodded. "I remember now. They were ruined by that privilege of theirs. They became depraved, or something. Incestuous, I think."

"It's only a theory," said Kessler. "We're straying again; you're an easy man to talk to. You were saying about this von Tiebolt daughter that life is difficult for her."

"For all of them. And more than difficult. It's crazy. They're running all the time. They have to live like fugitives."

"They're easy prey for fanatics," agreed Erich.

"Like the *Odessa* and the *Rache*?"

"Yes. Such organizations can't function within Germany itself; they're not allowed. So they operate in other countries where disaffected expatriates such as the *Verwünschte Kinder* have gravitated. They want only to stay alive and vital, waiting for the chance to return to Germany."

"*Return*?"

Kessler held up his hand. "Please God, they never will, but they can't accept that. The *Rache* once wanted the Bonn government to be an arm of the Comintern, but even Moscow rejected them; they've become nothing more or less than terrorists. The *Odessa* has always wanted to revive Nazism. They're scorned in Germany."

"Still, they go after the kids," said Noel. "Helden used the phrase, damned for what they were, damned for what they weren't."

"An apt judgement."

"They should be stopped. Some of that money in Geneva should be used to cripple the *Odessa*, break the *Rache*."

"I wouldn't disagree with you."

"I'm glad to hear that," said Holcroft. "Let's get back to Geneva."

"By all means."

Noel had covered the objectives of the covenant and defined the conditions demanded of the inheritors. It was time to concentrate on what had happened to *him*.

He began with the murder on the plane, the terror in New York, the rearranged apartment, the letter from the men of Wolfsschanze, the enigmatic telephone call from Peter Baldwin, and the subsequent brutal killings it engendered. He spoke of the flight to Rio and a man with thick eyebrows: Anthony Beaumont, *Odessa* agent. He told of the doctored records and the strange meeting with Maurice Graff. He dwelt on MI5's intrusion in London and the astonishing news that British Intelligence believed Johann von Tiebolt was the assassin they called the Tinamou.

"The Tinamou?" broke in Kessler, stunned, his face flushed. It was his first interruption of Holcroft's narrative.

"Yes. You know something about him?"

"Only what I've read."

I gather some people think he's been responsible for dozens of assassinations."

"And the British think it's *Johann von Tiebolt?*"

"They're wrong," said Noel. "I'm certain they know it now. Something happened yesterday afternoon that proves it. You'll understand when I come to it."

"Go on."

He touched briefly on the evening with Gretchen, the photograph of Anthony Beaumont. He went on to Helden and *Herr Oberst*, then to the death of Richard Holcroft. He described the calls between himself and a detective in New York named Miles, as well as his with his mother.

He told of the green Fiat that had followed them to Barbizon, and the man with the pockmarked face.

Then came the madness of the *Fêtes d'Hiver*. How he had tried to trap the man in the Fiat and had himself nearly been killed.

"I told you a few minutes ago the British were wrong about Tennyson . . ."

"Tennyson? Oh, the name von Tiebolt assumed."

"That's right. MI5 was convinced that everything that happened in Montereau, including the man with the pockmarked face who was following us, was the work of the Tinamou. But that man was killed; he *worked* for von Tiebolt, they *knew* that. Helden even confirmed it."

"And," interrupted Kessler, "the Tinamou would not kill his own man."

"Exactly."

"Then the agent will tell his superiors . . ."

"He can't," broke in Noel. "He was shot saving Helden's life. But identifications will be made; the British will piece it together."

"Will the British find the agent who died?"

"Word will get back to them. It has to. The police were everywhere; they'll find his body."

"Can he be traced to you?"

"It's possible. We fought in the square; people will remember. But as Helden put it, we were followed, we didn't do the following. There's no reason why we should *know* anything."

"You sound unsure."

"Before the agent died, I decided to mention Baldwin's name to him, see if I could learn anything. He reacted as if I'd fired a gun in front of his face. He pleaded with Helden and me to get in touch with a man named Payton-Jones. We were supposed to tell him everything that happened, tell him to find out who attacked us, who killed von Tiebolt's man, and, most important, to tell MI5 he believed it was all related to Peter Baldwin."

"To Baldwin? He'd been with MI6, you said?"

"Yes. He'd gone to them some time ago with information about the survivors of Wolfsschanze."

"Wolfsschanze?" Kessler repeated the name softly. "That was in the letter Manfredi gave you in Geneva, the one written over thirty years ago."

"That's right. The agent said we were to tell Payton-Jones to go back to Baldwin's file. To '*Code Wolfsschanze*'. That was the phrase he used."

"In his phone call to you in New York, did Baldwin mention Wolfsschanze?" asked Kessler.

"No. He said only that I should stay away from Geneva; that he knew things no one else knew. Then he went to answer the door and he never came back."

Kessler's eyes were colder now. "So Baldwin had learned about Geneva and this Wolfsschanze's commitment to it."

"How much he learned we don't know. It could be very little, just rumours."

"But enough to stop you from going to MI5. The price of eliminating Beaumont could be too great. The British would question you and the girl at length – there are a thousand ways, and they're experts. Baldwin's name might surface and they would go back to his file. You can't chance that."

"I came to the same conclusion," said Holcroft, impressed.

"Perhaps there's another way to remove Beaumont."

"How?"

"The *Odessa* is loathed here in Germany. Word to the proper people could result in his removal. You'd never have to reach the British yourself, never have to risk Baldwin's name coming to light."

"Could that be arranged?"

"Unquestionably. If Beaumont's really an *Odessa* agent, a brief message from the Bonn government to the Foreign Office would be enough. I know any number of men who could send it."

Relief swept over Holcroft. One more obstacle was being removed. "I'm glad we met . . . that you're you and not somebody else."

"Don't be too quick to make that judgement. You want my answer. Will I join you? Frankly, I . . ."

"I don't want your answer yet," interrupted Noel. "You were fair with me and I have to be fair with you. I'm not finished. There was tonight."

"Tonight?" Kessler was disturbed, impatient.

"Yes. The last couple of hours in fact."

"What happened . . . tonight?"

Noel leaned forward. "We know about the *Rache* and the *Odessa*. We're not sure how much *they* know about Geneva, but we're damned sure what they'd do if they knew enough. We know about the men of Wolfsschanze. Whoever they are they're crazy – no better than the others – but in their own strange way they're on our side; they want Geneva to succeed. But there's someone else. Someone – *something* – much more powerful than the others. I found that out tonight."

"What are you saying?" The tone of Kessler's voice did not change.

"A man followed me from my hotel. He was on a motorbike and stayed with my taxi across Berlin."

"A man on a motorbike?"

"Yes. Like a damned fool I led him here. I realized how stupid that was and knew I had to stop him. I managed to do it, but I never meant it to happen the way it did. He was no part of the *Rache*, no part of the *Odessa*. He hated them both, called them butchers and clowns . . ."

"He *called them* . . ." Kessler was silent for a moment. Then he continued, regaining part of the composure he had lost. "Tell me everything that happened, everything that was said."

"Do you have any ideas?"

"No . . . Not at all. I'm merely interested. Tell me."

Holcroft had no difficulty remembering it all. The chase, the trap, the exchange of words, the gunshot. When he had finished, Kessler asked him to go back to the words he and the man in the black leather jacket had said to one another. Then he asked Noel to repeat them again. And *again*.

"Who was he?" Holcroft knew that Kessler's mind was racing ahead of his. "Who *are* they?"

"There're several possibilities," said the German, "but obviously they're Nazis. Neo-Nazis, to be precise. Descendants of the Party, a splinter faction that has no use for the *Odessa*. It happens."

"But how would they know about Geneva?"

"Millions stolen from the occupied countries, from Wehrmacht payrolls, from the *Finanzministerium*. All banked in Switzerland. Such massive manipulations could not be kept completely secret."

Something bothered Noel, something Kessler had just said, but he could not put his finger on it. "But what good would it do them? They can't get the money. They could only tie it up in the courts for years. Where do they benefit?"

"You don't understand the hardcore Nazi. None of you ever did. It's not merely how he can benefit. It's of equal importance to him that others do *not* benefit. That was his essential destructiveness."

There was a sudden, loud commotion outside the booth. A single crash, then several; followed by a woman's scream that triggered other screams.

The curtain across the booth was yanked aside. The figure of a man loomed suddenly in the open space and plunged forward, falling over the table, his eyes wide and staring, blood streaming from his mouth and his neck. His face was contorted, his body racked with convulsions; his hands lurched over the surface of the table, gripping the sides between Holcroft and Kessler. He whispered, gasping for air, *"Wolfsschanze! Soldaten von Wolfsschanze!"*

He raised his head in the start of a scream; his breath was forced out of him and his head crashed down on the table. The man in the black leather jacket was dead.

26

The next moments were as bewildering to Noel as they were chaotic. The screaming and the shouting grew louder; waves of panic spread throughout the ratskeller. The blood-soaked man had slipped off the table and was now sprawled on the floor.

"Rudi! *Rudi!*"

"*Herr Kessler!* Come with me!"

"Quickly!" yelled Erich.

"What?"

"This way, my friend. You can't be seen here."

"But he's the one!"

"Say *nothing*, Noel. Please, take my arm."

"What? Where? . . ."

"Your *briefcase!* The papers!"

Holcroft grabbed the papers and shoved them into the case. He felt himself being pulled into the circle of onlookers. He was not sure where he was being taken, but that it was away from the dead man in the black leather jacket was enough. He followed blindly.

Kessler pulled him through the crowd. In front of Kessler was the manager, parting the bodies in their path that led to a closed door beneath and to the left of the staircase. The manager took a key from his pocket, opened the door, and rushed the three of them inside. He slammed the door shut and turned to Kessler.

"I don't know what to say, gentleman! It's terrible. A drunken brawl."

"No doubt, Rudi. And we thank you," replied Kessler.

"*Natürlich*. A man of your stature can't be involved."

"You're most kind. Is there a way outside?"

"Yes. My private entrance. Over here."

The entrance led into an alleyway. "This way," Kessler said. "My car's on the street."

They hurried out of the alley into the Kurfürstendamm, turning left on the street. To the right, an excited crowd had gathered in front of the ratskeller's entrance. Farther on, Noel could see a policeman running up the street.

"Quickly," said Kessler.

The car was a vintage Mercedes; they climbed in. Kessler started the engine, but did not idle it. Instead, he pulled the gearshift into drive and sped west.

"That man . . . in the jacket . . . he was the one who followed me," Holcroft whispered.

"I gathered as much," answered Kessler, "He found his way back, after all."

"My *God*," cried Noel. "What did I *do?*"

"You didn't kill him, if that's what you mean."

Holcroft stared at Kessler. "What?"

"You didn't kill that man."

"The gun went off! He was shot."

"I don't doubt it, but the bullet didn't kill him."

"What *did* then?"

"Obviously you didn't see his throat. He had been garrotted."

"Baldwin in New York!"

"Wolfsschanze in Berlin," answered Kessler. "His death was timed to the split second. Someone in that restaurant, outside the booth, brought him to within feet of our table and used the noise and the crowd to cover the execution."

"Oh, Jesus! Then whoever it was . . ." Noel could not finish the statement; fear was making him ill. He wanted to vomit.

"Whoever it was," completed Kessler, "knows now that I am part of Geneva. So, you have your answer, for I have no choice. I'm with you."

"I'm sorry," said Holcroft. "I wanted you to have a choice."

"I know you did and I thank you for it. However, I must insist on one condition."

"What's that?"

"My brother Hans, in Munich, must be made part of the covenant."

Noel recalled Manfredi's words; there were no restrictions in this respect. The only stipulation was that each family had one vote. "There's nothing to prevent him if he wants to."

"He'll want to. We're very close. You'll like him. He's a fine doctor."

"I'd say you were both fine doctors."

"He heals. I merely expound . . . I'm also driving aimlessly. I'd ask you out to my house, but under the circumstances I'd better not."

"I've done enough damage. But you should get back as soon as you can."

"Why?"

"If we're lucky, nobody'll give your name to the police and it won't matter. But if someone does – a waiter or anybody that knows you – you can say you were on your way out when it happened."

Kessler shook his head. "I'm a passive man. Such thoughts would not have occurred to me."

"Three weeks ago they wouldn't have occurred to me, either. Let me off near a taxi stand. I'll go to my hotel and get my suitcase."

"Nonsense. I'll drive you."

"We shouldn't be seen together any more. That's asking for complications."

"I must learn to listen to you. When will we see each other then?"

"I'll call you from Paris. I'm meeting von Tiebolt in a day or so. Then the three of us have to get to Geneva. There's very little time left."

"That man in New York? Miles?"

"Among other things. I'll explain when I see you again. There's a taxi on the corner."

"What will you do now? I doubt there are planes at this hour."

"Then I'll wait at the airport. I don't want to be isolated in a hotel room." Kessler stopped the car; Holcroft reached for the door. "Thank you, Erich. And I'm sorry."

"Don't be, my friend Noel. Call me."

The blond-haired man sat rigidly behind the desk in Kessler's library. His eyes were furious, his voice strained and intense as he spoke.

"Tell me again. Every *word*. Leave out nothing."

"What's the point?" replied Kessler from across the room. "We've gone over it ten times. I've remembered everything."

"Then we shall go over it ten more times!" shouted Johann von Tiebolt. "*Thirty* times, *forty* times! Who *was* he? Where did he come from? Who were the two men in Montereau? They're linked together; where did all *three* come from?"

"We don't know," said the scholar. "There's no way to tell."

"But there is! Don't you see? The answer's in what that man said to Holcroft in the alley. I'm certain of it. I've heard the words before. It's there!"

"For God's sake, you *had* the man." Kessler spoke firmly. "If you couldn't learn anything from him, what makes you think we can from anything Holcroft said? You should have broken him."

"He wouldn't break; he was far too gone for drugs."

"So you put a wire to his throat and threw him to the American. Madness!"

"Not madness," said Tennyson. "Consistency. Holcroft must be convinced that Wolfsschanze is everywhere. Prodding, threatening, protecting . . . Let's go back to what was said. According to Holcroft the man wasn't afraid to die. What was it?' . . . I am prepared. We are all prepared. We will stop you. We will stop Geneva. Kill me and another will take my place; kill him, another his.' The words of a fanatic, but he wasn't a fanatic, I saw that for myself. He was no *Odessa* agent, no *Rache* revolutionary. He was something else. Holcroft was right about that. Something *else*."

"We're at a dead end."

"Not entirely. I have a man in Paris checking on the identities of the bodies found in Montereau."

"*Sûreté?*"

"Yes. He's the best." Tennyson sighed. "It's all so incredible. After thirty years the first overt moves are made and within *two weeks* men come out of *nowhere*. As if they'd been waiting along with us for three decades. Yet they don't come out in the *open*. Why not? *That's* the sticking point. Why *not?*"

"The man said it to Holcroft in the alley. 'We can put that fortune to use.' They can't get it if they expose Geneva's sources."

"Too simple; the amount's too great. If it was money alone, nothing would prevent them from coming to us – to the bank's directors, for that matter – and negotiating from a position of strength. Nearly eight hundred million; from their point of view, they could demand two-thirds. They'd be dead after the fact, but they don't know that. No, Erich, it's not the money alone. We must look for something else."

"We must *look* at the *other crisis!*" Kessler shouted. "Whoever that man was tonight, whoever the two men were in Montereau – they're secondary to our most immediate concern! Face it, Johann! The British know you're the Tinamou! Don't sidetrack that any longer. They know you're the Tinamou!"

"Correction. They *suspect* I'm he, they don't know it. And as Holcroft so correctly put it, they'll soon be convinced they're wrong, if they're not convinced already. Actually, it's a very advantageous position."

"You're *mad!*" screamed Kessler. "You'll jeopardize *everything!*"

"On the contrary," said Tennyson calmly. "I'll solidify everything. What better ally could we have than MI5? To be certain we have men in British Intelligence, but none so high as Payton-Jones."

"What in the name of God are you *talking* about?" The scholar was perspiring, the veins pronounced in his neck.

"Sit down, Erich."

"*No!*"

"*Sit down!*"

Kessler sat. "I won't tolerate this, Johann."

"Don't tolerate anything, just listen." Tennyson leaned forward. "For a few moments let's reverse roles; I'll be the professor."

"Don't push me. We can handle intruders who won't show themselves; they have something to hide. We can't handle this. If you're taken, what's left?"

"That's flattering, but you mustn't think that way. If anything should happen to me there are the lists, names of our people everywhere. A man can be found among them, the Fourth Reich will have a leader in any event. But nothing *will* happen to me. The Tinamou is my shield, my protection. With his capture, I'm not only free of suspicion, I'm held in great respect."

"You've lost your senses! You *are* the Tinamou!"

Tennyson sat back, smiling. "Let's examine our assassin, shall we? Ten years ago you agreed he was my finest creation. I believe you said the Tinamou might well turn out to be our most vital weapon."

"In *theory*. Only in *theory*. It was an academic judgement; I also said that!"

"True, you often take refuge high up in your cloistered tower, and that's how it should be. But you were right, you know. In the last analysis, the millions in Switzerland cannot serve us unless they can be put to use. There are laws everywhere; they must be circumvented. It's not as simple as it once was to pay for a Reichstag, or a block of seats in Parliament, or to buy an election in America. But for us it's nowhere near as difficult as it would be for others; that was your point ten years ago, and it's more valid today. We're in a position to make extraordinary demands on the most influential men in every major government. They've *paid* the Tinamou to assassinate their adversaries. From Washington to Paris to Cairo; from Athens to Beirut to Madrid; from London to Warsaw and even to Moscow itself. The Tinamou is irresistible. He is our own nuclear bomb."

"And he can claim *us* in the fallout!"

"He could," agreed Tennyson, "but he won't. Years ago, Erich, we vowed to keep no secrets from each other and I've kept that vow in all matters except one. I won't apologize; it was, as they say, a decision of rank and I felt it was necessary."

"What did you do?" asked Kessler.

"Gave us that most vital weapon you spoke of ten years ago."

"How?"

"A few moments ago you were quite specific. You raised your voice and said I was the Tinamou."

"You *are!*"

"I'm not."

"*What?*"

"I'm one half of the Tinamou. To be sure, the better half, but still only *half.* For years I trained another; he is my alternative in the field. His expertise has been taught, his brilliance acquired; next to the real Tinamou, he's the best on earth."

The scholar stared at the blond man in astonishment . . . and awe. "He's one of us? A *Sonnenkind?*"

"Of course not! He's a paid killer; he knows nothing but an extraordinary life-style in which every need and appetite is gratified by the extraordinary sums he earns. He's also aware that one day he may have to pay the price for his way of living and he accepts that. He's a professional."

Kessler sank back in the chair, loosening his collar. "I must say, you never cease to amaze me."

"I'm not finished," replied Tennyson. "An event is taking place in London shortly, a gathering of heads of state. It's the perfect opportunity. The Tinamou will be caught."

"He'll be *what?*"

"You heard correctly." Tennyson smiled. "The Tinamou will be captured, a weapon in his hands, the odd calibre and the bore markings traceable to three previous assassinations. He will be caught and killed by the man who has been tracking him for nearly six years. A man who, for his own protection, wants no credit, wants no mention of his name. Who calls in the intelligence authorities of his adopted country. John Tennyson, European correspondent of *The Guardian.*"

"*My God,*" whispered Kessler. "How will you do it?"

"Even you can't know that. But there'll be a dividend as powerful as Geneva itself. The word will go out in print that the Tinamou kept private records. They haven't been found, and thus can be presumed to have been stolen by someone. That someone will be ourselves. So, in death, the Tinamou serves us still."

Kessler shook his head in wonder. "You think exotically, that's your essential gift."

"Among others," said the blond man matter-of-factly. "And our new-found alliance with MI5 may be helpful. Other intelligence services may be more sophisticated, but none are better." Tennyson slapped the arm of the chair. "*Now.* Let's get back to our unknown enemy. His identity is in the words spoken in that alley. I've *heard* them! I know it."

"We've exhausted that approach."

"We've only begun." The blond man reached for a pencil and paper. "Now, from the *beginning*. We'll write down everything he said, everything you can remember."

The scholar sighed. "From the beginning," he repeated. "Very well. According to Holcroft, the man's first words referred to the killing in France, the fact that Holcroft had not hesitated to fire his pistol then . . ."

Kessler spoke. Tennyson listened and interrupted and asked for repetitions of words and phrases. He wrote furiously. Forty minutes passed.

"I can't go on any longer," said Kessler. "There's no more I can tell you."

"Again the *eagles*," countered the blond man harshly. "Say the words exactly as Holcroft said them."

"Eagles? . . . 'You won't stop the eagles. Not this time.' Could he have meant the *Luftwaffe?* The *Wehrmacht?*"

"Not likely." Tennyson looked down at the pages in front of him. He tapped his finger at something he had written down. "Here. 'Your Wolfsschanze.' *Your* Wolfsschanze . . . Meaning ours, not *theirs.*"

"What are you talking about?" said Kessler. "We *are* Wolfsschanze; the men of Wolfsschanze are *Sonnenkinder!*"

Tennyson ignored the interruption. "Von Stauffenberg, Olbricht, von Falkenhausen and Hopner. Rommel called them the 'true eagles of Germany'. They were the insurrectionists, the Fuhrer's would-be assassins. All were shot, Rommel ordered to take his own life. *Those* are the eagles he referred to. *Their* Wolfsschanze, not *ours.*"

"Where does it lead us? For God's *sake*, Johann, I'm exhausted. I can't go on!"

Tennyson had covered a dozen pages of paper; now he shuffled them, underlining words, circling phrases. "You may have said enough," he replied. "It's here . . . in this section. He used the words 'butchers and clowns', and then 'you won't stop the eagles . . .' Only seconds later, Holcroft told him that the account would be tied up for years, that there were conditions . . . 'the money frozen, sent back into the ground'. The man repeated the phrase: 'back into the ground', saying it was the flaw. But then he added that there would be 'no scorched earth'. 'Scorched earth.' 'There will be no . . . *scorched earth.*'

The blond man's whole upper body tensed. He leaned back in the chair, his face twisted in concentration. "It couldn't be . . . after all these years. Operation Barbarossa! The *scorched earth* of Barbarossa! Oh, my God, the *Nachrichtendienst*. It's the *Nachrichtendienst!*"

"What are you talking about?" Kessler asked. "Barbarossa was Hitler's first invasion north, a magnificent victory."

"He called it a victory. The Prussians called it a disaster. A hollow victory, written in blood. Whole divisions unprepared, decimated . . . 'We took the land,' the generals said. 'We took the worthless, scorched earth of Barbarossa.' Out of it came the *Nachrichtendienst*."

"What was it?"

"An intelligence unit. Rarefied, exclusively Junker, a corps of aristocrats. Later, there were those who thought it was a Gehlen operation, designed to sow distrust between the Russians and the West, but it wasn't. It was solely its own. It loathed Hitler, it scorned the *Schutzstaffel* – SS garbage, was the term it used; it hated the commanders of the *Luftwaffe*. All were called butchers and clowns. It was above the war, above the party. It was only for Germany. *Their* Germany."

"Say what you mean, Johann!" shouted Kessler.

"The *Nachrichtendienst* survives. It's the intruder. It wants to destroy Geneva. It will stop at nothing to abort the Fourth Reich before it's born."

27

Noel waited on the bridge, watching the lights of Paris flicker on like exploding clusters of tiny candles. He had reached Helden at Gallimard; she had agreed to meet him after work on the Pont Neuf. He had tried to convince her to drive to the hotel in Argenteuil, but she had declined his offer.

"You promised me days, weeks, if I wished," he said.

"I promised us both, my darling, and we'll have them. But not Argenteuil. I'll explain when I see you."

It was barely 5.15; the winter night descended on Paris quickly, and the chill of the river wind penetrated him. He pulled up the collar of his second-hand overcoat to ward off the cold. He looked at his watch again; it had not moved. How could it? No more than ten seconds had elapsed.

He felt like a young man waiting for a girl he had met at a country club in the summer moonlight, and smiled to himself, feeling awkward and embarrassed, not wanting to acknowledge his anxiety. He was not in the moonlight on some warm summer's night. He was on a bridge in Paris, and the air was cold, and he carried a gun.

He saw her walking on to the bridge. She was wearing the black raincoat, her hair encased by a dark red scarf that framed her face. Her pace was steady, neither rapid nor casual; she was a lone woman going home from her place of work. Except for her striking features – only hinted at in the distance – she was like thousands of other women in Paris heading home in the early evening.

She saw him. He started walking towards her, but she held up her hand, a signal for him to remain where he was. He paid no attention, wanting to reach her quickly, his arms held out. She walked into them and they embraced, and he felt warm in the comfort of being with her again. She pulled her head back and looked at him, then pretended to be firm, but her eyes smiled.

"You must never run on a bridge," she said. "A man running across a bridge stands out. One strolls over the water, one doesn't race."

"I missed you. I don't give a damn."

"You must learn to. How was Berlin?"

He put his arm around her shoulder and they started towards the Quai Saint-Bernard and the Left Bank. "I've got a lot to tell you, some good, some not so good. But if learning something is progress, I think we've taken a couple of giant steps. Have you heard from your brother?"

"Yes. This afternoon. He called an hour after you did. His plans have changed; he can be in Paris tomorrow."

"That's the best news you could give me. At least, I think it is. I'll let you know tomorrow." They walked off the bridge and turned left along the river bank. "Did you miss me?"

"Noel, you're mad. You left yesterday afternoon. I barely had time to get home, bathe, have a very much needed night's sleep, and get to work."

"You went home? To your apartment?"

"No, I . . ." She stopped and looked up at him, smiling. "Very good, Noel Holcroft, new recruit. Interrogate casually."

"I don't feel casual."

"You promised not to ask that question."

"Not specifically. I asked you if you were married, or living with someone – to which I got a negative to the first and a very oblique answer to the second – but I never actually promised not to try and find out where you live."

"You implied it, my darling. One day I'll tell you and you'll see how foolish you are."

"Tell me now. I'm in love. I want to know where my girl lives."

The smile disappeared from her lips. Then it returned, and she glanced up at him again. "You're like a little boy practising a new word. You don't know me well enough to love me, I told you that."

"I forgot, you like women."

"They're among my best friends."

"But you wouldn't want to marry one."

"I don't want to marry anyone."

"Good. It's less complicated. Just move in with me for the next ten years, exercisable options on both sides."

"You say nice things."

They stopped at an intersection. He turned Helden to him, both his hands on her arms. "I say them because I mean them."

"I believe you," she said, looking at him curiously, her eyes part questioning, part fearful.

He saw the fear; it bothered him and so he smiled. "Love me a little?"

She could not bring the smile to her lips. "I think I love you more than a little. You're a problem I didn't want. I'm not sure I can handle it."

"That's even better." He laughed and took her hand to cross the street. "It's nice to know you don't have all the answers."

"Did you believe I did?"

"I thought you thought so."

"I don't."

The restaurant was half filled with diners. Helden asked for a table in the rear, out of sight of the entrance. The proprietor nodded. It was apparent that he could not quite accept such a *plus belle femme* coming into his establishment with such a poorly dressed companion.

"He doesn't approve of me," said Holcroft.

"There's hope for you, though. You grew in his estimation when you specified expensive whisky. He grinned, didn't you see?"

"He was looking at my jacket. It came from a somewhat better rack than the overcoat."

Helden laughed. "That overcoat's purpose was not high fashion. Did you use it in Berlin?"

"I used it. I wore it when I picked up a whore. Are you jealous?"

"Not of anyone accepting an offer from you dressed like that."

"She was a vision of loveliness."

"Probably an *Odessa* agent and you've come down with a social disease as planned. See a doctor before you see me again."

Noel took her hand. There was no humour in his voice when he spoke. "The *Odessa's* no concern of ours. Neither is the *Rache*. That's one – or two – of the things I learned in Berlin. It's doubtful either of them know anything about Geneva."

Helden was stunned. "But what about Beaumont? You said he was part of *Odessa*, that he followed you to Rio."

"I think he is *Odessa* and he did follow me, but not because of Geneva. He's tied in with Graff. Somehow he found out I was looking for Johann von Tiebolt; *that* was why he followed me. Not Geneva. I'll know more when I speak to your brother tomorrow. Anyway, Beaumont'll be out of the picture in a few days. Kessler's taking care of it. He said he'd make a call to someone in the Bonn government."

"It's that simple?"

"It's not that difficult. Any hint of *Odessa*, especially in the military, is enough to start a battery of inquiries. Beaumont'll be pulled in."

"If it's not the *Odessa*, or the *Rache*, who is it?"

"That's part of what I've got to tell you. I had to get rid of the Mackinaw and the cap."

"Oh?" Helden was confused by the *non sequitur*.

He told her why, minimizing the violence in the dark alleyway. Then he described the conversation with Kessler, realizing as he came to the end that he could not omit the murder of the unknown man in the leather jacket. He would tell her brother about it tomorrow; to withhold it from Helden now would serve no purpose. When he had finished, she shuddered, pressing her fingers into the palm of her hand.

"How *horrible*. Did Kessler have any idea who he was, where he came from?"

"Not really. We went over everything he said half a dozen times trying to figure it out, but there wasn't that much. In Kessler's opinion he was part of a neo-Nazi group – descendants of the party, Kessler called them. A splinter faction that has no use for the *Odessa*."

"How would they know about the account in Geneva?"

"I asked Kessler that. He said that the sort of manipulations required to get that money out of Germany couldn't have been kept as quiet as we think. That someone somewhere could have learned about it."

"But Geneva is *based* on secrecy. Without it, it would collapse."

"Then it's a question of degree. When is a secret a secret? What separates confidential information from highly classified data? A handful of people found out about Geneva and want to stop us from getting the money and using it the way it's supposed to be used. They want it for themselves, so they're not going to expose it."

"But if they've learned that much, they know they can't get it."

"Not necessarily."

"Then they should be told!"

"I said as much to the man in the alley. I didn't convince him. Even if I had, it wouldn't make any difference now."

"But don't you see? Someone has to reach these people – whoever they are – and convince them they gain nothing by stopping you and my brother and Erich Kessler."

Holcroft drank. "I'm not sure we should do that. Kessler said something that bothered me when I heard it, and it bothers me now. He said that we – the 'we', I guess, meaning all of us who haven't studied the subject that closely – never understood the hardcore Nazi. From the Nazi's point of view, it wasn't simply a question of how *he* could benefit, it was just as important to him that others don't benefit. Kessler called it the essential destructiveness."

Helden's frown returned. "So if they're told, they'll go after you. They'll kill the three of you, because without you there's no Geneva."

"Not for another generation. That's motive enough. The money goes back in the vaults for another thirty years."

Helden brought her hand to her mouth. "Wait a minute; there's something terribly wrong. They've tried to kill you. *You.* From the beginning . . . *you.*"

Holcroft shook his head. "We can't be certain . . ."

"Not *certain?* broke in Helden. "My God, what more do you want? You showed me your jacket. There was the strychnine on that plane, the shots in Rio. What more do you want?"

"I want to know who was really behind those things. That's why I have to talk to your brother."

"What can Johann tell you?"

"Whom he killed in Rio." Helden started to object; he took her hand again. "Let me explain. I think we're in the middle – I'm in the middle – of two fights, neither having anything to do with the other. Whatever happened to your brother in Rio has nothing to do with Geneva. That's where I made my mistake. I tied everything into Geneva."

"I tried to tell you that," said Helden.

"I was slow. But then, no one's ever fired a gun at me, or tried to poison me, or shoved a knife in my stomach. Those kind of things play hell with your thinking process. At least they do mine."

"Johann is a man of many interests, Noel," she said. "He can be very charming, very personable, but he can also be reticent. It's part of him. He's lived a strange life; sometimes I think of him as a gadfly. He darts quickly from one place to another, one interest to another, always brilliantly, always leaving his mark, but not always wishing that mark to be recognized."

"'He's here, he's there, he's everywhere'," interrupted Holcroft. "You're describing some sort of Scarlet Pimpernel."

"Exactly. Johann may not tell you what happened in Rio."

"But I have to know."

"Since it has nothing to do with Geneva, he may disagree."

"Then I'll try to convince him. We *have* to find out how vulnerable he is."

"Let's say he is vulnerable. What happens then?"

"He'd be disqualified from taking part in Geneva. We know he killed someone. You heard a man – a wealthy, influential man, you thought – say he wanted to see your brother hanged for murder. *I* know he tangled with Graff, and that means the *Odessa*. He ran for his life. He took you and your sister with him, but he ran for *his* life. He's mixed up in a lot of complications; people are after him and it's not unreasonable to think he could be blackmailed. That could shape Geneva; it could corrupt it."

"Do the bankers have to be told?" asked Helden.

Noel touched her cheek, forcing her to look at him. "I'd have to tell them. We're talking about 780 million dollars. About three men who did something remarkable. It was their gesture to history, I really believe that. If your brother puts it in jeopardy, or causes it to be misused, then maybe it's better those millions get locked up for the next generation. But it doesn't have to be that way. According to the rules, you're the one who'd be the von Tiebolt executor."

Helden gazed at him. "I can't accept that, Noel. It must be Johann. Not only is he more qualified to be a part of Geneva, he deserves it. I can't take that from him."

"And I can't give it to him. Not if he can hurt the covenant. Let's talk about it after I see him."

She studied his face; he felt awkward. She took his hand from her cheek and held it. "You're a moral man, aren't you?"

"Not necessarily. Just angry. I'm sick of corruption in the rarefied circles of finance. There's been an awful lot of it in my country."

"'Rarefied circles of finance'?"

"It's a phrase my father used in his letter to me."

"That's odd," said Helden.

"What is?"

"You've always called him Clausen, or Heinrich Clausen. Formal, rather distant."

Holcroft nodded, acknowledging the truth of her remark. "It's funny, because I really don't know any more about him now than I did before. But he's been described to me. The way he looked, the way he talked, how people listened to him and were affected by him."

"Then you do know more about him."

"Not actually. Only impressions. A child's impressions at that. But in a small way I think I've found him."

"When did your parents tell you about him?"

"Not my parents, not my . . . stepfather. Just Althene. It was a couple of weeks after my twenty-fifth birthday. I was working then, a certified professional."

"Professional?"

"I'm an architect, remember? I've almost forgotten."

"Your mother waited until you were twenty-five before she told you?"

"She was right. I don't think I could have handled it when I was younger. Good Lord. Noel Holcroft, American boy. Hot dogs and french fries, Shea Stadium and the Mets, the Garden and the Knicks; and college and friends whose fathers were soldiers in the big war, each one winning it in his own way. That fellow's told his real father was one of those heel-clicking sadists in the war movies. Christ, that kid would flip out."

"Why did she tell you at all then?"

"On the remote chance that I'd find out for myself one day and she didn't want that. She didn't think it would happen. She and Dick had covered the traces right down to a birth certificate which said I was their son. But there was another birth certificate. In Berlin. 'Clausen, male child. Mother – Althene. Father – Heinrich.' And there were people who knew she'd left him, left Germany. She wanted me to be prepared if it ever surfaced, if anyone for any reason ever remembered and tried to use the information. Prepared, incidentally, to deny it. To say there'd been another child – never mentioned in the house – who had died in infancy in England."

"Which means there was another certificate. A death certificate."

"Yes. Properly recorded somewhere in London."

Helden leaned back against the booth. "You and me are not so different after all. Our lives are full of false papers. What a luxury it must be not to live that way. Has it ever occurred to you – since you were twenty-five?"

"No. Papers don't mean much to me. I've never hired anyone because of them, and I've never fired anyone because someone else brought them to me." Noel finished his drink. "I ask the questions myself. And I'm going to ask your brother some very tough ones. I hope to God he has the answers I want to hear."

"So do I."

He leaned towards her, their shoulders touching. "Love me a little?"

"More than a little."

"Stay with me tonight."

"I intend to. Your hotel?"

"Not the one in rue Chevalle. That Mr Fresca we invented the other night has moved to better lodgings. You see, I've got a few friends in Paris, too. One's an assistant manager at the Georges Cinq."

"How extravagant."

"It's allowed. You're a very special woman and we don't know what's going to happen, starting tomorrow. By the way, why couldn't we go to Argenteuil? You said you'd tell me."

"We were seen there."

"What? By whom?"

"A man saw us – saw you, really. We don't know his name, but we know he was from Interpol. We have a source there. A bulletin was circulated from the Paris headquarters with your description. A trace was put out for you from New York. From a police officer named Miles."

28

John Tennyson walked out into Heathrow Airport's crowded arrivals area. He walked to a black Jaguar sedan waiting at the kerb. The driver was smoking a cigarette and reading a book. At the sight of the approaching blond man he got out of the car.

"Good afternoon, Mr Tennyson," said the man in a throaty Welsh accent.

"Have you been waiting long?" asked Tennyson without much interest.

"Not very," answered the driver, taking Tennyson's briefcase and overnight bag. "I presume you wish to drive."

"Yes, I'll drop you off along the way. Some place where you find a taxi."

"I can get one here."

"No, I want to talk for a few minutes." Tennyson climbed in behind the wheel; the Welshman opened the rear door and put the luggage inside. Within minutes they had passed the airport gates and were on the motorway to London.

"Did you have a good trip?" asked the Welshman.

"A busy one."

"I read your article about Bahrain. Most amusing."

"Bahrain's amusing. The Indian shopkeepers are the only economists on the archipelago."

"But you were kind to the sheiks."

"They were kind to me. What's the news from the Mediterranean? Have you stayed in touch with your brother on board Beaumont's ship?"

"Constantly. We use a radio phone off Cap Camarat. Everything's going according to schedule. The rumours have come back from the piers. The commander was seen going out in a small boat with a woman from Saint Tropez. Neither the boat nor the couple have been heard from in over forty-eight hours, and there were offshore squalls. My brother will report the incident tomorrow. He will assume command, of course."

"Of course. Then it all goes well. Beaumont's death will be clear-cut. An accident in bad weather."

"You don't care to tell me what happened?"

"Not specifically; it would be a burden to you. But basically, Beaumont over-reached himself. He was seen in the wrong places by the wrong people. It was speculated that our upstanding officer was actually connected to the *Odessa*."

The Welshman's expression conveyed his anger. "That's dangerous. The damn fool."

"There's something I must tell you," said Tennyson. "It's almost time."

The Welshman replied in awe. "It's happened then? It's come at last."

"Within two weeks, I'd guess."

"I can't believe it!"

"Why?" asked Tennyson. "Everything's on schedule. The cables must begin to go out. Everywhere."

"Everywhere ..." repeated the man.

"The code is Wolfsschanze."

"*Wolfsschanze?* ... Oh God, it's come!"

"It's here. Update a final master list of district leaders, one copy only of course. Take all the microdot files – country by country, city by city, each political connection – and seal them in the steel case. Bring the case personally to me, along with the master list, one week from today. Wednesday. We'll meet on the street outside my flat in Kensington. Eight o'clock at night."

"A week from today. Wednesday. Eight o'clock. With the case."

"And the master list. The leaders."

"Of course." The Welshman brought his clenched fist to his face, the knuckle of his index finger to his teeth. "It's really come," he whispered.

"There's a minor obstacle, but we'll surmount it."

"Can I help? I'll do anything."

"I know you will, Ian. You're one of the best. I'll tell you next week."

"*Anything.*"

"Of course." Tennyson slowed the Jaguar at the approach of an exit. "I'd drive you into London, but I'm heading towards Margate. It's imperative that I get there quickly."

"Don't worry about me. God, man, you must have so much on your mind!" Ian kept his eyes on Tennyson's face, on the strong; chiselled features that held such promise ... such power. "To be here now; to have the privilege to be present at the beginning. At the rebirth. There's no sacrifice I wouldn't make."

The blond man smiled. "Thank you," he said.

"Leave me anywhere. I'll find a taxi ... I didn't know we had people in Margate."

"We have people everywhere," said Tennyson, stopping the car.

Tennyson sped down the familiar road towards Portsea. He would reach Gretchen's house before eight o'clock and that was as it should be; she expected him at nine. He'd be able to make sure she had no visitors, no friendly male neighbours who might have dropped in for a drink.

The blond man smiled to himself. Even in her mid-forties, his sister drew men as the proverbial flame drew moths, scorched into satiety by the heat, saved from themselves by their inability to reach the flame itself. For Gretchen did not fulfil the promise of her sexuality unless told to do so. It was a weapon to be used, as all potentially lethal weapons were to be used – with discretion.

238

Tennyson did not relish what he had to do, but he knew he had no choice. All threads that led to Geneva had to be cut, and his sister was one of them. As Anthony Beaumont had been one. Gretchen simply knew too much; Wolfsschanze's enemies could break her – and they would.

There were three items of information the *Nachrichtendienst* did not have. The timetable, the methods of dispersing the millions, and the lists. Gretchen knew the timetable; she was familiar with the methods of dispersal; and, as the methods were tied to the names of recipients all over the world, she was all too aware of the lists.

His sister had to die.

As the Welshman had to make the sacrifice he spoke of so nobly. Once the airtight carton and the master list were delivered, the Welshman's contributions were finished. He remained only a liability, for except for the sons of Erich Kessler and Wilhelm von Tiebolt no one else alive would ever see those lists. Thousands of names in every country who were the true inheritors of Wolfsschanze, the perfect race, the *Sonnenkinder*.

PORTSEA-15M

The blond man pressed the accelerator; the Jaguar shot forward.

"So, at last it's here," said Gretchen Beaumont, sitting next to Tennyson on the soil leather couch, her hand caressing his face, her fingers darting in and out between his lips, arousing him as she had always been able to do since they were children. "And you're so beautiful. There's no other man like you; there never will be."

She leaned forward, her unbuttoned blouse exposing her breasts, inviting his caress. She opened her mouth and covered his, groaning in that throaty way that drove him wild.

But there were facts to be covered; he could not succumb. When he did, it would be the last act of a secret ritual that had kept him pure and untangled . . . since he was a child. He held her shoulders and gently pushed her back on the couch.

"It's here," he said. "I must learn everything that's happened while my mind's clear. We have lots of time. I'll leave about six in the morning for Heathrow, for the first plane to Paris. But now, is there anything you forgot to tell me about the American? Are you sure he never made the connection between you and New York?"

"Never. The dead woman across from his apartment was known to be a heavy smoker. I don't smoke and made a point of it when he was here. I also made it clear that I hadn't been anywhere in weeks. If he questioned that, I could have proved it, of course. And, obviously, I was very much alive."

"So when he left, he had no idea that the highly erotic, straying wife he went to bed with was the woman in New York."

"Of course not. And he didn't leave," said Gretchen, laughing, "He *fled*. Bewildered and panicked, convinced I was unbalanced – as we had planned – thus making you next in line for Geneva." She stopped laughing. "He also fled with Tony's photograph, which we had not planned. You're getting it back, I assume."

Tennyson nodded. "Yes."

"What will you tell Holcroft?"

"He believes Beaumont was an *Odessa* agent; that I was somehow embroiled with Graff and had to escape from Brazil or be shot. That's what he told Kessler. The truth is he's not at all sure what happened in Rio except that I killed someone; he's worried about it." Tennyson smiled. "I'll play on his assumptions. I'll think of something startling, something that will stun him, convince him I'm holier than John the Baptist. And, of course, I'll be grateful that our partner has caused the removal of the terrible Beaumont from our concerns."

Gretchen took his hand, pressing it between her legs, rubbing her stockings up and down against his flesh. "You are not only beautiful, you're brilliant."

"Then I'll turn the tables, make him feel he must convince me *he's* worthy of Geneva. *He* will be the one who must justify his part of the covenant. It's psychologically vital that he be put in that position; his dependency on me must grow."

Gretchen locked her legs against his hand and held his wrist; the grip was abrupt and sexual. "You can excite me with words, but you know that, don't you?"

"In a while, my love . . . my only love. We've got to talk." Tennyson dug his fingers into his sister's leg; she moaned. "Of course, I'll know more what to say after I've spoken to Helden."

"You'll see her before we meet with Holcroft, then?"

"Yes. I'll call her and tell her I've got to see her right away. For the first time in her life, she'll observe me in the throes of self-doubt, desperately needing to be convinced my actions are right."

"Brilliant again." She took his hand from between her legs and placed it under her breast. "And does our little sister still run with the flotsam and jetsam? The self-imposed *Verwünschte Kinder*, with their beards and bad teeth?"

"Of course. She has to feel need; it was always her weakness."

"She wasn't born in the Reich."

Tennyson laughed derisively. "To compound her striving for adequacy, she's become a nursemaid. She lives in *Herr Oberst's* house and cares for the crippled bastard. Two changes of cars each evening, so as not to lead the assassins of the *Rache* and the *Odessa* to him."

"One or the other may kill her one day," mused Gretchen. "That's something to think about. Soon, after the bank frees the account, she'll have to go. She's not stupid, Johann. One more murder laid at the foot of the *Rache*. Or the *Odessa*."

"It's crossed my mind . . . Speaking of murder, tell me. While Holcroft was here, did he mention Peter Baldwin?"

"Not a word. I never thought he would, not if I was playing my part right. I was an unbalanced, resentful wife. He didn't want to frighten me, nor did he wish to give me information dangerous to Geneva."

Tennyson nodded; they had projected accurately. "What was his reaction when you talked about me?"

"I gave him very little time to react," said Gretchen. "I simply told him you spoke for the von Tiebolts. Why did Baldwin try to intercept him in New York? Do you know?"

"I've pieced it together. Baldwin operated out of Prague, an MI6er whose allegiance, many said, was to the highest bidder. He sold information to anyone until his own people began to suspect him. They fired him, but didn't prosecute because they couldn't be sure; he'd operated as a double agent in the past and claimed it as his cover. He swore he was developing a two-way network. He also knew the name of every British contact in Middle Europe, and obviously let his superiors know that those names would surface if anything happened to him. He maintained his innocence, said he was being punished for doing his job too well."

"What's that got to do with Holcroft?"

"You have to see Baldwin for what he was to understand. He was good, his sources the best. In addition to which he could track anything. While in Prague he heard rumours of a great fortune being held in Geneva. Nazi spoils. The rumour wasn't unusual; such stories have been around since Berlin fell. The difference with this rumour was that Clausen's name was mentioned. Again, not completely startling; Clausen was the financial genius of the Reich. But Baldwin checked out everything to the finest point; it was the way he worked."

"He went back to the courier archives," interrupted Gretchen.

"Yes. Concentrating on the *Finanzministerium*. Hundreds of runs were made, Manfredi the recipient in dozens. Once he had Manfredi's name, the rest was patience and observation – and money spread cautiously within the bank. His break came when he got word that Manfredi was setting up a contact with a heretofore unheard-of American named Holcroft. *Why?* He studied Holcroft and found the mother."

"She was Manfredi's strategy," broke in Gretchen again.

"From the beginning," agreed Tennyson, nodding. "He convinced Clausen she had to leave Germany. She had money of her own and moved in monied circles; she could be of great use to us in America. With Clausen's help, she came to accept that, but she was essentially Manfredi's creation."

"Underneath that gnome's benign appearance," said Gretchen, "was a Machiavelli."

"Without that kindly innocence of his, I doubt he'd ever have got away with it. But Machiavelli isn't the parallel. Manfredi's interest was solely the money; it was the only power he wanted. He was a sworn companion of the gold quota. It was his intention to control the agency in Zurich; it's why we killed him."

"How much did Baldwin learn?"

"We'll never know exactly, but whatever it was, it was to be his vindication with British Intelligence. You see, he wasn't a double agent; he was exactly what he claimed to be. MI6's very effective man in Prague."

"He reached Manfredi?"

"Oh, yes. He implied that much by his knowledge of the Geneva meeting. He was just a little late, that's all." The blond man smiled. "I can picture the confrontation. Two specialists circling each other, both wanting something desperately. One to prise out information, the other to retain it at all costs, knowing he was dealing with a potentially catastrophic situation. Certain agreements must have been made, and, true to form, Manfredi broke his word, moved up the meeting with Holcroft, and then alerted us about Baldwin. He covered everything. If your husband had been caught killing Peter Baldwin, there was no connection with Ernst Manfredi. He was a man to be respected. He might have won."

"But not against Johann von Tiebolt," said Gretchen, squeezing his hand beneath her breast, moving it up. "Incidentally, I received another code from Graff in Rio. He's upset again. He says he's not being kept informed."

"His senility is showing. He, too, has served his purpose. Age makes him careless; it's no time for him to be sending messages to England. I'm afraid the moment has arrived for *der Alte* in Brazil."

"You'll send the order out?"

"In the morning. One more arm of the hated *Odessa* severed. He trained me too well." Tennyson leaned forward, his hand cupping his sister's breast. "I think we're finished talking. As always, talking with you clears my mind. I can't think of anything more to say, anything more to ask you."

"Then make demands instead. It's been so long for you, you must be bursting inside. I'll take care of you, as I always have."

"Since we were children," said Tennyson, his mouth covering hers, her hand groping for his trousers. Both were trembling.

Gretchen lay naked beside him, her breathing steady, her body drained and satisfied. The blond man raised his hand and looked at the radium dial of his watch. It was 2.30 in the morning. Time to do the terrible thing demanded of him by the covenant of Wolfsschanze. All traces to Geneva had to be removed.

He reached over the side of the bed for his shoes. He lifted one up, feeling the heel with his fingers in the darkness. There was a small metal disc in the centre. He pressed it, turning it to the left until a spring was released. He placed the disc on the bedside table, then tilted the shoe back and removed a steel needle ten inches long, concealed in a tiny bore drilled from heel to sole. The needle was flexible but unbreakable. Inserted properly between the fourth

242

and fifth ribs, it punctured the heart, leaving a mark more often missed than found, even during an autopsy.

He held it delicately between the thumb and index finger of his right hand, reaching for his sister with his left. He touched her right breast and then her naked shoulder. She opened her eyes.

"You are insatiable," she whispered, smiling.

"Only with you." He drew her up to him until their flesh touched. "You are my only love," he said, his right arm sliding behind her, extended a foot beyond her spine. He turned his wrist inwards; the needle was positioned. He thrust it forward.

The back-country roads were confusing but Tennyson had memorized the route. He knew the way to the hidden cottage that housed the ubiquitous *Herr Oberst*, that betrayer of the Reich. Even the title, *Oberst*, was an ironic comment in itself. The traitor had been no colonel; he was a general of the Wehrmacht, General Klaus Falkenheim, at one time fourth-in-command of all Germany. Praise had been lavished on him by his military peers, and even by the Führer himself. And all the while a jackal had lived in that shiny, hollow shell.

God, how Johann von Tielbolt loathed the misfit liar that was *Herr Oberst!* But John Tennyson would not show that loathing. On the contrary, Tennyson would fawn on the old man, proclaiming awe and respect. For if there was one certain way to get his younger sister's total cooperation, it was by showing such deference.

He had called Helden at Gallimard, telling her that he had to see where she lived. Yes, he knew she lived in *Herr Oberst's* small house; and again, yes, he knew where it was.

"I'm a newspaperman now. I wouldn't be a very good one if I didn't have sources."

She had been stunned. He insisted on seeing her in the late morning, before meeting Holcroft in the afternoon. No, he would *not* meet the American unless and until he saw her first. Perhaps *Herr Oberst* could help clarify the situation. Perhaps the old gentleman might allay any fears she might have.

He reached the dirt road that led through the overgrown grass into the untamed glen that protected *Herr Oberst's* house from prying eyes. Three minutes later he stopped in front of the path that led to the cottage. The door opened; Helden came out to greet him. How lovely she looked; so like Gretchen.

They exchanged a brother-and-sister embrace, both anxious to begin the meeting with *Herr Oberst*. Helden's eyes conveyed her bewilderment. She led him inside the small, spartan house. *Herr Oberst* stood by the fireplace. Helden introduced the two men.

"This is a moment I shall treasure throughout my life," said Tennyson. "You've earned the gratitude of Germans everywhere. If I can ever be of service to you, tell Helden, and I'll do whatever you ask."

"You're too kind, Herr von Tiebolt," replied the old man. "But according to your sister, it's you who seek something from me, and I can't imagine what it is. How can I help you?"

"My problem is the American. This Holcroft."

"What about him?" asked Helden.

"Thirty years ago a magnificent thing was done, an incredible feat engineered by three extraordinary men who wished to make restitution for the anguish inflicted by butchers and maniacs. Through circumstances that seemed right at the time, Holcroft was projected to be a key factor in the dissemination of millions throughout the world. I'm now asked to meet him, cooperate with him . . ." Tennyson stopped, as if the words eluded him.

'And?' *Herr Oberst* took a step forward.

"I don't trust him," said the blond man. "He's met Nazis. Men who would kill us, Helden. Men like Maurice Graff in Brazil."

"*What are you saying?*"

"The bloodlines re-emerge. Holcroft is a Nazi."

Helden's face was stretched in shock, her eyes a mixture of anger and disbelief. "That's absurd! Johann, that's insane."

"Is it? I don't think so."

Noel waited until Helden left for work before placing the phone call to Miles in New York. Their night had been filled with love and comfort. He knew he had to convince her they would go on; there was no predetermined ending to their being together. He would not accept that now.

The telephone rang. "Yes, operator, this is Mr Fresca calling Lieutenant Miles."

"I thought it had to be you," said Miles. "Interpol reach you?"

"*Reach* me? There are men following me, if that's what you mean. I think it's called a 'trace'. Put out by *you*."

"That's right."

"You gave me two weeks! What the hell are you doing?"

"Trying to find you. Trying to get you information I think you should have. It concerns your mother."

Noel felt a sharp pain in his chest. "What about my mother?"

"She ran." Miles paused. "I'll give her credit, she's damned good. It was a very professional skip. She went the Mexican route, and before you could say Althene Holcroft, she was a little old lady on her way to Lisbon with a new name and a new passport courtesy of dealers in Tulancingo. Unfortunately, those tactics are outdated. We know them all."

"Maybe she thought you were harassing her," said Noel with little conviction. "Maybe she just wanted to get away from you."

"There's no harassment. And whatever her reasons, she'd better realize that someone else is aware of them. Someone very serious."

"What are you telling me?"

"She was being followed by a man we couldn't place in any file anywhere. His papers were as counterfeit as hers. We had picked him up at the airport in Mexico City. Before anyone could question him, he slipped a cyanide capsule in his mouth."

29

A meeting ground was chosen. There was a vacant flat in Montmartre, on the top floor of an old building, its owner an artist currently in Italy. Helden telephoned, giving Noel the address and the time. She would be there to introduce her brother to him, but would not stay.

Noel climbed the last step and knocked on the door. He heard hurrying footsteps; the door opened; Helden was in the narrow foyer. "Hello, my darling," she said.

"Hello," he answered awkwardly as he met her lips, his eyes glancing behind her.

"Johann's on the terrace," she said, laughing. "A kiss is permitted in any event. I told him . . . how fond I am of you."

"Was that necessary?"

"Strangely enough, it was. I'm glad I did. It made me feel good." She closed the door, holding his arm. "I can't explain this," she said. "I haven't seen my brother in over a year. But he's changed. The situation in Geneva has affected him; he's profoundly committed to its success. I've never seen him so . . . oh, I don't know . . . so thoughtful."

"I still have questions, Helden."

"So does he. About you."

"Really?"

"At one point this morning, he didn't want to meet you. He didn't trust you. He believed you'd been reached, paid to betray Geneva."

"*Me?*"

"Think about it. He learned from people in Rio that you'd met Maurice Graff. From Graff you went straight to London, to Anthony Beaumont. You were right about him; he's *Odessa*." Helden stopped briefly. "He said you . . . spent the night with Gretchen, went to bed with her."

"Wait a minute," interrupted Noel.

"No, darling, it's not important. I told you, I know my sister. But there's a pattern, don't you see? To the *Odessa*, women are only conveniences. You were a friend of *Odessa*, you'd had a long, exhausting trip. It was perfectly natural that your needs should be fulfilled."

"That's barbarian!"

"It's the way Johann saw it."

"He's wrong."

"He knows that now. At least, I think he does. I told him about the things that had happened to you – to us – and how you'd nearly been killed. He was amazed. He may still have questions to ask you, but I think he's convinced."

Holcroft shook his head in bewilderment. *Nothing* is *as it was for you . . . nothing can ever be the same.* Not only was nothing the same, it wasn't even what it appeared *not* to be. There was no straight line from point A to point B.

"Let's get this over with," he said. "Can we meet later?"

"Of course."

"Are you going back to work?"

"I haven't been to work."

"I forgot. You were with your brother. You said you were going to work, but you were with him."

"It was a necessary lie."

"They're all necessary, aren't they?"

"Please, Noel. Shall I come back for you? Say in two hours?"

Holcroft considered. Part of his mind was still on the startling news Miles had given him. He had tried to reach Sam Buonoventura, in Curaçao, but Sam had been in the field. "You could do me a favour instead. I've told you about Buonoventura in the Caribbean. I put in a call to him from the hotel; he hasn't returned it. If you're free, would you wait in the room in case he does call? I wouldn't ask you, but it's urgent. Something happened; I'll tell you about it later. Will you?"

"Certainly. What shall I say to him?"

"Tell him to stay put for a few hours. Or to give you a number where I can call him later. Six to eight, Paris time. Tell him it's important." Noel reached in his pocket. "Here's the key. Remember my name's Fresca."

Helden took the key and then his arm, leading him into the studio. "And you remember, my brother's name is Tennyson. John Tennyson."

Holcroft saw Tennyson through thick panes of leaded glass windows that looked out on the terrace. If anything the glass magnified his features; they seemed larger than life. He wore a dark, pin-striped suit, no overcoat or hat, his hands on the railing, peering out at the Paris skyline. He was tall and slender, the body tapered almost too perfectly; it was the body of an athlete, a series of coiled springs, taut and contained. He turned slightly to his right; revealing his face. It was a face like no other Noel had seen. It was an artist's rendering, the features too idealized for actual skin and blood. And because it did not accept blemish, the face was cold. It was a face cast in marble, topped by glistening light blond hair, perfectly groomed, matching the stone.

Then von Tiebolt-Tennyson saw him through the window; their eyes met and the image of marble collapsed. The blond man's eyes were alive and penetrating. He pushed himself off the railing and walked towards the terrace door.

Stepping inside, he extended his hand.

"I'm the son of Wilhelm von Tiebolt."

"I'm . . . Noel Holcroft," said Noel. "My father was Heinrich Clausen."

"I know. Helden has told me a great deal about you. You've been through a lot."

"We both have," agreed Holcroft. "I mean your sister and I. I gather you've had your share, too."

"Our legacy, unfortunately." Tennyson smiled. "It's awkward meeting like this, isn't it?"

"I've been more comfortable."

"And I've not said a word," interjected Helden. "You were both quite capable of introducing yourselves. I'll leave now."

"You certainly don't have to," said Tennyson. "What we have to say to each other concerns you, I think."

"I'm not sure it does. Not for the moment. Besides, I have something to do," replied Helden. She started towards the foyer. "I think it's terribly important – for a great many people – that you trust each other. I hope you can." She opened the door and left.

Neither man spoke for several moments; both looked towards the spot where Helden had stood.

"She's remarkable," said Tennyson. "I love her very much."

Noel turned his head. "So do I."

Tennyson acknowledged the look as well as the statement. "I hope it's not a complication for you."

"It isn't, although it may be for her."

"I see." Tennyson walked to the window and gazed outside. "I'm not in a position to give you my blessing – Helden and I live very separate lives – and even if I could, I'm not sure I would."

"Thanks for your frankness."

The blond man turned. "Yes, I'm frank. I don't know you. I only know what Helden has told me about you and what I've learned for myself. What she tells me is basically what you've told her, coloured by her feelings, of course. What I've learned is not so clear-cut. Nor does the composite fit my sister's rather enthusiastic picture."

"We both have questions. Do you want to go first?"

"It doesn't really matter, does it? Mine are very few and very direct." Tennyson's voice was suddenly harsh. "What was your business with Maurice Graff?"

"I thought Helden told you."

"Again it was what you told *her*. Now, tell *me*. I'm somewhat more experienced than my sister. I don't accept things simply because you say them. Over the years, I've learned not to do that. Why did you go to see Graff?"

"I was looking for you."

"For *me?*"

"Not you specifically. For the von Tiebolts. For information about any of you."

"Why *Graff?*"

"His name was given to me."

"By whom?"

"I don't remember . . ."

"You don't *remember?* Of thousands and thousands of men in Rio de Janeiro, the name of Maurice Graff just *happens* to be the one casually given to you."

"It's the truth."

"It's ludicrous."

"Wait a minute." Noel tried to reconstruct the sequence of events that led him to Graff. "It started in New York . . ."

"*What* started? Graff was in New York?"

"No, the consulate. I went to the Brazilian Consulate and spoke to an attaché. I wanted to find out how I'd go about locating a family that no one had heard from in several years. A family that had immigrated to Brazil in the forties. The attaché put the facts together and figured out I was looking for Germans. He gave me a lecture about . . . well, there's a Spanish phrase for it."

"I speak Spanish," interrupted Tennyson. "What was it?"

"'*El lado de abajo alemán.*' It means the underside of the German; what's beneath his thinking."

"I'm aware of that. Go on."

"He told me there was a strong, close-knit German community in Rio run by a few powerful men. He warned me about looking for a German family that had disappeared; he said it could be dangerous. The immigrants protected each other from Nuremberg and Israeli hunters. Maybe he exaggerated because I wouldn't give him your name."

"Thank God you didn't."

"When I got to Rio, I couldn't find out anything. Even the immigration records were doctored."

"At great cost to a great many people," said Tennyson bitterly. "It was our only protection."

"I was stuck. Then I remembered what the attaché had said about the German community being run by a few powerful men. I went to a German bookstore, the kind that sells German newspapers and magazines, and asked a clerk about the houses. Large ones, mansions with a lot of acreage. I called them Bavarian, but he knew what I meant. I'm an architect and I figured . . ."

"I understand." Tennyson nodded. "Large German estates, the most influential leaders in the German community."

"That's right. The clerk gave me a couple of names. One was Jewish, the other was Graff. He said Graff's estate was among the most impressive in Brazil."

"It is."

"And that's it. That's how I came to go to Graff."

Tennyson stood motionless, his expression noncommittal. "It's not unreasonable."

"I'm glad you think so," said Noel.

"I said it was reasonable, I didn't say I believed you."

"I've no reason to lie."

"Even if you do, I'm not sure you have the talent. I'm very good at seeing through liars."

Noel was struck by the statement. "That's practically what Helden said the night I met her."

"I've trained her well. Lying is a craft; it must be developed. You're out of your depth."

"What the hell are you trying to say?"

"I'm saying you're a very convincing amateur. You built your story well, but it is not sufficiently professional. Your keystone is missing. As an architect, I'm sure you understand."

"I'll be goddamned if I do. Tell me."

"With pleasure. You left Brazil knowing the name von Tiebolt. You arrive in England and within twelve hours you're in a suburb of Portsmouth with my sister, *sleeping* with my sister. You didn't even have the name of Tennyson. How could you possibly have known about Beaumont?"

"But I *did* have the name of Tennyson."

"*How?* How did you get it?"

"I told Helden. This couple, a brother and sister named Cararra, came to see me at the hotel."

"Oh yes, Cararra. A very common name in Brazil. Did it mean anything to you?"

"Of course not."

"So these *Cararras* came to see you out of nowhere, claiming to be dear friends of ours. But as Helden told *you*, we've never heard of them. Come, Mr Holcroft, you'll have to do better than that." Tennyson raised his voice. "Graff gave you Beaumont's name, didn't he? *Odessa* to *Odessa*."

"No! Graff didn't know. He thinks you're still hiding somewhere in Brazil."

"He said that?"

"He implied it. The Cararras confirmed it. They mentioned some colonies in the south – Catarinas or something. A mountain region settled by Germans."

"You've done your homework well. The Santa Catarinas are German settlements. But again we're back to the elusive Cararras."

Noel remembered clearly the fear in the faces of the young brother and sister in Rio. "Maybe they're elusive to you, but not to me. You've either got a lousy memory or you're a lousy friend. They said they barely knew Helden, but knew you very well. They risked a hell of a lot to come and see me. Portuguese Jews who . . ."

"*Portuguese* . . ." interrupted Tennyson, suddenly alarmed. "Oh, my God! And they used the name Cararra . . . Describe them!"

When he had finished, Tennyson whispered, "Out of the past, Mr Holcroft. It all fits. The use of the name Cararra. Portuguese Jews, Santa Catarina . . . they came back to Rio."

"Who came back?"

"The Montealegres, that's their real name. Ten, twelve years ago . . . What

250

they told you was a cover, so you'd never be able to reveal their identities, even unconsciously."

"What happened twelve years ago?"

"The details aren't important, but we had to get them out of Rio, so we sent them to the Catarinas. Their parents helped the Israelis; they were killed for it. The two children were hunted; they would have been shot, too. They had to be taken south."

"Then there are people in the Catarinas who know about you?"

"Yes, a few. Our base of operations was in Santa Catarina. Rio was too dangerous."

"What operations? Who's we?"

"Those of us in Brazil who fought the *Odessa*." Tennyson shook his head. "I have an apology to make. Helden was right, I did you an injustice. You've told the truth."

Noel had the sensation of having been vindicated when no vindication was sought. He felt awkward questioning a man who fought the *Odessa*, who had rescued children from death as surely as if he'd taken them out of Auschwitz, or Belsen, who had trained the woman he loved to survive. But he *had* questions; it was no time to forget them.

"It's my turn now," he said. "You're very quick, and you know about things I've never heard of, but I'm not sure you've said a hell of a lot."

"If one of your questions concerns the Tinamou," said Tennyson, "I'm sorry, but I won't answer you. I won't even discuss it."

Holcroft was stunned. "You won't *what?*"

"You heard me. The Tinamou is a subject I won't discuss. It's not your business."

"I think it is! For starters, let's put it this way. If you won't discuss the Tinamou, we haven't anything to discuss."

Tennyson paused, startled. "You mean that, don't you?"

"Absolutely."

"Then try to understand me. Nothing can be left to chance now, to the offhand possibility – no matter how remote – that the wrong word might be dropped to the wrong person. If I'm right, and I think I am, you'll have your answer in a matter of days."

"That's not good enough!"

"Then I'll go one step further. The Tinamou was trained in Brazil. By the *Odessa*. I've studied him as thoroughly as any man on earth. I've been tracking him for six years."

It took several seconds for Noel to find his voice. "You've been . . . For six years?"

"Yes. It's time for the Tinamou to strike; there'll be another assassination. It's why the British contacted you; they know it, too."

"Why don't you *work* with them? For God's sake, do you know what they think?"

"I know what someone's tried to *make* them think. It's why I can't work with them. The Tinamou has sources everywhere; they don't know him, but he uses them."

"You said a matter of days."

"If I'm wrong I'll tell you everything. I'll even go to the British with you."

"A matter of days . . . Okay. We'll pass on the Tinamou – for a matter of days."

"Whatever else I can tell you, I will. I've nothing to hide."

"You knew Beaumont in Rio, knew he was part of the *Odessa*. You even accused me of having got his name from Graff. Yet in spite of all this, he married your sister. *Odessa* to *Odessa*? Are you one of them?"

Tennyson did not waver. "A question of priorities. Put simply, it was planned. My sister Gretchen is not the woman she once was, but she's never lost her hatred of the Nazis. She's made a sacrifice greater than any of us. We know every move that Beaumont makes."

"But he knows you're von Tiebolt! Why doesn't he tell Graff?"

"Ask him, if you like. He may tell you."

"*You* tell me."

"He's afraid to," replied Tennyson. "Beaumont is a pig. Even his commitments lack cleanliness. He works less and less for the *Odessa*, and only then when they threaten him."

"I don't understand."

"Gretchen has her own – shall we say, persuasive powers; I think you're aware of them. Beyond these, a large sum of untraceable money found its way into Beaumont's account. Added to both sets of circumstances, he fears exposure from Graff on one side . . . and from me to the other. He's useful to us both, more so to me than to Graff, of course. He checkmated."

"If you knew every move he made, you had to know he was on that plane to Rio. You had to know he was following me."

"How could I? I didn't know *you*."

"He was there. Someone sent him!"

"When Helden told me, I tried to find out who. What I learned was very little, but enough to alarm me. In my judgement our checkmated pig was reached by a third party. Someone who had unearthed his *Odessa* connection and was using him – as Graff used him. As I used him."

"Who?"

"I wish to heaven I knew! He was granted an emergency leave from his ship in the Mediterranean. He went to Geneva."

"*Geneva?*" Noel's memory raced back. *The station!* A fight had broken out; a man had arched backwards with blood on his shirt, another had gone after a third . . . A man in panic had raced by, his eyes wide in fright, beneath . . . thick eyebrows of *black-and-white* hair. "That was it," said Holcroft, astonished. "Beaumont was in Geneva."

"I just told you that."

"That's where I saw him! I couldn't remember where before. He followed me from *Geneva*."

"I'm afraid I don't know what you're talking about."

"Where's Beaumont now?" asked Noel.

"Back on board ship. Gretchen left several days ago to join him. In Saint Tropez, I think."

Tomorrow I go to the Mediterranean. To a man I loathe . . . Everything made so much more sense now. Perhaps Tennyson was not the only man in that room who had been unfair in his judgements.

"We've got to find out who sent Beaumont after me," said Noel, picturing the man in a black leather jacket. Tennyson was right; their conclusions were the same. There *was* someone else.

"I agree," said the blond man. "Shall we go together?"

Holcroft was tempted, but he had not finished. There could be no unanswered questions later. Not once the commitment had been made between them.

"Maybe," he replied. "There are two other things I want to ask you about. And I warn you, I want the answers now, not in a "matter of days"

"All right."

"You killed someone in Rio."

Tennyson's eyes narrowed. "Helden told you."

"I had to know, she understood that. There are conditions in Geneva that won't allow surprises. If you can be blackmailed, I can't let you go on."

Tennyson nodded. "I see."

"Who was it? Whom did you kill?"

"You mistake my reticence," replied the blond man. "I've no compunction whatsoever about telling you who it was. I'm trying to think how you can check up on what I say. There's no blackmail involved. There couldn't be; but how can you be sure?"

"Let's start with a name."

"Manuel Cararra."

"*Cararra?* . . ."

"Yes. It's why those two young people used it. They knew I'd see the political connection. Cararra was a leader in the Chamber of Deputies, one of the most powerful men in the country. But his allegiance was not to Brazil, it was to Graff. To the *Odessa*. I killed him seven years ago and I'd kill him tomorrow."

Noel studied Tennyson's face. "Who knew?"

"A few old men. Only one's still alive. I'll give you his name, if you like. He'd never say anything."

"Why not?"

"The shoe, as they say, was on the other foot. Before I left Rio de Janeiro, I met with them. My threat was clear. If ever they pursued me, I would make public what I knew about Cararra. The long-revered image of a conservative martyr would be shattered. The conservative cause in Brazil can't tolerate that."

"I want the name."

"I'll write it out for you." Tennyson did. "I'm sure you can reach him by transatlantic telephone. It won't take much; my name coupled with Cararra's should be enough."

"I may do that."

"By all means," said Tennyson. "He'll confirm what I've told you."

The two men faced each other, only feet apart. "There was an underground train accident in London," Noel went on. "A number of people were killed, including a man who worked for *The Guardian*. He was the man whose signature was on your employment records. The man who interviewed you, the only one who could shed any light on how or why you were hired."

Tennyson's eyes were suddenly cold again. "It was a shock I'll never get over. What's your question?"

"There was another accident. In New York. Only days ago. A number of innocent people were killed then, too, but one of them was the target. Someone I loved very much."

"I repeat! What's your *point*, Holcroft?"

"There's a certain similarity, wouldn't you say? MI5 doesn't know anything about the accident in New York, but it has very specific ideas about the one in London. I've put them together and come up with a disturbing connection. What do you know about that accident five years ago in London?"

Tennyson's body was rigid. "Watch out," he said. "The British go too far. What do you want of me? How far will you go to discredit me?"

"Cut the bullshit!" said Noel. "What happened on that train?"

"I was there!" the blond man thrust his hand up to his collar beneath the pin-striped suit. He yanked furiously, ripping his shirt half off his chest, exposing a scar that extended from the base of his throat to his breast. "I don't know anything about New York, but the experience in Charing Cross five years ago is one I'll live with for the rest of my life! Here it is; there's not a day when I'm not reminded of it. Forty-seven stitches, neck to thorax. I thought for a few moments – five years ago in London – that my head had been cut off from the rest of me. And that man you speak of so enigmatically was my dearest friend in England! He helped us get out of Brazil. If someone killed him, they tried to kill me, too! I was *with* him."

"I didn't know . . . the British didn't say anything. They didn't know you were *there*."

"Then I suggest someone look. There's a hospital record around somewhere. It shouldn't be hard to find." Tennyson shook his head in disgust. "I'm sorry, I shouldn't be angry at you. It's the British; they'll use anything."

"It's possible they really didn't know."

"I suppose so. Hundreds of people were taken off that train. A dozen clinics in London were filled that night; no one paid much attention to names. But you'd think they would have found mine. I was in the hospital for several days." Tennyson stopped abruptly. "You said someone you loved was killed in New York only a few days ago? What happened?"

Noel told him how Richard Holcroft had been run down in the streets, and

254

of the theory conceived by David Miles. It was pointless to withhold anything from this man he had come close to misjudging so completely.

In the telling was the conclusion both men had arrived at.

In my judgement, our checkmated pig has been reached by a third party.

Who?

I wish to heaven I knew.

Someone else.

A man in a black leather jacket. Defiant in a dark alley in Berlin. Willing to die ... asking to be shot. Refusing to say who he was or where he came from. Someone or something more powerful, more knowledgeable than, the Rache or the Odessa.

Someone else.

Noel told Tennyson everything, relieved that he could say it all.

When he had finished, Noel felt exhausted. "That's all I know," he said.

Tennyson nodded. "We've finally met, haven't we? We both had to say what was on our minds. We both thought the other was the enemy, and we were both wrong. Now, we have work to do."

"How long have you known about Geneva?" asked Holcroft. "Gretchen told me that you said a man would come one day and speak of a strange arrangement."

"Since I was a child. My mother told me there was an extraordinary sum of money that was to be used for great works, to make amends for the terrible things done in Germany's name, but not by true Germans. But only that fact, no specifics."

"You don't know Erich Kessler, then."

"I remember the name, but only vaguely. I was very young."

"You'll like him."

"As you describe him, I'm sure I will. You say he's bringing his brother to Geneva? Is that allowed?"

"Yes. I said I'd telephone him in Berlin and give him dates."

"Why not wait until tomorrow or the day after? Call him from Saint Tropez?"

"Beaumont?"

"Beaumont," said Tennyson, his mouth set. "I think we should meet with our checkmated pig. He has something to tell us. Specifically, who was his latest employer? Who sent him to that train station in Geneva? Who paid him for – or blackmailed him into – following you to New York and then to Rio de Janeiro? When we find this out, we'll know where your man in the black leather jacket came from."

Someone else.

Noel looked at his watch. It was nearly six o'clock; he and Tennyson had talked over two hours, yet there was still a great deal more to say. "Do you want to have dinner with your sister and me?" he asked.

Tennyson smiled. "No, my friend. We'll talk on our way south. I've calls to make and copy to file. I mustn't forget I'm a newspaperman. Where are you staying?"

"At the Georges Cinq. Under the name of Fresca."

"I'll phone you later this evening." Tennyson extended his hand. "Until tomorrow."

"Tomorrow."

"Incidentally, if my fraternal blessings mean anything, you have them."

Johann von Tiebolt stood at the railing of the terrace in the cold air of the early evening. Below on the street he could see Holcroft emerge from the building and walk east.

It had all been so easy. The orchestration of lies had been studiously thought out and arranged, the rendering underpinned with outraged conviction and sudden revelation that led to acceptance. An old man would be alerted in Rio; he knew what to say. A medical record would be placed in a London hospital, the dates and information corresponding to a tragic accident on the Charing Cross underground five years ago. And if all went according to schedule, a news item would be carried in the evening papers reporting another tragedy. A naval officer and his wife had disappeared in a small pleasure boat off the Mediterranean coast.

Von Tiebolt smiled. Everything was going as it was projected thirty years ago. Even the *Nachrichtendienst* could not stop them now. In a matter of days, the *Nachrichtendienst* would be castrated.

It was time for the Tinamou.

30

Noel hurried through the lobby of the Georges Cinq, eager to get to his room, to Helden; Geneva was closer now; it would be closer still when they met Anthony Beaumont in Saint Tropez and forced the truth from him.

Too, he was anxious to learn whether Buonoventura had returned his call. His mother had said she would let Sam know her plans. All Miles knew in New York was that Althene had left Mexico City for Lisbon. Why Lisbon? And who had followed her?

The image of the man in the black leather jacket came back to Holcroft. The steady look in his eyes, the acceptance of death . . . *kill me and another will take my place. Kill him, another his.*

The lift was empty, the ascent swift. The door opened; Noel caught his breath at the sight of the man standing in the corridor facing him. It was the *Verwünschtes Kind* from Sacré Coeur, the fashion plate who had searched him in front of the candles.

"Good evening, *monsieur.*"

"What are you doing here? Is Helden all right?"

"She can answer your questions."

"So can you." Holcroft grabbed the man's arm and turned him forcibly towards the door of the room.

"Take your hands off me!"

"When she tells me to let you go, I'll let you go. Come on." Noel propelled the man down the corridor to the door and knocked.

In seconds the door opened. Helden stood there, startled at the sight of the two of them. In her hand was a folded newspaper; in her eyes was something beyond her astonishment: sadness.

"What's the matter?" she asked.

"That's what I wanted to know, but he wouldn't tell me." Holcroft pushed the man through the door.

"Noel, *please.* He's one of us."

"I want to know why he's here."

"I called him; he had to know where I was. He told me he had to see me. I'm afraid he's brought us dreadful news."

"What?"

"Read the papers," said the man. "There are both French and English."

Holcroft picked up a copy of the *Herald–Tribune* from the coffee table.

"Page two," said the *Verwünschtes Kind.* "Top left."

Noel turned the page, snapping it flat. He read the words, a sense of anger . . . and fear . . . sweeping over him.

Naval Officer and Wife
Lost in Mediterranean

St Tropez – Commander Anthony Beaumont, captain of the patrol ship *Argo* and a highly decorated officer of Her Majesty's Royal Navy, along with his wife who had joined him in this resort town for the weekend, were feared drowned when their small boat foundered in an angry squall that blew up several miles south along this rock-bound coast. A capsized craft fitting the description of the small boat was sighted by low-flying coastal search planes. The commander and his wife had not been heard from in over forty-eight hours, prompting second-in-command of the *Argo*, Lt Morgan Llewellen, to issue search directives. The Admiralty has concluded that Commander and Mrs Beaumont lost their lives in the tragic accident. The couple had no children . . .

"Oh *God*," whispered Holcroft. "Did your brother tell you?"

"About Gretchen?" Helden asked. "Yes. She suffered so much, gave so much. It's why she wouldn't see me or talk to me. She never wanted me to know what she did, why she married him. She was afraid I might sense the truth."

"If what you *say* is true," said the well-dressed man, "that Beaumont was *Odessa*, we don't believe that newspaper story for a minute."

"He means your friend in Berlin," interrupted Helden. "I told him that you had a friend in Berlin who said he would transmit your suspicions to London."

Noel understood. She was telling him she had said nothing about Geneva. He turned to the *Verwünschtes Kind*. "What do you think happened?"

"If the British discovered an *Odessa* agent in the upper ranks of the navy, especially one commanding a coastal patrol vessel – a euphemism for an espionage ship – it would mean they had been duped again. There's just so much they can take; there'd be no inquiries. A swift execution is preferable."

"That's a pretty rough indictment," said Holcroft.

"It's an embarrassing situation."

"They'd kill an innocent woman?"

"Without thinking twice – on the possibility that she might not be innocent. The message would be clear, at any rate. The *Odessa* network would have its warning."

Noel turned away in disgust, and put his arms around Helden. "I'm sorry," he said. "I know how you must feel and I wish there was something I could do. Outside reaching your brother, I'm not sure there is."

Helden turned and looked at him, her eyes searching. "You trust each other?"

"Very much. We're working together now."

"Then there's no time for mourning, is there? I'm going to stay here tonight," she told the well-dressed man. "Is it all right? Can I be covered?"

"Of course," said the man. "I'll arrange it."

"Thank you. You're a good friend."

He smiled. "I don't think Mr Holcroft believes that. But then, he's got a great deal to learn." The man nodded and went to the door; he stopped, his hand on the knob, and turned to Noel. "I apologize if that appears cryptic to you, but be tolerant, *monsieur*. What's between you and Helden also seems cryptic to me, but I don't inquire. I trust. But, if that trust is found to be misplaced, we'll kill you. I just thought you ought to know."

The *Verwünschtes Kind* left quickly. Noel took an angry step after him, but Helden touched his arm. "Please, darling. He, too, has a lot to learn and we can't tell him. He is a friend."

"He's an insufferable little bastard." Holcroft paused. "I'm sorry. You've got enough on your mind, you don't need foolishness from me."

"A man threatened your life."

"Someone took your sister's. Under the circumstances, I was foolish."

"We've no time for such thoughts. Your friend Buonoventura returned your call. I wrote down the number where you can reach him. It's by the telephone."

Noel walked to the bedside table, and picked up the paper. "Your brother and I were going to Saint Tropez tomorrow. To make Beaumont tell us what he knew. The news'll be shattering to him. On both counts."

"You said you were going to call him. I think it's best that I do. He and Gretchen were very close: When they were younger they were inseparable."

"Actually, he said he'd phone me later this evening." Holcroft lifted the phone and gave Buonoventura's number to the operator.

"I'll speak to Johann when he calls," said Helden.

The transatlantic lines were light, the link to Curaçao made in less than a minute.

"You're a pistol, Noley! I'm glad I don't have to pay your phone bills. You're seeing the goddamn world, I'll say that for you."

"I'm seeing a lot more than that, Sam. Did my mother call you?"

"She did. She said to tell you she'll see you in Geneva in about a week. You're to stay at the Hotel D'Accord, but you're not to say anything to anyone."

"*Geneva?* She's going to Geneva? Why the hell did she even leave the country?"

"She said it was an emergency. You were to keep your mouth shut, and not do anything until you see her. She was one upset lady."

"I've got to get hold of her. Did she give you a telephone number – an address – where I could reach her?"

"Not a thing, pal. She didn't have much time to talk and the connection was rotten. It was out of Mexico. Anybody mind telling me what's going on?"

Holcroft shook his head as if Buonoventura were in the room facing him. "Sorry, Sam. Perhaps some day. I owe you."

"I think maybe you do. We'll cut a deck for it. Take care of yourself. You got a real nice mother. Be good to her."

Holcroft hung up. Buonoventura was a good friend to have. As good a friend as the well-dressed man was to Helden, he thought. He wondered what she meant when she asked the *Verwünschtes Kind* if she were covered. Covered for what? By whom?

"My mother's on her way to Geneva," he said.

Helden turned. "I heard you. You sounded upset."

"I am. A man followed her to Mexico. Miles had him picked up at the airport; he took a cyanide capsule before they could find out who he was or where he came from."

"'Kill me, another will take my place. Kill him, another his.' Weren't those the words?"

"Yes. I was thinking about them on the way up."

"Does Johann know?"

"I told him everything."

"What does he think?"

"He doesn't know what to think. The key was Beaumont. I don't know where we go now, except to Geneva and hope that no one stops us."

Helden came towards him. "Tell me something. What can they – whoever they are – really do? Once the three of you present yourselves to the bank in Geneva, each of you in agreement, all reasonable men, it's over. So what can they actually do?"

"You said it last night."

"What?"

"They can kill us."

The telephone rang. Holcroft reached for it. "Yes?"

"It's John Tennyson." The voice was strained.

"Your sister wants to talk to you," said Holcroft.

"In a moment," replied Tennyson. We must speak first. Does she know?"

"Yes. Obviously you do, too."

"My paper called me with the news. The night editor knew how close Gretchen and I were. It's horrible."

"I wish there was something I could say."

"I couldn't help you when you told me about your stepfather. We have to live with these things by ourselves. There's nothing anyone can do or say when they happen. Helden understands."

"Then you don't believe the story that was given out? About the boat and the storm?"

"That they went out in a boat and never came back, yes, I believe it. That he was responsible, of course not. It's not even plausible. Whatever else he was, Beaumont was a superb sailor. He could smell a storm twenty miles away. If he was in a light-weight craft, he'd have it in shore before any weather struck."

"Who then?"

"Come, my friend, we both know the answer. That someone else who hired him also killed him. They made him follow you to Rio. You spotted him; his usefulness had come to an end." Tennyson paused. "It was as if they'd known we were on our way to Saint Tropez. The unpardonable act was to kill Gretchen as well. For *appearances*."

"I'm sorry. *God*, I feel responsible."

"It was totally out of your control."

"Could it have been the British?" asked Holcroft. "I told Kessler; he said he was going to work through channels. Bonn to London. Maybe an *Odessa* agent commanding one of those electronic ships was too much of an embarrassment."

"The temptation might be there, but no one in authority would grant permission. The English would put him into isolation and break him on a rack if they had to get information, but they wouldn't kill him. They *had* him. He and Gretchen were killed by someone who could be damaged by what he knew, not by anyone who could benefit."

Tennyson's reasoning was persuasive. "You're right. The British wouldn't gain anything. They'd keep him under wraps."

"Exactly. And there's another factor, a moral one. I think MI6 is riddled with self-seekers, but I don't believe they kill to avoid embarrassment. It's not in their nature. But they'll go to extraordinary lengths to maintain a reputation. Or revive it. And I pray to God I'm right about that."

"What do you mean?"

"I'm flying to London tonight. In the morning I'll contact Payton-Jones at MI5. I've an exchange to offer him. One I think he'll find difficult to resist. I may be able to give him a ground-dwelling bird that moves rapidly from one place to another, its feathers blending in with the environment."

Holcroft was as surprised as he was bewildered. "I thought you said you couldn't work with them."

"*Him*. Only Payton-Jones, no one else. He must give me his assurance of that, or we go no farther."

"Do you think he will?"

"He really has no choice. That ground-dwelling bird has become an MI obsession."

"Suppose you do? What do you get in return?"

"Access to classified materials. The British have thousands of secret files. They concern the last years of the war and are embarrassing to a lot of people. But somewhere in those files is our answer. A man, a group of men, a band of fanatics – I don't know who or what, but it's there. Someone who had a connection with the *Finanzministerium* thirty years ago. Or with our fathers; someone they trusted and to whom they gave responsibility. It could even be a Loch Torridon infiltration."

"A what?"

"Loch Torridon. It was an espionage and sabotage operation mounted by the British from '41 to '44. Hundreds of former nationals were sent back to Germany and Italy to work in factories and railroads and government offices everywhere. It's common knowledge there were Loch Torridon personnel in the *Finanzministerium* ... The answer is in the archives."

"From those thousands of files you expect to find one identity? Even if it's there, it could take months"

"Not really. I know precisely what to look for. In your very detailed narrative this afternoon, you gave me what I need. I have the names, of course – ours and Manfredi's – but more than that I have approximate dates, the methods of transferring the funds, and, most important, *sources* from which the monies were stolen. I'll look for Geneva. I'll find it."

Tennyson spoke so rapidly, with such assurance, that Noel found it difficult to keep up with him. "Why are you so convinced the information is there to begin with?"

"Because it has to be. You made that clear to me this afternoon. The man who called you in New York, the one who was killed."

"Peter Baldwin?"

"Yes. MI6. He knew about Geneva. We start with him; he's our key now."

"Then go to the file called *Wolfsschanze*," said Holcroft. "*Code Wolfsschanze.* That may be it!"

Tennyson did not reply at first. He was either thinking or startled, Noel could not tell which. "Where did you hear that?" he asked. "You never mentioned it. Neither did Helden."

"Then we both forgot," Holcroft told him.

"We should be careful," said Tennyson, when Noel had finished. "If the name Wolfsschanze is tied to Geneva we must be extremely *careful*. The British can't learn about Geneva. It would be disastrous."

"I agree; but what reason will you give Payton-Jones for wanting access to the archives?"

"Part of the truth," answered Tennyson. "I want Gretchen's killer."

"And for that you're willing to give up the ... ground–dwelling bird you've been tracking for six years?"

"For that and for Geneva. With all my heart."

Noel was touched. "Do you want me to talk to Payton-Jones?"

"*No!*" Tennyson shouted, then lowered his voice. "I mean, it would be far too dangerous. Trust me. Do as I ask you, please. You and Helden must stay out of sight. *Completely.* Until I contact you, Helden must not return to work. She must stay with you and you both must remain invisible."

Holcroft looked at Helden. "I don't know if she'll agree to that."

"I'll convince her. Let me speak to her. You and I have finished our talk."

"You'll call me?"

"In a few days. If you change hotels, leave word at my message centre where Mr Fresca can be reached. Helden has the number. Let me talk to her now. In spite of our differences, we need each other now, perhaps as we've never needed each other before. And Noel?"

"Yes?"

"Be kind to her. Love her. She needs you, too."

Holcroft stood up and handed the phone to Helden.

"*Mein Bruder . . .*"

31

Code Wolfsschanze!

Von Tiebolt-Tennyson slammed his fist on the desk in the small, out-of-the-way office he used in Paris.

Code Wolfsschanze. That most sacrosanct of phrases had been *given* to Peter Baldwin by Ernst Manfredi! The banker had played a dangerous but ingenious game. He knew that Baldwin's mere use of the phrase was enough to guarantee his death. But Manfredi would never have given the Englishman more than that; it would not have been in the banker's interests. Still, Baldwin had possessed one of the best minds in Europe. Had he pieced more together than Manfredi had considered possible? How much had he really learned? What was contained in Baldin's file at MI5?

Or did it matter? The British had rejected whatever it was Baldwin had to offer. One file folder among thousands upon thousands. Buried in the archives, lost because it was one more insert of rejected information.

Code Wolfsschanze. It meant nothing to those who knew nothing, and the few hundred who did – those district leaders in every country – knew only that it was a signal. They were to make themselves ready; enormous funds would soon be sent to them, to be used for the cause.

Die Sonnenkinder. All over the world, prepared to rise and assert their birthright.

Baldwin's file could not contain that information; it was not possible. But those who held that file would be used. Above all else, the British wanted the Tinamou. His capture by MI5 would reassert English supremacy in intelligence operations – a supremacy lost through years of blunders and defections.

MI5 would be handed the Tinamou, and with that gift would come an obligation to the giver. That was the splendid irony; the hated British Intelligence, that quiet, serpentine monster which had wreaked such havoc on the Third Reich, would help create the Fourth.

For MI5 would be told that the *Nachrichtendienst* was involved in an extraordinary conspiracy. The British would believe the man who told them; he was giving them the Tinamou.

Tennyson walked through the London offices of *The Guardian*, receiving the congratulations of his colleagues and their subordinates. As always, he accepted the compliments modestly.

He studied the women casually. The secretaries and the receptionists invited this most beautiful of men to acknowledge them, inviting him, actually, to take whatever he wished.

It struck him that he might have to select one of these women. His beloved Gretchen was gone, but not his appetites. Yes, thought Tennyson as he walked towards the door of the senior editor's office, he would select a woman. The excitement was mounting, the intensity of Wolfsschanze growing with every passing hour. He would need sexual release; it was always this way; Gretchen had understood.

"John, it's good to see you," said the senior editor, getting up from behind the desk and extending his hand. "We're running the Bonn article tomorrow. Fine job."

Tennyson sat down in a chair in front of the desk. "Something has come up," he said. "If my sources are accurate, and I'm sure they are, a killing – killings – will be attempted that could provoke a world crisis."

"Good heavens, have you written it up?"

"No. We can't write about it. I don't think any responsible newspaper should."

The editor leaned forward. "What is it, John?"

"There's an economic summit conference called for next Tuesday . . ."

"Of course. Right here in London. Leaders from the East and West."

"That's the point. East and West. They're flying in from Moscow and Washington, from Peking and Paris. The most powerful on earth." Tennyson paused.

"And?"

"Two are to be assassinated."

"*What?*"

"Two are to be killed; which two is irrelevant as long as they are from opposing sides. The President of the United States and the Chairman of the People's Republic; or the Prime Minister and Premier of Soviet Russia."

"Impossible! Security measures will be airtight."

"Not really. There'll be crowds, processions, banquets, motorcades. Where's the absolute guarantee found?"

"It has to be!"

"Not against the Tinamou."

"The *Tinamou?*"

"He's accepted the highest fee in history."

"Good God, from *whom?*"

"An organization known as the *Nachrichtendienst*."

Harold Payton-Jones stared across the table at Tennyson in the dimly lit room that had no other furniture but the table and two chairs. The location had been selected by MI5; it was a deserted boarding house in east London.

"I repeat," said the grey-haired agent curtly, "you expect me to accept the things you say merely because you're willing to go on record? Preposterous!"

"It's my only *proof*," replied Tennyson. "Everything I've told you is true. We haven't time to fight each other any longer. Every hour is vital."

"Nor have I the inclination to be hoodwinked by an opportunistic journalist who may be much more than a correspondent! You're very clever. And quite possibly outrageous."

"For God's sake, if that's true why am I *here?* Listen to me! I'll say it for the last time. The Tinamou was trained by the *Odessa*. In the hills of Rio de Janeiro! I've fought the *Odessa* all my life; that's on my record if anyone cares to examine it. The *Odessa* forced us out of Brazil, cut us off from everything we'd built there. I want the Tinamou!"

Payton-Jones studied the blond man. The argument had been vicious, lasting nearly half an hour. The agent had been relentless, pounding Tennyson with a barrage of questions, lashing out at him with insults. It was a studied technique of MI5's designed to separate truth from falsehood. It was apparent that the Englishman was now satisfied. He lowered his voice.

"All right, Mr Tennyson. We can stop fighting each other. I gather we owe you an apology."

"The apologies are not one-sided. It's just that I knew I could work better alone. I had to pretend to be so many things. If ever anyone had seen me with a member of your service my effectiveness would have been destroyed."

"Then I'm sorry we called you in."

"They were dangerous moments for me. I could feel the Tinamou slipping away."

"We haven't caught him yet."

"We're close. It's only a matter of days now. We'll succeed if we're painstaking in every decision we make, every street the delegations travel – the locations of every meeting, every ceremony, every banquet. There's an advantage that's never existed before: we know he's there."

"You're absolutely convinced of your source?"

"Never more so in my life. That man in the rathskeller was the courier. Every courier used to reach the Tinamou has been killed. His last words were '*London. Next week. The summit. One from each side. A man with a tattoo of a rose on the back of his hand. Nachrichtendienst.*' "

Payton-Jones nodded. "We'll put out inquiries to Berlin as to the man's identity."

"I doubt you'll find anything. From what little I know about the *Nachrichtendienst*, it was extremely thorough."

"But it was neutral," Payton-Jones said, "and its information was always accurate. It spared no one. The prosecutors of Nuremberg were continuously fed data by the *Nachrichtendienst*."

"I suggest," said Tennyson, "that the prosecutors were given only what the *Nachrichtendienst* wanted to give them. You can't know what was withheld."

The Britisher nodded again. "It's possible. That's something we'll never know. The question is why? What's the motive?"

"If I may," replied the blond man . . . "A few old men about to die, taking their final vengeance. The Third Reich had two specific philosophical enemies, who allied themselves in spite of their antagonisms. The Communists and the democracies. Now each wants supremacy. What better revenge than for each to accuse the other of assassination? For each to destroy the other?"

"If we could establish that," interrupted Payton-Jones, "it could be the motive behind a number of assassinations during the past years."

"How does one establish it beyond doubt?" asked Tennyson. "Did British Intelligence ever have a direct connection with the *Nachrichtendienst?*"

"Oh yes. We insisted on identities – to be kept locked in the vaults, of course. We couldn't act on such information blindly."

"Are any alive today?"

"It's possible. It's been years since anyone mentioned the *Nachrichtendienst.* I'll check, of course."

"Will you give me their names?"

The MI5 man leaned back in the chair. "Is this one of the conditions you spoke of, Mr Tennyson?"

"Spoke of, but made clear that under the circumstances I could never insist upon."

"If we catch the Tinamou you'll have the gratitude of world governments; the names are minor. If we have them, so will you. Do you have other requests? Should I have brought a notebook?"

"They're limited," answered Tennyson, overlooking the insult, "and may surprise you. Out of gratitude to my employers, I should like a five-hour advance exclusive for *The Guardian.*"

"It's yours," said Payton-Jones. "What else?"

"In so far as MI5 has approached various people, implying that I was the subject of inquiries, I should like a letter from British Intelligence making it clear that my personal dossier is not only without blemish, but that I've made an active contribution to your efforts to maintain – shall we say – international stability."

"Quite unnecessary," said the Englishman. "Should the Tinamou be caught through the information you bring us, governments everywhere no doubt will decorate you with highest honours. A letter from us would be gratuitous. You won't need it."

"But you see, I will," said Tennyson. "For my next to last request is that my name never be mentioned."

"Never be . . ." Payton-Jones was stunned. "That's hardly in character, is it?"

"Please don't confuse my professional endeavours with my private way of life. I seek no credit. The von Tiebolts owe a debt; call this part payment."

The MI5 operative was silent for a moment. "I *have* misjudged you. I apologize again. Of course, you'll have your letter."

"Frankly, there's another reason for wanting anonymity. I realize that the Royal Navy and the French authorities are satisfied that my sister and her husband died accidentally while on holiday, and they're probably right. But I think you'll agree the timing was unfortunate. I have one sister left; she and I are the last of the von Tiebolts. If anything happened to her I'd never forgive myself."

"I understand."

"Needless to say, I'd like to offer you whatever assistance I can. I believe I know as much about the Tinamou as anyone alive. I've studied him for years. Every killing, every projected move he made before and after the acts. I think I can help. I'd like to be a part of your team."

"I'd be a damn fool to turn you down. What's your last request?"

"We'll get to it." Tennyson stood up. "The thing to realize about the Tinamou is that his technique is instant variation, practised improvisation. He doesn't have a single strategy, but ten or twelve – each methodically conceived and rehearsed so that it can be adapted to the moment."

"I'm not sure I know what you mean."

"Let me explain. The killing Madrid seven months ago, during the riots. Do you remember?"

"Of course. The rifle was fired from a fourth-floor window above the crowds."

"Exactly. A government building in a government square where the demonstrations were scheduled to take place. A *government* building. That bothered me. Suppose the guards were more alert, security measures more effective, people checked thoroughly for weapons? Suppose he could *not* have got to that window? It was an ideal spot, incidentally, for getting the target in his gunsight, but suppose there'd been people in that room?"

"He would have moved to another location."

"Naturally. But no matter how well-concealed the weapon – whether part of a crutch, or strapped to his leg, or sewn in sections into his clothing – it would have been awkward. He had to move quickly; timing was important; the demonstration wasn't going to last that long. The Tinamou had to have more than one location, more than one option; he had to have alternative positions available to him. And he did."

"How do you know?" asked the MI5 man, fascinated.

"I spent two days in Madrid, going over every building, every window, every rooftop in that square. The Tinamou removes only what's practical for him. After he kills, he gets away quickly. I found four weapons intact, and three other locations where floorboards had been ripped out, window sashes removed, and mouldings torn apart. Additional weapons had been concealed in those places. I even found two pounds of plastic explosives in a rubbish bin on the street. Fifty feet from the centre of the demonstration. *Eight* positions from which to kill. Alternative selections for him to choose, each designed to fit a projected moment during a specific timespan."

Payton-Jones sat forward, his hands on the table. "That complicates things.

Standard protective measures concentrate on a single location. Which of half a hundred possibilities is the most likely? The assumption is that the killer will have stationed himself in one location. The strategy you describe adds another dimension: instant mobility. Not a single pre-set hiding place, but several, selected at any given moment."

"Within a given timespan," completed the blond-haired man. "But as I mentioned, we have an advantage. We know he's there. There's also a second advantage, and it's one we should use immediately." Tennyson stopped.

"What is it?"

"I'll qualify that statement. We should use it only if we agree that the capture of the Tinamou is almost as vital as the ultimate safety of his targets."

The Englishman frowned. "That's a rather dangerous thing to say. There can be no risks – calculated or overlooked – where those men are concerned. Not on British soil."

"Hear me out, please. He's killed political leaders before, spreading suspicion, arousing hostilities between governments. And always steadier heads have prevailed; they've cooled things off. But the Tinamou must be stopped on the outside chance that one day the steadier heads will not be swift enough. I think we can stop him now if all consent."

"Consent to what?"

"To adhering to published schedules. Bring the leaders of the delegations together, tell them what you know. Tell them that extraordinary precautions will be mounted, but by keeping to schedules, there's a good chance that the Tinamou will at last be caught." Tennyson paused and leaned over the chair, his hands on the rim. "I think if you're honest, no one will disagree. After all, it's not much more than what political leaders face every day."

The frown on the MI5 man's face disappeared. "And no one will want to be called a coward. Now, what's this second advantage?"

"The Tinamou's technique requires him to pre-set concealed weapons in a number of locations. To do that he must begin days, perhaps weeks, before the designated assassination. He's no doubt already begun here in London. I suggest we start a very quiet but thorough search, staking out those areas that conform to the published reports of the summit's schedule."

Payton-Jones brought his hands together in a gesture of agreement. "Of course. We need only find one and we have not only the general location but the timespan."

"Exactly. We'll know that within a given number of minutes during a specific event in a precise area, the assassination will be attempted." Again the blond man paused. "I'd like to help in that search. I know what to look for, and, perhaps more important, where not to look. We haven't much time."

"Your offer's appreciated, sir," said the Englishman. "MI5 is grateful. Shall we begin tonight?"

"Let's give him one more day to set his guns. It'll increase our chances of finding something. Also, I'll need an innocuous sort of uniform and a permit that identifies me as a building inspector or some such title."

"Very good," said Payton-Jones. "I'm embarrassed to say we have a photo-graph of you on file; we'll use it for the permit. I'd imagine that you're a size forty-four, trousers long, waist thirty-three or four."

"Close enough. A civil service uniform should hardly be tailored."

"Quite so. We'll take care of both items in the morning." Payton-Jones got up. "You said you had one more request."

"I do. Since I left Brazil, I've not owned a weapon. I'm not even sure it's permitted, but I should like to have one now. Only for the duration of the summit, of course."

"I'll have one issued to you."

"That would need my signature, wouldn't it?"

"Yes."

"Forgive me, but I meant what I said before. As I want no credit for what I've brought you, I feel equally strongly about having my name listed anywhere as an associate of MI5. I wouldn't want anyone to know the nature of my contributions. My name on a weapon's file card could lead a curious person to the truth. Someone, perhaps, connected to the *Nachrichtendienst*."

"I see." The Englishman unbuttoned the jacket of his suit coat and reached underneath. "This is highly irregular but so are the circumstances." He withdrew a small, short-barrelled revolver and handed it to Tennyson. "Since we both know the source, take mine. I'll list it out for overhaul and replace it."

"Thank you," said the blond man, holding the weapon as if it were an unfamiliar object.

Tennyson entered a crowded pub off Soho Square. He scanned the room through the heavy layers of smoke and saw what he was looking for: a hand raised by a man at a table in the far corner. The man, as always, wore a brown raincoat made specifically for him. It looked like any other raincoat; the difference was found in the additional pockets and straps that often contained various handguns, silencers, and explosives. He had been trained by the Tinamou, trained so well that he often performed services contracted by the assassin when the Tinamou was unavailable.

His last assignment had been at Kennedy Airport during a rainswept night when a cordon of police surrounded the glistening fuselage of a British Airways 747. He had found his quarry in a fuel truck. He had done his job.

John Tennyson carried his pint to the table and joined the man in the brown raincoat. The table was round and small, the chairs so close together that their heads were only inches apart, allowing both men to keep their voices low.

"Is everything placed?" asked the blond man.

"Yes," replied his companion. "The motorcade goes south on the Strand, around Trafalgar Square, through the gates of Admiralty Arch, and into the Mall towards the palace. There are seven locations."

"Give me the sequence."

"From north to south in order of progression we start at the Strand Hotel, opposite Savoy Court. Third floor, Room 306. Automatic repeating rifle and scope are sewn into the mattress of the bed nearest the window. A block south, east side, fourth floor, the men's room of an accounting firm. The weapon is in the ceiling, above the tile to the left of the fluorescent light. Directly across the street, again on the fourth floor – there's a penny arcade on the first – the offices of a typing service. Rifle and scope are strapped to the undercarriage of a xerox copier. Moving on towards Trafalgar . . ."

The man in the brown raincoat went through the locations of the remaining caches of weapons. They were within a distance of approximately half a mile. From Savoy Court to Admiralty Arch.

"Excellent choices," said Tennyson, pushing the untouched pint of beer away. "You understand your moves fully?"

"I know what they are; I can't say I understand them."

"That's not really necessary, is it?" asked the blond man.

"Of course not, but I'm thinking of you. If you're hemmed in, or blocked, I could do the job. From any of the locations. Why not give me one?"

"Even you're not qualified for this. There can be no room whatsoever for the slightest error. A single misplaced bullet would be disastrous."

"May I remind you, I was trained by the best there is."

Tennyson smiled. "You're right. Very well, make the moves I gave you and position yourself in an eighth location. Choose a room in the Government Building, beyond Admiralty Arch, and let me know which. Can you do that?"

"Ducks in a gallery," replied the man, lifting his pint of beer to his lips. Tennyson could see the tattoo of a red rose on the back of his right hand.

"May I make a suggestion?" asked John Tennyson.

"Of course. What is it?"

"Wear gloves," said the Tinamou.

32

The blond man opened the door and reached for the light switch on the wall; two table lamps went on in the hotel room marked 306. He motioned for his middle-aged companion to follow him inside.

"It's all right," said Tennyson. "Even if the room is being watched, the shades are drawn and the hour corresponds to the time the maids turn down the beds. Over here."

Payton-Jones kept pace as Tennyson took a miniature metal detector from his overcoat pocket. He touched the button, holding the device over the bed. The tiny hum grew louder; the needle on the dial jumped to the right.

Carefully, he folded back the covers and undid the sheets. "It's there. You can feel the outlines," he said, pressing his fingers into the mattress.

"Remarkable," said Payton-Jones. "And the room has been leased for ten days?"

"By telegraph and postal money order, originating in Paris. The name is Le Fèvre, a meaningless pseudonym. No one's been here."

"It's there, all right." Payton-Jones removed his hands from the bed.

"I can make out the rifle," said Tennyson, "but what's the other object?"

"A telescopic sight," replied the Englishman. "We'll leave everything intact and post men in the corridor."

"The next location is down the street, in the lavatory of an accounting firm on the fourth floor. The gun's in the ceiling, wired to a suspension rod above a fluorescent light."

"Let's go," said Payton-Jones.

An hour and forty-five minutes later, the two men were on the roof of a building overlooking Trafalgar Square. Both knelt by the short wall that bordered the edge. Below was the route the summit motorcade would take on its way through Admiralty Arch and into the Mall.

"The fact that the Tinamou would put a weapon here," said Tennyson, his hand on the tar paper that bulged slightly next to the wall, "makes me think he'll be wearing a police uniform."

"I see what you mean," said Payton-Jones. "A policeman walking on to a roof where we've stationed a man wouldn't cause any great alarm."

"Exactly. He could kill your man and take up his position."

"But then he isolates himself. He has no way out."

"I'm not sure the Tinamou needs one in the conventional sense. A taut rope into a back alley; hysterical crowds below; stairwells jammed, general pandemonium. He's escaped under less dramatic conditions. Remember, he has more identities than a telephone directory. In Madrid I'm convinced he was one of the interrogators on the scene."

"We'll have two men up here, one out of sight. And four sharpshooters on adjacent rooftops." Payton-Jones crawled away from the wall; the blond man followed. "You've done extraordinary work, Tennyson," said the MI5 agent. "You've unearthed five locations in something over thirty-six hours. Are you satisfied these are all?"

"Not yet. However, I'm satisfied that we've established the parameters. From the Savoy Court to the end of Trafalgar; somewhere in those half a dozen blocks he'll make his move. Once the motorcade's through the arch and into the Mall we can breathe again. Until that moment, I'm not sure I will. Have the delegations been told?"

"Yes. Each head of state will be outfitted with chest, groin and leg plates, as well as crowns of bulletproof plastic in their hats. The President of the United States, naturally, objected to any hat at all, and the Russian wants the plastic fitted into his fur, but otherwise, we're in good shape. The risk is minimal."

Tennyson looked at Payton-Jones. "Do you really believe that?"

"Yes. Why?"

"I think you're wrong. The Tinamou is no mere marksman. He's capable of rapid-fire accuracy that would spin a shilling into figure-eights at five hundred yards. An expanse of flesh beneath a hat brim is no challenge for him. He'd go for the eyes and he wouldn't miss."

The Englishman glanced briefly at Tennyson. "I said the risk was minimal, not non-existent. At the first sign of disturbance, each head of state will be covered by human shields. You've found five locations so far; say there's another five. If you find no others, we've still reduced his efficiency by fifty per cent, and it's a good chance – at least fifty per cent – that he'll show up at one of those uncovered. The odds are decidedly against the Tinamou. We'll catch him. We've *got* to."

"His capture means a great deal to you, doesn't it?"

"As much as it does to you, Mr Tennyson. More than any single objective in over thirty years of service."

The blond man nodded. "I understand. I owe this country a great deal and I'll do whatever I can to help. But I'll be happy when that motorcade reaches Admiralty Arch."

By three in the morning on Tuesday, Tennyson had uncovered two additional weapons. There were now seven in all, forming a straight line down the Strand from the Savoy Court to the rooftop at the corner of Whitehall and Trafalgar. Every location was covered by a minimum of five agents hidden in corridors and on rooftops, rifles and handguns poised, prepared to fire at anyone who even approached the hidden weapons.

Still Tennyson was not satisfied. "There's something *wrong*," he kept repeating to Payton-Jones. "I don't know what it is, but something doesn't *fit*."

"You're overworked," said the agent in the room at the Savoy which was their base of operations. "And overwrought. You've done a splendid job."

"Not splendid enough. There's *something* and I can't put my finger on it!"

"Calm down. Look at what you *have* put your fingers on. Seven weapons. In all likelihood, that's all there are. He's bound to get near one of those guns, bound to betray the fact that he knows it's there. He's ours. Relax. We've got scores of men out there."

"But something's *wrong*."

The crowds lined the Strand, the pavements jammed from kerb to shopfronts. Stanchions were placed on both sides of the street, linked by thick steel cables. The London police stood in front of the cables, their eyes darting continuously in every direction, their truncheons at their sides.

Beyond the police and intermingling with the crowds were over a hundred operatives of British Intelligence, many flown back from posts overseas.

They were the experts Payton-Jones had insisted upon, his insurance against the master assassin who could spin a shilling into figure-eights at five hundred yards. They were linked by miniaturized radios on an ultra-high frequency that could neither be interfered with nor intercepted.

The operations room at the Savoy was tense, each man there an expert. Computer screens showed every yard of the gauntlet, graphs and grid marks signifying blocks and streets. The screens were connected to radios outside; they showed as tiny moving dots that lit up when activated. The time was near. The motorcade was in progress.

"I'm going back down on the street," said Tennyson, pulling out the small radio from his pocket. "I set the green arrow on the receiving position, is that correct?"

"Yes, but don't send any messages unless you feel they're vital," said Payton-Jones. "Once the motorcade reaches Waterloo Bridge, everything is on five-second report intervals each fifty yards – except for emergencies, of course. Keep the channels clear."

An agent sitting by a computer panel spoke in a loud voice. "Within five hundred feet of Waterloo, sir. Spread holding at eight mph."

The blond man hurried from the room. It was time to put into motion the swift moves that would destroy the *Nachrichtendienst* once and for all and cement the Wolfsschanze covenant.

He walked out into the Strand and looked at his watch. Within thirty seconds the man in the brown raincoat would appear in a window on the second floor of the Strand Hotel. The room was 206, directly beneath the room with the weapon concealed in the mattress. It was the first move.

Tennyson glanced around for one of Payton-Jones's specialists. They were not difficult to spot; they carried small radios identical to his. He approached an agent trying to keep his position by a shopfront against the jostling crowds, a man he had purposely spoken to; he had spoken to a number of them.

"Hello, there? How are things going?"

"I beg your pardon? Oh, it's you, sir." The agent was watching the people within the borders of his station. He had no time for idle conversation.

An eruption of noise came from the Strand near Waterloo Bridge. The motorcade was approaching. The crowd pushed nearer the kerb, waving miniature flags. The two lines of police in the street beyond the stanchions seemed to close ranks, as if anticipating a stampede.

"Over there!" yelled Tennyson, grabbing the agent's arm. Up *there!*"

"What? *Where?*"

"That window! It was closed a few seconds ago!"

They could not see the man in the brown raincoat clearly, but it was obvious that a figure stood in the shadows of the room.

The agent raised his radio. "Suspect possibility. Sector One, Strand Hotel, second floor, third window from south corner."

Static preceded the reply. "That's beneath 306. Security check immediately."

The man in the window disappeared.

"He's gone," said the agent quickly.

Five seconds later another voice came over the radio. "There's no one here. Room's empty."

"Sorry," said the blond man.

"Better safe than that, sir," said the agent.

Tennyson moved away, walking south through the crowds. He checked his watch again; twenty seconds to go. He approached another man holding a radio in his hand; he produced his own to establish the relationship.

"I'm one of you," he said. "Things all right?"

The agent faced him. "What?" He saw the radio in Tennyson's hand. "Oh yes, you were at the morning's briefing. Things are fine, sir."

"That *doorway!*" Tennyson put his hand on the agent's shoulder. "Across the street. The open doorway. You can see the staircase above the heads of the crowd. That *doorway.*"

"What about it? The man on the steps? The one running?"

"Yes! It's the same man."

"Who? What are you talking about?"

"In the hotel room. A few minutes ago. It's the same man, I *know* it! He was carrying a briefcase."

The agent spoke into his radio. "Security check requested. Sector Four, west flank. Doorway adjacent to jewellery shop. Man with briefcase. Up the stairs."

"In progress," came the reply.

Across the Strand Tennyson could see two men racing through the open door and up the dark steps. He looked to the left; the man in the brown raincoat was walking out of the jewellery shop into the crowd. There was a door on the first landing, normally locked – as it was locked now – that connected the two buildings.

A voice came over the radio. "No one with a briefcase on second to fifth floors. Will check the roof."

"Don't bother," ordered another voice. "We're up here and there's no sign of anyone."

Tennyson shrugged apologetically and moved away. He had three more alarms to raise as the motorcade made its stately way down the Strand. The last of these would cause the lead vehicle to stop, clearance required before it continued towards Trafalgar. This final alarm would be raised by him. It would precede the chaos.

Alarm One. An arm was grabbed; an arm whose hand held a radio.

"That *scaffold!* Up *there!*"

"*Where?*"

The entire side of a building opposite Charing Cross Station was in the middle of reconstruction. People had scaled the pipes, cheering and whistling as the international motorcade came into view.

"Up on the right. He went behind the plywood!"

"*Who*, sir?"

"The man in the hotel, on those steps in the doorway! The *briefcase.*"

"Security check. Sector Seven. Man on construction scaffold. With a briefcase."

Static. An eruption of voices.

"We're all *over* the scaffolds, mate!"

"No one here with a briefcase!"

"Dozens of cameras. No briefcases, or luggage of any sort."

"The plywood on the second level!"

"Man was changing film, mate. He's climbing down. No bird."

"I'm sorry."

"You gave us a start, sir."

"My apologies."

Alarm Two. Tennyson showed a policeman his temporary MI5 identification and rushed across the intersection into a packed Trafalgar Square.

"The lions! My *God*, the *lions!*"

The agent – one of those Tennyson had spoken to during the morning's briefing – stared at the base of the Lord Nelson monument. Scores of onlookers were perched on the lions surrounding the towering symbol of Nelson's victory at Trafalgar.

"What, sir?"

"He's there again! The man on the scaffold!"

"I heard that report just moments ago," said the agent. "Where is he?"

"He went behind the lion on the right. It's not a briefcase. It's a leather bag, but it's too large for a camera! Can't you *see?* It's too *large for a camera!*"

The agent did not hesitate; the radio was at his lips. "Security check. Sector Nine. North cat. Man with large leather bag."

The static crackled; two voices rode over each other.

"Man with two cameras, larger one at his feet . . ."

"Man checking light meter, corresponds . . . see no danger, no bird here."

"Man descending, setting camera focus. No bird."

The MI5 agent glanced at Tennyson, then looked away, his eyes scanning the crowds.

The moment had come. The start of the final alarm, the beginning of the end of the *Nachrichtendienst*.

"You're *wrong*," shouted Tennyson furiously. "You're *all* wrong! Every one of you!"

"What?"

The blond man ran as best he could, threading his way through the packed square towards the kerbside, the radio next to his ear. He could hear excited voices commenting upon his explosion.

He's mad as hell!

He says we're wrong.

About what?

Have no idea.

He ran.

Where?

I don't know. I can't see him.

Tennyson reached the iron fence that bordered the monument. He could see his colleague – the Tinamou's apprentice – dashing across the street towards the arch. The man in the raincoat held a small black plastic case in his hand. The identification card inside was an exact replica of the one in Tennyson's pocket – except that the photograph was different.

Now!

The blond man pressed the button and shouted into the radio.

"It's him! I know it!"

Who's that?

Respond.

It's from Sector Ten.

"I understand now! I see what it was that didn't fit."

Is that you, Tennyson? Payton-Jones's voice.

"Yes!"

Where are you?

"That's it! Now I see it."

See what? Tennyson, is that you? What's the matter? Respond.

"It's so clear now! That's where we made our mistake! It's not going to happen when we thought it would – *where* we thought it would."

What are you talking about? Where are you?

"We were wrong, don't you see? The weapons. The seven locations. They were *meant* to be found! That's what didn't fit!"

What? Push the red button, Tennyson. Clear all channels. What didn't fit?

"The hiding of the weapons. It wasn't good enough. We found them too easily."

For God's sake, what are you trying to say?

"I'm not sure yet," replied Tennyson, walking towards an opening in the gate. "I just know those weapons were meant to be found. It's in the progression!"

What progression? Push the red button. Where are you?

Somewhere between Sector Ten and back towards Nine, intruded another voice. *West flank. In Trafalgar.*

"The progression from one weapon to another!" shouted Tennyson. "Going from north to south! As each position is passed, we eliminate it. We shouldn't. They're open limousines!"

What do you mean?

"Stop the motorcade! In the name of all that's holy, stop it!"

Stop the motorcade. The command's been relayed. Now where are you?

The blond man crunched; two MI5 men passed within feet of him. "I think I've spotted him! The man on the scaffold! In the doorway. In the hotel window. It's him! He's doubling back; he's running now!"

Describe him. For God's sake, describe the man.

"He's wearing a jacket. A brown checked jacket."

All operatives alert. Pick up man in brown checked jacket. Running north past Sectors Nine, Eight, and Seven. West flank.

"It has to be another weapon! A weapon we never found. He's going to fire from behind! Distance is nothing to him. He'll hit the back of a neck from a thousand yards! Start the motorcade up again! Quickly!"

Vehicle One, proceed. Operatives mount trunks of all cars. Protect targets from rear fire.

"He's stopped!"

Tennyson, where are you? Give us your location.

Still between Sectors Nine and Ten, sir.

"He's not wearing the jacket now, but it's the same man! He's running across the Strand!"

Where?

There's no one crossing in Sector Eight.

Sector Nine?

No one, sir.

"Back further! Behind the motorcade!"

Sector Five reporting. Police have relaxed the lines..

Tighten them. Get everyone out of the street. Tennyson, what's he wearing? Describe him.

The blond man was silent; he walked through the square for a distance of twenty yards, then brought the radio to his lips again. "He's in a brown raincoat. He's heading back towards Trafalgar Square."

Sector Eight, sir. Transmission in Sector Eight.

Tennyson switched off the radio, shoved it into his pocket, and ran back to the iron fence. The motorcade had reached Charing Cross, perhaps four hundred yards away. The timing was perfect. The Tinamou's timing was always perfect.

The man in the brown raincoat positioned himself in a deserted office of the Government Building beyond Admiralty Arch, a room commandeered by the mocked-up MI5 identification card. The card was a licence; no one argued with it, not today. The line of fire from that room to the motorcade was difficult, but it was no problem for one trained by the Tinamou.

Tennyson leaped over the iron fence and raced diagonally across Trafalgar Square towards Admiralty Arch. Two police officers stopped him, their truncheons raised in unison; the motorcade was three hundred yards away.

"This is an emergency!" shouted the blond man, showing his identification. "Check your radios! MI5 frequency, Savoy operations. I've got to get to the Government Building!"

The police were confused. "Sorry, sir. We don't have radios."

"Then get them!" yelled Tennyson, rushing past.

At the Arch, he activated his radio. "It's the Mall! Once the motorcade's through the Arch, stop all vehicles. He's in the trees!"

Tennyson, where are you?

Sector Twelve, sir. He's in Sector Twelve. East flank.

Relay his instructions. Quickly, for God's sake.

Tennyson switched off the radio, put it in his pocket, and continued through the crowds. He entered the Mall and turned left, racing across the path to the first doorway of the Government Building. Two uniformed guards blocked him; he produced the MI5 card.

"Oh yes, sir," said the guard on the left. "Your team's on the second floor. I'm not sure which office."

"I am," said the blond man as he ran towards the staircase. The cheers in Trafalgar Square mounted; the motorcade approached Admiralty Arch.

He took the steps three at a time, crashing the corridor door open on the second floor, pausing in the hallway to shift his gun from his pocket to his belt. He walked swiftly to the second door on the left. There was no point in trying to open it; it was locked. Yet to break it down without warning was to ask for a bullet in his head.

"*Es ist Wolfsschanze!*" he shouted. "*Bleib beim Fenster!*"

"*Herein!*" was the reply.

Tennyson angled his shoulder, rushed forwards, and slammed his body against the fragile door; the door flew open, revealing the man in the raincoat crouched in front of the window, a long-barrelled rifle in his hands. His hands were encased in sheer, flesh-coloured gloves.

"*Johann?*"

"They found *everything*," said the blond man. "Every weapon, every *location!*"

"Impossible!" yelled the man in the raincoat. "One or two, perhaps. Not *all!*"

"Every one," said Tennyson, kneeling behind the man in front of the window. The advance security car had passed through Admiralty Arch; they would see the first limousine in seconds. The cheers from the crowds lining the Mall swelled like a mammoth chorus. "Give me the rifle!" Tennyson said. "Is the sight calibrated?"

"Of course," said the man, handing over the weapon.

Tennyson thrust his left hand through the strap, lashing it taut, then raised the rifle to his shoulder, the telescopic sight to his eye. The first limousine moved into the light-green circle, the Prime Minister of Great Britain in the cross-hairs. Tennyson moved the rifle slightly; the smiling face of the President of the United States was now in the gunsight, the cross-hairs intersecting the American's left temple. Tennyson shifted the weapon back and forth. It was important for him to know that with two squeezes of the trigger he could eliminate them both.

A third limousine came slowly into the green circle. The Chairman of the People's Republic of China was in the gunsight, the cross-hairs centred below the visor of his peasant's cap. A slight pressure against the trigger would blow the man's head apart.

"What are you *waiting* for?" asked the Tinamou's apprentice.

"I'm making my decision," replied Tennyson. "Time is relative. Half-seconds become half-hours." The fourth limousine was there now, the leader of Soviet Russia in the lethal green circle.

The exercise was over. In his mind he had done it. The transition between desire and the reality was a minor thing because it was so possible.

But this was not the way to destroy the *Nachrichtendienst*. The killing would come later; it would commence in a matter of weeks and continue for a matter of weeks. It was part of the Wolfsschanze covenant, an intrinsic part. So many of the leaders would die. But not now, not this afternoon.

The motorcade stopped; Payton-Jones had relayed Tennyson's instructions. No limousine entered the Mall. Dozens of agents began fanning out over the grass, guns drawn but held unobtrusively as they raced through the foliage, their eyes on the trees.

Tennyson held the rifle in the grip of his left hand, the strap taut from barrel to shoulder. He removed his finger from the trigger housing and lowered his right hand to his wrist, pulling the revolver from his belt.

"*Now*, Johann! They've stopped," whispered the apprentice. "Now, or they'll start up again. You'll lose them!"

"Yes, now," said Tennyson softly, turning to the man crouched beside him. "And I lose nothing."

He fired the gun, the explosion echoing through the deserted office. The man spun wildly off his feet, blood erupting from his forehead. He fell to the floor, his eyes wide and staring.

It was doubtful that the gunshot was heard for any distance over the noise of the outside crowds, but it didn't really matter. In seconds there'd be gunfire no one would miss. Tennyson sprang to his feet, removed the rifle from his arm, and took a folded slip of paper from his pocket. He knelt beside the dead man and shoved the paper into the bloodied, lifeless mouth, pushing it as far in as he could down the throat.

Strapping the weapon back on its owner's arm, he dragged the body over to the window. Pulling out a handkerchief, he wiped the rifle clean and forced the dead fingers into the trigger housing, tearing the fabric of the right-hand glove so he could see the tattoo.

Now.

He took out the radio and leaned out of the window.

"I think I've spotted him! It's the same as Madrid. That's it! Madrid!"

Madrid: Tennyson, where . . .

Sector Thirteen, sir. East flank.

Thirteen? Specify. Madrid? . . .

Tennyson pushed himself off the sill and back into the deserted office. It would be only seconds now. Seconds until the connection was made by Payton-Jones.

Tennyson placed the radio on the floor and he knelt by the dead man. He edged the dead arm and weapon up into the open window. He listened to the excited voices over the radio.

Sector Thirteen. East flank. Beyond the arch to the left, heading south.

All agents concentrate on Sector Thirteen. East flank. Converge.

All personnel converging, sir. Sector . . .

Madrid! . . . The Government Building. It's the Government Building.

Now.

The blond man yanked at the dead finger four times, firing indiscriminately into the crowds near the motorcade. He could hear the screams, see the bodies fall.

Get out. All vehicles move out. Alert One. Move out.

The engines of the limousines roared; the cars lurched forward. The sounds of sirens filled Saint James' Park.

Tennyson let the dead man fall back to the floor and sprang towards the doorway, the pistol in his hand. He pulled the trigger repeatedly until there were no more shells left in the chamber. The body of the dead man jerked as each new bullet hit.

The voices on the radio were now indistinguishable. He could hear the sounds of racing footsteps in the corridor.

Johann von Tiebolt walked to the wall and sank to the floor, his face drawn in exhaustion. It was the end of his performance. The Tinamou had been caught.

By the Tinamou.

33

Their final meeting took place twenty-seven and a half hours after the death of the unknown man presumed to be the Tinamou.

Since the first account of the momentous event – initially reported by *The Guardian* and subsequently confirmed by Downing Street – the news had electrified the world. And British Intelligence, which refused all comment on the operation other than to express gratitude to sources it would not reveal, regained the supremacy it had lost through years of defections and ineptitude.

Payton-Jones took two envelopes from his pocket and handed them to Tennyson. "These seem such inadequate compensation. The British Government owes you a debt it can never repay."

"I never sought payment," said Tennyson, accepting the envelopes. "It's enough that the Tinamou is gone. I assume one of these is the letter from MI5, and the other the names pulled from the *Nachrichtendienst* file?"

"They are."

"And my name has been removed from the operation?"

"It was never there. In the reports you are referred to as 'Source Able'. The letter, a copy of which remains in the files, states that your dossier is unblemished."

"What about those who heard my name used over the radios?"

"Indictable under the Official Secrets Act should they reveal it. Not that it makes much difference; they heard only the name Tennyson. There must be a dozen Tennysons under deep cover in British Intelligence, any one of which can be mocked up in the event it's necessary."

"Then I'd say our business is concluded."

"I imagine so," agreed Payton-Jones. "What will you do now?"

"Do? My job, of course. I'm a newspaperman. I might request a short leave of absence, however. My older sister's effects must sadly be taken care of, and then I'd like a brief holiday. Switzerland, perhaps. I like to ski."

"It's the season for it."

"Yes." Tennyson paused. "I hope it won't be necessary to have me followed any longer."

"Of course not. Only if you request it."

"Request it?"

"For protection." Payton-Jones gave Tennyson a xerox copy of a note. "The Tinamou was professional to the end. He tried to get rid of this, tried to swallow it. And you were right. It's the *Nachrichtendienst*."

Tennyson picked up the xerox. The words were blurred but legible.

Nachricht. 1360° 78K. Au 23°-22°.

"What does it mean?" he asked.

"Actually, it's rather simple," replied the agent. "The *Nachricht* is obviously the *Nachrichtendienst*. The figure 1360.78K is the metric equivalent of three thousand pounds, or one and a half tons. *Au* is the chemical symbol for gold. The 23°–22° we believe are the map coordinates in longitude and latitude of Johannesburg. The Tinamou was being paid out of Johannesburg in gold for his work yesterday. Something in the neighbourhood of three million, six hundred thousand pounds sterling, or over seven million American dollars."

"It's frightening to think the *Nachrichtendienst* has that kind of money."

"More frightening when one considers how it was being used."

"You're not going to release the information? Or the note?"

"We'd rather not. However, we realize we have no right to prevent you – especially you – from revealing it. In your *Guardian* story, you alluded to an unknown group of men who might have been responsible for the assassination attempt."

"I speculated on the possibility," corrected Tennyson, "in so far as it was the Tinamou's pattern. He was a hired assassin, not an avenger. Did you learn anything about the man himself?"

"Virtually nothing. The only identification on him, unfortunately, was an excellent forgery of an MI5 authorization card. His fingerprints aren't in any files anywhere – from Washington to Moscow. His suit was off a rack; we doubt it's English. There were no laundry marks on his underwear, and even his raincoat, which we traced to a shop on Old Bond Street, was paid for in cash."

"But he travelled continuously. He must have had papers."

"We don't know where to look. We don't even know his nationality. The laboratories have worked around the clock for something to go on: dental work, evidence of surgery, physical marks that a computer might pick up somewhere, *anything*. So far nothing."

"Then maybe he wasn't the Tinamou. The only evidence is the tattoo on the back of his hand and a similar calibre of weapons. Will it be enough?"

"It is now; you can add it to your story tomorrow. The ballistics are irrefutable. Two of the concealed rifles that were removed, plus the one on his person, match three guns used in previous assassinations."

Tennyson nodded. "There's a certain comfort in that, isn't there?"

"There certainly is." Payton-Jones gestured at the xerox paper. "What's your answer?"

"About what? The note?"

"The *Nachrichtendienst*. You brought it to us and now it's confirmed. It's an extraordinary story. You unearthed it; you have every right to print it."

"But you don't want me to."

"We can't stop you."

"On the other hand," said the blond man, "there's nothing to prevent you from including my name in your reports, and that's one thing *I* don't want."

The MI5 man cleared his throat. "Well, actually, there is something. I gave you my word, Mr Tennyson. I'd like to think it's good."

"I'm sure it is, but I'm equally sure your giving it could be reappraised should the situation warrant it. If not by you, then by someone else."

"I see no likelihood of that. You've dealt only with me, that was our understanding."

"So, 'Source Able' is anonymous. He has no identity."

"Right. Nor is it unusual at the levels in which I negotiate. I've spent my life in the service. My word's not questioned when it's given."

"I see." Tennyson stood. "Why don't you want the *Nachrichtendienst* identified?"

"I want time. A month or two. Time to get closer without alarming it."

"Do you think you'll be able to?" Tennyson pointed to one of the envelopes on the table. "Will those names help?"

"I'm not sure. I've just begun. There are only eight men listed; we're not even certain they're all alive. There's been no time to check them out."

"*Someone's* alive. Someone very wealthy and powerful."

"Obviously."

"So the compulsion to catch the Tinamou is replaced by an obsession with the *Nachrichtendienst*."

"A logical transfer, I'd say," agreed Payton-Jones. "And, I should add, there's another reason – quite professional, but also part personal. I'm convinced the *Nachrichtendienst* killed a young man I trained."

"Who was he?"

"My assistant. As committed as any man I've ever met in service. His body was found in a small village called Montereau some sixty miles south of Paris. He went to France initially to track Holcroft, but found that Holcroft was a dead-end. An Interpol report has the American nearly a hundred miles away at the time, *north* of Paris, in Argenteuil. Our man would not make such an error."

"What do you think happened?"

"I *know* what happened. Remember, he was after the Tinamou. When Holcroft proved to be only what he said he was – a man looking for you because of a minor inheritance . . ."

"Very minor," interrupted Tennyson.

". . .Our young man went underground. He was a first-rate professional; he made progress. More than that, he made a connection. He *had* to have made a connection. The Tinamou, the *Nachrichtendienst* . . . Paris. Everything fits."

"Why does it fit?"

"There's a name on that list. A man living near Paris – we don't know where – who was a general in the German High Command. Klaus Falkenheim. But he was more than that. We believe he was a prime mover of the *Nachricht-*

endienst, one of the original members. He's known as *Herr Oberst*."

John Tennyson stood rigidly by the chair. "You have my word," he said. "I'll print nothing."

Holcroft sat forward on the couch, the newspaper in his hand. The headline reached from border to border. It said it all.

ASSASSIN TRAPPED, KILLED IN LONDON

Nearly every article on the page was related to the dramatic capture and subsequent death of the Tinamou. There were stories reaching back fifteen years, linking the Tinamou to both Kennedys, and Martin Luther King, as well as Oswald and Ruby; more recent speculations touched on killings in Madrid, and Beirut, Paris and Lisbon, Prague, and even Moscow itself.

The unknown man was an instant legend. Tattoo parlours from cities everywhere reported a swelling upsurge in business.

"My God, he did it," said Noel.

"Yet his name isn't mentioned anywhere," Helden said. "It's unlike Johann to give up credit in something as extraordinary as this."

"You said he'd changed, that Geneva had affected him. I believe that. The man I talked to wasn't concerned with himself. I told him that the bank in Geneva didn't want complications. The directors would be looking for anything that might disqualify one of us, that would put the money in potentially compromising circumstances. A man who's placed himself in a dangerous situation, who's had to deal with the kind of people your brother's had to deal with in tracking the Tinamou, could scare the hell out of the bankers."

"But you and my brother say there's someone more powerful than the *Rache* or the *Odessa* – or Wolfsschanze – who's trying to stop you. How do you think the men in Geneva will accept all that?"

"They'll be told only what they have to be told," said Holcroft. "Which may be nothing, if your brother and I *can sort it out*."

"Can you?"

"Maybe. He thinks so, and God knows he's had more experience in these things than I've had. It's been a crazy process of elimination. First we're convinced it's one thing – one group – then another; then it turns out to be neither."

"You mean the *Odessa* and the *Rache?*"

"Yes. They're eliminated. Now we're looking for someone else. All we need is a name, an identity."

"What will you do when you find it?"

"I don't know," Holcroft said. "I hope your brother will tell me. I just know that whatever we do, we've got to do it quickly. Miles will get in in a few days. He's going to publicly connect me to homicides ranging from Kennedy Airport to the Plaza Hotel. He'll ask for extradition and he'll get it. If that

285

happens, Geneva's finished and for all intents and purposes so am I."

"If they can find you," said Helden. "We have ways . . ."

Noel stared at her. "No," he replied. "I'm not going to live with three changes of clothing and rubber-soled shoes and guns with silencers. I want you to be a part of my life, but I won't be a part of yours."

"You may not have a choice."

The telephone rang, startling them both. Holcroft picked it up.

"Good afternoon, Mr Fresca."

It was Tennyson.

"Can you talk?" asked Noel.

"Yes. This telephone is fine and I doubt whether the Georges Cinq switchboard is interested in a routine call from London. Still, we should be careful."

"I understand. Congratulations. You did what you said you would."

"I had a great deal of help."

"You worked with the British?"

"Yes. You were right. I should have done so a long time ago. They were splendid."

"I'm glad to hear it. It's nice to know we have friends."

"More than that. We have the identity of Geneva's enemy."

"*What?*"

"We have the names. We can move against them now. We *must* move against them; the killing must stop."

"How? . . ."

"I'll explain when I see you. Your friend, Kessler, was close to the truth."

"A splinter faction of *Odessa?*"

"Be careful," interrupted Tennyson. "Let's say a group of tired old men with too much money and a vendetta that goes back to the end of the war."

"What do we do?"

"Perhaps very little. The British may do it for us."

"They know about *Geneva?*"

"No. They simply understand a debt."

"It's more than we could ask for."

"No more than we deserve," said Tennyson. If I may say so."

"You may. These . . . old men. They were responsible for *everything*. Including New York?"

"Yes."

"Then I'm clear."

"You will be shortly."

"Thank *Christ!*" Noel looked at Helden across the room and smiled. "What do you want me to do?"

"It's Wednesday. Be in Geneva Friday night. I'll see you then. I'll take the late flight from Heathrow and get there by eleven-thirty or midnight. Call Kessler in Berlin; tell him to join us."

"Why not today, or tomorrow?"

"I've got things to do. They'll be helpful to us. Make it Friday. Do you have a hotel?"

"Yes. The D'Accord. My mother's flying to Geneva. She got word to me to stay there."

There was a silence on the line from London. Finally, Tennyson spoke, his voice a whisper. "What did you say?"

"My mother's flying to Geneva."

"We'll talk later," said Helden's brother, barely audible. "I've got to go."

Tennyson replaced the phone on the small table in his Kensington flat. As always, he detested the instrument when it was the carrier of unexpected news. News in this case that could be as dangerous as the emergence of the *Nachrichtendienst*.

What insanity made Althene Holcroft fly to Geneva? It was never part of the plan – as she understood the plan. Did the old woman think she could travel to *Switzerland* without arousing suspicions, especially *now?* Or perhaps the years had made her careless. In that event she would not live long enough to regret her indiscretion. Perhaps, again, she had divided loyalties – as she understood those loyalties. If so, she would be reminded of her priorities before she took leave of a life in which she had abused so many.

So be it. He had his own priorities; she would take her place among them. The covenant of Wolfsschanze was about to be fulfilled. Everything was timing now.

First the lists. There were two and they were the key to Wolfsschanze. One was eleven pages in length, with the names of nearly 1,600 men and women – powerful men and women in every country in the world. These were the elite of the *Sonnenkinder*, the leaders waiting for the signal from Geneva, waiting to receive the millions that would purchase influence, buy elections, shape policies. This was the primary list and with it would emerge the outlines of the Fourth Reich.

But outlines required substance, depth. Leaders needed followers. These would come with the second list, this one in the form of a hundred spools of film. The master list. Microdot records of their people in every part of the globe. By now thousands upon thousands, begat and recruited by the children sent out of the Reich by ship and plane and submarine.

Operation Sonnenkinder.

The lists, the names. One copy only, never to be duplicated, guarded as closely as any holy grail. For years they had been kept and updated by Maurice Graff in Brazil, then presented to Johann von Tiebolt on his twenty-fifth birthday. The ceremony signified the transfer of power; the chosen new absolute leader had exceeded all expectations.

John Tennyson had brought the lists to England, knowing it was imperative to find a repository safer than any bank, more removed from potential scrutiny than any vault in London. He had found his secret place in an obscure mining town in Wales, with a *Sonnenkind* who would gladly give his life to protect the precious documents.

Ian Llewellen, brother of Morgan – second-in-command of Beaumont's *Argo*.

And it was nearly time for the Welshman to arrive. After he had delivered his cargo, the loyal *Sonnenkind* would make the sacrifice he had pleaded to make only days ago when they drove down the motorway from Heathrow. His death was mandatory; no one could be aware of those lists, those names. When that sacrifice was made, only two men on earth would have the key to Wolfsschanze. One a quiet professor of history in Berlin, the other a man revered by British Intelligence – above suspicion.

Nachrichtendienst! The next priority.

Tennyson stared at the page of paper next to the telephone; it had been there for several hours. It was another list – light years away from the *Sonnenkinder* – given him by Payton-Jones. It was the *Nachrichtendienst*.

Eight names, eight men. And what the British had not learned in two days, he had learned in less than two hours. Five of those men were dead. Three remained, one of them now close to death in a sanatorium outside of Stuttgart. That left two: the traitor, Klaus Falkenheim, known as *Herr Oberst*, and a former diplomat of eighty-three named Werner Gerhardt, who lived quietly in a Swiss village on Lake Neuchatel.

But old men did not travel in transatlantic aircraft and put strychnine in glasses of whisky. They did not beat a man unconscious for a photograph. They did not fire guns at the same man in a French village or assault that man in a back alley in Berlin.

The *Nachrichtendienst* had indoctrinated younger, very capable disciples. Indoctrinated them to the point of absolute commitment . . . as the disciples of Wolfsschanze were committed.

Nachrichtendienst! Falkenheim, Gerhardt. How long had they known about Wolfsschanze?

Tomorrow he would find out. In the morning he would take a plane to Paris, and call on Falkenheim, on the hated *Herr Oberst*. Consummate actor, consummate garbage. Betrayer of the Reich.

Tomorrow he would call on Falkenheim and break him. Then kill him.

A car horn sounded from outside. Tennyson looked at his watch as he walked to the window. Eight o'clock precisely. Down in the street was the Welshman's car, and inside, sealed in a steel carton, were the lists.

Tennyson took a gun from a drawer and shoved it into the holster strapped to his shoulder.

He wished the events of the night were over and he was on the plane to Paris. He could barely wait to confront Klaus Falkenheim.

Holcroft sat silently on the couch in the semi-darkness, the glow of an unseen moon filling the windows. It was 4.00 in the morning. He smoked a cigarette.

He had opened his eyes fifteen minutes ago and had not been able to go back to sleep.

Helden. She was the woman he wanted to be with for the rest of his life, yet she would not tell him where she lived or whom she lived with. It was past flippancy now; he was not interested in games any longer.

"Noel?" Helden's voice floated across the shadows.

"Yes?"

"What's the matter, darling?"

"Nothing. Just thinking."

"I've been thinking, too."

"I thought you were asleep."

"I felt you get out of bed. What are you thinking about?"

"A lot of things," he said. "Mostly Geneva. It'll be over soon. You're going to be able to stop running; so will I."

"That's what I've been thinking about. I want to tell you my secret."

"Secret?"

"It's not much of one, but I want to see your face when I tell you. Come here."

She held out both her hands and he took them, sitting naked in front of her. "What's your secret?"

"It's your competition. The man I live with. Are you ready?"

"I'm ready."

"It's *Herr Oberst*. I love him."

"The old man?" Noel breathed again.

"Yes. Are you furious?"

"Beside myself. I'll have to challenge him to a duel." Holcroft took her in his arms.

Helden laughed and kissed him. "I've got to see him today."

"I'll go with you. I've got your brother's blessings. I'll see if I can get his."

"No. I must go alone. I'll only be an hour or so."

"Two hours. That's the limit."

"Two hours. I'll stand in front of his wheelchair and say: '*Herr Oberst*. I'm leaving you for another man.' Do you think he'll be crushed?"

"It'll kill him," whispered Noel. He pulled her gently down on the bed.

34

Tennyson walked into the parking lot at Orly Airport and saw the grey Renault. The driver of the car was the second highest ranking official of the *Sûreté*. He had been born in Düsseldorf, but grew up a Frenchman, sent out of Germany on a plane from a remote airfield north of Essen. He had been six years old at the time – 10 March 1945 – and he had no memories of the Fatherland. But he did have a commitment – he was a *Sonnenkind*.

Tennyson reached the door, opened it, and climbed inside.

"*Bonjour, monsieur,*" he said.

"*Bonjour,*" replied the Frenchman. "You look tired."

"It's been a long night. Did you bring everything I asked for? I have very little time."

"Everything." The *Sûreté* official reached for a file folder on the ledge under the dashboard and handed it to the blond man. "I think you'll find this complete."

"Give me a summary, I'll read it later. I want to know quickly where we stand."

"Very well." The Frenchman put the folder on his lap. "First things first. The man named Werner Gerhardt in Neuchatel cannot possibly be a functioning member of the *Nachrichtendienst*."

"Why not? Von Papen had his enemies in the diplomatic corps. Why couldn't this Gerhardt have been one of them?"

"He may very well have been. But I use the present tense; he is no longer. He's not only senile, he's feebleminded. He's been this way for years; he's a joke in the village where he lives. The old man who mumbles to himself and sings songs and feeds pigeons in the square."

"Senility can be faked," said Tennyson. "And 'feeble' is hardly a pathological term."

"There's proof. He's an outpatient at the local clinic with a bona fide medical record. He has the mentality of a child and is barely able to care for himself."

Tennyson nodded, smiling. "So much for Werner Gerhardt. Speaking of patients, what's the status of the traitor in Stuttgart?"

"Cerebral cancer, final stages. He won't last a week."

"So the *Nachrichtendienst* has but one functioning leader left," said Tennyson. "Klaus Falkenheim."

"It would appear so. However, he may have delegated authority to a younger man. He has soldiers available to him."

"Merely available? From the children he protects? The *Verwünschte Kinder?*"

"Hardly. They're sprinkled with a few idealists, but there's no essential strength in their ranks. Falkenheim has sympathy for them, but he keeps those interests separate from the *Nachrichtendienst*."

"Then where do the *Nachrichtendienst* soldiers come from?"

"They're Jews."

"*Jews!?*"

The Frenchman nodded. "As near as we can determine, they're recruited as they're needed, one assignment at a time. There's no organization, no structured group. Beyond being Jews, they have only one thing in common. Where they come from."

"Which is?"

"The Kibbutz *Har Sha'alav.* In the Negev."

"*Har Sha'alav?* . . . My God, how perfect," said Tennyson with cold, professional respect. "*Har Sha'alav.* The kibbutz in Israel with but one requirement for residency: the applicant had to be the sole survivor of a family destroyed in the camps."

"Right," said the Frenchman. "The kibbutz has over two hundred men – men now – who can be recruited."

Tennyson looked out of the window. "'Kill me, another will take my place. Kill him, another his.' The implication was an unseen army willing to accept a collective death sentence. The commitment's understandable, but this is no army. It's a series of patrols, selected at random." Tennyson turned back to the driver. "Are you sure of your information?"

"Yes. The breakthrough came with the two unknown men killed in Montereau. Our laboratories traced a number of things. Clothing, sediment in shoes and in skin pores, the alloys used in dental work, and especially earlier forensic surgery. Both men had been wounded; one had shell fragments in his shoulder. The Yom Kippur War. We narrowed the evidence to the southwest Negev and found the kibbutz. The rest was simple."

"You sent a man to *Har Sha'alav?*"

The Frenchman nodded again. "One of us. His report is in here. No one talks freely at *Har Sha'alav* but what's going on is clear. Someone sends a cablegram; a few men are chosen and given orders."

"Potential suicide squads committed to the destruction of anything related to the Nazis."

"Exactly. And to confirm our findings, we've established the fact that Falkenheim travelled to Israel three months ago. The computers picked up his name."

"Three months ago . . . At the time Manfredi first reached Holcroft to set up the meeting in Geneva. So Falkenheim not only know about Wolfsschanze, he projected the schedule. He recruited and prepared his army three months in advance. It's time he and I met each other in our proper roles: two sons of the Reich."

"To what should I attribute his death?"

"To the *Odessa*, of course. And call a strike on *Har Sha'alav.* I want every leader killed; prepare it carefully. Blame it on *Rache* terrorists. Let's go."

For the next minutes, he would not be John Tennyson, thought the blond man as he walked down the winding dirt road. Instead, he would be called by his rightful name, Johann von Tiebolt, son of Wilhelm, leader of the new Reich.

The cottage was in sight, the death of a traitor approaching. Von Tiebolt turned and looked back up the hill. The man from the *Sûreté* waved. He would remain there blocking the road until the job was done. Von Tiebolt continued walking until he was within ten yards of the stone path that led to the small house. He stopped, concealed by the foliage, and shifted his gun from the shoulder holster to his overcoat pocket. Crouching, he stepped through the overgrown grass towards the door and beyond it, then stood up, his face at the edge of the single front window.

In spite of the fact that the morning was bright with sunlight, a table lamp was turned on in the dark interior of the room. Beyond the lamp Klaus Falkenheim sat in his wheelchair. The old man's back was to him.

Von Tiebolt walked silently back to the door and considered for a moment whether or not to break it down, as a killer from the *Odessa* undoubtedly would do. He decided against it. *Herr Oberst* was old and decrepit, but he was no fool. Somewhere on his person, or in that wheelchair, was a weapon. At the first sound of a crash it would be levelled at the intruder.

Johann smiled at himself. There was no harm in a little game. One consummate actor on stage with another. Who would be applauded most? The answer was obvious: he who was there for the curtain call. It would not be Klaus Falkenheim.

He rapped on the door. "*Mein Herr*. Forgive me, it's Johann von Tiebolt. I'm afraid my car couldn't negotiate the hill."

At first there was only silence. If it continued beyond five seconds von Tiebolt realized he would have to take sterner measures; there could be no sudden telephone calls. Then he heard the old man's words.

"Von Tiebolt?"

"Yes. Helden's brother. I've come to speak with her. She's not at work so I assume she's here."

"She's not." The old man was silent again.

"Then I shan't disturb you, *Mein Herr*, but if I may, is is possible to use your telephone and call for a taxi?"

"The telephone?"

The blond man smiled. Falkenheim's confusion carried through the barrier between them. "I'll only be a moment. I really must find Helden by noon. I leave for Switzerland at two o'clock."

Again silence, but it was short-lived. He heard a bolt slide back and the door opened. *Herr Oberst* was there in the chair, wheeling backwards, a blanket on his lap. There had been no blanket moments ago.

"*Danke, Mein Herr*," said von Tiebolt, holding out his hand. "It's good to see you again."

Bewildered, the old man raised his hand in greeting. Johann wrapped his fingers swiftly around the bony hand, twisting it to the left. With his free hand, he reached down and yanked the blanket from Falkenheim's lap. He saw what he expected: a Luger across the emaciated legs. He removed it, kicking the door shut as he did.

"*Heil Hitler, General Falkenheim*," he said. "*Wo ist der Nachrichtendienst?*"

The old man remained motionless, staring up at his captor, no fear in his eyes. "I wondered when you would find out. I didn't think it would be so quickly. I commend you, *Sohn des Wilhelm von Tiebolt*."

"Yes, son of Wilhelm and something else as well."

"Oh, yes. The new *Reichführer*. That's your objective, but it won't happen. We'll stop you. If you've come to kill me, do so. I'm prepared."

"Why should I? Such a valuable hostage."

"I doubt you'd get much ransom."

Von Tiebolt spun the old man's chair towards the centre of the room. "I imagine that's true," he replied, abruptly stopping the chair. "I assume you have certain funds available, perhaps solicited by the wandering children you think so much of. However, pfennigs and francs are immaterial to me."

"I was sure of that. So fire the gun."

"*And*," said von Tiebolt, "it's doubtful that a man dying of cerebral cancer in a Stuttgart sanatorium could offer much. Wouldn't you say that, too, is true?"

Falkenheim controlled his surprise. "He was a very brave man," he said.

"I'm sure. You're all brave men. Successful traitors must be imbued with a certain warped courage. Werner Gerhardt, for instance."

"*Gerhardt?* . . ." This time the old man could not conceal his shock. "Where did you hear that name?"

"You wonder how I could know? How I even found out about you, perhaps?"

"Not about me. The risk I took was quite apparent. I arranged for a von Tiebolt to be near me. I considered that risk necessary."

"Yes, the beautiful Helden. But then, I'm told we're all beautiful. It has its advantages."

"She's no part of you; she never was."

"She's part of your wandering garbage. *Verwünschte Kinder*. A weak whore. She whores now with the American."

"Your judgements don't interest me. How did you find out about Gerhardt?"

"Why should I tell you?"

"I'm going to die. What difference does it make?"

"I'll strike a bargain. Where did you learn of Wolfsschanze?"

"Agreed. Gerhardt first."

"Why not. He's of no value. A senile, feeble-minded old man."

"Don't harm him!" shouted Falkenheim suddenly. "He's been through so much . . . so much *pain*."

"Your concern is touching."

"They broke him. Four months of torture; his mind snapped. Leave him in peace."

"Who broke him? The Allies? The British?"

"*Odessa.*"

"For once they served a useful purpose."

"Where did you hear his name? How did you find him?"

Von Tiebolt smiled. "The British. They have a file on the *Nachrichtendienst*. You see, they're very interested in the *Nachrichtendienst* right now. Their objective is to find you and destroy you."

"Destroy? There's no *reason* . . ."

"Oh, but there is. They have proof you hired the Tinamou."

"The Tinamou? Absurd!"

"Not at all. It was your final vengeance, the revenge of tired old men against their enemies. Take my word for it, the proof is irrefutable. I gave it to them."

The old man looked at Johann, his expression filled with revulsion. "You're obscene."

"About Wolfsschanze!" Von Tiebolt raised his voice. "Where? How? I'll know if you lie."

Falkenheim sank back in the wheelchair. "It doesn't matter now. For either of us. I'll die and you'll be stopped."

"Now it is I who am not interested in *your* judgements. Wolfsschanze!"

Falkenheim glanced up listlessly. "Althene Clausen," he said quietly. "Heinrich Clausen's nearly perfect strategy."

Von Tiebolt's face was frozen in astonishment. "Clausen's wife? . . ." He trailed off the words. "You found out about her?"

The old man turned back to Johann. "It wasn't difficult; we had informers everywhere. In New York as well as Berlin. We knew who Mrs Richard Holcroft was, and because we knew we sent out orders to protect her; that was the irony. To *protect* her. Then word came: at the height of the war, while her American husband was at sea, she flies in a private plane to Mexico. From Mexico she goes secretly on to Buenos Aires where the German Embassy takes over and she's flown under diplomatic cover to Lisbon. To *Lisbon*. Why?"

"Berlin gave you the answer?" asked von Tiebolt.

"Yes. Our people in the *Finanzministerium*. We'd learned that extraordinary sums of money were being siphoned out of Germany; it was in our interests not to interfere. Whatever helped cripple the Nazi machine, we sanctioned; peace and sanity would return sooner. But five days after Mrs Holcroft left New York for Lisbon, by way of Mexico and Buenos Aires, Heinrich Clausen, the genius of the *Finanzministerium*, flew covertly out of Berlin. He stopped first in Geneva to meet a banker named Manfredi, then he too went on to Lisbon. We knew he was no defector; above all men, he was a true believer in German – Aryan – supremacy. So much so that he couldn't stomach the flaws in Hitler's ranks of gangsters." *Herr Oberst* paused. "We made the simple addition. Clausen and his supposedly treasonous former wife in Lisbon together; millions upon millions banked in Switzerland . . . and the defeat of Germany now assured. We looked for the deeper meaning and found it in Geneva."

"You read the documents?"

"We read everything in the Grande Banque de Genève. The price was five hundred thousand Swiss francs."

"To Manfredi?"

"Naturally. He knew who we were; he thought we'd believe – and honour – the objectives espoused in those papers. We let him think so. Wolfsschanze! *Whose* Wolfsschanze? 'Amends must be made.'" Falkenheim spoke the words scathingly. "The furthest thought in any of their minds. That money was to be used to revive the Reich."

"What did you do then?"

The old soldier looked directly at von Tiebolt. "Returned to Berlin and executed your father, Kessler, and Heinrich Clausen. They never intended to take their own lives; they expected to find sanctuary in South America, oversee their plan, watch it come to fruition. We gave them their pact with death that Clausen wrote so movingly about to his son."

Von Tiebolt fingered the Luger in his hand. "So you learned the secret of Althene Clausen?"

"You spoke of whores. She's the whore of the world."

"I'm surprised you let her live."

"A second irony: we had no choice. With Clausen gone we realized she was the key to Wolfsschanze. *Your* Wolfsschanze. We knew that she and Clausen had refined every move that was to be made during the coming years. We had to learn; she'd never tell us, so we had to watch. When were the millions to be taken from Geneva? How specifically were they to be used? And by whom?"

"The *Sonnenkinder*," said von Tiebolt.

The old man's eyes were blank. "What did you say?"

"Never mind. So it was a question of waiting for Althene Clausen to make her move, whatever it might be?"

"Yes, but we learned nothing from her. Ever. As the years went by, we realized she had absorbed her husband's genius. In thirty years she never once betrayed the cause by word or action. One had to admire the sheer discipline. Our first signal came when Manfredi made contact with the son." Falkenheim winced. "The despicable thing is that she consented to the rape of her own child. Holcroft knows nothing."

The blond man laughed. "You're so out of touch. The renowned *Nachricht-endienst* is a collection of fools."

"You think so?"

"I *know* so. You watched the wrong horse in the wrong stable!"

"What?"

"For thirty years your eyes were focused on the one person who knew absolutely *nothing*. The whore of the world, as you call her, is secure in the knowledge that she and her son are truly part of a great apology. She's never thought otherwise!" Von Tiebolt's laughter echoed off the walls of the room. "That trip to Lisbon," he continued, "was Heinrich Clausen's most brilliant manipulation. The contrite sinner turned holy man with a holy cause. It must have been the performance of his life. Even down to his final instructions that she was not to give her instant approval. The son was to see for himself the justness of his martyred father's cause. And being convinced become committed beyond anything in his life." Von Tiebolt leaned against the table, his arms folded, the Luger in his hand. "Don't you see? None of *us* could *do* it. The document in Geneva was utterly correct about that. The fortunes stolen by the Third Reich are legendary. There could not be a single connection between that account in Geneva and a true son of Germany."

Falkenheim stared at Johann. "She never *knew?* . . ."

"Never! She was the ideal puppet. Even psychologically. The fact that Heinrich Clausen was revealed to be that holy man reaffirmed her confidence in her own judgements. She had married *that* man, not the Nazi."

"Incredible," whispered *Herr Oberst.*

"At least that," agreed von Tiebolt. "She followed his instructions to the letter. Every contingency was considered, including a death certificate of an infant male in a London hospital. All traces to Clausen were obliterated." The blond man laughed again, the sound unnerving. "So you see, you're no match for Wolfsschanze."

"Your Wolfsschanze, not mine." Falkenheim glanced away. "You are to be commended."

Suddenly von Tiebolt stopped laughing. Something was wrong. It was in the old man's eyes – flashed briefly, clouded, deep within that emaciated skull. "Look at me!" he shouted. "*Look* at me!"

Falkenheim turned. "What is it?"

"I said something just now . . . something you knew about. You *knew.*"

"What are you talking about?"

Von Tiebolt grabbed the old man by the throat. "I spoke of contingencies, of a death certificate! In a London hospital! You've heard it *before!*"

"I don't know what you mean." Falkenheim's trembling fingers were wrapped around the blond man's wrists, his voice rasping under the pressure of Johann's grip.

"I think you *do*. Everything I've just told you shocked you. Or did it? You pretended shock, but you're *not* shocked. The hospital. The death certificate. You didn't react at all! You've heard it *before.*"

"I've heard nothing," gasped Falkenheim.

"Don't lie to me!" Von Tiebolt whipped the Luger across *Herr Oberst's* face, lacerating the cheek. "You're not that good any more. You're too *old*. You have lapses! Your brain is atrophied. You pause at the wrong instant, *Herr General.*"

"You're a maniac . . ."

You're a liar! A *poor* liar at that. Traitor." Again he struck *Herr Oberst* in the face with the barrel of the weapon. Blood poured from the open wounds. "You lied about her! . . . My God, you *knew!*"

"Nothing . . . *nothing.*"

"Yes! *Everything!* That's why she's flying to Geneva. I asked myself. *Why?*" Von Tiebolt struck furiously again; the old man's lip was torn half off his face. "You! In your last desperate attempt to stop us, you reached her! You threatened her . . . and in those threats you told her what she never *knew!*"

"You're wrong. *Wrong.*"

"No," said von Tiebolt, suddenly lowering his voice. "There's no other reason for her to fly to Geneva . . . So that's how you think you'll stop us. The mother reaches the child and tells him to turn back. Her covenant is a *lie.*"

Falkenheim shook his bloodied head. "No . . . Nothing you say is true."

"It's all true and it answers a last question. If you so dearly wanted to destroy Geneva, all you had to do was let the word get out. Nazi treasure. Claims would be made against it from the Black Sea to the northern Elbe, from Moscow to Paris. But you don't do that. Again, *why?*" Von Tiebolt bent over further, inches from the battered face beneath him. "You think you can control Geneva, use the millions as *you* want them used. 'Amends must be made.' Holcroft learns the truth and becomes *your* soldier, his anger complete, his commitment tripled."

"He *will* find out," whispered Falkenheim. "He's better than you; we've both learned that, haven't we? You should find satisfaction in that. After all, in his own way he's a *Sonnenkind*"

"*Sonnen* . . ." Von Tiebolt swung the barrel of his pistol again across *Herr Oberst's* face. "You're filled with lies. I said the name; you showed nothing."

"Why should I lie now? *Operation Sonnenkinder,*" said Falkenheim, speaking German. "By ship, and plane, and submarine. Everywhere the children. We never got the lists, but we don't need them. They'll be stopped when you're stopped. When Geneva's stopped."

"For that to happen, Althene Clausen must reach her son. She won't expose Geneva for what it is, she's tried everything else. To do so would destroy her son, let the world know who he is. She'll do anything before she lets that happen. She'll try to reach him quietly. We'll stop her."

"*You'll* be stopped!" said Falkenheim, choking on the blood that flowed over his lips. "There'll be no vast sums dispensed to your *Sonnenkinder*. We, too, have an army, one you'll never know about. Each man will gladly give his life to stop you, expose you."

"Of course, *Herr General*." The blond man nodded. "The Jews of *Har Sha'alav.*"

The words were spoken softly, but they had the effect of a lash on the old man's wounds. "*No! . . .*"

"Yes," said von Tiebolt. "'Kill me, another will take my place. Kill him, another his.' The Jews of *Har Sha'alav.* Initiated into the *Nachrichtendienst* so thoroughly that they *became* the *Nachrichtendienst*. The living remains of Auschwitz."

"You're an *animal* . . ." Falkenheim's body trembled in a spasm of pain.

"I am Wolfsschanze, the true Wolfsschanze," said the blond man, raising the Luger. "Until you knew the truth, the Jews tried to kill the American, and now the Jews will die. Within the week *Har Sha'alav* will be destroyed, and with it the *Nachrichtendienst*. Wolfsschanze will triumph."

Von Tiebolt held the gun in front of the old man's head. He fired.

35

Tears streaked down Helden's cheeks. She cradled the body of Klaus Falkenheim, but could not bring herself to look at the head. Finally, she let go of the corpse and crawled away, filled with horror . . . and guilt. She lay curled up on the floor, her sobbing uncontrollable. In pain, she pushed herself to the wall, her forehead pressed against the moulding, and let the tears pour out. Gradually it became clear to her that her screams and sobs had not been heard. She had walked alone into the carnage, and had found signs of the hated *Odessa* everywhere. Swastikas scratched into wood, scrawled with soap on the window, painted with Falkenheim's blood on the floor. Beyond the despicable symbols, the room had been torn apart. Books ripped, shelves broken, furniture slashed; the house had been searched by maniacs. There was nothing left but ruins.

Yet there was something . . . not in the house. Outside. In the forest. Helden pressed her hands on the floor and raised herself against the wall, trying desperately to remember the words spoken by *Herr Oberst* only five mornings ago.

If anything should happen to me, you must not panic. Go alone into the woods where you took me for my brief walk the other day. Do you remember? I asked you to pick a cluster of wild flowers, as I remained by a tree. I pointed out to you that there was a perfect V formed by the limbs. Go to that tree. Wedged into the branches is a small canister. Inside, there is a message to be read only by you. .

Helden prised the small tubular receptacle from its recess and tore open the rubber top. Inside there was a rolled-up piece of paper; attached to it several bills, each worth 10,000 francs. She removed the money and read:

My dearest Helden –
  Time and danger to your person will not permit me to write here what you must know. Three months ago I arranged for you to come to me because I believed you were an arm of an enemy I have waited thirty years to confront. I have come to know you – and to love you – and with great relief to understand that you are not part of the horror that might once again be visited upon the world.
  Should I be killed, it will mean I have been found out. Further, it will signify that the time is near for the catastrophes to begin. Orders must be relayed to those courageous men who will stand at the final barricade.
  You must go alone – I repeat, alone – to Lake Neuchatel in Switzerland. Don't let anyone follow you. I know you can do this, you have been taught. In the village of Près-du-Lac there is a man named Werner Gerhardt. Find him. Give him the following

message: "The coin of Wolfsschanze has two sides." He will know what to do.

You must go quickly. There is very little time. Again, say nothing to anyone. Raise no alarms. Tell your employers and your friends that you have personal matters in England, a logical statement considering the fact that you lived there over five years.

Quickly now, my dearest Helden. To Neuchatel. To Près-du-Lac. To Werner Gerhardt. Memorize the name and burn this paper.

Godspeed,
Herr Oberst

Helden leaned against the tree and looked up at the sky. Wisps of thin clouds moved swiftly in an easterly course; the winds were strong. She wished she could be carried by them, and not have to run from point to point, every move a risk, every person she looked at a potential enemy.

Noel had said that it would all be over soon and she would be able to stop running.

He was wrong.

Holcroft pleaded over the telephone, trying to convince her not to go – at least for another day – but Helden would not be dissuaded. Word had reached her through Gallimard that her sister's personal effects were awaiting her inspection; decisions had to be considered, arrangements made.

"I'll call you in Geneva, my darling. You'll be staying at the D'Accord?"

"Yes." What was wrong with her? She'd been so happy, so elated barely two hours ago. She sounded tense now; her words were facile but her voice was strained.

"I'll phone you in a day or so. Under the name of Fresca."

"Do you want me to go with you? I don't have to be in Geneva until late tomorrow night. The Kesslers won't get there till ten, your brother even later."

"No, darling. It's a sad trip. I'd rather make it alone. Johann's in London now . . . I'll try to reach him."

"You've got some clothes here."

"A dress, a pair of slacks, shoes. It's quicker for me to stop at . . . *Herr Oberst's* . . . and pick up others more appropriate for Portsmouth."

"Quicker?"

"On the way to the airport. I have to go there at any rate. My passport, money."

"I have money . . ." interrupted Noel. "I thought you'd been to his place by now."

"*Please*, darling. Don't be difficult." Helden's voice cracked. "I told you, I stopped at the office."

"No, you didn't. You didn't say that. You said you got word." Holcroft was alarmed; she wasn't making sense. *Herr Oberst's* hidden cottage was *not* on the way to Orly. "Helden, what's the matter?"

"I love you, Noel. I'll call you tomorrow night. Hotel D'Accord, Geneva."
She hung up.

Holcroft replaced the phone, the sound of her echoing voice in his ears. It was possible she was going to London, but he doubted it. Where *was* she going? Why did she lie? Goddamn it! What was *wrong* with her? What had *happened*?

There was no point in staying in Paris. Since he had to reach Geneva on his own, he might as well get started.

He could not chance the airlines or the trains. Unseen men would be watching; he had to elude them. The assistant manager of the Georges Cinq could hire him a car under the name of Fresca. The route would be mapped for him. He would drive through the night to Geneva.

Althene Holcroft looked out the window of the TAP airliner at the lights of Lisbon below; they would be on the ground in minutes. She had a great deal to accomplish during the next twelve hours and she hoped to God she was capable of doing it. A man had followed her in Mexico, she knew that. But then he had disappeared at the airport, which meant that another had taken his place.

She had failed in Mexico. She had not dropped out of sight. Once in Lisbon, she would have to vanish; she could not fail again.

Lisbon.

Oh, *God*, Lisbon!

It had been in Lisbon where it had all begun. The lie of a lifetime, conceived in diabolical brilliance. What an imbecile she had been; what a performance Heinrich had given.

She had loved him again – during those brief few days in Lisbon – and in a rush of emotion had offered herself to him.

With tears in his eyes, he had refused. He was not worthy, he said.

It was the consummate deception! The ultimate irony!

For now, at this moment, the very threat that brought her to Lisbon thirty years ago was the threat that brought her here again. Noel *Holcroft* would be destroyed; he would become Noel *Clausen*, son of Heinrich, "instrument" of the new Reich.

A man had come to her in the middle of the night in Bedford Hills. A man who had gained entrance by invoking the name "Manfredi" behind the closed door; she had admitted him thinking her son perhaps had sent him. He had said that he was a Jew from a place called *Har Sha'alav* and that he was going to kill her. And then he would kill her son. There'd be no spectre of Wolfsschanze – the *false* Wolfsschanze – spreading from Zürich out of Geneva."

Althene had been furious. Did the man know to whom he was speaking? What she had *done*? What she *stood for*?

The man knew only about Geneva and Zurich . . . and Lisbon thirty years ago. It was all he had to know, to know what she stood for, and that stance

301

was an abomination to him and all men like him over the world.

Althene had seen the pain and anger in the dark eyes that held her at bay as surely as if a weapon had been levelled at her. In desperation, she had demanded that he tell her what he thought he knew.

He had told her that extraordinary sums were to be funnelled to committees and causes throughout all nations. To men and women who had been waiting for thirty years for the signal.

There would be killing and disruption and conflagrations in the streets; governments would be bewildered, their agencies internally crippled. Strong men and women with massive sums at their disposal would then assert themselves. Within months control would be theirs.

They were everywhere. In all countries, awaiting only the signal from Geneva.

Who were they?

The *Sonnenkinder*. The children of fanatics, sent out of Germany over thirty years ago by plane and ship and submarine. Sent out by men who knew their cause was lost – but believed that cause could live again.

They were everywhere. They could not be fought by ordinary men in ordinary ways through ordinary channels of authority. In too many instances the *Sonnenkinder* controlled those channels. But the Jews of *Har Sha'alav* were not ordinary men, nor did they fight in ordinary ways. They understood that to stop the false Wolfsschanze, they had to fight secretly, violently, never allowing the *Sonnenkinder* to know where they were – or where they would strike next. And the first order of business was to stop the massive infusion of funds.

Expose them now!

Who? Where? What are their identities? How will proof be furnished? Who can say this general or that admiral, this chief of police or that corporation president, this justice or that senator is a *Sonnenkind*?

They are everywhere. The Nazi is among us and we don't see him. He is cloaked in respectability and a pressed suit of clothes.

The Jew of *Har Sha'alav* had spoken passionately. "Even you, old woman. You and your son, instruments of the new Reich. Even you do not know who they are."

I know nothing. I swear on my life I know nothing. I'm not what you think I am. Kill me. For God's sake, kill me. Now! Take your vengeance out on me. You deserve that and so do I if what you say is true. But I implore you, reach my son. Take him. Explain to him. Stop him! Don't kill him, don't brand him. He's not what you think he is. Give him his life. Take mine, but give him his!

The Jew of *Har Sha'alav* had spoken. "Richard Holcroft was killed. It was no accident."

She had nearly collapsed, but she would not allow herself to fall. She could not permit the momentary oblivion that would have been so welcome.

302

Oh, my God . . .

"Wolfsschanze killed him. The false Wolfsschanze. As surely as if they had marched him in to a chamber at Auschwitz."

What is Wolfsschanze? Why do you call it false?

"Learn for yourself. We'll talk again. If you've lied, we'll kill you. Your son will live – for as long as the world lets him – but he will live with a swastika across his face."

Reach him. Tell him.

The man from *Har Sha'alav* left. Althene sat in a chair by the window, staring out at the snow-covered grounds throughout the night. Her beloved Richard, the husband who had given her and her son their lives again . . . what had she done?

But she knew what to do now.

The plan touched ground, the impact pushing Althene's reveries out of her mind, bringing her back to the moment at hand. To Lisbon.

She stood at the railing of the ferry, the waters of the Tagus River slapping against the hull as the old ship made its way across the bay. In her left hand was a lace handkerchief, fluttering in the wind.

She thought she saw him, but as instructed made no move until he approached her. She had never seen him before, of course, but that was not necessary. He was an old man in rumpled clothes, with heavy grey sideburns that met the stubble of a white beard. His eyes searched the passengers as if he were afraid one of them might yell for the police. He was the man; he stood behind her.

"The river looks cold today," he said.

The lace handkerchief flew away in the wind. "Oh, dear, I've lost it." Althene watched it plummet into the water.

"You've found it," said the man.

"Thank you."

"Please don't look at me. Look at the skyline across the lagoon."

"Very well."

"You spread money too generously, *Senhora*," the man said.

"I'm in a great hurry."

"You bring up names so long in the past there are no faces. Requests that have not been made in years."

"I can't believe times have changed that much."

"Oh, but they have, *Senhora*. Men and women still travel secretly, but not with such simple devices as doctored passports. It's the age of the computer. False papers are not what they once were. We go back to the war. To the escape routes."

"I have to get to Geneva as quickly as possible. No one must know I'm there."

"You'll get to Geneva, *Senhora*, and only those you inform will know you're there. But it will not be as quickly as you wish; it will not be a matter of a single flight on an airline."

"How long?"

"Two or three days. Otherwise there are no guarantees. You'll be picked up, either by the authorities or by those you care to avoid."

"How do I get there?"

"Across borders that are unpatrolled, or where the guards can be bribed. The northern route. Sierra de Gata across to Zaragoza on to the eastern Pyrenees. From there to Montpellier and Avignon. At Avignon a small plane will take you to Grenoble, another to Chambery and to Genève. It will cost."

"I can pay. When do we start?"

"Tonight."

36

The blond man signed the Hôtel D'Accord registration card and handed it to the desk clerk.

"Thank you, Mr Tennyson. You'll be staying fourteen days?"

"Perhaps longer, certainly no less. I appreciate your making a suite available."

The clerk smiled. "We received a call from your friend, the First Deputy of Canton Genève. We assured him we would do everything to make your stay pleasant."

"I'll inform him of my complete satisfaction."

"You're most kind."

"Incidentally, I'm expecting to meet an old friend here during the next few days. A Mrs Holcroft. Could you tell me when she's expected?"

The clerk took up a ledger and thumbed through the pages. "Did you say the name was Holcroft?"

"Yes. Althene Holcroft. An American. You might also have a reservation for her son. Mr N. Holcroft."

"I'm afraid we have no reservations in that name, sir. And I know there's no one named Holcroft presently a guest."

The muscles of the blond man's jaw tensed. "Surely an error has been made. My information's accurate. She's expected in Geneva, at this hotel. Perhaps not this evening, but certainly tomorrow or the day after. Please check again. Is there a confidential listing?"

"No, sir."

"If there were, I'm quite certain my friend, the First Deputy, would ask you to let me see it."

"If there were, that wouldn't be necessary, Mr Tennyson. We understood fully that we're to co-operate with you in all requests."

"Perhaps she's travelling incognito. She's been known to be eccentric that way."

The clerk turned the ledger around. "Please, look for yourself, sir. It's possible you'll recognize a name."

Tennyson did not. It was infuriating. "This is the complete list?" he asked again.

"Yes, sir. We're a small, and if I may say so, rather exclusive hotel. Most of our guests have been here previously. I'm familiar with nearly every one of those names."

"Which ones aren't you familiar with?" pressed the blond man.

The clerk placed his finger on two. "These are the only names I don't know," he said. "The gentlemen from Germany, two brothers named Kessler, and a Sir William Ellis from London. The last was made only hours ago."

Tennyson looked pointedly at the desk clerk. "I'm going to my rooms, but I need to ask you for an example of that co-operation the First Deputy spoke of. It's most urgent that I find out where Mrs Holcroft is staying in Geneva. I'd appreciate your calling the various hotels, but under no circumstances should my name be mentioned." He took out a 100-franc note. "Find her for me," he said.

By midnight Noel reached Châtillon-sur-Seine, where he made the phone call to an astonished Ellis in London.

"You'll do *what?*" Ellis said.

"You heard me, Willie. I'll pay you five hundred dollars and your expenses for one, maybe two days in Geneva. All I want you to do is take my mother back to London."

"I'm a dreadful nanny. And from what you've told me about your mother, she's the last person in the world who needs a travelling companion."

"She does now. Someone was following her. I'll tell you about it when I see you in Geneva. How about it, Willie? Will you do it?"

"Of course. But stuff your five hundred. I'm sure your mother and I'll have far more in common than we ever did. You may, however, pick up the tabs. I travel well, as you know."

"While we're on the subject, travel with a little cool, will you, please? I want you to call the Hotel D'Accord in Geneva and make a reservation for late this morning. The first plane should get you there by nine-thirty."

"I'll be on my best behaviour, befitting Louis Vuitton luggage. Perhaps a minor title . . ."

"*Willie.*"

"I know the Swiss better than you. They adore titles; they reek of money and money's their mistress."

"I'll phone you around ten, ten-thirty. I want to use your room until I know what's going on."

"That's extra," said Willie Ellis. "See you in Geneva."

Holcroft had decided to call on Willie because there was no one else he could think of who would not ask questions. Ellis was not the outrageous fool he pretended to be. Althene could do far worse for an escort out of Switzerland.

And she had to get out. The covenant's enemy had killed her husband; it would kill her, too. Because Geneva was where it was going to happen. In two or three days a meeting would take place, and papers signed, and money transferred to Zurich. The covenant's enemy would try everything to abort those negotiations. His mother could not stay in Geneva. There would be violence in Geneva; he could feel it.

He drove south to Dijon, arriving well after midnight. The small city was asleep and as he passed through the dark streets he knew he needed sleep, too; tomorrow he had to be alert. More alert than he had ever been in his life. He continued driving until he was back in the countryside and stopped the rented car on the side of a road. He smoked a cigarette, then crushed it out and put his feet on the seat, his head against the window, cushioned by his raincoat.

In a few hours he'd be at the border, crossing into Switzerland with the first wave of morning traffic. Once in Switzerland . . . He couldn't think any more. The mist was closing in on him, his breathing low and heavy. And then the face appeared, strong, angular, so unfamiliar yet so recognizable to him now.

It was the face of Heinrich Clausen and he was calling to him, telling him to hurry. The agony would be over soon, amends would be made.

He slept.

Erich Kessler watched as his younger brother, Hans, showed the airline security officer his medical bag. Since the Olympics of '72, when the Palestinians were presumed to have flown in with dismantled rifles and submachine guns, the airport's security measures had tripled.

It was a wasted effort, mused Erich. The Palestinians' weapons had been brought to Munich by Wolfsschanze – *their* Wolfsschanze.

Hans laughed with the airline official, sharing a joke. But, thought Erich, there would be no such jokes in Geneva, for there would be no inspection by the airlines or customs or anyone else. The First Deputy of Canton Genève would see to it. One of Munich's most highly regarded doctors, a specialist in internal medicine, was arriving as his guest.

Hans was all that and more, thought Erich, as his brother approached him at the gate. Hans was a medium-sized bull with maximum charm. A superb soccer player who captained his district team and later ministered to the opponents he had injured.

It was odd, but Hans was far better equipped that he to be the elder son. Save for the accident of time and chromosomes, it would be Hans who worked with Johann von Tiebolt, and he, the quiet scholar, the subordinate. Once, in a moment of self-doubt, he had said as much to Johann.

Von Tiebolt would not hear of it. A pure intellectual was demanded. A man who lived a bloodless life – someone never swayed by reasons of the heart or intemperate anger. Had that not been proved by those infrequent but vital moments when he – the quiet scholar – had stood up to the Tinamou and stated his reservations? Reservations that resulted in a change of strategy?

Yes, it was true, but it was not the essential truth. That truth was something Johann did not care to face: Hans was nearly von Tiebolt's equal. If they clashed, Johann might die.

That was the opinion of the quiet, bloodless intellectual.

"Everything proceeds," said Hans, as they walked through the gate on to the plane. "The American's as good as dead, and no laboratory will trace the cause."

Helden got off the train at Neuchâtel. She stood on the platform, adjusting her eyes to the shafts of sunlight that shot down from the roof of the railroad station. She knew she should mingle with the crowds that scrambled off the train, but for a moment she had to stand still and breathe the air. She had spent the past three hours in the darkness of a freight car, crouched behind crates of machinery. A door had been opened electronically for precisely sixty seconds at Besançon and she had gone inside. At exactly five minutes to noon the door was opened again; she had reached Neuchâtel unseen. Her legs ached and her head pounded, but she had made it. It had cost a great deal of money.

The air filled her lungs. She picked up her suitcase and started for the doors of the Neuchâtel station. The village of Près-du-Lac was on the west side of the lake, no more than twenty miles south. She found a taxi willing to make the trip.

The ride was jarring and filled with turns but it was like a calm, floating glide for her. She looked out of the window at the rolling hills and the blue waters of the lake. The diverse scenery had the effect of suspending everything. It gave her the precious moments she needed to try to understand. What had *Herr Oberst* meant when he wrote that he had arranged for her to be near him because he had believed she was "an arm of an enemy'? An enemy he had "waited thirty years to confront'. What enemy was that? And why herself?

What had she done? Or not done? Was it again the terrible dilemma? Damned for what she was and damned for what she wasn't. When in God's name would it *stop*?

Herr Oberst knew he was going to die. He had prepared her for his death as surely as if he had announced it, making sure she had the money to buy a secret passage to Switzerland, to a man named Werner Gerhardt in Neuchâtel. Who was he? What was he to Klaus Falkenheim, that he was to be contacted only in death?

The coin of Wolfsschanze has two sides.

Whatever the words meant, they had a special meaning for that man.

The taxi driver interrupted her thoughts. "The inn's down by the shoreline," he said. "It's not much of a hotel."

"It will do, I'm sure."

The room overlooked the waters of Lake Neuchâtel. It was so peaceful that Helden was tempted to sit at the window and do nothing but think about Noel, because when she thought about him she felt . . . comfortable. But there was a Werner Gerhardt to find. The telephone directory of Près-du-Lac had no such listing; God knew when it was last updated. But it was not a large village; she would begin casually with the concierge. Perhaps the name was familiar to him.

It was, but not in a way that gave her any confidence.

"Mad Gerhardt?" said the obese man, sitting in a wicker chair behind the counter. "You bring him greetings from old friends? You should bring him instead a potion to unscramble his doddering brains. He won't understand a thing you say."

"I didn't know," replied Helden, overwhelmed by a feeling of despair.

"See for yourself. It's mid-afternoon and the day is cool, but the sun is out. He'll no doubt be in the square singing his little songs and feeding the pigeons. They soil his clothes and he doesn't notice."

She saw him sitting on the stone ledge of the circular fountain in the village square. He was oblivious to the passers-by who intermittently glanced down at him, more often in revulsion than in tolerance. His clothes were frayed, the tattered overcoat soiled with droppings as the concierge had predicted. He was as old and as sickly as *Herr Oberst*, but much shorter and puffier in face and body. His skin was pallid and drawn, marred by spider veins, and he wore thick, steel-rimmed glasses that moved from side to side in rhythm with his trembling head. His hand shook as he reached into a paper bag, taking out breadcrumbs and scattering them, attracting scores of pigeons that cooed in counterpoint to the high-pitched, singsong words that came from the old man's lips.

Helden felt sick. He was only a remnant of a man. He was beyond senility; no other state could produce what she saw before her on the fountain's edge.

The coin of Wolfsschanze has two sides. The time is near for the catastrophe to begin . . . . It seemed pointless to repeat the words. Still, she'd come this far, knowing only that a great man had been butchered because his warning was real.

She approached the old man and sat beside him, aware that several people in the square looked at her as if she, too, were feeble-minded. She spoke quietly in German.

"Herr Gerhardt? I've travelled a long way to see you."

"Such a pretty lady . . . a pretty, pretty lady."

"I come from Herr Falkenheim. Do you remember him?"

"A falcon's home? Falcons don't like my pigeons. They hurt my pigeons. My friends and I don't like them, do we, sweet feathers?"

"You'd like this man, if you remembered him," said Helden.

"How can I like what I don't know? Would *you* like some bread? You can eat it, if you wish, but my friends might be hurt." The old man sat up with difficulty and dropped crumbs at Helden's feet.

"'The coin of Wolfsschanze has two sides,'" whispered Helden.

And then she heard the words. There was no break in the rhythm; the quiet, high-pitched singsong was the same, but there was meaning now. "He's dead, isn't he – don't answer me, just nod your head or shake it. You're talking to a foolish old man who makes very little sense. Remember that."

Helden was too stunned to move. And by her immobility, she gave the old man his answer. He continued in his singsong cadence. "Klaus is dead. So, finally, they found him and killed him."

"It was the *Odessa*," she said. "The *Odessa* killed him. There were swastikas everywhere."

"Wolfsschanze wanted us to believe that." Gerhardt threw crumbs in the air; the pigeons fought among themselves. "Here, sweet feathers! It's tea time for you." He turned to Helden, his eyes distant. "The *Odessa*, as always, is the scapegoat. Such an obvious one."

"You say Wolfsschanze," whispered Helden. "A letter was given to a man named Holcroft, threatening him. It was written thirty years ago, signed by men who called themselves the survivors of Wolfsschanze."

For an instant, Gerhardt's trembling stopped. "There were no survivors of Wolfsschanze, save one! Klaus Falkenheim. Others were there, and they lived, but they were not the eagles, they were filth. And now they think their time has come."

"I don't understand."

"I'll explain it to you, but not here. After dark, come to my house on the lake. South on the waterfront road, precisely three kilometres beyond the fork, is a path. . .' He gave her the directions as though they were words written to accompany a childish tune. When he had finished, he stood up painfully, tossing the last crumbs to the birds. "I don't think you'll be followed," he said with a senile smile, "but make sure of it. We have work to do, and it must be done quickly . . . Here, my sweet feathers! The last of your meal, my fluttering ones."

37

A small, single-engine plane circled in the night sky above the flat pasture in Chambéry. Its pilot waited for the dual line of flares to be ignited; his signal to land. On the ground was another aircraft, a seaplane with wheels encased in its pontoons, prepared for departure. It would be airborne minutes after the first plane came to the end of the primitive runway and would carry its valuable cargo north along the eastern leg of the Rhone River, crossing the Swiss border at Versoix, and landing on Lake Geneva twelve miles north of the city. The cargo had no name but that did not matter to the pilots. She paid as well as the highest-priced narcotics courier.

Only once had she shown any emotion and that was four minutes out of Avignon towards Saint Vallier when the small plane had run into an unexpected and dangerous hailstorm.

"The weather may be too much for this light aircraft," the pilot said. "It would be wiser to turn back."

"Fly above it."

"We haven't the power and we have no idea how extensive the front is."

"Then go through it. I'm paying for a schedule as well as transportation. I must get to Geneva tonight."

"If we're forced down on the river, we could be picked up by the patrols. We have no flight registration."

"If we're forced down on the river, I'll buy the patrols. They were bought at the border in Port-Bou; they can be bought again. Keep going."

"And if we crash, Madame?"

"Don't."

Below them in the darkness, the Chambéry flares were ignited successively, one row at a time. The pilot dipped his wing to the left and circled downwards for his final approach. Seconds later they touched ground.

"You're good," said the valuable cargo, reaching for the buckle of her seatbelt. "Is my next pilot your equal?"

"As good, Madame, and with an advantage I don't have. He knows the radar points within a tenth of an air mile in the darkness. One pays for such expertise."

"Gladly," replied Althene.

The seaplane lifted off against the night wind at exactly 10.57. The flight across the border at Versoix would be made at very low altitude and take very little time, no more than twenty minutes to half an hour. It was the specialist's leg of the journey, and the specialist in the cockpit was a stocky man with a red beard and thinning red hair. He chewed a half-smoked cigar between his teeth and spoke English in the harsh accent associated with Alsace-Lorraine. He said nothing for the first few minutes of the flight, but when he spoke Althene was stunned.

"I don't know what the merchandise is that you carry, Madame, but there is an alert for your whereabouts throughout Europe."

"*What?* Who put out this alert, and how would you know? My name hasn't been mentioned, I was guaranteed that!"

"An all-Europe bulletin circulated by Interpol is most descriptive. It's rare that the international police look for a woman of – shall we say – your age and appearance. I presume your name is Holcroft."

"Presume nothing." Althene gripped her seatbelt, trying to control her reaction. She did not know why it startled her – the Jew of *Har Sha'alav* had said they were everywhere – but the fact that this Wolfsschanze had sufficient influence with Interpol to use its apparatus was unnerving. She not only had to elude the Nazis of Wolfsschanze but also the network of legitimate law enforcement. It was a well-executed trap; her crimes were undeniable: travelling under a false passport and then with none. And she could give no explanation for those crimes. To do so would link her son – the son of Heinrich Clausen – to a conspiracy so massive he'd be destroyed. That extremity had to be faced; her son might have to be sacrificed. But the irony was found in the very real possibility that Wolfsschanze itself was deep within the legitimate authorities . . . *they were everywhere.* Once taken, Wolfsschanze would kill her before she could say what she knew.

Death was acceptable, stilling her voice was not. She turned to the bearded pilot. "How do you know about this bulletin?"

The man shrugged. "How do I know about the radar vectors? You pay me, I pay others. There's no such thing as a clear profit these days."

"Does the bulletin say why this . . . old woman . . . is wanted?"

"It's a strange alert, Madame. It states clearly that she's travelling with false papers, but she's not to be picked up. Her whereabouts are to be reported to Interpol-Paris, where they will be relayed to New York."

"New York?"

"That's where the request originated. The police in New York, a detective named Miles."

"Miles!" She closed her eyes. "How would you like to make a very clear profit?"

"I'm no Communist; the word doesn't offend me. How?"

"Hide me in Geneva. Help me reach someone."

The pilot checked his panel, then banked to the right. "It will cost you."

"I'll pay," she said.

Johann von Tiebolt paced the hotel suite, a graceful, angry animal consumed. His audience was the brothers Kessler, the First Deputy of Canton Genève having left minutes ago. The three were alone, the tension apparent.

"She's somewhere in Geneva," said von Tiebolt. "She *has* to be."

"Obviously under an assumed name," added Hans Kessler, his medical bag at his feet. "We'll find her. It's merely a question of fanning men out with a description. Our deputy has assured us it's no problem."

Von Tiebolt stopped his pacing. "No problem? I trust you and he have examined this 'no-problem'. According to our deputy, the Geneva police report an Interpol bulletin on her. Quite simply, that means she's travelled a minimum of four thousand miles without being found. Four thousand miles through banks of computers, on aircraft crossing borders and landing with manifests, through at least two immigration points. And there's nothing. Don't fool yourself, Hans. She's better than we thought she was."

"Tomorrow's Friday," said Erich. "Holcroft's due tomorrow, and he'll get in touch with us. When we have him, we have her."

"He said he was staying at the D'Accord but he's changed his mind. There's no reservation, and Mr Fresca has checked out of the Georges Cinq." Von Tiebolt stood by the window. "I don't like it. Something's wrong."

Hans reached for his drink. "I think you're overlooking the obvious."

"What?"

"By Holcroft's lights, a great deal's wrong. He thinks people are after him; he'll be cautious, and he'll travel cautiously. I'd be surprised if he did make a reservation in his own name."

"I assumed the name would be Fresca, or a derivation I'd recognize," said von Tiebolt, dismissing the young Kessler's observation. "There's nothing like it in any hotel in Geneva."

"Is there a Tennyson," asked Erich softly, "or anything like *it?*"

"Helden?" Johann turned.

"Helden." The older Kessler nodded. "She was with him in Paris. It's to be assumed she's helping him; you even suggested it."

Von Tiebolt stood motionless. "Helden and her filthy, wandering outcasts are preoccupied at the moment. They're scouring the *Odessa* for the killers of *Herr Oberst*."

"*Falkenheim?*" Hans sat forward. "Falkenheim's *dead?*"

"Falkenheim was the leader of the *Nachrichtendienst*, the last functioning member, to be precise. With his death Wolfsschanze is unopposed. His army of Jews will be headless, what little they know buried with *their* leaders."

"Jews? With *Nachrichtendienst?*" Erich was exasperated. "What in God's name are you *talking* about?"

"A strike's been called on the kibbutz *Har Sha'alav; Rache* terrorists were held responsible. I'm sure the name *Har Sha'alav* has meaning for you. At the last, the *Nachrichtendienst* turned to the Jews of *Har Sha'alav*. Garbage to garbage."

"I'd like a more specific explanation!" said Erich.

"Later. We must concentrate on the Holcrofts. We must . . ." Von Tiebolt stopped, a thought striking him. "Priorities. Always look to priorities." he added, as if talking to himself. "And the first priority is the document at the

Grande Banque de Genève, which means the son takes precedence. Find *him*, isolate *him*, keep him in absolute quarantine. For our purposes, it need only be for thirty-six hours."

"I don't follow you," interrupted Hans. "What happens in thirty-six hours?"

"The three of us will have met with the bank's directors," Erich said. "Everything will have been signed, executed in the presence of the Grande Banque attorney, all the laws of Switzerland observed. The money will be released to Zurich and we assume control Monday morning."

"But thirty-six hours from Friday morning is . . ."

"Saturday noon," completed von Tiebolt. "We meet with the directors Saturday morning at nine o'clock. There was never any question of our acceptance – except in Holcroft's mind. Manfredi took care of that months ago. We're not only acceptable, we're damn near holy men; my letter from MI5 is merely a final crown. By Saturday noon it will have been accomplished."

"They're so anxious to lose 780 million dollars they'll open the bank on a Saturday?"

The blond man smiled. "I made the request in Holcroft's name, for reasons of speed and confidentiality. The directors didn't object; they look for crumbs. And neither will Holcroft when we tell him. He has his own reasons for wanting everything over with. He's stretched to the limits of his capacities." Von Tiebolt glanced at Erich, his smile broader. "He looks upon us both as friends, as pillars of strength, as two men he desperately needs. The programming has exceeded our hopes."

Kessler nodded. "By noon Saturday he'll have signed the final condition."

"What final condition?" asked Hans, alarmed. "What does that mean? What does he sign?"

"We'll each have signed it," answered von Tiebolt, pausing for emphasis. "It's a *requirement* of Swiss law for the release of such accounts. We've met, and fully understand our responsibilities; we've come to know each other and to trust each other. Therefore, in the event one of us pre-deceases the others, each assigns all rights and privileges to his co-inheritors. Except, of course, the stipend of two million, which is to be distributed to the individual's heirs. That two million – legally assigned and prohibited from being given to the other executors – removes any motive for double-cross."

The younger Kessler whistled softly. "Utterly brilliant. So this final condition – this death clause wherein you each assign to the other your responsibility – never had to be made part of the document . . . because it's the law. If it had been included, Holcroft might have been suspicious from the beginning." The doctor shook his head in respect, his eyes bright. "But it never was, because it's the *law*."

"Precisely. And every legality must be observed. A month – six weeks – from now, it'll be irrelevant, but until we've made substantive progress, there can be no alarms."

"I understand that," said Hans. "But actually, by Saturday noon Holcroft's expendable, isn't he?"

Erich held up his hand. "Best put him under your drugs for a period of time, available for display, as it were. A functioning mental cripple . . . until a great portion of the funds is dispersed. By then it won't matter, the world will be too preoccupied to care about an accident in Zurich. Right now we must do as Johann says. We must find Holcroft before his mother does."

"And under one pretext or another," added von Tiebolt, "keep him isolated until our meeting the day after tomorrow. She'll undoubtedly try to reach him, and then we'll know where she is. We have men in Geneva who can take care of the rest." He hesitated. "As always, Hans, your brother addresses himself to what's optimum. But the answer to your question is yes. By noon Saturday, Holcroft is expendable. When I think about it, I'm not sure the additional weeks are even desirable."

"You annoy me again," said the scholar. "I defer to your exotic mind in many things, but a deviation in strategy at this juncture is hardly welcome. Holcroft *must* be available. In *your words*, until substantive progress is made, there can be no alarms."

"I don't think there will be," replied von Tiebolt. "The change I'm implementing would be approved by our fathers. I've moved up the timetable."

"You've *what* – ?"

"When I used the word 'alarms', I referred to legalities, not Holcroft. Legalities are constant, life-spans never."

"What timetable? Why?"

"Second question first, and you may answer it." Johann stood in front of the older Kessler's chair. "What was the single most effective weapon of war the Fatherland employed? What strategy would have brought England to her knees had there been no hesitation? What were the lightning bolts that shook the world?"

"*Blitzkrieg*," said the doctor, answering for his brother.

"Yes. Swift, sharp onslaughts out of nowhere. Men and weapons and machinery, sweeping across borders with extraordinary speed, leaving in their wakes confusion and devastation. Whole peoples divided, unable to reform ranks, incapable of making decisions. The *Blitzkrieg*, Erich. We must adapt it now; we can't hesitate."

"Abstractions, Johann! Give me specifics!"

"Very well. Specific One: John Tennyson has written an article that will be picked up by the wire services and flashed everywhere tomorrow. The Tinamou kept records and there is talk that they've been found. Names of those powerful men who've hired him, dates, sources of payments. It will have the effect of massive electric shocks throughout the world's power centres. Specific Two: On Saturday, the Geneva document is executed, the funds transferred to Zurich. Sunday, we move to our headquarters there – they've been prepared, all communications are functioning. If Holcroft is with us, Hans has him drugged; if not, he's dead. Specific Three: Monday, the assets are deemed liquid and in our control. Using the Greenwich time zones, we begin cabling funds to our people, concentrating on the primary targets. We start right here in Geneva. Then to Berlin, Paris, Madrid, Lisbon, London, Washington, New York, Chicago, Houston, Los Angeles, and San Francisco. By five, Zurich time, we move into the Pacific. Honolulu, the Marshalls, and the Gilberts. By eight, we go into New Zealand. Auckland and Wellington. By ten, it's Australia. Brisbane, Sydney, Adelaide, then to Perth and across to Singapore into the Far East. The first phase stops in New Delhi; on paper we're financed over three-quarters of the globe. Specific Four: At the end of another twenty-four hours – Tuesday – we receive confirmations that the funds have been received and converted into cash, ready for use. Specific Five: I will make twenty-three telephone calls from Zurich. They will be made to twenty-three men in various capitals who have employed the services of the Tinamou. They will be told that certain demands will be made of them during the next few weeks; they are expected to comply. Specific Six: On Wednesday, it begins. The first killing will be symbolic. The Chancellor in Berlin, the leader of the Bundestag. We sweep westward in a *Blitzkrieg*." Von Tiebolt stopped for precisely three seconds, and then concluded quietly. "On Wednesday, *Code Wolfsschanze* is activated."

The telephone rang; at first no one seemed to hear it. Then von Tiebolt crossed rapidly to the desk and answered it.

"Yes?"

He stared at the wall as he listened in silence. Finally he spoke. "Use the words I gave you," he said softly. "Kill them." He hung up.

"What is it?" asked the doctor.

Von Tiebolt, his hand still on the telephone, replied in a monotone. "It was only a guess . . . a possibility, but I sent a man to Neuchâtel. To observe someone. And that someone met with another. It's no matter; they're both dead."

It did not make sense, thought Holcroft as he listened to Willie Ellis's words over the phone. He had reached Willie at the D'Accord from a booth in Geneva's crowded Place Jueve, fully expecting the designer to have made contact with Althene by now. He hadn't; she wasn't there. But his mother had said the Hotel D'Accord. She would meet him at the *Hôtel D'Accord*.

"Did you describe her? An American, around seventy, tall for a woman?"

"Naturally. Everything you mentioned half an hour ago. There's no one here by the name of Holcroft or any woman fitting the description. There are no Americans at all."

"It's crazy." Noel tried to think. Tennyson and the Kesslers weren't due until evening; he had no one to turn to. Was his mother doing the same thing he was doing? Trying to reach *him* from outside the hotel, expecting *he'd* be there? "Willie, call up the front desk and say you just heard from me. Use my name. Tell them I asked you if there were any messages for me."

"I don't think you understand the rules in Geneva, Willie said. "Messages between two people aren't given to unknown third parties, and the D'Accord is no exception. Frankly, when I asked about your mother, I was given some very odd looks. Despite my Louis Vuitton, the little bastard couldn't wait for me to stop talking."

"Try it anyway."

"There's a better way. I think if I . . ." Willie stopped; from somewhere in the distance there was a tapping. "Just a minute, there's someone at the door. I'll get rid of whoever it is and be right back."

Noel could hear the sound of a door opening. There were voices, indistinct, questioning; a brief exchange took place, and then there were footsteps. Holcroft waited for Willie to get back on the line.

There was the sound of a cough, but more than a cough. What was it? The start of a cry? Was it the start of a *cry*?

"Willie?"

Silence. Then footsteps again.

"*Willie?*" Suddenly, Noel felt cold. And the pain came back to his stomach as he remembered the words. *The same words!*

. . . *There's someone at the door. I'll get rid of whoever it is and be right back . . . .*

Another Englishman. Four thousand miles away in New York. And a match flaring up in the window across the courtyard.

Peter Baldwin.

"*Willie! Willie,* where *are* you? *Willie!*"

There was a click. The line went dead.

Oh, Christ! What had he *done?* Willie!

Beads of sweat broke out on his forehead; his hands trembled.

He had to get to the D'Accord! He had to get there as fast as he could and find Willie, help Willie. Oh, *Jesus Christ*, he wished the hammering pain would get out of his eyes!

He ran out of the phone booth and down the street to his car. He started the engine, unsure for a moment where he was or where he was going. The D'Accord. *Hôtel D'Accord!* It was on the rue des Granges, near the Puits Saint Pierre; a street lined with enormous old houses – mansions. The D'Accord was the largest. On the hill . . . *what* hill? He had no idea how to get there!

He sped down to the corner; the traffic was stopped. He yelled through his window at a startled woman driving the car next to his.

"Please! The rue des Granges? Which way?"

The woman refused to acknowledge his shouts; she pulled her eyes away and looked straight ahead.

"*Please*, someone's been hurt. I think hurt badly. Please, lady! I can't speak French very well. Or German, or . . . *please!*"

The woman turned back to him, studying him for a moment. Then she leaned over and rolled down the window.

"Rue des Granges?"

"Yes, please!"

She gave him rapid instructions. Five streets down, turn right towards the bottom of the hill, then left . . .

The traffic started up. Perspiring, Noel tried to memorize every word, every number, every turn. He shouted his thanks and pressed the accelerator.

He would never know how he found the old street, but it was suddenly there. He drove up the steep incline towards the top and saw the flat gold lettering.

Hôtel D'Accord

His hands shaking, he parked the car and got out. He had to lock it; twice he tried to insert the key but could not hold his hand steady enough. So he held his breath and pressed his fingers against the metal until they stopped trembling. He had to control himself now; he *had to think*. Above all, he had to be careful. He had seen the enemy before and he had fought that enemy. He could do so again.

He looked up at the D'Accord's ornate entrance. Beyond the glass doors, he could see the doorman talking with someone in the lobby. He could not go through that entrance and into that lobby; if the enemy had trapped Willie Ellis, that enemy was waiting for him.

There was a narrow alley that sloped downwards at the side of the building. On the stone wall was a sign.

Livraisons

Somewhere in that alley was a delivery entrance. He pulled the collar of his raincoat up around his neck and walked across the pavement, putting his hands in his pockets, feeling the steel of the revolver in his right, the perforated cylinder of the silencer in his left. He thought briefly of the giver, of Helden. Where was she? What had happened?

Nothing is as it was for you . . .

Nothing at all.

He reached the door as a tradesman in a white smock coat was leaving. He held up his hand and smiled at the man.

"Excuse me. Do you speak English?"

"But of course, *monsieur*. This is Geneva."

It was a harmless joke, that's all, but the foolish American with the broad smile would pay fifty francs for the cheap coat, twice its value new. The exchange was made swiftly; this was Geneva. Holcroft removed his raincoat and folded it over his left arm. He put on the smock and went inside.

Willie had reserved a suite on the third floor, the last door in the corridor towards the street. He walked through a dark hallway that led to a darker staircase. At the landing, there was a cart against the wall, three small, unopened cases of hotel soap beneath one that was half empty. He removed the top carton, picked up the remaining three, and proceeded up the marble steps, hoping he looked even vaguely like someone who might belong there.

"Jacques? *C'est vous?*" The caller spoke from below, his voice pleasant.

Holcroft turned and shrugged.

"*Pardon. Je croyas que c'était Jacques de la fleuriste.*"

"*Non*," said Noel quickly, continuing up the stairs.

He reached the third floor, put the cartons of soap on the staircase, and removed the smock. He put on his raincoat, felt the revolver, and opened the door slowly; there was no one in the corridor.

He walked to the last door on the right, listening for sounds; there were none. He remembered listening at another doorway in another hallway light years away from this ivoried, ornamental corridor in which he stood now. In a place called Montereau . . . there had been gunfire then. And death.

Oh, *God*, had anything happened to *Willie?* Willie who had not refused him, who had been a friend when others could not be found. Holcroft took out the gun and reached for the knob. He stepped back as far as he could.

In one motion he twisted the knob and threw his full weight against the door, his shoulder a battering ram. The door sprang open unimpeded, crashing into the wall behind it; it had not been locked.

Noel crouched, the weapon levelled in front of him. There was no one in the room, but a window was open, the cold winter air billowing the curtains. He walked to it bewildered; why would a window be open in this weather?

Then he saw them: circles of blood on the sill; someone had been bleeding profusely. Outside the window was a fire escape. He could see streaks of red on the steps. Whoever had run down them had been severely wounded.

Willie?

"Willie? Willie, are you here?"

Silence.

Holcroft ran into the bedroom.

No one.

"*Willie?*"

He was about to turn around when he saw strange markings on the panelling of a closed door. The panelling was profuse with gold fluting and ornate *fleur de lis*, pink and white and light blue. But what he saw was not part of the rococo design.

They were blurred handprints outlined in blood.

He raced to the door, kicking it in with such force that the panelling cracked and splintered.

What he saw was the horror of a lifetime. Arched over the rim of the empty bathtub was the mutilated body of Willie Ellis, soaked in blood. There were huge punctures in his chest and stomach, intestines protruding over his red-drenched shirt, his throat slashed so deeply that his head was barely attached to his neck, his eyes open, glaring upwards in agony. He had been butchered by a maniac.

Noel collapsed, trying to swallow the air that would not fill his lungs.

And then he saw a word, scrawled in blood on the tiles above the mutilated corpse.

Nachrichtendienst

38

Helden found the path three kilometres beyond the fork in the road leading out of Près-du-Lac. She had borrowed a flashlight from the concierge, and now angled the beam of light in front of her as she began the trek through the woods to Werner Gerhardt's house.

It was not so much a house, thought Helden as she reached the strange-looking structure, as a miniature fortress. It was very small – smaller than *Herr Oberst's* cottage – but from where she stood the walls appeared to be extremely thick. The beam of the flashlight caught bulging rocks that had been cemented together along the two sides she could see; and the roof, too, was heavy. The few windows were high off the ground and narrow. She had never seen a house like it before. It seemed to belong in a children's fairytale, subject to magic incantations.

It answered a question provoked by the concierge's remarks when she had returned from the village square several hours ago.

"Did you find Mad Gerhardt? They say he was once a great diplomat before the marbles rattled in his head. It's rumoured old friends still care for him, although none come to see him any more. They cared once, though. They built him a strong cottage on the lake. No Christmas wind will ever knock it down."

No wind, no storm, no winter snows could have any effect on this house. Someone had cared deeply.

She heard the sound of a door opening. It startled Helden because there was no door at the side or rear walls. Then the beam of light caught the short figure of Werner Gerhardt; he stood on the edge of the lakeside porch and raised his hand.

How could the old man possibly have heard her?

"You've come, I see," said Gerhardt, no madness in his voice. "Quickly now, these woods are cold. Get inside in front of the fire. We'll have tea."

The room seemed larger than the outside structure would indicate. The heavy furniture was old but comfortable, a profusion of leather and wood. Helden sat on an ottoman, warmed by the fire and the tea. She had not realized how cold she'd been.

They had talked for a few minutes, Gerhardt answering the first question before she'd had a chance to ask it.

"I came here from Berlin five years ago, by way of Munich, where my cover was established. I was a 'victim' of *Odessa*, a broken man, living out his years

321

in senility and solitude. I'm a figure of ridicule; a doctor at the clinic keeps my records. His name is Litvak, should you ever need him. He's the only one who knows I'm perfectly sane."

"But why was your cover necessary?"

"You'll understand as we talk. Incidentally, you were surprised that I knew you were outside." Gerhardt smiled. "This primitive lakeside cottage is very sophisticated. No one approaches without my knowing it. A hum is heard." The old man's smile vanished. "Now, what happened to Klaus?"

She told him. Gerhardt was silent for a while, pain in his eyes.

"*Animals*," he said. "They can't even execute a man with any semblance of decency; they must mutilate. May God *damn* them!"

"Who?"

"The false Wolfsschanze. The animals. Not the eagles."

"Eagles? I don't understand."

"The plot to kill Hitler in July of '45 was a conspiracy of the generals. Military men – by and large decent men – who came to see the horrors committed by the Fuhrer. It was not the Germany they cared to fight for. Their objective was to assassinate Hitler, sue for a just peace, and expose the killers and sadists who'd functioned in the name of the Reich. Rommel called these men the true eagles of Germany."

"The eagles . . ." Helden repeated. "'You won't stop the eagles'. . ."

"I beg your pardon?" asked the old man.

"Nothing. Go on, please."

"Of course, the generals failed and a bloodbath followed. Two hundred and twelve officers, many only vaguely suspect, were tortured and put to death. Then suddenly Wolfsschanze became the excuse to still all dissent within the Reich. Thousands who had voiced even the most minor political or military criticisms were arrested on fabricated evidence and executed. The vast majority had never heard of a staff headquarters called Wolfsschanze, much less any attempt on Hitler's life. Rommel was ordered to kill himself, the penalty for refusal to carry out an additional five thousand *indiscriminate* executions. The worst fears of the generals were borne out: the maniacs were in total control of Germany. It was what they had hoped to stop at Wolfsschanze. *Their* Wolfsschanze, the true Wolfsschanze."

"*Their* . . . Wolfsschanze?" asked Helden. "'The coin of Wolfsschanze has two sides.'"

"Yes," said Gerhardt. "There was another Wolfsschanze, another group of men who also wanted Hitler killed. But for an entirely different reason. These men thought he had failed. They saw his weaknesses, his diminished capacities. They wanted to supplant the madness that *was* for another madness far more efficient. There were no appeals for peace in their plans, only the fullest prosecution of the war. Their strategies included tactics unheard of since the Mongol armies swept through Asia centuries ago. Whole peoples held as hostages, mass executions for the slightest infractions, a reign of abuse so terrible the world would seek a truce, if only in the name of humanity."

322

Gerhardt paused; when he continued his voice was filled with loathing. "This was the false Wolfsschanze, the Wolfsschanze that was never meant to be. It wanted Hitler dead, but not for peace and whatever honour might survive him. Instead, for continued holocaust and victory. They – the men of *that* Wolfsschanze – are committed still."

"Yet these same men were part of the conspiracy to kill Hitler." Helden asked, "How did they escape?"

"By becoming the fiercest of Hitler's loyalists. They regrouped quickly, feigned revulsion at the treachery, and turned on the others. As always, zealousness and ferocity impressed the Fuhrer; he was essentially a physical coward, you see. He put some of them in charge of the executions and delighted in their devotion."

Helden moved to the edge of the seat. "You say these men – this other Wolfsschanze – are still committed. Surely most of them are dead by now."

The old man sighed. "You really don't know, do you? Klaus said you didn't."

"You know who I am?" asked Helden.

"Of course. You yourself mailed the letters."

"I mailed a lot of letters for *Herr Oberst*. But none to Neuchâtel."

"Those that were meant for me, I received."

"He wrote to you about me?"

"Often. He loved you very much." Gerhardt's smile was warm. It faded as he spoke. "You asked me how the men of the false Wolfsschanze could still be committed after so many years. You're right, of course. Most of them are dead. So it's not they; it's the children."

"The *children?*"

"Yes. They're everywhere, in every city, province and country. In every profession, every political group. Their function is to apply pressure constantly, convincing people that their lives could be so much better if strong men protested weakness. Angry voices are being substituted for genuine remedies; rancour supplants reason. It's happening everywhere and only a few of us know what it is: a massive preparation. The children have grown up."

"Where did they come from?"

"Now we come to the heart of the matter. It will answer other questions for you." The old man leaned forward. "It was called *Operation Sonnenkinder*, and took place during the months of January, February, and March of 1945. Thousands of children between the ages of six months and sixteen years were sent out of Germany. To all parts of the world . . ."

As Gerhardt told the story, Helden felt sick, physically sick.

"A plan was devised," continued Gerhardt, "wherein millions upon millions of dollars would be available to the *Sonnenkinder* after a given period of time. The time was calculated by projections of the normal economic cycles; it was thirty years."

Helden's sharp intake of breath interrupted him, but only briefly.

"It was a plan conceived by three men . . ."

A cry emerged from Helden's throat.

" . . . these three men had access to funds beyond calculation; and one of them was perhaps the most brilliant financial manipulator of our time. It was he and he alone who brought the international economic forces together that ensured the rise of Adolf Hitler. And when his Reich failed him, he set about creating another."

"Heinrich Clausen . . ." whispered Helden. "Oh, *God*, no! . . . Noel; oh, God, *Noel*."

"He was never more than a device, a conduit for money. He knows nothing."

"Then . . ." Helden's eyes grew wide; the pain in her temples increased.

"Yes," said Gerhardt, reaching for her hand. "A young boy was chosen, another of the sons. An extraordinary child, a fanatically devoted member of the Hitler Youth. Brilliant, beautiful. He was watched, developed, trained for his mission in life."

"Johann . . . Oh, God in heaven, it's *Johann*."

"Yes. Johann von Tiebolt. It is he who expects to lead the *Sonnenkinder* into power all over the world."

The sound of an echoing drum grew louder inside her temples, the percussive beats jarring and thunderous. Images went out of focus; the room spun and darkness descended. Helden fell into a void.

She opened her eyes, not knowing how long she had been unconscious. Gerhardt had managed to prop her up against the ottoman and was holding a glass of brandy beneath her nostrils. She gripped the glass and swallowed, the alcohol spreading quickly, bringing her back to the terrible moment.

"*Johann*," she whispered, the name itself a cry of pain. "That's why *Herr Oberst* . . ."

"Yes," said the old man, anticipating her. "It's why Klaus had you brought to him. The rebellious von Tiebolt daughter, born in Rio, estranged from her brother and sister. Was that estrangement real, or were you being used to infiltrate the ranks of wandering, disaffected German youth? We had to know."

"Used, then killed," added Helden, shuddering. "They tried to kill me in Montereau. Oh, God, my *brother*."

The old man stood up. "I'm afraid you're wrong," he said. "It was a tragic afternoon, filled with errors. The two men who came after you were from us. Their instructions were clear: learn everything there was to learn about Holcroft. He was still an unknown factor then. Was he part of Wolfsschanze – their Wolfsschanze? If an unknowing conduit, he was to live and we would convince him to come with us. If part of Wolfsschanze, he was to be killed. If that was the case, you were to be taken away before you were harmed, before you were implicated. For reasons we don't know, our men decided to kill him."

Helden lowered her eyes. "Johann sent a man to follow us that afternoon. To learn about *you*."

Gerhardt sat down. "So our people thought it was a rendezvous with von Tiebolt, with an emissary of the *Sonnenkinder*. For them it meant Holcroft *was* part of Wolfsschanze. They needed nothing else."

"It's my fault," said Helden. "When that man took my arm in the crowd, I was frightened. He told me I had to go with him. He spoke German. I thought he was *Odessa*."

"He was the furthest thing from it. He was a Jew from a place called *Har Sha'alav*."

"A Jew?"

Gerhardt told her briefly of the strange kibbutz in the Negev desert. "They are our small army. A cable is sent; men are dispatched. It's as simple as that."

Orders must be relayed . . . to the courageous men who will stand at the final barricade. Helden understood *Herr Oberst's* words. "You'll send that cable now?"

"*You* will send it. A while ago, I mentioned a Dr Litvak at the clinic. He keeps my medical records for any who may be curious. He's one of us; he has long-range radio equipment and checks with me every day. It's too dangerous to have a telephone here. Go to him tonight. He knows the codes and will reach *Har Sha'alav.* A team must be sent to Geneva; you must tell them what to do. Von Tiebolt, Kessler, even Noel Holcroft, if he's beyond pulling out, must be killed. Those funds must not be dispersed."

"I'll convince Noel."

"For your sake, I hope you can. It may not be as simple as you think. He's been manipulated brilliantly. He believes deeply, even to the point of vindicating a father he never knew."

"How did you learn?"

"From his mother. For years we believed she was part of Clausen's plan and for years we waited. Then we confronted her and learned she was never part of it. She was the bridge to – as well as the source of – the perfect conduit. Who else but a Noel Clausen Holcroft – whose origins had been obliterated from every record but his own mind – would accept the conditions of secrecy demanded by the Geneva document? A normal man would have asked for legal and financial advice. But Holcroft, believing in his covenant, kept everything to himself."

"But he had to be *convinced*," said Helden. "He's a strong man, a very moral man. How could they do it?"

"How is anyone convinced his cause is just?" asked the old man rhetorically. "By seeing that there are those who desperately wish to stop him. We've read the reports out of Rio, Holcroft's experience with Maurice Graff, the charges he registered with the embassy. It was all a sham; no one tried to kill him in Rio, but Graff wanted him to think so."

"He's *Odessa*."

"Never. He's one of the leaders of the false Wolfsschanze . . . the only Wolfsschanze now. I should say he was; he's dead."

"What?"

"Shot yesterday by a man who left a note claiming vengeance from Portuguese Jews. Your brother's work, of course. Graff was too old; too cantankerous. He'd served his purpose."

Helden placed the glass of brandy on the floor. The question had to be asked. "Herr Gerhardt, why haven't you ever exposed Geneva for what it was?"

The old man returned her inquisitive stare. "Because exposing Geneva would be only half the story. As soon as we did, we'd be killed, but that's inconsequential. It's the rest."

"The rest?"

"The second half. Who are the *Sonnenkinder?* What are their names? Where are they? A master list was made thirty years ago; your brother must have it. It's huge, hundreds of pages, and has to be hidden somewhere. Von Tiebolt would die in fire before revealing its whereabouts. But there *has* to be another list! A short one − a few pages perhaps. It's either on his person or near him. The identities of all those receiving funds. These will be the trusted manipulators of Wolfsschanze. This is the list that can and must be found. You must tell the soldiers of *Har Sha'alav* to find it. Stop the money and find the list. It's our only hope."

"I'll tell them," said Helden. "They'll find it." She looked away, lost in another thought. "Wolfsschanze. Even the letter written to Noel Holcroft over thirty years ago, pleading with him, threatening him . . . was part of it."

"They appealed and threatened in the name of eagles, but their commitment was to animals."

"He couldn't know that."

"No. He couldn't. The name Wolfsschanze is awesome, a symbol of bravery. That was the only Wolfsschanze Holcroft could relate to. He had no knowledge of the other Wolfsschanze, the filth. No one did. Save one."

"*Herr Oberst?*"

"Falkenheim, yes."

"How did he escape?"

"By the most basic of coincidences. A confusion of identities." Gerhardt walked to the fireplace and prodded the logs with a poker. "Among the giants of Wolfsschanze was the commander of the Belgian sector, Alexander von Falkenhausen. Falken*hausen*, Falkenheim. Klaus Falkenheim had left East Prussia for a meeting in Berlin. When the assassination attempt failed, Falkenhausen somehow managed to reach Falkenheim by radio to tell him of the disaster. He begged Klaus to stay away. He would be the 'falcon' who was caught; the other 'falcon' was loyal to Hitler, he would make that clear. Klaus objected, but understood. He had work to do. Someone had to survive."

"Where is Noel's mother?" Helden asked. "What has she learned?"

"She knows everything now. Let's hope she hasn't panicked. We lost her in

Mexico; we think she's trying to reach her son in Geneva. She'll fail. The instant she's spotted, she's a dead woman."

"We've got to find her,"

"Not at the expense of the other priorities," said the old man. "Remember, there is only one Wolfsschanze now. *Crippling* it is all that matters." Gerhardt put the poker down. "You'll see Dr Litvak tonight. His house is near the clinic, above it, on a hill two kilometres north. The hill is quite steep; the radio functions well there. I'll give you. . ."

A sharp humming sound filled the room. It echoed off the walls so loudly that Helden felt the vibrations going through her and jumped to her feet. Gerhardt turned from the fireplace and stared up at a narrow window high in the left wall. He seemed to be studying the panes of glass that were too far above him to see through.

"There's a night mirror that picks up images in the black light," he said, watching intently. "It's a man. I recognize him, but I don't know him." He walked to the desk, took out a small pistol, and handed it to Helden.

"What should I do?" she asked.

"Hide it under your skirt."

"You don't know who it is?" Helden lifted her skirt and sat down in a chair facing the door, the weapon hidden.

"No. He arrived yesterday; I saw him in the square. He may be one of us; he may not. I don't know."

Helden could hear footsteps outside the door. They stopped; there was a moment of silence, then rapid knocking.

"Herr Gerhardt?"

The old man answered, his voice now high-pitched and in the singsong cadence he had used in the square. "Good heavens, who is it? It's very late; I'm in the middle of my prayers."

"I bring you news from *Har Sha'alav*."

The old man exhaled in relief, and nodded to Helden. "He's one of us," he said, unlatching the bolt. "No one but we know about *Har Sha'alav*."

The door opened. For the briefest instant Helden froze, then spun out of the chair and lunged for the floor. The figure in the doorway held a large-barrelled gun in his hand; its explosion was thunderous. Gerhardt arched backwards, blown off his feet, his body a contorted bloody mass, suspended in the air before it fell into the desk.

Helden lurched behind the leather armchair, reaching for the pistol under her skirt.

There was another gunshot as thunderous as the first. The leather back of the chair exploded out of its shell. *Another*, and she felt an ice-like pain in her leg. Blood spread over her stocking.

She raised the pistol and squeezed the trigger repeatedly, aiming – and not aiming – at the huge figure in shadows by the door.

She heard the man scream. In panic, she crashed into the wall, a cornered insect, trapped, about to lose its insignificant life. Tears streamed down her face as she aimed again and pulled the trigger until the firing stopped, replaced by the sickening clicks of the empty gun. She screamed in terror; there were no bullets left. She hoped to God her death would come quickly.

She heard screams – she *heard* them – as if she were floating in the sky, looking below at chaos and smoke.

There *was* smoke. Everywhere. It filled the room, the acrid fumes stinging her eyes, blinding her. She did not understand; nothing happened.

Then she heard faint, whispered words.

"My child . . ."

It was Gerhardt! Sobbing, she pressed her hand against the wall and pushed herself away. Dragging her bloodied leg, she crawled towards the source of the whisper.

The smoke was beginning to clear. She could see the figure of the killer. He was lying on his back, small red circles in his throat and forehead. He was dead.

Gerhardt was dying. She crept to him and put her face on his face, her tears falling on his flesh.

"My child . . . get to Litvak. Cable *Har Sha'alav.* Stay away from Geneva."

"Stay *away?*"

"You, child. They know you came to me. Wolfsschanze has seen you . . . You're all that's left. *Nachricht . . .*"

"What?"

"You are . . . *Nachrichtendienst.*"

Gerhardt's head slipped away from her face. He was gone.

39

The red-bearded pilot walked rapidly down the rue des Granges towards the parked car. Inside, Althene saw him approaching. She was alarmed. Why hadn't the pilot brought her son with him? And why was he hurrying so?

The pilot climbed in behind the wheel, pausing for a moment to catch his breath.

"There's great confusion at the D'Accord, Madame. A killing."

Althene gasped. "*Noel?* Is it my *son?*"

"No. An Englishman."

"Who was it?"

"A man named Ellis. A William Ellis."

"Dear God!" Althene gripped her purse. "Noel had a friend in London named Ellis. He talked about him frequently. I must reach my son!"

"Not in there, Madame. Not if there's a connection between your son and the Englishman. The police are everywhere and there's an alert out for you."

"Get to a telephone."

"I'll make the call. It may be the last thing I do for you, Madame. I've no wish to be associated with killing; that's not part of any agreement between us."

They drove for nearly fifteen minutes before the pilot was satisfied no one had followed them.

"Why should anyone follow us?" Althene asked. "Nobody saw me; you didn't mention my name. Or Noel's."

"Not you, Madame. Me. I don't make it a point to fraternize with the Geneva police. I've run into a few now and then, off and on. We don't get along very well."

They entered the lake-front district, the pilot scanning the streets for an out-of-the-way telephone. He found one, swerved the car to the kerb, and dashed outside to the booth. Althene watched him make the call. Then he returned, got behind the wheel with less alacrity than he had left it, and sat for a moment, scowling.

"For heaven's sake, what happened?"

"I don't like it," he said. "They expected a call from you."

"Of course. My son arranged it."

"But it was not you on the phone. It was me."

"What difference does it make? I had someone call for me. What did they say?"

"Not they. He. And what he said was far too specific. In this city, one is not that free with information. Specifics are exchanged when ears recognize voices, or when certain words are used that mean the caller has a right to know."

"What *was* the information?" asked Althene, irritated.

"A rendezvous. As soon as possible. Ten kilometres north on the road to Vèsenaz. It's on the east side of the lake. He said your son would be there."

"Then we'll go."

"'We,' Madame?"

"I'd like to negotiate further with you."

She offered him five hundred American dollars. "You're crazy," he said.

"We have an agreement then?"

"On the condition that until you and your son are together, you do exactly as I say," he replied. "I don't accept such money for failure. However, if he's not there, that's no concern of mine. I get paid."

"You'll get paid. Let's go."

"Very well." The pilot started the car.

"Why are you suspicious? It all seems quite logical to me," said Althene.

"I told you. This city has its own code of behaviour. In Geneva, the telephone is the courier. A second number should have been given, so that you yourself could talk with your son. When I suggested it, I was told there wasn't time."

"All quite possible."

"Perhaps, but I don't like it. The switchboard said they were connecting me to the front desk, but the man I talked to was no clerk."

"How do you know that?"

"Desk clerks can be arrogant and often are, but they aren't demanding. The man I spoke to was. And he wasn't from Geneva. He had an accent I couldn't place. You'll do exactly as I say, Madame."

Von Tiebolt replaced the phone and smiled in satisfaction. "We have her," he said simply, walking to the couch where Hans Kessler lay holding an ice pack to his right cheek, his face bruised where it had not been stitched by the First Deputy's personal physician.

"I'll go with you," said Hans, his voice strained in anger and pain.

"I don't think so," interjected his brother from a nearby armchair.

"You can't be seen," added von Tiebolt. "We'll tell Holcroft you were delayed."

"No!" roared the doctor, slamming his fist on the coffee table. "Tell Holcroft anything you like, but I'm going with you tonight. That bitch is responsible for this!"

"I'd say *you* were," said von Tiebolt. "There was a job to do and you wanted to do it. You were most anxious. You always are in such matters; you're a very physical man."

"He wouldn't die! That faggot wouldn't *die!*" Hans yelled. "He had the strength of five lions. Look at my stomach!" He ripped the shirt below his face, revealing a curving pattern of crisscrossed black threads. "He tore it with his hands! With his *hands!*"

Erich Kessler turned his eyes away from his brother's wound. "You were lucky to get away without being seen. And now we must get you out of this hotel. The police are questioning everyone."

"They won't come here," countered Hans angrily. "Our deputy's taken care of that."

"Nevertheless, one curious policeman walking through the door could lead to complications," von Tiebolt said, looking at Erich. "Hans must go. Dark glasses, a muffler, his hat. The deputy's in the lobby." The blond man shifted his gaze to the wounded brother. "If you can move, you'll have your chance at Mrs Holcroft. That may make you feel better."

"I can move," said Hans, his face contorted in pain.

Johann turned back to the older Kessler. "You'll stay here, Erich. Holcroft will start calling soon, but he won't identify himself until he recognizes your voice. Be solicitous, be concerned. Say I reached you in Berlin and asked you to get here early – that I tried to call *him* in Paris but he'd gone. Then tell him that we're both shocked at what happened here this afternoon. The man who was killed had been asking about him; we're both concerned for his safety. He must *not* be seen at the D'Accord."

"I could say that someone fitting his description was seen leaving by the service entrance," added the scholar. "He was in a state of shock; he'll accept that. It will add to his panic."

"Excellent. Meet him and take him to the Excelsior. Register under the name of . . ." The blond man thought for a moment. "Under the name of Fresca. If he has any lingering doubts, that will convince him. He never used the name with you; he'll know we've met and talked."

"Fine," said Erich. "And at the Excelsior, I'll explain that because of everything that's happened you reached the bank's directors and set up the conference for tomorrow morning. The quicker it's over, the quicker we can get to Zurich and set up proper security measures."

"Excellent again, Herr Professor."

"Come, Hans," von Tiebolt said, "I'll help you."

"It's not necessary," said Hans. "Just get my bag."

"Of course." Von Tiebolt picked up the physician's leather case. "I'm fascinated. You must tell me what you intend to inject. Remember, we want a death, but not a killing."

"Don't worry," Hans said. "Everything's clearly coded. There'll be no mistakes."

"After our meeting with Mrs Holcroft," said von Tiebolt, draping an overcoat over Hans's shoulders, "we'll decide where Hans should stay tonight. Perhaps at the deputy's house."

"Good idea," agreed the scholar. "The doctor would be available."

"I don't *need* him," argued Hans, his breath escaping between clenched teeth, his walk hesitant and painful. "I could have sewn myself up; he's not very good. *Auf Wiedersehen*, Erich."

"*Auf Wiedersehen, Hans.*"

Von Tiebolt opened the door and escorted the wounded Hans out into the corridor. "You say each vial is coded?"

"Yes. For the woman the serum will accelerate her heart to the point . . ."

The door closed. The older Kessler shifted his bulk in the chair. It was the way of Wolfsschanze; there was no other decision. The physician who had tended Hans made it clear that there was internal bleeding – the organs had been severely damaged, as if torn by claws possessing extraordinary strength. Unless Hans were taken to the hospital he could easily die. But his brother could not be admitted to a hospital; questions would be asked. A man had been killed that afternoon at the D'Accord; the wounded patient had been at the D'Accord. Too many questions. Besides, Hans's contributions were in the black leather case Johann carried. The Tinamou would learn everything they had to know. Hans Kessler, *Sonnenkind*, was no longer needed; he was a liability.

The telephone rang. Kessler picked it up.

"Erich?"

It was Holcroft.

"Yes?"

"I'm in Geneva. You got here early, I thought I'd try."

"Yes, von Tiebolt called me this morning in Berlin, he tried to reach you in Paris. He suggested . . ."

"Has he arrived?" interrupted the American.

"Yes. He's out making the final arrangements for tomorrow. We've got a great deal to tell you."

"And I've got a great deal to tell *you*," said Holcroft. "Do you know what's happened?"

"Yes, it's horrible." *Where was the panic? Where was the anxiety of a man stretched to the limit of his capacities? The voice on the phone was not that of someone drowning, grasping for a lifeline.* "He was a friend of yours. They say he asked for you."

There was a pause. "He asked for my mother."

"I didn't understand. We know only that he used the name Holcroft."

"What does *Nach* . . . *Nach – rich* . . . I can't pronounce it."

"*Nachrichtendienst?*"

"Yes. What does it mean?"

Kessler was startled. The American was in control of himself; it was not to be expected. "What can I tell you? It's Geneva's enemy."

"That's what von Tiebolt found out in London?"

"Yes. Where are you, Noel? I must see you, but you can't come here."

"I know that. Listen to me. Do you have money?"

"Some."

332

"A thousand Swiss francs?"

"A thousand? . . . Yes, I imagine so."

"Go downstairs to the front desk and talk to the desk clerk privately. Get his name and give him the money. Tell him it's from me and that I'll be calling him in a few minutes."

"But how? . . ."

"Let me finish. After you pay him and get his name, go to the pay telephones near the lifts. Stand by the one on the left towards the entrance. When it rings, pick it up. It'll be me."

"How do you know the number?"

"I paid someone to go inside and get it."

This was not a man in panic. It was a rational man with a deadly purpose . . . It was what Erich Kessler had feared. But for the accident of chromosomes — and a headstrong woman — the man on the phone might be one of them. A Sonnenkind.

"What will you say to the clerk?"

"I'll tell you later, there's no time now. How long will it take you?"

"I don't know. Not long."

"Ten minutes?"

"Yes, I think so. But Noel, perhaps we should wait until Johann returns."

"When's that?"

"No more than an hour or two."

"Can't do it. I'll call you in the lobby in ten minutes. My watch says eight forty-five, how about yours?"

"The same." Kessler did not bother to look at his watch; his mind was racing. Holcroft's spine was too dangerously firm. "I really think we should wait."

"I can't. They killed him — God! *How* they killed him! They want her, but they won't find her."

"Her? Your mother? . . . Von Tiebolt told me."

"They won't find her," repeated Holcroft. "They'll find *me*; that's who they really want. And I *want them.* I'm going to trap them, Erich."

"Control yourself. You don't know what you're doing."

"I know exactly."

"The Geneva police are in the hotel. If you speak to the desk clerk, he may say something. They'll be looking for you."

"They can have me in a few hours. In fact, I'll be looking for them."

"*What?* Noel, I *must* see you!"

"Ten minutes, Erich. It's eight forty-six." Holcroft went off the line.

Kessler replaced the phone, knowing that he had no choice but to follow instructions. To do anything else would be suspect. But what did Holcroft expect to accomplish? What would he say to the desk clerk? It pro-

333

bably did not matter. With the mother gone, it was only necessary to keep Holcroft functioning until tomorrow morning. By noon, he was expendable.

Noel waited on the dark street corner at the base of rue des Granges. He was not proud of what he was about to do, but the rage inside him numbed any feelings of morality. The sight of Willie Ellis had caused something to snap in his head. That sight gave rise to other images: Richard Holcroft, crushed into a stone building by a car gone wild by design. Strychnine in the air, and death in a French village, and murder in Berlin. And a man who had followed his mother . . . he would not let them *near her!*

It was a question now of using every available resource, every strength he had, every fact he could recall that would work for him. And it was the murder in Berlin that provided him with the single fact that could work for him now. In Berlin he had led killers to Erich Kessler. Stupidly, carelessly – to a ratskeller on the Kurfurstendamm. *Kessler* and *Holcroft; Holcroft* and *Kessler.* If those killers were looking for Holcroft, they would keep Kessler in their sights. And if Kessler left the hotel they would follow him.

Holcroft looked at his watch. It was time to call; he started across the pavement towards the booth.

He hoped Erich would answer.

And later understand.

Kessler stood in the hotel lobby, in front of the pay phone, a slip of paper in his hand. On it the astonished desk clerk had written his name; the man's hand had shaken when he had taken the money. Professor Kessler would appreciate knowing the gist of Mr Holcroft's message to the clerk. For Mr Holcroft's benefit. And the clerk's, in so far as an additional 500 francs would be his.

The telephone rang; Erich had it off the hook before the ring was finished. "Noel?"

"What's the desk clerk's name?"

Kessler gave it.

"Fine."

"Now, I must insist we meet," said Erich. "There's a great deal you should know. Tomorrow's a very important day."

"Only if we get through tonight. If I find her tonight."

"Where are you? We *must* meet."

"We will. Listen carefully. Wait by that phone for five minutes. I may have to call you again. If I don't – after five minutes – go outside and begin walking down the hill. Just keep walking. When you get to the bottom, turn left and keep going. I'll join you in the street."

"Good! Five minutes then." Kessler smiled. Whatever games the amateur indulged in were worthless. He would undoubtedly ask the desk clerk to relay a message or a telephone number to his mother if and when she called him – the unregistered guest; so much for that. Perhaps Johann was right, perhaps Holcroft had reached the limits of his capacity. Perhaps the American was not a potential *Sonnenkind* after all.

Police were still in the D'Accord's lobby, and several journalists, sensing a story behind the clouded story of robbery the police had given out; this was Geneva. And the curious – guests milling around, talking to each other, reassuring each other, some afraid, some seeking sensation.

Erich stayed to the side, avoiding the crowd, remaining as inconspicuous as possible. He did not like being in the lobby at all; he preferred the anonymity of the hotel room upstairs.

He looked at his watch; four minutes had passed since Holcroft's call. If the American did not call again during the next minute, he would find the desk clerk and . . .

The desk clerk approached. "Professor?"

"Yes, my friend." Kessler put his hand in his pocket.

The message Holcroft left was not what Erich had expected. Noel's mother was to remain hidden and leave a telephone number where her son could reach *her*. The clerk had sworn not to reveal that number, of course, but then prior commitments always took precedence. When and if the lady called, the number would be left on a piece of paper in Herr Kessler's box.

"Paging Mr Kessler! Professor Erich Kessler."

A bellboy was walking through the lobby, shouting his name. *Shouting* it! It was *impossible*. No one knew he was here!

"Yes? Yes, I'm Professor Kessler," said Erich. "What *is* it?" He tried to keep his voice low, his presence unobtrusive. People were *looking* at him.

"The message is to be delivered verbally, sir," said the bellboy. "The caller said there was no time for a note. It's from Mr H. He says you're to start out now, sir."

"What?"

"That's all he said, sir. I spoke to him myself. To Mr H. You're to start out now. That's what he told me to tell you."

Kessler held his breath. It was suddenly, unexpectedly clear. Holcroft was using *him* as the *bait*.

From the American's point of view, whoever killed the man in the black leather jacket in Berlin knew that Noel Holcroft had been with Erich Kessler.

The strategy was simple but ingenious. Expose Erich Kessler, have Erich Kessler receive a message from *Mr H.*, and leave the hotel for the dark streets of Geneva.

Again, from Holcroft's viewpoint, those stalking him would surely not allow Erich Kessler out of sight. They would follow anyone who had received a message from Mr H.

And if *no one* followed, the disparity between cause and effect might be difficult to explain. So difficult that Holcroft might re-examine his bait. Questions might surface that could blow Geneva apart.

Noel Holcroft was a potential *Sonnenkind* after all.

40

Helden crawled through Gerhardt's house, over the smashed furniture and the blood on the floor, opening drawers and panels until she had found a small tin box of first-aid supplies. Trying desperately not to think of anything but becoming mobile, rejecting the pain as an unwanted state of mind, she strapped her wound as tightly as she could and struggled to her feet. Using Gerhardt's cane for support, she managed to walk up the path and north three kilometres to the fork.

A vintage car driven by a farmer picked her up. Could he drive her to a Dr Litvak on the hill near the clinic?

He could. It was not far out of his way.

Would he please *hurry?*

Walther Litvak was in his late forties, with a balding head and clear eyes and a penchant for short, precise sentences. Being slender, he moved quickly, wasting as few motions as he did words. Being highly intelligent, he made observations before replies, and being a Jew hidden by Dutch Catholics as a child and brought up by sympathetic Lutherans, he had no tolerance for intolerance.

He had one bias, and it was understandable. His father and mother, two sisters and a brother, had been gassed at Auschwitz. Save for an appeal of a Swiss doctor who spoke of a district in the hills of Neuchâtel without medical care, Walther Litvak would be living in Kibbutz *Har Sha'alav* in the Negev desert.

He had intended to spend three years at the clinic; that was five years ago. And then, after several months in Neuchâtel, he was told who his recruiter was: one of a group of men who fought the resurgence of Nazism. They knew things other men did not know. About thousands of grown-up children — everywhere. And of untold millions that could reach those unknown people — everywhere. There was much non-medical work to be done. His contact was a man named Werner Gerhardt, and the group was called *Nachrichtendienst.*

Walther Litvak stayed in Neuchâtel.

"Come inside, quickly," he said to Helden. "Let me help you. I have an officer here."

He removed her coat and half carried her into a room with an examination table.

"I was shot." It was all Helden could think of to say.

Litvak placed her on the table, and removed her skirt and half-slip. "Don't waste your strength trying to talk." He scissored the bandage and studied the wound, then took a hypodermic needle from a sterilizer. "I'm going to let you sleep for a few minutes."

"You *can't*. There isn't time! I have to tell you . . ."

"I said a few minutes," interrupted the doctor, inserting the needle into Helden's arm.

She opened her eyes, the shapes around her out of focus, a numb sensation in her leg. As her vision cleared, she saw the doctor across the room. She tried to sit up; Litvak heard her and turned.

"These are antibiotics," he said, handing her a bottle of pills. "Every two hours for a day, then every four. What happened? Tell me quickly. I'll go down to the cottage and take care of things."

"The cottage? You knew?"

"While you were under you talked; people generally do after trauma. You repeated *Nachrichtendienst* several times. Then 'Johann'. I assume that's von Tiebolt, and you're his sister; the one who's been with Falkenheim. It's happening, isn't it? The inheritors are closing ranks in Geneva."

"Yes."

"I thought as much this morning. The news bulletins from the Negev are horrible. They found out, God knows how."

"What bulletins?"

"*Har Sha'alav.*" The doctor gripped the bottle in his hands; veins swelled on his forearm. "A raid. Houses bombed, people massacred, fields burned to the ground. The death count isn't complete yet, but the estimates exceed one hundred and seventy. Men mostly, but women and children too."

Helden closed her eyes; there were no words. Litvak went on.

"To a man, the elders were killed, butchered in the gardens. They say it was the work of terrorists, of the *Rache*. But that's not true. It's Wolfsschanze. *Rache* fighters would never attack *Har Sha'alav*; they know what would happen. Jews from every kibbutz, every commando unit, would go after them."

"Gerhardt said you were supposed to cable *Har Sha'alav*," whispered Helden.

Litvak's eyes clouded. "There's nothing to cable now. There's no one left. Now, tell me what happened down at the lake."

She did. When she had finished, the doctor helped her off the table and carried her into the large Alpine living room. He lowered her on the couch and summarized.

"Geneva's the battleground and there's not an hour to be lost. Even if *Har Sha'alav* could be reached, it would be useless. But there is a man from *Har Sha'alav* in London; he's been ordered to stay there. He followed Holcroft to Portsmouth. He was the one who took the photograph from Holcroft's pocket."

"It was a picture of Beaumont," said Helden. "*Odessa*."

"Wolfsschanze," corrected Litvak. "A *Sonnenkind*. One of thousands, but also one of the few to work with von Tiebolt."

Helden raised herself, frowning. "The records. Beaumont's *records*. They didn't make sense."

"What records?"

She told the angry doctor about the obscure and contradictory information found in Beaumont's naval records. And of the similar type of public dossier belonging to Beaumont's second-in-command, Ian Llewellen.

Litvak wrote down the name on a note pad. "How convenient. Two men of Wolfsschanze commanding an electronic espionage vessel. How many more are there like them? In how many places?"

"Llewellen was quoted in the papers the other day. When Beaumont and Gretchen . . ." She could not finish.

"Don't dwell on it," said the doctor. "The *Sonnenkinder* have their own rules. Llewellen is a name to add to the list that must be found in Geneva. Gerhardt was right: above all, that list must be found. It's as vital as stopping the money. In some ways, more vital."

"Why?"

"The funds are a means to the Fourth Reich, but the people are that Reich; they'll be there whether or not the funds are dispersed. We've got to find out who they are."

Helden leaned back. "My . . . Johann von Tiebolt can be killed. So, too, can Kessler and . . . if it's necessary . . . even Noel. The money can be stopped. But how can we be sure the list will be found?"

"The man from *Har Sha'alav* in London will have ideas. He has many talents." Litvak glanced briefly away. "You should know because you'll have to work with him. He's called a killer and a terrorist. He doesn't consider himself either, but the laws he's broken and the crimes he's committed would tend to dispute that judgement." The doctor glanced at his watch. "It's three minutes to nine; he lives less than a mile from Heathrow. If I can contact him, he can be in Geneva by midnight. Do you know where Holcroft is staying?"

"Yes. At the D'Accord. You understand, he knows nothing. He believes deeply in what he's doing. He thinks it's right."

"I understand. Unfortunately, that may be irrelevant in terms of his life. The first thing, however, is to reach him."

"I said I'd call him tonight."

"Good. Let me help you to the telephone. Be careful what you say. He'll be watched; his line will be tapped." Litvak helped her to the table with the phone.

"Hotel D'Accord. *Bonsoir*," said the operator.

"Good evening. Mr Noel Holcroft, please?"

"Monsieur Holcroft? . . ." The operator hesitated. "Just one minute, Madame."

There was a silence, a click, and a man spoke. "Mrs Holcroft?"

"What?"

"This is Mrs Holcroft, is it not?"

Helden was surprised. Something was wrong; the switchboard had not even tried to ring Noel's room. "You were expecting me, then?" she asked.

"But of course, Madame," replied the desk clerk with confidentiality. "Your son was most generous. He said to tell you it's imperative you remain out of sight, but you are to leave a telephone number where he can reach you."

"I see. Just one minute, please." Helden cupped the phone and turned to Litvak. "They think I'm Mrs Holcroft. He's paid them to take a number where he can reach her."

The doctor nodded and walked quickly to a desk. "Keep talking. Say you want to make sure this number will not be given to anyone else. Offer money. Anything to stall them." Litvak took out a worn address book.

"Before I give you a number I'd like to be certain . . ." Helden paused; the desk clerk swore on his mother's grave he would give the number only to Holcroft. The doctor rushed back to the table, a number written on a slip of paper. Helden repeated it to the desk clerk and hung up. "Where is this?" she asked.

"It reaches an empty apartment on the avenue de la Paix, but the apartment is not at the address listed with the telephone exchange. Here it is." Litvak wrote the address beneath the number. "Memorize them both."

"I will."

"Now, I'll try our man in London," said the doctor, heading for the staircase. "I have radio equipment here. It links me with a routine mobile telephone service." He stopped on the bottom step. "I'll get you to Geneva. You won't be able to move around much, but the wound isn't deep; your stitches will hold under the pressure of the bandage, and you'll have the chance to reach Holcroft. I hope you do and I hope you're successful. Noel Holcroft must walk away from von Tiebolt and Kessler. If he fights you, if he even hesitates, he must be killed."

"I know."

"Knowing it may not be enough. I'm afraid the decision won't be yours to make."

"Whose then? Yours?"

"I can't leave Neuchâtel. It will be up to the man in London."

"The terrorist? The killer who has only to hear the word Nazi and he fires a gun?"

"He'll be objective," said Litvak, continuing up the staircase. "He won't have other pressures on him. You'll meet him at the apartment."

"How will I get to Geneva? I . . ." Helden stopped.

"What?"

"I asked how I would get to Geneva. Are there trains?"

"There's no time for trains. You'll fly."

"Fine. It will be quicker."

"Much quicker."

And far better, thought Helden. For the one thing she had not relayed to the doctor was Werner Gerhardt's final warning. To her.

My child. Stay away from Geneva . . . Wolfsschanze has seen you.

"Who'll take me?"

"There are pilots who fly the lakes at night," said Litvak.

Althene was irritated, but she had agreed to the condition. The pilot had asked her a single question.

"Do you know by sight the people who are looking for you?"

She had replied that she did not.

"You may before the night is over."

Which was why she was standing now beside a tree in the dark woods above the road in sight of the car. It was a sloping forest of pine that rose above the lakeside highway. She had been guided to her watchpost by the pilot.

"If your son is there, I'll send him to you," he had said.

"Of course he'll be there. Why wouldn't he?"

"We'll see."

For a moment his doubts had disturbed her. "If he's not, what then?"

"Then you'll know who it is who's looking for you." He had started back towards the road.

"What about you?" she had called after him. "If my son isn't there?"

"Me?" The pilot laughed. "I've been through many such negotiations. If your son isn't there, it will mean they're desperate to find you, won't it? Without me, they can't have you."

She waited now by the tree, no more than forty yards away, the line of sight reasonably clear considering the profusion of limbs and branches. The car was off the side of the road, pointing north, its parking lights on. The pilot had told the man at the D'Accord to be there in one hour, not before, and to approach from the south, blinking his lights repeatedly within a quarter of a mile of the rendezvous.

"Can you hear me, Madame?" The pilot stood by the car and spoke in a normal tone of voice.

"Yes."

"Good. They're coming. Lights are flashing on and off down the road. Stay where you are; watch and listen, but don't show yourself. If your son steps out, say nothing until I send him to you." The pilot paused. "If they force me to go with them, get to the landing on the west side of the lake where we flew in. It's called *Atterrissage Médoc*. I'll reach you there. I don't like this."

"Why? What is it?"

"There are two men in the car. The one next to the driver holds up a weapon; he checks it perhaps."

"How would I get there?" asked Althene.

"There's a second set of keys in a small magnet box under the hood." The bearded man raised one hand to his mouth, speaking loudly above the roar of the approaching car. "On the right side. Be still!"

A long black car came to a stop ten yards in front of the pilot. A man on the passenger side got out, but it was not her son. He was stocky, wearing an overcoat with the lapels pulled up, a heavy muffler around his throat. Large-framed dark glasses covered his eyes, giving him the appearance of a huge insect. He limped as he walked into the spill of the headlights.

The driver remained behind the wheel. Althene stared at him, hoping to recognize Noel. It was not him; she could not see the man's face clearly, but the hair was blond.

"Mrs Holcroft's in the car, I presume," said the man with the dark glasses to the pilot. The language was English, but the accent unmistakably German.

"Her son is in yours, then?" replied the pilot.

"Please ask Mrs Holcroft to step out."

"Please ask her son to do the same."

"Don't be difficult. We have a schedule to keep."

"So do we. There's only one other person in your car, Monsieur. He doesn't fit the description of her son."

"We'll take Mrs Holcroft to him."

"We'll take *him* to Mrs Holcroft."

"Stop it!"

"Stop what, Monsieur? I am paid, as I'm sure you are paid. We both do our jobs, do we not?"

"I've no time for you!" the German shouted, limping past the pilot towards the car.

The pilot nodded. "May I suggest you find the time. For you won't find Mrs Holcroft."

"*Du Sauhund! Wo ist die Frau?*"

"May I further suggest, Monsieur, that you don't call me names. I come from Châlons-sur-Marne. Twice you won there and I was brought up with a certain distaste for your name-calling."

"Where's the *woman?*"

"Where's the son?"

The German took his right hand from his overcoat pocket. He was holding a gun. "You're not paid so much that it's worth your life. Where is she?"

"And you, Monsieur? Perhaps you're paid too much to shoot me and not find out."

The gunshot was deafening. Dirt at the pilot's feet exploded. Althene gripped the tree in shock.

"Now, Frenchman, perhaps *you* see that payment is not so important to me as the woman. Where *is* she?"

"The *Boche,*" said the pilot in disgust. "Give you a gun and you go mad. You never change. If you want the woman, you'll produce the son and I'll take him to her."

"You'll tell me where she is now!" The German raised his gun, levelling it at the pilot's head. "*Now!*"

Althene could see the car door open. A gunshot exploded, then another. The pilot lunged to the dirt; the German screamed, his eyes bulging.

"Johann? *Johann.*"

There was a third explosion. The German collapsed on the road; the pilot scrambled to his feet.

"He was going to *kill* you," yelled the driver, his voice incredulous. "We knew he was sick, but not insane. What can I say?"

"He would have *killed* me? . . ." The pilot asked the question no less incredulously. "It doesn't make sense."

"Of course it didn't," said the blond man. "Your *request* made sense. First, help me pull him into the woods and remove his identification. Then come with me."

"Who are you?"

"A friend of Holcroft's."

"I'd like to believe that."

"You will."

It was all Althene could do to hold her place. Her legs were weak, her throat dry and the ache in her eyes caused her to shut them repeatedly.

The blond man and the pilot dragged the body into the woods not twenty feet below her. The pilot's instructions meant a great deal to her now. He had been right.

"Shall I take my car, Monsieur?"

"No. Shut off the lights and come with me. We'll pick it up in the morning."

The pilot did as he was told, then hesitated. "I don't like to leave it so near a corpse."

"We'll get it before daybreak. Have you your keys?"

"Yes."

"Hurry!" said the blond man.

The pilot's relief was in his silence; he made no further protest. In seconds, they had sped away.

Althene pushed herself away from the tree. She tried to recall the pilot's exact words. *There's a second set of keys . . . a small magnet box . . . under the hood . . . get to the landing . . . where we flew in. Atterrissage Médoc.*

Atterrissage Médoc. On the west side of the lake.

Five minutes later, her hands covered with grease, she was travelling south on the lakeside highway towards Geneva. As the moments passed, her foot became firmer on the accelerator, her grip on the steering wheel less frantic. She began to think again.

Atterrissage Médoc. On the west side of the lake . . . ten or twelve miles north of the city. If she thought only of that, of the small, obscure stretch of lake-front with the petrol pumps on the single dock, she might slow her heart-beat and breathe again.

Atterrissage Médoc. Please, God, let me find it! Let me live to find it and reach my son! Dear God! What have I done? A lie of thirty years . . . a betrayal so horrible, a stigma so terrifying . . . I must find him!

Helden sat directly behind the pilot in the small seaplane. She felt the bandage beneath her skirt; it was tight, but did not cut off circulation. The wound throbbed now and then but the pills reduced the pain; she could walk adequately. Even if she could not, she would force herself to.

The pilot leaned back towards her. "Half an hour after landing you'll be driven to a restaurant on the lake where you can get a taxi into the city," he said. "Should you require our services within the next two weeks, our base for this period is a private marina called *Atterrissage Médoc*. It's been a pleasure having you on board."

41

Erich Kessler was not a physical man, yet he approved of physical violence when that violence brought about practical objectives. He approved of it as observer and theoretician, not participant. However, there was no alternative now, and no time to seek one. He would have to become a part of the violence.

Holcroft had left him no choice. The amateur had sorted out his own priorities and acted on them with alarming perception. The chromosomes of Heinrich Clausen were in the son. He had to be controlled again, remanoeuvred again.

Erich chose the person he needed among the clusters of people in the lobby: a newspaperman and, from the ease of his manner and his expertise with notebook and pencil, probably a good one.

Kessler approached the man, keeping his voice low. "You're the journalist from . . . what paper is it?"

"*Le Gené Soir*," said the reporter.

"Dreadful, what happened. That poor man. A tragedy. I've been standing here quite a while trying to decide whether to say anything. But I simply can't get involved."

"You're staying at the hotel?"

"Yes. I'm from Berlin. I come to Geneva often. My conscience tells me to go right over to the police and tell them what I know. But my attorney says it could be misconstrued. I'm here on business; it could be detrimental. Still they should have it"

"What kind of information?"

Erich looked at the journalist sadly. "Let's say I knew the man who was killed very well."

"And?"

"Not here. My attorney says I should stay out of it."

"Are you telling me you *were* involved?"

"Oh, good heavens, *no*. Not like that, not at all. It's just that I have . . . information. Perhaps even a name or two. There are *raisons des coeurs*."

"If you're not involved, I'll protect you as a source."

"That's all I ask. Give me two or three minutes to go upstairs and get my coat. I'll come down and head outside. Follow me down the hill. I'll find a secluded spot where we can talk. Don't approach me until I call for you."

The journalist nodded. Kessler turned towards the lifts. He would get his overcoat and two revolvers, both untraceable. The minor delay would heighten Holcroft's anxieties and that was fine.

Noel waited in the doorway across the street from the Hotel D'Accord. Kessler should have received the message five minutes ago. What was holding him up?

There he was! The corpulent figure walking slowly down the short steps of the D'Accord's entrance could be no one else. The bulk, the deliberate pace . . . and the heavy overcoat. That was it; Kessler had gone back to his room for the coat.

Holcroft watched as Erich made his stately way down the hill, nodding pleasantly to the passers-by. Kessler was a gentle person, thought Noel, and probably would not understand why he was being used as the lure; it wasn't in his nature to think that way. Nor had it ever been in Holcroft's to use a man this way, but *nothing is as it was*. It was natural for him now.

And it was successful. Goddamn it, it worked! A man in his mid-thirties, perhaps, reached the bottom step of the D'Accord and looked directly at Kessler's receding figure. He began walking slowly – too slowly for someone going somewhere – and took up his position far enough behind Erich not to be seen.

Now if only Kessler would do as he was told. The intersecting avenue at the bottom of the rue des Granges was made up of old, three-storey office buildings, manicured and expensive, but after five o'clock in the evening essentially deserted. Noel had done his homework; on it depended his trapping a killer of the *Nachrichtendienst*. Just one killer was enough; he'd lead him to others. It was not out of the question to break that man's neck to get the information. Or fire bullets across that man's eyes.

Noel felt the gun in his pocket and took up slow pursuit, staying on his side of the street.

Four minutes later Kessler reached the bottom of the hill and turned left. The man behind him did the same. Holcroft waited until the traffic passed and both men were out of sight. Then crossed the intersection, still keeping on the opposite side, his view clear.

Suddenly he stopped, gripped by a sharp pain in his stomach. Kessler was nowhere in sight.

Neither was the man who had followed him.

Noel began running.

Kessler turned left into a dimly lit street, walked about a hundred and fifty feet, and held up a small mirror. The journalist was behind him, Holcroft was not. It was the moment to move quickly.

On the left was a cul de sac, designed for parking two or three cars, a chain across the front denoting its private ownership. There were no cars and it was dark. Very dark. Ideal. With difficulty, he stepped over the chain and walked rapidly to the wall at the rear. He put his hand into his right pocket and took out the first gun – the first gun he would use. He had to tug at it; the silencer was caught momentarily in the cloth.

"In here!" he said, loud enough to be heard by the newspaperman. "We can talk here and no one will see us."

The journalist climbed over the chain, his eyes squinting into the shadows. "Where are you?"

"Over here." Erich raised the gun as the journalist approached. When he was within several feet, Kessler fired into the dim silhouette of the man's neck. The spit had a hollow sound; the explosion of air from the punctured throat echoed between the two buildings. The newspaperman collapsed. Erich pulled the trigger once again, shooting him in the head.

He unscrewed the silencer from the pistol, rummaged through the dead man's clothes, extracting a billfold and the notebook, throwing them into the shadows. He took out the second gun from his left pocket and pressed the weapon into the reporter's hand, the index finger around the trigger.

Still kneeling, Kessler tore in front of his shirt and ripped two buttons off his overcoat. He rubbed the flat of his hand harshly over the oil and dirt of the parking lot and soiled his face with the residue.

He was ready. He rose to his feet and lurched towards the chain. At first he could not see Holcroft, but then he did. The American was running in the street; he stopped briefly in front of a streetlight, and then continued.

Now.

Kessler walked back to the dead man, leaned over, and grabbed the hand with the gun, holding it up towards the sky and pressing the dead finger against the trigger.

The small-calibre gunshot was amplified by the surrounding stone. Erich yanked at the frozen finger twice more, let it drop, and swiftly removed the gun from his own pocket.

"Noel! *Noel!*" he screamed, throwing himself against the wall, his heavy body sinking to the concrete. "Noel, where *are* you?"

"Erich?! For God's sake . . . *Erich?*" Holcroft's voice was not far distant; in seconds it was closer.

Kessler aimed his unsilenced gun towards the clump of dead flesh in the shadows. It was the last shot he had to fire . . . and he did so the instant he saw the silhouette of Noel Holcroft in the dim spill of the light.

"Erich!"

"*Here*. He tried to *kill* me! Noel, he tried to *kill me!*"

Holcroft felt the chain, jumped over it and raced to Kessler. He knelt down in the darkness. "*Who? Where?*"

"Over there! Johann made me carry a gun . . . I had to shoot it. I had *no choice!*"

"Are you all right?"

"I think so. He came *after* me. He knew about you. 'Where is he?' he kept saying. 'Where is H.? Where's Holcroft?' He threw me to the ground . . .''

"Oh, *Christ!*" Noel leaped up and lunged towards the body in the shadows. He pulled his lighter from his pocket and snapped it on; the flame spread light over the corpse. Noel searched the pockets of the outer clothes, then rolled the body over to check the trousers. "Goddamn it, there's *nothing!*"

"Nothing? What do you mean nothing? Noel, we've got to get out of here. Think of tomorrow."

"There's no wallet, no licence, *nothing!*"

"*Tomorrow.* We must think about tomorrow."

"*Tonight!*" roared Holcroft. "I wanted them tonight!"

Kessler was silent for several seconds, then spoke softly, incredulity in his voice. "You planned this . . ."

Holcroft got up angrily, the anger lessened by Erich's words. "I'm sorry," he said. "I didn't want you to get hurt. 1 thought I had everything under control."

"Why did you do it?"

"Because they'll kill her if they find her. Just as they killed Willie Ellis and . . . Richard Holcroft. So many others."

"Who?"

"Geneva's enemy. This *Nachrichtendienst*. I wanted just one of them! Alive, *goddamn* it!"

"Help me up," said Kessler.

"Can you understand?" Holcroft found Erich's hand and lifted him up.

"Yes, of course. But I don't think you should have acted alone."

"I was going to trap him, get the names of others from him if I had to blind him for them. Then turn him over to the police, ask them to help me find my mother, protect her."

"We can't do that now. He's dead; there'd be too many questions we can't answer. But Johann can help."

"Von Tiebolt?"

"Yes. He told me he had an influential friend here in Geneva. A first deputy. He said when I found you to take you to the Excelsior. Register under the name of Fresca. I don't know why that name."

"It's one we're used to," said Noel. "He'll reach us there?"

"Yes. He's making the final arrangements for tomorrow. At the bank."

"The *bank?*"

"It'll be over tomorrow, that's what I tried to tell you. Come, we must hurry. We can't stay here; someone may pass by. Johann told me to tell you that if your mother was in Geneva, *we'll* find her. She'll be protected."

Holcroft helped Kessler towards the chain. The scholar looked back into the dark recesses of the walled enclosure and shuddered.

"Don't think about it," said Noel.

"It was horrible."

"It was necessary."

Yes, it was, thought Kessler.

Noel smiled at his friend, his gentle friend who had been called upon to act so brutally because brutality had been inflicted on him. "What did you say in Berlin? That you were a 'veritable lion'? I believe it."

Believe what you will, American. I am a Sonnenkind.

Helden saw the old woman sitting on a bench at the base of the dock, looking out at the water, oblivious to the few mechanics and passengers who walked to and from the seaplanes.

As she drew near, she was struck by the woman's face, the angular features and the high cheekbones that set off the wide eyes in the moonlight. She was lost in thought, strong and distant. The old woman was so alone, so out of place, so . . .

Helden limped in front of the bench and stared at the face below. My *God*, she was looking down at a face that, but for years and gender, could belong to Noel Holcroft. It was his *mother!*

What was she doing *here?* Of all places in the world, why *here?* The answer was obvious: Noel's mother was flying into Geneva secretly!

The old woman looked up, then looked away, uninterested, and Helden hurried as best she could across the path that led to a small building that was both waiting room and radio base. She went inside and limped up to a man standing behind a makeshift counter beyond which were telephones and radio equipment. "The woman outside. Who is she?"

The man looked up briefly from a clipboard, studying her. "No names are mentioned here," he said. "You should know that."

"But it's terribly important! If she's who I think she is, she's in great danger. I say this to you because I know you know Dr Litvak."

At the name, the man looked up again. It was apparent that at *Atterrissage Médoc* they lived with risk and danger but avoided both where possible. Dr Litvak was obviously a trusted customer. "She's waiting for a phone call."

"From whom?"

The man studied her again. "From one of our pilots. *Le chat rouge.* Has she trouble with the police?"

"No."

"The Corsicans? Mafia?"

Helden shook her head. "Worse."

"You're a friend of Dr Litvak?"

"Yes. He booked the flight from Neuchâtel for me. Check if you like."

"I don't have to. We don't want trouble here. Get her out."

"How? A car's supposed to drive me to a restaurant on the lake where I'm to wait for a taxi. It'll be half an hour, I'm told."

"Not now." He took a set of car keys from under the counter. "Go talk to the old woman. Tell her she must leave."

"She may not listen."

"She has to. You'll have your transportation."

Helden went back outside as quickly as her wound permitted. Mrs Holcroft was not on the bench and for an instant Helden panicked. Then she saw her, out on the now-deserted dock, standing motionless in the moonlight. Helden started towards her.

The old woman turned at the sound of Helden's footsteps. She held her place and offered no greeting.

"You're Mrs Holcroft," said Helden. "Noel's mother."

At the mention of her son's name, Althene Holcroft brought her hands together; she seemed to stop breathing. "Who are you?"

"A friend. Please believe that. More than you know."

"Since I know nothing, it can be neither more nor less."

"My name's von Tiebolt."

"Then get out of my sight!" The old woman's words were lashes in the night air. "Men here have been paid. They'll not let you interfere with me. They'll kill you first. Go join your wolfpack!"

"I'm no part of Wolfsschanze, Mrs Holcroft."

"You're a von Tiebolt!"

"If I were part of Wolfsschanze, I woudn't come near you. Surely you understand that."

"I understand the filth you represent . . ."

"I've lived with that judgement in one form or another all my life, but you're wrong! You must believe me. You can't stay here, it's not safe for you. I can hide you, I can help you . . ."

"*You?* How. Through the barrel of a gun? Under the wheels of a car?"

"*Please!* I know why you've come to Geneva. I'm here for the same reason. We've got to reach him, tell him before it's too late. The funds must be stopped!"

The old woman seemed stunned by Helden's words. Then she frowned, as if the words were a trap.

"Must they? Or must *I?* Well, I won't be. I'm going to call out, and when I do, men will come. If they kill you, it means nothing to me. You're thirty years of a lie! All of you! You won't reach *anyone.*"

"Mrs Holcroft! I love your son. I love him so much.. and if we don't reach him, he'll be killed. By either side! Neither can let him live! You've got to *understand.*"

"Liar!" said Althene. "You're all liars!"

"Damn you!" cried Helden. "No one will come to help you. They want you out of here! And there's a *bullet* in my leg! It's there because I'm trying to reach Noel! You don't know what we've been through! You have no right to . . ."

There was a loud commotion from the small building on the waterfront. The two women could hear the words . . . as they were meant to hear them.

"You're not welcome here, Monsieur! There's no such women as you describe! Please leave."

"Don't give me orders! She's here!"

Helden gasped. It was a voice she'd heard all her life.

"This is a private marina. I ask you again to leave!"

"Open that door!"

"What? What door?"

"Behind you!"

Helden turned to Althene Holcroft. "I've no time to explain. I can only tell you I'm your friend. Get into the water! Out of sight. *Now.*"

"Why should I believe you?" The old woman stared beyond Helden to the base of the dock and the building; she was alarmed, indecisive. "You're young and strong. You could easily kill me."

"That man wants to kill you," whispered Helden. "He tried to kill me."

"Who is he?"

"My brother. In the name of God, be quiet!"

Helden grabbed Althene around the waist and forced the old woman down to the wood of the dock. As gently as possible she rolled both of them over the edge and into the water. Althene trembled, her mouth full of water; she coughed and thrashed her hands. Helden kept her arm around the old woman's waist, holding her up, scissoring the water below.

"Don't cough! We can't make a noise. Put the strap of your purse around your neck. I'll help you."

"Dear God, what are you *doing?*"

"Be *quiet.*"

There was a small outboard motorboat moored thirty feet from the dock. Helden pulled Althene towards the protective shadows of its hull. They were halfway there when they heard the crash of a door and saw the beam of a powerful flashlight. It danced in ominous figures as the blond man ran towards the pier, then stopped and shot the light out at the water. Helden struggled, her leg in agony now, trying to reach the boat.

She could not do it; she had no strength in the leg and the weight of the wet clothes was too much.

"Try to get to the boat," she whispered. "I'll head back . . . he'll see me and . . ."

"Be still!" said the old woman, her arms now spreading out in quick, floating motions, easing the burden on Helden. "It's the same man. Your brother. He has a gun. *Hurry.*"

"I can't."

"You will."

Together, each supporting the other, they propelled themselves towards the boat.

The blond man was on the dock, the beam of the flashlight crisscrossing the water's surface in methodical patterns. In seconds the light would hit them; it was moving out like a deadly laser beam. The instant it centred on them, a fusillade of bullets would come next and it would all be over.

Johann von Tiebolt was a superb marksman and his sister knew it.

The blinding beam came; the hull was above them. Instinctively, both women put their faces in the water and surged underneath. The beam passed; they were behind the boat, the chain tangled in their clothes. They held on to it, a lifeline, filling their exhausted lungs with air.

Silence. Footsteps; at first slow and deliberate, then suddenly gathering momentum as Johann von Tiebolt left the dock. And then the crash of a door again, and voices again.

"Where did she go?"

"You're mad"

"You're dead!"

A gunshot echoed through the waterfront. It was followed by a scream of pain, then a second gunshot. And then silence.

Minutes passed; the two women in the water looked at each other under the wash of moonlight. Tears filled the eyes of Helden von Tiebolt. The old woman touched the girl's face and said nothing.

The roar of an engine broke the terror of the silence. Then spinning tyres and the sound of erupting gravel from an unseen drive came from the shore. The two women nodded at each other, and once more, each holding the other, started for the dock.

They crawled up a ladder and knelt in the darkness, breathing deeply.

"Isn't it odd," said Althene, "At one point I thought about my shoes. I didn't want to lose them."

"Did you?"

"No. That's even stranger, I imagine."

"Mine are gone," said Helden aimlessly. She stood up. "We must leave. He may come back." She looked towards the building. "I don't want to go in there but I think we have to. There was a set of car keys . . ." She reached down to help the old woman up.

Helden opened the door and instantly closed her eyes. The man was slumped over the counter, his face blown off. For a moment, the image of the mutilated head of Klaus Falkenheim flashed across her mind and she wanted to scream. Instead, she whispered.

"*Mein Bruder . . .*"

"Come, child. Quickly now!" Unbelievably, it was the old woman who spoke, giving the order with authority. She had spotted a ring of keys. "It's better to take their car. I have one, but it's been seen."

And then Helden saw the word, printed clearly in a heavy crayon on the floor beneath the dead man.

"*No!* It's a lie!"

"What is it?" The old woman grabbed the keys and rushed over to the girl.

"*There.* It's a lie!"

The word on the floor was written hastily, the letters large.

Helden limped towards it, sank to her knees, and tried to rub the letters away, her hands moving furiously, the tears streaming down her face. "A lie! A *lie!* They were great men!"

Althene touched the hysterical girl's shoulder, then took her arm and pulled her off the floor. "There's no time for this! You said it yourself. We must leave here."

Gently but firmly, the older woman led the younger out to the drive. A single light was on above the door, creating as much shadow as illumination. There were two cars, the one Althene had driven and a nondescript grey one with a licence plate wired to the bumper. She guided Helden towards it.

And then stopped. Whatever control she had managed to summon was shattered.

The body of her red-haired pilot lay in the gravel. He was dead, his hands tied behind his back. All over his face − around his eyes and mouth − were slashes made by the blade of a knife.

He had been tortured and shot.

They drove in silence, each with her own agonizing thoughts. "There's an apartment." said Helden finally. "I've been given directions. We'll be safe there. A man has flown in from London to help us. He should be there by now."

"Who is he?"

"A Jew from a place called *Har Sha'alav.*"

Althene looked at the girl through the racing shadows.

"A Jew from *Har Sha'alav* came to see me. It's why I'm here."

"I know."

The door of the apartment was opened by a slender man with dark skin and very dark eyes. He was neither tall nor short but he emanated raw physical power. What conveyed it were enormous shoulders, accentuated by the stretched cloth of his white shirt, open at the neck, with the sleeves rolled up displaying a pair of muscular arms. His black hair was trimmed, his face striking, as much for its rigid solemnity as for its features.

He studied the two women, then nodded, gesturing them inside. He watched Helden's limp without comment, observed their drenched clothing in the same manner.

"I am Yakov Ben-Gadíz," he said. "So that we understand one another, it's I who will make the decisions."

"On what basis?" asked Althene.

Ben-Gadíz looked at her. "You're the mother?"

353

"Yes."

"I didn't expect you."

"I didn't expect to be here. I'd be dead if it weren't for this girl."

"Then you have a further obligation in addition to your overwhelming one."

"I asked you a question. On whose authority do you make decisions for me? No one does."

"I've been in contact with Neuchâtel. There's work to be done tonight."

"There's only one thing *I* must do. That's reach my son."

"Later," said Yakov Ben-Gadíz. "There's something else first. A list must be found. We think it's in the Hôtel D'Accord."

"It's vital," interrupted Helden, her hand on Althene's arm.

"As vital as reaching your son," continued Yakov. "And I need a decoy."

42

Von Tiebolt spoke into the telephone, Kessler's note in his free hand. On the other end of the line was the First Deputy of Canton Genève. "I tell you the address is wrong! It's an old deserted building, no telephone wires going through it. I'd say the *Nachrichtendienst* rather successfully invaded your state telephone service. Now, find me the right one!"

The blond man listened for several moments and then exploded. "You idiot, I *can't* call the number! The clerk swore he'd give it to no one but Holcroft. No matter what I might say, she'd be alarmed. Now, find me that address! I don't care if you have to wake up the prime minister to do it. I expect you to call me back within the hour." He slammed down the phone and looked again at Kessler's note.

Erich had gone to meet Holcroft. Undoubtedly they were at the Excelsior by now, registered under the name of Fresca. He could phone to make sure but calling might lead to complications. The American had to be pushed to the edge of sanity. His friend from London murdered, his mother nowhere to be found; it was even possible he'd heard of Helden's death in Neuchâtel. Holcroft would be close to breaking; he might demand a meeting.

Johann was not prepared to agree to one yet. It was shortly past three o'clock in the morning and the mother had not been located. He had to find her, kill her. There were six hours to go before the conference at the bank. At any moment – from out of a crowd, from a taxi in traffic, on a staircase or a corner – she might confront her son and scream the warning: *Betrayal! Stop, abandon Geneva.*

That could not happen! Her voice had to be stilled, the programming of her son carried out. Quite simply, she had to die tonight, all risks eliminated with her death. And then another death would follow quickly, quietly. The son of Heinrich Clausen would have fulfilled his function.

But his mother first. Before daybreak. The infuriating thing was that she was out there. At the end of a telephone line whose accurate address was buried in some bureaucrat's file!

The blond man sat down and took a long, double-edged knife from a scabbard sewn into his coat. He'd have to wash it. The red-bearded pilot had soiled it; the man's blood was still on the blade.

Noel opened his suitcase on the luggage rack and looked at the rumpled mass of clothes inside. Then his eyes scanned the white walls with the flock paper and the French doors and the small overly ornate chandelier in the ceiling. Hotel rooms were all beginning to look alike; he remembered the seedy exception in Berlin with a certain fondness. That he even remembered it under the circumstances was a little startling. He had settled into his unsettling new world with his faculties intact. He was not sure whether that was good or bad, only that it was so.

Erich was on the phone, trying to reach von Tiebolt at the D'Accord. Where the hell was Johann? It was 3.30 in the morning. Kessler hung up and turned to Noel. "He left a message saying we weren't to be alarmed. He's with the First Deputy. They're doing everything they can to find your mother."

"No call from her then?"

"No."

"It doesn't make sense. Is the desk clerk still there?"

"Yes. You paid him two weeks' wages. The least he could do is to stay through the night." Kessler's expression grew pensive. "You know, it's quite possible she's simply delayed. Missed connections, a fog-bound airport, difficulties with immigration somewhere."

"Anything's possible, but it still doesn't make sense. I know her; she'd get word to me."

"Perhaps she's being detained."

"I thought about that; it's the best thing that could happen. She's travelling under a false passport. Let's hope she's arrested and thrown into a cell for a couple of days. No call from Helden, either?"

"No calls at all," replied the German.

Holcroft stretched, shaving kit in hand. "It's the waiting without knowing that drives me crazy." He gestured at the bathroom door. "I'm going to wash."

"Good idea. Then why don't you rest for a while? You must be exhausted. We have less than five hours to go and I do believe Johann's a very capable man."

"I'm banking on it," said Noel.

He took off his shirt and ran the hot water at full force, generating steam. The vapour rose, clouding the mirror and fogging the area above the sink. He put his face into the moist heat, supporting himself on the edge of the basin, and stayed there until sweat poured down his forehead. The practice was one he had learned from Sam Buonoventura several years ago. It was no substitute for a steam bath, but it helped.

Sam? Sam! For Christ's sake why hadn't he thought of him? If his mother had changed her plans, or something had happened, it was entirely possible she'd call Sam. Especially if there was no one at the D'Accord named Noel Holcroft.

He looked at his watch; it was 3.35 Geneva time, 10.35 Caribbean. If Sam had something to tell him, he'd stay by the telephone.

Noel turned off the tap. He could hear Kessler's voice from the bedroom, but there was no one else there. Who was he talking to, and why was he keeping his voice so low?

Holcroft turned to the door and opened it less than an inch. Kessler was across the room, his back to the bathroom door, speaking into the telephone. Noel heard the words and stepped out.

"I tell you, that's our answer. She's travelling with a false passport. Check immigration records for . . ."

"*Erich!*"

Yakov Ben-Gadíz closed the first-aid kit, stood up beside the bed, and surveyed his handiwork. Helden's wound was inflamed, but there was no infection. He had replaced the soiled bandage with a clean one.

"There," he said, "that will do for a while. The swelling will go down in an hour or so, but you must stay off your feet. Keep the leg elevated."

"Don't tell me you're a doctor," said Helden.

"One doesn't have to be a doctor to treat bullet wounds. You just have to get used to them." The Israeli crossed to the door. "Stay here. I want to talk to Mrs Holcroft."

"No!"

Yakov Ben-Gadíz stopped. "What did you say?"

"Don't send her out alone. She's beside herself with guilt and frightened for her son. She can't think clearly; she won't have a chance. Don't do it."

"And if I do, you'll stop me?"

"There's a better way. You want my brother. Use *me*."

"I want the *Sonnenkinder* list first. We've got three days to kill von Tiebolt."

"Three days?"

"Banks are closed tomorrow and Sunday. Monday would be the earliest they could meet the bank's directors. The list comes first. I agree with Litvak; *it's* the priority."

"If it's so important, he's surely got it *with* him."

"I doubt it. Men like your brother don't take chances like that. An accident, a robber in the streets . . . someone like me. No, he wouldn't carry that list around. Neither would he put it in a hotel vault; it's in his room. In a better vault. I want to get in that room, get him out of there for a while."

"Then all the more reason to use me!" said Helden. "He thinks I'm *dead*. He didn't see me at the seaplane base; he was looking for *her*, not *me*. The shock will stun him; he'll be confused. He'll go anywhere I say to find me. All I have to do is say the word *Nachrichtendienst*. I'm *sure* of it."

"And I'm counting on it," replied Yakov. "But for tomorrow. Not tonight. You're not the one he wants tonight. Holcroft's mother is."

"I'll tell him she's *with* me! It's perfect!"

"He'd never believe you. You, who went to Neuchâtel to meet Werner Gerhardt? Who escaped? You're synonymous with a trap."

"Then at least let me go with her," pleaded Helden. "Set up a meeting and

I'll stay out of sight. Give her *some* protection. I have a gun."

Ben-Gadíz thought a moment before answering. "I know what you're offering and I admire you for it. But I can't risk the two of you. You see, I need her tonight, and I'll need you tomorrow. She'll draw him away tonight, you'll draw him out tomorrow. It has to be that way."

"You can accomplish *both* tonight!" pressed Helden. "Get your *list*. I'll *kill* him. I swear it!"

"I believe you, but you're missing a point. I give your brother more credit than you do. No matter how we plan, he'll control the meeting with Mrs Holcroft tonight. He has the numbers, the methods. We don't."

Helden stared at the Israeli. "You're not only using her, you're sacrificing her."

"I'll use *each* of us, *sacrifice* each of us, to do what has to be done. If you interfere, I'll kill you." Yakov walked to the bedroom door and let himself out.

Althene was sitting at a desk at the far end of the room, its small lamp the only source of light. She wore Yakov's bathrobe which she'd found in a closet; it was too large and deep red. The drenched clothes she and Helden had worn were draped over radiators, drying out. She was writing on a sheet of stationery; at the sound of Yakov's footsteps she turned.

"I borrowed some paper from your desk," she said.

"It's not my paper, not my desk," answered the Israeli. "Are you writing a letter?"

"Yes. To my son."

"Why? With any luck we'll reach him. You'll talk."

Althene leaned back in the chair, her gaze steady on Ben-Gadíz. "I think we both know that there's little chance I'll see him again."

"Do we?"

"Of course. There's no point in deceiving myself . . . or you trying to deceive me. Von Tiebolt has to meet me. When he does, he won't let me go. Not alive; why would he?"

"We'll take precautions as best we can."

"I'll take a gun, thank you. I've no intention of standing there, telling him to fire away."

"It would be better if you were sitting."

They smiled at each other. "We're both practical, aren't we? Survivors."

Yakov shrugged. "It's easier that way."

"Tell me. This list you want so badly. The *Sonnenkinder*. It must be enormous. Volumes. Names of people and families everywhere."

"That's not the list we're after; that's the master list. I doubt we'll ever see it. The list we *can* find – we've *got* to find – is the practical one. The names of the leaders who'll receive the funds, who'll distribute them in strategic areas. That list has to be where von Tiebolt can get at it readily."

"And with it, you'll have the identity of Wolfsschanze's leaders."

"Everywhere."

"Why are you so sure it's at the D'Accord?"

"It's the only place it could be. Von Tiebolt trusts no one. He lets others deal in fragments; he controls the whole. He wouldn't leave the list in a vault, nor would he carry it on him. It will be in his hotel room, the room itself filled with traps. And he would only leave it for the most dire of circumstances."

"We agree I'm that circumstance."

"Yes. He fears you as he fears no one else, for no one else could convince your son to walk away from Geneva. They need him, they always have. The laws must be observed for the funds to be released."

"What about my son? Will you kill him?"

"I don't want to."

"I'd like something more concrete."

"There'll be no reason to, if he comes with us. If he can be convinced of the truth and not think he's being tricked, there's a good reason to keep him alive. Wolfsschanze won't end with the collapse of the funds. The *Sonnenkinder* are out there. They'll be crippled but not exposed. Or destroyed. We'll need every voice that can be raised against them. Your son will have a vital story to tell. Together we'll reach the right people."

"How will you convince him . . . if I don't come back from my meeting with von Tiebolt?"

The Israeli saw the hint of a smile on Althene's lips and understood her pause. His assumption had been clear: she would not come back.

"As the contact in Neuchâtel and I see it, we have today and tomorrow; the moves at the Grande Banque will no doubt begin Monday. They'll keep him isolated, out of reach. It's my job to break that isolation, get him away."

"And when you do, what will you say?"

"I'll tell him the truth, explain everything we learned at *Har Sha'alav.* Helden can be extremely helpful – if she's alive, frankly. And then there's the list. If I can find it, I'll show it to him."

"Show him this letter," interrupted Althene, turning back to the paper on the desk.

"It, too, would be helpful," said the Israeli.

"*Erich!*"

Kessler whipped around, his obese body rigid. He started to lower the phone, but Holcroft stopped him.

"Hold it! Who are you talking to?" Noel grabbed the telephone; he spoke into it. "Who is this?"

Silence.

"Who is this?"

"*Please*," said Kessler, regaining his composure. "We're trying to *protect* you. You can't be seen on the streets, you know that. They'll kill you. You're the key to Geneva."

"You weren't talking about me!"

"We're trying to find your mother! You said she was travelling on a false passport, out of Lisbon. We didn't understand that. Johann knows people who provide such papers; we were discussing it now."

Holcroft spoke again into the phone. "Von Tiebolt? Is that you?"

"Yes, Noel," came the calm reply. "Erich's right. I have friends here who are trying to help us. Your mother could be in danger. You can't be a part of the search. You must stay out of sight."

"Can't?" Holcroft said the word sharply. "*Must?* Let's get something straight – both of you." Noel spoke into the phone, his eyes on Kessler. "I'll decide what I do and what I don't do. Is that clear?"

The scholar nodded. Von Tiebolt said nothing. Holcroft raised his voice. "I asked you if that was *clear.*"

"Yes, of course," said Johann finally. "As Erich's told you, we only want to help. This information about your mother travelling on a passport that's not her own could be helpful. I know men who deal in such matters. I'll make calls and keep you informed."

"Please."

"If I don't see you before morning, we'll meet at the bank. I assume Erich's explained."

"Yes, he has. And, Johann . . . I'm sorry I blew, I know you're trying to help. The people we're after are called the *Nachrichtendienst*, aren't they? That's what you found out in London."

There was a pause on the line. Then, "How did you know?"

"They left a calling card. I want those bastards."

"So do we."

"Thanks. Call me the minute you hear anything." Noel hung up. "Don't ever do that again," he told Kessler.

"I apologize. I thought I was doing the right thing. Just as I think you believed you were doing the right thing to have me followed from the D'Accord."

"It's a lousy world these days," Noel said, reaching for the phone.

"What are you doing?"

"There's a man in Curaçao I want to talk to. He may know something."

"Oh, yes. The engineer who's been relaying your messages."

"I owe him." Noel reached the overseas operator and gave her the number in Curaçao. "Shall I stay on the line, or will you call me back?"

"The cables are not crowded at this hour, sir."

"I'll stay on." He sat on the bed and waited. Before ninety seconds had passed, he heard the ring of Buonoventura's phone.

A male voice answered. But it was not Sam's voice.

"Yeah?"

"Sam Buonoventura, please."

"Who wants him?"

"A personal friend. I'm calling from Europe."

"He ain't gonna come runnin', mister. He ain't takin' no more phone calls."

"What are you talking about?"

"Sam bought it, mister. Some fuckin' nigger native put a wire through his throat. We're beating the high grass and the beaches for that son of a bitch."

Holcroft lowered his head, his eyes closed, his breath suspended. His moves had been traced to Sam and Sam's help could not be tolerated. Buonoventura was his information centre; he had to be killed, no more messages relayed. The *Nachrichtendienst* was trying to isolate him. He had owed Sam a debt and that debt had been paid with death. Everything he touched was touched with death; he was its carrier.

"Don't bother with the high grass," he said, barely aware he was talking. "I killed him."

43

"Did your son ever mention the name Tennyson?" asked Ben-Gadíz.

"No."

"Damn it! When was the last time you talked to him?"

"After my husband's death. He was in Paris."

Yakov unfolded his arms; he had heard something he wanted to hear. "Was it the first time you'd spoken since your husband's death?"

"His murder," corrected Althene. "Although I didn't know it then."

"Answer my question. Was it the first time you'd talked since your husband had died?"

"Yes."

"It was a sad conversation then."

"Obviously. I had to tell him."

"Good. Such times cloud the mind; things are said that are rarely recalled with clarity. *That's* when he mentioned the name Tennyson. He told you he was on his way to Geneva, probably with a man named *Tennyson*. Can you convey that to von Tiebolt?"

"Certainly, but will he accept it?"

"He has no choice. He wants you."

"I want him."

"Make the call. And remember, you're close to hysterics; a panicked woman is unmanageable. Throw him off balance with your voice. Shout, whisper, stutter. Tell him you were to call your pilot at the seaplane base. There'd been a killing; it was swarming with police and you're frightened out of your mind. Can you do it?"

"Just listen," said Althene, reaching for the phone.

The D'Accord switchboard connected her to the room of its very important guest, Mr John Tennyson.

And Yakov listened in admiration as Althene performed.

"You must get a hold of yourself, Mrs Holcroft," said the stranger at the D'Accord.

"Then you *are* the Tennyson my son referred to?"

"Yes. I'm a friend. We met in Paris."

"For the love of God, can you help me?"

"Of course. It would be a privilege."

"Where's Noel?"

"I'm afraid I don't know . . . He has business in Geneva with which I'm not involved."

"You're not?" A statement made in relief.

"Oh no. We had dinner earlier, last night actually, and he left to see his associates."

"Did he say where he was going?"

"I'm afraid he didn't. You see, I'm on my way to Milan . . . In Paris, I told Noel I'd stop over with him in Geneva and show him the city. He's never been here, of course."

"Can you meet with me, Mr Tennyson?"

"Certainly. Where are you?"

"We must be careful. I can't let you take risks."

"There's no risk for me, Mrs Holcroft. I move freely in Geneva."

"I don't. That dreadful business at Médoc."

"Come now, you're overwrought. Whatever it was, I'm sure it doesn't concern you. Where are you? Where can we meet?"

"The train station. The north entrance waiting room. In forty-five minutes. God bless you."

She hung up abruptly. Yakov Ben-Gadíz smiled in approval.

"He'll be very careful," said the Israeli. "He'll mount his defences and that will give us more time. I'll head for the D'Accord. I'll need every minute."

Von Tiebolt replaced the phone slowly. The possibilities of a trap were more rather than less, he thought, but the evidence was not conclusive. He had purposely made the statement that Holcroft had never been to Geneva; it was a lie and the old woman knew it. On the other hand, she sounded genuinely panicked, and a woman of her age in panic did not so much listen as wish to be listened to. It was conceivable that she had not heard the remark or, if she had, considered it subordinate to her own concerns.

Holcroft's using the name Tennyson – if true – was not out of character for the American. He was subject to quick emotional outbursts, often speaking without thinking. The news of Richard Holcroft's death in New York could easily have put him in such an emotional state that the name Tennyson slipped out without his realizing it.

On the other hand, the American had displayed strengths where strengths had not been thought to exist. Giving the name Tennyson to his mother contradicted the discipline he had developed. And further, Johann knew that he was dealing with a woman who was capable of obtaining false papers, who had disappeared in Lisbon. He would take extraordinary precautions. He would not be trapped by an old woman in panic – or who pretended to be in panic.

The telephone rang, breaking his concentration.

"Yes?"

It was the First Deputy. They were still trying to locate the accurate address of the telephone number given the D'Accord by Mrs Holcroft. A bureaucrat was on his way to the state telephone office to open a file. Von Tiebolt replied icily.

"By the time he finds it, it'll be of no use to us. I've made contact with the woman. Send a policeman driving an official car to the D'Accord immediately. Tell him I'm a visitor of state who requires a personal courtesy. Have him in the lobby in fifteen minutes." Von Tiebolt did not wait for a reply. He replaced the phone and went back to the table where there were two handguns. They had been broken down for cleaning; he would reassemble them quickly. They were two of the Tinamou's favourite weapons.

If Althene Holcroft had the audacity to bait a trap, she would learn she was no match for the leader of Wolfsschanze. Her trap would snap back, crushing her in its teeth.

The Israeli stayed out of sight in the alleyway across from the D'Accord. On the hotel steps, von Tiebolt was talking quietly with a police officer, giving him instructions.

When they had finished, the officer ran to his car. The blond man walked to a black limousine at the kerb and climbed in behind the wheel. Von Tiebolt wanted no chauffeur for the trip he was about to make.

Both cars drove off down the rue des Granges. Yakov waited until he could see neither, then, briefcase in hand, walked across the street to the D'Accord.

He approached the front desk, the picture of weary officialdom. He sighed as he spoke to the clerk. "Police examiners. I've been rousted from my bed to take additional scrapings from the dead man's room. That Ellis fellow. The inspectors never have ideas until everyone they need is asleep. What's the number?"

"Third floor. Room 31," said the clerk, grinning sympathetically. "There's an officer on duty outside."

"Thanks." Ben-Gadíz walked to the lift, pressing 5. John Tennyson was in Room 512.

The policeman walked through the north entrance of the railway station, his leather heels clacking against the stone. He approached the old woman seated at the far end of the first row of benches.

"Mrs Althene Holcroft?"

"Yes?"

"Please come with me, Madame."

"May I ask why?"

"I'm to escort you to Mr Tennyson."

"Is that necessary?"

"It is a courtesy of the city of Geneva."

The old woman got to her feet and accompanied the man in uniform. As they walked towards the double doors of the north entrance, four additional policemen emerged from the outside and took positions in front of the doors.

No one would pass by them until permission was granted.

Outside on the platform flanking a police car at the kerb, were two more uniformed men. The one near the hood opened the door for the woman. She climbed in; her escort addressed his subordinates.

"As instructed, no private cars or taxis are to leave the terminal for a period of twenty minutes. Should any attempt to do so, get the identification and have the information radioed to my car."

"Yes, sir."

"If there are no incidents, the men may go back to their posts in twenty minutes." The police officer got inside the car and started the engine.

"Where are we going?" asked Althene.

"To a guest house on the estate of the First Deputy of Geneva. This Mr Tennyson must be a very important man."

"In many ways," she replied.

Von Tiebolt waited behind the wheel of the black limousine. He was parked fifty yards from the ramp that led out of the station's north entrance, the limousine's motor idling. He watched as the police car drove out on to the street and turned right, then waited until he saw the two police officers take up their positions.

He pulled out into the street. As planned, he would follow the police car at a discreet distance, keeping alert for signs of other cars showing interest in the police car. All contingencies had to be considered, including the possibility that somewhere on her person the old woman had concealed an electronic homing device that would send out signals attracting the carrion she employed.

The last obstacle for *Code Wolfsschanze* would be eliminated within the hour.

Yakov Ben-Gadíz stood in front of von Tiebolt's door with the Do Not Disturb sign on it, then knelt down and opened his briefcase. He took out an odd-shaped flashlight and snapped it on; the glow was barely perceptible and light green. He pointed the light at the bottom left of the door, walked across, and up, and over the top. He was looking for strands of thread or human hair. Tiny alarms that if removed told the occupant his room had been entered. The light identified two threads below, three vertical, and one above. Yakov removed a tiny pin recessed in the handle of the flashlight. Delicately, he touched the wood beside each thread, the pin markings infinitesimal – unseen by the naked eye, picked up, however, by the green light – and then knelt down again and took out a small metal cylinder from his briefcase. It was a highly sophisticated, electronic lock-picking instrument developed in the counter-terrorist laboratories at Tel Aviv.

He placed the mouth of the cylinder over the lock and activated the tumbler probes. The lock sprung, and Yakov carefully slid the fingers of his left hand along the borders of the door, removing the threads. Slowly he pushed the door open. He reached for his briefcase, stepped inside, and closed the door. There was a small table by the wall; he put the threads down carefully on it, weighting them with the cylinder, and again snapped on the flashlight.

He looked at his watch. Conservatively, he had no more than thirty minutes to deactivate whatever alarms von Tiebolt had set and find the *Sonnenkinder* list. The fact that threads had been planted in the door was a good sign. They were there for a reason.

He angled the beam of green light around the sitting room. There were two closets and the bedroom door, all closed. He eliminated the closets first. No thread, no bolted locks, nothing.

He approached the door to the bedroom and threw the beam along the edges. There were no threads, but there was something else. The wash of green light picked up the reflection of a tiny yellow light recessed between the door and the frame approximately two feet above the floor. Ben-Gadíz knew immediately what he was looking at: a miniature photoelectric cell, making contact with another drilled into the wood of the door's edging.

If the door was opened the contact would be broken and the alarm triggered. It was as foolproof as modern technology allowed; there was no way to immobilize the device. Yakov had seen them before, tiny cells with built-in timers. Once implanted they were there for the specific durations called for, rarely less than five hours. No one, including the person who set them, could neutralize them before the timers ran down.

Which meant that Johann von Tiebolt expected to break the contact if he wanted to enter the room. Emergencies might arise that required his setting off the alarm.

What kind of alarm was it? Sound had to be ruled out; any loud noise would draw attention to the room. Radio signals were a possibility, but signals had too limited a range.

No, the alarm itself had to release a deterrent within the immediate vicinity of the protected area. A deterrent that would immobilize an intruder, but which could be defused by von Tiebolt himself.

Electric shock was not dependable. Acid was uncontrollable; von Tiebolt might sustain permanent injury and disfigurement. Was it a gas? A vapour? . . .

Toxin. A vaporized poison. Toxic *fumes*. Powerful enough to render a trespasser unconscious. An oxygen mask would be protection against the vapour. If von Tiebolt used one, he could enter the room at will.

Tear gas and mace were not unknown in Yakov's line of work. He returned to his briefcase, knelt down, and pulled out a gas mask with a small canister of oxygen. He put it on, inserted the mouthpiece, and went back to the door. He pushed the door open quickly, and stepped back.

A burst of vapour filled the doorframe. It was suspended for several seconds and then evaporated rapidly, leaving the space as clear as if it had never appeared. Ben-Gadíz felt a minor stinging around his eyes. It was an irritant, not blinding, but Yakov knew that if inhaled the chemicals which produced that stinging would inflame the lungs and cause his instant collapse. It was proof he was looking for. The *Sonnenkinder* list was somewhere in that room.

He stepped through the doorway, past a tripod with a cylinder of gas attached to the top. To remove whatever traces might remain of the fumes, he opened a window, cold winter air rushed in, billowing the curtains.

Ben-Gadíz went back into the sitting room, picked up his briefcase, and returned to the bedroom to begin the search. Assuming that the list would be protected by a fire-resistant steel container of some sort, he took out a small metal scanner with a luminous dial. He started at the bed area and began working his way around the room.

The needle of the detector leaped forward in front of the clothes closet. The green light picked up the familiar, tiny yellow dots in the door-frame.

He had found the vault.

He opened the door; vapour burst forth, filling the closet as it had filled the space of the bedroom door. Only now it remained longer than before, the cloud denser. If the first canister had malfunctioned, this one contained enough toxin to kill a man. On the floor of the closet was an overnight suitcase, its dark brown leather soft and expensive, but Yakov knew it was not an ordinary piece of luggage. There were no wrinkles on the front or back, as there were across the top and down the sides. The leather was reinforced with steel.

He checked for threads and markings with the green light; there were none. He lifted the suitcase to the bed, then punched a second button on the flashlight. The green light was replaced with a sharp beam of yellowish white. He studied the two locks. They were different; undoubtedly each triggered a different alarm.

He removed a thin pick from his pocket and inserted it in the lock on the right, careful to keep his hand as far back as possible.

There was a rush of air; a long needle shot out from the left of the lock. Fluid oozed from the point, globules dripping to the carpet. Yakov took out a handkerchief, wiped the needle clean and slowly, cautiously, pushed it back into its recess, using his pick to press it through the tiny orifice.

He turned his attention to the lock on the left. Standing to the side he repeated the manipulations with the pick; the latch snapped up; there was a second rush of air. Instead of a needle, something shot out, embedding itself in the fabric of an armchair across the room. Ben-Gadíz rushed over, shining the light on the point of entry. There was a circle of dampness where the object had entered the cloth. With the pick, he dug it out.

It was a gelatinous capsule, its tip made of steel. It would enter flesh as easily as it had broken the threads of fabric. The fluid was a powerful narcotic of one sort or another.

Satisfied, Ben-Gadíz put the capsule in his pocket, returned to the suitcase and opened it. Inside was a flat metal envelope attached to the steel reinforcement. He had reached the safety box beyond the alarms, within the successive deadly vaults, and it was his.

He looked at his watch; the operation had taken eighteen minutes.

He lifted the flap of the metal envelope and took out the papers. There were eleven pages, each page containing six columns – names, cable addresses, and cities – perhaps 150 entries per page. Approximately 1,650 identities.

The élite of the *Sonnenkinder*. The manipulators of Wolfsschanze.

Yakov Ben-Gadíz knelt down over his open briefcase and removed a camera.

"Vous êtes trés affable. Nous vous appelons encore en une demi-heure. Merci." Kessler hung up the telephone, shaking his head at Noel who stood by the window. "Nothing. Your mother didn't call."

"They're certain?"

"There've been no calls at all for a Mr Holcroft. I even checked the switchboard in case the desk clerk had stepped out for a moment or two. You heard me."

"I *don't* understand her. Where *is* she? She should have called hours ago. And Helden. She said she'd phone me Friday night; goddamn it, it's Saturday morning!"

"Nearly four o'clock," said Erich. "You really should get some rest. Johann's doing everything he can to find your mother. He's got the best people in Geneva working for us."

"I can't rest," said Noel. "You forget, I just killed a man in Curaçao. His crime was helping me, and I killed him."

"You didn't. The *Nachrichtendienst* did."

"Then let's *do* something!" cried Holcroft. "Von Tiebolt has friends in high places? Tell them about it! British Intelligence owes him one hell of a debt; he gave them the Tinamou! Call in that debt! Now! Let the whole goddamn world know about those *bastards!* What are we *waiting* for?"

Kessler took several steps towards Noel, his eyes level and compassionate. "We're waiting for the most important thing of all. The meeting at the bank. The covenant. Once that's over with there's nothing we can't do. And then we do it, the 'whole goddamn world', as you put it, will have to listen. Look to our covenant, Noel. It's the answer to so much. For you, your mother, Helden . . . so much. I think you know that."

Holcroft nodded. "I do. It's the not knowing, not hearing, that drives me crazy."

"I know it's been difficult for you. But it will be over soon; everything will be fine." Erich smiled. "I'm going to wash up."

Noel went to the window. Geneva was asleep – as Paris had been asleep, and Berlin and London and Rio. Through how many windows had he looked out at the sleeping cities at night? Too many. *Nothing is as it was for you . . .*

Nothing.

Holcroft frowned. *Nothing.* Not even his name. His *name.* He was registered as Fresca. Not Holcroft, but *Fresca.*

Fresca.

He spun around towards the telephone. There was no point in having Erich make the call; the D'Accord operator spoke English and he knew the number. He dialled.

"Hotel D'Accord. *Bonsoir.*"

"Operator, this is Mr Holcroft. Dr Kessler spoke to you a few minutes ago about the messages I was expecting."

"I beg your pardon, Monsieur. Dr Kessler? You wish Dr Kessler?"

"No, you don't understand. Dr Kessler spoke to you just a few minutes ago about my messages. There's another name I want to ask you about. *Fresca.* N. Fresca. Have there been any messages for N. Fresca?"

The operator paused. "There's no Fresca at the D'Accord, Monsieur. Do you wish me to ring Dr Kessler's room?"

"No, he's *here.* He just spoke to you!" Goddamn it, thought Noel, the woman couldn't understand English. Then he remembered the name of the desk clerk; he gave it to the operator. "May I speak to him, please?"

"I'm sorry, Monsieur. He left over three hours ago. He's off duty at midnight."

Holcroft held his breath, his eyes on the bathroom door. He could hear water running; Erich could not hear him. And the operator understood English perfectly. "Wait a minute, miss. Let me get this straight. You didn't talk to Dr Kessler a few minutes ago?"

"No, Monsieur."

"Is there another operator on the switchboard?"

"No. There are very few calls during these hours."

"And the desk clerk left at midnight?"

"Yes, I just told you."

"And there've been no calls for Mr Holcroft?"

Again the operator paused. When she spoke, she was hesitant as if remembering. "I think there was, Monsieur. Shortly after I came on duty. A woman called. I was instructed to give the call to the head clerk."

"Thank you," said Noel softly, hanging up.

The water in the bathroom stopped running. Kessler stepped out. He saw Holcroft's hand on the telephone; the scholar's eyes were no longer gentle.

"What the hell's going on?" asked Noel. "You didn't talk to the clerk. *Or* the switchboard. My mother called hours ago. You never told me. You *lied.*"

"You must not get upset, Noel."

"You lied to me!" roared Holcroft, grabbing his jacket off the chair and going to the bed where he had thrown his raincoat – the raincoat with the gun in the pocket. "She *called* me, you son of a bitch!"

Kessler ran to the foyer and placed himself in front of the door. "She wasn't where she said she'd be! We're worried. We're trying to find her, *protect* her. Protect you! Von Tiebolt understands these things; he's lived with them. Let *him* make the decisions."

"*Decisions?* What goddamn decisions? He doesn't make decisions for me! Neither do you! Get out of my way!"

Kessler did not move, so Noel grabbed him by the shoulders and threw him across the room.

Holcroft raced into the hallway towards the staircase.

44

The gates of the estate parted; the official vehicle drove through. The police-
man nodded to the guard and glanced warily through the window at the
Dobermann, straining on its leash, prepared to attack. He turned to Mrs
Holcroft.

"The guest house is four kilometres from the gate. We take the road that
veers to the right off the main drive."

"I'll take your word for it," said Althene.

"I tell you because I've never been here before, Madame. I trust I'll find
my way in the dark."

"I'm sure you will."

"I'm to leave you there and return to my official duties," he said. "There's
no one at the guest house, but the front entrance, I'm told, will be open."

"I see. Mr Tennyson is waiting for me?"

The police officer seemed to hesitate. "He'll be along shortly. He'll drive
you back, of course."

"Of course. Tell me, do your orders come from Mr Tennyson?"

"My present instructions, yes. Not the orders. They come from the First
Deputy, through the prefect of police."

"The First Deputy? The prefect? They're friends of Mr Tennyson?"

"I imagine so, Madame. As I mentioned, Mr Tennyson must be a very
important man. Yes, I'd say they're friends."

"But you're not?"

The man laughed. "Me? Oh no, Madame. I only met the gentleman briefly.
As I said to you, this is merely a municipal courtesy."

"I see. Do you think you might extend a courtesy to me?" asked Althene,
pointedly opening her purse. "On a confidential basis."

"That would depend, Madame . . ."

"It's only a telephone call to a friend who may be worried about me. I
forgot to call her from the railway station."

"Gladly," said the officer. "As a friend of Mr Tennyson, I assume you're
also an important visitor to Genève."

"I'll write out the number. A young lady will answer. Tell her exactly where
you've taken me."

The guest house was high-ceilinged, with tapestries on the walls and French
provincial furniture. It belonged in the Loire Valley, an adjunct to a great
château.

Althene sat in a large chair, the pistol belonging to Yakov Ben-Gadíz wedged between the pillow and the base of the arm. The police officer had left five minutes ago; she waited now for Johann von Tiebolt.

He had arrived; the low, vibrating sound of a car motor outside was proof. She had heard that powerful engine hours before as it came to a stop on a deserted stretch of highway above Lake Geneva. She had watched through the trees as the blond man killed. As he had killed ruthlessly hours later at *Atterrissage Médoc*. To bring about his death would be a privilege. She touched the handle of the gun, secure in her purpose.

The door opened and the tall man with the shining blond hair and the sculptured features walked inside. He closed the door; his movements in the soft, indirect lighting were supple.

"Mrs Holcroft, how good of you to come."

"It was I who asked for the meeting. How good of you to arrange it. Your precautions were commendable."

"You seemed to feel they were called for."

"No car could have followed us from the station."

"None did. We're alone."

"This is a pleasant house. My son would find it interesting. As an architect, he'd call it an example of something-or-other, and point out the various influences."

"I'm sure he would; his mind works that way."

"Yes," said Althene, smiling. "He'll be walking down a street and suddenly stop and stare up at a window or a cornice, seeing a detail others don't see. He's quite devoted to his work. I never knew where he got it from. I have no talents in that direction and his late father was a banker."

The blond man stood motionless. "Then both fathers were associated with money."

"You know, then?" Althene asked.

"Of course. Heinrich Clausen's son. I think we can stop lying to each other, Mrs Holcroft."

"I understood it was a lie on your part, Herr von Tiebolt. I wasn't sure you knew it was one on mine."

"To be frank, until this moment I didn't. If your objective was to set a trap, I'm sorry to have spoiled it for you. But then, I'm sure you knew the risk."

"Yes, I did."

"Why did you take it? You must have considered the consequences."

"I considered them. But I felt it was only fair to let you know the consequences of a previous action on my part. Knowing it, perhaps an accommodation can be reached between us."

"Really? And what would this accommodation entail?"

"Abandoning Geneva. Dismantling Wolfsschanze."

"Is that all?" The blond man smiled. "You're mad."

"Suppose I told you that I had written a very long letter detailing a lie I have lived with for over thirty years. A letter in which I identify the participants and their strategy by name and family and bank."

"And destroyed your son in so doing."

"He'd be the first to agree with what I did, if he knew."

Von Tiebolt folded his arms. "You said 'suppose I told you' . . . about this letter of yours. Well, you've told me. And I'm afraid I'd have to say that you wrote about something you know nothing about. All the laws have been observed, and the pitifully few facts you claim to have would be called the ramblings of a crazy old woman who's been the object of official surveillance for a very long time. But this is irrelevant. You never wrote such a letter."

"You don't know that."

"Please," said von Tiebolt. "We have copies of every bit of correspondence, every will, every legal document you've written . . . as well as the substance of every phone call you've made during the past five years."

"You've *what?*"

"There's a file in your Federal Bureau of Investigation with the code name 'Mother Goddamn'. It's one that will never be released by the Freedom of Information Act because it deals with national security. No one's quite sure why, but it does, and certain latitudes are permitted. That file is also at the Central Intelligence Agency and the Defense Intelligence Agency and in the computer banks of Army G-Two." Von Tiebolt smiled again. "We are *everywhere*, Mrs Holcroft. Can't you understand that? You should know it before you leave this world; your remaining here would change nothing. You can't stop us. No one can."

"You'll be stopped because you offer lies! You always did. And when the lies fail, you kill. It was your way then; it's your way now."

"Lies are palliatives, death often the answer for irritating problems that interfere with progress."

"The problems being people."

"Always."

"You are the most contemptible man on earth. You're *insane!*"

The blond killer put his hand in his jacket pocket. "You make my work pleasant," he said, withdrawing a pistol. "Another woman said those words to me. She was no less headstrong than you. I put a bullet in her head – through a car window. At night. In Rio de Janeiro. She was my mother and she called me insane, called our work contemptible. She never grasped the necessity – the beauty – of our cause. When she found out, she tried to interfere." The blond man raised the gun. "A few old men – devoted lovers of the whore – suspected me of killing her and in their feeble way tried to have me charged. Can you imagine? Have me *charged*. It sounds so official. What they didn't realize was that we controlled the courts. *No one* can stop us."

"Noel will stop you!" cried Althene, her hand edging towards the concealed weapon at her side.

"Your son will be dead in a day or two. But even if we don't kill him, others would. He's left a trail of murder from which he could never extricate himself. A former member of British Intelligence, Peter Baldwin, was garrotted in New York. His last conversation was with your son. A man named Graff was killed in Rio; your son threatened him. A construction engineer in the Caribbean died tonight, also garrotted. He relayed confidential messages to Noel Holcroft from Rio to Paris and stops in between. Tomorrow morning a New York detective named Miles will be slain in the streets. The current case file that's obsessed him has been altered somewhat, but not its subject, not Noel Holcroft. In fact, for Noel's own peace of mind it would probably be better if we killed him after all. He has no life now." Von Tiebolt raised his weapon further, then stretched out his arm slowly, the object of aim his target's head. "So you see, Mrs Holcroft, you can't possibly stop us. We are *everywhere*."

Althene suddenly twisted in her chair, thrusting her hand towards the gun.

Johann von Tiebolt fired. Then he fired again. And again.

Outside, men walked up the path to the door. They would dispose of the garbage.

Yakov Ben-Gadíz rearranged von Tiebolt's suite, leaving it exactly as he had found it, reloading the traps and airing the rooms so that there was no evidence of entry.

Were he alive Klaus Falkenheim would be appalled at what he was doing. *Get the list. The identities. Once the names are yours, expose the account for what it is. Cause the distribution of the millions to be abandoned. Cripple the* Sonnenkinder. Those had been Falkenheim's instructions.

But there was another way. It had been discussed quietly among the elders at *Har Sha'alav*. They'd never had time to bring it to Falkenheim's attention, but it was their intention to do so. They called it the option of *Har Sha'alav*.

It was dangerous, but it could be done.

Get the list and control the millions. Don't expose the account; steal it. Use the great fortune to fight the Sonnenkinder. *Everywhere*.

The strategy had not been perfected because not enough was known. But Yakov knew enough now. Of the three sons who would present themselves to the bank, one was not what the others were.

In the beginning, Noel Holcroft was the key to fulfilling the Wolfsschanze covenant. At the end, he would be its undoing.

Falkenheim was dead, Yakov reflected. The elders of *Har Sha'alav* were dead; there was no one else. The decision was his alone.

The option of *Har Sha'alav*.

Could it be done?

He would know within the next twenty-four hours.

His eyes fell on every object in the room. Everything was in place, everything as it had been. Except that in his briefcase now were eleven photographs that could signify the beginning of the end of Wolfsschanze. Eleven pages of names, the identities of the most trusted, most powerful *Sonnenkinder* across the world. Men and women who had lived the Nazi lie in deep cover for thirty years.

Never again.

Yakov picked up his briefcase. He would re-thread the outer door and . . .

He stopped all movement, all thought, and concentrated on the sudden intrusion from beyond the door. He could hear footsteps, racing footsteps muffled by the carpet but distinguishable, running up the hotel corridor. They drew near, then came to an abrupt stop. Silence, followed by the sound of a key in the lock and the frantic turning of both knob and key. The inside latch held firm. A fist pounded against the door inches from Ben-Gadíz.

"Von Tiebolt! Let me in!"

It was the American. In seconds he would break down the door.

Kessler crawled to the bed, held on to the post, and pulled his large frame off the floor. His glasses had flown off his face under the force of Holcroft's attack. He would find them in a few minutes, but right now he had to think, to analyse his immediate course of action.

Holcroft would go to the D'Accord to confront Johann; there was nothing else he *could* do. But Johann was not there and it was no time for the American to create a scene.

Nor *would* he, thought Kessler, smiling in spite of his anxiety. Holcroft had only to gain admittance to von Tiebolt's suite. A simple hotel key was the answer. Once inside, the American would open the bedroom door. The instant he did, he would collapse, no longer an immediate problem.

An antidote and several ice packs would revive him sufficiently for the conference at the bank; a dozen explanations could be given to him. It was only a matter of getting Johann's room key to him.

The clerks at the D'Accord would not give him one on the strength of another guest's request, but they would if the First Deputy told them to. Von Tiebolt was his personal friend; accommodations were to be granted in all things.

Kessler picked up the phone.

Helden limped about the apartment, forcing her leg to get used to the movement, angry that she had been left behind, but knowing it was the sensible thing to do – the only thing. The Israeli did not think Noel would call, but it was a contingency that had to be considered. Yakov was convinced Noel was being isolated, all messages intercepted, but there was a remote chance . . .

The telephone rang; Helden thought the blood would burst from her throat. She swallowed and limped across the room to pick it up. *Oh, God! Let it be Noel!*

It was an unfamiliar voice belonging to someone who would not identify himself.

"Mrs Holcroft was driven to a guest house on an estate thirteen kilometres south of the city. I'll give you directions."

He did. Helden wrote them down. When he had finished, the stranger added, "There is a guard at the main gate. He has an attack dog."

Yakov could not let the pounding continue, nor Holcroft's shouted commands. The disturbance would be reported; it could not be allowed to happen.

The Israeli twisted the latch and pressed himself against the wall. The door crashed open, the tall American filling the frame, lunging into the room, his arms in front of him as if prepared to repel an assault.

"*Von Tiebolt!* Where *are* you?"

Holcroft was obviously startled by the darkness. Ben-Gadíz stepped silently to the side, the flashlight in his hand. He spoke rapidly, completing two sentences in a single breath.

"Von Tiebolt's not here and I mean you no harm. We are not on opposite sides."

Holcroft spun around, his hands extended. "Who are you? What the hell are you *doing* here? Turn on the light!"

"No lights! Just listen."

The American stepped forward angrily. Yakov pressed the button on his flashlight; the wash of green spread over Holcroft, causing him to cover his eyes. "Turn that off!"

"No. Listen to me first."

Holcroft lashed his right foot out, catching Ben-Gadíz in the knee, and at the contact sprang forward, his eyes shut, his hands clutching for the Israeli's body.

Yakov crouched and threw his shoulder up into the American's chest; Holcroft would not be stopped. He brought his knee into Ben-Gadíz's temple; his fist smashed into Yakov's face.

There could be no lacerations. No traces of blood on the floor! Yakov dropped the light and held on to the American's arms; he was amazed at Holcroft's strength. He spoke as loudly as he dared to.

"You must *listen!* I'm not your enemy. I've got news of your mother. I have a letter. She's been with *me.*"

The American struggled; he was breaking the grip. "Who *are* you?"

"*Nachrichtendienst,*" whispered Ben-Gadíz.

At the sound of the name, Holcroft went wild. He roared, his arms and legs battering rams that would not, could not be repulsed.

"I'll kill *you* . . ."

Yakov had no choice. He surged through the hammering attack, his fingers centring in on the American's neck, his thumbs grinding into the pronounced veins of the stiffened throat. By touch he found a nerve and pressed with all his strength. Holcroft screamed and then collapsed.

Noel opened his eyes in the darkness, but the darkness was not complete. Angled against the wall was a wash of green light – the same green light that had blinded him before – and at the sight of it, his outrage returned.

He was being pressed against the floor, a knee sunk into his shoulder, the barrel of a gun against his head. His throat was in agony, but still he twisted, trying to rise from the carpet, away from the weapon. His neck could not take the strain. He fell back, and heard the intense whisper of the man above him.

"Be very clear in this. If I were your enemy, I would have killed you. Can you understand that?"

"You *are* my enemy," answered Noel, barely able to speak through the bruised muscles of his throat. "You said you were *Nachrichtendienst*. Geneva's enemy . . . *my* enemy!"

"The first absolutely, but not the second. Not you."

"You're *lying!*"

"*Think!* Why haven't I pulled this trigger? Geneva's stopped, you're stopped, no funds are transferred. If I'm your enemy what prevents me from blowing your head off? I can't use you as a hostage, there's no point. You have to *be* there. So I'd gain nothing by letting you live . . . if I'm your enemy."

Holcroft tried to grasp the words, tried to find the meaning behind them, but he could not. He wanted only to strike out at the man holding him captive. "What do you want? Where have you got my mother? You said you had a letter."

"We'll take all things in order. What I want first is to leave here. With *you*. Together we can do what Wolfsschanze never believed possible."

"Wolfsschanze? . . . Do *what?*"

"Make the laws work for us. Make amends."

"Make? . . . Whoever you are, you're out of your mind!"

"It's the option of *Har Sha'alav*. Control the millions. Fight them. *Everywhere*. I'm prepared to offer you the only proof I have." Yakov Ben-Gadíz took the pistol away from Noel's head. "Here's my gun. He offered it to Holcroft."

Noel studied the stranger's face in the odd shadows produced by the macabre green light. The eyes above him belonged to a man who was speaking the truth.

"Help me up," he said. "There's a back staircase. I know the way."

"First we have to straighten up anything that's out of place. Everything must be as it was."

Nothing is as it was . . .

"Where are we going?"

"To an apartment in rue de la Paix. The letter's there. So is the girl."

"The girl?"
"Von Tiebolt's sister. He thinks she's dead. He ordered her killed."
"*Helden?*"
"Later."

45

They raced out of the alley and down the rue des Granges to the Israeli's car. They climbed in, Ben-Gadíz behind the wheel. Holcroft held his throat; he thought the veins were ruptured, so intense was the pain.

"You left me no choice," said Yakov, seeing Holcroft's agony.

"You left me one," replied Noel. "You gave the gun. What's your name?"

"Yakov."

"What kind of name is that?"

"Israeli . . . Jacob, to you. Ben-Gadíz."

"Ben-who?"

"Gadíz."

"Spanish?"

"Moorish," said Yakov speeding down the street, across the intersection, towards the lake. "My family immigrated to Krakow in the early 1900s. Everyone else was leaving; they had to save the temples."

Yakov swung the car to the right in a small, unfamiliar square.

"I thought you were Kessler's brother," said Holcroft. "The doctor from Munich."

"I know nothing about a doctor from Munich."

"He's here somewhere. When I got to the D'Accord, the front desk gave me von Tiebolt's key, then asked if I wanted Hans Kessler."

"What's that got to do with me?"

"The clerk knew that the Kesslers and von Tiebolt had dinner together in Johann's suite. He thought Kessler's brother was still there."

"Wait a minute!" broke in Yakov. "The brother is a stocky man? Short? Strong?"

"I've no idea. Could be; Kessler said he was a soccer player."

"He's dead. Your mother told us. Von Tiebolt killed him. I think he was injured by your friend Ellis; they couldn't carry him any longer."

Noel stared at the Israeli. "Are you saying he was the one who did that to Willie? Killed him and knifed him like that?"

"It's only a guess."

"Oh, *Christ!* . . . Tell me about my mother. Where is she?"

"Later."

"*Now.*"

"There's a telephone. I have to call the apartment. Helden's there." Ben-Gadíz swung the car to the kerb.

"I said *now!*" Holcroft levelled the gun at Yakov.

"If you decide to kill me now," said Yakov, "I deserve to die and so do you.

379

I'd ask you to make the call yourself, but we haven't time for emotion."

"We've all the time we need," answered Noel. "The bank can be postponed."

"The *bank?* The Grande Banque de *Genève?*"

"Nine o'clock this morning."

"My God!" Ben-Gadíz grabbed Holcroft's shoulder and lowered his voice; it was the voice of a man pleading for more than his life. "Give the option of *Har Sha'alav* a chance. It will never come again. Trust me. I've killed too many people not to have killed you twenty minutes ago. We must know every moment where we stand. Helden may have learned something."

Again Noel studied the face. "Make the call. Tell her I'm here and I want explanations from both of you."

They sped down the country road past the gates of the estate, driver and passenger oblivious to the sounds of an angry dog suddenly disturbed from its sleep by the racing car. The road curved to the left, gradually. Yakov coasted to a stop off the shoulder, into the underbrush.

"Dogs' ears pick up engines that stop quickly. A diminuendo is more difficult for them."

"Are you a musician?"

"I was a violinist."

"Any good?"

"Tel Aviv Symphony."

"What made you? . . ."

"I found more suitable work," interrupted Ben-Gadíz. "Get out quickly. Press the door closed; make no sound. The guest house will be back quite a way, but we'll find it. Remove your overcoat; take your weapon."

There was a thick brick wall bordering the grounds, a string of coiled barbed wire on the top of it. Yakov scaled a tree to study the wire and the wall. "There are no alarms," he said. "Small animals would trigger them too frequently. But it's messy; the coil's nearly two feet wide. We'll have to jump."

The Israeli came down, crouched next to the wall and cupped his hands. "Step up," he ordered Noel.

The ring of wired barbs on the top of the wall was impossible to avoid; there was no space on the ledge untouched by it.

Straining, Holcroft managed to get his left toe on the edge, then sprang up, vaulting the ominous coil and plummeting to the ground. His jacket had been caught, his ankles badly scraped, but he had made it. He stood up only vaguely aware that he was breathing heavily, the pain in his throat and shins merely irritations. If the stranger had given Helden the right information on the phone, he was within a few hundred yards of Althene.

On top of the wall, the silhouette of the Israeli loomed like a large bird in the night sky; he vaulted over the coiled wire and spun down to the ground. He rolled once, as a tumbler might roll to break a fall, and sprang up next to

Noel, lifting his wrist in front of him to look at his watch.

"It's nearly six. It'll be light soon. Hurry."

They sliced through the forest, side-stepping branches, leaping over the tangled foliage until they found the dirt road that led towards the guest house. In the distance, they could see a dim glow of lights that shone from small cathedral windows.

"*Stop!*" Ben-Gadíz said.

"What?" Yakov's hand gripped Noel's shoulder. The Israeli fell on him, dragging Holcroft to the ground. "What are you *doing?*"

"Be still! There's activity in the house. People."

Noel peered through the grass at the house no more than a hundred yards away. He could see no movement, no figure in the windows. "I don't see anyone."

"Look at the lights. They're not steady. People are moving in front of lamps."

Holcroft saw instantly what Ben-Gadíz had seen. There *were* subtle changes of shading. The normal eye – especially the normal eye of an anxious runner – would not notice them, but they were there. "You're right," he whispered.

"Come," said Yakov, "we'll cut through the woods and approach from the side."

They went back into the forest and emerged at the edge of a small croquet course, grass and wickets cold and rigid in the winter night. Beyond the flat ground were the windows of the house.

"I'll run across and signal you to follow," Yakov whispered. "Remember, no noise."

The Israeli dashed across the lawn and crouched at the side of a window. Slowly he stood up and peered inside. Noel got to his knees, prepared to race out from the foliage.

The signal did not come. Ben-Gadíz stood motionless at the side of the window, but made no move to raise his hand. What was wrong? Why didn't the signal come?

Holcroft could wait no longer. He sprang up and ran over the stretch of grass.

The Israeli turned, his eyes glaring. "Get away!" he whispered.

"What are you talking about? She's in there!"

Ben-Gadíz grabbed Holcroft by the shoulders, pushing him backwards. "I said go *back!* We must get out of here . . ."

"The hell we will!" Noel swung both arms up violently, breaking the Israeli's grip. He leaped to the window and looked inside.

The universe went up in fire. His mind burst open. He tried to scream, but no scream would come, only pure, raw horror, beyond sound, beyond sanity.

Inside the dimly lit room he saw the body of his mother arched diagonally in death across the back of a chair. The graceful, wondrous head was streaked with blood, scores of red rivers over wrinkled flesh.

Noel raised his hands, his arms, his whole being in the process of exploding. He could feel the air. His fists plunged towards the panes of glass.

The impact never came. Instead an arm was around his neck, a hand clasped over his mouth, both were giant tentacles pulling his head back viciously, lifting him off his feet, his spine arching, his legs crumbling beneath him as he was forced to the ground. His face was being pushed into dirt until there was no air. And then a sharp agonizing pain shot through his throat, and the fire returned.

He knew he was moving but he did not know how or why. Branches kept slapping his face, hands hammered at his back, propelling him forward into the darkness. He could not know how long he was in the suspended state of chaos, but finally there was a stone wall. Harsh commands barked into his ear.

"Get up! Over the wire!"

Cognizance began to return. He felt the sharp metal points stabbing him, scraping his skin, ripping his clothes. Then he was being dragged across a hard surface and slammed against the door of an automobile.

The next thing he knew he was in the seat of a car, staring through the glass of a windscreen. Dawn was coming up.

He sat in the chair, drained, numb, and read the letter from Althene.

Dearest Noel

It is unlikely that we shall see each other, but I beg you, do not mourn me. Later, perhaps, but not now. There is no time.

I do what I have to do for the simple reason that it must be done and I am the most logical person to do it. Even if there were another, I'm not at all sure I would allow him to do what has been reserved for me.

I'll not dwell on the lie I have lived for over thirty years. My new friend, Mr Ben-Gadíz, will explain it fully to you. Suffice it to say I was never aware of the lie, nor – God-in-heaven – the terrible role you would be called upon to play.

I come from another era, one in which debts were called by their rightful name, and honour was not held to be an anachronism. I willingly pay my debt in hopes that a vestige of honour may be restored.

If we do not meet again, know that you have brought great joy to my life. If ever man needed proof that we are better than our sources, you are that proof.

I add a word about your friend Helden. I think she is the lovely daughter I might have had. It's in her eyes, in her strength. I've known her but a few hours, during which time she saved my life, prepared to sacrifice her own in doing so. It is true that we often perceive a lifetime in a moment of clarity. The moment was there for me, and she has my deep affection.

God speed you, my Noel.

My love,
Althene

Holcroft looked up at Yakov, who was standing by the apartment window looking out at the grey light of the early winter morning.

"What was it she wouldn't let anyone else do?" he asked.

"Meet my brother," answered Helden from across the room.

Noel clenched his fist and closed his eyes.

"Ben-Gadíz said he ordered you killed."

"Yes. He's had many people killed."

Holcroft turned to the Israeli. "My mother wrote that you would explain the lie."

"I defer to Helden. I know a great deal of the story, but she knows it all."

"This is what you went to London for?" asked Noel.

"It's why I left Paris," she replied. "But it wasn't to London, it was to a small village on Lake Neuchâtel."

She told him the story of Werner Gerhardt, of Wolfsschanze – the coin that had two sides. She tried to remember every detail given her by the last of the *Nachrichtendienst*.

When she had finished, Holcroft got out of the chair. "So all along I've been the figurehead for the lie. For the other side of Wolfsschanze."

"You are the code numbers that open the *Sonnenkinder* vaults," said Ben-Gadíz. "You were the one who made all the laws work for them. Such massive funds cannot spring from the earth without a structure. The chain of legalities must be met, or they are challenged. Wolfsschanze could not afford that. It was a brilliant deception."

Noel stared at the wall by the bedroom door. He stood facing it, facing the dimly lit wallpaper, the obscure figures in the pattern a series of concentric circles engulfing themselves. The muted light – or his own unbalanced sight – made them spin with dizzying speed, black dots disappearing, only to become large circles again. *Circles. Circles of deception.* There were no straight lines of truth in those circles, only deceit. Only lies!

He heard the scream come out of his throat and felt the impact of his hands upon the wall, pounding furiously, wanting only to destroy the terrible circles.

Other hands touched him. Gentle hands.

A man in agony had cried out to him. And that man was false!

Where was he? What had he done?

He felt tears in his eyes and knew they were his because the circles became blurs, meaningless designs. And Helden was holding him, pulling his face to hers, her gentle fingers brushing away the tears.

"My darling. My only darling . . ."

"*I . . . will . . . kill!*" Again, he heard the sound of his own scream, the horrible conviction of his own words.

"You *will*," a voice answered, echoing in the chambers of his mind. It was loud and resonant, and it belonged to Yakov Ben-Gadíz, who had pushed Helden aside and had spun him around, pinning his shoulders to the wall. "You *will!*"

Noel tried to focus his burning eyes, tried to control his trembling. "You tried to stop me from seeing her!"

"I knew I couldn't," said Yakov quietly. "I knew it when you lunged. I've been trained as few others on this earth, but you have something extraordinary inside you. I'm not sure I care to speculate, but I'm grateful you're not my enemy."

"I don't understand you."

"I give you the option of *Har Sha'alav*. It will demand the most extraordinary discipline of which you are capable. I'll be frank. I couldn't do it, but perhaps you can."

"What is it?"

"Go through with the meeting at the bank. With the killers of your mother, with the man who ordered Helden's death, Richard Holcroft's death. Face him, face them. Sign the papers."

"You're out of your mind! Out of your fucking *mind!*"

"I'm not! We've studied the laws. You'll be required to sign a release. In it, in the event of your death, you assign all rights and privileges to the coinheritors. When you do, you'll sign a death warrant. *Sign it!* It won't be your death warrant, but *theirs!*"

Noel looked into Yakov's dark, imploring eyes. There it was again, the straight line of truth. No one spoke for a while, and slowly Holcroft began to find the control he had lost. Ben-Gadíz released his shoulders; balance returned.

"They'll be looking for me," said Noel. "They think I went to von Tiebolt's rooms."

"You did; the door wasn't rethreaded. You saw that no one was there, so you left."

"Where did I go? They'll want to know."

"Are you familiar with the city?"

"Not really."

"Then you took taxis; you travelled along the waterfront, stopping at a dozen piers and marinas, looking for anyone who might have seen your mother. It's plausible; they think you were in panic."

"It's almost seven-thirty," Noel said. "An hour and a half left. I'll go back to the hotel. We'll meet after the conference at the bank."

"Where?" asked Yakov.

"Take a room at the Excelsior as a married couple. Get there after nine-thirty, but long before noon. I'm in 412."

He stood outside the hotel door; it was three minutes past eight. He could hear angry voices from inside. Von Tiebolt dominated whatever conversation was taking place, his tone incisive, on the edge of violence.

Violence. Holcroft took a deep breath and forced himself to reject the instincts that seared through him. He would face the man who killed his mother and his father and look that man in the eyes and not betray his rage.

He knocked on the door, grateful that his hand did not tremble.

The door opened and he stared into the eyes of the blond-haired killer of loved ones.

"Noel! Where have you *been?* We've been looking *everywhere!*"

"So have I," said Holcroft, the weariness not difficult to feign, the control of outrage nearly impossible. "I've spent the night looking for her. I couldn't find her. I don't think she ever got here."

"We'll keep trying," said von Tiebolt.

"Have some coffee. We'll be off to the bank soon, and it will all be over."

"Yes, it will, won't it?" said Noel.

The three of them sat on one side of the long conference table, Holcroft in the centre, Kessler to his left, von Tiebolt on his right. Facing them were the two directors of the Grande Banque de Genève.

In front of each man was a neat pile of legal pages, all identical and arranged in sequence. Eyes followed the typed words, pages were turned, and over an hour passed before the precious document had been read aloud in its entirety.

There were two remaining articles-of-record, their cover pages bordered in dark blue. The director on the left spoke.

"As I'm sure you're aware, with an account of this magnitude and the objectives contained therein, the Grande Banque de Genève cannot legally assume responsibility for dispersals once the funds are released and are no longer under our control. The document is specific as to the burden of that responsibility. It is equally divided among the three participants. Therefore, the law requires that each of you assign all rights and privileges to your co-inheritors-in-trust in the event you pre-decease them. These rights and privileges, however, do not affect the individual bequests; they are to be distributed to your estates in the event of your death." The director put on his spectacles. "Please read the pages in front of you to see that they conform to what I've represented, and sign above your names in the presence of one another. Exchange papers so that all signatures appear on each."

The reading was rapid; the signatures followed and the pages exchanged. As Noel handed his signed paper to Kessler, he spoke casually.

"You know, I forgot to ask you, Erich. Where's your brother? I thought he was going to be here in Geneva."

"With all the excitement, I forgot to tell you," Kessler said, smiling. "Hans was delayed in Munich. I'm sure we'll see him in Zürich."

"Zürich?"

The scholar looked past Holcroft towards von Tiebolt. "Well, yes. Zürich. I thought we planned to be there Monday morning."

Noel turned to the blond man. "You didn't mention it."

"We've had no time to talk. Is Monday inconvenient for you?"

"Not at all. Maybe I'll have heard from her by then."

"What?"

"My mother. Or even Helden. She should be calling."

"Yes, of course. I'm sure they'll both reach you."

The last article-of-record was the formal release of the account. A computer had been pre-set. Upon the signatures of everyone in the room, the codes would be punched, the funds made liquid and transferred to the Staats Bank, Zürich.

All signed. The director on the right picked up a telephone. "Enter the following numbers on computer bank eleven. Are you ready? . . . Six, one, four, four, two. Break four. Eight, one, zero, zero. Break zero . . . Repeat, please." The director listened, then nodded. "Correct. Thank you."

"Is it complete then?" asked his colleague.

"It is," answered the director. "Gentlemen, as of this moment, the sum of 780 million American dollars is in your collective names at the Staats Bank, Zürich. May you have the wisdom of prophets, and may your decisions be guided by God."

Outside on the street, von Tiebolt turned to Holcroft. "What are your plans, Noel? We must still be careful, you know. The *Nachrichtendienst* won't take this easily."

"I know . . . Plans? I'm going to keep trying to find my mother. She's somewhere – she's got to be."

"I've arranged through my friend, the First Deputy, for the three of us to receive police protection. Your detail will pick you up at the Excelsior, ours at the D'Accord. Unless, of course, you'd prefer to move in with us."

"That's too much work," said Holcroft. "I'm half settled now. I'll stay at the Excelsior."

"Shall we go to Zürich in the morning?" asked Kessler, deferring the decision to von Tiebolt.

"It might be a good idea," said Holcroft, "for us to travel separately. If the police have no objections, I'd just as soon go by car."

"Very good thinking, my friend," said von Tiebolt. "The police won't object and travelling separately makes sense. You take the train, Erich, I'll fly, and Noel will drive. I'll make us reservations at the Columbine."

Holcroft nodded. "If I don't hear from my mother or Helden by tomorrow, I'll leave word for them to reach me there," he said. "I'll grab a cab." He walked rapidly to the corner. Another minute and the rage within him would have exploded. He would have killed von Tiebolt with his bare hands.

Johann spoke quietly. "He knows – how much, I'm not certain – but he knows."

"How can you be sure?" Kessler asked.

"At first I merely sensed it, then I knew. He asked about Hans and accepted your answer that he was still in Munich. He knows that's not true. A clerk at the D'Accord offered to ring Hans's room for him last night."

"Oh, my God . . ."

"Don't be upset. Our American colleague will die on the road to Zürich."

46

The attempt on Noel's life – if it was going to be made – would take place on the roads north of Fribourg, south of Koniz. That was the judgement of Yakov Ben-Gadíz. The distance was something over twenty kilometres, with stretches in the hills which rarely had traffic this time of year. It was winter, and although the climate was not Alpine, light snows were frequent, the roads not the best; drivers were discouraged from them. But Holcroft had mapped out a route that avoided the highways, concentrating on rural towns with architecture he claimed he wanted to see.

That was to say, Yakov mapped it out and Noel had delivered it to police who were under orders from the First Deputy to act as his escort north. The fact that no one discouraged this particular driver from this chosen route lent substance to the Israeli's judgement.

Yakov further speculated on the method of killing. Neither von Tiebolt nor Kessler would be near the area; they would be very much in evidence somewhere else. And if there was to be an execution, it would be carried out by as few men as possible – paid killers in no way associated with Wolfsschanze. No chances would be taken so soon after the meeting at the Grande Banque de Genève. The killer, or killers, would in turn be murdered by *Sonnenkinder*; all traces to Wolfsschanze obliterated.

That was the strategy as Ben-Gadíz saw it, and a counter-strategy had to be mounted. One that got Noel to Zürich; that was all that mattered. Once in Zürich it would be *their* strategy. There were a dozen ways to kill in a large city and Yakov was an expert in all of them.

The trip began, the counter-strategy put in play. Holcroft drove a heavy car rented from Bonfils, Geneva, the most expensive leasing firm in Switzerland, specializing in the unusual car for the unusual client. It was a Rolls-Royce, outfitted with armour plate, bulletproof glass, and puncture-proof tyres.

Helden was a mile in front of Noel, driving a nondescript but manoeuvrable Renault; Ben-Gadíz was behind, never more than half a mile, and his car was a Maserati, common among the wealthy of Geneva and capable of very high speeds. Between Yakov and Holcroft was the two-man police car assigned to the American as protection. The police knew nothing.

"They'll be immobilized en route," the Israeli had said while the three of them studied maps in Noel's hotel room. "They won't be sacrificed; there'd be too many questions. They're legitimate police. I got the numbers off their helmets and called Litvak. We checked; they're first-year men from the Central Headquarters Barracks. As such, not very experienced."

"Will they be the same men tomorrow?"

"Yes. Their orders read that they're to stay with you until the Zürich police take over. Which I think means that they'll find themselves with a malfunctioning vehicle, call their superiors, and be told to return to Geneva. The order for your protection will evaporate."

"Then they're just window dressing."

"Exactly. Actually, they'll serve a purpose. As long as you can see them, you're safe. No one will try anything."

They were in sight now, thought Noel, glancing at the rear-view mirror, applying the brakes to the Rolls-Royce for the long curving descent at the side of the hill. Far below, he could see Helden's car come out of a turn. In two more minutes she would slow down and wait until they were in plain sight of each other before resuming speed; that, too, was part of the plan. She had done so three minutes ago. Every five minutes they were to be in eye contact. He wished he could *speak* to her. Just talk . . . simple talk, quiet talk . . . having nothing to do with death or the contemplation of death, or the strategies demanded to avoid it.

But that talk could only come after Zürich. There would be death in Zürich, but not like any death Holcroft had ever thought about. Because he would be the killer, no one else. *No one.* He demanded the right. He would look into the eyes of Johann von Tiebolt and tell him he was about to die.

He was going too fast; his anger had caused him to press too hard on the accelerator. He slowed down; it was no time to do von Tiebolt's work for him. It had started to snow and the downhill road was slippery.

Yakov cursed the light snowfall, not because it made the driving difficult, but because it reduced visibility. They relied on sight; radio communication was out of the question, the signals too easily intercepted.

The Israeli's hand touched several items on the seat beside him; similar items were in Holcroft's Rolls. They were part of the counter-strategy – the most effective part.

Explosives. Eight in all. Four charges, wrapped in plastic, timed to detonate precisely three seconds after impact; and four anti-tank grenades. In addition there were two weapons: a US Army Colt automatic and a carbine rifle, each loaded, safeties off, prepared for firing.

All were purchased through Litvak's contacts in Geneva.

Ben-Gadíz peered through the windscreen. If it happened, it would happen shortly. The police car several hundred yards in front would be immobilized, the result, probably, of cleats coated with acid, timed to eat through tyres; or a defective radiator filled with a coagulant that would clog the hoses – there were so many ways. But the police car would suddenly not be there and Holcroft would be isolated.

Yakov hoped Noel remembered precisely what he was to do if a strange car approached. He was to start zigzagging over the road while Yakov accelerated, braking his Maserati within feet of the unknown car, hurling first the plastic charges at it waiting the precious seconds for the explosions to take place as Holcroft got out of firing range. If there were problems – defective charges, no explosives – the grenades were a backup.

It would be enough. Von Tiebolt would not risk more than one execution car. The possibility of stray drivers, unwitting observers, would be considerable; the killers would be few and professional. The leader of the *Sonnenkinder* was no idiot; if Holcroft's death did not take place on the road to Koniz, it would take place in Zürich.

That was the *Sonnenkind's* mistake, thought the Israeli, filled with a sense of satisfaction. Von Tiebolt did not know about him. Also no idiot, also professional. The American *would* get to Zürich, and once in Zürich Johann von Tiebolt was a dead man, as Erich Kessler was a dead man, killed by the son filled with rage.

Yakov swore again. The snow was heavier, the flakes larger, which meant the fall would not last long, but for the time being it was an interruption he did not like.

He could not see the police car! Where was it? The road was filled with sharp curves and offshoots. The police car was nowhere to be seen. He had lost it! How in God's name *could* he have?

And then it was there and he breathed again, pressing his foot on the accelerator to get closer. He could not allow his mind to wander so. The police car was the key; he could not let it out of his sight for a moment.

He was going faster than he thought; the speedometer read seventy-three kilometres, much too fast for this road. Why?

Then he knew why. He was closing the gap between himself and the Geneva police car, but the police car was accelerating. It was going faster than it had before; it was racing into the curves, speeding through the snowfall . . . closing in on Holcroft!

Was the driver *insane?*

Ben-Gadíz stared through the windscreen trying to understand. Something bothered him and he was not sure what it was. What were they *doing?*

Then he saw it; it had not been there before.

A dent in the boot of the police car. A dent! There'd been no dent in the boot of the car he had followed for the past three hours!

It was a different police car.

From one of the offshoots on the maze of curves, a radio command had been given ordering the original car off the road. Another had taken its place. Which meant the men in that car now were aware of the Maserati, and . . . infinitely more dangerous . . . Holcroft was not aware of *them*.

The police car swung into a long curve; Yakov could hear continuous blasts of its horn through the snow and the wind. It was *signalling* Holcroft. It was pulling alongside.

"*No!* Don't *do* it!" screamed Yakov at the glass, holding his thumbs on the horn, gripping the wheel as his tyres skidded over the surface of the curve.

He hurled the Maserati towards the police car fifty yards away. "*Holcroft! Don't!*"

Suddenly, his windscreen shattered. Tiny circles of death appeared everywhere; he could feel glass slice his cheeks, his fingers. He was hit. A submachine gun had fired at him from the smashed rear window of the police car.

There was a billow of smoke from the hood; the radiator exploded. An instant later the tyres were pierced, strips of rubber blown off. The Maserati lurched to the right, crashing into an embankment.

Ben-Gadíz roared to the heavens, hammering his shoulder against a door that would not open. Behind him the petrol fires started.

Holcroft saw the police car in the rear-view mirror. It was suddenly coming closer, its headlights flickering on and off. For some reason the police were signalling him.

There was no place to stop on the curve; there had to be a lay-by several hundred yards down the road. He slowed the Rolls as the police car came alongside, the figure of the young officer blurred by the snow.

He heard the blasts of the horn and saw the continuous, now rapid flashing of the lights. He rolled down the window.

"I'll pull over as soon as . . ."

He saw the face. And the expression on that face. It was not one of the young policemen from Geneva! It was a face he had never seen before. Then the barrel of a rifle was there.

Desperately, he tried to roll up the window. It was too late. He heard the gunfire, saw the blinding flashes of light, and could feel a hundred razors slashing his skin. He saw his own blood splattered against glass and sensed his own screams echoing through a car gone wild.

Metal crunched against metal, groaning under the force of a thousand impacts. The dashboard was upside down, the pedals where the roof should be; and he was against that roof, and then he was not, now plummeted over the back of the seat, now hurled against glass and away from glass, now impaled on the steering wheel, then lifted in space and thrown into more space.

There was peace in that space. The pain of the razors went away and he walked through the mists of his mind into a void.

Yakov smashed the glass of the remaining windscreen with his pistol. The carbine had been jarred to the floor; the plastic explosives remained strapped in their box, the grenades nowhere to be seen.

All the weapons were useless save one, because it was available, and in his hand, and he would use it until the ammunition was gone – and his life was gone.

There were three men in the false police car, the third, the marksman, once again crouched in the back. Ben-Gadíz could see his head in the rear window! Now! He took careful aim through the blankets of steam and squeezed the trigger. A scream followed as a face whipped diagonally up and then fell back into the jagged glass of the window.

Yakov crashed his shoulder once more against the door; it loosened. It *had* to; the fires behind guaranteed the explosion of the fuel tank. Up ahead, the driver of the police car was slamming it into the Rolls; the second man was on the road, reaching into Holcroft's window, yanking at the steering wheel. They were trying to send the car over the embankment.

Ben-Gadíz hammered his whole upper body against the door; it swung open. The Israeli lunged out on the snow-covered surface of the road, his wounds producing a hundred red streaks on the white powder. He raised his pistol and fired one shot after another, his eyes blurred, his aim imperfect.

And then two terrible things happened at the same moment.

The Rolls went over the embankment, and a roar of gunfire filled the snow-laden air. A line of bullets kicked up the road and cut across Yakov's legs. He was beyond pain.

There was no feeling left but he twisted and turned and rolled wherever he could. His hands touched the slashed rubber of the tyres, then steel and more steel, and cold patches of glass and snow.

The explosion came; the fuel tank of the Maserati burst into flames. And Ben-Gadíz heard the words, shouted in the distance. "They're dead! Turn around! Get out of here!"

The attackers fled.

Helden had slowed down the car well over a minute ago. Noel should have been in sight by now. Where was he? She stopped at the side of the road and waited. Another two minutes went by; she could not wait any longer.

She swung the car into a U-turn and started back up the hill. Pushing the accelerator to the floor, she passed the half-mile mark; still there was no sign of him. Her hands began to tremble and her breath came in short, erratic gasps.

Something had happened. She knew it, she could feel it!

She saw the Maserati! It was demolished! On fire!

Oh, *God!* Where was Noel's car? Where was *Noel? Yakov?*

She slammed on the brakes and ran out, screaming. She fell on the slippery road, unaware that her own wounded leg had caused the fall, and pushed herself up, and screamed again, and ran again.

"*Noel! Noel!*"

Tears streaked down her face in the cold air; her screams tore the raw nerves of her throat. She could not cope with her own hysteria.

She heard the command out of nowhere.

"*Helden!* Stop it. Here . . ."

A voice. Yakov's voice! From where? Where was it *coming* from? She heard it again.

"Helden! Down here!"

The embankment. She raced to the embankment and her world collapsed. Below was the Rolls-Royce – overturned and smoking, crushed metal everywhere. In horror she saw the figure of Yakov Ben-Gadíz on the ground next to the Rolls. And then she saw the streaks of red on the snow that formed a path across the road and down the embankment to where Yakov lay.

Helden lunged over the embankment, rolling in the snow and over the rocks, screaming at the death she knew awaited her. She fell by Ben-Gadíz and stared through the open window at her love. He was sprawled out, immobile, his face drenched with blood.

"No! . . . *No!*"

Yakov grabbed her arm and pulled her to him. He could barely speak, but his commands were clear. "Get back to your car. There's a small village south of Treyvaux, no more than three miles from here. Call Litvak. Près-du-Lac's not so far away . . . twelve, fourteen miles. He can hire pilots, fast cars. Reach him, tell him."

Helden could not take her eyes off Noel. "He's dead . . . He's *dead!*"

"He may not be. Hurry!"

"I can't. I can't *leave* him!"

Ben-Gadíz raised his pistol. "Unless you do, I'll kill him now."

Litvak walked into the room where Ben-Gadíz lay on the bed, his lower body encased in bandages. Yakov was staring out the window at the snow-covered fields and the mountains beyond; he continued to stare, taking no notice of the doctor's entrance.

"Do you want the truth?"

The Israeli turned his head slowly. "There's no point in avoiding it, is there? At any rate, I can see it in your face."

"I could bring you worse news. You'll not walk very well ever again, the damage is too extensive. But, in time, you'll get around. At first with the help of crutches; later, perhaps, with a cane."

"Not exactly the physical prognosis needed for my work, is it?"

"No, but your mind's intact and your hands will heal. It won't affect your music."

Yakov smiled sadly. "I was never that good. My mind wandered too frequently. I was not as fine a professional as I was in my other life."

"That mind can be put to other uses."

The Israeli frowned, looking again out the window. "We'll see when we know what's left out there."

"It's changing out there, Yakov. It's happening quickly," said the doctor.

"What about Holcroft?"

"I don't know what to say. He should have died. But he's still alive. Not that it makes much difference in terms of his life. He can't go back to who he was. He's wanted in half a dozen countries for murder. The death penalty's been restored everywhere. Everywhere. He'd be shot on sight."

"They've won," said Yakov, his eyes filling with tears. "The *Sonnenkinder* have won."

"We'll see," said Litvak. "When we know what's left out there."

Epilogue

Images. Shapeless, unfocused, without meaning or definition, outlines etched in vapour. There was only awareness. Then the shapeless images began to take form, the mists cleared, turning awareness into recognition. Thought would come later; it was enough to be able to see and to remember.

Noel saw her face above him, framed by the cascading blonde hair that touched his face. There were tears in her eyes; they ran down her cheeks. He tried to wipe away the tears, but he could not reach the lovely, tired face above. His hand fell and she took it in hers.

"My darling . . ."

He heard her. He was able to hear. Sight and sound had meaning. He closed his eyes, knowing that somehow thought would come soon, too.

Litvak stood in the doorway, watching Helden sponge Noel's chest and neck. There was a newspaper under his arm. He examined Holcroft's face, the face that had taken such punishment from the fusillade of bullets. There were scars on his left cheek and across his forehead and all over his neck. But the healing process had begun. From somewhere inside the house were the sounds of a violin being played by a very professional musician.

"I'd like to recommend a raise for your nurse," said Noel weakly.

"For which duties?" laughed Litvak.

"Physician, heal thyself." Helden joined the laughter.

"I wish I could. I wish I could heal a lot of things," replied the doctor, dropping the newspaper at Holcroft's side. It was the Paris edition of the *Herald-Tribune*. "I picked this up for you in Neuchâtel. I'm not sure you want to read it."

"What's the lesson for today?"

"The consequences of dissent would be a fair title, I imagine. The editorial staff of the *New York Times* have been enjoined by your Supreme Court from any further coverage of the Pentagon. The issue, of course, is national security. Said Supreme Court also upheld the legality of the multiple executions in your state of Michigan. The court's opinion expresses the profound thought that when minorities threaten the well-being of the general public, swift and visible examples are to be made in the cause of deterrence."

"Today John Q. Public is a minority," said Noel weakly, his head resting back on the pillow. "Boom, he's dead."

This was the world news, reported by the BBC in London. Since the wave of assassinations that took the lives of political figures across the globe, security measures of unparalleled severity have been mounted in the nations' capitals. It is to the military and police authorities everywhere that falls the greatest responsibility, and so that international co-operation at the highest levels may be achieved, an agency has been formed in Zürich, Switzerland. This agency, to be called Anvil, will facilitate the swift, accurate, and confidential exchange of information between member military and police forces . . .

Yakov Ben-Gadíz was halfway through the *scherzo* of Mendelssohn's Violin Concerto when he found his mind wandering again. Noel Holcroft was stretched out on the couch across the room, Helden sitting on the floor beside him.

The plastic surgeon who had flown from Los Angeles to operate on his unidentified patient had done a remarkable job. The face was still Holcroft's, and yet it wasn't. The scars that had resulted from the facial wounds were gone, in their place slight indentations that lent a chiselled look to the features. The lines on his forehead were deeper, the wrinkles about his eyes more pronounced. There was no innocence in the slightly altered, restored face; instead there was a touch of cruelty. Perhaps more than a touch.

In addition to the changes, Noel had grown older, the ageing process swift and painful. It had been four months since they had taken him out of the embankment on the road north of Fribourg, but looking at him one might judge the time to be nearer in years.

Still he had his life and his body had sprung back under the care of Helden, and the never-ending exercises ordered by Litvak, supervised by a once-formidable commando from *Har Sha'alav*.

Yakov took pleasure in these sessions. He demanded excellence and Holcroft met the demands; full health was required in the physical instrument before the real training could begin.

It would begin tomorrow. High in the spring hills and mountains, beyond the scrutiny of prying eyes, but under the harshest scrutiny of Yakov Ben-Gadíz. The pupil would do what the master could do no longer; the pupil would be put through the rigours of hell until he excelled the master.

Tomorrow it would begin.

Deutsche Zeitung

Berlin, 4 July – The Bundestag today gave its formal consent to the establishment of rehabilitation centres patterned after those in America in the states of Arizona and Texas. These centres will be, as their US Counterparts, primarily educational in nature and will be under the supervision of the military.

Those sentenced for rehabilitation terms will have been judged by the courts to be guilty of crimes against the German people . . .

"Wire! Rope! Chain!"

"Use your fingers! They're weapons, never forget it . . ."

"Scale that tree again, you were too slow . . ."

"Climb the hill and get back down without my seeing you . . ."

"I *saw* you. Your head was blown off!"

"Press the *nerve*, not the vein! There are five nerve points. Find them. With your blindfold on. *Feel* them . . ."

"*Roll* out of a fall, don't crouch . . ."

"Every action must have two alternative, split-second options. Train yourself to think in those terms. *Instinctively* . . ."

"Accuracy is a question of zero-sighting, immobility, and breathing. Fire again, seven shots; they *must* be within a two-inch diameter . . . ."

"Escape, escape, *escape! Use* your surroundings, *melt* into them! Don't be afraid to stay still. A man standing motionless is often the last person seen . . . ."

The summer months passed and Yakov Ben-Gadíz was pleased. The pupil was now better than the master. He was ready.

As was his colleague; she was ready, too. Together they would form the team.

The *Sonnenkinder* were marked.

The list was taken out and studied.

The Herald-Tribune
European Edition
Paris, 10 Oct. – The international agency in Zürich known as Anvil today announced the formation of an independent Board of Chancellors selected by secret ballot from member nations. The first Anvil Congress will be held on the 25th of the month . . .

The couple walked down the street in Zürich's Lindenhof district, on the left bank of the Linmat River. The man was fairly tall, but stooped, a pronounced limp impeding his progress through the crowds, the shabby suitcase in his hand a further hindrance. The woman held his arm, more as though guiding an irritable responsibility than with affection. Neither spoke; they were a couple grown to an indeterminate age together in mutual loathing.

They reached an office building and went inside, the man limping after the woman towards the lifts. They stopped in front of the starter; the woman asked in decidedly middle-class German the office number of a small accounting firm.

She was give a number on the twelfth floor, the top floor, but as it was the lunch hour the starter doubted anyone was there. It did not matter; the couple would wait.

They stepped out of the lift on the twelfth floor; the hallway was deserted. The moment the lift door closed, the couple ran to the staircase at the right end of the corridor. Gone was the limp, gone the sombre faces. They raced up the steps to the door of the roof and stopped on the landing. The man set down the suitcase, knelt, and opened it. Inside were the barrel and stock of a

397

rifle, a telescopic sight clamped to the former, a strap to the latter.

He took them out and attached them. Then he removed his hat with the wig sewn into the crown and threw it into the suitcase. He stood up and helped the woman take off her coat, pulling the sleeves through, reversing the cloth. It was now a well-cut, expensive beige topcoat, purchased at one of the better shops in Paris.

Then the woman helped the man reverse his overcoat. It was transformed into a fashionable gentleman's winter coat, trimmed in suede. The woman took off her kerchief, removed several pins, and let her blonde hair fall down over her shoulders. She opened her purse and took out a revolver.

"I'll be here," said Helden. "Good hunting."

"Thanks," said Noel, opening the door to the roof.

He crouched against the wall by an out-of-use chimney, inserted his arm through the sling, and pulled the strap taut. He reached into his pocket and took out three shells; he pressed them into the chamber and slapped the bolt into firing position. *Every action must have two alternative, split-second options.*

He would not need them. He would not miss.

He turned and knelt by the wall. He edged the rifle over the top and put his eye to the telescopic sight.

Twelve stories below, across the street, crowds were cheering various men coming out of the huge glass doors of the Lindenhof Hotel. They walked into the sunlight under banners hailing the first Anvil Congress.

There he was. In the gunsight, the cross-hairs centred on the sculptured face beneath the shining blond hair.

Holcroft squeezed the trigger. Twelve stories below, the face erupted into a mass of blood and shattered flesh.

The Tinamou was killed at last.

By the Tinamou.

They were everywhere. It had only begun.

The Rhinemann Exchange

For Norma and Ed Marcum —
for so many things, my thanks

Preface

MARCH 20, 1944

WASHINGTON, D.C.

"David?"

The girl came into the room and stood silently for a moment, watching the tall army officer as he stared out the hotel window. The March rain fell through a March chill, creating pockets of wind and mist over the Washington skyline.

Spaulding turned, aware of her presence, not of her voice. "I'm sorry. Did you say something?" He saw that she held his raincoat. He saw, too, the concern in her eyes – and the fear she tried to conceal.

"It's over," she said softly.

"It's over," he replied. "Or will be in an hour from now."

"Will they all be there?" she asked as she approached him, holding the coat in front of her as though it were a shield.

"Yes. They have no choice. . . . I have no choice." Spaulding's left shoulder was encased in bandages under his tunic, the arm in a wide, black sling. "Help me on with that, will you? The rain's not going to let up."

Jean Cameron unfolded the coat reluctantly and opened it.

She stopped, her eyes fixed on the collar of his army shirt. Then on the lapels of his uniform.

All the insignia had been removed.

There were only slight discolorations in the cloth where the emblems had been.

There was no rank, no identifying brass or silver. Not even the gold initials of the country he served.

Had served.

He saw that she had seen.

"It's the way I began," he said quietly. "No name, no rank, no history. Only a number. Followed by a letter. I want them to remember that."

The girl stood motionless, gripping the coat. "They'll kill you, David." Her words were barely audible.

"That's the one thing they won't do," he said calmly. "There'll be no assassins, no accidents, no sudden orders flying me out to Burma or Dar es Salaam. That's finished. . . . They can't know what I've done."

He smiled gently and touched her face. Her lovely face. She breathed deeply and imposed a control on herself he knew she did not feel. She slipped the raincoat carefully over his left shoulder as he reached around for the right sleeve. She pressed her face briefly against his back; he could feel the slight trembling as she spoke.

"I won't be afraid. I promised you that."

He walked out the glass entrance of the Shoreham Hotel and shook his head at the doorman under the canopy. He did not want a taxi; he wanted to walk. To let the dying fires of rage finally subside and burn themselves out. A long walk.

It would be the last hour of his life that he would wear the uniform.

The uniform now with no insignia, no identification.

He would walk through the second set of doors at the War Department and give his name to the military police.

David Spaulding.

That's all he would say. It would be enough; no one would stop him, none would interfere.

Orders would be left by unnamed commanders – divisional recognition only – that would allow him to proceed down the grey corridors to an unmarked room.

Those orders would be at that security desk because another order had been given. An order no one could trace. No one comprehended. . . .

They claimed. In outrage.

But none with an outrage matching his.

They knew that, too, the unknown commanders.

Names meaning nothing to him only months ago would be in the unmarked room. Names that now were symbols of an abyss of deceit that so revolted him, he honestly believed he had lost his mind.

Howard Oliver.

Jonathan Craft.

Walter Kendall.

The names were innocuous-sounding in themselves. They could belong to untold hundreds of thousands. There was something so. . . . American about them.

Yet these names, these men, had brought him to the brink of insanity.

They would be there in the unmarked room, and he would remind them of those who were absent.

Erich Rhinemann. Buenos Aires.

Alan Swanson. Washington.

Franz Altmüller. Berlin.

Other symbols. Other threads. . . .

The abyss of deceit into which he had been plunged by . . . enemies.

How in God's name had it *happened?*

How *could* it have happened?

But it did happen. And he had written down the facts as he knew them.

Written them down and placed . . . the document in an archive case inside a deposit box within a bank vault in Colorado.

Untraceable. Locked in the earth for a millennium . . . for it was better that way.

Unless the men in the unmarked room forced him to do otherwise.

If they did . . . if they forced him . . . the sanities of millions would be tested. The revulsion would not acknowledge national boundaries or the cause of any global tribe.

The leaders would become pariahs.

As he was a pariah now.

A number followed by a letter.

He reached the steps of the War Department; the tan stone pillars did not signify strength to him now. Only the appearance of light brown paste.

No longer substance.

He walked through the sets of double doors up to the security desk, manned by a middle-aged lieutenant colonel flanked by two sergeants.

"Spaulding, David," he said quietly.

"Your I.D. . . ." the lieutenant colonel looked at the shoulders of the raincoat, then at the collar, "Spaulding. . . ."

"My name is David Spaulding. My source is Fairfax," repeated David softly. "Check your papers, soldier."

The lieutenant colonel's head snapped up in anger, gradually replaced by bewilderment as he looked at Spaulding. For David had not spoken harshly, or even impolitely. Just factually.

The sergeant to the left of the lieutenant colonel shoved a page of paper in front of the officer without interrupting. The lieutenant colonel looked at it.

He glanced back up at David – briefly – and waved him through.

As he walked down the grey corridor, his raincoat over his arm, Spaulding could feel the eyes on him, scanning the uniform devoid of rank or identification. Several salutes were rendered hesitantly.

None was acknowledged.

Men turned; others stared from doorways.

This was the . . . officer, their looks were telling him. They'd heard the rumors, spoken in whispers, in hushed voices in out-of-the-way corners. This was the man.

An order had been given. . . .

The *man*.

Prologue

Prologue

One

The two army officers, their uniforms creased into steel, their hats removed, watched the group of informally dressed men and women through the glass partition. The room in which the officers sat was dark.

A red light flashed; the sounds of an organ thundered out of the two webbed boxes at each corner of the glass-fronted, light-less cubicle. There followed the distant howling of dogs – large, rapacious dogs – and then a voice – deep, clear, forbidding spoke over the interweaving sounds of the organ and the animals.

Wherever madness exists, wherever the cries of the helpless can be heard, there you will find the tall figure of Jonathan Tyne – waiting, watching in shadows, prepared to do battle with the forces of hell. The seen and the unseen . . . .

Suddenly there was a piercing, mind-splitting scream. "Eeaagh!" Inside the lighted, inner room an obese woman winked at the short man in thick glasses who had been reading from a typed script and walked away from the microphone, chewing her gum rapidly.

The deep voice continued. *Tonight we find Jonathan Tyne coming to the aid of the terror-stricken Lady Ashcroft, whose husband disappeared into the misty Scottish moors at precisely midnight three weeks ago. And each night at precisely midnight, the howls of unknown dogs bay across the darkened fields. They seem to be challenging the very man who now walks stealthily into the enveloping mist. Jonathan Tyne. The seeker of evil; the nemesis of Lucifer. The champion of the helpless victims of darkness . . . .*

The organ music swelled once more to a crescendo; the sound of the baying dogs grew more vicious.

The older officer, a colonel, glanced at his companion, a first lieutenant. The younger man, his eyes betraying his concern, was staring at the group of nonchalant actors inside the lighted studio.

The colonel winced.

"Interesting, isn't it?" he said.

"What?' . . . Oh, yes, sir. Yes, sir, very interesting. Which one is he?"

"The tall fellow over in the corner. The one reading a newspaper.

"Does he play Tyne?"

"Who? Oh, no, lieutenant. He has a small role, I think. In a Spanish dialect."

"A small role ... in a Spanish dialect." The lieutenant repeated the colonel's words, his voice hesitant, his look bewildered. "Forgive me, sir, I'm confused. I'm not sure what we're *doing* here; what *he's* doing here. I thought he was a construction engineer."

"He is."

The organ music subsided to pianissimo; the sound of the howling dogs faded away. Now another voice – this one lighter, friendlier, with no undercurrent of impending drama – came out of the two webbed boxes.

Pilgrim. The soap with the scent of flowers in May; the Mayflower soap. Pilgrim brings you once again ... "The Adventures of Jonathan Tyne."

The thick corked door of the dark cubicle opened and a balding man, erect, dressed in a conservative business suit, entered. He carried a manila envelope in his left hand; he reached over and extended his right hand to the colonel. He spoke quietly, but not in a whisper. "Hello, Ed. Nice to see you again. I don't have to tell you your call was a surprise."

"I guess it was. How are you, Jack. . . . Lieutenant, meet Mr. John Ryan; formerly Major John N. M. I. Ryan of Six Corps."

The officer rose to his feet.

"Sit down, lieutenant," said Ryan, shaking the young man's hand.

"Nice to meet you, sir. Thank you, sir."

Ryan edged his way around the rows of black leather armchairs and sat down next to the colonel in front of the glass partition. The organ music once more swelled, matching the reintroduced sounds of the howling dogs. Several actors and actresses crowded around two microphones, all watching a man behind a panel in another glass booth – this one lighted – on the other side of the studio.

"How's Jane?" asked Ryan. "And the children?"

"She hates Washington; so does the boy. They'd rather be back in Oahu. Cynthia loves it, though. She's eighteen, now; all those D.C. dances."

A hand signal was given by the man in the lighted booth across the way. The actors began their dialogue.

Ryan continued. "How about you? 'Washington' looks good on the roster sheet."

"I suppose it does, but nobody knows I'm there. That won't help me."

"Oh?"

"G-2."

"Yes, I gathered that."

"You look as though you're thriving, Jack."

Ryan smiled a little awkwardly. "No sweat. Ten other guys in the agency could do what I'm doing ... better. But they don't have the Point on their résumés. I'm an agency symbol, strong-integrity version. The clients sort of fall in for muster."

The colonel laughed. "Horseshit. You were always good with the beady-bags. Even the high brass used to turn the congressmen over to you."

"You flatter me. At least I *think* you're flattering me."

"Eeaagh!" The obese actress, still chewing her gum, had screeched into the second microphone. She backed away, goosing a thin, effeminate-looking actor who was about to speak.

"There's a lot of screaming, isn't there." The colonel wasn't really asking a question.

"And dogs barking and off-key organ music and a hell of a lot of groaning and heavy breathing. 'Tyne's' the most popular program we have."

"I admit I've listened to it. The whole family has; since we've been back."

"You wouldn't believe it if I told you who writes most of the scripts."

"What do you mean?"

"A Pulitzer poet. Under another name, of course."

"That seems strange."

"Not at all. Survival. We pay. Poetry doesn't."

"Is that why *he's* on?" The colonel gestured with a nod of his head toward the tall, dark-haired man who had put down the newspaper but still remained in the corner of the studio, away from the other actors, leaning against the white corked wall.

"Beats the hell out of me. I mean, I didn't know who he was – that is, I knew who he *was*, but I didn't know anything about him – until you called." Ryan handed the colonel the manila envelope. "Here's a list of the shows and the agencies he's worked for. I called around; implied that we were considering him for a running lead. The Hammerts use him a lot. . . ."

"The who?"

"They're packagers. They've got about fifteen programs; day-time serials and evening shows. They say he's reliable; no sauce problems. He's used exclusively for dialects, it seems. And language fluency when it's called for."

"German and Spanish." It was a statement.

"That's right. . . ."

"Only it's not Spanish, it's Portuguese."

"Who can tell the difference? You know who his parents are. Another statement, only agreement anticipated."

"Richard and Margo Spaulding. Concert pianists, very big in England and the Continent. Current status: semi-retirement in Costa del Santiago, Portugal."

"They're American, though, aren't they?"

"Very. Made sure their son was born here. Sent him to American settlement schools wherever they lived. Shipped him back here for his final two years in prep school and college."

"How come Portugal, then?"

"Who knows? They had their first successes in Europe and decided to stay there. A fact I *think* we're going to be grateful for. They only return here for tours; which aren't very frequent anymore. . . . Did you know that he's a construction engineer?"

"No, I didn't. That's interesting."

"Interesting? Just 'interesting'?"

Ryan smiled; there was a trace of sadness in his eyes. "Well, during the last six years or so there hasn't been a lot of building, has there? I mean, there's no great call for engineers . . . outside of the CCC and the NRA." He lifted his right hand and waved it laterally in front of him, encompassing the group of men and women inside the studio. "Do you know what's in there? A trial lawyer whose clients – when he can get a few – can't pay him; a Rolls-Royce executive who's been laid off since thirty-eight; and a former state senator whose campaign a few years ago not only cost him his job but also a lot of potential employers. They think he's a Red. Don't fool yourself, Ed. You've got it good. The Depression isn't over by a long shot. These people are the lucky ones. They found avocations they've turned into careers. . . . As long as they last."

"If I do *my* job, *his* career won't last any longer than a month from now."

"I figured it was something like that. The storm's building, isn't it? We'll be in it pretty soon. And I'll be back, too. . . ."

Where do you want to use him?"

"Lisbon."

David Spaulding pushed himself away from the white studio wall. He held up the pages of his script as he approached the microphone, preparing for his cue.

Pace watched him through the glass partition, wondering how Spaulding's voice would sound. He noticed that as Spaulding came closer to the group of actors clustered around the microphone, there was a conscious – or it seemed conscious – parting of bodies, as if the new participant was in some way a stranger. Perhaps it was only normal courtesy, allowing the new performer a chance to position himself, but the colonel didn't think so. There were no smiles, no looks, no indications of familiarity as there seemed to be among the others.

No one winked. Even the obese woman who screamed and chewed gum and goosed her fellow actors just stood and watched Spaulding, her gum immobile in her mouth.

And then it happened; a curious moment.

Spaulding grinned, and the others, even the thin, effeminate man who was in the middle of a monologue, responded with bright smiles and nods. The obese woman winked.

A curious moment, thought Colonel Pace.

Spaulding's voice – mid-deep, incisive, heavily accented – came through the webbed boxes. His role was that of a mad doctor and bordered on the comic. It *would* have been comic, thought Pace, except for the authority Spaulding gave the writer's words. Pace didn't know anything about acting, but he knew when a man was being convincing. Spaulding was convincing.

That would be necessary in Lisbon.

In a few minutes Spaulding's role was obviously over. The obese woman screamed again; Spaulding retreated to the corner and quietly, making sure the pages did not rustle, picked up his folded newspaper. He leaned against the wall and withdrew a pencil from his pocket. He appeared to be doing *The New York Times* crossword puzzle.

Pace couldn't take his eyes off Spaulding. It was important for him to observe closely any subject with whom he had to make contact whenever possible. Observe the small things: the way a man walked; the way he held his head; the steadiness or lack of it in his eyes. The clothes, the watch, the cuff links; whether the shoes were shined, if the heels were worn down; the quality or lack of quality – in a man's posture.

Pace tried to match the human being leaning against the wall, writing on the newspaper, with the dossier in his Washington office.

His name first surfaced from the files of the Army Corps of Engineers. David Spaulding had inquired about the possibilities of a commission – not volunteered: what would his opportunities be? were there any challenging construction projects? what about the length-of-service commitments? The sort of questions thousands of men – skilled men – were asking, knowing that the Selective Service Act would become law within a week or two. If enlistment meant a shorter commitment and/or the continued practice of their professional skills, then better an enlistment than be drafted with the mobs.

Spaulding had filled out all the appropriate forms and had been told the army would contact him. That had been six weeks ago and no one had done so. Not that the Corps wasn't interested; it was. The word from the Roosevelt men was that the draft law would be passed by Congress any day now, and the projected expansion of the army camps was so enormous, so incredibly massive, that an engineer – especially a *construction* engineer of Spaulding's qualifications – was target material.

But those high up in the Corps of Engineers were aware of the search being conducted by the Intelligence Division of the Joint Chiefs of Staff and the War Department.

Quietly, slowly. No mistakes could be made.

So they passed along David Spaulding's forms to G-2 and were told in turn to stay away from him.

The man ID was seeking had to have three basic qualifications. Once these were established, the rest of the portrait could be microscopically scrutinized to see if the whole being possessed the other desirable requirements. The three basics were difficult enough in themselves: the first was fluency in the Portuguese language; the second, an equal mastery of German; the third, sufficient professional experience in structural engineering to enable swift and accurate understanding of blueprints, photographs – even verbal descriptions – of the widest variety of industrial designs. From bridges and factories to warehousing and railroad complexes.

The man in Lisbon would need each of these basic requirements. He would employ them throughout the war that was to be; the war that the United States inevitably would have to fight.

The man in Lisbon would be responsible for developing an Intelligence network primarily concerned with the destruction of the enemy's installations deep within its own territories.

Certain men – and women – traveled back and forth through hostile territories, basing their undefined activities in neutral countries. These were the people the man in Lisbon would use . . . before others used them.

These plus those he would train for infiltration. Espionage units. Teams of bi- and trilingual agents he would send up through France into the borders of Germany. To bring back their observations; eventually to inflict destruction themselves.

The English agreed that such an American was needed in Lisbon. British Intelligence admitted its Portuguese weakness; they had simply been around too long, too obviously. And there were current, very serious lapses of security in London. MI-5 had been infiltrated.

Lisbon would become an American project.

If such an American could be found.

David Spaulding's preapplication forms listed the primary requisites. He spoke three languages, had spoken them since he was a child. His parents, the renowned Richard and Margo Spaulding, maintained three residences: a small, elegant Belgravia flat in London; a winter retreat in Germany's Baden-Baden; and a sprawling oceanside house in the artists' colony of Costa del Santiago in Portugal. Spaulding had grown up in these environs. When he was sixteen, his father – over the objections of his mother – insisted that he complete his secondary education in the United States and enter an American university.

Andover in Massachusetts; Dartmouth in New Hampshire; finally Carnegie Institute in Pennsylvania.

Of course, the Intelligence Division hadn't discovered *all* of the above information from Spaulding's application forms. These supplementary facts – and a great deal more – were revealed by a man named Aaron Mandel in New York.

Pace, his eyes still riveted on the tall, lean man who had put down his newspaper and was now watching the actors around the microphones with detached amusement, recalled his single meeting with Mandel. Again, he matched Mandel's information with the man he saw before him.

Mandel had been listed on the application under "References. *Power-of-attorney, parents' concert manager.* An address was given: a suite of rooms in the Chrysler Building. Mandel was a very successful artists' representative, a Russian Jew who rivaled Sol Hurok for clients, though not as prone to attract attention or as desirous of it."

"David has been as a son to me," Mandel told Pace. "But I must presume you know that."

"Why must you? I know only what I've read on his application forms. And some scattered information; academic records, employment references."

"Let's say I've been expecting you. Or someone like you."

"I beg your pardon?"

"Oh, come. David spent a great many years in Germany; you might say he almost grew up there."

"His application . . . as a matter of fact his passport information, also includes family residences in London and a place called Costa del Santiago in Portugal."

"I said almost. He converses easily in the German language."

"Also Portuguese, I understand."

"Equally so. And its sister tongue, Spanish. . . . I wasn't aware that a man's enlistment in the army engineers called for a full colonel's interest. And passport research." Mandel, the flesh creased around his eyes, smiled.

"I wasn't prepared for you." The colonel's reply had been stated simply. "Most people take this sort of thing as routine. Or they convince themselves it's routine . . . with a little help."

"Most people did not live as Jews in tsarist Kiev. . . . What do you want from me?"

"To begin with, did you tell Spaulding you expected us? Or someone"

"Of course not," Mandel interrupted gently. "I told you, he is as a son to me. I wouldn't care to give him such ideas."

"I'm relieved. Nothing may come of it anyway."

"However, you hope it will."

"Frankly, yes. But there are questions we need answered. His background isn't just unusual, it seems filled with contradictions. To begin with, you don't expect the son of well-known musicians . . . I mean . . .

"Concert artists." Mandel had supplied the term Pace sought.

"Yes, concert artists. You don't expect the children of such people to become engineers. Or accountants, if you know what I mean. And then – and I'm sure you'll understand this – it seems highly illogical that once that fact is accepted, the son *is* an engineer, we find that the major portion of his income is currently earned as a . . . as a radio performer. The pattern indicates a degree of instability. Perhaps more than a degree."

"You suffer from the American mania for consistency. I don't say this unkindly. I would be less than adequate as a neurosurgeon; you may play the piano quite well, but I doubt that I'd represent you at Covent Garden. . . . The questions you raise are easily answered. And, perhaps, the word *stability* can be found at the core. . . . Have you any idea, any *conception*, of what the world of the concert stage is like? *Madness*. . . . David lived in this world for nearly twenty years; I suspect . . . no, I don't suspect, I know . . . he found it quite distasteful . . . And so often people overlook certain fundamental characteristics of musicianship. Characteristics easily inherited. A great musician is often, in his own way, an exceptional mathematician. Take Bach. A genius at mathematics. . . ."

According to Aaron Mandel, David Spaulding found his future profession while in his second year in college. The solidity, the permanence of structural creation combined with the precision of engineering detail were at once his answer to and escape from the mercurial world of the "concert stage." But there were other inherited characteristics equally at work inside him. Spaulding had an ego, a sense of independence. He needed approval, wanted recognition. And such rewards were not easily come by for a junior engineer, just out of graduate school, in a large New York firm during the late thirties. There simply wasn't that much to do; or the capital to do it with.

"He left the New York firm," Mandel continued, "to accept a number of individual construction projects where he believed the money would grow faster, the jobs be his own. He had no ties; he could travel. Several in the Midwest, one . . . no, two, in Central America; four in Canada, I think. He got the first few right out of the newspapers; they led to the others. He returned to New York about eighteen months ago. The money didn't really grow, as I told him it wouldn't. The projects were not his own; provincial . . . local interference."

"And somehow this led to the radio work?"

Mandel had laughed and leaned back in his chair. "As you may know, Colonel Pace, I've diversified. The concert stage and a European war – soon to reach these shores, as we all realize – do not go well together. These last few years my clients have gone into other performing areas, including the highly paid radio field. David quickly saw opportunities for himself and I agreed. He's done extremely well, you know."

"But he's not a trained professional."

"No, he's not. He has something else, however . . . Think. Most children of well-known performers, or leading politicians, or the immensely rich, for that matter, have it. It's a public confidence, an assurance, if you will; no matter their private insecurities. After all, they've generally been on display since the time they could walk and talk. David certainly has it. And he has a good ear; as do both of his parents, obviously. An aural memory for musical or linguistic rhythms. . . . He doesn't act, he *reads*. Almost exclusively in the dialects or the foreign languages he knows fluently. . . ."

David Spaulding's excursion into the "highly paid radio field' was solely motivated by money; he was used to living well. At a time when owners of engineering companies found it difficult to guarantee themselves a hundred dollars a week, Spaulding was earning three or four hundred from his "radio work' alone.

"As you may have surmised," said Mandel, "David's immediate objective is to bank sufficient monies to start his own company. Immediate, that is, unless otherwise shaped by world or national conditions. He's not blind; anyone who can read a newspaper sees that we are being drawn into the war."

"Do you think we should be?"

"I'm a Jew. As far as I'm concerned, we're late."

"This Spaulding. You've described what seems to me a very resourceful man."

"I've described only what you could have found out from any number of sources. And *you* have described the conclusion you have drawn from that surface information. It's not the whole picture." At this point, Pace recalled, Mandel had gotten out of his chair, avoiding any eye contact, and walked about his office. He was searching for negatives; he was trying to find the words that would disqualify "his son' from the government's interests. And Pace had been aware of it. "What certainly must have struck you – from what I've told you – is David's preoccupation with himself, with his comforts, if you wish. Now, in a business sense this might be applauded; therefore, I disabused you of your concerns for stability. However, I would not be candid if I didn't tell you that David is abnormally headstrong. He operates – I think – quite poorly under authority. In a word, he's a selfish man, not given to discipline. It pains me to say this; I love him dearly. . . ."

And the more Mandel had talked, the more indelibly did Pace imprint the word *affirmative* on Spaulding's file. Not that he believed for a minute the extremes of behavior Mandel suddenly ascribed to David Spaulding – no man could function as "stably" as Spaulding had if it were true. But if it were only half true, it was no detriment; it was an asset.

The last of the requirements.

For if there were any soldier in the United States Army – in or out of uniform – who would be called upon to operate solely on his own, without the comfort of the chain of command, without the knowledge that difficult decisions could be made by his superiors, it was the Intelligence officer in Portugal.

The man in Lisbon.

OCTOBER 8,1939

FAIRFAX, VIRGINIA

There were no names.

Only numbers and letters.

Numbers followed by letters.

Two-Six-B. Three-Five-Y. Five-One-C.

There were no personal histories, no individual backgrounds . . . no references to wives, children, fathers, mothers . . . no countries; cities, hometowns, schools, universities; there were only bodies and minds and separate, specific, reacting intelligences.

The location was deep in the Virginia hunt country, 220 acres of fields and hills and mountain streams. There were sections of dense forest bordering stretches of flat grasslands. Swamps – dangerous with body-sucking earth and hostile inhabitants, reptile and insect – were but feet from sudden masses of Virginia boulders fronting abrupt inclines.

The area had been selected with care, with precision. It was bordered by a fifteen-foot-high hurricane fence through which a paralyzing not lethal – electrical current flowed continuously; and every twelve feet there was a forbidding sign that warned observers that this particular section of the land . . . forest, swamp, grassland and hill . . . was the exclusive property of the United States government. Trespassers were duly informed that entry was not only prohibited, it was exceedingly dangerous. Titles and sections of the specific laws pertaining to the exclusivity were spelled out along with the voltage in the fence.

The terrain was as diverse as could be found within a reasonable distance from Washington. In one way or another – one place or another – it conformed remarkably to the topography of the locations projected for those training inside the enormous compound.

The numbers followed by the letters.

No names.

There was a single gate at the center of the north perimeter, reached by a back country road. Over the gate, between the opposing guard houses, was a metal sign. In block letters it read: FIELD DIVISION HEADQUARTERS – FAIRFAX.

No other description was given, no purpose identified.

On the front of each guard house were identical signs, duplicates of the warnings placed every twelve feet in the fence, proclaiming the exclusivity, the laws and the voltage.

No room for error.

David Spaulding was assigned an identity – his Fairfax identity. He was Two-Five-L.

No name. Only a number followed by a letter.

Two-Five-L.

Translation: his training was to be completed by the fifth day of the second month. His destination: Lisbon.

It was incredible. In the space of four months a new way of life – of *living* – was to be absorbed with such totality that it strained acceptance.

"You probably won't make it," said Colonel Edmund Pace.

"I'm not sure I want to," had been Spaulding's reply.

But part of the training was motivation. Deep, solid, ingrained beyond doubt . . . but not beyond the psychological reality as perceived by the candidate.

With Two-Five-L, the United States government did not wave flags and roar espousals of patriotic causes. Such methods would not be meaningful; the candidate had spent his formative years outside the country in a sophisticated, international environment. He spoke the language of the enemy-to-be; he knew them as people – taxi drivers, grocers, bankers, lawyers – and the vast majority of those he knew were not the Germans fictionalized by the propaganda machines. Instead – and this was Fairfax's legitimate hook – they were goddamned fools being led by psychopathic criminals. The leaders were, indeed, fanatics, and the overwhelming evidence clearly established their crimes

420

beyond doubt. Those crimes included wanton, indiscriminate murder, torture and genocide.

Beyond doubt.

Criminals.

Psychopaths.

Too, there was Adolf Hitler.

Adolf Hitler killed Jews. By the thousands – soon to be millions if his *final solutions* were read accurately.

Aaron Mandel was a Jew. His other "father' was a Jew; the "father" he loved more than the parent. And the goddamned fools tolerated an exclamation point after the word *Juden!*

David Spaulding could bring himself to hate the goddamned fools – the taxi drivers, the grocers, the bankers, the lawyers – without much compunction under the circumstances.

Beyond this very rational approach, Fairfax utilized a secondary psychological "weapon" that was standard in the compound; for some more than others, but it was never absent.

The trainees at Fairfax had a common gift – or flaw – depending on one's approach. None was accepted without it.

A highly developed sense of competition; a thrust to win.

There was no question about it; arrogance was not a despised commodity at Fairfax.

With David Spaulding's psychological profile – a dossier increasingly accepted by the Intelligence Division – the Fairfax commanders recognized that the candidate-in-training for Lisbon had a soft core which the field might harden – undoubtedly *would* harden if he lived that long – but whatever advances could be made in the compound, so much the better. Especially for the subject.

Spaulding was confident, independent, extremely versatile in his surroundings . . . all to the very good; but Two–Five–L had a weakness. There was within his psyche a slowness to take immediate advantage, a hesitancy to spring to the kill when the odds were his. Both verbally and physically.

Colonel Edmund Pace saw this inadequacy by the third week of training. Two–Five–L's abstract code of fairness would never do in Lisbon. And Colonel Pace knew the answer.

The mental adjustment would be made through the physical processes.

"Seizures, Holds and Releases" was the insipid title of the course. It disguised the most arduous physical training at Fairfax: hand-to-hand combat. Knife, chain, wire, needle, rope, fingers, knees, elbows . . . never a gun.

Reaction, reaction, reaction.

Except when one initiated the assault.

Two–Five–L had progressed nicely. He was a large man but possessed the quick coordination usually associated with a more compact person. Therefore his progress had to be stymied; the man himself humiliated. He would learn the practical advantages of the odds.

From smaller, more arrogant men.

Colonel Edmund Pace "borrowed' from the British commando units the best they had in uniform. They were flown over by the Bomber Ferry Command; three bewildered "specialists' who were subtly introduced to the Fairfax compound and given their instructions.

"Kick the shit out of Two–Five–L."

They did. For many weeks of sessions.

And then they could not do so with impunity any longer.

David Spaulding would not accept the humiliation; he was becoming as good as the "specialists."

The man for Lisbon was progressing.

Colonel Edmund Pace received the reports in his War Department office. Everything was on schedule.

The weeks became months. Every known portable offensive and defensive weapon, every sabotage device, every conceivable method of ingress and egress – apparent and covert – was exhaustively studied by the Fairfax trainees. Codes and variations became fluent languages; instant fabrications second nature. And Two–Five–L continued to advance. Whenever there appeared a slackening, harsher instructions were given to the "specialists' in "Seizures, Holds and Releases." The psychological key was in the observable, physical humiliation.

Until it was no longer viable. The commandos were bested.

Everything on schedule.

"You may make it after all," said the colonel.

"I'm not sure what I've made," replied David in his first lieutenant's uniform, over a drink in the Mayflower Cocktail Lounge. And then he laughed quietly. "I suppose if they gave degrees in Advanced Criminal Activities, I'd probably qualify."

Two–Five–L's training would be completed in ten days. His twenty-four-hour pass was an irregularity, but Pace had demanded it. He had to talk with Spaulding.

"Does it bother you?" asked Pace.

Spaulding looked across the small table at the colonel. "If I had time to think about it, I'm sure it would. Doesn't it bother you?"

"No . . . Because I understand the reasons."

"O.K. Then so do I."

"They'll become clearer in the field."

"Sure," agreed David tersely.

Pace watched Spaulding closely. As was to be expected, the young man had changed. Gone was the slightly soft, slightly pampered grace of inflection and gesture. These had been replaced by a tautness, a conciseness of movement and speech. The transformation was not complete, but it was well in progress.

The patina of the professional was beginning to show through. Lisbon would harden it further.

"Are you impressed by the fact that Fairfax skips you a rank? It took me eighteen months to get that silver bar."

"Again, time. I haven't had time to react. I haven't worn a uniform before today; I think it's uncomfortable." Spaulding flicked his hand over his tunic.

"Good. Don't get used to it."

"That's a strange thing to say."

"How do you feel?" said Pace, interrupting.

David looked at the colonel. For a moment or two, the grace, the softness – even the wry humor – returned. "I'm not sure." ... As though I'd been manufactured on a very fast assembly line. A sort of high-speed treadmill, if you know what I mean.

"In some ways that's an accurate description. Except that you brought a lot to the factory."

Spaulding revolved his glass slowly. He stared at the floating cubes, then up at Pace. "I wish I could accept that as a compliment," he said softly. "I don't think I can. I know the people I've been training with. They're quite a collection."

"They're highly motivated."

"The Europeans are as crazy as those they want to fight. They've got their reasons; I can't question them . . ."

"Well," interrupted the colonel, "we don't have that many Americans. Not yet."

"Those you do are two steps from a penitentiary."

"They're not army."

"I didn't know that," said Spaulding quickly, adding the obvious with a smile. "Naturally."

Pace was annoyed with himself. The indiscretion was minor but still an indiscretion. "It's not important. In ten days you'll be finished in Virginia. The uniform comes off then. To tell you the truth, it was a mistake to issue you one in the first place. We're still new at this kind of thing; rules of requisition and supply are hard to change." Pace drank and avoided Spaulding's eyes.

"I thought I was supposed to be a military attaché at the embassy. One of several."

"For the record, yes. They'll build a file on you. But there's a difference; it's part of the cover. You're not partial to uniforms. We don't think you should wear one. Ever." Pace put down his glass and looked at David. "You hustled yourself a very safe, very comfortable job because of the languages, your residences and your family connections. In a nutshell, you ran as fast as you could when you thought there was a chance your pretty neck might be in the real army."

Spaulding thought for a moment. "That sounds logical. Why does it bother you?"

"Because only one man at the embassy will know the truth. He'll identify himself. . . . After a while others may suspect – after a long while. But they won't know. Not the ambassador, not the staff. . . . What I'm trying to tell you is, you won't be very popular."

David laughed quietly. "I trust you'll rotate me before I'm lynched."

Pace's reply was swift and quiet, almost curt. "Others will be rotated. Not you."

Spaulding was silent as he responded to the colonel's look. "I don't understand."

"I'm not sure I can be clear about it." Pace put down his drink on the small cocktail table. "You'll have to start slowly, with extreme caution. British MI-5 has given us a few names – not many but something to start with. You'll have to build up your own network, however. People who will maintain contact only with you, no one else. This will entail a great deal of traveling. We think you'll gravitate to the north country, across the borders into Spain. Basque country . . . by and large anti-Falangist. We think those areas south of the Pyrenees will become the data and escape routes. . . .We're not kidding ourselves: the Maginot won't hold. France will fall. . . ."

"*Jesus*," interrupted David softly. "You've done a lot of projecting."

"That's almost *all* we do. It's the reason for Fairfax."

Spaulding leaned back in the chair, once more revolving his glass. "I understand about the network; in one form or another it's what the compound's training all of us for. This is the first I've heard about the north of Spain, the Basque areas. I know that country."

"We could be wrong. It's only a theory. You might find the water routes . . . Mediterranean, Málaga, or Biscay, or the Portuguese coast . . . more feasible. That's you for to decide. And develop."

"All right. I understand. . . . What's that got to do with rotation?"

Pace smiled. "You haven't reached your post. Are you angling for a leave already?"

"You brought it up. Sort of abruptly, I think."

"Yes, I did." The colonel shifted his position in the small chair. Spaulding was very quick; he locked in on words and used brief time spans to maximize their effectiveness. He would be good in interrogations. Quick, harsh inquiries. In the field. "We've decided that you're to remain in Portugal for the duration. Whatever normal and 'abnormal' leaves you take should be spent in the south. There's a string of colonies along the coast. . ." "Costa del Santiago among them," interjected Spaulding under his breath. "Retreats for the international rich."

"That's right. Develop covers down there. Be seen with your parents. Become a fixture." Pace smiled again; the smile was hesitant. "I could think of worse duty."

"You don't know those colonies. . . . If I read you – as we say in Fairfax –

Candidate Two–Five–L had better take a good, hard look at the streets of Washington and New York because he's not going to see them again for a very long time."

"We can't risk bringing you back once you've developed a network, assuming you *do* develop one. If, for whatever reason, you flew out of Lisbon to Allied territory, there'd be an enemy scramble to microscopically trace every movement you made for months. It would jeopardize everything. *You're* safest – *our interests* are safest – if you remain permanent. The British taught us this. Some of their operatives have been local fixtures for years."

"That's not very comforting."

"You're not in MI-5. Your tour is for the duration. The war won't last forever."

It was Spaulding's turn to smile; the smile of a man caught in a matrix he had not defined. "There's something insane about that statement. . . . The war won't last forever. . . ."

"Why?"

"We're not in it yet."

"You are," Pace said.

Two

The man in the pinstriped suit, styled by tailors in Alte Strasse, stared in disbelief at the three men across the table. He would have objected strenuously had the three laboratory experts not worn the square, red, metal insignias on the lapels of their starched white laboratory jackets, badges that said these three scientists were permitted to walk through passageways forbidden to all but the elite of Peenemünde. He, too, had such a badge attached to his pinstriped lapel; it was a temporary clearance he was not sure he wanted.

Certainly he did not want it now.

"I can't accept your evaluation," he said quietly. "It's preposterous."

"Come with us," replied the scientist in the center, nodding to his companion on the right.

"There's no point procrastinating," added the third man.

The four men got out of their chairs and approached the steel door that was the single entrance to the room. Each man in succession unclipped his red badge and pressed it against a grey plate in the wall. At the instant of contact, a small white bulb was lighted, remained so for two seconds and then went off; a photograph had been taken. The last man – one of the Peenemünde personnel – then opened the door and each went into the hallway.

Had only three men gone out, or five, or any number not corresponding to the photographs, alarms would have been triggered.

They walked in silence down the long, starched-white corridor, the Berliner in front with the scientist who sat between the other two at the table, and was obviously the spokesman; his companions were behind.

They reached a bank of elevators and once more went through the ritual of the red tags, the grey plate and the tiny white light that went on for precisely two seconds. Below the plate a number was also lighted.

Six.

From elevator number six there was the sound of a single muted bell as the thick steel panel slid open. One by one each man walked inside.

The elevator descended eight stories, four below the surface of the earth, to the deepest levels of Peenemnde. As the four men emerged into yet another white corridor, they were met by a tall man in tight-fitting green coveralls, an outsized holster in his wide brown belt. The holster held a Lüger *Sternlicht*, a specially designed arm pistol with a telescopic sight. As the man's visor cap indicated, such weapons were made for the Gestapo.

The Gestapo officer obviously recognized the three scientists. He smiled perfunctorily and turned his attention to the man in the pinstriped suit. He held out his hand, motioning the Berliner to remove the red badge.

The Berliner did so. The Gestapo man took it, walked over to a telephone on the corridor wall and pushed a combination of buttons. He spoke the Berliner's name and waited, perhaps ten seconds.

He replaced the phone and crossed back to the man in the pinstriped suit. Gone was the arrogance he had displayed moments ago.

"I apologize for the delay, Herr Strasser. I should have realized. . . ." He gave the Berliner his badge.

"No need for apologies, Herr Oberleutnant. They would be necessary only if you overlooked your duties."

"*Danke*," said the Gestapo man, gesturing the four men beyond his point of security.

They proceeded towards a set of double doors; clicks could be heard as locks were released. Small white bulbs were lighted above the mouldings; again photographs were taken of those going through the double doors.

They turned right into a bisecting corridor – this one not white, but instead, brownish black; so dark that Strasser's eyes took several seconds to adjust from the pristine brightness of the main halls to the sudden night quality of the passageway. Tiny ceiling lights gave what illumination there was.

"You've not been here before," said the scientist-spokesman to the Berliner. "This hallway was designed by an optics engineer. It supposedly prepares the eyes for the high-intensity microscope lights. Most of us think it was a waste."

There was a steel door at the end of the long-dark tunnel. Strasser reached for his red metal insignia automatically; the scientist shook his head and spoke with a slight wave of his hand.

"Insufficient light for photographs. The guard inside has been alerted."

The door opened and the four men entered a large laboratory. Along the right wall was a row of stools, each in front of a powerful microscope, all the microscopes equidistant from one another on top of a built-in workbench. Behind each microscope was a high-intensity light, projected and shaded on a goose-necked stem coming out of the immaculate white surface. The left wall was a variation of the right. There were no stools, however, and fewer microscopes. The work shelf was higher: it was obviously used for conferences, where many pairs of eyes peered through the same sets of lenses; stools would only interfere, men stood as they conferred over magnified particles.

At the far end of the room was another door, not an entrance. A vault. A seven-foot-high, four-foot-wide, heavy steel vault. It was black; the two levers and the combination wheel were in glistening silver.

The spokesman-scientist approached it.

"We have fifteen minutes before the timer seals the panel and the drawers.

427

I've requested closure for a week. I'll need your counter-authorization, of course."

"And you're sure I'll give it, aren't you?"

"I am." The scientist spun the wheel right and left for the desired locations. "The numbers change automatically every twenty-four hours," he said as he held the wheel steady at its final mark and reached for the silver levers. He pulled the top one down to the accompaniment of a barely audible whirring sound, and seconds later, pulled the lower one up.

The whirring stopped, metallic clicks could be heard and the scientist pulled open the thick steel door. He turned to Strasser. "These are the tools for Peenemünde. See for yourself."

Strasser approached the vault. Inside were five rows of removable glass trays, top to bottom; each row had a total of one hundred trays, five hundred in all.

The trays that were empty were marked with a white strip across the facing glass, the word *Auffüllen* printed clearly.

The trays that were full were so designated by strips of black across their fronts.

There were four and a half rows of white trays. Empty.

Strasser looked closely, pulled open several trays, shut them and stared at the Peenemünde scientist.

"This is the sole repository?" he asked quietly.

"It is. We have six thousand casings completed; God knows how many will go in experimentation Estimate for yourself how much further we can proceed."

Strasser held the scientist's eyes with his own. "Do you realize what you're saying?"

"I do. We'll deliver only a fraction of the required schedules. Nowhere near enough. Peenemünde is a disaster."

SEPTEMBER 9, 1943

THE NORTH SEA

The fleet of B-17 bombers had aborted the primary target of Essen due to cloud cover. The squadron commander, over the objections of his fellow pilots, ordered the secondary mission into operation: the shipyards north of Bremerhaven. No one liked the Bremerhaven run; Messerschmitt and Stuka interceptor wings were devastating. They were called the Luftwaffe suicide squads, maniacal young Nazis who might as easily collide with enemy aircraft as fire at them. Not necessarily due to outrageous bravery; often it was merely inexperience or worse: poor training.

Bremerhaven-north was a terrible secondary. When it was a primary objective, the Eighth Air Force fighter escorts took the sting out of the run; they were not there when Bremerhaven was a secondary.

The squadron commander, however, was a hardnose. Worse, he was West Point: the secondary would not only be hit, it would be hit at an altitude that guaranteed maximum accuracy. He did not tolerate the very vocal criticism of his second-in-command aboard the flanking aircraft, who made it clear that such an altitude was barely logical *with* fighter escorts; *without* them, considering the heavy ack-ack fire, it was ridiculous. The squadron commander had replied with a terse recital of the new navigational headings and termination of radio contact.

Once they were into the Bremerhaven corridors, the German interceptors came from all points; the antiaircraft guns were murderous. And the squadron commander took his lead plane directly down into maximum-accuracy altitude and was blown out of the sky.

The second-in-command valued life and the price of aircraft more than his West Point superior. He ordered the squadron to scramble altitudes, telling his bombardiers to unload on anything below but for-God's-sake-release-the-goddamn-weight so all planes could reach their maximum heights and reduce antiaircraft and interceptor fire.

In several instances it was too late. One bomber caught fire and went into a spin; only three chutes emerged from it. Two aircraft were riddled so badly both planes began immediate descents. Pilots and crew bailed out. Most of them.

The remainder kept climbing; the Messerschmitts climbed with them. They went higher and still higher, past the safe altitude range. Oxygen masks were ordered; not all functioned.

But in four minutes, what was left of the squadron was in the middle of the clear midnight sky, made stunningly clearer by the substratosphere absence of air particles. The stars were extraordinary in their flickering brightness, the moon more a bombers' moon than ever before.

Escape was in these regions.

"Chart man!" said the exhausted, relieved second-in-command into his radio, "give us headings! Back to Lakenheath, if you'd he so kind."

The reply on the radio soured the moment of relief. It came from an aerial gunner aft of navigation. "He's dead, colonel. Nelson's dead."

There was no time in the air for comment, "Take it, aircraft three. It's your chart," said the colonel in aircraft two.

The headings were given. The formation grouped and, as it descended into safe altitude with cloud cover above, sped toward the North Sea.

The minutes reached five, then seven, then twelve. Finally twenty. There was relatively little cloud cover below; the coast of England should have come into sighting range at least two minutes ago. A number of pilots were concerned. Several said so.

"Did you give accurate headings, aircraft three?" asked the now squadron commander.

"Affirmative, colonel," was the radioed answer.

"Any of you chart men disagree?"

A variety of negatives was heard from the remaining aircraft.

"No sweat on the headings, colonel," came the voice of the captain of aircraft five. "I fault your execution, though."

"What the hell are you talking about?"

"You pointed two-three-niner by my reading. I figured my equipment was shot up. . . ."

Suddenly there were interruptions from every pilot in the decimated squadron.

"I read one-seven "

"My heading was a goddamned two-niner-two. We took a direct hit on. . . ."

"*Jesus!* I had sixer-four. . . ."

"Most of our middle took a load. I discounted my readings totally!"

And then there was silence. All understood.

Or understood what they could not comprehend.

"Stay off all frequencies," said the squadron commander, "I'll try to reach base."

The cloud cover above broke; not for long, but long enough. The voice over the radio was the captain of aircraft three.

"A quick judgment, colonel, says we're heading due northwest."

Silence again.

After a few moments, the commander spoke. "I'll reach somebody. Do all your gauges read as mine? Fuel for roughly ten to fifteen minutes?"

"It's been a long haul, colonel," said aircraft seven. "No more than that, it's for sure."

"I figured we'd be circling, if we had to, five minutes ago," said aircraft eight.

"We're not," said aircraft four.

The colonel in aircraft two raised Lakenheath on an emergency frequency.

"As near as we can determine," came the strained, agitated, yet controlled English voice, "and by that I mean open lines throughout the coastal defense areas – water and land – you're approaching the Dunbar sector. That's the Scottish border, colonel. What in blazes are you doing there?"

"For Christ's sake, I don't *know!* Are there any fields?"

"Not for *your* aircraft. Certainly not a formation; perhaps, one or two. . . ."

"I don't want to hear that, you son of a bitch! Give me emergency instructions!"

"We're really quite unprepared.."

"Do you *read me?!* I have what's left of a very chopped-up squadron! We have less than six minutes' fuel! Now you *give!*"

The silence lasted precisely four seconds. Lakenheath conferred swiftly. With finality.

"We believe you'll sight the coast, probably Scotland. Put your aircraft down at sea. . . . We'll do our best, lads."

"We're eleven *bombers*, Lakenheath! We're not a bunch of ducks!"

"There isn't time, squadron Leader. . . . The logistics are insurmountable. After all, we didn't guide you there. Put down at sea. We'll do our best . . . Godspeed."

Part One

1

Reichsminister of Armaments Albert Speer raced up the steps of the Air Ministry on the Tiergarten. He did not feel the harsh, diagonal sheets of rain that plummeted down from the grey sky; he did not notice that his raincoat – unbuttoned – had fallen away, exposing his tunic and shirt to the inundation of the September storm. The pitch of his fury swept everything but the immediate crisis out of his mind.

Insanity! Sheer, unmitigated, unforgivable insanity!

The industrial reserves of all Germany were about exhausted; but he could handle that immense problem. Handle it by properly utilizing the manufacturing potential of the occupied countries; reverse the unmanageable practices of importing the labor forces. Labor forces? Slaves!

Productivity disastrous; sabotage continuous, unending.

What did they expect?

It was a time for sacrifice! Hitler could not continue to be all things to all people! He could not provide outsized Duesenbergs and grand operas and populated restaurants; he had to provide, instead, tanks, munitions, ships, aircraft! *These* were the priorities!

But the Führer could never erase the memory of the 1918 revolution.

How totally inconsistent! The sole man whose will was shaping history, who was close to the preposterous dream of a thousand-year Reich, was petrified of a long-ago memory of unruly mobs, of unsatisfied masses.

Speer wondered if future historians would record the fact. If they would comprehend just how weak Hitler really was when it came to his own countrymen. How he buckled in fear when consumer production fell below anticipated schedules.

Insanity!

But still *he*, the Reichsminister of Armaments, could control this calamitous inconsistency as long as he was convinced it was just a question of time. A few months; perhaps six at the outside.

For there was Peenemünde.

The rockets.

Everything reduced itself to Peenemünde!

Peenemünde was irresistible. Peenemünde would cause the collapse of

435

London and Washington. Both governments would see the futility of continuing the exercise of wholesale annihilation.

Reasonable men could then sit down and create reasonable treaties.

Even if it meant the silencing of *un*reasonable men. Silencing Hitler.

Speer knew there were others who thought that way, too. The Führer was manifestly beginning to show unhealthy signs of pressure – fatigue. He now surrounded himself with mediocrity – an ill-disguised desire to remain in the comfortable company of his intellectual equals. But it went too far when the Reich itself was affected. A wine merchant, the foreign minister A third-rate party propagandizer, the minister of eastern affairs! An erstwhile fighter pilot, the overseer of the *entire economy!*

Even himself. Even the quiet, shy architect; now the minister of armaments.

All that would change with Peenemünde.

Even himself. Thank *God!*

But first there *had* to be Peenemünde. There could be no *question of* its operational success. For without Peenemünde, the war was lost.

And now they were telling him there *was a* question. A flaw that might well be the precursor of Germany's defeat.

A vacuous-looking corporal opened the door of the cabinet room. Speer walked in and saw that the long conference table was about two-thirds filled, the chairs in cliquish separation, as if the groups were suspect of one another. As, indeed, they were in these times of progressively sharpened rivalries within the Reich.

He walked to the head of the table, where – to his right – sat the only man in the room he could trust. Franz Altmüller.

Altmüller was a forty-two-year-old cynic. Tall, blond, aristocratic; the vision of the Third Reich Aryan who did not, for a minute, subscribe to the racial nonsense proclaimed by the Third Reich. He did, however, subscribe to the theory of acquiring whatever benefits came his way by pretending to agree with anyone who might do him some good.

In public.

In private, among his *very* close associates, he told the truth.

When that truth might also benefit him.

Speer was not only Altmüller's associate, he was his friend. Their families had been more than neighbors; the two fathers had often gone into joint merchandising ventures; the mothers had been school chums.

Altmüller had taken after his father. He was an extremely capable businessman; his expertise was in production administration.

"Good morning," said Altmüller, flicking an imaginary thread off his tunic lapel. He wore his party uniform far more often than was necessary, preferring to err on the side of the archangel.

"That seems unlikely," replied Speer, sitting down rapidly. The groups – and they were groups – around the table kept talking among themselves but the voices were perceptibly quieter. Eyes kept darting over in Speer's direction, then swiftly away; everyone was prepared for immediate silence yet none wished to appear apprehensive, guilty.

Silence would come when either Altmüller or Speer himself rose from his chair to address the gathering. That would be the signal. Not before. To render attention before that movement might give the appearance of fear. Fear was equivalent to an admission of error. No one at the conference table could afford that.

Altmüller opened a brown manila folder and placed it in front of Speer. It was a list of those summoned to the meeting. There were essentially three distinct factions with subdivisions within each, and each with its spokesman. Speer read the names and unobtrusively – he thought – looked up to ascertain the presence and the location of the three leaders.

At the far end of the table, resplendent in his general's uniform, his tunic a field of decorations going back thirty years, sat Ernst Leeb, Chief of the Army Ordnance Office. He was of medium height but excessively muscular, a condition he maintained well into his sixties. He smoked his cigarette through an ivory holder which he used to cut off his various subordinates' conversations at will. In some ways Leeb was a caricature, yet still a powerful one. Hitler liked him, as much for his imperious military bearing as for his abilities.

At the midpoint of the table, on the left, sat Albert Vögler, the sharp, aggressive general manager of Reich's Industry. Vögler was a stout man, the image of a burgomaster; the soft flesh of his face constantly creased into a questioning scowl. He laughed a great deal, but his laughter was hard; a device, not an enjoyment. He was well suited to his position. Vögler liked nothing better than hammering out negotiations between industrial adversaries. He was a superb mediator because all parties were usually frightened of him.

Across from Vögler and slightly to the right, toward Altmüller and Speer, was Wilhelm Zangen, the Reich official of the German Industrial Association. Zangen was thin-lipped, painfully slender, humorless; a fleshed-out skeleton happiest over his charts and graphs. A precise man who was given to perspiring at the edge of his receding hairline and below the nostrils and on his chin when nervous. He was perspiring now, and continuously brought his handkerchief up to blot the embarrassing moisture. Somewhat in contradiction to his appearance, however, Zangen was a persuasive debater. For he never argued without the facts.

They were all persuasive, thought Speer. And if it were not for his anger, he knew such men could – probably would – intimidate him. Albert Speer was honest in self-assessment; he realized that he had no substantial sense of authority. He found it difficult to express his thoughts forthrightly among such potentially hostile men. But now the potentially hostile men were in a defensive position. He could not allow his anger to cause them to panic, to seek only absolution for themselves.

They needed a remedy. Germany needed a remedy.

Peenemünde had to be saved.

"How would you suggest we begin?" Speer asked Altmüller, shading his voice so no one else at the table could hear him.

"I don't think it makes a particle of difference. It will take an hour of very loud, very boring, very obtuse explanations before we reach anything concrete."

"I'm not interested in explanations."

"Excuses, then."

"Least of all, excuses. I want a solution."

"If it's to be found at this table – which, frankly, 1 doubt – you'll have to sit through the excess verbiage. Perhaps something will come of it. Again, I doubt it."

"Would you care to explain that?"

Altmüller looked directly into Speer's eyes. "Ultimately, I'm not sure there is a solution. But if there is, I don't think it's at this table. . . . Perhaps I'm wrong. Why don't we listen first?"

"All right. Would you please open with the summary you prepared? I'm afraid I'd lose my temper midway through."

"May I suggest," Altmüller whispered "that it will be necessary for you to lose your temper at some point during this meeting. I don't see how you can avoid it."

"I understand."

Altmüller pushed back his chair and stood up. Grouping by grouping the voices trailed off around the table.

"Gentlemen. This emergency session was called for reasons of which we assume you are aware. At least you should be aware of them. Apparently it is only the Reichsminister of Armaments and his staff who were not informed; a fact which the Reichsminister and his staff find appalling. . . . In short words, the Peenemünde operation faces a crisis of unparalleled severity. In spite of the millions poured into this most vital weaponry development, in spite of the assurances consistently offered by your respective departments, we now learn that production may be brought to a complete halt within a matter of weeks. Several months prior to the *agreed-upon* date for the first operational rockets. That date has never been questioned. It has been the keystone for whole military strategies; entire armies have been maneuvered to coordinate with it. Germany's victory is predicated on it. . . . But now Peenemünde is threatened; Germany is threatened. . . . If the projections the Reichsminister's staff have compiled – *unearthed* and compiled – are valid, the Peenemünde complex will exhaust its supply of industrial diamonds in less than ninety days. Without industrial diamonds the precision tooling in Peenemünde cannot continue."

The babble of voices – excited, guttural, vying for attention – erupted the second Altmüller sat down. General Leeb's cigarette holder slashed the air in front of him as though it were a saber; Albert Vögler scowled and wrinkled his flesh-puffed eyes, placed his bulky hands on the table and spoke harshly in a loud monotone; Wilhelm Zangen's handkerchief was working furiously around his face and his neck, his high-pitched voice in conflict with the more masculine tones around him.

Franz Altmüller leaned toward Speer. "You've seen cages of angry ocelots in the zoo? The zookeeper can't let them hurl themselves into the bars. I suggest you lose your benign temper far earlier than we discussed. Perhaps now."

"This is not the way."

"Don't let them think you are cowed . . ."

"Nor that I am cowering." Speer interrupted his friend, the slightest trace of a smile on his lips. He stood up. "Gentlemen."

The voices trailed off.

"Herr Altmüller speaks harshly; he does so, I'm sure, because I spoke harshly with him. That was this morning, very early this morning. There is greater perspective now; it is no time for recriminations. This is not to lessen the critical aspects of the situation, for they are great. But anger will solve nothing. And we need solutions. . . . Therefore, I propose to seek your assistance – the assistance of the finest industrial and military minds in the Reich. First, of course, we need to know the specifics. I shall start with Herr Vögler. As manager of Reich's Industry, would you give us your estimate?"

Vögler was upset; he didn't wish to be the first called. "I'm not sure I can be of much enlightenment, Herr Reichsminister. I, too, am subject to the reports given me. They have been optimistic; until the other week there was no suggestion of difficulty."

"How do you mean, optimistic?" asked Speer.

"The quantities of bortz and carbonado diamonds were said to be sufficient. Beyond this there are the continuing experiments with lithicum, carbon and paraffin. Our intelligence tells us that the Englishman Storey at the British Museum reverified the Hannay-Moissan theories. Diamonds *were* produced in this fashion."

"Who verified the Englishman?" Franz Altmüller did not speak kindly. "Had it occurred to you that such data was meant to be passed?"

"Such verification is a matter for Intelligence. I am not with Intelligence, Herr Altmüller."

"Go on," said Speer quickly. "What else?"

"There is an Anglo-American experiment under the supervision of the Bridgemann team They are subjecting graphite to pressures in excess of six million pounds per square inch. So far there is no word of success."

"Is there word of failure?" Altmüller raised his aristocratic eyebrows, his tone polite.

"I remind you again, I am not with Intelligence. I have received no word whatsoever."

"Food for thought, isn't it," said Altmüller, without asking a question.

"Nevertheless," interrupted Speer before Vögler could respond, "you had reason to assume that the quantities of bortz and carbonado were sufficient. Is that not so?"

"Sufficient. Or at least obtainable, Herr Reichsminister."

"How so obtainable?"

"I believe General Leeb might be more knowledgeable on that subject."

Leeb nearly dropped his ivory cigarette holder. Altmüller noted his surprise and cut in swiftly. "Why would the army ordnance officer have that information, Herr Vögler? I ask merely for my own curiosity."

"The reports, once more. It is my understanding that the Ordnance Office is responsible for evaluating the industrial, agricultural and mineral potentials of occupied territories. Or those territories so projected."

Ernst Leeb was not entirely unprepared. He *was* unprepared for Vögler's insinuations, not for the subject. He turned to an aide, who shuffled papers top to bottom as Speer inquired.

"The Ordnance Office is under enormous pressure these days as is your department, of course, Herr Vögler. I wonder if General Leeb has had the time."

"We *made* the time," said Leeb, his sharp military bearing pitted in counterpoint to Vögler's burgomaster gruffness. "When we received word – from Herr Vögler's subordinates – that a crisis was imminent – not upon us, but imminent – we immediately researched the possibilities for extrication."

Franz Altmüller brought his hand to his mouth to cover an involuntary smile. He looked at Speer, who was too annoyed to find any humor in the situation.

"I'm relieved the Ordnance Office is so confident, general," said Speer. The Reichsminister of Armaments had *little* confidence in the military and had difficulty disguising it. "Please, your extrication?"

"I said *possibilities*, Herr Speer. To arrive at practical solutions *will* take more time than we've been given."

"Very well. Your possibilities?"

"There is an immediate remedy with historical precedent." Leeb paused to remove his cigarette, crushing it out, aware that everyone around the table watched him intently. "I have taken the liberty of recommending preliminary studies to the General Staff. It involves an expeditionary force of less than four battalions . . . Africa. The diamond mines east of Tanganyika."

"*What?*" Altmüller leaned forward; he obviously could not help himself. "You're not serious."

"Please!" Speer would not allow his friend to interrupt. If Leeb had even conceived of such drastic action, it might have merit. No military man, knowing the thin line of combat strength – chewed up on the Eastern Front, under murderous assault by the Allies in Italy – could suggest such an absurdity unless he had a realistic hope of success. "Go ahead, general."

"The Williamson Mines at Mwadui. Between the districts of Tanganyika and Zanzibar in the central sector. The mines at Mwadui produce over a million carats of the carbonado diamond annually. Intelligence – the intelligence that is forwarded regularly to me at my insistence informs us that there are supplies going back several months. Our agents in Dar es Salaam are convinced such an incursion would be successful."

Franz Altmüller passed a sheet of paper to Speer. On it he had scribbled: "He's lost his senses!"

"What is the historical precedent to which you refer?" asked Speer, holding his hand over Altmüller's paper.

"All of the districts east of Dar es Salaam rightfully belong to the Third Reich, German West Africa. They were taken from the fatherland after the Great War. The Führer himself made that clear four years ago."

There was silence around the table. An embarrassed silence. The eyes of even his aides avoided the old soldier. Finyall Speer spoke quietly.

"That is justification, not precedent, general. The world cares little for our justifications, and although I question the logistics of moving battalions halfway around the globe, you may have raised a valid point. Where else nearer . . . in *East* Africa, perhaps, can the bortz or the carbonado he found?"

Leeb looked to his aides; Wilhelm Zangen lifted his handkerchief to his nostrils and bowed his thin head in the direction of the general. He spoke as if exhaling, his high voice irritating.

"I'll answer you, Herr Reichsminister. And then, I believe, you will see how fruitless this discussion is . . . Sixty per cent of the world's crushing-bortz diamonds are in the Belgian Congo. The two principal deposits are in the Kasai and the Bakwanga fields, between the Kanshi and the Bushimaie rivers. The district's governor-general is Pierre Ryckmans; he is devoted to the Belgian government in exile in London. I can assure Leeb that the Congo's allegiances to Belgium are far greater than ours ever were in Dar es Salaam."

Leeb lit a cigarette angrily. Speer leaned back in his chair and addressed Zangen.

"All right. Sixty per cent crushing-bortz; what of carbonado and the rest?"

"French Equatorial: totally allied to de Gaulle's Free French. Gold Coast and Sierra Leone: the tightest of British controls."

Angola: Portuguese domination and their neutrality's inviolate; we know that beyond doubt. French West Africa: not only under Free French mandate but with Allied forces manning the outposts. . . . Here, there was only one possibility and we lost it a year and a half ago. Vichy abandoned the Ivory Coast. . . . There is no access in Africa, Reichsminister. None of a military nature."

"I see." Speer doodled on top of the paper Altmüller had passed to him. "You are recommending a nonmilitary solution?"

"There is no other. The question is what."

Speer turned to Franz Altmüller. His tall, blond associate was staring at them all. Their faces were blank. Baffled.

2

Brigadier General Alan Swanson got out of the taxi and looked up at the huge oak door of the Georgetown residence. The ride over the cobblestone streets had seemed like a continuous roll of hammering drums.

Prelude to execution.

Up those steps, inside that door, somewhere within that five-story brownstone and brick aristocratic home, was a large room. And inside that room thousands of executions would be pronounced, unrelated to any around the table within that room.

Prelude to annihilation.

If the schedules were kept. And it was inconceivable that they would be altered.

Wholesale murder.

In line with his orders he glanced up and down the street to make sure he hadn't been followed. Asinine! CIC had all of them under constant surveillance. Which of the pedestrians or slowly moving automobiles had him in their sights? It didn't matter; the choice of the meeting place was asinine, too. Did they really believe they could keep the crisis a secret? Did they think that holding conferences in secluded Georgetown houses would help?

Asses!

He was oblivious to the rain; it came down steadily, in straight lines. An autumn rainstorm in Washington. His raincoat was open, the jacket of his uniform damp and wrinkled. He didn't give a damn about such things; he couldn't think about them.

The only thing he could think about was packaged in a metal casing no more than seven inches wide, five high, and perhaps a foot long. It was designed for those dimensions; it had the appearance of sophisticated technology; it was tooled to operate on the fundamental properties of inertia and precision.

And it wasn't functional; it didn't work.

It failed test after test.

Ten thousand high-altitude B-17 bomber aircraft were emerging from production lines across the country. Without high-altitude, radio-beam gyroscopes to guide them, they might as well stay on the ground!

And without those aircraft, Operation Overlord was in serious jeopardy. The invasion of Europe would extract a price so great as to be obscene.

442

Yet to send the aircraft up on massive, round-the-clock, night and day bombing strikes throughout Germany without the cover of higher altitudes was to consign the majority to destruction, their crews to death. Examples were constant reminders ... whenever the big planes soared too high. The labels of pilot error, enemy fire and instrument fatigue were not so. It was the higher altitudes. ... Only twenty-four hours ago a squadron of bombers on the Bremerhaven run had scrambled out of the strike, exacting the maximum from their aircraft and regrouped far above oxygen levels. From what could be determined, the guidance Systems went crazy; the squadron ended up in the Dunbar sector near the Scottish border. All but one plane crashed into the sea. Three survivors were picked up by coastal patrols. Three out of God knows how many that had made it out of Bremerhaven. The one aircraft that attempted a ground landing had blown up on the outskirts of a town. ... No survivors.

Germany was in the curve of inevitable defeat, but it would not die easily. It was ready for counterstrike. The Russian lesson had been learned; Hitler's generals were prepared. They realized that ultimately their only hope for any surrender other than *unconditional* lay in their ability to make the cost of an Allied victory so high it would stagger imagination and sicken the conscience of humanity.

Accommodation would then be reached.

And *that* was unacceptable to the Allies. *Unconditional surrender* was now a tripartite policy; the absolute had been so inculcated that it dared not be tampered with. The fever of total victory had swept the lands; the leaders had shaped that, too. And at this pitch of frenzy, the leaders stared into blank walls seeing nothing others could see and said heroically that losses would be tolerated.

Swanson walked up the steps of the Georgetown house. As if on cue, the door opened, a major saluted and Swanson was admitted quickly. Inside the hallway were four noncommissioned officers in paratroop leggings standing at ready-at-ease; Swanson recognized the shoulder patches of the Ranger battalions. The War Department had set the scene effectively.

A sergeant ushered Swanson into a small, brass-grilled elevator. Two stories up the elevator stopped and Swanson stepped out into the corridor. He recognized the face of the colonel who stood by a closed door at the end of the short hallway. He could not recall his name, however. The man worked in Clandestine Operations and was never much in evidence. The colonel stepped forward, saluting.

"General Swanson? Colonel Pace."

Swanson nodded his salute, offering his hand instead. "Oh, yes. Ed Pace, right?"

"Yes, sir."

"So they pulled you out of the cellars. I didn't know this was your territory."

"It's not, sir. Just that I've had occasion to meet the men you're seeing. Security clearances."

"And with you here they know we're serious." Swanson smiled.

"I'm sure we are, but I don't know what we're serious about."

"You're lucky. Who's inside?"

"Howard Oliver from Meridian. Jonathan Craft from Packard. And the lab man, Spinelli, from ATCO."

"They'll make my day; I can't wait. Who's presiding? Christ, there should be *one* person on our side."

"Vandamm."

Swanson's lips formed a quiet whistle; the colonel nodded in agreement. Frederic Vandamm was undersecretary of state and rumored to be Cordell Hull's closest associate. If one wanted to reach Roosevelt, the best way was through Hull; if that avenue was closed, one pursued Vandamm.

"That's impressive artillery," Swanson said.

"When they saw him, I think he scared the hell out of Craft and Oliver. Spinelli's in a perpetual daze. He'd figure Patton for a doorman."

"I don't know Spinelli, except by rep. He's supposed to be the best gyro man in the labs. . . . Oliver and Craft I know *too* well. I wish to hell you boys had never cleared them for road maps."

"Not much you can do when they own the roads, sir." The colonel shrugged. It was obvious he agreed with Swanson's estimate.

"I'll give you a clue, Pace. Craft's a social-register flunky. Oliver's the bad meat."

"He's got a lot of it on him," replied the colonel, laughing softly.

Swanson took off his raincoat. "If you hear gunfire, colonel, it's only me fooling around. Walk the other way."

"I accept that as an order, general. I'm deaf," answered Pace as he reached for the handle and opened the door swiftly for his superior.

Swanson walked rapidly into the room. It was a library with the furniture pushed back against the walls and a conference table placed in the center. At the head of the table sat the white-haired, aristocratic Frederic Vandamm. On his left was the obese, balding Howard Oliver, a sheaf of notes in front of him. Opposite Oliver were Craft and a short, dark, bespectacled man Swanson assumed was Gian Spinelli.

The empty chair at the end of the table, facing Vandamm, was obviously for him. It was good positioning on Vandamm's part.

"I'm sorry to be late, Mr. Undersecretary. A staff car would have prevented it. A taxi wasn't the easiest thing to find . . . Gentlemen?"

The trio of corporate men nodded; Craft and Oliver each uttered a muted "General." Spinelli just stared from behind the thick lenses of his glasses.

"I apologize, General Swanson," said Vandamm in the precise, Anglicized speech that bespoke a background of wealth. "For obvious reasons we did not want this conference to take place in a government office, nor, if known, did we wish any significance attached to the meeting itself. These gentlemen represent War Department gossip, I don't have to tell you that. The absence of urgency was desirable. Staff cars speeding through Washington – don't ask

444

me why, but they never seem to slow down – have a tendency to arouse concern. Do you see?"

Swanson returned the old gentleman's veiled look. Vandamm was a smart one, he thought. It was an impetuous gamble referring to the taxi, but Vandamm had understood. He'd picked it up and used it well, even impartially.

The three corporate men were on notice. At this conference, they were the enemy.

"I've been discreet, Mr. Undersecretary."

"I'm sure you have. Shall we get down to points? Mr. Oliver has asked that he be permitted to open with a general statement of Meridian Aircraft's position."

Swanson watched the heavy-jowled Oliver sort out his notes. He disliked Oliver intensely; there was a fundamental gluttony about him. He was a manipulator; there were so many of them these days. They were everywhere in Washington, piling up huge sums of money from the war; proclaiming the power of the deal, the price of the deal, the price of the power-which they held.

Oliver's rough voice shot out from his thick lips. "Thank you. It's our feeling at Meridian that the . . . *assumed* gravity of the present situation has obscured the real advancements that *have* been made. The aircraft in question has proved beyond doubt its superior capabilities. The new, improved Fortress is ready for operational combat; it's merely a question of desired altitudes."

Oliver abruptly stopped and put his obese hands in front of him, over his papers. He had finished his statement; Craft nodded in agreement. Both men looked noncommittally at Vandamm. Gian Spinelli simply stared at Oliver, his brown eyes magnified by his glasses.

Alan Swanson was astounded. Not necessarily by the brevity of the statement but by the ingenuousness of the lie.

"If that's a position statement, I find it wholly unacceptable. The aircraft in question has *not* proved its capabilities until it's operational at the altitudes specified in the government contracts."

"It's operational," replied Oliver curtly.

"Operational. Not functional, Mr. Oliver. It is not functional until it can be guided from point A to point B at the altitudes called for in the specifications."

"*Specified* as 'intended maximum,' General Swanson," shot back Oliver, smiling an obsequious smile that conveyed anything but courtesy.

"What the hell does that mean?" Swanson looked at Undersecretary Vandamm.

"Mr. Oliver is concerned with a contractual interpretation."

"I'm *not*."

"I *have* to be," replied Oliver. "The War Department has refused payment to Meridian Aircraft Corporation. We have a contract. . . ."

"Take the goddammed contract up with someone else!"

"Anger won't solve anything." Vandamm spoke harshly.

"I'm sorry, Mr. Undersecretary, but I'm not here to discuss *contractual interpretations.*"

"I'm afraid you'll have to, General Swanson." Vandamm now spoke calmly. "The Disbursement Office has withheld payment to Meridian on *your* negative authorization. You haven't cleared it."

"Why should I? The aircraft can't do the job we expected."

"It *can* do the job you contracted for," said Oliver, moving his thick neck from Vandamm to the brigadier general. "Rest assured, general, our best efforts are being poured into the *intended* maximum guidance system. We're expending all our resources. We'll reach a breakthrough, we're convinced of that. But until we do, we expect the contracts to be honored. We've met the guarantees."

"Are you suggesting that we take the aircraft *as is?*"

"It's the finest bomber in the air." Jonathan Craft spoke. His soft, high voice was a weak exclamation that floated to a stop. He pressed his delicate fingers together in what he believed was emphasis.

Swanson disregarded Craft and stared at the small face and magnified eyes of the ATCO scientist, Gian Spinelli. "What about the *gyros?* Can you give me an answer, Mr. Spinelli?"

Howard Oliver intruded bluntly. "Use the existing systems. Get the aircraft into combat."

"*No!*" Swanson could not help himself. His was the roar of disgust, let Undersecretary Vandamm say what he liked. "Our strategies call for round-the-clock strikes into the deepest regions of Germany. From all points – known and unknown. Fields in England, Italy, Greece . . . yes, even unlisted bases in Turkey and Yugoslavia; carriers in the Mediterranean and, goddamn it, the Black Sea! Thousands and thousands of planes crowding the air corridors for space. We need that extra altitude! We need the guidance systems to operate at those altitudes! Anything less is unthinkable! . . . I'm sorry, Mr. Vandamm. I believe I'm justifiably upset."

"I understand," said the white-haired undersecretary of state. "That's why we're here this afternoon. To look for solutions . . . as well as money." The old gentleman shifted his gaze to Craft. "Can you add to Mr. Oliver's remarks, from Packard's vantage point?"

Craft disengaged his lean, manicured fingers and took a deep breath through his nostrils as if he were about to deliver essential wisdom. The executive font of knowledge, thought Alan Swanson, jockeying for a chairman's approval.

"Of course, Mr. Undersecretary. As the major subcontractor for Meridian, we've been as disturbed as the general over the lack of guidance results. We've spared nothing to accommodate. Mr. Spinelli's presence is proof of that. After all, we're the ones who brought in ATCO. . . .' here Craft smiled heroically, a touch sadly. "As we all know, ATCO is the finest – and most costly. We've spared *nothing.*"

"You brought in ATCO," said Swanson wearily, "because your own laboratories couldn't do the job. You submitted cost overruns to Meridian which were passed on to us. I don't see that you spared a hell of a lot."

"Good Lord, general!" exclaimed Craft with very little conviction. "The *time*, the *negotiations* . . . time is money, sir; make no mistake about *that*. I could show you. . . ."

"The general asked *me* a question. I should like to answer him."

The words, spoken with a trace of dialect, came from the tiny scientist, who was either dismissing Craft's nonsense, or oblivious to it, or., somehow, both.

"I'd be grateful, Mr. Spinelli."

"Our progress has been consistent, steady if you like. Not rapid. The problems are great. We believe the distortion of the radio beams beyond certain altitudes varies with temperatures and land-mass curvatures. The solutions lie in alternating compensations. Our experiments continuously narrow that field . . . Our rate of progress would be more rapid were it not for constant interferences."

Gian Spinelli stopped and shifted his grotesquely magnified eyes to Howard Oliver, whose thick neck and jowled face were suddenly flushed with anger.

"You've had no interference from *us!*"

"And certainly not from Packard!" chimed in Craft. "We've stayed in almost daily contact. Our concerns have never flagged!"

Spinelli turned to Craft. "Your concerns . . . as those of Meridian.. have been exclusively budgetary, as far as I can see."

"That's preposterous! Whatever financial inquiries were made, were made at the request of the . . . contractor's audit division. . . ."

"And totally necessary!" Oliver could not conceal his fury at the small Italian. "You *laboratory* . . . people don't reconcile! You're *children!*"

For the next thirty seconds the three agitated men babbled excitedly in counterpoint. Swanson looked over at Vandamm. Their eyes met in understanding.

Oliver was the first to recognize the trap. He held up his hand . . . a corporate command, thought Swanson.

"Mr. Undersecretary." Oliver spoke, stifling the pitch of his anger. "Don't let our squabbling convey the wrong impression. We turn out the products."

"You're not turning out this one," said Swanson. "I recall vividly the projections in your bids for the contract. You had everything *turned out then*."

When Oliver looked at him, Alan Swanson instinctively felt he should reach for a weapon to protect himself. The Meridian executive was close to exploding.

"We relied on subordinates' evaluations," said Oliver slowly, with hostility. "I think the military has had its share of staff errors."

"Subordinates don't plan major strategies."

"Vandamm raised his voice. "Mr. Oliver. Suppose General Swanson were convinced it served no purpose withholding funds. What kind of time limits could you *now* guarantee?"

Oliver looked at Spinelli. "What would you estimate?" he asked coldly.

Spinelli's large eyes swept the ceiling. "In candor, I cannot give you an answer. We *could* solve it next week. Or next year."

Swanson quickly reached into his tunic pocket and withdrew a folded page of paper. He spread it out in front of him and spoke swiftly. "According to this memorandum . . . our last communication from ATCO . . . once the guidance system *is* perfected, you state you need six weeks of inflight experimentation. The Montana Proving Grounds."

"That's correct, general. I dictated that myself," said Spinelli.

"Six weeks from next week. Or next year. And assuming the Montana experiments are positive, another month to equip the fleets."

"Yes."

Swanson looked over at Vandamm. "In light of this, Mr. Undersecretary, there's no other course but to alter immediate priorities. Or at least the projections. We can't meet the logistics."

"Unacceptable, General Swanson. We have to meet them."

Swanson stared at the old man. Each knew precisely what the other referred to.

Overlord. The invasion of Europe.

"We must postpone, sir."

"Impossible. That's the word, general."

Swanson looked at the three men around the table.

The enemy.

"We'll he in touch, gentlemen," he said.

3

David Spaulding waited in the shadows of the thick, gnarled tree on the rocky slope above the ravine. It was Basque country and the air was damp and cold. The late afternoon sun washed over the hills; his back was to it. He had years ago – it seemed a millennium but it wasn't – learned the advantage of catching the reflections of the sun off the steel of small weapons. His own rifle was dulled with burnt, crushed cork.

Four.

Strange, but the number four kept coming to mind as he scanned the distance.

Four.

Four years and four days ago exactly. And this afternoon's contact was scheduled for precisely four o'clock in the afternoon.

Four years and four days ago he had first seen the creased brown uniforms behind the thick glass Partition in the radio studio in New York. Four years and four days ago since he had walked toward that glass wall to pick up his raincoat off the back of a chair and realized that the eyes of the older officer were looking at him. Steadily. Coldly. The younger man avoided him, as if guilty of intrusion, but not his superior, not the lieutenant colonel.

The lieutenant colonel had been studying him.

That was the beginning.

He wondered now – as he watched the ravine for signs of movement – when it would end. Would he be alive to see it end?

He intended to be.

He had called it a treadmill once. Over a drink at the Mayflower in Washington. Fairfax had *been* a treadmill; still, he had not known at the time how completely accurate that word would continue to be; a racing treadmill that never stopped.

It slowed down occasionally. The physical and mental pressures demanded deceleration at certain recognizable times – recognizable to him. Times when he realized he was getting careless . . . or too sure of himself. Or too absolute with regard to decisions that took human life.

Or might take his.

They were often too easily arrived at. And sometimes that frightened him. Profoundly.

During such times he would take himself away. He would travel south along the Portuguese coast where the enclaves of the temporarily inconvenienced rich denied the existence of war. Or he would stay in Costa del Santiago – with his perplexed parents. Or he would remain within the confines of the embassy in Lisbon and engross himself in the meaningless chores of neutral diplomacy. A minor military attaché who did not wear a uniform. It was not expected in the streets; it was inside the "territory." He did not wear one, however; no one cared. lie was not liked very much. He socialized too frequently, had too many prewar friends. By and large, he was ignored . . . with a certain disdain.

At such times he rested. Forced his mind to go blank; to recharge itself.

Four years and four days ago such thoughts would have been inconceivable. Now they consumed him. When he had the time for such thoughts.

Which he did not have now.

There was still no movement in the ravine. Something was wrong. He checked his watch; the team from San Sebastián was too far behind schedule. It was an abnormal delay. Only six hours ago the French underground had radioed that everything was secure; there were no complications, the team had started out.

The runners from San Sebastián were bringing out photographs of the German airfield installations north of Mont-de-Marsan. The strategists in London had been screaming for them for months. Those photographs had cost the lives of four . . . again, that goddamned number . . . four underground agents.

If anything, the team should have been early; the runners should have been waiting for the man from Lisbon.

Then he saw it in the distance; perhaps a half a mile away, it was difficult to tell. Over the ravine, beyond the opposite slope, from one of the miniature hills. A flashing.

An intermittent but rhythmic flashing. The measured spacing was a mark of intent, not accident.

They were being signaled. *He* was being signaled by someone who knew his methods of operation well; perhaps someone he had trained. It was a warning.

Spaulding slung the rifle over his shoulder and pulled the strap taut, then tighter still so that it became a fixed but flexible appendage to his upper body. He felt the hasp of his belt holster; it was in place, the weapon secure. He pushed himself away from the trunk of the old tree and, in a crouching position, scrambled up the remainder of the rock-hewn slope.

On the ridge he ran to his left, into the tall grass toward the remains of a dying pear orchard. Two men in mud-caked clothes, rifles at their sides, were sitting on the ground playing trick knife, passing the time in silence. They snapped their heads up, their hands reaching for their guns.

Spaulding gestured to them to remain on the ground. He approached and spoke quietly in Spanish.

"Do either of you know who's on the team coming in?"

"Bergeron, I think," said the man on the right. "And probably Chivier. That old man has a way with patrols; forty years he's peddled across the border."

"Then it's Bergeron," said Spaulding.

"What is?" asked the second man.

"We're being signaled. They're late and someone is using what's left of the sun to get our attention."

"Perhaps to tell you they're on their way." The first man put the knife back in his scabbard as he spoke.

"Possible but not likely. We wouldn't go anywhere. Not for a couple of hours yet." Spaulding raised himself partially off the ground and looked eastward. "Come on! We'll head down past the rim of the orchard. We can get a cross view there."

The three men in single file, separated but within hearing of each other, raced across the field below the high ground for nearly four hundred yards. Spaulding positioned himself behind a low rock that jutted over the edge of the ravine. He waited for the other two. The waters below were about a hundred feet straight down, he judged. The team from San Sebastián would cross them approximately two hundred yards west, through the shallow, narrow passage they always used.

The two other men arrived within seconds of each other. "The old tree where you stood was the mark, wasn't it?" asked the first man.

"Yes," answered Spaulding, removing his binoculars from a case opposite his belt holster. They were powerful, with Zeiss Ikon lenses, the best Germany produced. Taken from a dead German at the Tejo River.

"Then why come down here? If there's a problem, your line of vision was best where you were. It's more direct."

"If there's a problem, they'll know that. They'll flank to their left. East. To the west the ravine heads *away* from the mark. Maybe it's nothing. Perhaps you were right; they just want us to know they're coming."

A little more than two hundred yards away, just west of the shallow passage, two men came into view. The Spaniard who knelt on Spaulding's left touched the American's shoulder.

"It's Bergeron and Chivier," he said quietly.

Spaulding held up his hand for silence and scanned the area with the binoculars. Abruptly he fixed them in one position. With his left hand he directed the attention of his subordinates to the spot.

Below them, perhaps fifty yards, four soldiers in Wehrmacht uniforms were struggling with the foliage, approaching the waters of the ravine.

Spaulding moved his binoculars back to the two Frenchmen, now crossing the water. He held the glasses steady against the rock until he could see in the woods behind the two men what he knew was there.

A fifth German. an officer, was half concealed in the tangled mass of weeds and low branches. He held a rifle on the two Frenchmen crossing the ravine.

Spaulding passed the binoculars quickly to the first Spaniard. He whispered. "Behind Chivier."

The man looked, then gave the glasses to his countryman.

Each knew what had to be done; even the methods were clear. It was merely a question of timing, precision. From a scabbard behind his right hip, Spaulding withdrew a short carbine bayonet, shortened further by grinding. His two associates did the same. Each peered over the rock at the Wehrmacht men below.

The four Germans, faced with waters waist high and a current – though not excessively strong, nevertheless considerable – strapped their rifles across their shoulders laterally and separated in a downstream column. The lead man started across, testing the depths as he did so.

Spaulding and the two Spaniards came from behind the rock swiftly and slid down the incline, concealed by the foliage, their sounds muffled by the rushing water. In less than half a minute they were within thirty feet of the Wehrmacht men, hidden by fallen tree limbs and overgrowth. David entered the water, hugging the embankment. He was relieved to see that the fourth man – now only fifteen feet in front of him – was having the most difficulty keeping his balance on the slippery rocks. The other three, spaced about ten yards apart, were concentrating on the Frenchmen upstream. Concentrating intently.

The Nazi saw him; the fear, the bewilderment was in the German's eyes. The split second he took to assimilate the shock was the time David needed. Covered by the sounds of the water, Spaulding leaped on the man, his knife penetrating the Wehrmacht throat, the head pushed violently under the surface, the blood mingling with the rushing stream.

There was no time, no second to waste. David released the lifeless form and saw that the two Spaniards were parallel with him on the embankment. The first man, crouched and hidden, gestured toward the lead soldier; the second nodded his head toward the next man. And David knew that the third Wehrmacht soldier was his.

It took no more than the time necessary for Bergeron and Chivier to reach the south bank. The three soldiers were dispatched, their blood-soaked bodies floating downstream, careening off rocks, filling the waters with streaks of magenta.

Spaulding signaled the Spaniards to cross the water to the north embankment. The first man pulled himself up beside David, his right hand bloodied from a deep cut across his palm.

"Are you all right?" whispered Spaulding.

"The blade slipped. I lost my knife." The man swore.

"Get out of the area," said David. "Get the wound dressed at the Valdero farm."

"I can put on a tight bandage. I'll be fine."

The second Spaniard joined them. He winced at the sight of his countryman's hand, an action Spaulding thought inconsistent for a guerrilla who had just minutes ago plunged a blade into the neck of a man, slicing most of his head off.

"That looks bad," he said.

"You can't function," added Spaulding, "and we don't have time to argue."

"I can. . . ."

"You *can't*." David spoke peremptorily. "Go back to Valdero's. I'll see you in a week or two. Get going and stay out of sight!"

"Very well." The Spaniard was upset but it was apparent that he would not, could not, disobey the American's commands. He started to crawl into the woods to the east.

Spaulding called quietly, just above the rush of the water. "Thank you. Fine work today."

The Spaniard grinned and raced into the forest, holding his wrist.

Just as swiftly, David touched the arm of the second man, beckoning him to follow. They sidestepped their way along the bank upstream. Spaulding stopped by a fallen tree whose trunk dipped down into the ravine waters. He turned and crouched, ordering the Spaniard to do the same. He spoke words quietly.

"I want him alive. I want to question him."

"I'll get him."

"No, I will. I just don't want you to fire. There could be a backup patrol." Spaulding realized as he whispered that the man couldn't help but smile. He knew why: his Spanish had the soft lilt of Castilian, a foreigner's Castilian at that. It was out of place in Basque country.

As he was out of place, really.

"As you wish, good friend," said the man. "Shall I cross farther back and reach Bergeron? He's probably sick to his stomach by now."

"No, not yet. Wait'll we're secure over here. He and the old man will just keep walking." David raised his head over the fallen tree trunk and estimated distances. The German officer was about sixty yards away, hidden in the woods. "I'll head in there, get behind him. I'll see if I can spot any signs of another patrol. If I do, I'll come back and we'll get out. If not, I'll try to grab him . . . If anything goes wrong, if he hears me, he'll probably head for the water. Take him."

The Spaniard nodded. Spaulding checked the tautness of his rifle strap, giving it a last-second hitch. He gave his subordinate a tentative smile and saw that the man's hands – huge, calloused – were spread on the ground like claws. If the Wehrmacht officer headed this way, he'd never get by those hands, thought David.

He crept swiftly, silently into the woods, his arms and feet working like a primitive hunter's, warding off branches, sidestepping rocks and tangled foliage.

In less than three minutes he had gone thirty yards behind the German on the Nazi's left flank. He stood immobile and withdrew his binoculars. He scanned the forest and the trail. There were no other patrols. He doubled back cautiously, blending every movement of his body with his surroundings.

When he was within ten feet of the German, who was kneeling on the ground, David silently unlatched his holster and withdrew his pistol. He spoke sharply, though not impolitely, in German.

"Stay where you are or I'll blow your head off."

The Nazi whipped around and awkwardly fumbled for his weapon. Spaulding took several rapid steps and kicked it out of his hands. The man started to rise, and David brought his heavy leather boot up into the side of the German's head. The officer's visor hat fell to the ground; blood poured out of the man's temple, spreading throughout the hairline, streaking down across his face. He was unconscious.

Spaulding reached down and tore at the Nazi's tunic. Strapped across the Oberleutnant's chest was a traveling pouch. David pulled the steel zipper laterally over the waterproofed canvas and found what he was sure he would find.

The photographs of the hidden Luftwaffe installations north of Mont-de-Marsan. Along with the photographs were amateurish drawings that were, in essence, basic blueprints. At least, schematics. Taken from Bergeron, who had then led the German into the trap.

If he could make sense out of them – along with the photographs – he would alert London that sabotage units could inflict the necessary destruction, immobilizing the Luftwaffe complex. He would send in the units himself.

The Allied air strategists were manic when it came to bombing runs. The planes dove from the skies, reducing to rubble and crater everything that was – and was not – a target, taking as much innocent life as enemy. If Spaulding could prevent air strikes north of Mont-de-Marsan, it might somehow . . . abstractly make up for the decision he now had to face.

There were no prisoners of war in the Galician hills, no internment centers in the Basque country.

The Wehrmacht lieutenant, who was so ineffectual in his role of the hunter . . . who might have had a life in some peaceful German town in a peaceful world . . . had to die. And he, the man from Lisbon, would be the executioner. He would revive the young officer, interrogate him at the point of a knife to learn how deeply the Nazis had penetrated the underground in San Sebastián. Then kill him.

For the Wehrmacht officer had seen the man from Lisbon; he could identify that man as David Spaulding.

The fact that the execution would be mercifully quick – unlike a death in partisan hands – was of small comfort to David. He knew that at the instant he pulled the trigger, the world would spin insanely for a moment or two. He would be sick to his stomach and want to vomit, his whole being in a state of revulsion.

But he would not show these things. He would say nothing, indicate

454

nothing . . . silence. And so the legend would continue to grow. For that was part of the treadmill.

The man in Lisbon was a killer.

4

Wilhelm Zangen brought the handkerchief to his chin, and then to the skin beneath his nostrils, and finally to the border of his receding hairline. The sweat was profuse; a rash had formed in the cleft below his lips, aggravated by the daily necessity to shave and the continuous pressure.

His whole face was stinging, his embarrassment compounded by Franz Altmüller's final words:

"Really, Wilhelm, you should see a doctor. It's most unattractive."

With that objective solicitousness, Altmüller had gotten up from the table and walked out the door. Slowly, deliberately, his briefcase – the briefcase containing the reports – held down at arm's length as though it had been some diseased appendage.

They had been alone. Altmüller had dismissed the group of scientists without acknowledging any progress whatsoever. He had not even allowed him, the Reich official of German Industry, to thank them for their contributions. Altmüller knew that these were the finest scientific minds in Germany, but he had no understanding of how to handle them. They were sensitive, they were volatile in their own quiet way; they needed praise constantly. He had no patience for tact.

And there *had* been progress.

The Krupp laboratories were convinced that the answer lay in the graphite experiments. Essen had worked around the clock for nearly a month, its managers undergoing one sleepless night after another. They had actually *produced carbon particles* in sealed iron tubes and were convinced these carbons held all the properties required for precision tooling. It was merely a question of time; time to create larger particles, sufficient for tolerance placement within existing machinery.

Franz Altmüller had listened to the Krupp team without the slightest indication of enthusiasm, although enthusiasm certainly had been called for under the circumstances. Instead, when the Krupp spokesman had finished his summary, Altmüller had asked one question. Asked it with the most bored expression imaginable!

"Have these . . . particles been subjected to the pressures of operational tooling?"

Of course they hadn't! How could they have been? They *had* been subjected to artificial, substitute pressures; it was all that was possible at the moment.

That answer had been unacceptable; Altmüller dismissed the most scientifically creative minds in the Reich without a single sentence of appreciation, only ill-disguised hostility.

"Gentlemen, you've brought me words. We don't need words, we need diamonds. We need them, we *must have* them within weeks. Two months at the outside. I suggest you return to your laboratories and consider our problem once again. Good day, gentlemen."

Altmüller was impossible!

After the scientists had left, Altmüller had become even more abrasive.

"Wilhelm," he had said with a voice bordering on contempt, "was *this* the nonmilitary solution of which you spoke to the minister of armaments?"

Why hadn't he used Speer's name? Was it necessary to threaten with the use of titles?

"Of course. Certainly more realistic than that insane march into the Congo. The mines at the Bushimaie River! Madness!"

"The comparison is odious. I overestimated you; I gave you more credit than you deserve. You understand, of course, that you failed." It was not a question.

"I disagree. The results aren't in yet. You can't make such a judgment."

"I can and I have!" Altmüller had slammed the flat of his hand against the tabletop; a crack of soft flesh against hard wood. An intolerable insult. "We have no time! We can't waste weeks while your laboratory misfits play with their bunsen burners, creating little stones that could fall apart at the first contact with steel! We need the *product!*"

"You'll have it!" The surface of Zangen's chin became an oily mixture of sweat and stubble. "The finest minds in all Germany are . . ."

"Are *experimenting.*" Altmüller had interrupted quietly, with scornful emphasis. "Get us the *product*. That's my order to you. Our powerful companies have long histories that go back many years. Certainly one of them can find an old friend."

Wilhelm Zangen had blotted his chin; the rash was agonizing. "We've covered those areas. Impossible."

"Cover them again." Altmüller had pointed an elegant finger at Zangen's handkerchief. "Really, Wilhelm, you should see a doctor. It's most unattractive."

SEPTEMBER 24, 1943

NEW YORK CITY

Jonathan Craft walked up Park Avenue and checked his wristwatch under the spill of a streetlamp. His long, thin fingers trembled; the last vestige of too many martinis, which he had stopped drinking twenty-four hours ago in Ann

Arbor. Unfortunately, he had been drunk for the three previous days. He had not been to the office. The office reminded him of General Alan Swanson; he could not bear that memory. Now he had to.

It was a quarter to nine; another fifteen minutes and he would walk into 800 Park Avenue, smile at the doorman and go to the elevator. He did not want to be early, dared not be late. He had been inside the apartment house exactly seven times, and each occasion had been traumatic for him. Always for the same reason: he was the bearer of bad news.

But they needed him. He was the impeccable man. His family was old, fine money; he had been to the right schools, the best cotillions. He had access into areas – social and institutional – the *merchants* would never possess. No matter he was stuck in Ann Arbor; it was a temporary situation, a wartime inconvenience. A sacrifice.

He would be back in New York on the Exchange as soon as the damn thing was over.

He had to keep these thoughts in mind tonight because in a few minutes he would have to repeat the words Swanson had screamed at him in his Packard office. He had written a confidential report of the conversation . . . the *unbelievable* conversation . . . and sent it to Howard Oliver at Meridian.

If you've done what I think you've done, it falls under the heading of treasonable acts! And we're at war!

Swanson.

Madness.

He wondered how many would be there, in the apartment. It was always better if there were quite a few, say a dozen. Then they argued among themselves; he was almost forgotten. Except for his information.

He walked around the block, breathing deeply, calming himself . . . killing ten minutes.

Treasonable acts!

And we are at war!

His watch read five minutes to nine. He entered the building, smiled at the doorman, gave the floor to the elevator operator and, when the brass grill opened, he walked into the private foyer of the penthouse.

A butler took his overcoat and ushered him across the hall, through the door and down three steps into the huge sunken living room.

There were only two men in the room. Craft felt an immediate sharp pain in his stomach. It was an instinctive reaction partly brought on by the fact that there were only two people for this extremely vital conference, but mainly caused by the sight of Walter Kendall.

Kendall was a man in shadows, a manipulator of figures who was kept out of sight. He was fiftyish, medium-sized, with thinning, unwashed hair, a rasping voice and an undistinguished – shoddy – appearance. His eyes darted continuously, almost never returning another man's look. It was said his mind concentrated incessantly on schemes and counterschemes; his whole purpose in life was apparently to outmaneuver other human beings – friend or enemy,

458

it made no difference to Kendall, for he did not categorize people with such labels.

All were vague opponents.

But Walter Kendall was brilliant at what he did. As long as he could be kept in the background, his manipulations served his clients. And made him a great deal of money – which he hoarded, attested to by ill-fitting suits that bagged at the knees and sagged below the buttocks. But he was always kept out of sight; his presence signified crisis.

Jonathan Craft despised Kendall because he was frightened by him.

The second man was to be expected under the circumstances. He was Howard Oliver, Meridian Aircraft's obese debater of War Department contracts.

"You're on time," said Walter Kendall curtly, sitting down in an armchair, reaching for papers in an open, filthy briefcase at his feet.

"Hello, Jon." Oliver approached and offered a short, neutral handshake.

"Where are the others?" asked Craft.

"No one wanted to be here," answered Kendall with a furtive glance at Oliver. "Howard has to be, and I'm paid to be. You had one hell of a meeting with this Swanson."

"You've read my report?"

"He's read it," said Oliver, crossing to a copper-topped wheel-cart in the corner on which there were bottles and glasses. "He's got questions."

"I made everything perfectly clear. . . ."

"Those aren't the questions," interrupted Kendall while squeezing the tip of a cigarette before inserting it into his mouth. As he struck a match, Craft walked to a large velvet chair across from the accountant and sat down. Oliver had poured himself a whisky and remained standing.

"If you want a drink, Jon, it's over there," said Oliver.

At the mention of alcohol", Kendall glanced up at him from his papers with ferret-like eyes. "No thank you," Craft replied. "I'd like to get this over with as soon as possible."

"Suit yourself' Oliver looked at the accountant. "Ask your questions."

Kendall, sucking on his cigarette, spoke as the smoke curled around his nostrils. "This Spinelli over at ATCO. Have you talked to him since you saw Swanson?"

"No. There was nothing to say; nothing I could say . . . without instructions. As you know, I spoke with Howard on the phone. He told me to wait; write a report and do nothing."

"Craft's the funnel to ATCO," said Oliver. "I didn't want him running scared, trying to smooth things over. It'd look like we were hiding something."

"We are," Kendall removed his cigarette, the ash falling on his trousers. He continued while slowly shuffling the papers on his lap. "Let's go over Spinelli's complaints. As Swanson brought them up."

The accountant touched briefly, concisely on each point raised. They covered Spinelli's statements regarding delayed deliveries, personnel transfers, blueprint holdups, a dozen other minor grievances. Craft replied with equal brevity, answering when he could, stating ignorance when he could not. There was no reason to hide anything.

He had been carrying out instructions, not issuing them.

"Can Spinelli substantiate these charges? And don't kid yourselves, these are charges, not complaints."

"What *charges*?" Oliver spat out the words. "That guinea bastard's fucked up everything! Who's he to make charges?"

"Get off it," said Kendall in his rasping voice. "Don't play games. Save them for a congressional committee, unless I can figure something."

At Kendall's words the sharp pain returned to Craft's stomach. The prospects of disgrace – even remotely associated – could ruin his life. The life be expected to lead back in New York. The financial boors, the *merchants*, could never understand. "That's going a little far. . . ."

Kendall looked over at Craft. "Maybe you didn't *hear* Swanson. It's not going far enough. You got the Fortress contracts because your *projections* said you could do the job."

"Just a minute!" yelled Oliver "We . . ."

"*Screw* the legal crap!" countered Kendall, shouting over Oliver's interruption. "My firm . . . *me*, I . . . squared those projections. I know what they say, what they implied. You left the other companies at the gate. They wouldn't *say* what you said. Not Douglas, not Boeing, not Lockheed. You were hungry and you got the meat and now you're not delivering. . . .So what else is new? Let's go back: can Spinelli substantiate?"

"*Shit*," exploded Oliver, heading for the bar.

"How do you mean . . . substantiate?" asked Jonathan Craft, his stomach in agony.

"Are there any memorandums floating around," Kendall tapped the pages in his hand, "that bear on any of this?"

"Well . . ." Craft hesitated; he couldn't stand the pain in his stomach." When personnel transfers were expedited, they were put into interoffice. . . ."

"The answer's yes," interrupted Oliver in disgust, pouring himself a drink.

"What about financial cutbacks?"

Oliver once again replied. "We obscured those. Spinelli's requisitions just got lost in the paper shuffle."

"Didn't he scream? Didn't *he* shoot off memos?"

"That's Craft's department," answered Oliver, drinking most of his whisky in one swallow. "Spinelli was his little guinea boy."

"Well?" Kendall looked at Craft.

"Well . . . he sent numerous communications." Craft leaned forward in the chair, as much to relieve the pain as to appear confidential. "I removed everything from the files," he said softly.

460

"*Christ*," exploded Kendall quietly. "I don't give a *shit* what *you* removed. He's got copies. Dates."

"Well, I couldn't say. . . ."

"He didn't type the goddamned things *himself* did he? You didn't take away the fucking secretaries, *too*, did you?"

"There's no call to be offensive. . . ."

"*Offensive!* You're a funny man! Maybe they've got fancy stripes for you in Leavenworth." The accountant snorted and turned his attention to Howard Oliver. "Swanson's got a case; he'll hang you. Nobody has to be a lawyer to see that. You held back. *You figured to use the existing guidance systems.*"

"Only because the new gyroscopes couldn't be developed! Because that guinea bastard fell so far behind he couldn't catch up!"

"Also it saved you a couple of hundred million. . . . You should have primed the pumps, not cut off the water. You're big ducks in a short gallery; a blind man could knock you off."

Oliver put his glass down and spoke slowly, "We don't pay you for that kind of judgment, Walter. You'd better have something else."

Kendall crushed out his mutilated cigarette, his dirty fingernails covered with ash. "I do," he said. "You need company; you're in the middle of a very emotional issue. It'll cost you but you don't have a choice. You've got to make deals, ring in everybody. Get hold of Sperry Rand, GM, Chrysler, Lockheed, Douglas, Rolls-Royce, if you have to . . . every son of a bitch with an engineering laboratory. A patriotic crash program. Cross-reference your data, open up everything you've got."

"They'll steal us blind!" roared Oliver. "Millions!"

"Cost you more if you don't . . . I'll prepare supplementary financial stats. I'll pack the sheets with so much ice, it'll take ten years to thaw. That'll cost you, too." Kendall smirked, baring soiled teeth.

Howard Oliver stared at the unkempt accountant. "It's crazy, he said quietly. "We'll be giving away fortunes for something that can't be bought because it doesn't exist."

"But you said it *did* exist. You told Swanson it existed – at least a hell of a lot more confidently than anybody else. You sold your great industrial know-how, and when you couldn't deliver, you covered up. Swanson's right. You're a menace to the war effort. Maybe you *should* be shot."

Jonathan Craft watched the filthy, grinning bookkeeper with bad teeth and wanted to vomit. But he was their only hope.

5

Wilhelm Zangen stood by the window overlooking Stuttgart's Reichssieg Platz, holding a handkerchief against his inflamed, perspiring chin. This outlying section of the city had been spared the bombing; it was residential, even peaceful. The Neckar River could be seen in the distance, its waters rolling calmly, oblivious to the destruction that had been wrought on the other side of the city.

Zangen realized he was expected to speak, to answer von Schnitzler, who spoke for all of I. G. Farben. The two other men were as anxious to hear his words as was von Schnitzler. There was no point in procrastinating. He had to carry out Altmüller's orders.

"The Krupp laboratories have failed. No matter what Essen says, there is no time for experimentation. The Ministry of Armaments has made that clear; Altmüller is resolute. He speaks for Speer." Zangen turned and looked at the three men. "He holds you responsible."

"How can that be?" asked von Schnitzler, his guttural lisp pronounced, his voice angry. How can we be responsible for something we know nothing about? It's illogical. Ridiculous!"

"Would you wish me to convey that judgment to the ministry?"

"I'll convey it myself thank you," replied von Schnitzler. "Farben is not involved."

"We are all involved," said Zangen quietly.

"How can *our* company be?" asked Heinrich Krepps, Direktor of Schreibwaren, the largest printing complex in Germany. "Our work with Peenemünde has been practically nothing; and what there was, obscured to the point of foolishness. Secrecy is one thing; lying to ourselves, something else again. Do not include us, Herr Zangen."

"You *are* included."

"I reject your conclusion. I've studied our communications with Peenemünde."

"Perhaps you were not cleared for all the facts."

"Asinine!"

"Quite possibly. Nevertheless . . ."

"Such a condition would hardly apply to *me*, Herr Reich official," said Johann Dietricht, the middle-aged effeminate son of the Dietricht Chemikalien empire. Dietricht's family had contributed heavily to Hitler's National Socialist coffers; when the father and uncle had died, Johann Dietricht was allowed to continue the management – more in name than in fact. "Nothing occurs at Dietricht of which I am unaware. We've had nothing to do with Peenemünde!"

Johann Dietricht smiled, his fat lips curling, his blinking eyes betraying an excess of alcohol, his partially plucked eyebrows his sexual proclivity – excess, again. Zangen couldn't stand Dietricht; the man – although no man – was a disgrace, his life-style an insult to German industry. Again, felt Zangen, there was no point in procrastinating. The information would come as no surprise to von Schnitzler and Krepps.

"There are many aspects of the Dietricht Chemikalien of which you know *nothing*. Your own laboratories have worked consistently with Peenemünde in the field of chemical detonation."

Dietricht blanched; Krepps interrupted.

"What is your purpose, Herr Reich official? You call us here only to insult us? You tell us, directors, that we are not the masters of our own companies? I don't know Herr Dietricht so well, but I can assure you that von Schnitzler and myself are not puppets."

Von Schnitzier had been watching Zangen closely, observing the Reich official's use of his handkerchief. Zangen kept blotting his chin nervously. "I presume you have specific information – such as you've just delivered to Herr Dietricht – that will confirm your statements."

"I have."

"Then you're saying that isolated operations – within our own factories – were withheld from us."

"I am."

"Then how can we be held responsible? These are insane accusations."

"They are made for practical reasons."

"Now you're talking in circles!" shouted Dietricht, barely recovered from Zangen's insult.

"I must agree," said Krepps, as if agreement with the obvious homosexual was distasteful, yet mandatory.

"Come, gentlemen. Must I draw pictures? These are *your companies*. Farben has supplied eighty-three per cent of all chemicals for the rockets; Schreibwaren has processed every blueprint; Dietricht, the majority of detonating compounds for the casing explosives. We're in a crisis. If we don't overcome that crisis, no protestations of ignorance will serve you. I might go so far as to say that there are those in the ministry and elsewhere who will deny that anything was withheld. You simply buried your collective heads. I'm not even sure myself that such a judgment is in error."

"Lies!" screamed Dietricht.

"Absurd!" added Krepps.

"But obscenely practical," concluded von Schnitzler slowly, staring at Zangen. "So this is what you're telling us, isn't it? What Altmüller tells us.

We either employ our resources to find a solution – to come to the aid of our industrial *Schwachling* – or we face equilateral disposition in the eyes of the ministry."

"And in the eyes of the Fuhrer; the judgment of the Reich itself."

"But *how?*" asked the frightened Johann Dietricht.

Zangen remembered Altmüller's words precisely. "Your companies have long histories that go back many years. Corporate and individual. From the Baltic to the Mediterranean, from New York to Rio de Janeiro, from Saudi Arabia to Johannesburg."

"And from Shanghai down through Malaysia to the ports in Australia and the Tasman Sea," said von Schnitzler quietly.

"They don't concern us."

"I thought not."

"Are you suggesting, Herr Reich official, that the solution for Peenemünde lies in our past associations?" Von Schnitzler leaned forward in his chair, his hands and eyes on the table.

"It's a crisis. No avenues can be overlooked. Communications can be expedited."

"No doubt. What makes you think they'd be exchanged?" continued the head of I. G. Farben.

"Profits," replied Zangen.

"Difficult to spend facing a firing squad." Von Schnitzler shifted his large bulk and looked up at the window, his expression pensive.

"You assume the commission of specific transactions. I refer more to acts of *omission.*"

"Clarify that, please." Krepps's eyes remained on the tabletop.

"There are perhaps twenty-five acceptable sources for the bortz and carbonado diamonds – acceptable in the sense that sufficient quantities can be obtained in a single purchase. Africa and South America; one or two locations in Central America. These mines are run by companies under fiat security conditions: British, American, Free French, Belgian . . . you know them. Shipments are controlled, destinations cleared. . . . We are suggesting that the shipments can be sidetracked, destinations altered in neutral territories. By the expedient of omitting normal security precautions. Acts of incompetence, if you will; human error, not betrayal."

"Extraordinarily profitable mistakes," summed up von Schnitzler.

"Precisely," said Wilhelm Zangen.

"Where do you find such men?" asked Johann Dietricht in his high-pitched voice.

"Everywhere," replied Heinrich Krepps.

Zangen blotted his chin with his handkerchief.

6

Spaulding raced across the foot of the hill until he saw the converging limbs of the two trees. They were the mark. He turned right and started up the steep incline, counting off an approximate 125 yards; the second mark. He turned left and walked slowly around to the west slope, his body low, his eyes darting constantly in all directions; he gripped his pistol firmly.

On the west slope he looked for a single rock – one among so many on the rock-strewn Galician hill – that had been chipped on its downward side. Chipped carefully with three indentations. It was the third and final mark.

He found it, spotting first the bent reeds of the stiff hill grass. He knelt down and looked at his watch: two forty-five.

He was fifteen minutes early, as he had planned to be. In fifteen minutes he would walk down the west slope, directly in front of the chipped rock. There he would find a pile of branches. Underneath the branches would be a short-walled cave; in that cave – if all went as planned – would be three men. One was a member of an infiltration team. The other two were *Wissenschaftler* – German scientists who had been attached to the Kindorf laboratories in the Ruhr Valley. Their defections – escape – had been an objective of long planning.

The obstacles were always the same.

Gestapo.

The Gestapo had broken an underground agent and was on to the *Wissenschaftler*. But, typical of the SS elite, it kept its knowledge to itself looking for bigger game than two disaffected laboratory men. Gestapo *Agenten* had given the scientists wide latitude; surveillance dismissed, laboratory patrols relaxed to the point of inefficiency, routine interrogation disregarded.

Contradictions.

The Gestapo was neither inefficient nor careless. The SS was setting a trap.

Spaulding's instructions to the underground had been terse, simple: let the trap be sprung. With no quarry in its net.

Word was leaked that the scientists, granted a weekend leave to Stuttgart, were in reality heading due north through underground routing to Bremerhaven. There contact was being made with a high-ranking defecting German naval officer who had commandeered a small craft and would make a dramatic run to the Allies. It was common knowledge that the German navy was rife

465

with unrest. It was a recruiting ground for the anti-Hitler factions springing up throughout the Reich.

The *word* would give everyone something to think about, reasoned Spaulding. And the Gestapo would be following two men it assumed were the *Wissenschaftler* from Kindorf. when actually they were two middle-aged Wehrmacht security patrols sent on a false surveillance.

Games and countergames.

So much, so alien. The expanded interests of the man in Lisbon.

This afternoon was a concession. Demanded by the German underground. He was to make the final contact alone. The underground claimed the man in Lisbon had created too many complications; there was too much room for error and counter-infiltration. There wasn't, thought David, but if a solo run would calm the nervous stomachs of the anti-Reichists, it was little enough to grant them.

He had his own Valdero team a half mile away in the upper hills. Two shots and they would come to his help on the fastest horses Castilian money could buy.

It was time. He could start toward the cave for the final contact.

He slid down the hard surface, his heels digging into the earth and rocks of the steep incline until he was above the pile of branches and limbs that signified the hideout's opening. He picked up a handful of loose dirt and threw it down into the broken foliage.

The response was as instructed: a momentary thrashing of a stick against the piled branches. The fluttering of bird's wings, driven from the bush.

Spaulding quickly sidestepped his way to the base of the enclosure and stood by the camouflage.

"*Alles in Ordnung. Kommen Sie,*" he said quietly but firmly. "There isn't much traveling time left."

"*Halt,*" was the unexpected shout from the cave.

David spun around, pressed his back into the hill and raised his Colt. The voice from inside spoke again. In English.

"Are you . . . Lisbon?"

"For God's sake, yes! Don't *do* that! You'll get your head shot off!" *Christ*, thought Spaulding, the infiltration team must have used a child, or an imbecile, or both as its runner. "Come on out."

"I am with apologies, Lisbon," said the voice, as the branches were separated and the pile dislodged. "We've had a bad time of it."

The runner emerged. He was obviously not anyone David had trained. He was short, very muscular, no more than twenty-five or twenty-six; nervous fear was in his eyes.

"In the future," said Spaulding, "don't acknowledge signals, then question the signaler at the very last moment. Unless you intend to kill him. *Es ist Schwarztuch-chiffre.*"

"*Was ist das?* Black . . ."

"Black drape, friend. Before our time. It means . . . confirm and terminate.

Never mind, just don't do it again. Where are the others?"

"Inside. They are all right; very tired and very afraid, but not injured." The runner turned and pulled off more branches. "Come out. It's the man from Lisbon."

The two frightened, middle-aged scientists crawled out of the cave cautiously, blinking at the hot, harsh sun. They looked gratefully at David; the taller one spoke in halting English.

"This is a . . . minute we have waited for. Our very much thanks."

Spaulding smiled. "Well, we're not out of the woods, yet. *Frei*. Both terms apply. You're brave men. We'll do all we can for you."

"There was . . . *nichts* . . . remaining," said the shorter laboratory man. "My friend's socialist . . . *Politik* . . . was unpopular. My late wife. . . . . *eine Jüdin*."

"No children?"

"Nein," answered the man. "*Gott sel dank*."

"I have one son," said the taller scientist coldly. "*Er . . . ist Gestapo*."

There was no more to be said, thought Spaulding. He turned to the runner, who was scanning the hill and the forests below. "I'll take over now. Get back to Base Four as soon as you can. We've got a large contingent coming in from Koblenz in a few days. We'll need everyone. Get some rest."

The runner hesitated; David had seen his expression before . . . so often. The man was now going to travel alone. No company, pleasant or unpleasant. Just alone.

"That is not my understanding, Lisbon. I am to stay with you. . . ."

"Why?" interrupted Spaulding.

"My instructions. . . ."

"From whom?"

"From those in San Sebastián. Herr Bergeron and his men. Weren't you informed?"

David looked at the runner. The man's fear was making him a poor liar, thought Spaulding. Or he was something else. Something completely unexpected because it was not logical; it was not, at this point, even remotely to be considered. Unless . . .

David gave the runner's frayed young nerves the benefit of the doubt. A benefit, not an exoneration. That would come later.

"No, I wasn't told," he said. "Come on. We'll head to Beta camp. We'll stay there until morning." Spaulding gestured and they started across the foot of the slope.

"I haven't worked this far south," said the runner, positioning himself behind David. "Don't you travel at night, Lisbon?"

"Sometimes," answered Spaulding, looking back at the scientists, who were walking side by side. "Not if we can help it. The Basque shoot indiscriminately at night. They have too many dogs off their leashes at night."

"I see."

"Let's walk single file. Flank our guests," said David to the runner.

The four traveled several miles east. Spaulding kept up a rapid pace; the middle-aged scientists did not complain but they obviously found the going difficult. A number of times David told the others to remain where they were while he entered the woods at various sections of the forest and returned minutes later. Each time he did so, the older men rested, grateful for the pauses. The runner did not. He appeared frightened – as if the American might not come back. Spaulding did not encourage conversation, but after one such disappearance, the young German could not restrain himself.

"What are you *doing*?" he asked.

David looked at the *Widerstandskämpfer* and smiled. "Picking up messages."

"Messages?"

"These are drops. Along our route. We establish marks for leaving off information we don't want sent by radio. Too dangerous if intercepted."

They continued along a narrow path at the edge of the woods until there was a break in the Basque forest. It was a grazing field, a lower plateau centered beneath the surrounding hills. The *Wissenschaftler* were perspiring heavily, their breaths short, their legs aching.

"We'll rest here for a while," said Spaulding, to the obvious relief of the older men. "It's time I made contact anyway."

"*Was ist los?*" asked the young runner. "Contact?"

"Zeroing our position," replied David, taking out a small metal mirror from his field jacket. "The scouts can relax if they know where we are. . . . If you're going to work the north country – what you call south – you'd better remember all this."

"I shall, I shall."

David caught the reflection of the sun on the mirror and beamed it up to a northern hill. He made a series of motions with his wrist, and the metal plate moved back and forth in rhythmic precision.

Seconds later there was a reply from halfway up the highest hill in the north. Flashes of light shafted out of an infinitesimal spot in the brackish green distance. Spaulding turned to the others.

"We're not going to Beta," he said. "Falangist patrols are in the area. We'll stay here until we're given clearance. You can relax."

The heavyset Basque put down the knapsack mirror. His companion still focused his binoculars on the field several miles below, where the American and his three charges were now seated on the ground.

"He says they are being followed. We are to take up counter-positions and stay out of sight," said the man with the metal mirror. "We go down for the scientists tomorrow night. He will signal us."

"What's *he* going to do?"

"I don't know. He says to get word to Lisbon. He's going to stay in the hills."

"He's a cold one," the Basque said.

DECEMBER 2, 1943

WASHINGTON, D.C.

Alan Swanson sat in the back of the army car trying his best to remain calm. He looked out the window; the late morning traffic was slight. The immense Washington labor force was at its appointed destinations; machines were humming, telephones ringing, men were shouting and whispering and, in too many places, having the first drink of the day. The exhilaration that was apparent during the first hours of the working day faded as noon approached. By eleven thirty a great many people thought the war was dull and were bored by their mechanical chores, the unending duplicates, triplicates and quadruplicates. They could not understand the necessity of painstaking logistics, of disseminating information to innumerable chains of command.

They could not understand because they could not be given whole pictures, only fragments, repetitious statistics. Of course they were bored.

They were weary. As he had been weary fourteen hours ago in Pasadena, California.

Everything had failed.

Meridian Aircraft had initiated – was *forced* to initiate – a crash program, but the finest scientific minds in the country could not eliminate the errors inside the small box that was the guidance system. The tiny, whirling spheroid discs would not spin true at maximum altitudes. They were erratic; absolute one second, deviant the next.

The most infinitesimal deviation could result in the midair collision of giant aircraft. And with the numbers projected for the saturation bombing prior to Overlord – scheduled to commence in less than four months – collisions *would* occur.

But this morning everything was different.

Could be different, if there was substance to what he had been told. He hadn't been able to sleep on the plane, hardly been able to eat. Upon landing at Andrews, he had hurried to his Washington apartment, showered, shaved, changed uniforms and called his wife in Scarsdale, where she was staying with a sister. He didn't remember the conversation between them; the usual endearments were absent, the questions perfunctory. He had no time for her.

The army car entered the Virginia highway and accelerated. They were going to Fairfax; they'd be there in twenty minutes or so. In less than a half hour he would find out if the impossible was, conversely, entirely possible. The news had come as a last-minute stay of execution; the cavalry in the distant hills – the sounds of muted bugles signaling reprieve.

Muted, indeed, thought Swanson as the army car veered off the highway onto a back Virginia road. In Fairfax, covering some two hundred acres in the middle of the hunt country, was a fenced-off area housing Quonset huts beside huge radar screens and radio signal towers that sprang from the ground like giant steel malformities. It was the Field Division Headquarters of Clandestine Operations; next to the underground rooms at the White House, the most sensitive processing location of the Allied Intelligence services.

Late yesterday afternoon, FDHQ-Fairfax had received confirmation of an Intelligence probe long since abandoned as negative. It came out of Johannesburg, South Africa. It had not been proved out, but there was sufficient evidence to believe that it could be.

High-altitude directional gyroscopes had been perfected. Their designs could be had.

DECEMBER 2, 1943

BERLIN, GERMANY

Altmüller sped out of Berlin on the Spandau highway toward Falkensee in the open Duesenberg. It was early in the morning and the air was cold and that was good.

He was so exhilarated that he forgave the theatrically secretive ploys of the Nachrichtendienst, code name for a select unit of the espionage service known to only a few of the upper-echelon ministers, not to many of the High Command itself. A Gehlen specialty.

For this reason it never held conferences within Berlin proper; always outside the city, always in some remote, secluded area or town and even then in private surroundings, away from the potentially curious.

The location this morning was Falkensee, twenty-odd miles northwest of Berlin. The meeting was to take place in a guest house on the estate belonging to Gregor Strasser.

Altmüller would have flown to Stalingrad itself if what he'd been led to believe was true.

The Nachrichtendienst had found the solution for Peenemünde.!

The solution *was* true; it was up to others to expedite it.

The solution that had eluded teams of "negotiators' sent to all parts of the world to explore – unearth – prewar "relationships." Capetown, Dar es Salaam, Johannesburg, Buenos Aires . . .

Failure.

No company, no individual would touch German negotiations. Germany was in the beginning of a death struggle. It would go down to defeat.

That was the opinion in Zürich. And what Zürich held to be true, international business did not debate.

But the Nachrichtendienst had found another truth.

So he was told.

The Duesenberg's powerful engine hummed; the car reached high speed; the passing autumn foliage blurred.

470

The stone gates of Strasser's estate came into view on the left, Wehrmacht eagles in bronze above each post. He swung into the long, winding drive and stopped at the gate guarded by two soldiers and snarling shepherd dogs. Altmüller thrust his papers at the first guard, who obviously expected him.

"Good morning, Herr Unterstaatssekretär. Please follow the drive to the right beyond the main house."

"Have the others arrived?"

"They are waiting, sir."

Altmüller maneuvered the car past the main house, reached the sloping drive and slowed down. Beyond the wooded bend was the guest cottage; it looked more like a hunting lodge than a residence. Heavy dark-brown beams everywhere; a part of the forest.

In the graveled area were four limousines. He parked and got out, pulling his tunic down, checking his lapels for lint. He stood erect and started toward the path to the door.

No names were ever used during a Nachrichtendienst conference; if identities were known – and certainly they had to be – they were never referred to in a meeting. One simply addressed his peer by looking at him, the group by gesture.

There was no long conference table as Altmüller had expected; no formal seating arrangement by some hidden protocol. Instead, a half dozen informally dressed men in their fifties and sixties were standing around the small room with the high Bavarian ceiling, chatting calmly, drinking coffee. Altmüller was welcomed as "Herr Unterstaatssekretär' and told that the morning's conference would be short. It would begin with the arrival of the final expected member."

Altmüller accepted a cup of coffee and tried to fall into the casual atmosphere. He was unable to do so; he wanted to roar his disapproval and demand immediate and serious talk. Couldn't they *understand*?

But this was the Nachrichtendienst. One didn't yell; one didn't demand.

Finally, after what seemed an eternity to his churning stomach, Altmüller heard an automobile outside the lodge. A few moments later the door opened; he nearly dropped his cup of coffee. The man who entered was known to him from the few times he bad accompanied Speer to Berchtesgaden. He was the Führer's valet, but he had no subservient look of a valet now.

Without announcement, the men fell silent. Several sat in armchairs, others leaned against walls or stayed by the coffee table. An elderly man in a heavy tweed jacket stood in front of the fireplace and spoke. He looked at Franz, who remained by himself behind a leather couch.

"There is no reason for lengthy discussions. We believe we have the information you seek. I say 'believe,' for we gather information, we do not act upon it. The ministry may not care to act."

"That would seem inconceivable to me," said Altmüller.

"Very well. Several questions then. So there is no conflict, no misrepresentation." The old man paused and lit a thick meerschaum pipe. "You have

471

exhausted all normal Intelligence channels? Through Zürich and Lisbon?"

"We have. And in numerous other locations – occupied, enemy and neutral."

"I was referring to the acknowledged conduits, Swiss, Scandinavian and Portuguese, primarily."

"We made no concentrated efforts in the Scandinavian countries. Herr Zangen did not think . . ."

"No names, please. Except in the area of Intelligence confrontation or public knowledge. Use governmental descriptions, if you like. Not individuals."

"The Reichsamt of Industry – which has continuous dealings in the Baltic areas – was convinced there was nothing to be gained there. I assume the reasons were geographical. There are no diamonds in the Baltic."

"Or they've been burnt too often," said a nondescript middle-aged man below Altmüller on the leather sofa. "If you want London and Washington to know what you're doing before you do it, deal with the Scandinavians."

"An accurate analysis," concurred another member of the Nachrichtendienst, this one standing by the coffee table, cup in hand. "I returned from Stockholm last week. We can't trust even those who publicly endorse us."

"Those least of all," said the old man in front of the fireplace, smiling and returning his eyes to Franz. "We gather you've made substantial offers? In Swiss currency, of course."

"Substantial is a modest term for the figures we've spoken of," replied Altmüller. "I'll be frank. No one will touch us. Those who could, subscribe to Zürich's judgment that we shall be defeated. They fear retribution; they even speak of postwar bank deposit reclamations."

"If such whispers reach the High Command there'll be a panic." The statement was made humorously by the Fuhrer's valet, sitting in an armchair. The spokesman by the fireplace continued.

"So you must eliminate money as an incentive . . . even extraordinary sums of money."

"The negotiating teams were not successful. You know that." Altmüller had to suppress his irritation. Why didn't they get to the *point?*

"And there are no ideologically motivated defectors on the horizon. Certainly none who have access to industrial diamonds."

"Obviously, *mein Herr.*"

"So you must look for another motive. Another incentive."

"I fail to see the point of this. I was told . . ."

"You will," interrupted the old man, tapping his pipe on the mantel. "You see, we've uncovered a panic as great as yours. . . . The enemy's panic. We've found the most logical motive for all concerned. Each side possesses the other's solution."

Franz Altmüller was suddenly afraid. He could not be sure he fully understood the spokesman's implications. "What are you saying?"

"Peenemünde has perfected a high-altitude, directional guidance system, is this correct?"

"Certainly. Indigenous to the basic operation of the rockets."

472

"But there'll be no rockets – or at best, a pitiful few – without shipments of industrial diamonds."

"Obviously."

"There are business interests in the United States who face insurmountable ... ," the old man paused for precisely one second and continued, "*insurmountable* problems that can only be resolved by the acquisition of functional high-altitude gyroscopes."

"Are you suggesting . . ."

"The Nachrichtendienst does not suggest, Herr Unterstaatssekretär. We say what is." The spokesman removed the meerschaum from his lips. "When the occasion warrants, we transmit concrete information to diverse recipients. Again, only what is. We did so in Johannesburg. When the man I. G. Farben sent in to purchase diamonds from the Koening mines met with failure, we stepped in and confirmed a long-standing Intelligence probe we knew would be carried back to Washington. Our agents in California had apprised us of the crisis in the aircraft industry. We believe the timing was propitious."

"I'm not sure I understand . . ."

"Unless we're mistaken, an attempt will be made to reestablish contact with one of the Farben men. We assume contingencies were made for such possibilities."

"Of course. Geneva. The acknowledged conduits."

"Then our business with you is concluded, sir. May we wish you a pleasant drive back to Berlin."

DECEMBER 2, 1943

FAIRFAX, VIRGINIA

The interior of the Quonset belied its stark outside. To begin with, it was five times larger than the usual Quonset structure, and its metal casing was insulated with a sound-absorbing material that swept seamless down from the high ceiling. The appearance was not so much that of an airplane hangar – as it should have been – as of a huge, windowless shell with substantial walls. All around the immense room were banks of complicated high-frequency radio panels; opposite each panel were glass-enclosed casings with dozens of detailed maps, changeable by the push of a button. Suspended above the maps were delicate, thin steel arms – markers, not unlike polygraph needles – that were manipulated by the radio operators, observed by men holding clipboards. The entire staff was military, army, none below the rank of first lieutenant.

Three-quarters into the building was a floor-to-ceiling wall that obviously was not the end of the structure. There was a single door, centered and closed. The door was made of heavy steel.

Swanson had never been inside this particular building. He had driven down to Field Division, Fairfax, many times – to get briefed on highly classified Intelligence findings, to observe the training of particular insurgence or espionage teams – but for all his brigadier's rank and regardless of the secrets he carried around in his head, he had not been cleared for this particular building. Those who were, remained within the two-hundred-acre compound for weeks, months at a time; leaves were rare and taken only in emergency and with escort.

It was fascinating, thought Swanson, who honestly believed he had lost all sense of awe. No elevators, no back staircases, no windows; he could see a washroom door in the left wall and without going inside, knew it was machine ventilated. And there was only a single entrance. Once inside there was no place for a person to conceal himself for any length of time, or to exit without being checked out and scrutinized. Personal items were left at the entrance; no briefcases, envelopes, papers or materials were removed from the building without signed authorization by Colonel Edmund Pace and with the colonel personally at the side of the individual in question.

If there was ever total security, it was here.

Swanson approached the steel door; his lieutenant escort pushed a button. A small red light flashed above a wall intercom, and the lieutenant spoke.

"General Swanson, colonel."

"Thank you, lieutenant," were the words that came from the webbed circle below the light. There was a click in the door's lock and the lieutenant reached for the knob.

Inside, Pace's office looked like any other Intelligence headquarters – huge maps on the walls, sharp lighting on the maps, lights and maps changeable by push-buttons on the desk. Teletype machines were equidistant from one another below printed signs designating theaters of operation – all the usual furnishings Except the furniture itself. It was simple to the point of primitiveness. No easy chairs, no sofas, nothing comfortable. Just plain metal straight-backed chairs, a desk that was more a table than a desk, and a rugless hardwood floor. It was a room for concentrated activity; a man did not relax in such a room.

Edmund Pace, Commander of Field Division, Fairfax, got up from his chair, came around his table and saluted Alan Swanson.

There was one other man in the room, a civilian, Frederic Vandamm, Undersecretary of State.

"General. Good to see you again. The last time was at Mr. Vandamm's house, if I remember."

"Yes, it was. How are things here?"

"A little isolated."

"I'm sure." Swanson turned to Vandamm. "Mr. Undersecretary? I got back here as soon as I could. I don't have to tell you how anxious I am. It's been a difficult month."

"I'm aware of that," said the aristocratic Vandamm, smiling a cautious smile, shaking Swanson's hand perfunctorily. "We'll get right to it. Colonel Pace, will you brief the general as we discussed?"

"Yes, sir. And then I'll leave." Pace spoke noncommittally; it was the military's way of telegraphing a message to a fellow officer: be careful.

Pace crossed to a wall map, present with markings. It was an enlarged, detailed section of Johannesburg, South Africa. Frederic Vandamm sat in a chair in front of the desk; Swanson followed Pace and stood beside him.

"You never know when a probe will get picked up. Or where." Pace took a wooden pointer from a table and indicated a blue marker on the map. "Or even if the location is important. In this case it *may* be. A week ago a member of the Johannesburg legislature, an attorney and a former director of Koening Mines, Ltd., was contacted by what he believed were two men from the Zürich Staats-Bank. They wanted him to middle-man a negotiation with Koening: simple transaction of Swiss francs for diamonds – on a large scale, with the anticipation that the diamond standard would remain more constant than the gold fluctuations." Pace turned to Swanson. "So far, so good. With lendlease, and monetary systems going up in smoke everywhere, there's a lot of speculation in the diamond market. Postwar killings could be made. When he accepted the contact, you can imagine his shock when he arrived for the meeting and found that one of the 'Swiss' was an old friend – a very old and good friend – from the prewar days. A German he'd gone to school with – the Afrikaner's mother was Austrian, father, a Boer. The two men had kept in close touch until thirty-nine. The German worked for I. G. Farben."

"What was the point of the meeting?" Swanson was impatient.

"I'll get to that. This background's important."

"O.K. Go on."

"There was no diamond market speculation involved, no transaction with any Zürich bank. It was a simple purchase. The Farben man wanted to buy large shipments of bortz and carbonado. . . ."

"Industrial diamonds?" interrupted Swanson.

Pace nodded. "He offered a fortune to his old friend if he could pull it off. The Afrikaner refused; but his long-standing friendship with the German kept him from reporting the incident. Until three days ago." Pace put down the pointer and started for his desk. Swanson understood that the colonel had additional information, written information, that he had to refer to; the general crossed to the chair beside Vandamm and sat down.

"Three days ago," continued Pace, standing behind the desk, "the Afrikaner was contacted again. This time there was no attempt to conceal identities. The caller said he was German and had information the Allies wanted; had wanted for a long time."

"The probe?" asked Swanson, whose impatience was carried by his tone of voice.

"Not exactly the probe we expected. . . . The German said he would come to the Afrikaner's office, but he protected himself. He told the lawyer that if any attempt was made to hold him, his old friend at I. G. Farben would be executed back in Germany." Pace picked up a sheet of paper from his desk. He spoke as he leaned across and handed it to Swanson. "This is the information, the report Sown in by courier."

Swanson read the typewritten words below the Military Intelligence letterhead; above the large, stamped *Top Secret. Eyes Only. Fairfax 4–0.*

Nov. 28, 1943. Johannesburg: Confirmed by Nachrichtendienst. Substratospheric directional gyroscopes perfected. All tests positive. Peenemünde. Subsequent contact: Geneva. Johannesburg contingent.

Swanson let the information sink in; he read the statement over several times. He asked a question of Edmund Pace with a single word: "Geneva?"

"The conduit. Neutral channel. Unofficial, of course."

"What is this . . . Nachrichtendienst?"

"Intelligence unit. Small, specialized; so rarefied it's above even the most classified crowds. Sometimes we wonder if it takes sides. It often appears more interested in observing than participating; more concerned with after the war than now. We suspect that it's a Gehlen operation. But it's never been wrong. Never misleading."

"I see." Swanson held out the paper for Pace.

The colonel did not take it. Instead, he walked around the desk toward the steel door. "I'll leave you gentlemen. When you're finished, please signify by pushing the white button on my desk." He opened the door and left quickly. The heavy steel frame closed into an airtight position; a subsequent click could be heard in the lock housing.

Frederic Vandamm looked at Swanson. "There is your solution, general. Your gyroscope. In Peenemünde. All you have to do is send a man to Geneva. Someone wants to sell it."

Alan Swanson stared at the paper in his hand.

7

Altmüller stared at the paper in his hand. It was after midnight, the city in darkness. Berlin had withstood another night of murderous bombardment; it was over now. There would be no further raids until late morning, that was the usual pattern. Still, the black curtains were pulled tight against the windows. As they were everywhere in the ministry.

Speed was everything now. Yet in the swiftness of the planning, mandatory precautions could not be overlooked. The meeting in Geneva with the conduit was only the first step, the prelude, but it had to be handled delicately. Not so much *what* was said but *who* said it. The *what* could be transmitted by anyone with the proper credentials or acknowledged authority. But in the event of Germany's collapse, that *someone* could not represent the Third Reich. Speer had been adamant.

And Altmüller understood: if the war was lost, the label of traitor could not be traced to the Reichsministry. Or to those leaders Germany would need in defeat. In 1918 after Versailles, there had been mass internal recriminations. Polarization ran deep, unchecked, and the nation's paranoia over betrayal from within laid the groundwork for the fanaticism of the twenties. Germany had not been able to accept defeat, could not tolerate the destruction of its identity by traitors.

Excuses, of course.

But the prospects of repetition, no matter how remote, were to be avoided at all costs. Speer was himself fanatic on the subject. The Geneva representative was to be a figure isolated from the High Command. Someone from the ranks of German industry, in no way associated with the rulers of the Third Reich. Someone expendable.

Altmüller tried to point out the inconsistency of Speer's manipulation: high-altitude gyroscopic designs would hardly be given to an expendable mediocrity from German business. Peenemünde was buried – literally buried in the earth; its military security measures absolute.

But Speer would not listen, and Altmüller suddenly grasped the Reichsminister's logic. He was shifting the problem precisely where it belonged: to those whose lies and concealments had brought Peenemünde to the brink of disaster. And as with so much in the wartime Reich – the labor forces, the death camps, the massacres – Albert Speer conveniently looked away. He wanted positive results, but he would not dirty his tunic.

In this particular case, mused Altmüller, Speer was right. If there were to be risks of great disgrace, let German industry take them. Let the German businessman assume complete responsibility.

Geneva was vital only in the sense that it served as an introduction. Cautious words would be spoken that could – or could not lead to the second stage of the incredible negotiation.

Stage two was geographical: the location of the exchange, should it actually take place.

For the past week, day and night, Altmüller had done little else but concentrate on this. He approached the problem from the enemy's viewpoint as well as his own. His worktable was covered with maps, his desk filled with scores of reports detailing the current political climates of every neutral territory on earth.

For the location had to be neutral; there had to be sufficient safeguards each side could investigate and respect. And perhaps most important of all, it had to be thousands of miles away ... from either enemy's corridors of power.

Distance.

Remote.

Yet possessing means of instant communication.

South America.

Buenos Aires.

An inspired choice, thought Franz Altmüller. The Americans might actually consider it advantageous to them. It was unlikely that they would reject it. Buenos Aires had much each enemy considered its own; both had enormous influence, yet neither controlled with any real authority.

The third stage, as he conceived of it, was concerned with the human factor, defined by the word *Schiedsrichter.*

Referee.

A man who was capable of overseeing the exchange, powerful enough within the neutral territory to engineer the logistics. Someone who had the appearance of impartiality ... above all, acceptable to the Americans.

Buenos Aires had such a man.

One of Hitler's gargantuan errors.

His name was Erich Rhinemann. A Jew, forced into exile, disgraced by Goebbels's insane propaganda machine, his lands and companies expropriated by the Reich.

Those lands and companies he had not converted before the misplaced thunderbolts struck. A minor percentage of his holdings, sufficient for the manic screams of the anti-Semitic press, but hardly a dent in his immense wealth.

Erich Rhinemann lived in exiled splendor in Buenos Aires, his fortunes secure in Swiss banks, his interests expanding throughout South America.

And what few people knew was that Erich Rhinemann was a more dedicated fascist than Hitler's core. He was a supremacist in all things financial and military, an elitist with regard to the human condition. He was an empire builder who remained strangely – stoically – silent

He had reason to be.

He would be returned to Germany regardless of the outcome of the war. He knew it.

If the Third Reich was victorious, Hitler's asinine edict would be revoked – as, indeed, might be the Führer's powers should he continue to disintegrate. If Germany went down to defeat – as Zürich projected – Rhinemann's expertise and Swiss accounts would be needed to rebuild the nation.

But these things were in the future. It was the present that mattered, and presently Erich Rhinemann was a Jew, forced into exile by his own countrymen, Washington's enemy.

He would be acceptable to the Americans.

And he would look after the Reich's interests in Buenos Aires.

Stages two and three, then, felt Altmüller, had the ring of clarity. But they were meaningless without an accord in Geneva. The prelude had to be successfully played by the minor instruments.

What was needed was a man for Geneva. An individual no one could link to the leaders of the Reich, but still one who had a certain recognition in the market place.

Altmüller continued to stare at the pages under the desk lamp. His eyes were weary, as he was weary, but he knew he could not leave his office or sleep until he had made the decision.

His decision; it was his alone. To be approved by Speer in the morning with only a glance. A name. Not discussed; someone instantly acceptable.

He would never know whether it was the letters in Johannesburg or the subconscious process of elimination, but his eyes riveted on one name, and he circled it. He recognized immediately that it was, again, an inspired choice.

Johann Dietricht, the bilious heir of Dietricht Fabriken; the unattractive homosexual given to alcoholic excess and sudden panic. A completely expendable member of the industrial community; even the most cynical would be reluctant to consider him a liaison to the High Command.

An expendable mediocrity.

A messenger.

DECEMBER 5, 1943

WASHINGTON, D.C.

The bass-toned chimes of the clock on the mantel marked the hour somberly. It was six in the morning and Alan Swanson stared out the window at the dark buildings that were Washington. His apartment was on the twelfth floor, affording a pretty fair view of the capital's skyline, especially from the living room, where he now stood in his bathrobe, no slippers on his feet.

He had been looking at Washington's skyline most of the night . . . most of the hours of the night for the past three days. God knew what sleep he managed was fitful, subject to sudden torments and awakenings; and always there was the damp pillow that absorbed the constant perspiration that seeped from the pores in the back of his neck.

If his wife were with him, she would insist that he turn himself in to Walter Reed for a checkup. She would force the issue with constant repetition until he was nagged into submission. But she was *not* with him; he had been adamant. She was to remain with her sister in Scarsdale. The nature of his current activities was such that his hours were indeterminate. Translation: the army man had no time for his army wife. The army wife understood: there was a severe crisis and her husband could not cope with even her minor demands and the crisis, too. He did not like her to observe him in these situations; he knew she knew that. She would stay in Scarsdale.

Oh, Christ! It was beyond belief!

None said the words; perhaps no one allowed himself to think them.

That was it, of course. The few – and there were *very* few – who had access to the data turned their eyes and their minds away from the ultimate judgment. They cut off the transaction at midpoint, refusing to acknowledge the final half of the bargain. That half was for others to contend with. Not them.

As the wily old aristocrat Frederic Vandamm had done.

There's your solution, general. Your guidance system. In Peenemünde. . . . Someone wants to sell it.

That's all.

Buy it.

None wanted to know the price. The price was insignificant . . . let others concern themselves with details. Under no circumstances – *no circumstances* – were insignificant details to be brought up for discussion! They were merely to be expedited.

Translation: the chain of command depended upon the execution of general orders. It did not – repeat, *not* – require undue elaboration, clarification or justification. Specifics were an anathema; they consumed time. And by all that was military holy writ, the highest echelons *had* no time. Goddamn it, man, there was a *war on!* We must tend to the great military issues of state!

The garbage will be sorted out by lesser men . . . whose hands may on occasion reek with the stench of their lesser duties, but that's what the chain of command is all about.

Buy it!

We have no time. Our eyes are turned. Our minds are occupied elsewhere.

Carry out the order on your own initiative as a good soldier should who understands the chain of command. No one will be inquisitive; it is the result that matters. We all know that; the chain of command, old boy.

Insanity.

By the *strangest coincidence* an Intelligence probe is returned by a man in Johannesburg through which the purchase of industrial diamonds was sought. A purchase for which a fortune in Swiss currency was tendered by Germany's I. G. Farben, the armaments giant of the Third Reich.

Peenemünde had the guidance system; it could be had. For a price.

It did not take a major intellect to arrive at that price.

Industrial diamonds.

Insanity.

For reasons beyond inquiry, Germany desperately needed the diamonds. For reasons all too clear, the Allies desperately needed the high-altitude guidance system.

An exchange between enemies at the height of the bitterest war in the history of mankind.

Insanity. Beyond comprehension.

And so General Alan Swanson removed it from his immediate . . . totality.

The single deep chime of the clock intruded, signifying the quarter hour. Here and there throughout the maze of dark concrete outside, lights were being turned on in a scattering of tiny windows. A greyish purple slowly began to impose itself on the black sky; vague outlines of cloud wisps could be discerned above.

In the higher altitudes.

Swanson walked away from the window to the couch facing the fireplace and sat down. It had been twelve hours ago . . . eleven hours and forty-five minutes, to be precise . . . when he had taken the first step of *removal*.

He had placed . . . delegated the insanity where it belonged. To the men who had created the crisis; whose lies and manipulations had brought Overlord to the precipice of obscenity.

He had ordered Howard Oliver and Jonathan Craft to be in his apartment at six o'clock. Twelve hours and fifteen minutes ago. He had telephoned them on the previous day, making it clear that he would tolerate no excuses. If transportation were a problem, he would resolve it, but they were to be in Washington, in his apartment, by six o'clock.

Exposure was a viable alternative.

They had arrived at precisely six, as the somber chimes of the mantel clock were ringing. At that moment Swanson knew he was dealing from absolute strength. Men like Oliver and Craft – especially Oliver – did not adhere to such punctuality unless they were afraid. It certainly was not courtesy.

The transference had been made with utter simplicity.

There was a telephone number in Geneva, Switzerland. There was a man at that number who would respond to a given code phrase and bring together two disparate parties, act as an interpreter, if necessary. It was understood that the second party – for purposes of definition – had access to a perfected high-altitude guidance system. The first party, in turn, should have knowledge of . . . perhaps access to . . . shipments of industrial diamonds. The Koening mines of Johannesburg might be a place to start.

That was all the information they had.

It was recommended that Mr. Oliver and Mr. Craft act on this information immediately.

If they failed to do so, extremely serious charges involving individual and corporate deceit relative to armaments contracts would be levelled by the War Department.

There had been a long period of silence. The implications of his statement – with all its ramifications – were accepted gradually by both men.

Alan Swanson then added the subtle confirmation of their worst projections: whoever was chosen to go to Geneva, it could *not* be anyone known to him. Or to any War Department liaison with *any* of their companies. That was paramount.

The Geneva meeting was exploratory. Whoever went to Switzerland should be knowledgeable and, if possible, capable of spotting deception. Obviously a man who practiced deception.

That shouldn't be difficult for them; not in the circles they traveled. Surely they knew such a man.

They did. An accountant named Walter Kendall.

Swanson looked up at the clock on the mantel. It was twenty minutes past six.

Why did the time go so slowly? On the other hand, why didn't it stop? Why didn't everything stop but the sunlight? Why did there have to be the nights to go through?

In another hour he would go to his office and quietly make arrangements for one Walter Kendall to be flown on neutral routes to Geneva, Switzerland. He would bury the orders in a blue pouch along with scores of other transport directives and clearances. There would be no signature on the orders, only the official stamp of Field Division, Fairfax; standard procedure with conduits.

Oh, Christ! thought Swanson. If there could be control . . . *without participation*.

But he knew that was not possible. Sooner or later he would have to face the reality of what he had done.

8

He had been in the north country for eight days. He had not expected it to be this long, but Spaulding knew it was necessary . . . an unexpected dividend. What had begun as a routine escape involving two defecting scientists from the Ruhr Valley had turned into something else.

The scientists were throwaway bait. Gestapo bait. The runner who had made their escape possible out of the Rurh was not a member of the German underground. He was Gestapo.

It had taken Spaulding three days to be absolutely sure. The Gestapo man was one of the best he had ever encountered, but his mistakes fell into a pattern: he was *not* an experienced runner. When David *was* sure, he knew exactly what had to be done.

For five days he led his "underground" companion through the hills and mountain passes to the east as far as Sierra de Guara, nearly a hundred miles from the clandestine escape routes. He entered remote villages and held "conferences" with men he knew were Falangists – but who did *not* know him – and then told the Gestapo man they were partisans. He traveled over primitive roads and down the Guayardo River and explained that these routes were the avenues of escape. . . . Contrary to what the Germans believed, the routes were to the *east*, into the *Mediterranean, not* the Atlantic. This confusion was the prime reason for the success of the Pyrenees network. On two occasions he sent the Nazi into towns for supplies – both times he followed and observed the Gestapo man entering buildings that had thick telephone wires sagging into the roofs.

The information was being transmitted back to Germany. That was reason enough for the investment of five additional days. The German interceptors would be tied up for months concentrating on the eastern "routes"; the network to the west would be relatively unencumbered.

But now the game was coming to an end. it was just as well, thought David; he had work to do in Ortegal, on the Biscay coast.

The small campfire was reduced to embers, the night air cold. Spaulding looked at his watch. It was two in the morning. He had ordered the "runner" to stay on guard quite far from the campsite . . . out of the glow of the fire. In darkness. He had given the Gestapo man enough time and isolation to

483

make his move, but the German had *not* made his move; he had remained at his post.

So be it, thought David. Perhaps the man wasn't as expert as be thought he was. Or perhaps the information his own men in the hills had given him was not accurate. There was no squad of German soldiers – suspected Alpine troops heading down from the mountain borders to take out the Gestapo agent.

And him.

He approached the rock on which the German sat. "Get some rest. I'll take over."

"*Danke*," said the man, getting to his feet. "First, nature calls; I must relieve my bowels. I'll take a spade into the field."

"Use the woods. Animals graze here. The winds carry."

"Of course. You're thorough."

"I try to be," said David.

The German crossed back toward the fire, to his pack. He removed a camp shovel and started for the woods bordering the field. Spaulding watched him, now aware that his first impression was the correct one. The Gestapo agent *was* expert. The Nazi had not forgotten that six days ago the two Ruhr scientists had disappeared during the night – at a moment of the night when he had dozed. David had seen the fury in the German's eyes and knew the Nazi was now remembering the incident.

If Spaulding assessed the current situation accurately, the Gestapo man would wait at least an hour into his watch, to be sure he, David, was not making contact with unseen partisans in the darkness. Only then would the German give the signal that would bring the Alpine troops out of the forest. With rifles leveled.

But the Gestapo man had made a mistake. He had accepted too readily – without comment – Spaulding's statement about the field and the wind and the suggestion that he relieve himself in the woods.

They had reached the field during late daylight; it was barren, the grass was sour, the slope rocky. Nothing would graze here, not even goats.

And there was no wind at all. The night air was cold, but dead.

An experienced runner would have objected, no doubt humorously, and say he'd be damned if he'd take a crap in the pitch-black woods. But the Gestapo agent could not resist the gratuitous opportunity to make his own contact.

If there *was* such a contact to be made, thought Spaulding. He would know in a few minutes.

David waited thirty seconds after the man had disappeared into the forest. Then he swiftly, silently threw himself to the ground and began rolling his body over and over again, away from the rock, at a sharp angle from the point where the runner had entered the forest.

When he had progressed thirty-five to forty feet into the grass, he stood up, crouching, and raced to the border of the woods, judging himself to be about sixty yards away from the German.

He entered the dense foliage and noiselessly closed the distance between them. He could not see the man but he knew he would soon find him.

Then he saw it. The German's signal. A match was struck, cupped, and extinguished swiftly.

Another. This one allowed to burn for several seconds, then snuffed out with a short spit of breath.

From deep in the woods came two separate, brief replies. Two matches struck. In opposite directions.

David estimated the distance to be, perhaps, a hundred feet. The German, unfamiliar with the Basque forest, stayed close to the edge of the field. The men he had signaled were approaching. Spaulding – making no sound that disturbed the hum of the woods – crawled closer.

He heard the voices whispering. Only isolated words were distinguishable. But they were enough.

He made his way rapidly back through the overgrowth to his original point of entry. He raced to his sentry post, the rock. He removed a small flashlight from his field jacket, clamped separated fingers over the glass and aimed it southwest. He pressed the switch five times in rapid succession. He then replaced the instrument in his pocket and waited.

It wouldn't be long now.

It wasn't.

The German came out of the woods carrying the shovel, smoking a cigarette. The night was black, the moon breaking only intermittently through the thick cover of clouds; the darkness was nearly total. David got up from the rock and signaled the German with a short whistle. He approached him.

"What is it, Lisbon?"

Spaulding spoke quietly. Two words.

"Heil Hitler."

And plunged his short bayonet into the Nazi's stomach, ripping it downward, killing the man instantly.

The body fell to the ground, the face contorted; the only sound was a swallow of air, the start of a scream, blocked by rigid fingers thrust into the dead man's mouth, yanked downward, as the knife had been, shorting out the passage of breath.

David raced across the grass to the edge of the woods, to the left of his previous entry. Nearer, but not much, to the point where the Nazi had spoken in whispers to his two confederates. He dove into a cluster of winter fern as the moon suddenly broke through the clouds. He remained immobile for several seconds, listening for sounds of alarm.

There were none. The moon was hidden again, the darkness returned. The corpse in the field had not been spotted in the brief illumination. And that fact revealed to David a very important bit of knowledge.

Whatever Alpine troops were in the woods, they were not on the *edge* of the woods. Or if they were, they were not concentrating on the field.

They were waiting. Concentrating in other directions.

Or just waiting.

He rose to his knees and scrambled rapidly west through the dense underbrush, flexing his body and limbs to every bend in the foliage, making sounds compatible to the forest's tones. He reached the point where the three men had conferred but minutes ago, feeling no presence, seeing nothing.

He took out a box of waterproof matches from his pocket and removed two. He struck the first one, and the instant it flared, he blew it out. He then struck the second match and allowed it to burn for a moment or two before he extinguished it.

About forty feet into the woods there was a responding flash of a match. Directly north.

Almost simultaneously came a second response. This one to the west, perhaps fifty or sixty feet away.

No more.

But enough.

Spaulding quickly crawled into the forest at an angle. Northeast. He went no more than fifteen feet and crouched against the trunk of an ant-ridden ceiba tree.

He waited. And while he waited, he removed a thin, short, flexible coil of wire from his field jacket pocket. At each end of the wire was a wooden handle, notched for the human hand.

The German soldier made too much noise for an Alpiner, thought David. He was actually hurrying, anxious to accommodate the unexpected command for rendezvous. That told Spaulding something else: the Gestapo agent he had killed was a demanding man. That meant the remaining troops would stay in position, awaiting orders. There would be a minimum of individual initiative.

There was no time to think of them now. The German soldier was passing the ceiba tree.

David sprang up silently, the coil held high with both hands. The loop fell over the soldier's helmet, the reverse pull so swift and brutally sudden that the wire sliced into the flesh of the neck with complete finality.

There was no sound but the expunging of air again.

David Spaulding had heard that sound so often it no longer mesmerized him. As it once had done.

Silence.

And then the unmistakable breaking of branches; footsteps crushing the ground cover of an unfamiliar path. Rushing, impatient, as the dead man at his feet had been impatient.

Spaulding put the bloody coil of wire back into his pocket and removed the shortened carbine bayonet from the scabbard on his belt. He knew there was no reason to hurry; the third man would be waiting. Confused, frightened perhaps . . . but probably not, if he was an Alpiner. The Alpine troops were rougher than the Gestapo. The rumors were that the Alpiners were chosen primarily for streaks of sadism. Robots who could live in mountain passes and nurture their hostilities in freezing isolation until the order for attack were given.

There was no question about it, thought David. There was a certain pleasure in killing Alpiners.

The treadmill.

He edged his way forward, his knife leveled.

"*Wer? . . . Wer ist dort?*" The figure in darkness whispered in agitation.

"*Hier, mein Soldat,*" replied David. His carbine bayonet slashed into the German's chest.

The partisans came down from the hills. There were five men, four Basque and one Catalonian. The leader was a Basque, heavyset and blunt.

"You gave us a wild trip, Lisbon. There were times we thought you were *loco*. Mother of God! We've traveled a hundred miles."

"The Germans will travel many times that, I assure you. What's north?"

"A string of Alpiners. Perhaps twenty. Every six kilometers, right to the border. Shall we let them sit in their wastes?"

"No," said Spaulding thoughtfully. "Kill them. . . . All but the last three; harass them back. They'll confirm what we want the Gestapo to believe."

"I don't understand."

"You don't have to." David walked to the dying fire and kicked at the coals. He had to get to Ortegal. It was all he could think about.

Suddenly he realized that the heavyset Basque had followed him. The man stood across the diminished campfire; he wanted to say something. He looked hard at David and spoke over the glow.

"We thought you should know now. We learned how the pigs made the contact. Eight days ago."

"What are you talking about?" Spaulding was irritated. Chains of command in the north country were at best a calculated risk. He would get the written reports; he did not want conversation. He wanted to sleep, wake up, and get to Ortegal. But the Basque seemed hurt; there was no point in that. "Go on, *amigo.*"

"We did not tell you before. We thought your anger would cause you to act rashly."

"How so? Why?"

"It was Bergeron."

"I don't believe that. . . ."

"It is so. They took him in San Sebastián. He did not break easily, but they broke him. Ten days of torture . . . wires in the genitals, among other devices, including hypodermics of the drug. We are told he died spitting at them."

David looked at the man. He found himself accepting the information without feeling. *Without feeling.* And that lack of feeling warned him . . . to be on guard. He had trained the man named Bergeron, lived in the hills with him, talked for hours on end about things only isolation produces between men. Bergeron had fought with him, sacrificed for him. Bergeron was the closest friend he had in the north country.

Two years ago such news would have sent him into furious anger. He would have pounded the earth and called for a strike somewhere across the borders, demanding that retribution be made.

"A year ago he would have walked away from the bearer of such news and demanded a few minutes to be by himself. A brief silence to consider . . . by himself . . . the whole of the man who had given his life, and the memories that man conjured up."

Yet now he felt nothing.

Nothing at all.

And it was a terrible feeling to feel nothing at all.

"Don't make that mistake again," he said to the Basque. "Tell me next time. I don't act rashly."

9

DECEMBER 13, 1943

BERLIN, GERMANY

Johann Dietrich shifted his immense soft bulk in the leather chair in front of Altmüller's desk. It was ten thirty at night and he had not had dinner; there had been no time. The Messerschmitt flight from Geneva had been cramped, petrifying; and all things considered, Dietricht was in a state of aggravated exhaustion. A fact he conveyed a number of times to the Unterstaatssekretär.

"We appreciate everything you've been through, Herr Dietricht. And the extraordinary service you've rendered to your country." Altmüller spoke solicitously. "This will take only a few minutes longer, and then I'll have you driven anywhere you like."

"A decent restaurant, if you can find one open at this hour," said Dietricht petulantly.

"We apologize for rushing you away. Perhaps a pleasant evening; a really good meal. Schnapps, good company. Heaven knows you deserve it. . . . There's an inn several miles outside the city. Its patronage is restricted; mostly young flight lieutenants, graduates in training. The kitchen is really excellent."

There was no need for Johann Dietricht to return Altmüller's smiling look; he accepted certain things as indigenous to his life-style. He had been catered to for years. He was a very important man, and other men were invariably trying to please him. As Herr Altmüller was trying to please him now.

"That might be most relaxing. It's been a dreadful day. Days, really."

"Of course, if you've some other . . ."

"No, no. I'll accept your recommendation. . . .Let's get on with it, shall we?"

"Very well. Going back over several points so there's no room for error. . . . The American was not upset with regard to Buenos Aires?"

"He jumped at it. Revolting man; couldn't look you in the eye, but he meant what he said. Simply revolting, though. His clothes, even his fingernails. Dirty fellow!"

"Yes, of course. But you couldn't have misinterpreted?"

"My English is fluent. I understand even the nuances. He was very pleased. I gathered that it served a dual purpose: far removed – thousands of miles away – and in a city nominally controlled by American interests."

"Yes, we anticipated that reaction. Did he have the authority to confirm it?"

"Indeed, yes. There was no question. For all his uncouth manner, he's obviously highly placed, very decisive. Unquestionably devious, but most anxious to make the exchange."

"Did you discuss – even peripherally – either's motives?"

"My word, it was unavoidable! This Kendall was most direct. It was a financial matter, pure and simple. There were no other considerations. And I believe him totally; he talks only figures. He reduces everything to numbers. I doubt he has capacities for anything else. I'm extremely perceptive."

"We counted on that. And Rhinemann? He, too, was acceptable?"

"Immaterial. I pointed out the calculated risk we were taking in an effort to allay suspicions; that Rhinemann was in forced exile. This Kendall was impressed only by Rhinemann's wealth."

"And the time element; we must be thoroughly accurate. Let's go over the projected dates. It would be disastrous if I made any mistake. As I understand you, the American had graduated estimates of carbonado and bortz shipping requirements . . ."

"Yes, yes," broke in Dietrich, as if enlightening a child. "After all, he had no idea of our needs. I settled on the maximum, of course; there was not that much difference in terms of time. They must divert shipments from points of origin; too great a risk in commandeering existing supplies."

"I'm not sure I understand that. It could be a ploy."

"They're trapped in their own security measures. As of a month ago, every repository of industrial diamonds has excessive controls, dozens of signatures for every kiloweight. To extract our requirements would be massive, lead to exposure."

"The inconvenience of the democratic operation. The underlings are given responsibility. And once given, difficult to divest. Incredible."

"As this Kendall phrased it, there would be too many questions, far too many people would be involved. It would be very sensitive. Their security is filled with Turks."

"We have to accept the condition." said Altmüller with resignation – his own, not for the benefit of Dietrich. "And the anticipated time for these shipment diversions is four to six weeks. It can't be done in less?"

"Certainly. If we are willing to process the ore ourselves."

"Impossible. We could end up with tons of worthless dirt. We must have the finished products, of course."

"Naturally. I made that clear."

"It strikes me as an unnecessary delay. I have to look for inconsistencies, Herr Dietrich. And you said this Kendall was devious."

"But anxious. I said he was anxious, too. He drew an analogy that lends weight to his statements. He said that their problem was no less than that of a man entering the national vaults in the state of Kentucky and walking out with crates of gold bullion. . . .Are we concluded?"

490

"Just about. The conduit in Geneva will be given the name of the man in Buenos Aires? The man with whom we make contact?"

"Yes. In three or four days. Kendall believed it might be a scientist named Spinelli. An expert in gyroscopics."

"That title could be questioned, I should think. He's Italian?"

"A citizen, however."

"I see. That's to be expected. The designs will be subject to scrutiny, of course. What remains now are the checks and counterchecks each of us employ up to the moment of the exchange. A ritual dance."

"*Ach!* That's for your people. I'm out of it. I have made the initial and, I believe, the most important contribution."

"There's no question about it. And, I assume, you have abided by the Führer's trust in you, conveyed through this office. You have spoken to no one of the Geneva trip?"

"No one. The Führer's trust is not misplaced. He knows that. As my father and his brother, my uncle, the Dietricht loyalty and obedience are unswerving."

"He's mentioned that often. We are finished, *mein Herr.*"

"Good! It's been absolutely nerve-wracking! . . . I'll accept your recommendation of the restaurant. If you'll make arrangements, I'll telephone for my car."

"As you wish, but I can easily have my personal driver take you there. As I said, it's somewhat restricted; my chauffeur is a young man who knows his way around." Altmüller glanced at Dietricht. Their eyes met for the briefest instant. "The Führer would be upset if he thought I inconvenienced you."

"Oh, very well. I suppose it *would* be easier. And we don't want the Führer upset." Dietricht struggled out of the chair as Altmüller rose and walked around the desk.

"Thank you, Herr Dietricht," said the Unterstaatssekretär, extending his hand. "When the time comes we will make known your extraordinary contribution. You are a hero of the Reich, *mein Herr.* It is a privilege to know you. The adjutant outside will take you down to the car. The chauffeur is waiting."

"Such a relief! Good evening, Herr Altmüller." Johann Dietricht waddled toward the door as Franz reached over and pushed a button on his desk.

In the morning Dietricht would be dead, the circumstances so embarrassing no one would care to elaborate on them except in whispers.

Dietricht, the misfit, would be eliminated.

And all traces of the Geneva manipulation to the leaders of the Reich canceled with him. Buenos Aires was now in the hands of Erich Rhinemann and his former brothers in German industry.

Except for him – for Franz Altmüller.

The true manipulator.

Swanson disliked the methods he was forced to employ. They were the beginnings, he felt, of an unending string of deceits. And he was not a deceitful man. Perhaps better than most at spotting deceitful men, but that was due to continuous exposure, not intrinsic characteristics.

The methods were distasteful: observing men who did not know they were being watched and listened to; who spoke without the inhibitions they certainly would have experienced had they any idea there were eyes and ears and wire recorders eavesdropping. It all belonged to that other world, Edmund Pace's world.

It had been easy enough to manipulate. Army Intelligence had interrogation rooms all over Washington. In the most unlikely places. Pace had given him a list of locations; he'd chosen one at the Sheraton Hotel. Fourth floor, Suite 4-M; two rooms in evidence and a third room that was not. This unseen room was behind the wall with openings of unidirectional glass in the two rooms of the suite. These observation holes were fronted by impressionist paintings hung permanently in the bedroom and the sitting room. Wire recorders with plug-in jacks were on shelves beneath the openings within the unseen room. Speakers amplified the conversation with minor distortion. The only visual obstructions were the light pastel colors of the paintings.

Not obstructions at all, really.

Neither had it been difficult to maneuver the three men to this room at the Sheraton. Swanson had telephoned Packard's Jonathan Craft and informed him that Walter Kendall was due in on an early afternoon flight from Geneva. The authoritative general also told the frightened civilian that it was possible the military might want to be in telephone communication. Therefore he suggested that Craft reserve a room at a busy, commercial hotel in the center of town. He recommended the Sheraton.

Craft was solicitous; he was running for his life. If the War Department suggested the Sheraton, then the Sheraton it would be. He had booked it without bothering to tell Meridian Aircraft's Howard Oliver.

The front desk took care of the rest.

When Walter Kendall had arrived an hour ago, Swanson was struck by the accountant's disheveled appearance. It was innate untidiness, not the result of traveling. A slovenliness that extended to his gestures, to his constantly darting eyes. He was an outsized rodent in the body of a medium-sized man. It seemed incongruous that men like Oliver and Craft – especially Craft – would associate with a Walter Kendall. Which only pointed up Kendall's value, he supposed. Kendall owned a New York auditing firm. He was a financial analyst, hired by companies to manipulate projections and statistics.

The accountant had not shaken hands with either man. He had gone straight to an easy chair opposite the sofa, sat down, and opened his briefcase. He had begun his report succinctly,

"The son of a bitch was a homo, I swear to Christ!"

As the hour wore on, Kendall described in minute detail everything that had taken place in Geneva. The quantities of bortz and carbonado agreed upon; the quality certifications; Buenos Aires; Gian Spinelli, the gyroscopic designs – *their* certifications and delivery; and the liaison, Erich Rhinemann, exiled Jew. Kendall was an authoritative rodent who was not awkward in the tunnels of negotiated filth. He was, in fact, very much at home.

"How can we be sure they'll bargain in good faith:' asked Craft."

"Good *faith?*" Kendall smirked and winced and grinned at the Packard executive. "You're too goddamned much. Good *faith!*"

"They might not give us the proper designs," continued Craft, "They could pass off substitutes, worthless substitutes!"

"He's got a point," said the jowled Oliver, his lips taut.

"And we could package crates of cut glass. You think that hasn't crossed their minds? . . . But they won't and we won't. For the same shit-eating reason. Our respective necks are on chopping blocks. We've got a common enemy and it's not each other."

Oliver, sitting across from Kendall, stared at the accountant. "Hitler's generals there; the War Department here."

"That's right. We're both lines of supply. For God, country and a dollar or two. And we're both in a lousy position. We don't tell the goddamned generals how to fight a war, and they don't tell us how to keep up production. If they screw up strategy or lose a battle, no screams come from us. But if we're caught short, if we don't deliver, those fuckers go after our necks. It's goddamned unfair. This homo Dietricht, he sees it like I do. We have to protect ourselves."

Craft rose from the couch; it was a nervous action, a gesture of doubt. He spoke softly, hesitantly. "This isn't exactly protecting ourselves in any normal fashion. We're dealing with the enemy."

"Which enemy?" Kendall shuffled papers on his lap; he did not look up at Craft. "But right, again. It's better than 'normal.' No matter who wins, we've each got a little something going when it's over. We agreed on that, too."

There was silence for several moments. Oliver leaned forward in his chair, his eyes still riveted on Kendall. "That's a dividend, Walter. There could be a lot of common sense in that."

"A lot," replied the accountant, allowing a short glance at Oliver. "We're kicking the crap out of their cities, bombing factories right off the map; railroads, highways – they're going up in smoke. It'll get worse. There's going to be a lot of money made putting it all back together. Reconstruction money."

"Suppose Germany wins?" asked Craft, by the window.

"Goddamned unlikely," answered Kendall. "It's just a question of how much damage is done to both sides, and we've got the hardware. The more damage, the more it'll cost to repair. That includes England. If you boys are smart, you'll be prepared to convert and pick up some of the post-war change."

"The diamonds. . . ." Craft turned from the window. "What are they for?"

"What difference does it make?" Kendall separated a page on his lap and wrote on it. "They ran out; their asses are in a sling. Same as yours with the guidance system. . . . By the way, Howard, did you have a preliminary talk with the mines?"

Oliver was deep in thought. He blinked and raised his eyes. "Yes. Koening. New York offices."

"How did you put it?"

"That it was top secret, War Department approval. The authorization would come from Swanson's office but even *he* wasn't cleared."

"They bought that?" The accountant was still writing.

"I said the money would be up front. They stand to make a few million. We met at the Bankers' Club."

"They bought it." A statement.

"Walter . . . ", continued Oliver, "you said Spinelli before. I don't like it. He's a bad choice."

Kendall stopped writing and looked up at the Meridian man. "I didn't figure to tell him anything. Just that we were buying; he was to clear everything before we paid, make sure the designs were authentic."

"No good. He wouldn't be taken off the project. Not now; too many questions. Find somebody else."

"I see what you mean." Kendall put down the pencil. He picked his nose; it was a gesture of thought. "Wait a minute. . . . There *is* someone. Right in Pasadena. He's a weird son of a bitch, but he could be perfect." Kendall laughed while breathing through his mouth. "He doesn't even talk; I mean he *can't* talk."

"Is he any good?" asked Oliver.

"He's got problems but he may be better than Spinelli," replied Kendall, writing on a separate piece of paper. "I'll take care of It. . . . It'll cost you."

Oliver shrugged. "Include it in the overruns, you prick. What's next?"

"A contact in Buenos Aires. Someone who can deal with Rhinemann, work out the details of the transfer."

"Who?" asked Craft apprehensively, both hands clasped in front of him.

The accountant grinned, baring his discolored teeth. "You volunteering? You look like a priest."

"Good Lord, no! I was simply . . ."

"How much, Kendall?" interrupted Oliver.

"More than you want to pay but I don't think you've got a choice. I'll pass on what I can to Uncle Sam; I'll save you what I can."

"You do that."

"There's a lot of military down in Buenos Aires. Swanson will have to run some interference."

"He won't touch it," said Oliver quickly. "He was specific. He doesn't want to hear or see your name again."

"I don't give a shit if he does. But this Rhinemann's going to want certain guarantees. I can tell you that right now."

"Swanson will be upset." Craft's voice was high and intense. "We don't *want* him upset."

"Upset, shit! He wants to keep that pretty uniform nice and clean. . . . Tell you what, don't push him now. Give me some time; I've got a lot of things to figure out. Maybe I'll come up with a way to keep his uniform clean after all. Maybe I'll send him a bill."

He wants to keep that pretty uniform nice and clean . . .

So devoutly to be wished, Mr. Kendall, thought Swanson as he approached the bank of elevators.

But not possible now. "The uniform had to get dirty. The emergence of a man named Erich Rhinemann made that necessary."

Rhinemann was one of Hitler's fiascos. Berlin knew it; London and Washington knew it. Rhinemann was a man totally committed to power: financial, political, military. For him all authority must emanate from a single source and he would ultimately settle for nothing less than being at the core of that source.

The fact that he was a Jew was incidental. An inconvenience to end with the end of the war.

When the war was over, Erich Rhinemann would be called back. What might be left of German industry would demand it; the world's financial leaders would demand it.

Rhinemann would reenter the international market place with more power than ever before.

Without the Buenos Aires manipulation.

With it his leverage would be extraordinary.

His knowledge, his participation in the exchange would provide him with an unparalleled weapon to be used against all sides, all governments.

Especially Washington.

Erich Rhinemann would have to be eliminated.

After the exchange.

And if only for this reason, Washington had to have another man in Buenos Aires.

10

It was unusual for the ranking officer of Fairfax to leave the compound for any reason, but Colonel Edmund Pace was so ordered.

Pace stood in front of General Swanson's desk and began to understand. Swanson's instructions were brief, but covered more territory than their brevity implied. Intelligence files would have to be culled from dozens of double-locked cabinets, a number examined minutely.

Swanson knew that at first Pace disapproved. The Fairfax commander could not conceal his astonishment – at first. The agent in question had to be fluent in both German and Spanish. He had to have a working knowledge – not expert but certainly more than conversational – of aircraft engineering, including metallurgical dynamics and navigational systems. He had to be a man capable of sustaining a cover perhaps on the embassy level. That meant an individual possessing the necessary graces to function easily in monied circles, in the diplomatic arena.

At this juncture Pace had balked. His knowledge of the Johannesburg probe and the Geneva conduit caused him to object. He interrupted Swanson, only to be told to hold his remarks until his superior had finished.

The last qualification of the man for Buenos Aires – and the general conceded its inconsistency when included with the previous technical qualifications – was that the agent be experienced in "swift dispatch."

The man was to be no stranger to killing. Not combat fire with its adversaries separated, pitched into frenzy by the sights and sounds of battle. But a man who could kill in silence, facing his target. Alone.

This last qualification mollified Pace. His expression conveyed the fact that whatever his superiors were involved in, it was not wholly what he suspected it to be – might be. The War Department did not request such a man if it intended to keep surface agreements.

The ranking officer of Fairfax made no comment. It was understood that he, alone, would make the file search. He asked for a code, a name to which he could refer in any communications.

Swanson had leaned forward in his chair and stared at the map on his desk. The map that had been there for over three hours.

"Call it 'Tortugas,'" he said.

DECEMBER 18, 1943

BERLIN, GERMANY

Altmüller stared at the unbroken seal on the wide, brown manila envelope. He moved it under his desk lamp and took a magnifying glass from his top drawer. He examined the seal under the magnification; he was satisfied. It had not been tampered with.

The embassy courier had Sown in from Buenos Aires – by way of Senegal and Lisbon – and delivered the envelope in person, as instructed. Since the courier was based permanently in Argentina, Altmüller did not want him carrying back gossip, so he indulged the man in innocuous conversation, referring to the communication several times in an offhand, derogatory manner. He implied it was a nuisance – a memorandum concerned with embassy finances and really belonged at the Finanzministerium, but what could he do? The ambassador was reputed to be an old friend of Speer's.

Now that the courier was gone and the door shut, Altmüller riveted his attention on the envelope. It was from Erich Rhinemann.

He sliced open the top edge. The letter was written by hand, in Rhinemann's barely decipherable script.

My Dear Altmüller:
   To serve the Reich is a privilege I undertake with enthusiasm. I am, of course, grateful for your assurances that my efforts will be made known to my many old friends. I assumed you would do no less under the circumstances.
   You will be pleased to know that in the coastal waters from Punta Delgada north to the Caribbean, my ships are honored under the neutrality of the Paraguayan flag. This convenience may be of service to you. Further, I have a number of vessels, notably small and medium-sized craft converted with high-performance engines. They are capable of traveling swiftly through the coastal waters, and there are refueling depots, thus enabling considerable distances to be traversed rapidly. Certainly no comparison to the airplane, but then the trips are made in utter secrecy, away from the prying eyes that surround all airfields these days. Even we neutrals must constantly outflank the blockades.
   This information should answer the curiously obscure questions you raised.
   I beg you to be more precise in future communications. Regardless, you may be assured of my commitment to the Reich.
   Along these lines, associates in Berne inform me that your Führer is showing marked signs of fatigue. It was to be expected, was it not?
   Remember, my dear Franz, the concept is always a greater monument than the man. In the current situation, the concept came *before* the man. *It* is the monument.
   I await word from you.

                                                                Erich Rhinemann

How delicately unsubtle was Rhinemann! . . . *commitment to the Reich* . . . *associates in Berne . . . marked signs of fatigue . . . to be expected* . . .
   . . . a greater monument than the man. . . .

497

Rhinemann spelled out his abilities, his financial power, his "legitimate" concerns and his unequivocal commitment to Germany. By including, *juxtaposing* these factors, he elevated himself above even the Führer. And by so doing, condemned Hitler – for the greater glory of the Reich. No doubt Rhinemann had photostats made of his letter: Rhinemann would start a very complete file of the Buenos Aires operation. And one day he would use it to maneuver himself to the top of postwar Germany. Perhaps of all Europe. For he would have the weapon to guarantee his acceptance.

In victory *or* defeat. Unswerving devotion or, conversely, blackmail of such proportions the Allies would tremble at the thought of it.

So be it, thought Altmüller. He had no brief with Rhinemann. Rhinemann was an expert at whatever he entered into. He was methodical to the point of excess; conservative in progress – only in the sense of mastering all details before going forward. Above everything, he was boldly imaginative.

Altmüller's eyes fell on Rhinemann's words:

I beg you to be more precise in future communications.

Franz smiled. Rhinemann was right. He *had* been obscure. But for a sound reason: he wasn't sure where he was going; where he was being led, perhaps. He only knew that the crates of carbonado diamonds had to be thoroughly examined, and that would take time. More time than Rhinemann realized if the information he had received from Peenemünde was accurate. According to Peenemünde, it would be a simple matter for the Americans to pack thousands of low-quality bortz that, to the inexperienced eye, would be undetectable. Stones that would crack at the first touch to steel.

If the operation was in the hands of the British, that would be the expected maneuver.

And even the Americans had decent Intelligence manipulators. *If* the Intelligence services were intrinsic to the exchange. Yet Altmüller doubted their active involvement. The Americans were governmentally hypocritical. They would make demands of their industrialists and expect those demands to be met. However, they would close their eyes to the methods; the unsophisticated Puritan streak was given extraordinary lip service in Washington.

Such children. Yet angry, frustrated children were dangerous.

The crates would have to be examined minutely.

In Buenos Aires.

And once accepted, no risks could be taken that the crates would be blown out of the sky or the water. So it seemed logical to ask Rhinemann what avenues of escape were available. For somewhere, somehow, the crates would have to make rendezvous with the most logical method of transportation back to Germany.

Submarine.

Rhinemann would understand; he might even applaud the precision of future communications.

Altmüller got up from his desk and stretched. He walked absently around his office, trying to rid his back of the cramps resulting from sitting too long.

He approached the leather armchair in which Johann Dietricht had sat several days ago.

Dietricht was dead. The expendable, misfit messenger had been found in a blood-soaked bed, the stories of the evening's debauchery so demeaning that it was decided to bury them and the body without delay.

Altmüller wondered if the Americans had the stomach for such decisions. He doubted it.

DECEMBER 19, 1943

FAIRFAX, VIRGINIA

Swanson stood silently in front of the heavy steel door inside the Quonset structure. The security lieutenant was on the wall intercom for only the length of time it took for him to give the general's name. The lieutenant nodded, replaced the phone, saluted the general for a second time. The heavy steel door clicked and Swanson knew he could enter.

The Fairfax commander was alone, as Swanson had ordered. He was standing to the right of his table-desk, a file folder in his hand. He saluted his superior.

"Good morning, general."

"Morning. You worked fast; I appreciate it."

"It may not be everything you want but it's the best we can come up with. . . . Sit down, sir. I'll describe the qualifications. If they meet with your approval, the file's yours. If not, it'll go back into the vaults."

Swanson walked to one of the straight-backed chairs in front of the colonel's desk and sat down. He did so with a touch of annoyance. Ed Pace, as so many of his subordinates in Clandestine Operations, functioned as though he were responsible to no one but God; and even *he* had to be cleared by Fairfax. It struck Swanson that it would be much simpler if Pace simply gave him the file and let him read it for himself.

On the other hand, Fairfax's indoctrination had at its core the possibility – however remote – that any pair of eyes might be captured by the enemy. A man could be in Washington one week, Anzio or the Solomons the next. There was logic in Pace's methods; a geographical network of underground agents could be exposed with a single break in the security chain.

Still, it was annoying as hell. Pace seemed to enjoy his role; be was humorless, thought Swanson.

"The subject under consideration is a proven field man. He's acted as independently as anyone in one of our touchiest locations. Languages: acceptable fluency. Deportment and cover: extremely flexible. He moves about the civilian spectrum facilely, from embassy teacups to bricklayers' saloons – he's very mobile and convincing."

"You're coming up with a positive print, colonel."

"If I am, I'm sorry. He's valuable where he is. But you haven't beard the rest. You may change your mind."

"Go on."

"On the negative side, he's not army. I don't mean he's a civilian – he holds the rank of captain, as a matter of fact, but I don't think he's ever used it. What I'm saying is that he's never operated within a chain of command. He set up the network; he *is* the command. He has been for nearly four years now."

"Why is that negative?"

"There's no way to tell how he reacts to discipline. Taking orders."

"There won't be much latitude for deviation. It's cut and dried."

"That *is* important!" Swanson spoke harshly; Pace was wasting his time. The man in Buenos Aires had to understand what the hell was going on; perhaps more than understand.

"He's in a related field, sir. One that our people say primes him for crash instructions."

"What is it?"

"He's a construction engineer. With considerable experience in mechanical, electrical and metal design. His background includes full responsibility for whole structures from foundations through the finished productions. He's a blueprint expert."

Swanson paused, then nodded noncommittally. "All right. Go on."

"The most difficult part of your request was to find someone – someone with these technical qualifications – who had practical experience in 'dispatch.' You even conceded that."

"I know." Swanson felt it was the time to show a little more humanity. Pace looked exhausted; the search had not been easy. "I handed you a tough one. Does your nonmilitary, mobile engineer have any 'dispatches' of record?"

"We try to avoid records, because . . ."

"You know what I mean."

"Yes. He's stationed where it's unavoidable, I'm sorry to say. Except for the men in Burma and India, he's had more occasions to use last-extremity solutions than anyone in the field. To our knowledge, he's never hesitated to implement them."

Swanson started to speak, then hesitated. He creased his brow above his questioning eyes. "You can't help but wonder about such men, can you?"

"They're trained. Like anyone else they do a job . . . for a purpose. He's not a killer by nature. Very few of our really good men are."

"I've never understood your work, Ed. Isn't that strange?"

"Not at all. I couldn't possibly function in your end of the War Department. Those charts and graphs and civilian double-talkers confuse me. . . .How does the subject sound to you?"

"You have no alternates?"

"Several. But with each there's the same negative. Those that have the languages *and* the aeronautical training have no experience in 'dispatch'. No records of . . . extreme prejudice. I worked on the assumption that it was as important as the other factors."

"Your assumption was correct. . . . Tell me, do you know him?"

"Very well. I recruited him, I observed every phase of his training. I've seen him in the field. He's a pro."

"I want one."

"Then maybe he's your man. But before I say it, I'd like to ask you a question. I have to ask it, actually; I'll be asked the same question myself."

"I hope I can give an answer."

"It's within bounds. It's not specific."

"What is it?"

Pace came to the edge of the desk toward Swanson. He leaned his back against it and folded his arms. It was another army signal: *I'm your subordinate but this puts us on equal footing right now — at the moment.*

"I said the subject was valuable where he is. That's not strong enough. He's invaluable, essential. By removing him from his station we jeopardize a very sensitive operation. We can handle it, but the risks are considerable. What I have to know is, does the assignment justify his transfer?"

"Let me put it this way, colonel," said Swanson, the tone of his voice gentle but strong. "The assignment has no priority equal, with the possible exception of the Manhattan Project. You've heard of the Manhattan Project, I assume."

"I have." Pace got off his desk, "And the War Department through your office — will confirm this priority?"

"It will."

"Then here he is, general." Pace handed Swanson the file folder. "He's one of the best we've got. He's our man in Lisbon. . . . Spaulding. Captain David Spaulding."

11

David sped south on the motorcycle along the dirt road paralleling the Minho River. It was the fastest route to the border, just below Ribadavia. Once across he would swing west to an airfield outside Valença. The flight to Lisbon would take another two hours, if the weather held and if an aircraft was available. Valença didn't expect him for another two days; its planes might all be in use.

His anxiety matched the intensity of the spinning, careening wheels beneath him. It was all so extraordinary; it made no *sense* to him. There was *no one* in *Lisbon* who could issue such orders as he had received from Ortegal!

What had *happened*?

He felt suddenly as though a vitally important part of his existence was being threatened. And then he wondered at his own reaction.He had no love for his temporary world; he took no pleasure in the countless manipulations and counter-manipulations. In fact, he despised most of his day-to-day activities, was sick of the constant fear, the unending high-risk factors to be evaluated with every decision.

Yet he recognized what bothered him so: he had grown in his work. He had arrived in Lisbon centuries ago, beginning a new life, and he had mastered it. Somehow it signified all the buildings he wanted to build, all the blueprints he wanted to turn into mortar and steel. There was precision and finality in his work; the results were there every day. Often many times every day. Like the hundreds of details in construction specifications, the information came to him and he put it all together and emerged with reality.

And it was this reality that others depended upon.

Now someone wanted him out of Lisbon! Out of Portugal and Spain! Was it as simple as that? Had his reports angered one general too many? Had a strategy session been nullified because he sent back the truth of a supposedly successful operation? Were the London and Washington brass finally annoyed to the point of removing a critical thorn? It was possible; he had been told often enough that the men in the underground rooms in London's Tower Road had exploded more than once over his assessments. He knew that Washington's Office of Strategic Services felt he was encroaching on their territory; even G-2, ostensibly his own agency, criticized his involvement with the escape teams.

But beyond the complaints there was one evaluation that overrode them all: he was good. He had welded together the best network in Europe.

Which was why David was confused. And not a little disturbed, for a reason he tried not to admit: he needed praise.

There were no buildings of consequence, no extraordinary blueprints turned into more extraordinary edifices. Perhaps there never would be. He would be a middle-aged engineer when it was over. A middle-aged engineer who had not practiced his profession in years, not even in the vast army of the United States, whose Corps of Engineers was the largest construction crew in history.

He tried not to think about it.

He crossed the border at Mendoso, where the guards knew him as a rich, irresponsible ex-patriot avoiding the risks of war. They accepted his gratuities and waved him over.

The flight from Valença to the tiny airfield outside Lisbon was hampered by heavy rains. It was necessary to put down twice – at Águeda and Pombal – before the final leg. He was met by an embassy vehicle; the driver, a cryptographer named Marshall, was the only man in the embassy who knew his real function

"Rotton weather, isn't it?" said the code man, settling behind the wheel as David threw his pack in the back seat. "I don't envy you up in a crate like that. Not in this rain."

"Those grass pilots fly so low you could jump down. I worry more about the trees."

"I'd just worry." Marshall started up and drove toward the broken-down pasture gate that served as the field's entrance. On the road he switched on his high beams; it was not yet six o'clock, but the sky was dark, headlights necessary. "I thought you might flatter me and ask why an expert of my standing was acting as chauffeur. I've been here since four. Go on, ask me. It was a hell of a long wait."

Spaulding grinned. "Jesus, Marsh, I just figured you were trying to get in my good graces. So I'd take you north on the next trip. Or have I been made a brigadier?"

"You've been made something, David." Marshall spoke seriously. "I took the D.C. message myself. It was that high up in the codes: eyes-only, senior cryp."

"I'm flattered," said Spaulding softly, relieved that he could talk to someone about the preposterous news of his transfer. "What the hell is it all about?"

"I have no idea what they want you for, of course, but I can spell out one conclusion: they want you yesterday. They've covered all avenues of delay. The orders were to compile a list of your contacts with complete histories of each: motives, dates, repeats, currency, routings, codes . . . everything. Nothing left out. Subsequent order: alert the whole network that you're out of strategy."

"*Out of* . . ." David trailed off the words in disbelief. *Out of strategy* was a phrase used as often for defectors as it was for transfers. Its connotation was final, complete break-off. "That's insane! This is *my network!*"

"Not anymore. They flew a man in from London this morning. I think he's Cuban; rich, too. Studied architecture in Berlin before the war. He's been holed up in an office studying your files. He's your replacement. . . . I wanted you to know."

David stared at the windshield, streaked with the harsh Lisbon rain. They were on the hard-surfaced road that led through the Alfama district, with its winding, hilly streets below the cathedral towers of the Moorish St. George and the Gothic Sé. The American embassy was in the Baixa, past the Terreiro do Paço. Another twenty minutes.

So it was really over, thought Spaulding. They were sending him out. A Cuban architect was now the man in Lisbon. The feeling of being dispossessed took hold of him again. So much was being taken away and under such extraordinary conditions. *Out of strategy* . . .

"Who signed the orders?"

"That's part of the craziness. The use of high codes presumes supreme authority; no one else has access. But no one signed them, either. No name other than yours was in the cable."

"What am I supposed to do?"

"You get on a plane tomorrow. The flight time will be posted by tonight. The bird makes one stop. At Lajes Field on Terceira, the Azores. You pick up your orders there."

12

Swanson reached for the tiny lever on his desk intercom and spoke: "Send Mr. Kendall in." He stood up, remaining where he was, waiting for the door to open. He would not walk around his desk to greet the man; he would not offer his hand in even a symbol of welcome. He recalled that Walter Kendall had avoided shaking hands with Craft and Oliver at the Sheraton. The handshake would not be missed; his avoidance of it, however, might be noted.

Kendall entered; the door closed. Swanson saw that the accountant's appearance had changed little since the afternoon conference he had observed from the unseen room two days ago. Kendall wore the same suit, conceivably the same soiled shirt. God knew about his underwear; it wasn't a pleasant thought to dwell on. There was the slightest curl on Kendall's upper lip. It did not convey anger or even disdain. It was merely the way the man breathed: mouth and nostrils simultaneously. As an animal might breathe.

"Come in, Mr. Kendall. Sit down."

Kendall did so without comment. His eyes locked briefly with Swanson's but only briefly.

"You're listed on my appointment calendar as being called in to clarify a specific overrun on a Meridian contract," said the general, sitting down promptly. "Not to justify, simply enumerate. As the . . . outside auditing firm you can do that."

"But that's not why I'm here, is it?" Kendall reached into his pocket for a crumpled pack of cigarettes. He squeezed the end before lighting one. Swanson noted that the accountant's fingernails were unkempt, ragged, soiled at the tips. The brigadier began to see – but would not ponder it – that there was a sickness about Walter Kendall, the surface appearance merely one manifestation.

"No, that's not why you're here," he answered curtly. "I want to set up ground rules so neither of us misunderstands. . . . So *you* don't misunderstand, primarily."

"Ground rules mean a game. What's the game we're playing, general?"

"Perhaps . . . 'Clean Uniforms' might be a good name for it. Or how to run some "Interference in Buenos Aires.' That might strike you as more inclusive."

Kendall, who had been gazing at his cigarette, abruptly shifted his eyes to the general, "So Oliver and Craft couldn't wait. They had to bring their teacher his big fat apple. I didn't think you wanted it."

"Neither Craft nor Howard Oliver have been in touch with this office – or with me – in over a week. Since you left for Geneva."

Kendall paused before speaking. "Then your uniform's pretty goddamned dirty now. . . . The Sheraton. I thought that was a little unritzy for Craft; he's the Waldorf type. . . . So you had the place *wired*. You trapped those fuckers." Kendall's voice was hoarse, not angry, not loud. "Well, you just remember how I got to where I was going. How I got to Geneva. You got that on the wire, too."

"We accommodated a request of the War Production Board; relative to a business negotiation with a firm in Geneva. It's done frequently. However, we often follow up if there's reason to think *any thing prejudicial*. . . ."

"Horseshit!"

Swanson exhaled an audible breath. "That reaction is pointless. I don't want to argue with you. The *point* had been *made*. I have an . . . edited spool of wire that could send you straight to the hangman or the electric chair. Oliver, too. . . .Craft might get off with a life sentence. You ridiculed his doubts; you didn't let him talk. . . . The point, however, *has been made*."

Kendall leaned forward and crushed out his cigarette in an ashtray on Swanson's desk. His sudden fear made him look at the general; he was searching. "But you're more interested in Buenos Aires than the electric chair. That's right, isn't it?"

"I'm forced to be, As distasteful as it may be to me. As loathsome. . . ."

"Cut out the horseshit," Kendall interrupted sharply; he was no amateur in such discussions. He knew when to assert himself and his contributions. "As you said, the point's been made. I think you're in the barnyard with the rest of us pigs. . . . So don't play Jesus. Your halo smells."

"Fair enough. But don't you forget, I've got a dozen different pigsties to run to. A great big War Department that could get me to Burma or Sicily in forty-eight hours. You don't. You're right out there . . . in the barnyard. For everyone to see. And I've got a spool of wire that would make you *special*. *That's* the understanding I want you to have clear in your mind. I hope it is."

Kendall squeezed the tip of a second cigarette and lit the opposite end. The smoke drifted over his nostrils; he was about to speak, then stopped, staring at the general, his look a mixture of fear and hostility.

Swanson found himself consciously avoiding Kendall's eyes. To acknowledge the man at that moment was to acknowledge the pact. And then he realized what would make the pact bearable. It was the answer, *his* answer; at least a surface one. He was amazed it had not occurred to him before this moment.

Walter Kendall would have to be eliminated.

As Erich Rhinemann would be eliminated.

When Buenos Aires was in reach of completion, Kendall's death was mandatory.

And then all specific traces to the government of the United States would be covered.

He wondered briefly if the men in Berlin had the foresight for such abrupt decisions. He doubted it.

He looked up at the filthy – sick – accountant and returned his stare in full measure. General Alan Swanson was no longer afraid. Or consumed with guilt.

He was a soldier.

"Shall we continue, Mr. Kendall?"

The accountant's projections for Buenos Aires were well thought out. Swanson found himself fascinated by Walter Kendall's sense of maneuver and counter-measure. The man thought like a sewer rat: instinctively, probing sources of smell and light; his strength in his suspicions, in his constantly varying estimates of his adversaries. He was indeed an animal: predator and evader.

The Germans' prime concerns could be reduced to three: the quality of the bortz and carbonado diamonds; the quantity of the shipment; and finally the methods of safe transport to Germany. Unless these factors could be guaranteed, there would be no delivery of the gyroscopic designs – the guidance system.

Kendall assumed that the shipment of diamonds would be inspected by a team of experts – not one man or even two.

A team, then, three to five men, would be employed; the length of time required might extend to the better part of a week depending upon the sophistication of the instruments used. This information he had learned from Koening in New York, During this period simultaneous arrangements would be agreed to that allowed an aerophysicist to evaluate the gyroscopic designs brought from Peenemünde. If the Nazis were as cautious as Kendall assumed they would be, the designs would be delivered in stages, timed to the schedule the inspection team considered adequate for its examination of the diamonds. The gyroscope scientist would no doubt be fed step-blueprints in isolation, with no chance of photostats or duplication until the diamond team had completed its work.

Once both sides were satisfied with the deliveries, Kendall anticipated that an ultimate threat would be imposed that guaranteed safe transport to the respective destinations. And it was logical that this "weapon" be identical for each party; threat of exposure. Betrayal of cause and country.

Penalties: death.

The same "weapon" the general held on him, on Walter Kendall.

What else was new?

Did Kendall think it was possible to get the designs and subsequently sabotage or reclaim the diamond shipment?

No. Not as long as it remained a civilian exchange. The threat of exposure was too complete; there was too much proof of contact. Neither crisis could be denied and names were known. The taint of collaboration could ruin men and corporations. "Authenticated" rumors could be circulated easily,

And if the military moved in, the civilians would move out instantly – the responsibility of delivery no longer theirs.

Swanson should know this; it was precisely the situation he had engineered. Swanson knew it.

Where would the diamonds be inspected? Where was the most advantageous location?

Kendall's reply was succinct: any location that seemed advantageous to one side would be rejected by the other. He thought the Germans foresaw this accurately and for that reason suggested Buenos Aires. It was on the spool of wire. Didn't Swanson listen?

Powerful men in Argentina were unquestionably, if quietly, pro-Axis, but the government's dependency on Allied economics took precedence. The neutrality essentially was controlled by the economic factors. Each side, therefore, had something: the Germans would find a sympathetic environment, but the Americans were capable of exerting a strong enough influence to counteract that sympathy – without eliminating it.

Kendall respected the men in Berlin who centered in on Buenos Aires. They understood the necessity of balancing the psychological elements, the need to give up, yet still retain spheres of influence. They were good.

Each side would be extremely cautious; the environment demanded it. Timing would be everything.

Swanson knew how the designs would be gotten out: a string of pursuit aircraft flying up the coastal bases under diplomatic cover. This cover would extend to the military. Only *he* would be aware of the operation; no one else in the services or, for that matter, in the government would be apprised. He would make the arrangements and give them to Kendall at the proper time.

What transport would the Germans arrive at? asked the general.

"They've got a bigger problem. They recognize it so they'll probably make some kind of airtight demands. They could ask for a hostage, but I don't think so."

"Why not?"

"Who've we got – that's involved – that's not expendable? Christ! If it was me, you'd be the first to say, 'Shoot the son of a bitch!'" Kendall again locked his eyes briefly with Swanson's. "Of course, you wouldn't know what particular safeguards I took; a lot of uniforms would be dirty as hell."

Swanson recognized Kendall's threat for what it was. He also knew he could handle it. It would take some thought, but such consideration could come later. It would be no insurmountable hurdle to prepare for Kendall's dispatch. The isolation would come first; then an elaborate dossier. . . .

"Let's concentrate on how they expect to ship out the bortz and carbonado. There's no point in going after each other," said Swanson.

"We're beyond that, then?"

"I think we are."

"Good. Just don't forget it," said Kendall.

"The diamonds will be brought to Buenos Aires. Have those arrangements been made?"

"They're being made. Delivery date in three, three-and-a-half weeks. Unless there's a fuck-up in the South Atlantic. We don't expect any."

"The inspection team does its work in Buenos Aires. We send the physicist . . . who will it be? Spinelli?"

"No. For both our sakes we ruled him out. But you know that . . ."

"Yes. Who, then?"

"Man named Lyons. Eugene Lyons. I'll get you a file on him. You'll sweat bullets when you read it, but if there's anyone better than Spinelli, it's him. We wouldn't take any chances. He's in New York now."

Swanson made a note. "What about the German transport? Any ideas?"

"A couple. Neutral cargo plane north to Recife in Brazil, across east to Palmas or someplace in Guinea on the African coast. Then straight up to Lisbon and out. That's the fastest routing. But they may not want to chance the air corridors."

"You sound military."

"When I do a job, it's thorough."

"What else?"

"I think they'll probably settle for a submarine. Maybe two, for diversion purposes. It's slower but the safest."

"Subs can't enter Argentine ports. Our southern patrols would blow them out of the water. If they put in, they're impounded. We're not going to change those rules."

"You may have to."

"Impossible. There has to be another way."

"You may have to find it. Don't forget those clean uniforms."

Swanson looked away. "What about Rhinemann?"

"What about him? He's on his way back. With his kind of money, even Hitler can't freeze him out."

"I don't trust him."

"You'd be a goddamned fool if you did. But the worst he can do is hold out for market concessions – or money – from both sides. So what? He'll deliver. Why wouldn't he?"

"I'm sure he'll deliver; that's the one thing I'm positive about. . . . Which brings me to the main point of this meeting. I want a man in Buenos Aires. At the embassy."

Kendall absorbed Swanson's statement before replying. He reached for the ashtray and put it on the arm of his chair. "One of your men or one of ours? We need someone; we figured you'd have us supply him."

"You figured wrong. I've picked him."

"That could be dangerous. I tell you this with no charge . . . since I already said it."

"If we move in, the civilian contingent moves out?" A question.

509

"It makes sense . . ."

"Only if the man I send *knows* about the diamonds. You're to make sure he doesn't." A statement. "Make *very* sure, Kendall. Your life depends on it."

The accountant watched Swanson closely. "What's the point?"

"There are six thousand miles between Buenos Aires and the Meridian Aircraft plants. I want that trip made without any mishaps. I want those designs brought back by a professional."

"You're taking a chance on dirtying up the uniforms, aren't you, general?"

"No. The man will be told that Rhinemann made a deal for the designs out of Peenemünde. We'll say Rhinemann brought in the German underground. For escape routings."

"Full of holes! Since when does the underground work for a price? Why would they go three thousand miles out of their way? Or work with Rhinemann?"

"Because they need him and he needs them. Rhinemann was exiled as a Jew; it was a mistake. He rivaled Krupp. There are many in German industry still loyal to him; and he maintains offices in Berne. . . . Our crisis in gyroscopics is no secret, we know that. Rhinemann would use that knowledge; make deals in Berne."

"Why even bring in the underground?"

"I have my own reasons. They're not your concern." Swanson spoke curtly, clipping his words. It crossed his mind – fleetingly – that he was getting overtired again. He had to watch that; his strength was hollow when he was tired. And now he had to be convincing. He had to make Kendall obey without question. The important thing was to get Spaulding within reach of Erich Rhinemann. Rhinemann was the target.

The brigadier watched the filthy man in front of him. It sickened him to think that such a human slug was so necessary to the moment. Or was it, he wondered, that he was reduced to using such a man? Using him and then ordering his execution. It made their worlds closer.

"All right, Mr. Kendall, I'll spell it out. . . . The man I've picked for Buenos Aires is one of the best Intelligence agents we've got. He'll bring those designs back. But I don't want to take the slightest chance that he could learn of the diamond transfer. Rhinemann operating alone is suspect; the inclusion of the German underground puts it above suspicion."

Swanson had done his homework; everyone spoke of the French and Balkan undergrounds, but the *German* underground had worked harder and more effectively, with greater sacrifice, than all the others combined. The former man in Lisbon would know that. It would make the Buenos Aires assignment palatable and legitimate.

"Wait a minute. . . . Jesus Christ! *Wait* a minute." Kendall's disagreeable expression abruptly changed. It was as it suddenly – with reluctant enthusiasm – he had found merit in something Swanson said. "That could be a good device."

"What do you mean, *device?*"

"Just that. You say you're going to use it for this agent. The underground's above suspicion and all that shit . . . O.K., let's go further. You just spelled out the guarantee we have to give."

"What guarantee?"

"That the shipment of Koening diamonds can get *out* of Buenos Aires. It's going to be *the* ball-breaker. . . . Let me ask you a couple of questions. And give me straight answers."

The *sewer rat*, thought Swanson, looking at the excited, disheveled figure-man. "Go ahead."

"This underground. They've gotten a lot of people out of Germany, very important people. I mean everybody knows that."

"They've – it's – been very effective."

"Does it have any hooks into the German *navy?*"

"I imagine so. Allied Central Intelligence would know specifically. . . ."

"But you don't want to go to them. Or do you?"

"Out of the question."

"But is it possible?"

"What?"

"The German *navy*, goddamn it! The submarine fleet!" Kendall was leaning forward, his eyes now boring into Swanson's.

"I would think so. I'm not . . . not primarily an Intelligence man. The German underground has an extensive network. I assume it has contacts in the naval command."

"Then it *is* possible."

"Yes, *anything's* possible." Swanson lowered his voice, turning away from his own words. "This is possible."

Kendall leaned back in the chair and crushed out his cigarette. He grinned his unattractive grin and wagged his forefinger at Swanson. "Then there's your story. Clean as a goddamned whistle and way above any goddamned suspicion. . . . While we're buying those designs, it just so happens that a German submarine is floating around, ready to surface and bring out one – even two, if you like – very important defectors. Courtesy of the underground. What better reason for a submarine to surface in hostile waters? Protected from patrols. . . . Only nobody gets off. Instead, some fresh cargo gets put on board."

Swanson tried to assimilate Kendall's rapidly delivered maneuvers. "There'd be complications. . . ."

"Wrong! It's *isolated. One* has nothing to do with the *other!* It's just talk, anyway."

Brigadier General Alan Swanson knew when he had met a man more capable in the field than himself. "It's possible. Radio blackout; Allied Central instructions."

Kendall rose from his chair; he spoke softly. "Details. I'll work them out. . . . And you'll pay me. Christ, will you pay."

13

The island of Terceira in the Azores, 837 miles due west of Lisbon, was a familiar stop to the trans-Atlantic pilots flying the southern route to the United States mainland. As they descended there was always the comfortable feeling that they would encounter minor traffic to be serviced by efficient ground crews who allowed them to be rapidly airborne again. Lajes Field was good duty; those assigned there recognized that and performed well.

Which was why the major in command of the B-17 cargo and personnel carrier which had a Captain David Spaulding as its single passenger couldn't understand the delay. It had begun at descent altitude, fourteen thousand feet. The Lajes tower had interrupted its approach instructions and ordered the pilot to enter a holding pattern. The major had objected; there was no necessity from his point of view. The field was clear. The Lajes tower radioman agreed with the major but said he was only repeating telephone instructions from American headquarters in Ponta Delgada on the adjacent island of São Miguel. Az-Am-HQ gave the orders; apparently it was expecting someone to meet the plane and that someone hadn't arrived. The tower would keep the major posted and, incidentally, was the major carrying some kind of priority cargo? Just curiosity.

Certainly not. There was *no* cargo; only a military attaché named Spaulding from the Lisbon embassy. One of those god-damned diplomatic tea-party boys. The trip was a routine return flight to Norfolk, and why the hell couldn't he land?

The tower would keep the major posted.

The B-17 landed at 1300 hours precisely, its holding pattern lasting twenty-seven minutes.

David got up from the removable seat, held to the deck by clamps, and stretched. The pilot, an aggressive major who looked roughly thirteen years old to Spaulding, emerged from the enclosed cockpit and told him a jeep was outside – or would be outside shortly – to drive the captain off the base.

"I'd like to maintain a decent schedule," said the young pilot, addressing his outranked elder humorlessly. "I realize you diplomatic people have a lot

512

of friends in these social posts, but we've got a long lap to fly. Bear it in mind, please."

"I'll try to keep the polo match down to three chukkers," replied David wearily.

"Yeah, you do that." The major turned and walked to the rear of the cabin, where an air force sergeant had sprung open the cargo hatch used for the aircraft's exit. Spaulding followed, wondering who would meet him outside.

"My name's Ballantyne, captain," said the middle-aged civilian behind the wheel of the jeep, extending his hand to Spaulding. "I'm with Azores–American. Hop in; we'll only be a few minutes. We're driving to the provost's house, a few hundred yards beyond the fence."

David noticed that the guards at the gate did not bother to stop Ballantyne, they just waved him through. The civilian turned right on the road paralleling the field and accelerated. In less time than it took to adequately light a cigarette, the jeep entered the driveway of a one-story Spanish hacienda and proceeded past the house to what could only be described as an out-of-place gazebo.

"Here we are. Come on, captain," said Ballantyne getting out, indicating the screen door of the screened enclosure. "My associate, Paul Hollander, is waiting for us."

Hollander was another middle-aged civilian. He was nearly bald and wore steel-rimmed spectacles that gave him an appearance beyond his years. As with Ballantyne, there was a look of intelligence about him. Both small and capital I. Hollander smiled genuinely.

"This is a distinct pleasure, Spaulding. As so many others, I've admired the work of the man in Lisbon."

Capital *I*, thought David.

"Thank you. I'd like to know why I'm not him any longer."

"I can't answer that. Neither can Ballantyne, I'm afraid."

"Perhaps they thought you deserved a rest," offered Ballantyne. "Good Lord, you've been there – how long is it now? Three years with no break."

"Nearer four," answered David. "And there were plenty of 'breaks'. The Costa Brava beats the hell out of Palm Beach. I was told that you – I assume it's you – have my orders. . . . I don't mean to seem impatient but there's a nasty teenager with a major's rank flying the plane. *He's* impatient."

"Tell him to go to blazes," laughed the man named Hollander. "We *do* have your orders and also a little surprise for you: you're a lieutenant colonel. Tell the major to get his uniform pressed."

"Seems I jumped one."

"Not really. You got your majority last year. Apparently you don't have much use for titles in Lisbon."

"Or military associations," interjected Ballantyne.

"Neither, actually," said David. "At least I wasn't broken. I had premonitions of walking guard duty around latrines."

"Hardly." Hollander sat down in one of the four deck chairs, gesturing

David to do the same. It was his way of indicating that their meeting might not be as short as Spaulding had thought. "If it was a time for parades or revelations, I'm sure you'd be honored in the front ranks."

"Thanks," said David, sitting down. "That removes a very real concern. What's this all about?"

"Again, we don't have answers, only ex cathedra instructions. We're to ask you several questions – only one of which could preclude our delivering your orders. Let's get that over with first; I'm sure you'd like to know at least where you're going." Hollander smiled his genuine smile again.

"I would. Go on."

"Since you were relieved of your duties in Lisbon, have you made contact – intentional or otherwise – with *anyone* outside the embassy? I mean by this, even the most innocuous good-bye? Or a settling of a bill – a restaurant, a store; or a chance run-in with an acquaintance at the airport, or on the way to the airport?"

"No. And I had my luggage sent in diplomatic cartons; no suitcases, no traveling gear."

"You're thorough," said Ballantyne, still standing.

"I've had reason to be. Naturally, I had engagements for the week after I returned from the north country. . . ."

"From *where?*" asked Hollander.

"Basque and Navarre. Contact points below the border. I always scheduled engagements right after; it kept a continuity. Not many, just enough to keep in sight. Part of the cover. I had two this week; lunch and cocktails."

"What about them?" Ballantyne sat down next to David.

"I instructed Marshall – he's the cryp who took my orders – to call each just before I was supposed to show up. Say I'd be delayed. That was all."

"Not that you wouldn't *be* there?" Hollander seemed fascinated.

"No. Just delayed. It fit the cover."

"I'll take your word for it," laughed Hollander. "You answered affirmatively and then some. How does New York strike you?"

"As it always has: pleasantly for limited periods."

"I don't know for how long but that's your assignment. And out of uniform, colonel."

"I lived in New York. I know a lot of people there."

"Your new cover is simplicity itself. You've been discharged most honorably after service in Italy. Medical reasons, minor wounds." Hollander took out an envelope from the inside pocket of his jacket and handed it across to David. "It's all here. Terribly simple, papers . . . everything."

"O.K.," said David, accepting the envelope. "I'm a ruptured duck in New York. So far, very nice. You couldn't make it the real thing, could you?"

"The papers are simple, I didn't say authentic. Sorry."

"So am I. What happens then?"

"Someone's very solicitous of you. You have an excellent job; good pay, too. With Meridian Aircraft."

"Meridian?"

"Blueprint Division."

"I thought Meridian was in the Midwest. Illinois or Michigan."

"It has a New York office. Or it does now."

"Aircraft blueprints, I assume."

"I should think so."

"Is it counterespionage?"

"We don't know," answered Ballantyne. "We weren't given any data except the names of the two men you'll report to."

"They're in the envelope?"

"No," said Hollander. "They're verbal and to be committed. Nothing written until you're on the premises."

"Oh, Christ, this all sounds like Ed Pace. He loves this kind of nonsense."

"Sorry, again. It's above Pace."

"What? ... I didn't think anything was, except maybe Holy Communion. ... Then how do *you* report? And to whom?"

"Priority courier straight through to an address in Washington. No department listing, but transmission *and* priority cleared through Field Division, Fairfax."

Spaulding emitted a soft, nearly inaudible whistle. "What are the two names?"

"The first is Lyons. Eugene Lyons. He's an aerophysicist. We're to tell you that he's a bit strange, but a goddamned genius."

"In other words, reject the man; accept the genius."

"Something like that. I suppose you're used to it," said Ballantyne.

"Yes," answered Spaulding. "And the other?"

"A man named Kendall." Hollander crossed his legs. "Nothing on him; he's just a name. Walter Kendall. Have no idea what he does."

David pulled the strap across his waist in the removable seat. The B-17's engines were revving at high speed, sending vibrations through the huge fuselage. He looked about in a way he hadn't looked at an airplane before, trying to reduce the spans and the plating to some kind of imaginary blueprint. If Hollander's description of his assignment was accurate – and why shouldn't it be? – he'd be studying aircraft blueprints within a few days.

What struck him as strange were the methods of precaution. In a word, they were unreasonable; they went beyond even abnormal concerns for security. It would have been a simple matter for him to report to Washington, be reassigned, and be given an in-depth briefing. Instead, apparently there would be *no* briefing.

Why not?

Was he to accept open-ended orders from two men he'd never met before? Without the sanction of recognition – even introduction from any military authority? What the hell was Ed Pace doing?

Sorry. . . .It's above Pace.

Those were the words Hollander had used.

. . . .cleared through Field Division, Fairfax.

Hollander again.

Except for the White House itself David realized that Fairfax was about as high up as one could go. But Fairfax was still *military*. And he wasn't being instructed by Fairfax, simply "cleared."

Hollander's remaining "questions" had not been questions at all, really. They had been introduced with interrogatory words: *do you, have you, can you*. But not questions; merely further instructions.

"Do you have friends in any of the aircraft companies? On the executive level?"

He didn't know, for God's sake. He'd been out of the country so damned long he wasn't sure he had any friends, period.

Regardless, Hollander had said, he was to avoid any such "friends" – should they exist. Report their names to Walter Kendall, if he ran across them.

"Have you any women in New York who are in the public eye?"

What kind of question was *that*? Silliest goddamned thing he'd ever heard of! What the hell did Hollander mean?

The balding, bespectacled Az-Am agent had clarified succintly. It was listed in David's file that he had supplemented his civilian income as a radio performer. That meant he knew actresses.

And actors, Spaulding suggested. And so what?

Friendships with well-known actresses could lead to newspaper photographs, Hollander rejoined. Or speculations in columns; his name in print. That, too, was to be avoided.

David recalled that he did know – knew – several girls who'd done well in pictures since he'd left. He'd had a short-lived affair with an actress who was currently a major star for Warner Brothers. Reluctantly he agreed with Hollander; the agent was right. Such contacts would be avoided.

"Can you absorb quickly, commit to memory, blueprint specifications unrelated to industrial design?"

Given a breakdown key of correlative symbols and material factors, the answer was probably yes.

Then he was to prepare himself – however it was done – for aircraft design.

That, thought Spaulding, was obvious.

That, Hollander had said, was all he could tell him.

The B-17 taxied to the west extreme of the Lajes runway and turned for takeoff. The disagreeable major had made it a point to be standing by the cargo hatch looking at his wristwatch when Spaulding returned. David had climbed out of the jeep, shaken hands with Ballantyne and held up three fingers to the major.

"The timer lost count during the last chukker," he said to the pilot. "You know how it is with these striped-pants boys."

The major had not been amused.

The aircraft gathered speed, the ground beneath hammered against the landing gear with increasing ferocity. In seconds the plane would be airborne. David bent over to pick up an Azores newspaper that Hollander had given him and which he'd placed at his feet when strapping himself in.

Suddenly it happened. An explosion of such force that the removable seat flew out of its clamps and jettisoned into the right wall of the plane, carrying David, bent over, with it. And he'd never know but often speculate on whether that Azores newspaper had saved his life.

Smoke was everywhere; the aircraft careened off the ground and spun laterally. The sound of twisting metal filled the cabin with a continuous, unending scream; steel ribs whipped downward from the top and sides of the fuselage – snapping, contorted, sprung from their mountings.

A second explosion blew out the front cabin; sprays of blood and pieces of flesh spat against the crumbling, spinning walls. A section of human scalp with traces of burnt hairline under the bright, viscous red fluid slapped into Spaulding's forearm. Through the smoke David could see the bright sunlight streaming through the front section of the careening plane.

The aircraft had been severed!

David knew instantly that he had only one chance of survival. The fuel tanks were filled to capacity fox the long Atlantic flight; they'd go up in seconds. He reached for the buckle at his waist and ripped at it with all his strength. It was locked; the hurling fall had caused the strap to bunch and crowd the housing with cloth. He tugged and twisted, the snap sprung and he was free.

The plane – what was left of it – began a series of thundering convulsions signifying the final struggle to come to a halt on the rushing, hilly ground beyond the runway. David crashed backward, crawling as best he could toward the rear. Once he was forced to stop and hug the deck, his face covered by his arms, a jagged piece of metal piercing the back of his right shoulder.

The cargo hatch was blown open; the air force sergeant lay half out of the steel frame, dead, his chest ripped open from throat to rib cage.

David judged the distance to the ground as best his panic would allow and hurled himself out of the plane, coiling as he did so for the impact of the fall and the necessary roll away from the onrushing tail assembly.

The earth was hard and filled with rocks, but he was *free*. He kept rolling, rolling, crawling, digging, gripping his bloodied hands into the dry, hard soil until the breath in his lungs was exhausted.

He lay on the ground and heard the screaming sirens far in the distance.

And then the explosion that filled the air and shook the earth.

Priority high-frequency radio messages were sent back and forth between the operations room of Lajes Airfield and Field Division, Fairfax.

David Spaulding was to be airlifted out of Terceira on the next flight to Newfoundland, leaving in less than an hour. At Newfoundland he would be met by a pursuit fighter plane at the air force base and flown directly to Mitchell Field, New York. In light of the fact that Lieutenant Colonel Spaulding had suffered no major physical disability, there would be no change in the orders delivered to him.

The cause of the B-17 explosions and resultant killings was, without question, sabotage. Timed out of Lisbon or set during the refueling process at Lajes. An intensive investigation was implemented immediately.

Hollander and Ballantyne had been with David when he was examined and treated by the British army doctor. Bandages around the sutures in his right shoulder, the cuts on his hands and forearms cleaned, Spaulding pronounced himself shaken but operable. The doctor left after administering an intravenous sedative that would make it possible for David to rest thoroughly on the final legs of his trip to New York.

"I'm sure it will be quite acceptable for you to take a leave for a week or so," said Hollander. "My God, you're lucky to be among us!"

"*Alive* is the word," added Ballantyne.

"Am I a mark?" asked Spaulding. "Was it connected with me?"

"Fairfax doesn't think so," answered the balding Hollander. "They think it's coincidental sabotage."

Spaulding watched the Az-Am agent as he spoke. It seemed to David that Hollander hesitated, as if concealing something.

"Narrow coincidence, isn't it? I *was* the only passenger"

"If the enemy can eliminate a large aircraft and a pilot in the bargain, well, I imagine he considers that progress. And Lisbon security *is* rotten."

"Not where I've been. Not generally."

"Well, perhaps here at Terceira, then . . . I'm only telling you what Fairfax thinks."

There was a knock on the dispensary door and Ballantyne opened it. A first lieutenant stood erect and spoke gently, addressing David, obviously aware that Spaulding had come very close to death.

"It's preparation time, sir. We should be airborne in twenty minutes. Can I help you with anything?"

"I haven't *got* anything, lieutenant. Whatever I had is in that mass of burnt rubble in the south forty."

"Yes, of course. I'm sorry."

"Don't be. Better it than me . . . I'll be right with you." David turned to Ballantyne and Hollander, shaking their hands.

As he said his last good-bye to Hollander, he saw it in the agent's eyes.

Hollander *was* hiding something.

The British naval commander opened the screen door of the gazebo and walked in. Paul Hollander rose from the deck chair.

"Did you bring it?" he asked the officer.

"Yes." The commander placed his attache case on the single wrought-iron

518

table and snapped up the hasps. He took out an envelope and handed it to the American. "The photo lab did a rather fine job. Well lighted, front and rear views. Almost as good as having the real item."

Hollander unwound the string on the envelope's flap and removed a photograph. It was an enlargement of a small medallion, a star with six points.

It was the Star of David.

In the center of the face was the scrolled flow of a Hebrew inscription. On the back was the bas-relief of a knife with a streak of lightning intersecting the blade.

"The Hebrew spells out the name of a prophet named Haggai; he's the symbol of an organization of Jewish fanatics operating out of Palestine. They call themselves the Haganah. Their business, they claim, is vengeance – two thousand years' worth. We anticipate quite a bit of trouble from them in the years to come; they've made that clear, I'm afraid."

"But you say it was welded to the bottom main strut of the rear cabin."

"In such a way as to escape damage from all but a direct explosion. Your aircraft was blown up by the Haganah."

Hollander sat down staring at the photograph. He looked up at the British commander. "Why? For God's sake, *why?*"

"I can't answer that."

"Neither can Fairfax. I don't think they even want to acknowledge it. They want it buried."

14

When the words came over his intercom in the soft, compensating voice of the WAC lieutenant who was his secretary, Swanson knew it was no routine communication.

"Fairfax on line one, sir. It's Colonel Pace. He says to interrupt you."

Since delivering David Spaulding's file, the Fairfax commander had been reluctant to call personally. He hadn't spoken of his reluctance, he simply relegated messages to subordinates. And since they all concerned the progress of getting Spaulding out of Portugal, Pace's point was clear: he would expedite but not personally acknowledge his participation.

Edmund Pace was still not satisfied with the murky "highest priority" explanations regarding his man in Lisbon. He would follow orders once-removed.

"General, there's a radio emergency from Lajes Field in Terceira," said Pace urgently.

"What the hell does that mean? *Where?*"

"Azores. The B-17 carrier with Spaulding on it was sabotaged. Blown up on takeoff."

"Jesus!"

"May I suggest you come out here, sir?"

"Is Spaulding dead?"

"Preliminary reports indicate negative, but I don't want to guarantee anything. Everything's unclear. I wanted to wait till I had further confirmations but I can't now. An unexpected development. Please, come out, general."

"On my way. Get the information on Spaulding!"

Swanson gathered the papers on his desk – the information from Kendall – that had to be clipped together, sealed in a thin metal box and locked in a file cabinet with two combinations and a key.

If there was ever a reason for total security, it was symbolized by those papers.

He spun the two combination wheels, turned the key and then thought for a second that he might reverse the process and take the papers with him. . . . No, that was unsound. They were safer in the cabinet. A file cabinet riveted to the floor was better than a cloth pocket on a man who walked in the street and drove in automobiles. A file cabinet could not have accidents; was not subject to the frailties of a tired, fifty-three-year-old brigadier.

He saluted the guard on duty at the entrance and walked rapidly down the steps to the curb. His driver was waiting, alerted by the WAC secretary, whose efficiency overcame her continuous attempts to be more than an efficient secretary to him. He knew that one day when the pressures became too much, he'd ask her in, lock the door and hump the ass off her on the brown leather couch.

Why was he thinking about his secretary? He didn't give a goddamn about the WAC lieutenant who sat so protectively outside his office door.

He sat back in the seat and removed his hat. He knew why he thought about his secretary: it gave him momentary relief. It postponed thoughts about the complications that may or may not have exploded on a runway in the Azores.

Oh *Christ!* The thought of rebuilding what he'd managed to put together was abhorrent to him. To go back, to reconstruct, to research for the right man was impossible. It was difficult enough for him to go over the details as they now stood.

The details supplied by the sewer rat.

Kendall.

An enigma. An unattractive puzzle even G-2 couldn't piece together. Swanson had run a routine check on him, based on the fact that the accountant was privy to Meridian's aircraft contracts; the Intelligence boys and Hoover's tight-lipped maniacs had returned virtually nothing but names and dates. They'd been instructed *not* to interview Meridian personnel or anyone connected with ATCO or Packard; orders that apparently made their task close to impossible.

Kendall was forty-six, severely asthmatic and a CPA. He was unmarried, had few if any friends and lived two blocks from his firm, which he solely owned, in mid-Manhattan.

The personal evaluations were fairly uniform: Kendall was a disagreeable, antisocial individualist who happened to be a brilliant statistician.

The dossier might have told a desolate story – paternal abandonment, lack of privilege, the usual – but it didn't. There was no indication of poverty, no record of deprivation or hardship anywhere near that suffered by millions: especially during the Depression years.

No records of depth on anything, for that matter.

An enigma.

But there was nothing enigmatic about Walter Kendall's "details" for Buenos Aires. They were clarity itself. Kendall's sense of manipulation had been triggered; the challenge stimulated his already primed instincts for maneuvering. It was as if he had found the ultimate "deal" – and indeed, thought Swanson, he had.

The operation was divided into three isolated exercises: the arrival and inspection of the diamond shipment; the simultaneous analysis of the gyroscopic blueprints, as they, too, arrived; and the submarine transfer. The crates of bortz and carbonado from the Koening mines would be secretly cordoned off in a warehouse in the Dársena Norte district of the Puerto Nuevo. The Germans assigned to the warehouse would report only to Erich Rhinemann.

The aerophysicist, Eugene Lyons, would be billeted in a guarded apartment in the San Telmo district, an area roughly equivalent to New York's Gramercy Park – rich, secluded, ideal for surveillance. As the step-blueprints were delivered, he would report to Spaulding.

Spaulding would precede Lyons to Buenos Aires and be attached to the embassy on whatever pretext Swanson thought feasible. His assignment – as *Spaulding* thought it to be – was to coordinate the purchase of the gyroscopic designs, and if their authenticity was confirmed, authorize payment. This authorization would be made by a code radioed to Washington that supposedly cleared a transfer of funds to Rhinemann in Switzerland.

Spaulding would then stand by at a mutually agreed-upon airfield, prepared to be flown out of Argentina. He would be given airborne clearance when Rhinemann received word that "payment" had been made.

In reality, the code sent by Spaulding was to be a signal for the German submarine to surface at a prearranged destination at sea and make rendezvous with a small craft carrying the shipment of diamonds. Ocean and air patrols would be kept out of the area; if the order was questioned – and it was unlikely – the cover story of the underground defectors would be employed.

When the transfer at sea was made, the submarine would radio confirmation – Rhinemann's "payment". It would dive and start its journey back to Germany. Spaulding would then be cleared for takeoff to the United States.

These safeguards were the best either side could expect. Kendall was convinced he could sell the operation to Erich Rhinemann. He and Rhinemann possessed a certain objectivity lacking in the others.

Swanson did not dispute the similarity; it was another viable reason for Kendall's death.

The accountant would fly to Buenos Aires in a week and make the final arrangements with the German ex-patriot. Rhinemann would be made to understand that Spaulding was acting as an experienced courier, a custodian for the eccentric Eugene Lyons – a position Kendall admitted was desirable. But Spaulding was nothing else. He was not part of the diamond transfer; he knew nothing of the submarine. He would provide the codes necessary for the transfer, but he'd never know it. There was no way he could learn of it.

Airtight, ironclad: acceptable.

Swanson had read and reread Kendall's "details"; he could not fault them. The ferret-like accountant had reduced an enormously complicated negotiation to a series of simple procedures and separate motives. In a way Kendall had created an extraordinary deception. Each step had a checkpoint, each move a countermove.

And Swanson would add the last deceit: David Spaulding would kill Erich Rhinemann.

Origin of command: instructions from Allied Central Intelligence. By the nature of Rhinemann's involvement, he was too great a liability to the German underground. The former man in Lisbon could employ whatever methods he thought best. Hire the killers, do it himself; whatever the situation called for. Just make sure it was done.

Spaulding would understand. The shadow world of agents and double agents had been his life for the past several years. David Spaulding – if his dossier was to be believed – would accept the order for what it was: a reasonable, professional solution.

If Spaulding was alive.

Oh, Christ! What had *happened?* Where was it? Lapess, Lajes. Some goddamned airfield in the Azores! Sabotage. Blown up on takeoff!

What the hell did it *mean?*

The driver swung off the highway onto the back Virginia road. They were fifteen minutes from the Fairfax compound; Swanson found himself sucking his lower lip between his teeth. He had actually bitten into the soft tissue; he could taste a trickle of blood.

"We have further information," said Colonel Edmund Pace, standing in front of a photograph map frame. The map was the island of Terceira in the Azores. "Spaulding's all right. Shaken up, of course. Minor sutures, bruises; nothing broken, though. I tell you he pulled off a miracle. Pilot, co–pilot, a crewman: all dead. Only survivors were Spaulding and a rear aerial gunner who probably won't make it."

"Is he mobile? Spaulding?"

"Yes. Hollander and Ballantyne are with him now. I assumed you wanted him out. . . ."

"Jesus, *yes*," interrupted Swanson.

"I got him on a Newfoundland transfer. Unless you want to switch orders, a coastal patrol flight will pick him up there and bring him south. Mitchell Field."

"When will he get in?"

"Late tonight, weather permitting. Otherwise, early morning. Shall I have him flown down here?"

Swanson hesitated. "No. . . . Have a doctor at Mitchell give him a thorough going-over. But keep him in New York. If he needs a few days' rest, put him up at a hotel. Otherwise, everything remains."

"Well . . ." Pace seemed slightly annoyed with his superior. "Someone's going to have to see him."

"Why?"

"His papers. Everything we prepared went up with the plane. They're a packet of ashes."

"Oh. Yes, of course. I didn't think about that." Swanson walked away from Pace to the chair in front of the stark, plain desk. He sat down.

The colonel watched the brigadier. He was obviously concerned with Swanson's lack of focus, his inadequate concentration. "We can prepare new ones easily enough, that's no problem."

"Good. Do that, will you? Then have someone meet him at Mitchell and give them to him."

"O.K. . . . But it's possible you may want to change your mind." Pace crossed to his desk chair but remained standing.

"Why? About what?"

"Whatever it is. . . . The plane was sabotaged, I told you that. If you recall, I asked you to come out here because of an unexpected development."

Swanson stared up at his subordinate. "I've had a difficult week. And I've told *you* the gravity of this project. Now, don't play Fairfax games with me. I make no claims of expertise in your field. I asked only for assistance; ordered it, if you like. Say what you mean without the preamble, please."

"I've tried to give you that assistance." Pace's tone was rigidly polite. "It's not easy, sir. And I've just bought you twelve hours to consider alternatives. That plane was blown up by the Haganah."

"The *what?*"

Pace explained the Jewish organization operating out of Palestine. He watched Swanson closely as he did so.

"That's insane! It doesn't make sense! How do you *know?*"

"The first thing an inspection team does at the site of sabotage is to water down, pick over debris, look for evidence that might melt from the heat, or burn, if explosives are used. It's a preliminary check and it's done fast. . . . A Haganah medallion was found riveted to the tail assembly. They wanted full credit."

"Good God! What did you say to the Azores people?"

"I bought you a day, general. I instructed Hollander to minimize any connection, keep it away from Spaulding. Frankly, to imply coincidence if the subject got out of hand. The Haganah is independent, fanatic. Most Zionist organizations won't touch it. They call it a group of savages."

"How could it get out of hand?" Swanson was disturbed on another level.

"I'm sure you're aware that the Azores are under British control. An old Portuguese treaty gives them the right to military installations."

"I know that," said Swanson testily.

"The British found the medallion."

"What will they do?"

"Think about it. Eventually make a report to Allied Central."

"But you know about it *now*."

"Hollander's a good man. He does favors; gets favors in return."

Swanson got out of the chair and walked aimlessly around it. "What do you think, Ed? Was it meant for Spaulding?" he looked at the colonel.

The expression on Pace's face let Swanson know that Pace was beginning to understand his anxiety. Not so much about the project — that was out of bounds and he accepted it — but that a fellow officer was forced to deal in an area he was out-of-sync with; territory he was not trained to cross. At such times a decent army man had sympathy.

"All I can give you are conjectures, very loose, not even good guesses. . . . It could be Spaulding. And even if it was, it doesn't necessarily mean it's connected with *your* project."

"What?"

"I don't know what Spaulding's field activities have been. Not specifically. And the Haganah is filled with psychopaths – deadly variety. They're about as rational as Julius Streicher's units. Spaulding may have had to kill a Portuguese or Spanish Jew. Or use one in a 'cover trap.' In a Catholic country that's all a Haganah cell would need. . . . Or it could be someone else on the plane. An officer or crewman with an anti-Zionist relative, especially a *Jewish* anti-Zionist relative. I'd have to run a check . . . Unless you'd read the book, you couldn't possibly understand those kikes."

Swanson remained silent for several moments. When he spoke he did so acknowledging Pace's attitude. "Thank you. . . . But it probably isn't any of those things, is it? I mean, Spanish Jews or 'cover traps' or some pilot's uncle . . . it's Spaulding."

"You don't *know* that. Speculate, sure; don't assume."

"I can't understand *how.*" Swanson sat down again, thinking aloud, really. "All things considered . . ." His thoughts drifted off into silence.

"May I make a suggestion?" Pace went to his chair. It was no time to talk down to a bewildered superior.

"By all means," said Swanson, looking over at the colonel, his eyes conveying gratitude to this hard-nosed, confident Intelligence man.

"I'm not cleared for your project, let's face it, I don't want to be. It's a DW exercise, and that's where it belongs. I said a few minutes ago that you should consider alternatives . . . maybe you should. But *only* if you see a direct connection. I watched you and you didn't."

"Because there isn't any."

"You're not involved – and even I don't see how, considering what I *do* know from the probe and Johannesburg – with the concentration camps? Auschwitz? Belsen?"

"Not even remotely."

Pace leaned forward, his elbows on the desk. "Those are Haganah concerns. Along with the 'Spanish Jews' and 'cover traps.' . . . Don't make any new decisions now, general. You'd be making them too fast, without supportive cause."

"*Support.* . . ." Swanson looked incredulous. "A plane was blown up. Men were killed!"

"And a medallion could be planted on a tail assembly by anyone. It's quite possible you're being tested."

"By *whom?*"

"I couldn't answer that. Warn Spaulding; it'll strike him as funny, he was *on* that aircraft. But let my man at Mitchell Field tell him there could be a recurrence; to be careful. . . . He's been there, general. He'll handle himself properly. . . . And in the meantime, may I also suggest you look for a replacement."

"A replacement?"

"For Spaulding. If there *is* a recurrence, it could be successful. He'd be taken out."

"You mean he'd be killed."

"Yes."

"What kind of world do you people live in?" asked Swanson softly.

"It's complicated," said Pace.

15

Spaulding watched the traffic below from the hotel window overlooking Fifth Avenue and Central Park. The Montgomery was one of those small, elegant hotels his parents had used while in New York, and there was a pleasant sense of nostalgia in his being there again. The old desk clerk had actually wept discreet tears while registering him. Spaulding had forgotten – fortunately he remembered before his signature was dry – that the old man years ago had taken him for walks in the park. Over a quarter of a century ago!

Walks in the park. Governesses. Chauffeurs standing in foyers, prepared to whisk his parents away to a train, a concert, a rehearsal. Music critics. Record company executives. Endless dinner parties where he'd make his usual "appearance" before bed time and be prompted by his father to tell some guest at what age Mozart composed the Fortieth; dates and facts he was forced to memorize and which he gave not one goddamn about. Arguments. Hysterics over an inadequate conductor or a bad performance or a worse review.

Madness.

And always the figure of Aaron Mandel, soothing, placating – so often fatherly to his overbearing father while his mother faded, waiting in a secondary status that belied her natural strength.

And the quiet times. The Sundays – except for concert Sundays – when his parents would suddenly remember his existence and try to make up in one day the attention they thought they had allocated improperly to governesses, chauffeurs and nice, polite hotel managements. At these times, the quiet times, he had felt his father's honest yet artificial attempts; had wanted to tell him it was all right, he wasn't deprived. They didn't have to spend autumn days wandering around zoos and museums; the zoos and museums were much better in Europe, anyway. It wasn't necessary that he be taken to Coney Island or the beaches of New Jersey in summer. What were they, compared to the Lido or Costa del Santiago? But whenever they were in America, there was this parental compulsion to fit into a mold labeled "An American Father and Mother".

Sad, funny, inconsistent, impossible, really.

And for some buried reason, he had never come back to this small, elegant hotel during the later years. There was rarely a need, of course, but he could have made the effort; the management was genuinely fond of the Spaulding

527

family. Now it seemed right, somehow. After the years away he wanted a secure base in a strange land, secure at least in memories.

Spaulding walked away from the window to the bed where the bellboy had placed his new suitcase with the new civilian clothes he had purchased at Rogers Peet. Everything, including the suitcase. Pace had had the foresight to send money with the major who had brought him duplicates of the papers destroyed in Terceira. He had to sign for the money, not nor the papers; that amused him.

The major who met him at Mitchell Field – on the field – had escorted him to the base infirmary, where a bored army doctor pronounced him fit but "run down"; had professionally criticized the sutures implanted by the British doctor in the Azores but saw no reason to change them; and suggested that David take two APCs every four hours and rest.

Caveat patient.

The courier-major had played a tune on the Fairfax piano and told him Field Division was still analyzing the Lajes sabotage; it could have been aimed at him for misdeeds out of Lisbon. He should be careful and report any unusual incidents directly to Colonel Pace at Fairfax. Further, Spaulding was to commit the name of Brigadier General Alan Swanson, DW. Swanson was his source control and would make contact in a matter of days, ten at the outside.

Why call Pace then? Regarding any "incidents." Why not get in touch directly with this Swanson? Since he was the SC.

Pace's instructions, replied the major – until the brigadier took over; just simpler that way.

Or further concealment, thought David, remembering the clouded eyes of Paul Hollander, the Az-Am agent in Terceira.

Something was happening. The source control transfer was being handled in a very unorthodox manner. From the unsigned, high-priority codes received in Lisbon to the extraordinary command: out of strategy. From the mid-ocean delivery of papers from Az-Am agents who said they had to question him first, to the strange orders that had him reporting to two civilians in New York without prior briefing.

It was all like a hesitation waltz. It was either very professional or terribly amateur; really, he suspected, a combination of both. It would be interesting to meet this General Swanson. He had never heard of him.

He lay down on the hotel bed. He would rest for an hour and then shower and shave and see New York at night for the first time in over three years. See what the war had done to a Manhattan evening; it had done little or nothing to the daylight hours, from what he'd seen – only the posters. It would be good to have a woman tonight. But if it happened, he'd want it to be comfortable, without struggle or urgency. A happy coincidence would be just right; a likable, really likable interlude. On the other hand, he wasn't about to browse through a telephone directory to create one. Three years and nine months had passed since he last picked up a telephone in New York City.

During that time he had learned to be wary of the changes taking place over a matter of days, to say nothing of three years and nine months.

And he recalled pleasantly how the Stateside transfers to the embassy in Lisbon often spoke of the easy accessibility of the women back home. Especially in Washington and New York, where the numbers and the absence of permanency worked in favor of one-night stands. Then he remembered, with a touch of amused resignation, that these same reports usually spoke of the irresistible magnetism of an officer's uniform, especially captain and over.

He had worn a uniform exactly three times in the past four years: at the Mayflower Hotel lounge with Ed Pace, the day he arrived in Portugal and the day he left Portugal.

He didn't even own one now.

His telephone rang and it startled him. Only Fairfax and, he assumed, this brigadier, Swanson, knew where he was. He had called the Montgomery from the Mitchell Field infirmary and secured the reservation; the major had said to take seventy-two hours. He needed the rest; no one would bother him. Now someone was bothering him.

"Hello?"

"*David!*" It was a girl's voice; low, cultivated at the Plaza. "David *Spaulding!*"

"Who is this?" He wondered for a second if his just-released fantasies were playing tricks on reality.

"*Leslie*, darling! Leslie *Jenner!* My God, it must be nearly *five years!*"

Spaulding's mind raced. Leslie Jenner was part of the New York scene but not the radio world; she was the up-from-college crowd. Meetings under the clock at the Biltmore; late nights at LaRue; the cotillions – which he'd been invited to, not so much from social bloodlines as for the fact that he was the son of the concert Spauldings. Leslie was Miss Porter's, Finch and the Junior League.

Only her name had been changed to something else. She had married a boy from Yale. He didn't remember the name.

"Leslie, this is . . . well, Jesus, a surprise. How did you know I was here?" Spaulding wasn't engaging in idle small talk.

"*Nothing* happens in New York that I don't know about! I have eyes and ears everywhere, darling! A veritable spy network!"

David Spaulding could feel the blood draining from his face; he didn't like the girl's joke. "I'm serious, Leslie. . . . Only because I haven't called anyone. Not even Aaron. How did you find out?"

"If you must know, Cindy Bonner – she was Cindy Tottle, married Paul Bonner – Cindy was exchanging some dreary Christmas gifts for Paul at Rogers Peet and she *swore* she saw you trying on a suit. Well, you know Cindy! Just too shy for *words* . . ."

David *didn't* know Cindy. He couldn't even recall the name, much less a face. Leslie Jenner went on as he thought about that.

" . . . and so she ran to the nearest phone and called me. After all, darling, we *were* a major item!"

If a "major item" described a couple of summer months of weekending at East Hampton and bedding the daughter of the house, then David had to agree. But he didn't subscribe to the definition; it had been damned transient, discreet and before the girl's very social marriage.

"I'd just as soon you kept that information from your husband. . . ."

"Oh, *God*, you poor lamb! It's *Jenner*, darling, not Hawkwood! Didn't even keep the *name*. Damned if I would."

That was it, thought David. She'd married a man named Hawkwood: Roger or Ralph; something like that. A football player, or was it tennis?

"I'm sorry. I didn't know. . . ."

"Richard and I called it quits simply *centuries* ago. It was a *disaster*. The son of a bitch couldn't even keep his hands off my best friends! He's in London now; air corps, but very hush-hush, I think. I'm sure the English girls are getting their fill of him . . . and I do mean fill! I *know!*"

There was a slight stirring in David's groin. Leslie Jenner was proffering an invitation.

'Well, they're allies," said Spaulding humorously. "But you didn't tell me, how did you find me here?"

"It took exactly four telephone calls, my lamb. I tried the usual: Commodore, Biltmore and the Waldorf; and then 1 remembered that your dad and mum always stopped off at the Montgomery. Very Old World, darling. . . . I thought, with reservations simply *hell*, you might have thought of it."

"You'd make a good detective, Leslie."

"Only when the object of my detecting is worthwhile, lamb. . . .We *did* have fun."

"Yes, we did," said Spaulding, his thoughts on an entirely different subject. "And we can't let your memory prowess go to waste. Dinner?"

"If you hadn't asked, I would have *screamed*."

"Shall I pick you up at your apartment? What's the address?"

Leslie hesitated a fraction of a moment. "Let's meet at a restaurant. We'd never get out of here."

An invitation, indeed.

David named a small Fifty-first Street cafe he remembered. It was on Park. "At seven thirty? Eight?"

"Seven thirty's lovely, but not *there*, darling. It closed simply years ago. Why not the Gallery? It's on Forty-sixth. I'll make reservations; they know me."

"Fine."

"You poor lamb, you've been away so *long*. You don't know *anything*. I'll take you in tow."

"I'd like that. Seven thirty, then."

"Can't wait. And I promise not to cry."

Spaulding replaced the telephone; he was bewildered – on several levels.

To begin with, a girl didn't call a former lover after nearly four war years without asking – especially in these times – where he'd been, how he was; at least the length of his stay in town. It wasn't natural, it denied curiosity in these curiosity-prone days.

Another reason was profoundly disturbing.

The last time his parents had been at the Montgomery was in 1934. And he had not returned since then. He'd met the girl in 1936; in October of 1936 in New Haven at the Yale Bowl. He remembered distinctly.

Leslie Jenner couldn't possibly know about the Montgomery Hotel. Not as it was related to his parents.

She was lying.

16

The Gallery was exactly as David thought it would be: a lot of deep-red velvet with a generous sprinkling of palms in varying shapes and sizes, reflecting the soft-yellow pools of light from dozens of wall sconces far enough above the tables to make the menus unreadable. The clientele was equally predictable: young, rich, deliberately casual; a profusion of wrinkled eyebrows and crooked smiles and very bright teeth. The voices rose and subsided, words running together, the diction glossy.

Leslie Jenner was there when he arrived. She ran into his arms in front of the cloak room; she held him fiercely, in silence, for several minutes – or it seemed like minutes to Spaulding; at any rate, too long a time. When she tilted her head back, the tears had formed rivulets on her cheeks. The tears were genuine, but there was something – was it the tautness of her full mouth? the eyes themselves? something artificial about the girl. Or was it him? The years away from places like the Gallery and girls like Leslie Jenner.

In all other respects she was as he remembered her. Perhaps older, certainly more sensual – the unmistakable look of experience. Her dark blonde hair was more a light brown now, her wide brown eyes had added subtlety to her innate provocativeness, her face was a touch lined but still sculptured, aristocratic. And he could feel her body against his; the memories were sharpened by it. Lithe, strong, full breasted; a body that centered on sex. Shaped by it and for it.

"God, God, God! Oh, *David!*" She pressed her lips against his ear.

They went to their table; she held his hand firmly, releasing it only to light a cigarette, taking it back again. They talked rapidly. He wasn't sure she listened, but she nodded incessantly and wouldn't take her eyes off him. He repeated the simple outlines of his cover: Italy, minor wounds; they were letting him out to go back into an essential industry where he'd do more good than carrying a rifle. He wasn't sure how long he'd be in New York. (He was honest about that, he thought to himself. He had no idea how long he'd be in town; he wished he did know.) He was glad to see her again.

The dinner was a prelude to bed. They both knew it; neither bothered to conceal the excitement of reviving the most pleasant of experiences: young sex that was taken in shadows, beyond the reprimands of elders. Enjoyed more because it was prohibited, dangerous.

"Your apartment?" he asked.

"No, lamb. I share it with my aunt, mum's younger sister. It's very chic these days to share an apartment; very patriotic."

The reasoning escaped David. "Then my place," he said firmly.

"David?" Leslie squeezed his hand and paused before speaking. "Those old family retainers who run the Montgomery, they know so many in our crowd. For instance, the Allcotts have a suite there, so do the Dewhursts. . . . I have a key to Peggy Webster's place in the Village. Remember Peggy? You were at their wedding. Jack Webster? You know Jack. He's in the navy; she went out to see him in San Diego. Let's go to Peggy's place."

Spaulding watched the girl closely. He hadn't forgotten her odd behavior on the telephone, her lie about the old hotel and his parents. Yet it was possible that his imagination was overworking – the years in Lisbon made one cautious. There could be explanations, memory lapses on his part; but now he was as curious as he was stimulated.

He was very curious. Very stimulated.

"Peggy's place," he said.

If there was anything beyond the sexual objective, it escaped him.

Their coats off, Leslie made drinks in the kitchen while David bunched newspapers beneath the fireplace grill and watched the kindling catch.

Leslie stood in the kitchen doorway looking down at him separating the logs, creating an airflow. She held their drinks and smiled. "In two days it's New Year's Eve. We'll jump and call this ours. Our New Year's. The start of many, I hope."

"Of many," he replied, standing up and going to her. He took both glasses, not the one extended. "I'll put them over here." He carried them to the coffee table in front of the small couch that faced the fireplace. He turned rapidly, politely to watch her eyes. She wasn't looking at the glasses. Or his placement of them.

Instead, she approached the fire and removed her blouse. She dropped it on the floor and turned around, her large breasts accentuated by a tight, transparent brassiere that had webbed stitching at the tips.

"Take off your shirt, David."

He did so and came to her. She winced at his bandages and gently touched them with her fingers. She pressed herself against him, her pelvis firm against his thighs, moving laterally, expertly. He reached around her back and undid the hasps of the brassiere; she hunched slightly as he pulled it away; then she turned, arching her breasts upward into his flesh. He cupped her left breast with his right hand; she reached down, stepping partially away, and undid his trousers.

"The drinks can wait, David. It's New Year's Eve. Ours, anyway."

Still holding her breast, he put his lips to her eyes, her ears. She felt him and moaned.

"Here, David," she said. "Right here on the floor." She sank to her knees, her skirt pulled up to her thighs, the tops of her stockings visible.

He lay down beside her and they kissed.

"I remember," he whispered with a gentle laugh. "The first time; the cottage by the boathouse. The floor. I remember."

"I wondered if you would. I've never forgotten."

It was only one forty-five in the morning when he took her home. They had made love twice, drunk a great deal of Jack and Peggy Webster's good whiskey and spoken of the "old days" mostly. Leslie had no inhibitions regarding her marriage. Richard Hawkwood, ex-husband, was simply not a man who could sustain a permanent relationship. He was a sexual glutton as long as the sex was spread around; not much otherwise. He was also a failure – as much as his family would allow – in the business world. Hawkwood was a man brought up to enjoy fifty thousand a year with the ability to make, perhaps, six.

The war was created, she felt, for men like Richard. They would excel in it, as her ex-husband had done. He should "go down in flames" somewhere, exiting brilliantly rather than returning to the frustrations of civilian inadequacy. Spaulding thought that was harsh; she claimed she was being considerate. And they laughed and made love.

Throughout the evening David kept alert, waiting for her to say something, reveal something, ask something unusual. Anything to clarify – if nothing else – the reasons behind her earlier lies about finding him. There was nothing.

He asked her again, claiming incredulity that she would remember his parents and the Montgomery. She stuck to her infallible memory, adding only that "love makes any search more thorough."

She was lying again; he knew that. What they had was not love.

She left him in the taxi; she didn't want him to come up. Her aunt would be asleep; it was better this way.

They'd meet again tomorrow. At the Websters'. Ten o'clock in the evening; she had a dinner date she'd get rid of early. And she'd break her engagement for the real New Year's Eve. They'd have the whole day to themselves.

As the doorman let her in and the taxi started up toward Fifth Avenue, he thought for the first time that Fairfax had him beginning his assignment at Meridian Aircraft the day after tomorrow. New Year's Eve. He expected it would be a half-day.

It was strange. New Year's Eve. Christmas.

He hadn't even thought about Christmas. He'd remembered to send his parents' gifts to Santiago, but he'd done that before his trip to the north country. To Basque and Navarre.

Christmas had no meaning. The Santa Clauses ringing their clinking bells on the New York streets, the decorations in the store windows – none had meaning for him.

He was sad about that. He had always enjoyed the holidays.

534

David paid the driver, said hello to the Montgomery night clerk and took the elevator to his floor. He got off and approached his door. Automatically, because his eyes were tired, he flipped his finger above the Do Not Disturb sign beneath the lock.

Then he felt the wood and looked down, punching his cigarette lighter for better vision.

The field thread was gone.

Second nature and the instructions from Fairfax to stay alert had caused him to "thread" his hotel room. Strands of invisible tan and black silk placed in a half-dozen locations, that if missing or broken meant a trespasser.

He carried no weapon and he could not know if anyone was still inside.

He returned to the elevator and pushed the button. He asked the operator if he had a passkey; his door wouldn't open. The man did not; he was taken to the lobby.

The night clerk obliged, ordering the elevator operator to remain at the desk while he went to the aid of Mr. Spaulding and his difficult lock.

As the two men walked out of the elevator and down the corridor, Spaulding heard the distinct sound of a latch being turned, snapped shut quietly but unmistakably. He rapidly turned his head in both directions, up and down the corridor, trying to locate the origin of the sound.

Nothing but closed hotel doors.

The desk clerk had no trouble opening the door. He had more difficulty understanding Mr. Spaulding's arm around his shoulder ushering him into the single room with him.

David looked around quickly. The bathroom and closet doors were open as he had left them. There were no other places of concealment. He released the desk clerk and tipped him with a five-dollar bill.

"Thank you very much. I'm embarrassed; I'm afraid I had too much to drink."

"Not at all, sir. *Thank* you, sir." The man left, pulling the door shut behind him.

David rapidly began his thread check. In the closet: his jacket breast pocket, leafed out, centered.

No thread.

The bureau: the first and third drawers, inserted.

Both threads out of place. The first inside on top of a handkerchief; the second, wedged between shirts.

The bed: laterally placed along the spread in line with the pattern.

Nowhere. Nothing.

He went to his suitcase, which lay on a luggage rack by the window. He knelt down and inspected the right lock; the thread had been clamped inside the metal hasp up under the tiny hinge. If the suitcase was opened, it had to break.

It was broken, only one half remaining.

The inside of the suitcase housed a single strand at the rear, crossing the elastic flap three fingers from the left side.

It was gone.

David stood up. He crossed to the bedside table and reached underneath for the telephone directory. There was no point in delay; what advantage he had was in surprise. His room had been searched professionally; he was not expected to know.

He would get Leslie Jenner's number, return to her apartment house and find a telephone booth near the entrance – with luck, in sight of it. He would then call her, tell her some wildly incredible story about anything and ask to see her. No mention of the search, nothing of his borne-out suspicions. Throw her off completely and listen acutely to her reaction. If she agreed to see him, all well and good. If she didn't, he'd keep her apartment under surveillance throughout the night, if necessary.

Leslie Jenner had a story to tell and he'd find out what it was. The man in Lisbon had not spent three years in the north provinces without gaining expertise.

There was no Jenner at the address of the apartment building.

There were six Jenners listed in Manhattan.

One by one he gave the hotel switchboard the numbers, and one by one – in varying stages of sleep and anger – the replies were the same.

No Leslie Jenner. None known.

Spaulding hung up. He'd been sitting on the bed; he got up and walked around the room.

He would go to the apartment building and ask the doorman. It was possible the apartment was in the aunt's name but it wasn't plausible. Leslie Jenner would put her name and number in the Yellow Pages, if she could; for her the telephone was an instrument of existence, not convenience. And if he went to the apartment and started asking questions, he would be announcing unreasonable concern. He wasn't prepared to do that.

Who was the girl at Rogers Peet? The one exchanging Christmas gifts. Cynthia? Cindy? ... Cindy. Cindy Tuttle ... Tottle. But not Tottle ... Bonner. Married to Paul Bonner, exchanging "dreary gifts for Paul."

He crossed to the bed and picked up the telephone directory.

Paul Bonner was listed: 480 Park Avenue. The address was appropriate. He gave the number to the switchboard.

The voice of a girl more asleep than awake answered.

"Yes? ... Hello?"

"Mrs. Bonner?"

"Yes. What is it? This is Mrs. Bonner."

"I'm David Spaulding. You saw me this afternoon at Rogers Peet; you were exchanging gifts for your husband and I was buying a suit. . . . Forgive me for disturbing you but it's important. I had dinner with Leslie . . . Leslie Jenner; you called her. I just left her at her apartment; we were to meet tomorrow and now I find that I may not be able to. It's foolish but I forgot to get her telephone number, and I can't find it in the book. I wondered . . ."

"Mr. Spaulding." The girl interrupted him, her tone sharp, no longer blurred with sleep. "If this is a joke, I think it's in bad taste. I do remember your name. . . .I did *not* see you this afternoon and I wasn't exchanging . . . I wasn't in Rogers Peet. My husband was killed four months ago. In Sicily. . . . I haven't spoken to Leslie Jenner . . . Hawkwood, I think now . . . in over a year. She moved to California, Pasadena, I believe. . . .We haven't been in touch. Nor is it likely we would be."

David heard the abrupt click of the broken connection.

17

It was the morning of New Year's Eve.

His first day of "employment" for Meridian Aircraft, Blueprint Division.

He had stayed most of the previous day in his hotel room, going out briefly for lunch and magazines, dinner through room service, and finally a pointless taxi to Greenwich Village, where he knew he would not find Leslie Jenner at ten o'clock.

He had remained confined for two reasons. The first was a confirmation of the Mitchell Field doctor's diagnosis: he was exhausted. The second reason was equally important. Fairfax was running cheeks on Leslie Jenner Hawkwood, Cindy Tottle Bonner, and a naval officer named Jack or John Webster, whose wife was conveniently in California. David wanted this data before progressing further, and Ed Pace had promised to be as thorough as forty-eight hours allowed.

Spaulding had been struck by Cindy Bonner's words concerning Leslie Jenner.

She moved to California. Pasadena, I believe . . .

And a routine phone call to the Greenwich Village apartment's superintendent had confirmed that, indeed, the Websters *did* live there; the husband was in the navy, the wife was visiting him someplace in California. The superintendent was holding the mail.

Someplace in California.

She moved to California . . .

Was there a connection? Or simple coincidence.

Spaulding looked at his watch. It was eight o'clock. The morning of New Year's Eve. Tomorrow would be 1944.

This morning, however, he was to report to one Walter Kendall and one Eugene Lyons at Meridian's temporary offices on Thirty-eighth Street.

Why would one of the largest aircraft companies in the United States have "temporary" offices?

The telephone rang. David reached for it.

"Spaulding?"

"Hello, Ed."

"I got what I could. It doesn't make a hell of a lot of sense. To begin with, there's no record of a divorce between the Hawkwoods. And he *is* in England.

538

Eighth Air Force, but nothing classified. He's a pilot, Tenth Bomber Command down in Surrey."

"What about her living in California?"

"Eighteen months ago she left New York and moved in with an aunt in Pasadena. Very rich aunt, married to a man named Goldsmith; he's a banker – Social Register, polo set. From what we've learned – and it's sketchy – she just likes California."

'O.K. What about this Webster?"

"Checks out. He's a gunner officer on the *Saratoga*. It pulled into San Diego for combat repairs. It's scheduled for sea duty in two weeks, and the date holds. Until then there are a lot of forty-eights, seventy-twos; no extended leaves, though. The wife Margaret joined her lieutenant a couple of days ago. She's at the Greenbrier Hotel."

"Anything on the Bonners?"

"Only what you know, except that he was a bona fide hero. Posthumous Silver Star, Infantry. Killed on a scout patrol covering an ambush evacuation. Sicily invasion."

"And that's it?"

"That's it. Obviously they all know each other, but I can't find anything to relate to your DW assignment."

"But you're not the control, Ed. You said you didn't know what the assignment was."

"True. But from the fragments I *do* know about, I can't find anything."

"My room was searched. I'm not mistaken about that."

"Maybe theft. Rich soldier in a rich hotel, home from an extended tour. Could be someone figured you were carrying a lot of back pay, discharge money."

"I doubt that. It was too pro."

"A lot of pros work those hotels. They wait for guys to start off on an alcoholic evening and . . ."

Spaulding interrupted. "I want to follow up something."

"What?"

"The Bonner girl said 'it wasn't likely' she'd be in touch with Leslie Jenner, and she wasn't kidding. That's an odd thing to say, isn't it? I'd like to know why she said it."

"Go ahead. It was your hotel room, not mine. . . . You know what I think? And I've thought about it; I've had to."

"What?"

"That New York crowd plays a fast game of musical beds. Now, you didn't elaborate, but isn't it logical the lady was in New York for a few days, perhaps saw you herself or knew someone who had, and figured, why not? I mean, what the hell, she's headed back to California; probably never see you again . . ."

"No, it's not logical. She was too complicated; she didn't have to be. She was keeping me away from the hotel."

"Well, you were there . . ."

"I certainly was. You know, it's funny. According to your major at Mitchell Field, you think the Azores thing was directed at me . . ."

"I said *might* be," interjected Pace.

"And I don't. Yet here I am, convinced the other night was, and *you* don't. Maybe we're both getting tired."

"Maybe I'm also concerned for your source control. This Swanson, he's very nervous; this isn't his ball park. I don't think he can take many more complications."

"Then let's not give him any. Not now. I'll know if I should."

Spaulding watched the disheveled accountant as he outlined the Buenos Aires operation. He had never met anyone quite like Walter Kendall. The man was positively unclean. His body odor was only partially disguised by liberal doses of bay rum. His shirt collar was dirty, his suit unpressed, and David was fascinated to watch the man breathe simultaneously through his mouth and nostrils. The agent in Terceira had said Eugene Lyons was "odd"; if this Kendall was "normal," he couldn't wait to meet the scientist.

The Buenos Aires operation seemed simple enough, far less complicated than most of the Lisbon work. So simple, in fact, that it angered him to think he had been removed from Lisbon for it. Had anyone bothered to fill him in a few weeks ago, he could have saved Washington a lot of planning, and probably money. He had been dealing with the German underground since that organization had consolidated its diverse factions and become an effective force. If this Erich Rhinemann was capable of buying the designs, removing them from the Peenemünde complex, he – the man in Lisbon – could have gotten them out of the country. Probably with more security than trying to slip them out of North Sea or Channel ports. Those ports were clamped tight, obsessively patrolled. Had they not been, much of his own work would have been unnecessary. The only really remarkable aspect of the operation was that Rhinemann *could* get blueprints – on *anything* – related to Peenemünde. That *was* extraordinary. Peenemünde was a concrete and steel vault buried in the earth. With the most complex system of safeguards and backups ever devised. It would be easier to get a man out – for any number of invented reasons – than to remove a single page of paper.

Further, Peenemünde kept its laboratories separate, vital stages coordinated by only a handful of elite scientific personnel under Gestapo check. In Buenos Aires terms, this meant that Erich Rhinemann was able to (1) reach and buy diverse laboratory heads in a systematic order; (2) circumvent or buy (impossible) the Gestapo; or (3) enlist the cooperation of those handful of scientists who crossed laboratory lines.

David's experience led him to disqualify the last two possibilities; there was too much room for betrayal. Rhinemann must have concentrated on the laboratory heads; that was dangerous enough but more feasible.

As Kendall talked, David decided to keep his conclusions to himself. He would ask several questions, one or two of which he really wanted answered, but he would not form a partnership with Walter Kendall at this time. It was an easy decision to make. Kendall was one of the least likable men he'd ever met.

"Is there any particular reason why the designs have to be delivered in stages?" Spaulding asked.

"They may not be. But Rhinemann's smuggling them out section by section. Everybody's got a schedule; he says it's safer that way. From his projections, we figure a period of a week."

"All right, that makes sense. . . . And this Lyons fellow can authenticate them?"

"There's no one better. I'll get to him in a few minutes; there are a couple of things you'll have to know. Once in Argentina, he's your property."

"That sounds ominous."

"You can handle him. You'll have help. . . . The point is, as soon as he's cleared those blueprints, you send the codes and Rhinemann gets paid. Not before."

"I don't understand. Why so complicated? If they check out, why not pay him off in Buenos Aires?"

"He doesn't want that money in an Argentine bank."

"It must be a bundle."

"It is."

"From what little I know of this Rhinemann, isn't it unusual for him to be working with the German underground?"

"He's a Jew."

"Don't tell any graduates of Auschwitz. They won't believe you."

"War makes necessary relationships. Look at us. We're working with the Reds. Same thing: common goals, forget the disagreements."

"In this case, that's a little cold-blooded."

"Their problem, not ours."

"I won't pursue it. . . . One obvious question. Since I'm on my way to Buenos Aires, the embassy, why this stop in New York? Wouldn't it have been easier to just rotate from Lisbon to Argentina?"

"A last-minute decision, I'm afraid. Awkward, huh?"

"Not too smooth. Am I on a transfer list?"

"A what?"

"Foreign Service transfer sheet. State Department. Military attaché."

"I don't know. Why?"

"I'd like to find out if it's common knowledge that I left Lisbon. Or could be common knowledge. I didn't think it was supposed to be."

"Then it wasn't. *Why?*"

"So I know how to behave, that's all."

"We thought you should spend a few days getting familiar with everything. Meet Lyons, me; go over the schedule. What we're after, that sort of thing."

"Very considerate." David saw the questioning look on Kendall's face. "No, I mean that. So often we get thrown field problems knowing too little background. I've done it to men myself. Then this discharge, the combat in Italy, they're the cover for my Lisbon activities? For New York only."

"Yeah, I guess that's right." Kendall, who'd been sitting on the edge of his desk, got up and walked around to his chair.

"How far am I to carry it?"

"Carry what?" Kendall avoided looking at David, who was leaning forward on an office couch.

"The cover. The papers mention Fifth Army – that's Clark; Thirty-Fourth Division, One Hundred and Twelfth Battalion, et cetera. Should I bone up? I don't know much about the Italian Theater. Apparently I got hit beyond Salerno; are there circumstances?"

"That's army stuff. As far as I'm concerned you'll be here five, six days, then Swanson will see you and send you down to Buenos Aires."

"All right, I'll wait for General Swanson." David realized there was no point in pursuing G-2 rituals with Kendall. . . . Part professional, part amateur. The hesitation waltz.

"Until you leave you'll spend whatever time you think is necessary with Lyons. In his office."

"Fine. I'd like to meet him." David stood up.

"Sit down, he's not here today. Nobody's here today but the receptionist. Till one o'clock. It's New Year's Eve." Kendall slumped into his chair and took out a cigarette, which he squeezed. "I've got to tell you about Lyons."

"All right." David returned to the couch.

"He's a drunk. He spent four years in jail, in a penitentiary. He can hardly talk because his throat got burned out with raw alcohol. . . . He's also the smartest son of a bitch in aerophysics."

Spaulding stared at Kendall without replying for several moments. When he did speak, he made no attempt to conceal his shock. "That's kind of a contradictory recommendation, isn't it?"

"I said he's smart."

"So are half the lunatics in Bellevue. Can he *function*? Since he's going to be my 'property' – as you put it – I'd like to know what the hell you've given me. And *why*, not incidentally."

"He's the best."

"That doesn't answer my question. Questions."

"You're a soldier. You take orders."

"I give them, too. Don't start that way."

"All right. . . . O.K. You're entitled, I guess."

"I'd say so."

"Eugene Lyons wrote the book on physical aerodynamics; he was the youngest full professor at the Massachusetts Institute of Technology. Maybe he was too young; he went downhill fast. Bum marriage, a lot of drinking, a lot of debts; the debts did it, they usually do. That and too many brains no one wants to pay for."

"Did what?"

"He went out of his skull, a week's bender. When he woke up in a South Side Boston hotel room, the girl he was with was dead. He'd beaten her to death. . . . She was a whore so nobody cared too much; still, he did it. They called it unpremeditated murder and MIT got him a good lawyer. He served four years, got out and nobody would hire him, wouldn't touch him. . . . That was 1936. He gave up; joined the skid row bums. I mean he really joined them." Kendall paused and grinned.

David was disturbed by the accountant's smile; there was nothing funny in the story. "Obviously he didn't stay there." It was all he could think to say.

"Did for damn near three years. Got his throat burned out right down on Houston Street."

"That's very sad."

"Best thing that happened to him. In the hospital ward they took his history and a doctor got interested. He was shipped off to the goddamned CCC, was reasonably rehabilitated, and what with the war coming he got into defense work."

"Then he's all right now." Spaulding made the statement positively. Again, it was all he could think to say.

"You don't clean out a man like that overnight. Or in a couple of years. . . . He has lapses, falls into the booze barrel now and then. Since working on classified stuff he's cooped up with his own personal wardens. For instance, here in New York he's got a room at St. Luke's Hospital. He's taken back and forth just like your socialite drunks. . . . In California, Lockheed's got him in a garden apartment with male nurses round the clock, when he's away from the plants. Actually, he's got it pretty good."

"He must be valuable. That's a lot of trouble. . . ."

"I told you," interrupted Kendall. "He's *the best*. He's just got to be watched."

"What happens when he's on his own? I mean, I've known alcoholics; they can slip away, often ingeniously."

"That's no problem. He'll get liquor – when he wants it; he'll be ingenious about that. But he doesn't go outside by himself. He won't go where there are any people, if you know what I mean."

"I'm not sure I do."

"He doesn't talk. The best he can manage is a hoarse whisper; remember, his throat was boiled out. He stays away from people. . . . Which is fine. When he's not drinking – which is most of the time – he's reading and working. He'll spend days in a laboratory stone sober and never go outside. It's just fine."

"How does he communicate? In the lab? In a meeting?"

"Pad and pencil, a few whispers, his hands. Mostly a pad and pencil. It's just numbers, equations, diagrams. That's his language."

"His entire language?"

"That's right. . . . If you're thinking about holding a conversation with him, forget it. He hasn't had a conversation with anyone in ten years."

18

DECEMBER 31, 1943

NEW YORK CITY

Spaulding hurried down Madison Avenue to the northeast corner of B. Altman's. There was a light snow falling; taxis rushed past the few pedestrians signaling in the middle of the block. The better fares were at the department store's entrance, carrying last-minute purchases for New Year's Eve. People who shopped at Altman's on the afternoon of New Year's Eve were prime passengers. Why waste gas on less?

David found himself walking faster than he had reason to; he wasn't going anywhere, to any specific place that required his presence at a specific time; he was getting away from Walter Kendall as fast as he could.

Kendall had finished his briefing on Eugene Lyons with the statement that "two hulks" would accompany the scientist to Buenos Aires. There'd be no liquor for the hermit-mute with his throat burned out; the male nurses carried "horse pills" at all times. Eugene Lyons, with no drink available, would spend hours over the work problems. Why not? He didn't do anything *else*. No conversations, David mused.

David turned down Kendall's offer of lunch on the pretext of looking up family friends. After all, it had been over three years. . . . He'd be in the office on January 2.

The truth was that Spaulding just wanted to get away from the man. And there was another reason: Leslie Jenner Hawkwood.

He didn't know where he'd begin, but he had to begin quickly.

He had roughly a week to learn the story behind that incredible evening two nights ago. The beginning would include a widow named Bonner, that much he knew.

Perhaps Aaron Mandel could help him.

He took a dollar bill from his pocket and approached the doorman in front of Altman's. A taxi was found in less than a minute.

The ride uptown was made to the accompanying loquaciousness of the driver, who seemed to have an opinion on most any subject. David found the man annoying; he wanted to think and it was difficult. Then suddenly he was grateful to him.

"I was gonna catch the New Year's Eve crowds, like up at the Plaza, you know what I mean? There's big tips over at those war relief things. But the wife said no. She said come home, drink a little wine, pray to God our boy

545

gets through the year. Now, I gotta. I mean if anything happened, I'd figure it was the tips I made New Year's Eve. Superstitions! What the hell, the kid's a typist in Fort Dix."

David had forgotten the obvious. No, not forgotten; he just hadn't considered the possibilities because they did not relate to him. On he to them. He was in New York. On New Year's Eve. And that meant parties, dances, charity balls and an infinite variety of war-created celebrations in a dozen ballrooms and scores of townhouses.

Mrs. Paul Bonner would be at one of those places, at one of those parties. It had been four months since her husband had been killed. It was sufficient mourning under the circumstances, for the times. Friends – other women like Leslie Jenner, but of course not Leslie Jenner – would make that clear to her. It was the way social Manhattan behaved. And quite reasonable, all things considered.

It shouldn't be too difficult to find out where she was going. And if he found her, he'd find others . . . it was a place to start.

He tipped the driver and walked rapidly into the Montgomery lobby.

"Oh, Mr. Spaulding!" The old desk clerk's voice echoed in the marble enclosure. "There's a message for you."

He crossed to the counter. "Thank you." He unfolded the paper; *Mr. Fairfax had telephoned. Would he return the call as soon us possible?*

Ed Pace wanted to reach him.

The thread was intact under the door lock. He entered his room and went directly to the telephone.

"We got something in on the Hawkwood girl," Pace said. "Thought you'd want to know."

"What is it?" Why, oh *why*, did Pace *always* start conversations like that? Did he expect him to say, no, I don't want to know anything, and hang up?

"It fits in, I'm afraid, with my opinion of the other night. Your antenna's been working overtime."

"For Christ's sake, Ed, I'll pin a medal on you whenever you like. What *is* it?"

"She plays around. She's got a wide sex life in the Los Angeles area. Discreet but busy. A high–class whore, if I don't offend you."

"You don't offend me. What's the source?"

"Several brother officers to begin with; navy and air force. Then some of the movie people, actors and a couple of studio executives. And the social-industrial crowd: Lockheed, Sperry Rand. She's not the most welcome guest at the Santa Monica Yacht Club."

"Is there a G-2 pattern?"

"First thing we looked for. Negative. No classified personnel in her bed. Just rank: military and civilian. And she *is* in New York. Careful inquiry says she went back to visit her parents for Christmas."

"There are no Jenners listed in the phone book who've ever heard of her."

"In Bernardsville, New Jersey?"

"No," said David wearily. "Manhattan. You *did* say New York."

"Try Bernardsville. If you want to find her. But don't hand in any expense vouchers; you're not on a courier run in the north country."

"No. Bernardsville is hunt country."

"What?"

"Very social territory. Stables and stirrup cups. . . . Thanks, Ed. You just saved me a lot of work."

"Think nothing of it. All you've had is the conduit center of Allied Intelligence solving the problems of your sex life. We try to please our employees."

"I promise to re-enlist when it's all over. Thanks again."

"Dave?"

"Yes?"

"I'm not cleared for the Swanson job, so no specifics, but how does it strike you?"

"I'll be damned if I know why you're *not* cleared. It's a simple purchase being handled by some oddballs – at least one . . . no, two that I know about. The one I've met is a winner. It seems to me they've complicated the deal, but that's because they're new at it. . . . We could have done it better."

"Have you met Swanson?"

"Not yet. After the holidays, I'm told. What the hell, we wouldn't want to interfere with the brigadier's Christmas vacation. School doesn't start until the first week in January."

Pace laughed on the other end of the line. "Happy New Year, Dave."

"The same, Ed. And thanks."

Spaulding replaced the receiver. He looked at his watch, it was one fifteen. He could requisition an army vehicle somewhere, he supposed, or borrow a car from Aaron Mandel. Bernardsville was about an hour outside New York, west of the Oranges, if he remembered correctly. It might be best to take Leslie Jenner by surprise, giving her no chance to run. On the other hand, on the premise he had considered before Pace's call, Leslie was probably in New York, preparing for the New Year's Eve she'd promised him. Somewhere, someplace. In an apartment or a brownstone or a hotel room like his own.

Spaulding wondered for a moment whether Pace had a point. Was he trying to find Leslie for reasons quite apart from his suspicions? The lies, the search. . . . It was possible. Why not? But a two-to three-hour drive to west Jersey and back would bring him no closer to either objective, investigatory or Freudian. If she wasn't there.

He asked the Montgomery switchboard to get him the number of the Jenner residence in Bernardsville, New Jersey. Not to place the call, just get the telephone number. And the address. Then he called Aaron Mandel.

He had postponed it for as long as he could; Aaron would be filled with tears and questions and offers of anything under the Manhattan sun and moon. Ed Pace told him he had interviewed the old concert manager four years ago before approaching David for Lisbon; that would mean he could reasonably avoid any lengthy discussions about his work.

And Aaron might be able to help him, should he need the old man's particular kind of assistance. Mandel's New York contacts were damn near inexhaustible. David would know more after he reached Bernardsville; and it would be less awkward to have made his duty call to Aaron before asking favors.

At first Spaulding thought the old man would have a coronary over the telephone. Aaron's voice choked, conveying his shock, his concern . . . and his love. The questions came faster than David could answer them; his mother, his father, his own well-being.

Mandel did not ask him about his work, but neither would he be satisfied that David was as healthy as he claimed. Aaron insisted on a meeting, if not this evening then certainly tomorrow.

David agreed. In the morning, late morning. They would have a drink together, perhaps a light lunch; welcome the New Year together.

"God be praised. You are well. You'll come around tomorrow?"

"I promise," David said.

"And you've never broken a promise to me."

"I won't. Tomorrow. And Aaron . . ."

"Yes?"

"It's possible I may need to find someone tonight. I'm not sure where to look but probably among the Social Register crowd. How are your Park Avenue connections?"

The old man chuckled in the quiet, good-humored, slightly arrogant way David remembered so well. "I'm the only Jew with a Torah stand in St. John the Divine. Everybody wants an artist—for nothing, of course. Red Cross, green cross; debutantes for war bandages, dances for fancy-sounding French medal winners. You name it, Mandel's on the hook for it. I got three coloraturas, two pianists and five Broadway baritones making appearances for 'our boys' tonight. All on the Upper East Side."

"I may call you in a little while. Will you still be at the office?"

"Where else? For soldiers and concert managers, when are the holidays?"

"You haven't changed."

"The main thing is that you're well. . . ."

No sooner had David hung up the phone than it rang.

"I have the telephone number and the address of your party in Bernardsville, Mr. Spaulding."

"May I have them, please?"

The operator gave him the information and he wrote it down on the ever-present stationery next to the phone.

"Shall I put the call through, sir?"

David hesitated, then said, "Yes, please. I'll stay on the line. Ask for a Mrs. Hawkwood, please."

548

"Mrs. Hawkwood. Very well, sir. But I can call you back when I have the party."

"I'd rather stay on an open circuit. . . ." David caught himself, but not in time. The blunder was minor but confirmed by the operator. She replied in a knowing voice.

"Of course, Mr. Spaulding. I assume if someone other than Mrs. Hawkwood answers, you'll wish to terminate the call?"

"I'll let you know."

The operator, now part of some sexual conspiracy, acted her role with firm efficiency. She dialed the outside operator and in moments a phone could be heard ringing in Bernardsville, New Jersey. A woman answered; it was not Leslie.

"Mrs. Hawkwood, please."

"Mrs. . . ." The voice on the Bernardsville line seemed hesitant.

"Mrs. Hawkwood, please. Long distance calling," said the Montgomery operator, as if she were from the telephone company, expediting a person-to-person call.

"Mrs. Hawkwood isn't here, operator."

"Can you tell me what time she's expected, please?"

"What time? Good heavens, she's not expected. At least, I didn't think she was. . . ."

Not fazed, the Montgomery employee continued, interrupting politely. "Do you have a number where Mrs. Hawkwood can be reached, please?"

"Well . . ." The voice in Bernardsville was now bewildered. "I suppose in California. . . ."

David knew it was time to intercede. "I'll speak to the party on the line, operator."

"Very well, sir." There was a *ther-ump* sound indicating the switchboard's disengagement from the circuit.

"Mrs. Jenner?"

"Yes, this is Mrs. Jenner," answered Bernardsville, obviously relieved with the more familiar name.

"My name is David Spaulding, I'm a friend of Leslie's and . . ." *Jesus!* He'd forgotten the husband's first name. " . . . Captain Hawkwood's. I was given this number. . . ."

"Well, *David Spaulding!* How are you, dear? This is Madge Jenner, you silly boy! Good heavens, it must be eight, ten years ago. How's your father and mother? I hear they're living in London. So very brave!"

Christ! thought Spaulding, it never occurred to him that Leslie's mother would remember two East Hampton months almost a decade ago. "Oh, Mrs. Jenner. . . . They're fine. I'm sorry to disturb you. . . ."

"You could never disturb us, you dear boy. We're just a couple of old stablehands out here. James has doubled our colors; no one wants to keep horses anymore. . . . You thought Leslie was here?"

"Yes, that's what I was told."

"I'm sorry to say she's not. To be quite frank, we rarely hear from her. She moved to California, you know."

"Yes, with her aunt."

"Only half-aunt, dear. My stepsister; we've not gotten along too well, I'm afraid. She married a Jew. He calls himself Goldsmith – hardly a disguise for Goldberg or Goldstein, is it? We're convinced he's in the black market and all that profiteering, if you know what I mean."

"Oh? Yes, I see.... Then Leslie didn't come East to visit you for Christmas?"

"Good heavens, no! She barely managed to send us a card...."

He was tempted to call Ed Pace in Fairfax; inform the Intelligence head that California G-2 had come up with a Bernardsville zero. But there was no point. Leslie Jenner Hawkwood was in New York.

He had to find out why.

He called Mandel back and gave him two names: Leslie's and Cindy Tottle Bonner, widow of Paul Bonner, hero. Without saying so, David indicated that his curiosity might well be more professional than personal. Mandel did not question; he went to work.

Spaulding realized that he could easily phone Cindy Bonner, apologize and ask to see her. But he couldn't risk her turning him down; which she probably would do in light of the crude telephone call he had placed two nights ago. There simply wasn't the time. He'd have to see her, trust the personal contact.

And even then she might not be able to tell him anything. Yet there were certain instincts one developed and came to recognize. Inverted, convoluted, irrational.... Atavistic.

Twenty minutes passed; it was quarter to three. His telephone rang.

"David?"

"Aaron."

"This Hawkwood lady, there's absolutely nothing. Everyone says she moved to California and nobody's heard a word... Mrs. Paul Bonner: there's a private party tonight, on Sixty-second Street, name of Warfield. Number 212."

"Thanks. I'll wait outside and crash it with my best manners."

"No need for that. You have an invitation. Personal from the lady of the house. Her name's Andrea and she's delighted to entertain the soldier son of the famous you-know-who. She also wants a soprano in February, but that's my problem."

19

The dinner clientele from the Gallery could have moved intact to the Warfield brownstone on Sixty-second Street. David mixed easily. The little gold emblem in his lapel served its purpose; he was accepted more readily, he was also more available. The drinks and buffet were generous, the small Negro jazz combo better than good.

And he found Cindy Bonner in a corner, waiting for her escort – an army lieutenant – to come back from the bar. She was petite, with reddish hair and very light, almost pale skin. Her posture was Vogue, her body slender, supporting very expensive, very subdued clothes. There was a pensive look about her; not sad, however. Not the vision of a hero's widow, not heroic at all. A rich little girl.

"I have a sincere apology to make," he told her. "I hope you'll accept it."

"I can't imagine what for. I don't think we've met." She smiled but not completely, as if his presence triggered a memory she could not define. Spaulding saw the look and understood. It was his voice. The voice that once had made him a good deal of money.

"My name is Spaulding. David . . ."

"You telephoned the other night," interrupted the girl, her eyes angry. "The Christmas gifts for Paul. Leslie . . ."

"That's why I'm apologizing. It was all a terrible misunderstanding. Please forgive me. It's not the sort of joke I'd enter into willingly; I was as angry as you were." He spoke calmly, holding her eyes with his own. It was sufficient; she blinked, trying to understand, her anger fading. She looked briefly at the tiny brass eagle in his lapel, the small insignia that could mean just about anything.

"I think I believe you."

"You should. It was sick; I'm not sick."

The army lieutenant returned carrying two glasses. He was drunk and hostile. Cindy made a short introduction; the lieutenant barely acknowledged the civilian in front of him. He wanted to dance; Cindy did not. The situation – abruptly created – was about to deteriorate.

David spoke with a trace of melancholy. "I served with Mrs. Bonner's husband. I'd like to speak with her for just a few minutes, I'll have to leave shortly, my wife's waiting for me uptown."

The combination of facts – reassurances – bewildered the drunken lieutenant as well as mollified him. His gallantry was called; he bowed tipsily and walked back toward the bar.

"Nicely done," Cindy said. "If there *is* a Mrs. Spaulding uptown, it wouldn't surprise me. You said you were out with Leslie; that's par for her course."

David looked at the girl. *Trust the developed instincts*, he thought to himself. "There is no Mrs. Spaulding. But there was a Mrs. Hawkwood the other night. I gather you're not very fond of her."

"She and my husband were what is politely referred to as 'an item.' A long-standing one. There are some people who say I forced her to move to California."

"Then I'll ask the obvious question. Under the circumstances, I wonder why she used your name? And then disappeared. She'd know I'd try to reach you."

"I think you used the term *sick*. She's sick."

"Or else she was trying to tell me something."

David left the Warfields' shortly before the New Year arrive He reached the corner of Lexington Avenue and turned south. There was nothing to do but walk, think, try to piece together what he had learned; find a pattern that made sense.

He couldn't. Cindy Bonner was a bitter widow; her husband's death on the battlefield robbed her of any chance to strike back at Leslie. She wanted, according to her, simply to forget. But the hurt had been major. Leslie and Paul Bonner had been more than an "item". They had reached – again, according to Cindy – the stage where the Bonners had mutually sued for divorce. A confrontation between the two women, however, did not confirm Paul Bonner's story; Leslie Jenner Hawkwood had no *intention* of divorcing *her* husband.

It was all a messy, disagreeable Social Register foul-up; Ed Pace's "musical beds."

Why, then, would Leslie use Cindy's name? It was not only provocative and tasteless, it was senseless.

Midnight arrived as he crossed Fifty-second Street. A few horns blared from passing automobiles. In the distance could be heard tower bells and whistles; from inside bars came the shrill bleats of noisemakers and a cacophony of shouting. Three sailors, their uniforms filthy, were singing loudly off key to the amusement of pedestrians.

He walked west toward the string of cafes between Madison and Fifth. He considered stopping in at Shor's or 21 . . . in ten minutes or so. Enough time for the celebrations to have somewhat subsided.

"Happy New Year, Colonel Spaulding."

The voice was sharp and came from a darkened doorway.

"What?" David stopped and looked into the shadows. A tall man in a light

552

grey overcoat, his face obscured by the brim of his hat, stood immobile. "What did you say?"

"I wished you a Happy New Year," said the man. "Needless to say, I've been following you. I overtook you several minutes ago."

The voice was lined with an accent, but David couldn't place it. The English was British tutored, the origin somewhere in Middle Europe. Perhaps the Balkans.

"I find that a very unusual statement and . . . needless to say . . . quite disturbing." Spaulding held his place; he had no weapon and wondered if the man recessed in the doorway was, conversely, armed. He couldn't tell. "What do you want?"

"To welcome you home, to begin with. You've been away a long time."

"Thank you. . . . Now, if you don't mind . . ."

"I mind! Don't move, colonel! Just stand there as if you were talking with an old friend. Don't back away; I'm holding a .45 leveled at your chest."

Several passersby walked around David on the curb side. A couple came out of an apartment entrance ten yards to the right of the shadowed doorway; they were in a hurry and crossed rapidly between Spaulding and the tall man with the unseen gun. David was first tempted to use them, but two considerations prevented him. The first was the grave danger to the couple, the second, the fact that the man with the gun had something to say. If he'd wanted to kill him, he would have done so by now.

"I won't move. . . . What is it?"

"Take two steps forward. Just *two*. No more."

David did so. He could see the face better now, but not clearly. It was a thin face, gaunt and lined. The eyes were deep-set with hollows underneath. Tired eyes. The dull finish of the pistol's barrel was the clearest object David could distinguish. The man kept shifting his eyes to his left, behind Spaulding. He was looking for someone. Waiting.

"All right. Two steps. Now no one can walk between us. . . . Are you expecting someone?"

"I'd heard that the main agent in Lisbon was very controlled. You bear that out. Yes, I'm waiting; I'll be picked up shortly."

"Am I to go with you?"

"It won't be necessary. I'm delivering a message, that is all. . . . The incident at Lajes. It is to be regretted, the work of zealots. Nevertheless, accept it as a warning. We can't always control deep angers; surely you must know that. Fairfax should know it. Fairfax *will* know it before this first day of the New Year is over. Perhaps by now. . . . There is my car. Move to my right, your *left*." David did so as the man edged toward the sidewalk, hiding the pistol under the cloth of his coat. "Heed us, colonel. There are to be no negotiations with Franz Altmüller. They are finished!"

"Wait a minute! I don't know what you're talking about. I don't *know* any Altmüller!"

"*Finished!* Heed the lesson of Fairfax!"

553

A dark brown sedan with bright headlights pulled up to the curb. It stopped, the rear door was thrown open, and the tall man raced across the sidewalk between the pedestrians and climbed in. The car sped away.

David rushed to the curb. The least he could do was get the vehicle's license number.

There was none. The rear license plate was missing.

Instead, above the trunk in the oblong rear window, a face looked back at him. His shock caused him to lose his breath. For the briefest of moments he wondered if his eyes, his senses were playing tricks on him, transporting his imagination back to Lisbon.

He started after the car, running in the street, dodging automobiles and the goddamned New Year's Eve revelers.

The brown sedan turned north on Madison Avenue and sped off. He stood in the street, breathless.

The face in the rear window was that of a man he had worked with in the most classified operations out of Portugal and Spain.

Marshall. Lisbon's master cryptographer.

The taxi driver accepted David's challenge to get him to the Montgomery in five minutes or less. It took seven, but considering the traffic on Fifth Avenue, Spaulding gave him five dollars and raced into the lobby.

There were no messages.

He hadn't bothered to thread his door lock; a conscious oversight, he considered. In addition to the maid service, if he could have offered an open invitation to those who had searched his room two nights ago, he would have done so. A recurrence might cause carelessness, some clues to identities.

He threw off his coat and went to his dresser, where he kept a bottle of Scotch. Two clean glasses stood on a silver tray next to the liquor. He'd take the necessary seconds to pour himself a drink before calling Fairfax.

"A very Happy New Year," he said slowly as he lifted the glass to his lips.

He crossed to the bed, picked up the telephone and gave the Virginia number to the switchboard. The circuits to the Washington area were crowded; it would take several minutes to get through.

What in God's name did the man mean? *Heed the lesson of Fairfax.* What the hell was he talking about? Who was Altmüller? . . . What was the first name? . . . Franz. Franz Altmüller.

Who was he?

So the Lajes Field "incident" *was* aimed at him. For Christ's sake, what *for?*

And *Marshall.* It *was* Marshall in that rear window! He *hadn't* been mistaken!

"Field Division Headquarters" were the monotoned words from the State of Virginia, County of Fairfax.

"Colonel Edmund Pace, please."

There was a slight pause at the other end of the line. David's ears picked up a tiny rush of air he knew very well.

It was a telephone intercept, usually attached to a wire recorder.

"Who's calling Colonel Pace?"

It was David's turn to hesitate. He did so thinking that perhaps he'd missed the interceptor sound before. It was entirely possible, and Fairfax was, after all . . . well, Fairfax.

"Spaulding. Lieutenant Colonel David Spaulding."

"Can I give the colonel a message, sir? He's in conference.

"No, you may not. You may and can give me the colonel."

"I'm sorry, sir." Fairfax's hesitation was now awkward. "Let me have a telephone number. . . ."

"Look, soldier, my name is Spaulding. My clearance is four-zero and this is a four-zero priority call. If those numbers don't mean anything to you, ask the son of a bitch on your intercept. Now, it's an emergency. Put me through to Colonel Pace!"

There was a loud double click on the line. A deep, hard voice came over the wire.

"And this is Colonel Barden, Colonel Spaulding. I'm also four-zero and any four-zeros will be cleared with this son of a bitch. Now, I'm in no mood for any rank horseshit. What do you want?"

"I like your directness, colonel," said David, smiling in spite of his urgency. "Put me through to Ed. It's really priority. It concerns Fairfax."

"I can't put you through, colonel. We don't have any circuits, and I'm not trying to be funny. Ed Pace is dead. He was shot through the head an hour ago. Some goddammed son of a bitch killed him right here in the compound."

20

It was four-thirty in the morning when the army car carrying Spaulding reached the Fairfax gate.

The guards had been alerted; Spaulding, in civilian clothes, possessing no papers of authorization, was matched against his file photograph and waved through. David had been tempted to ask to see the photograph; to the best of his knowledge, it was four years old. Once inside, the automobile swung left and headed to the south area of the huge compound. About a half mile down the gravel road, past rows of metal Quonset huts, the car pulled up in from of a barracks structure. It was the Fairfax Administration Building.

Two corporals flanked the door. The sergeant driver climbed out of the car and signaled the noncoms to let Spaulding through; be was already in front of them.

David was shown to an office on the second floor. Inside were two men: Colonel Ira Barden and a doctor named McCleod, a captain. Barden was a thick, short man with the build of a foot-ball tackle and close-cropped black hair. McCleod was stooped, slender, bespectacled – the essence of the thoughtful academician.

Barden wasted the minimum time with introductions. Completed, he went immediately to the questions at hand.

"We've doubled patrols everywhere, put men with K-9s all along the fences. I'd like to think no one could get out. What bothers us is whether someone got out beforehand."

"How did it happen?"

"Pace had a few people over for New Year's. Twelve, to be exact. Four were from his own Quonset, three from Records, the rest from Administration. Very subdued . . . what the hell, this is Fairfax. As near as we can determine, he went out his back door at about twenty minutes past midnight. Carrying out garbage, we think; maybe just to get some air. He didn't come back. . . . A guard down the road came to the door, saying he'd heard a shot. No one else had. At least, not inside."

"That's unusual. These quarters are hardly soundproof."

"Someone had turned up the phonograph."

"I thought it was a subdued party."

Barden looked hard at Spaulding. His glare was not anger, it was his way

556

of telegraphing his deep concern. "That record player was turned up for no more than thirty seconds. The rifle used – and ballistics confirms this – was a training weapon, .22 caliber."

"A sharp crack, no louder," said David.

"Exactly. The phonograph was a signal."

"Inside. At the party," added Spaulding.

"Yes. . . . McCleod here is the base psychiatrist. We've been going over everyone who was inside. . . ."

"Psychiatrist?" David was confused. It was a security problem, not medical.

"Ed was a hardnose, you know that as well as I do. He trained you. . . . I looked you up, Lisbon. It's one angle. We're covering the others."

"Look," interrupted the doctor, "you two want to talk, and I've got files to go over. I'll call you in the morning; later this morning, Ira. Nice to meet you, Spaulding. Wish it wasn't this way."

"Agreed," said Spaulding, shaking the man's hand.

The psychiatrist gathered up the twelve file folders on the colonel's desk and left.

The door closed. Barden indicated a chair to Spaulding. David sat down, rubbing his eyes. "One hell of a New Year's, isn't it?" said Barden.

"I've seen better," Spaulding replied.

"Do you want to go over what happened to you?"

"I don't think there's any point. I was stopped; I told you what was said. Ed Pace was obviously the 'Fairfax lesson.' It's tied to a brigadier named Swanson at DW."

"I'm afraid it isn't."

"It has to be."

"Negative. Pace wasn't involved with the DW thing. His only tie was recruiting you; a simple transfer."

David remembered Ed Pace's words: *I'm not cleared . . . how does it strike you? Have you met Swanson?* He looked at Barden. "Then someone thinks be was. Same motive. Related to the sabotage at Lajes. In the Azores."

"How?"

"The son of a bitch said so on Fifty-second Street! Five *hours* ago. . . . Look, Pace is dead; that gives you certain latitude under the circumstances. I want to check Ed's four-zero flies. Everything connected to my transfer."

"I've already done that. After your call there was no point in waiting for an inspector general. Ed was about my closest friend. . . ."

"And?"

"There are no files. Nothing."

"There *has* to be! There's got to be a record for Lisbon. For *me*."

"There is. It states simple transfer to DW. No names. Just a word. A single word: 'Tortugas'."

"What about the papers you prepared? The discharge, the medical record; Fifth Army, One Hundred and Twelfth Battalion? Italy? . . . Those papers aren't manufactured without a Fairfax file!"

"This is the first I've heard of them. There's nothing about them in Ed's vaults."

"A major – Winston, I think his name is – met me at Mitchell Field. I flew in from Newfoundland on a coastal patrol. He brought me the papers."

"He brought you a sealed envelope and gave you verbal instructions. That's all he knows."

"*Jesus!* What the hell happened to the so–called Fairfax efficiency?"

"You tell me. And while you're at it, who murdered Ed Pace?"

David looked over at Barden. The word *murder* hadn't occurred to him. One didn't commit *murder*; one killed, yes, that was part of it. But murder? Yet it *was* murder.

"I can't tell you that. But I can tell you where to start asking questions."

"Please do."

"Raise Lisbon. Find out what happened to a cryptographer named Marshall."

JANUARY 1, 1944

WASHINGTON, D.C.

The news of Pace's murder reached Alan Swanson indirectly; the effect was numbing.

He had been in Arlington, at a small New Year's Eve dinner party given by the ranking general of Ordnance when the telephone call came. It was an emergency communication for another guest, a lieutenant general on the staff of the Joint Chiefs. Swanson had been near the library door when the man emerged; the staffer had been white, his voice incredulous.

"My God!" he had said to no one in particular. "Someone shot Pace over at Fairfax. He's dead!"

Those few in that small gathering in Arlington comprised the highest echelons of the military; there was no need for concealing the news; they would all, sooner or later, be told.

Swanson's hysterical first thoughts were of Buenos Aires. Was there *any possible connection?*

He listened as the brigadiers and the two- and three-stars joined in controlled but excited speculations. He heard the words ... *infiltrators, hired assassins, double agents.* He was stunned by the wild theories ... advanced rationally ... that one of Pace's undercover agents had to be behind the murder. Somewhere a defector had been paid to make his way back to Fairfax; somewhere there was a weak link in a chain of Intelligence that had been bought.

Pace was not just a crack Intelligence man, he was one of the best in Allied Central. So much so that he twice had requested that his brigadier star be officially recorded but not issued, thus protecting his low profile.

But the profile was not low enough. An extraordinary man like Pace would have an extraordinary price on his head. From Shanghai to Berne; with Fairfax's rigid security the killing had to have been planned for months. Conceived as a long-range project, to be executed internally. There was no other way it could have been accomplished. And there were currently over five hundred personnel in the compound, including a rotating force of espionage units-in-training – nationals from many countries. No security system could be that absolute under the circumstances. All that was needed was one man to slip through.

Planned for months ... a defector who had made his way back to Fairfax ... a double agent ... a weak Intelligence link paid a fortune. Berne to Shanghai.

A long-range project!

These were the specific words and terms and judgments that Swanson heard clearly because he wanted to hear them.

They removed the motive from Buenos Aires. Pace's death had nothing to *do* with Buenos Aires because the time element prohibited it.

The Rhinemann exchange had been conceived barely three weeks ago; it was inconceivable that Pace's murder was related. For it to be so would mean that he, himself had broken the silence.

No one else on earth knew of Pace's contribution. And even Pace had known precious little.

Only fragments.

And all the background papers concerning the man in Lisbon had been removed from Pace's vault. Only the War Department transfer remained.

A fragment.

Then Alan Swanson thought of something and he marveled at his own cold sense of the devious. In a way, it was chilling that it could escape the recesses of his mind. With Edmund Pace's death, not even Fairfax could piece together the events leading up to Buenos Aires. The government of the United States was removed one step further.

As if abstractly seeking support, he ventured aloud to the small group of his peers that he recently had been in communication with Fairfax, with Pace as a matter of fact, over a minor matter of clearance. It was insignificant really, but he hoped to Christ ...

He found his support instantly. The lieutenant general from staff, two brigs and a three-star all volunteered that they, too, had used Pace.

Frequently. Obviously more than he did.

"You could save a lot of time dealing directly with Ed," said the staffer. "He cut tape and shot you off a clearance right away."

One step further removed.

Once back in his Washington apartment, Swanson experienced the doubts again. Doubts and opportunities alike. Pace's murder was potentially a problem because of the shock waves it would produce. There would be a major investigation, all avenues explored. On the other hand, the concentration would be on Fairfax. It would consume Allied Central Intelligence. At least for a while. He had to move now. Walter Kendall had to get to Buenos Aires and conclude the arrangements with Rhinemann.

The guidance designs from Peenemünde. Only the designs were important.

But first tonight, this morning. David Spaulding. It was time to give the former man in Lisbon his assignment.

Swanson picked up the telephone. His hand shook.

The guilt was becoming unbearable.

JANUARY 1, 1944

FAIRFAX, VIRGINIA

"Marshall was killed several miles from a place called Valdero's. In the Basque province. It was an ambush."

"That's horseshit! Marshall never went into the north country! He wasn't trained, he wouldn't know what to do!" David was out of the chair, confronting Barden.

"Rules change. You're not the man in Lisbon now. . . . He went, he was killed."

"Source?"

"The ambassador himself."

"*His* source?"

"Your normal channels, I assume. He said it was confirmed. Identification was brought back."

"Meaningless!"

"What do you want? A body?"

"This may surprise you, Barden, but a hand or a finger isn't out of the question. *That's* identification. . . . Any photographs? Close shots, wounds, the eyes? Even those can be doctored."

"He didn't indicate any. What the hell's eating you? This is *confirmed*."

"Really?" David stared at Barden.

"For Christ's sake, Spaulding! What the hell is . . . 'Tortugas'? If it killed Ed Pace, I want to know! And I'm going to goddamned well find out! I don't give a shit about Lisbon cryps!"

The telephone rang on Barden's desk; the colonel looked briefly at it, then pulled his eyes back to Spaulding.

"Answer it," said David. "One of those calls is going to be Casualty. Pace has a family. . . . Had."

"Don't complicate my life any more than you have." Barden crossed to his desk. "Ed was due for an escort leave this Friday. I'm putting off calling – till morning. . . . Yes?" The colonel listened to the phone for several seconds, then looked at Spaulding. "It's the trip–line operator in New York; the one we've got covering you. This General Swanson's been trying to reach you. He's got him holding now. Do you want him to put the old man through?"

David remembered Pace's appraisal of the nervous brigadier. "Do you have to tell him I'm here?"

"Hell, no."

"Then put him through."

Barden walked from behind the desk as Spaulding took the phone and repeated the phrase "Yes, sir" a number of times. Finally he replaced the instrument. "Swanson wants me in his office this morning."

"I want to know why the hell they ripped you out of Lisbon," Barden said.

David sat down in the chair without at first answering. When he spoke he tried not to sound military or officious. "I'm not sure it has anything to do with ... anything. I don't want to duck; on the other hand, in a way I have to. But I want to keep a couple of options open. Call it instinct, I don't know. . . . There's a man named Altmüller. Franz Altmüller. . . . Who he is, where he is – I have no idea. German, Swiss, I don't know. . . . Find out what you can on a four-zero basis. Call me at the Hotel Montgomery in New York. I'll be there for at least the rest of the week. Then I go to Buenos Aires."

"I will if you flex the clearances . . . tell me what the hell is going on."

"You won't like it. Because if I do, and if it *is* connected, it'll mean Fairfax has open code lines in Berlin."

JANUARY 1, 1944

NEW YORK CITY

The commercial passenger plane began its descent toward La Guardia Airport. David looked at his watch, It was a little past noon. It had all happened in twelve hours: Cindy Bonner, the stranger on Fifty-second Street, Marshall, Pace's murder, Barden, the news from Valdero's . . . and finally the awkward conference with the amateur source control, Brigadier General Alan Swanson, DW.

Twelve hours.

He hadn't slept in nearly forty-eight. He needed sleep to find some kind of perspective, to piece together the elusive pattern. Not the one that was clear.

Erich Rhinemann was to be killed.

Of *course* he had to be killed. The only surprise for David was the bumbling manner in which the brigadier had given the order. It didn't require elaboration or apology. And it – at *last* – explained his transfer from Lisbon. It filled in the gaping hole of *why*. He was no gyroscope specialist; it hadn't made sense. But now it did. He was a good selection; Pace had made a thoroughly professional choice. It was a job for which he was suited – in addition to being a bilingual liaison between the mute gyroscopic scientist, Eugene Lyons, and Rhinemann's blueprint man.

That picture was clear; he was relieved to see it come into focus.

What bothered him was the unfocused picture.

The embassy's Marshall, the cryp who five days ago picked him up at a rain-soaked airfield outside of Lisbon. The man he *had* seen looking at him through the automobile window on Fifty-second Street; the man supposedly killed in an ambush in the north country, into which he never had ventured. Or would venture.

Leslie Jenner Hawkwood. The resourceful ex-lover who had lied and kept him away from his hotel room, who foolishly used the ploy of Cindy Bonner and the exchange of gifts for a dead husband she had stolen. Leslie was not an idiot. She *was* telling him something.

But what?

And Pace. Poor, humorless Ed Pace cut down within the most security-conscious enclosure in the United States.

The *lesson of Fairfax*, predicted with incredible accuracy – nearly to the moment – by a tall, sad-eyed man in shadows on Fifty-second Street.

That . . . *they* were the figures in the unfocused picture.

David had been harsh with the brigadier. He had demanded – professionally, of course – to know the exact date the decision had been reached to eliminate Erich Rhinemann. Who had arrived at it? How was the order transmitted? Did the general know a cryptographer named Marshall? Had Pace ever mentioned him? Had *anyone* ever mentioned him? And a man named Altmüller. Franz Altmüller. Did that name mean anything?

The answers were no help. And God knew Swanson wasn't lying. He wasn't pro enough to get away with it.

The names Marshall and Altmüller were unknown to him. The decision to execute Rhinemann was made within hours. There was absolutely no way Ed Pace could have known; he was not consulted, nor was anyone at Fairfax. It was a decision emanating from the cellars of the White House; no one at Fairfax or Lisbon could have been involved. For David that absence of involvement was the important factor. It meant simply that the whole unfocused picture had nothing to do with Erich Rhinemann. And thus, as far as could be determined, was unrelated to Buenos Aires. David made the quick decision not to confide in the nervous brigadier. Pace had been right: the man couldn't take any more complications. He'd use Fairfax, source control be damned.

The plane landed; Spaulding walked into the passenger terminal and looked for the signs that read Taxis. He went through the double doors to the platform and heard the porters shouting the various destinations of the unfilled cabs. It was funny, but the shared taxis were the only things that caused him to think La Guardia Airport knew there was a war going on somewhere.

Simultaneously he recognized the foolishness of his thoughts. And the pretentiousness of them.

A soldier with no legs was being helped into a cab. Porters and civilians were touched, helpful.

The soldier was drunk. What was left of him, unstable.

Spaulding shared a taxi with three other men, and they talked of little but the latest reports out of Italy. David decided to forget his cover in case the inevitable questions came up. He wasn't about to discuss any mythical combat in Salerno. But the questions did not arise. And then he saw why.

The man next to him was blind; the man shifted his weight and the afternoon sun caused a reflection in his lapel. It was a tiny metal replica of a ribbon: South Pacific.

David considered again that he was terribly tired. He was about the most unobservant agent ever to have been given an operation, he thought.

He got out of the cab on Fifth Avenue, three blocks north of the Montgomery. He had overpaid his share; he hoped the other two men would apply it to the blind veteran whose clothes were one hell of a long way from Leslie Jenner's Rogers Peet.

Leslie Jenner . . . Hawkwood.

A cryptographer named Marshall.

The unfocused picture.

He had to put it all out of his mind. He had to sleep, forget; let everything settle before he thought again. Tomorrow morning he would meet Eugene Lyons and begin . . . again. He had to be ready for the man who'd burned his throat out with raw alcohol and had not had a conversation in ten years.

The elevator stopped at the sixth floor. His was the seventh. He was about to tell the elevator operator when he realized the doors were not opening.

Instead, the operator turned in place. In his hand he gripped a short-barreled Smith & Wesson revolver. He reached behind him to the lever control and pushed it to the left, the enclosed box jerked and edged itself up between floors.

"The lobby lights go out this way, Colonel Spaulding. We may hear buzzers, but there's a second elevator used in emergencies. We won't be disturbed."

The accent was the same, thought David. British overlay. Middle Europe.

"I'm glad of that. I mean, Jesus, it's been so long."

"I don't find you amusing."

"Nor I, you . . . obviously."

"You've been to Fairfax, Virginia. Did you have a pleasant journey?"

"You've got an extraordinary pipeline." Spaulding wasn't only buying time with conversation. He and Ira Barden had taken the required precautions. Even if the Montgomery switchboard reported everything he said, there was no evidence that he had flown to Virginia. The arrangements were made from telephone booths, the flight from Mitchell to Andrews under an assumed name on a crew sheet. Even the Manhattan number he had left with the Montgomery desk had a New York address under constant surveillance. And *in* the Fairfax compound, only the security gate had his name; he had been seen by only four, perhaps five men.

"We have reliable sources of information. . . . Now you have learned first-hand the lesson of Fairfax, no?"

"I've learned that a good man was murdered. I imagine his wife and children have been told by now."

563

"There is no murder in war, colonel. A misapplication of the word. And don't speak to us. . . ."

A buzzer interrupted the man. It was short, a polite ring.

"Who is 'us'?" asked David.

"You'll know in time, if you cooperate. If you don't cooperate, it will make no difference; you'll be killed. . . . We don't make idle threats. Witness Fairfax."

The buzzer sounded again. This time prolonged, not quite polite.

"How am I supposed to cooperate? What about?"

"We must know the precise location of Tortugas."

Spaulding's mind raced back to five o'clock that morning. In Fairfax. Ira Barden had said that the name "Tortugas" was the single word opposite his transfer specification. No other data, nothing but the word "Tortugas." And it had been buried in Pace's "vaults." Cabinets kept behind steel doors, accessible only to the highest-echelon Intelligence personnel.

"Tortugas is part of an island complex off the coast of Florida. It's usually referred to as the Dry Tortugas. It's on any map."

The buzzer again. Now repeated; in short, angry spurts.

"Don't be foolish, colonel."

"I'm not being anything. I don't know what you're talking about."

The man stared at Spaulding. David saw that he was unsure, controlling his anger. The elevator buzzer was incessant now; voices could be heard from above and below.

"I'd prefer not to have to kill you but I will. *Where is Tortugas?*"

Suddenly a loud male voice, no more than ten feet from the enclosure, on the sixth floor, shouted.

"*It's up here! It's stuck!* Are you all *right* up there?"

The man blinked, the shouting had unnerved him. It was the instant David was waiting for. He lashed his right hand out in a diagonal thrust and gripped the man's forearm, hammering it against the metal door. He slammed his body into the man's chest and brought his knee up in a single, crushing assault against the groin. The man screamed in agony; Spaulding grabbed the arched throat with his left hand and tore at the veins around the larynx. He hammered the man twice more in the groin, until the pain was so excruciating that no more screams could emerge, only low, wailing moans of anguish. The body went limp, the revolver fell to the floor, and the man slid downward against the wall.

Spaulding kicked the weapon away and gripped the man's neck with both hands, shaking the head back and forth to keep him conscious.

"Now, you tell *me*, you son of a bitch! What *is* 'Tortugas'?"

The shouting outside the elevator was now deafening. There was a cacophony of hysteria brought on by the screams of the battered operator. There were cries for the hotel management. For the police.

The man looked up at David, tears of terrible pain streaming from his eyes.

564

"Why not kill me, pig," he said between agonizing chokes of breath. " . . . You've tried before."

David was bewildered. He'd never *seen* the man. The north country? Basque? Navarre?

There was no time to think.

"What is '*Tortugas*'?"

"Altmüller, pig. The pig Altmüller . . ." The man fell into unconsciousness.

There was the name again.

Altmüller.

Spaulding rose from the unconscious body and grabbed the control lever of the elevator. He swung it to the far left, accelerating the speed as fast as possible. There were ten floors in the Montgomery; the panel lights indicated that the first-, third-, and sixth-floor buttons had been activated. If he could reach the tenth before the hysterical voices followed him up the stairs, it was possible that he could get out of the elevator, race down the corridor to one of the corners, then double back into the crowd which surely would gather around the open elevator doors.

Around the unconscious man on the floor.

It *had* to be possible! This was no time for him to be involved with the New York police.

The man was carried away on a stretcher; the questions were brief.

No, he didn't know the elevator operator. The man had dropped him off at his floor ten or twelve minutes ago. He'd been in his room and came out when he'd heard all the shouting.

The same as everyone else.

What was New York coming to?

David reached his room on seven, closed the door and stared at the bed. Christ, he was exhausted! But his mind refused to stop racing.

He would postpone everything until he had rested, except for two items. He had to consider those now. They could not wait for sleep because a telephone might ring, or someone might come to his hotel room. And he had to make his decisions in advance. Be prepared.

The first item was that Fairfax no longer could be used as a source. It was riddled, infiltrated. He had to function without Fairfax, which, in a way, was akin to telling a cripple he had to walk without braces.

On the other hand, he was no cripple.

The second item was a man named Altmüller. He had to find a man named Franz Altmüller; find out who he was, what he meant to the unfocused picture.

David lay down on the bed; he didn't have the energy to remove his clothes, even his shoes. He brought his arm up to shade his eyes from the afternoon sun streaming in the hotel windows. The afternoon sun of the first day of the new year, 1944.

Suddenly, he opened his eyes in the black void of tweed cloth. There was a third item. Inextricably bound to the man named Altmüller.

What the hell did "Tortugas" mean?

21

NEW YORK CITY

Eugene Lyons sat at a drafting board in the bare office. He was in shirtsleeves. There were blueprints strewn about on tables. The bright morning sun bouncing off the white walls gave the room the antiseptic appearance of a large hospital cubicle.

And Eugene Lyons's face and body did nothing to discourage such thoughts.

David had followed Kendall through the door, apprehensive at the forthcoming introduction. He would have preferred not knowing anything about Lyons.

The scientist turned on the stool. He was among the thinnest men Spaulding had ever seen. The bones were surrounded by flesh, not protected by it. Light blue veins were in evidence throughout the hands, arms, neck and temples. The skin wasn't old, it was worn out. The eyes were deep-set but in no way dull or flat; they were alert and, in their own way, penetrating. His straight grey hair was thinned out before its time; he could have been any age within a twenty-year span.

There was, however, one quality about the man that seemed specific: disinterest. He acknowledged the intrusion, obviously knew who David was, but made no move to interrupt his concentration.

Kendall forced the break. "Eugene, this is Spaulding. You show him where to start."

And with those words Kendall turned on his heel and went out the door, closing it behind him.

David stood across the room from Lyons. He took the necessary steps and extended his hand. He knew exactly what he was going to say.

"It's an honor to meet you, Dr. Lyons. I'm no expert in your field, but I've heard about your work at MIT. I'm lucky to have you spread the wealth, even if it's only for a short time."

There was a slight, momentary flicker of interest in the eyes. David had gambled on a simple greeting that told the emaciated scientist several things, among which was the fact that David was aware of Lyons's tragedy in Boston – thus, undoubtedly, the rest of his story – and was not inhibited by it.

Lyons's grip was limp; the disinterest quickly returned. Disinterest, not necessarily rudeness. On the borderline.

"I know we haven't much time and I'm a neophyte in gyroscopics," said

567

Spaulding, releasing the hand, backing off to the side of the drafting board. "But I'm told I don't have to recognize much more than pretty basic stuff; be able to verbalize in German the terms and formulas you write out for me."

David emphasized – with the barest rise in his voice – the words *verbalize . . . you write out for me.* He watched Lyons to see if there was any reaction to his open acknowledgment of the scientist's vocal problem. He thought he detected a small hint of relief.

Lyons looked up at him. The thin lips flattened slightly against the teeth; there was a short extension at the corners of the mouth and the scientist nodded. There was even an infinitesimal glint of appreciation in the deep-set eyes. He got up from his stool and crossed to the nearest table where several books lay on blueprints. He picked up the top volume and handed it to Spaulding. The title on the cover was *Diagrammatics: Inertia and Precession.*

David knew it would be all right.

It was past six o'clock.

Kendall had gone; the receptionist had bolted at the stroke of five, asking David to close the doors if he was the last person to leave. If not, tell one of the others.

The "others" were Eugene Lyons and his two male nurses.

Spaulding met them – the male nurses – briefly in the reception room. Their names were Hal and Johnny. Both were large men; the talkative one was Hal, the leader was Johnny, an ex-marine.

"The old guy is on his real good behavior," said Hal. "Nothing to worry about."

"It's time to get him back to St. Luke's," said Johnny. "They get pissed off if he's too late for the night meal."

Together the men went into Lyons's office and brought him out. They were polite with the cadaverous physicist, but firm. Eugene Lyons looked indifferently at Spaulding, shrugged and walked silently out the door with his two keepers.

David waited until he heard the sound of the elevator in the hallway. Then he put down the *Diagrammatics* volume the physicist had given him on the receptionist's desk and crossed to Walter Kendall's office.

The door was locked, which struck him as strange. Kendall was on his way to Buenos Aires, he might not be back for several weeks. Spaulding withdrew a small object from his pocket and knelt down. At first glance, the instrument in David's hand appeared to be an expensive silver pocket knife, the sort so often found at the end of an expensive key chain, especially in very expensive men's clubs. It wasn't. It was a locksmith's pick designed to give that appearance. It had been made in London's Silver Vaults, a gift from an MI-5 counterpart in Lisbon.

David spun out a tiny cylinder with a flat tip and inserted it into the lock housing. In less than thirty seconds the appropriate clicks were heard and Spaulding opened the door. He walked in, leaving it ajar.

Kendall's office had no file cabinets, no closets, no bookshelves; no recesses whatsoever other than the desk drawers. David turned on the fluorescent reading lamp at the far edge of the blotter and opened the top center drawer.

He had to stifle a genuine laugh. Surrounded by an odd assortment of paper clips, toothpicks, loose Lifesavers, and note paper were two pornographic magazines. Although marked with dirty fingerprints, both were fairly new.

Merry Christmas, Walter Kendall, thought David a little sadly. The side drawers were empty, at least there was nothing of interest. In the bottom drawer lay crumpled yellow pages of note paper, meaningless doodles drawn with a hard pencil, piercing the pages.

He was about to get up and leave when he decided to look once more at the incoherent patterns on the crumpled paper. There was nothing else; Kendall had locked his office door out of reflex, not necessity. And again by reflex, perhaps, he had put the yellow pages – not in a wastebasket, which had only the contents of emptied ashtrays – but in a drawer. Out of sight.

David knew he was reaching. There was no choice; he wasn't sure what he was looking for, if anything.

He spread two of the pages on top of the blotter, pressing the surfaces flat. Nothing.

Well, something. Outlines of women's breasts and genitalia. Assorted circles and arrows, diagrams: a psychoanalyst's paradise.

He removed another single page and pressed it out. More circles, arrows, breasts. Then to one side, childlike outlines of clouds – billowy, shaded; diagonal marks that could be rain or multiple sheets of thin lightning.

Nothing.

Another page.

It caught David's eye. On the bottom of the soiled yellow page, barely distinguishable between criss-cross penciling, was the outline of a large swastika. He looked at it closely. The swastika had circles at the right-hand points of the insignia, circles that spun off as if the artist were duplicating the ovals of a Palmer writing exercise. And flowing out of these ovals were unmistakable initials. *JD*. Then *Joh D., J Diet*. . . . The letters appeared at the end of each oval line. And beyond the final letters in each area were elaborately drawn ???

? ? ?

David folded the paper carefully and put it in his jacket pocket.

There were two remaining pages, so he took them out simultaneously. The page to the left had only one large, indecipherable scribble – once more circular, now angry – and meaningless. But on the second paper, again toward the bottom of the page, was a series of scroll–like markings that could be interpreted as Js and Ds, similar in flow to the letters after the swastika points on the second page. And opposite the final *D* was a strange horizontal obelisk, its taper on the right. There were lines on the side as though they were edges. . . . A bullet, perhaps, with bore markings. Underneath, on the next line of the paper to the left, were the same oval motions that brought to mind the Palmer exercise. Only they were firmer here, pressed harder into the yellow paper.

Suddenly David realized what he was staring at.

Walter Kendall had subconsciously outlined an obscene caricature of an erect penis and testicles.

Happy New Year, Mr. Kendall, thought Spaulding.

He put the page carefully into his pocket with its partner, returned the others and shut the drawer. He switched off the lamp, walked to the open door, turning to see if he had left everything as it was, and crossed into the reception room. He pulled Kendall's door shut and considered briefly whether to lock the tumblers in place.

It would be pointless to waste the time. The lock was old, simple; janitorial personnel in just about any building in New York would have a key, and it was more difficult inserting tumblers than releasing them. To hell with it.

A half hour later it occurred to him – in an instant of reflection – that this decision probably saved his life. The sixty, or ninety, or one-hundred-odd seconds he eliminated from his departure placed him in the position of an observer, not a target.

He put on the Rogers Peet overcoat, turned off the lights, and walked into the corridor to the bank of elevators. It was nearly seven, the day after New Year's, and the building was practically deserted. A single elevator was working. It had passed his floor, ascending to the upper stories, where it seemed to linger. He was about to use the stairs – the offices were on the third floor, it might be quicker – when he heard rapid, multiple footsteps coming up the staircase. The sound was incongruous. Moments ago the elevator had been in the lobby; why would two – more than two? – people be racing up the stairs at seven at night? There could be a dozen reasonable explanations, but his instincts made him consider *un*reasonable ones.

Silently, he ran to the opposite end of the short floor, where an intersecting corridor led to additional offices on the south side of the building. He rounded the corner and pressed himself against the wall. Since the assault in the Montgomery elevator, he carried a weapon – a small Beretta revolver – strapped to his chest, under his clothes. He flipped open his overcoat and undid the buttons of his jacket and shirt. Access to the pistol would be swift and efficient, should it be necessary.

It probably wouldn't be, he thought, as he heard the footsteps disappear.

Then he realized that they had not disappeared, they had faded, slowed down to a walk – a quiet, cautious walk. And then he heard the voices: whisper-like, indistinguishable. They came from around the edge of the wall, in the vicinity of the unmarked Meridian office, no more than thirty feet away.

He inched the flat of his face to the sharp, concrete corner and simultaneously reached his right hand under his shirt to the handle of the Beretta.

There were two men with their backs to him, facing the darkened glass of the unmarked office door. The shorter of the two put his face against the pane, hands to both temples to shut out the light from the corridor. He pulled back and looked at his partner, shaking his head negatively.

The taller man turned slightly, enough for Spaulding to recognize him.

It was the stranger in the recessed, darkened doorway on Fifty-second Street. The tall, sad-eyed man who spoke gently, in bastardized British-out-of-the-Balkans, and held him under the barrel of a thick, powerful weapon.

The man reached into his left overcoat pocket and gave a key to his friend. With his right hand he removed a pistol from his belt. It was a heavy-duty .45, army issue. At close range, David knew it would blow a person into the air and off the earth. The man nodded and spoke softly but clearly.

"He has to be. He didn't leave. I want him."

With these words the shorter man inserted the key and shoved at the door. It swung back slowly. Together, both men walked in.

At that precise moment the elevator grill could be heard opening, its metal frames ringing throughout the corridor. David could see the two men in the darkened reception room freeze, turn toward the open door and quickly shut it.

"*Chee-ryst Almighty!*" was the irate shout from the angry elevator operator as the grill rang shut with a clamor.

David knew it was the instant to move. Within seconds one or both men inside the deserted Meridian offices would realize that the elevator had stopped on the third floor because someone had pushed the button. Someone not in evidence, someone they had not met on the stairs. Someone still on the floor.

He spun around the edge of the wall and raced down the corridor toward the staircase. He didn't look back; he didn't bother to muffle his steps – it would have reduced his speed. His only concern was to get down those steps and out of the building. He leaped down the right-angled staircase to the in-between landing and whipped around the corner.

And then he stopped.

Below him, leaning against the railing, was the third man. He *knew* he'd heard more than two sets of feet racing up the staircase minutes ago. The man was startled, his eyes widened in shocked recognition and his right hand jerked backwards toward his coat pocket. Spaulding didn't have to be told what he was reaching for.

David sprang off the landing straight down at the man, making contact in midair, his hands clawing for the man's throat and right arm. He gripped the skin on the neck below the left ear and tore at it, slamming the man's head into the concrete wall as he did so. David's heavier body crushed into the would-be sentry's chest; he twisted the right arm nearly out of its shoulder socket.

The man screamed and collapsed; the scalp was lacerated, blood flowing out of the section of his skull that had crashed into the wall.

David could hear the sounds of a door being thrown open and men running. Above him, of course, one floor above him.

He freed his entangled legs from the unconscious body and raced down the remaining flight of stairs to the lobby. The elevator had, moments ago, let out its cargo of passengers; the last few were going out the front entrance. If any had heard the prolonged scream from the battered man sixty feet away up the staircase, none acknowledged it.

David rushed into the stragglers, elbowing his way through the wide double doors and onto the sidewalk. He turned east and ran as fast as he could.

He had walked over forty city blocks – some two miles in Basque country, but here infinitely less pleasant.

He had come to several decisions. The problem was how to implement them.

He could not stay in New York; not without facing risks, palpably unacceptable. And he had to get to Buenos Aires at once, before any of those hunting him in New York knew he was gone.

For they were hunting him now; that much was clear.

It would be suicide to return to the Montgomery. Or for that matter, to the unmarked Meridian offices in the morning. He could handle both with telephone calls. He would tell the hotel that he had been suddenly transferred to Pennsylvania; could the Montgomery management pack and hold his things? He'd call later about his bill. . . .

Kendall was on his way to Argentina. It wouldn't make any difference what the Meridian office was told.

Suddenly, he thought of Eugene Lyons.

He was a little sad about Lyons. Not the man (of course the man, he reconsidered quickly, but not the man's affliction, in this instance), but the fact that he would have little chance to develop any sense of rapport before Buenos Aires. Lyons might take his sudden absence as one more rejection in a long series. And the scientist might really need his help in Buenos Aires, at least in the area of German translation. David decided that he had to have the books Lyons selected for him; he had to have as solid a grasp of Lyons's language as was possible.

And then David realized where his thoughts were leading him.

For the next few hours the safest places in New York were the Meridian offices and St. Luke's Hospital.

After his visits to both locations he'd get out to Mitchell Field and telephone Brigadier General Swanson.

The answer to the violent enigma of the past seven days – from the Azores to a staircase on Thirty-eighth Street and everything in between – was in Buenos Aires.

Swanson did not know it and could not help; Fairfax was infiltrated and could not be told. And *that* told *him* something.

He was on his own. A man had two choices in such a dilemma: take himself out of strategy, or dig for identities and blow the covers off.

The first choice would be denied him. The brigadier, Swanson, was paranoid on the subject of the gyroscopic designs. And Rhinemann. There'd be no out of strategy.

That left the second: the identity of those behind the enigma.

A feeling swept over him, one he had not experienced in several years: the fear of sudden inadequacy. He was confronted with an extraordinary problem for which there was no pat – or complicated – solution in the north country. No unraveling that came with moves or countermoves whose strategies he had mastered in Basque and Navarre.

He was suddenly in another war. One he was not familiar with; one that raised doubts about himself.

He saw an unoccupied taxi, its roof light dimly lit, as if embarrassed to announce its emptiness. He looked up at the street sign; he was on Sheridan Square – it accounted for the muted sounds of jazz that floated up from cellars and surged down crowded side streets. The Village was warming up for another evening.

He raised his hand for the taxi; the driver did not see him. He started running as the cab proceeded up the street to the corner traffic light. Suddenly he realized that someone else on the other side of the square was rushing toward the empty taxi; the man was closer to it than Spaulding, his right hand was gesturing.

It was now terribly important to David that he reach the car first. He gathered speed and ran into the street, dodging pedestrians, momentarily blocked by two automobiles that were bumper to bumper. He spread his hands from hood to trunk and jumped over into the middle of the street and continued racing toward his objective.

Objective.

He reached the taxi no more than half a second after the other man.

Goddamn it! It was the obstruction of the two automobiles!

Obstruction.

He slammed his hand on the door panel, preventing the other man from pulling it open. The man looked up at Spaulding's face, at Spaulding's eyes.

"Christ, fella. I'll wait for another one," the man said quickly.

David was embarrassed. What the hell was he *doing*?

The doubts? The goddamned doubts.

"No, really, I'm terribly sorry." He mumbled the words, smiling apologetically. "You take it. I'm in no hurry. . . . Sorry again."

He turned and walked rapidly across the street into the crowds of Sheridan Square.

He could have had the taxi. That was the important thing.

Jesus! The treadmill never let up.

Part Two

22

BUENOS AIRES, ARGENTINA

The Pan American Clipper left Tampa at eight in the morning, with scheduled coastline stops at Caracas, São Luis, Salvador, and Rio de Janeiro before the final twelve hundred miles to Buenos Aires. David was listed on the passenger invoice as Mr. Donald Scanlan of Cincinnati, Ohio; occupation: mining surveyor. It was a temporary cover for the journey only. "Donald Scanlan" would disappear after the Clipper landed at the Aeroparque in Buenos Aires. The initials were the same as his own for the simple reason that it was so easy to forget a monogrammed gift or the first letter of a hastily written signature. Especially if one was preoccupied or tired . . . or afraid.

Swanson had been close to panic when David reached him from the Mitchell Field Operations Room in New York. As a source control, Swanson was about as decisive as a bewildered bird dog. Any deviation from Kendall's schedule Kendall's instructions, really – was abhorrent to him. And Kendall wasn't even *leaving* for Buenos Aires until the following morning.

David had not wasted complicated explanations on the general. As far as he was concerned, three attempts had been made on his life at least, they could be so interpreted and if the general wanted his "services" in Buenos Aires, he'd better get down there while he was still in one piece and functioning.

Were the attempts – the attacks – related to Buenos Aires? Swanson had asked the question as though he were afraid to name the Argentine city.

David was honest: there was no way to tell. The answer was in Buenos Aires. It was reasonable to consider the possibility, but not to assume it.

"That's what Pace said," had been Swanson's reply. "Consider, don't assume."

"Ed was generally right about such things."

"He said when you operated in Lisbon, you were often involved in messy situations in the field."

"True. I doubt that Ed knew the particulars, though. But he was right in what he was trying to tell you. There are a lot of people in Portugal and Spain who'd rather see me dead than alive. Or at least they think they would. They could never be sure. Standard procedure, general."

There had been a prolonged pause on the Washington line. Finally, Swanson

577

had said the words. "You realize, Spaulding, that we may have to replace you."

"Of course. You can do so right now, if you like." David had been sincere. He wanted very much to return to Lisbon. To go into the north country. To Valdero's. To find out about a cryp named Marshall.

"No. . . .No, everything's too far along. The designs. They're the important thing. Nothing else matters."

The remainder of the conversation concerned the details of transportation, American and Argentine currency, replenishing of a basic wardrobe, and luggage. Logistics which were not in the general's frame of reference and for which David took responsibility. The final command – request – was delivered, not by the general, but by Spaulding.

Fairfax was not to be informed of his whereabouts. Nor was anyone else for that matter, except the embassy in Buenos Aires; but make every effort to keep the information from Fairfax.

Why? Did Spaulding think . . .

"There's a leak in Fairfax, general. You might pass that on to the White House cellars."

"That's impossible!"

"Tell that to Ed Pace's widow."

David looked out the Clipper window. The pilot, moments ago, had informed the passengers that they were passing over the huge coastal lake of Mirim in Uruguay. Soon they'd be over Montevideo, forty minutes from Buenos Aires.

Buenos Aires. The unfocused picture, the blurred figures of Leslie Jenner Hawkwood, the cryptographer Marshall, a man named Franz Altmüller; strange but committed men on Fifty-second and Thirty-eighth streets – in a darkened doorway, in a building after office hours, on a staircase. A man in an elevator who was so unafraid to die. An enemy who displayed enormous courage . . . or misguided zealousness. A maniac.

The answer to the enigma was in Buenos Aires, less than an hour away. The city was an hour away, the answer much longer. But no more than three weeks if his instincts were right. By the time the gyroscopic designs were delivered.

He would begin slowly, as he always did with a new field problem. Trying first to melt into the surroundings, absorb his cover; be comfortable, facile in his relationships. It shouldn't be difficult. His cover was merely an extension of Lisbon's: the wealthy trilingual attaché whose background, parents, and prewar associations in the fashionable centers of Europe made him a desirable social buffer for any ambassador's dinner table. He was an attractive addition to the delicate world of a neutral capital; and if there were those who thought someone, somewhere, had used money and influence to secure him such combat-exempt employment, so be it. It was denied emphatically, but not vehemently; there was a difference.

The "extension" for Buenos Aires was direct and afforded him top-secret classification. He was acting as a liaison between New York-London banking circles and the German ex-patriot Erich Rhinemann. Washington approved, of course; postwar financing in areas of reconstruction and industrial rebuilding were going to be international problems. Rhinemann could not be overlooked, not in the civilized marble halls of Berne and Geneva.

David's thoughts returned to the book on his lap. It was the second of six volumes Eugene Lyons had chosen for him.

"Donald Scanlan" went through the Aeroparque customs without difficulty. Even the embassy liaison, who checked in all Americans, seemed unaware of his identity.

His single suitcase in hand, David walked to the taxi station and stood on the cement platform looking at the drivers standing beside their vehicles. He wasn't prepared to assume the name of Spaulding or to be taken directly to the embassy just yet. He wanted to assure himself that "Donald Scanlan" was accepted for what he was – a mining surveyor, nothing more, that there was no unusual interest in such a man. For if there were, it would point to David Spaulding, Military Intelligence, Fairfax and Lisbon graduate.

He selected an obese, pleasant-looking driver in the fourth cab from the front of the line. There were protests from those in front, but David pretended not to understand. "Donald Scanlan" might know a smattering of Spanish, but certainly not the epithets employed by the disgruntled drivers cheated out of a fare.

Once inside he settled back and gave instructions to the unctuous driver. He told the man he had nearly an hour to waste before he was to be met – the meeting place not mentioned – and asked if the driver would give him a short tour of the city. The tour would serve two purposes: he could position himself so that he could constantly check for surveillance, and he would learn the main points of the city.

The driver, impressed by David's educated, grammatical Spanish, assumed the role of tour director and drove out of the airport's winding lanes to the exit of the huge Parque 3 de Febrero in which the field was centered.

Thirty minutes later David had filled a down pages with notes. The city was like a European insert on the southern continent. It was a strange mixture of Paris, Rome and middle Spain. The streets were not city streets, they were boulevards: wide, lined with color. Fountains and statuary everywhere. The Avenida 9 de Julio might have been a larger Via Veneto or Saint-Germain-des-Près. The sidewalk cafes, profuse with brightly decorated awnings and greenery from hundreds of planter boxes, were doing a brisk summer afternoon business. The fact that it *was* summer in Argentina was emphasized for David by the perspiration on his neck and shirt front. The driver admitted that the day was inordinately warm, in the high seventies.

David asked to be driven – among other places – to a district called San Telmo. The cab owner nodded appreciatively, as if he had accurately assessed the rich American. Soon Spaulding understood. San Telmo was as Kendall had noted: elegant, secluded, beautifully kept old houses and apartment buildings with wrought-iron balustrades and brilliantly blossoming flowers lining the spotless streets.

Lyons would be comfortable.

From San Telmo the driver doubled back into the inner city and began the tour from the banks of the Rio de la Plata.

The Plaza de Mayo, the Cabildo, the Casa Rosada, Calle Rivadavia. The names filled David's notebook; these were the streets, the squares, the locations he would absorb quickly.

La Boca. The waterfront, south of the city; this, the driver said, was no place for the tourist.

The Calle Florida. Here was the finest shopping area in all South America. The driver could take his American to several store owners personally known to him and extraordinary purchases could be made.

Sorry, there was no time. But David wrote in his notebook that traffic was banned at the borders of the Calle Florida.

The driver then sped out the Avenida Santa Fé toward, the Palermo. No sight in Buenos Aires was as beautiful as the Palermo.

What interested David more than the beauty was the huge park – or series of individual parks; the quiet, immense, artificial lake. The acres of botanical gardens; the enormous zoo complex with rows of cages and buildings.

Beauty, yes. Secure areas of contact, more so. The Palermo might come in handy.

An hour had passed; there were no automobiles following the taxi. "Donald Scanlan" had not been under surveillance; David Spaulding could emerge.

Quietly.

He instructed the driver to leave him off at the cabstand outside the entrance to the Palermo zoo. He was to meet his party there. The driver looked crestfallen. Was there no hotel? No place of residence?

Spaulding did not reply, he simply asked the fare and quickly held out the amount. No more questions were in order.

David spent an additional fifteen minutes inside the zoo, actually enjoying it. He bought an ice from a vendor, wandered past the cages of marmosets and orangutans – finding extraordinary resemblances to friends and enemies – and when he felt comfortable (as only a field man can feel comfortable), walked out to the cabstand.

He waited another five minutes while mothers and governesses and children entered the available taxis. It was his turn.

"The American embassy, *par favor*."

Ambassador Henderson Granville allowed the new attaché a half hour. There would be other days when they could sit and chat at length, but Sundays were hectic. The rest of Buenos Aires might be at church or at play; the diplomatic corps was at work. He had two garden parties still to attend – telephone calls would be made detailing the departures and arrivals of the

German and the Japanese guests; *his* arrivals and departures would be timed accordingly. And after the second garden-bore there was dinner at the Brazilian embassy, neither German nor Japanese interference was anticipated. Brazil was close to an open break.

"The Italians, you realize," said Granville, smiling at David, "don't count any longer. Never did really; not down here. They spend most of their time cornering us in restaurants, or calling from public phones, explaining how Mussolini ruined the country."

"Not too different from Lisbon."

"I'm afraid they're the only pleasant similarity. . . .I won't bore you with a tedious account of the upheavals we've experienced here, but a quick sketch – and emphasis – will help you adjust. You've read up, I assume."

"I haven't had much time. I left Lisbon only a week ago. I know that the Castillo government was overthrown."

"Last June. Inevitable. . . .Ramón Castillo was as inept a president as Argentina ever had, and it's had its share of buffoons. The economy was disastrous: agriculture and industry came virtually to a halt; his cabinet never made provisions to fill the beef market void created by the British struggle, even though the lot of them figured John Bull was finished. He deserved to be thrown out. . . .Unfortunately, what came in the front door – marched in phalanx up the Rivadavia, to be more precise hardly makes our lives easier."

"That's the military council, isn't it? The junta?"

Granville gestured with his delicate hands, the chiseled features of his aging, aristocratic face formed a sardonic grimace. "The Grupo de Oficiales Unidos! As unpleasant a band of goose-stepping opportunists as you will meet . . . I daresay, anywhere. You know, of course, the entire army was trained by the Wehrmacht officer corps. Add to that jovial premise the hot Latin temperament, economic chaos, a neutrality that's enforced but not believed in, and what have you got? A suspension of the political apparatus; no checks and balances. A police state rife with corruption."

"What maintains the neutrality?"

"The infighting, primarily. The GOU – that's what we call it – has more factions than the '29 Reichstag. They're all jockeying for the power spots. And naturally, the cold fear of an American fleet and air force right up the street, so to speak. . . .The GOU has been reappraising its judgments during the past five months. The colonels are beginning to wonder about their mentors' thousand-year crusade; extremely impressed by our supply and production lines."

"They should be. We've . . ."

"And there's another aspect," interrupted Granville thoughtfully. "There's a small, very wealthy community of Jews here. Your Erich Rhinemann, for example. The GOU isn't prepared to openly advocate the solutions of Julius Streicher . . . It's already used Jewish money to keep alive lines of credit pretty well chewed up by Castillo. The colonels are afraid of financial manipulations, most military people are. But there's a great deal of money to be made in this war. The colonels intend to make it. . . .Do I sketch a recognizable picture?"

"A complicated one."

"I daresay. . . .We have a maxim here that serves quite well. Today's friend will probably be on the Axis payroll tomorrow; conversely, yesterday's Berlin courier might be for sale next week. Keep your options open and your opinions private. And publicly . . . allow for a touch more flexibility than might be approved of at another post. It's tolerated."

"And expected?" asked David.

"Both."

David lit a cigarette. He wanted to shift the conversation; old Granville was one of those ambassadors, professorial by nature, who would go on analyzing the subtleties of his station all day if someone listened. Such men were usually the best diplomats but not always the most desirable liaisons in times of active practicality. Henderson Granville was a good man, though his concerns shone in his eyes, and they were fair concerns.

"I imagine Washington has outlined my purpose here."

"Yes. I wish I could say I approved. Not of you; you've got your instructions. And I suppose international finance will continue long after Herr Hitler has shrieked his last scream. . . .Perhaps I'm no better than the GOU. Money matters can be most distasteful."

"These in particular, I gather."

"Again, yes. Erich Rhinemann is a sworn companion of the wind. A powerful companion, make no mistake, but totally without conscience; a hurricane's morality. Unquestionably the least honorable man I've ever met. I think it's criminal that his resources make him acceptable to London and New York."

"Perhaps necessary is a more appropriate term."

"I'm sure that's the rationalization, at any rate."

"It's mine."

"Of course. Forgive an old man's obsolete limits of necessity. But we have no quarrel. You have an assignment. What can I do for you? I understand it's very little."

"Very little indeed, sir. Just have me listed on the embassy index; any kind of office space will do as long as it has a door and a telephone. And I'd like to meet your cryp. I'll have codes to send."

"My word, that sounds ominous," said Granville, smiling without humor.

"Routine, sir. Washington relay; simple Yes and Nos."

"Very well. Our head cryptographer is named Ballard. Nice fellow; speaks seven or eight languages and is an absolute whiz at parlor games. You'll meet him directly. What else?"

"I'd like an apartment . . ."

"Yes, we know," interrupted Granville gently, snatching a brief look at the wall clock. "Mrs. Cameron has scouted one she thinks you'll approve. . . .Of course, Washington gave us no indication of your length of stay. So Mrs. Cameron took it for three months."

"That's far too long. I'll straighten it out. . . .I think that's almost all, Mr. Ambassador. I know you're in a hurry."

"I'm afraid I am."

David got out of his chair, as did Granville. "Oh, one thing, sir. Would this Ballard have an embassy index? I'd like to learn the names here."

"There aren't that many," said Granville, leveling his gaze at David, a subtle note of disapproval in his voice. "Eight or ten would be those you'd normally come in contact with. And I can assure you we have our own security measures."

David accepted the rebuke. "That wasn't my point, sir. I really *do* like to familiarize myself with the names."

"Yes, of course." Granville came around the desk and walked Spaulding to the door. "Chat with my secretary for a few minutes. I'll get hold of Ballard; he'll show you around."

"Thank you, sir." Spaulding extended his hand to Granville, and as he did so he realized for the first time how tall the man was.

"You know," said the ambassador, releasing David's hand, "there was a question I wanted to ask you, but the answer will have to wait for another time. I'm late already."

"What was that?"

"I've been wondering why the boys on Wall Street and the Strand sent *you*. I can't imagine there being a dearth of experienced bankers in New York or London, can you?"

"There probably isn't. But then I'm only a liaison carrying messages; information best kept private, I gather. I *have* had experience in those areas . . . in a neutral country."

Granville smiled once more and once more there was no humor conveyed. "Yes, of course. I was sure there was a reason."

23

Ballard shared two traits common to most cryptographers, thought David. He was a casual cynic and a fount of information. Qualities, Spaulding believed, developed over years of deciphering other men's secrets only to find the great majority unimportant. He was also cursed with the first name of Robert, by itself acceptable but when followed by Ballard, invariably reduced to Bobby. Bobby Ballard. It had the ring of a 1920s socialite or the name in a cereal box cartoon.

He was neither. He was a linguist with a mathematical mind and a shock of red hair on top of a medium-sized, muscular body; a pleasant man.

"That's our home," Ballard was saying. "You've seen the working sections; big, rambling, baroque and goddamned hot this time of year. I hope you're smart and have your own apartment."

"Don't you? Do you live *here?*"

"It's easier. My dials are very inconsiderate, they hum at all hours. Better than scrambling down from Chacarita or Telmo. And it's not bad; we stay out of each other's way pretty much."

"Oh? A lot of you here?"

"No. They alternate. Six, usually. In the two wings, east and south. Granville has the north apartments. Besides him, Jean Cameron and I are the only permanents. You'll meet Jean tomorrow, unless we run into her on the way out with the old man. She generally goes with him to the diplobores."

"The what?"

"Diplo-bores. The old man's word . . . contraction. I'm surprised he didn't use it with you. He's proud of it. Diplobore is an embassy duty bash." They were in a large empty reception room; Ballard was opening a pair of French doors leading out onto a short balcony. In the distance could be seen the waters of the Rio de la Plata and the estuary basin of the Puerto Nuevo, Buenos Aires' main port. "Nice view, isn't it?"

"Certainly is." David joined the cryptographer on the balcony. "Does this Jean Cameron and the ambassador . . . 1 mean, are they . . . ?"

"Jean and the old *man?*" Ballard laughed loud and good-naturedly. "Christ, no! . . . Come to think of it, I don't know why it strikes me so funny. I suppose there're a lot of people who think that. And *that's* funny."

"Why?"

"Sad-funny, I guess I should say," continued Ballard without interruption. "The old man and the Cameron family go back to the original Maryland money. Eastern Shore yacht clubs, blazer jackets, tennis in the morning – you know: diplomat territory. Jean's family was part of it, too. She married this

Cameron; knew him since they could play doctor together in their Abercrombie pup tents. A rich-people romance, childhood sweethearts. They got married; the war came; he chucked his law books for a TBF – aircraft carrier pilot. He was killed in the Leyte Gulf. That was last year. She went a little crazy; maybe more than a little."

"So the . . . Granville brought her down here?"

"That's right."

"Nice therapy, if you can afford it."

"She'd probably agree with that." Ballard walked back into the reception room; Spaulding followed. "But most people will tell you she pays her dues for the treatment. She works damned hard and knows what she's doing. Has rotten hours, too; what with the diplobores."

"Where's *Mrs.* Granville?"

"No idea. She divorced the old man ten, fifteen years ago."

"I still say it's nice work if you can get it." David was thinking, In an offhand way, of several hundred thousand other women whose husbands had been killed, living with reminders every day. He dismissed his thoughts; they weren't his concerns.

"Well, she's qualified."

"What?" David was looking at a rococo-styled corner pillar in the wall, not really listening.

"Jean spent four years – off and on – down here as a kid. Her father was in Foreign Service; probably would have been an ambassador by now if he'd stuck with it. . . .Come on, I'll show you the office Granville assigned you. Maintenance should have it tidied up by now," Ballard smiled.

"You've been employing a diversion," laughed David, following the cryp out the door into another hallway.

"I had to. You've got a room in the back. So far back it's been used for storage, I think."

"Obviously I made points with Granville."

"You sure did. He can't figure you out. . . .Me? I don't try." Ballard turned left into still another intersecting hallway. "This is the south wing. Offices on the first and second floors; not many, three on each. Apartments on the third and fourth. The roof is great for sunbathing, if you like that sort of thing."

"Depends on the company, I suppose."

The two men approached a wide staircase, preparing to veer to the left beyond it, when a feminine voice called down from the second landing.

"Bobby, is that you?"

"It's Jean," said Ballard. "Yes," he called out. "I'm with Spaulding. Come on down and meet the new recruit with enough influence to get his own apartment right off."

"Wait'll he sees the apartment!"

Jean Cameron came into sight from around the corner landing. She was a moderately tall woman, slender and dressed in a floor-length cocktail gown at once vivid with color yet simple in design. Her light brown hair was shoulder length, full and casual. Her face was a combination of striking features blended into a soft whole; wide, alive blue eyes; a thin, sharply etched nose; lips medium full and set as if in a half-smile. Her very clear skin was bronzed by the Argentine sun.

David saw that Ballard was watching him, anticipating his reaction to the girl's loveliness. Ballard's expression was humorously sardonic, and Spaulding read the message: Ballard had been to the font and found it empty – for those seeking other than a few drops of cool water. Ballard was now a friend to the lady; he knew better than to try being anything else.

Jean Cameron seemed embarrassed by her introduction on the staircase. She descended rapidly, her lips parted into one of the most genuine smiles David had seen in years. Genuine and totally devoid of innuendo.

"Welcome," she said, extending her hand. "Thank heavens I have a chance to apologize before you walk into that place. You may change your mind and move right back here."

"It's that bad?" David saw that Jean wasn't quite as young at close range as she seemed on the staircase. She was past thirty; comfortably past. And she seemed aware of his inspection, the approbation – or lack of it – unimportant to her.

"Oh, it's all right for a limited stay. You can't get anything else on that basis, not if you're American. But it's small."

Her handshake was firm, almost masculine, thought Spaulding. "I appreciate your taking the trouble. I'm sorry to have caused it."

"No one else here could have gotten you anything but a hotel," said Ballard, touching the girl's shoulder; was the contact protective? wondered David. "The *porteños* trust Mother Cameron. Not the rest of us."

"*Porteños*," said Jean in response to Spaulding's questioning expression, "are the people who live in BA. . . ."

"And BA – don't tell me – stands for Montevideo," replied David.

"Aw, they sent us a *bright* one," said Ballard.

"You'll get used to it," continued Jean. "Everyone in the American and English settlements calls it BA. Montevideo, of course," she added, smiling. "I think we see it so often on reports, we just do it automatically."

"Wrong," interjected Ballard. "The vowel juxtaposition in 'Buenos Aires' is uncomfortable for British speech."

"That's something else you'll learn during your stay, Mr. Spaulding," said Jean Cameron, looking affectionately at Ballard. "Be careful offering opinions around Bobby. He has a penchant for disagreeing."

"Never so," answered the cryp. "I simply care enough for my fellow prisoners to want to enlighten them. Prepare them for the outside when they get paroled."

'Well, I've got a temporary pass right now, and if I don't get over to the ambassador's office, he'll start on that damned address system. . . .Welcome again, Mr. Spaulding."

"Please. The name's David."

"Mine's Jean. Bye," said the girl, dashing down the hallway, calling back to Ballard. "Bobby? You've got the address and the key? For . . . David's place?"

"Yep. Go get irresponsibly drunk, I'll handle everything."

Jean Cameron disappeared through a door in the right wall.

"She's very attractive," said Spaulding, "and you two are good friends. I should apologize for . . ."

"No, you shouldn't," interrupted Ballard. "Nothing to apologize for. You formed a quick judgment on isolated facts. I'd've done the same, thought the same. Not that you've changed your mind; no reason to, really."

"She's right. You disagree . . . before you know what you're disagreeing to; and then you debate your disagreement. And if you go on, you'll probably challenge your last position."

"You know what? I can follow that. Isn't it frightening?"

"You guys are a separate breed," said David, chuckling, following Ballard beyond the stairs into a smaller corridor.

"Let's take a quick look at your Siberian cubicle and then head over to your other cell. It's on Córdoba; we're on Corrientes. It's about ten minutes from here."

David thanked Bobby Ballard once again and shut the apartment door. He had pleaded exhaustion from the trip, preceded by too much welcome home in New York – and God knew that was the truth – and would Ballard take a raincheck for dinner?

Alone now, he inspected the apartment; it wasn't intolerable at all. It was small: a bedroom, a sitting room-kitchen, and a bath. But there was a dividend Jean Cameron hadn't mentioned. The rooms were on the first floor, and at the rear was a tiny brick-leveled patio surrounded by a tall concrete wall, profuse with hanging vines and drooping flowers from immense pots on the ledge. In the center of the enclosure was a gnarled fruit-bearing tree he could not identify; around the trunk were three rope-webbed chairs that had seen better days but looked extremely comfortable. As far as he was concerned, the dividend made the dwelling.

Ballard had pointed out that his section of the Avenida Córdoba was just over the borderline from the commercial area, the "downtown" complex of Buenos Aires. Quasi residential, yet near enough to stores and restaurants to be easy for a newcomer.

David picked up the telephone; the dial tone was delayed but eventually there. He replaced it and walked across the small room to the refrigerator, an American Sears Roebuck. He opened it and smiled. The Cameron girl had provided – or had somebody provide – several basic items: milk, butter, bread, eggs, coffee. Then happily he spotted two bottles of wine: an Orfila *tinto* and a Colón *blanco*. He closed the refrigerator and went back into the bedroom.

He unpacked his single suitcase, unwrapping a bottle of Scotch, and remembered that he'd have to buy additional clothes in the morning. Ballard had offered to go with him to a men's shop in the Calle Florida – if his goddamned dials weren't "humming." He placed the books Eugene Lyons had given him on the bedside table. He had gone through two of them; he was beginning to gain confidence in the aerophysicists' language. He would need comparable studies in German to be really secure. He would cruise around the bookshops in the German settlement tomorrow; he wasn't looking for definitive texts, just enough to understand the terms. It was really a minor part of his assignment, he understood that.

Suddenly, David remembered Walter Kendall. Kendall was either in Buenos Aires by now or would be arriving within hours. The accountant had left the United States at approximately the same time he had, but Kendall's flight from New York was more direct, with far fewer stopovers.

He wondered whether it would be feasible to go out to the airport and trace Kendall. If he hadn't arrived, he could wait for him; if he had, it would be simple enough to check the hotels according to Ballard there were only three or four good ones.

On the other hand, any additional time – more than absolutely essential – spent with the manipulating accountant was not a pleasant prospect. Kendall would be upset at finding him in Buenos Aires before he'd given the order to Swanson. Kendall, no doubt, would demand explanations beyond those David wished to give; probably send angry cables to an already strung-out brigadier general.

There were no benefits in hunting down Walter Kendall until Kendall expected to find him. Only liabilities.

He had other things to do: the unfocused picture. He could begin that search far better alone.

David walked back into the living room-kitchen carrying the Scotch and took out a tray of ice from the refrigerator. He made himself a drink and looked over at the double doors leading to his miniature patio. He would spend a few quiet twilight moments in the January summertime breeze of Buenos Aires.

The sun was fighting its final descent beyond the city; the last orange rays were filtering through the thick foliage of the unidentified fruit tree. Underneath, David stretched his legs and leaned back in the rope-webbed chair. He realized that if he kept his eyes closed for any length of time, they would not reopen for a number of hours. He had to watch that; long experience in the field had taught him to eat something before sleeping.

Eating had long since lost its pleasure for him – it was merely a necessity directly related to his energy level. He wondered if the pleasure would ever come back; whether so much he had put aside would return. Lisbon had probably the best accommodations – food, shelter, comfort – of all the major cities, excepting New York, on both continents. And now he was on a third continent, in a city that boasted undiluted luxury.

But for him it was the field – as much as was the north country in Spain. As much as Basque and Navarre, and the freezing nights in the Galician hills or the sweat-prone silences in ravines, waiting for patrols – waiting to kill.

So much. So alien.

He brought his head forward, took a long drink from the glass and let his neck arch back into the frame of the chair. A small bird was chattering away in the midsection of the tree, annoyed at his intrusion. It reminded David of how he would listen for such birds in the north country. They telegraphed the approach of men unseen, often falling into different rhythms that he began to identify – or thought he identified – with the numbers of the unseen, approaching patrols.

Then David realized that the small chattering bird was not concerned with him. It hopped upward, still screeching its harsh little screech, only faster now, more strident.

There was someone else.

Through half-closed eyes, David focused above, beyond the foliage. He did so without moving any part of his body or head, as if the last moments were approaching before sleep took over.

The apartment house had four stories and a roof that appeared to have a gentle slope covered in a terra-cotta tile of sorts – brownish pink in color. The windows of the rooms above him were mostly open to the breezes off the Rio de la Plata. He could hear snatches of subdued conversation, nothing threatening, no loud vibrations. It was the Buenos Aires siesta hour, according to Ballard; quite different from Rome's afternoon or the Paris lunch. Dinner in BA was very late, by the rest of the world's schedule. Ten, ten-thirty, even midnight was not out of the question.

The screeching bird was not bothered by the inhabitants of the Córdoba apartment house; yet still he kept up his strident alarms.

And then David saw why.

On the roof, obscured but not hidden by the branches of the fruit tree, were the outlines of two men.

They were crouched, staring downward; staring, he was sure, at him.

Spaulding judged the position of the main intersecting tree limb and rolled his head slightly, as if the long-awaited sleep were upon him, his neck resting in exhaustion on his right shoulder, the drink barely held by a relaxed hand, millimeters from the brick pavement.

It helped; he could see better, not well. Enough, however, to make out the sharp, straight silhouette of a rifle barrel, the orange sun careening off its black steel. It was stationary, in an arrest position under the arm of the man on the right. No movement was made to raise it, to aim it; it remained immobile, cradled.

Somehow, it was more ominous that way, thought Spaulding. As though in the arms of a killer guard who was sure his prisoner could not possibly vault the stockade; there was plenty of time to shoulder and fire.

David carried through his charade. He raised his hand slightly and let his drink fall. The sound of the minor crash "awakened" him; he shook the pretended sleep from his head and rubbed his eyes with his fingers. As he did so, he maneuvered his face casually upward. The figures on the roof had stepped back on the terracotta tiles. There would be no shots. Not directed at him.

He picked up a few pieces of the glass, rose from the chair and walked into the apartment as a tired man does when annoyed with his own carelessness. Slowly, with barely controlled irritation.

Once he crossed the saddle of the door, beneath the sightline of the roof, he threw the glass fragments into a wastebasket and walked rapidly into the bedroom. He opened the top drawer of the bureau, separated some handkerchiefs and withdrew his revolver.

He clamped it inside his belt and picked up his jacket from the chair in which he'd thrown it earlier. He put it on, satisfied that it concealed the weapon.

He crossed out into the living room, to the apartment door, and opened it silently.

The staircase was against the left wall and David swore to himself, cursing the architect of this particular Avenida Córdoba building – or the profuseness of lumber in Argentina. The stairs were made of wood, the brightly polished wax not concealing the obvious fact that they were ancient and probably squeaked like hell.

He closed his apartment door and approached the staircase, putting his feet on the first step.

It creaked the solid creak of antique shops.

He had four flights to go; the first three were unimportant. He took the steps two at a time, discovering that if he hugged the wall, the noise of his ascent was minimized.

Sixty seconds later he faced a closed door marked with a sign in goddamned curlicued Castilian lettering:

El Techo.

The roof.

The door, as the stairs, was old. Decades of seasonal heat and humidity had caused the wood to swell about the hinges; the borders were forced into the frame.

It, too, would scream his arrival if he opened it slowly.

There was no other way: he slipped the weapon out of his belt and took one step back on the tiny platform. He judged the frame – the concrete walls surrounding the old wooden door and with an adequate intake of breath, he pulled at the handle, yanked the door open and jumped diagonally into the right wall, slamming his back against the concrete.

The two men whirled around, stunned. They were thirty feet from David at the edge of the sloping roof. The man with the rifle hesitated, then raised the weapon into waist-firing position. Spaulding had his pistol aimed directly into the man's chest. However, the man with the gun did not have the look of one about to fire at a target; the hesitation was deliberate, not the result of panic or indecision.

The second man shouted in Spanish; David recognized the accent as southern Spain, not Argentine. *"Por favor, señor!"*

Spaulding replied in English to establish their understanding, or lack of it. "Lower that rifle. *Now!*"

The first man did so, holding it by the stock. "You are in error, he said in halting English. "There have been . . . how do you say, *ladrones* . . . thieves in the neighborhood."

David walked over the metal transom onto the roof, holding his pistol on the two men. "You're not very convincing. *Se dan corte, amigos.* You're not from Buenos Aires."

"There are a great many people in this neighborhood who are as we: displaced, *señor.* This is a community of . . . not the native born," said the second man.

"You're telling me you weren't up here for my benefit? You weren't watching me?"

"It was coincidental, I assure you," said the man with the rifle.

"Es la verdad," added the other. "Two *habitaciones* have been broken into during the past week. The police do not help; we are . . . *extranjeros*, foreigners to them. We protect ourselves."

Spaulding watched the men closely. There was no waver in either man's expression, no hint of lies. No essential fear.

"I'm with the American embassy," said David curtly. There was no reaction from either *extranjero.* "I must ask you for identification."

"Qué cosa?" The man with the gun.

"Papers. Your names. . . .*Certificados."*

"Por cierto, en seguida." The second man reached back into his trousers pocket; Spaulding raised the pistol slightly, in warning.

The man hesitated, now showing his fear. "Only a *registro, señor.* We all must carry them. . . .Please. In my *cartera."*

David held out his left hand as the second man gave him a cheap leather wallet. He flipped it open with minor feelings of regret. There was a kind of helplessness about the two *extranjeros*; he'd seen the look thousands of times. Franco's Falangistas were experts at provoking it.

He looked quickly down at the cellophane window of the billfold; it was cracked with age.

Suddenly, the barrel of the rifle came crashing across his right wrist; the pain was excruciating. Then his hand was being twisted expertly inward and down; he had no choice but to release the weapon and try to kick it away on the sloping roof. To hold it would mean breaking his wrist.

He did so as his left arm was being hammerlocked – again expertly – up over his neck. He lashed his foot out at the unarmed *extranjero*, who had hold of his hand. He caught him in the stomach and as the man bent forward, David crossed his weight and kicked again, sending the man tumbling down on the tiled incline.

David fell in the thrust direction of the hammerlock – downward, to his rear – and as the first man countered the position, Spaulding brought his right elbow back up, crushing into the man's groin. The arm was released as the *extranjero* tried to regain his balance.

He wasn't quick enough; Spaulding whipped to his left and brought his knee up into the man's throat. The rifle clattered on the tiles and rolled downward on the slope. The man sank, blood dribbling from his mouth where his teeth had punctured the skin.

Spaulding heard the sound behind him and turned.

He was too late. The second *extranjero* was over him, and David could hear the whistling of his own pistol piercing the air above him, crashing down into his skull.

All was black. Void.

"They described the right attitude but the wrong section of town," said Ballard, sitting across the room from David, who held an ice pack to his head. "The *extranjeros* are concentrated in the west areas of the La Boca district. They've got a hell of a crime rate over there; the *policia* prefer strolling the parks rather than those streets. And the Grupo – the GOU – has no love for *extranjeros*."

"You're no help," said Spaulding, shifting the ice pack around in circles on the back of his head.

"Well, they weren't out to kill you. They could have thrown you off or just left you on the edge; five to one you'd've rolled over and down four flights."

"I knew they weren't intent on killing me. . . ."

"How?"

"They could have done that easily before. I think they were waiting for me to go out. I'd unpacked; they'd have the apartment to themselves."

"What for?"

"To search my things. They *have* done that before."

"Who?"

"Dammed if I know."

"Now who's no help?"

"Sorry. . . . Tell me, Bobby, who exactly knew I was flying in? How was it handled?"

"First question: three people. I did, of course; I'm on the dials. Granville, obviously. And Jean Cameron; the old man asked her to follow up on an apartment . . . but you know that. Question two: very confidentially. Remember, your orders came through at night. From Washington. Jean was playing chess with Granville in his quarters when I brought him the eggs. . . ."

"The what?" interrupted David.

"The scrambler; it's marked. Washington had your sheet radioed in on a scrambler code. That means only myself or my head man can handle it, deliver it to the ambassador."

"O.K. Then what?"

"Nothing. I mean nothing you don't know about."

"Tell me anyway."

Ballard exhaled a long, condescending breath. "Well, the three of us were alone; what the hell, I'd read the scramble and the instructions were clear about the apartment. So Granville figured – apparently – that Jean was the logical one to scout one up. He told her you were coming in; to do what she could on such short notice." Ballard looked about the room and over at the patio doors. "She didn't do badly, either."

"Then that's it; they've got a network fanned out over the city; nothing unusual. They keep tabs on unoccupied places: apartments, rooming houses; hotels are the easiest."

"I'm not sure I follow you," said Ballard, trying to.

"We can all be smart as whips, Bobby, but we can't change a couple of basics: we have to have a place to sleep and take a bath."

"Oh, I follow *that*, but you can't apply it here. Starting tomorrow you're no secret; until then you are. D.C. said you were coming down on your own; we had no idea precisely when or how. . . .Jean didn't get this apartment for *you*. Not in *your name*."

"Oh?" David was far more concerned than his expression indicated. The two *extranjeros* had to have been on the roof before he arrived. Or, at least, within minutes after he did so. "How did she lease it then? Whose name did she use? I didn't want a cover; we didn't ask for one."

"Jesus, I thought I talked fast. Sunday is *Sunday*, Monday is *Monday*. Sunday we don't know you; Monday we do. That's what Washington spelled out. They wanted no advance notice of your arrival and, incidentally, if *you* decided to stay out of sight, we were to adhere to your wishes. I'm sure Granville will ask you what you want to do in the morning. . . .How did Jean lease the place? Knowing her, she probably implied the ambassador had a girl on the side, or something. The *porteños* are very *simpático* with that sort of thing; the Paris of South America and all that. . . .One thing I *do* know, she wouldn't have used your name. Or any obvious cover. She'd use her own first."

"Oh, boy," said Spaulding wearily, removing the ice pack and feeling the back of his head. He looked at his fingers. Smudges of blood were apparent.

"I hope you're not going to play hero with that gash. You should see a doctor."

"No hero." David smiled. "I've got to have some sutures removed, anyway. Might as well be tonight, if you can arrange it."

"I can arrange it. Where did you get the stitches?"

"I had an accident in the Azores."

"Christ, you travel, don't you?"

"So does something ahead of me."

24

"Mrs. Cameron is here at my request, Spaulding. Come in. I've talked with Ballard and the doctor. Stitches taken out and new ones put in; you must feel like a pincushion."

Granville was behind his baroque desk, reclining comfortably in his high-backed chair. Jean Cameron sat on the couch against the left wall; one of the chairs in front of the desk was obviously meant for David. He decided to wait until Granville said so before sitting down. He remained standing; he wasn't sure he liked the ambassador. The office assigned to him was, indeed, far back and used for storage.

"Nothing serious, sir. If it was, I'd say so." Spaulding nodded to Jean and saw her concern. Or, at least, that's what he thought he read in her eyes.

"You'd be foolish not to. The doctor says the blow to the head fortunately fell between concussion areas. Otherwise, you'd be in rather bad shape."

"It was delivered by an experienced man."

"Yes, I see. . . .Our doctor didn't think much of the sutures he removed."

"That seems to be a general medical opinion. They served their purpose; the shoulder's fine. He strapped it."

"Yes. . . .Sit down, sit down."

David sat down. "Thank you, sir."

"I gather the two men who attacked you last evening were *provincianos*. Not *porteños*."

Spaulding gave a short, defeated smile and turned to Jean Cameron. "I got to *porteños*; I guess *provincianos* means what it says. The country folk? Outside the cities."

"Yes," said the girl softly. "*The* city. BA."

"Two entirely different cultures," continued Granville. "The *provincianos* are hostile and with much legitimacy. They're really quite exploited; the resentments are flaring up. The GOU has done nothing to ease matters, it only conscripts them in the lowest ranks."

"The *provincianos* are native to Argentina, though, aren't they?"

"Certainly. From their point of view, much more so than Buenos Airens, *porteños*. Less Italian and German blood, to say nothing of Portuguese, Balkan and Jewish. There were waves of immigrations, you see. . . ."

"Then, Mr. Ambassador," interrupted David, hoping to stem another post analysis by the pedagogical diplomat, "these were not *provincianos*. They called themselves *extranjeros*. Displaced persons, I gathered."

"*Extranjero* is a rather sarcastic term. Inverse morbidity. As though employed by a reservation Indian in our Washington. A foreigner in his own native land, you see what I mean?"

"These men were not from Argentina," said David quietly, dismissing Granville's question. "Their speech pattern was considerably alien."

"Oh? Are you an expert?"

"Yes, I am. In these matters."

"I see." Granville leaned forward. "Do you ascribe the attack to embassy concerns? Allied concerns?"

"I'm not sure. It's my opinion I was the target. I'd like to know how they knew I was here."

Jean Cameron spoke from the couch. "I've gone over everything I said, David." She stopped and paused briefly, aware that the ambassador had shot her a look at her use of Spaulding's first name. "Your place was the fourth apartment I checked into. I started at ten in the morning and got there around two o'clock. And leased it immediately. I'm sorry to say it was the patio that convinced me."

David smiled at her.

"Anyway, I went to a real estate office at Viamonte. Geraldo Baldez is the owner; we all know him. He's partisan; has no use for Germans. I made it clear that I wanted to rent the apartment for one of our people who was living here and who, frankly, found the embassy restrictions too limiting. He laughed and said he was sure it was Bobby. I didn't disagree."

"But it was a short lease," said David.

"I used it as an excuse in case you didn't like the apartment. It's a standard three-month clause."

"Why wouldn't Bobby – or anyone else – get his own place?"

"Any number of reasons. Also standard . . . here." Jean smiled, a touch embarrassed, thought David. "I know the city better than most; I lived here for several years. Also there's a little matter of expense allowance; I'm a pretty good bargainer. And men like Bobby have urgent work to do. My hours are more flexible; I have the time."

"Mrs. Cameron is too modest, Spaulding. She's an enormous asset to our small community."

"I'm sure she is, sir. . . . Then you don't think anyone had reason to suspect you were finding a place for an incoming attaché."

"Absolutely not. It was all done in such a . . . lighthearted way, if you know what I mean."

"What about the owner of the building?" David asked.

"I never saw him. Most apartments are owned by wealthy people who live in the Telmo or Palermo districts. Everything's done through rental agencies."

David turned to Granville. "Have there been any calls for me? Messages?"

"No. Not that I'm aware of and I'm sure I would be. You would have been contacted, of course."

"A man named Kendall. . . ."

"Kendall?" interrupted the ambassador. "I know that name . . . Kendall. Yes, Kendall." Granville riffled through some papers on his desk. "Here. A Walter Kendall came in last night. Ten thirty flight. He's staying at the Alvear; that's near the Palermo Park. Fine old hotel." Granville suddenly looked over at Spaulding. "He's listed on the sheet as an industrial economist. Now that's a rather all-inclusive description, isn't it? Would he be the banker I referred to yesterday?"

"He'll make certain arrangements relative to my instructions." David did not conceal his reluctance to go into the matter of Walter Kendall. On the other hand, he instinctively found himself offering a token clarification to Jean Cameron. "My primary job here is to act as liaison between financial people in New York and London and banking interests here in Buenos . . . BA." David smiled; he hoped as genuinely as Jean smiled. "I think it's a little silly. I don't know a debit from an asset. But Washington okayed me. The ambassador is worried that I'm too inexperienced."

Spaulding quickly shifted his gaze to Granville, reminding the old man that "banking interests" was the limit of identities. The name of Erich Rhinemann was out of bounds.

"Yes, I admit, I was. . . .But that's neither here nor there. What do you wish to do about last night? I think we should lodge a formal complaint with the police. Not that it will do a damn bit of good."

David fell silent for a few moments, trying to consider the pros and cons of Granville's suggestion. "Would we get press coverage?"

"Very little, I'd think," answered Jean.

"Embassy attachés usually have money," said Granville. "They've been robbed. It will be called an attempted robbery. Probably was."

"But the Grupo doesn't like that kind of news. It doesn't fit in with the colonels' view of things, and they control the press. Jean was thinking out loud, looking at David. "They'll play it down."

"And if we don't complain – assuming it was not robbery we're admitting we think it was something else. Which I'm not prepared to do," said Spaulding.

"Then by all means, a formal complaint will be registered this morning. Will you dictate a report of the incident and sign it, please?" Obviously, Granville wished to terminate the meeting. "And to be frank with you, Spaulding, unless I'm considerably in the dark, I believe it *was* an attempt to rob a newly arrived rich American. I'm told the airport taxi drivers have formed a veritable thieves' carnival. *Extranjeros* would be perfectly logical participants."

David stood up; he was pleased to see that Jean did the same. "I'll accept that, Mr. Ambassador. The years in Lisbon have made me overly . . . concerned. I'll adjust."

"I daresay. Do write up the report."

"Yes, sir."

"I'll get in a stenographer," said Jean. "Bilingual."

"Not necessary. I'll dictate it in Spanish."

"I forgot." Jean smiled. "Bobby said they'd sent us a bright one."

David supposed it began with that first lunch. Later she told him it was before, but he didn't believe her. She claimed it was when he said that BA stood for Montevideo; that was silly, it didn't make sense.

What made sense – and they both recognized it without any attempt to verbalize it – was the total relaxation each felt in the other's company. It was as simple as that. It was a splendid comfort; the silences never awkward, the laughter easy and based in communicated humor, not forced response.

It was remarkable. Made more so, David believed, because neither expected it, neither sought it. Both had good and sufficient reasons to avoid any relationships other than surface or slightly below. He was an impermanent man, hoping only to survive and start somewhere again with a clear head and suppressed memories. That was important to him. And he knew she still mourned a man so deeply she couldn't possibly – without intolerable guilt – push that man's face and body and mind behind her.

She told him partially why herself. Her husband had not been the image of the dashing carrier pilot so often depicted by navy public relations. He'd had an extraordinary fear – not for himself – but of taking lives. Were it not for the abuse he knew would have been directed at his Maryland wife and Maryland family, Cameron would have sought conscientious objector status. Then, too, perhaps he hadn't the courage of his own convictions.

Why a pilot?

Cameron had been flying since he was in his teens. It seemed natural and he believed his civilian training might lead to a Stateside instructor's berth. He rejected military law; too many of his fellow attorneys had gone after it and found themselves in the infantry and on the decks of battleships. The military had enough lawyers; they wanted pilots.

David thought he understood why Jean told him so much about her dead husband. There were two reasons. The first was that by doing so openly, she was adjusting to what she felt was happening between them; atoning, perhaps. The second was less clear but in no way less important. Jean Cameron hated the war; hated it for what it had taken away from her. She wanted him to know that.

Because – David realized – her instincts told her he was very much involved. And she would have no part of that involvement; she owed that much to Cameron's memory.

They'd gone to lunch at a restaurant overlooking the waters of the Riachúelo Basin near the piers of Dársena Sud. She had suggested it – the restaurant and the lunch. She saw that he was still exhausted; what sleep he'd managed had been interrupted constantly with pain. She insisted that he needed a long, relaxing lunch, then home to bed and a day's recuperation.

She hadn't meant to go with him.

He hadn't meant for her to.

"Ballard's a nice guy," said Spaulding, pouring a clear white Colón.

"Bobby's a dear," she agreed. "He's a kind person."

"He's very fond of you."

"And I of him. . . .What you're speculating on is perfectly natural, and I'm sorry to spoil the wilder melody. Is melody right? Granville told me who your parents were. I'm impressed."

"I've refused to read music since the age of eight. But 'melody's' fine. I just wondered."

"Bobby gave me a thoroughly professional try, with enormous charm and good humor. A better girl would have responded. He had every right to be angry. . . .I wanted his company but gave very little in return for it."

"He accepted your terms," said David affirmatively.

"I said he was kind."

"There must be ten other fellows here. . . ."

"Plus the marine guard," interjected Jean, feigning a lovely, unmilitary salute. "Don't forget them."

"A hundred and ten, then. You're Deanna Durbin."

"Hardly. The marines rotate off the FMF base south of La Boca; the staff – those without wives and kinder – are plagued with the embassy syndrome."

"What's that?"

"State Department-eye-tis. . . .The quivers. You seem to be singularly lacking in them."

"I don't know whether I am or not. I don't know what they are."

"Which tells me something about you, doesn't it?"

"What does it tell you?"

"You're not a State Department climber. The 'eye-tis' syndrome is treading lightly and making damned sure everybody above you – especially the ambassador – is happy with your *sincerest efforts*." Jean grimaced like a boxer puppy, her delicate chin forward, her eyebrows down – mocking the words. Spaulding broke out laughing; the girl had captured the embassy look and voice with devastating accuracy.

"Christ, I'm going to put you on the radio." He laughed again. "You've described the syndrome. I see it, Lord! I see it!"

"But you're not infected by it." Jean stopped her mimicry and looked into his eyes. "I watched you with Granville; you were just barely polite. You weren't looking for a fitness report, were you?"

He returned her gaze. "No, I wasn't. . . .To answer the question that's rattling around that lovely head of yours so loud it vibrates – I'm not a Foreign Service career officer. I'm strictly wartime. I *do* work out of embassies on a variety of related assignments for a couple of related reasons. I speak four languages and because of those parents that impressed you so, I have what is euphemistically described as access to important people in government, commerce, those areas. Since I'm not a complete idiot, I often circulate confidential information among corporations in various countries. The market place doesn't stop humming for such inconveniences as war. . . .That's my contribution. I'm not very proud of it, but it's what they handed me."

She smiled her genuine smile and reached for his hand. "I think you do whatever you do very intelligently and well. There aren't many people who can say that. And God knows you can't choose."

" 'What did you do in the war, daddy?' . . . 'Well, son,' " David tried his own caricature. " 'I went from place to place telling friends of the Chase Bank to sell high and buy low and clear a decent profit margin.' " He kept her hand in his.

"And got attacked on Argentine rooftops and . . . and what were those stitches in your shoulder?"

"The cargo plane I was on in the Azores made a rotten landing. I think the pilot and his whole crew were plastered."

"There. See? You live as dangerously as any man at the front. . . .If I meet that boy you're talking to, I'll tell him that."

Their eyes were locked; Jean withdrew her hand, embarrassed. But for Spaulding the important thing was that she believed him. She accepted his cover extension without question. It occurred to him that he was at once greatly relieved and yet, in a way, quite sorry. He found no professional pride in lying to her successfully.

"So now you know how I've avoided the State Department syndrome. I'm still not sure why it's relevant. What the hell, with a hundred and ten men and marines. . . ."

"The marines don't count. They have sundry interests down here in La Boca."

"Then the staff – those without the 'Wives and kinder' – they can't all be quivering."

"But they do and I've been grateful. They'd like to get to the Court of St. James's someday."

"Now you're playing mental gymnastics. I'm not following you."

"No, I'm not. I wanted to see if Bobby had told you. He hasn't. I said he was kind. . . .He was giving me the chance to tell you myself."

"Tell me what?"

"My husband was Henderson Granville's stepson. They were very close."

They left the restaurant shortly past four and walked around the docks of the Dársena Sud waterfront, breathing in the salt air. It seemed to David that Jean was enjoying herself in a way she hadn't in too long a time. That it was part of the instant comfort between them, he realized, but it went further. As if some splendid relief had swept over her.

Her loveliness had been evident from those first moments on the staircase, but as he thought back on that brief introduction, he knew what the difference was. Jean Cameron had been outgoing, good-natured . . . welcoming charm itself. But there'd been something else: a detachment born of self-control.

Total control. A patina of authority that had nothing to do with her status at the embassy or whatever other benefits derived from her marriage to the ambassador's stepson. It was related solely to her own decisions, her own outlook.

He had seen that detached authority throughout the morning – when she introduced him to various embassy employees; when she gave directions to her secretary; when she answered her telephone and rendered quick instructions.

Even in the byplay with Bobby Ballard she glided firmly, with the assurance of knowing her own pattern. Ballard could shout humorously that she could "get irresponsibly drunk" because by no stretch of the imagination would she allow herself to do that.

Jean kept a tight rein on herself.

The rein was loosening now.

Yesterday he had looked at her closely, finding the years; and she was completely unconcerned, without vanity. Now, walking along the docks, holding his arm, she was pleasantly aware of the looks she received from the scores of waterfront *Bocamos*. Spaulding knew she hoped he was aware of those looks.

"Look, David," she said excitedly. "Those boats are going to crash head on."

Several hundred yards out in the bay, two trawlers were on a collision course, both steam whistles filling the air with aggressive warnings, both crews shouting at each other from port and starboard railings.

"The one on the right will veer."

It did. At the last moment, amid dozens of guttural oaths and gestures.

"How did you know?" she said.

"Simple right of way; the owner would get clobbered with damages. There'll be a brawl on one of these piers pretty soon, though."

"Let's not wait for it. You've had enough of that."

They walked out of the dock area into the narrow La Boca streets, teeming with small fish markets, profuse with fat merchants in bloodied aprons and shouting customers. The afternoon catch was in, the day's labor on the water over. The rest was selling and drinking and retelling the misadventures of the past twelve hours.

They reached a miniature square called – for no apparent reason – Plaza Ocho Calle; there was no street number eight, no plaza to speak of. A taxi hesitantly came to a stop at the corner, let out its fare and started up again, blocked by pedestrians unconcerned with such vehicles. David looked at Jean and she nodded, smiling. He shouted at the driver.

Inside the taxi he gave his address. It didn't occur to him to do otherwise.

They rode in silence for several minutes, their shoulders touching, her hand underneath his arm.

"What are you thinking of?" David asked, seeing the distant but happy expression on her face.

"Oh, the way I pictured you when Henderson read the scramble the other night. . . . Yes, I call him Henderson; I always have."

"I can't imagine anyone, even the president, calling him Henderson."

"You don't know him. Underneath that Racquet Club jacket is lovable Henderson."

"How did you picture me?"

"Very differently."

"From what?"

"You. . . . I thought you'd be terribly short, to begin with. An attaché named David Spaulding who's some kind of financial whiz and is going to have conferences with the banks and the colonels about money things is short, at least fifty years old and has *very* little hair. He also wears spectacles — not glasses — and has a thin nose. Probably has an allergy as well — he sneezes a lot and blows his nose all the time. And he speaks in short, clipped sentences; very precise and quite disagreeable."

"He chases secretaries, too; don't leave that out."

"My David Spaulding doesn't chase secretaries. He reads dirty books."

David felt a twinge. Throw in an unkempt appearance, a soiled handkerchief and replace the spectacles with glasses — worn occasionally — and Jean was describing Walter Kendall.

"Your Spaulding's an unpleasant fellow."

"Not the new one," she said, tightening her grip on his arm.

The taxi drew up to the curb in front of the entrance on Córdoba. Jean Cameron hesitated, staring momentarily at the apartment house door. David spoke softly, without emphasis.

"Shall I take you to the embassy?"

She turned to him. "No."

He paid the driver and they went inside.

The field thread was invisibly protruding from the knob; he felt it.

He inserted the key in the lock and instinctively, gently shouldered her aside as he pushed the door open. The apartment was as he had left it that morning; he knew she felt his relief. He held the door for her. Jean entered and looked around.

"It really *isn't* so bad, is it?" she said.

"Humble but home," He left the door open and with a smile, a gesture — without words — he asked her to stay where she was. He walked rapidly into the bedroom, returned and went through the double doors onto his miniature, high-walled patio. He looked up, scanning the windows and the roof carefully. He smiled again at her from under the branches of the fruit tree. She understood, closed the door and came out to him.

"You did that very professionally Mr. Spaulding."

"In the best traditions of extreme cowardice, Mrs. Cameron."

He realized his mistake the minute he'd made it. It was not the moment to use the married title. And yet, in some oblique way she seemed grateful that he had. She moved again and stood directly in front of him.

"Mrs. Cameron thanks you."

He reached out and held her by the waist. Her arms slowly, haltingly, went up to his shoulders; her hands cupped his face and she stared into his eyes.

He did not move. The decision, the first step, had to be hers; he understood that.

She brought her lips to his. The touch was soft and lovely and meant for earthbound angels. And then she trembled with an almost uncontrollable sense of urgency. Her lips parted and she pressed her body with extraordinary strength into his, her arms clutched about his neck.

She pulled her lips away from his and buried her face into his chest, holding him with fierce possession.

"Don't say anything," she whispered. "Don't say anything at all. . . . *Just take me.*"

He picked her up silently and carried her into the bedroom. She kept her face pressed into his chest, as if she were afraid to see light or even him. He lowered her gently onto the bed and closed the door.

In a few moments they were naked and he pulled the blankets over them. It was a moist and beautiful darkness. A splendid comfort.

"I want to say something," she said, tracing her finger over his lips, her face above his, her breasts innocently on his chest. And smiling her genuine smile.

"I know. You want the other Spaulding. The thin one with spectacles." He kissed her fingers.

"He disappeared in an explosion of sorts."

"You're positively descriptive, young lady."

"And not so young. . . . That's what I want to talk about."

"A pension. You're angling for Social Security. I'll see what I can do."

"Be serious, silly boy."

"And not so silly. . . ."

"There's no commitment, David," she said, interrupting him. I want you to know that. . . . I don't know how else to say it. Everything happened so fast."

"Everything happened very naturally. Explanations aren't required."

"Well, I think some are. I didn't expect to be here."

"I didn't expect that you would be. I suppose I hoped, I'll admit that. . . . I didn't plan; neither of us did."

"I don't know; I think I did. I think I saw you yesterday and somewhere in the back of my mind I made a decision. Does that sound brazen of me?"

"If you did, the decision was long overdue."

"Yes, I imagine it was." She lay back, pulling the sheet over her. "I've been very selfish. Spoiled and selfish and behaving really quite badly."

"Because you haven't slept around?" It was his turn to roll over and touch her face. He kissed both her eyes, now open; the deep speckles of blue made bluer, deeper, by the late afternoon sun streaming through the blinds. She smiled; her perfect white teeth glistening with the moisture of her mouth, her lips curved in that genuine curve of humor.

"That's funny. I must be unpatriotic. I've withheld my charms only to deliver them to a noncombatant."

"The Visigoths wouldn't have approved. The warriors came first, I'm told."

"Let's not tell them." She reached up for his face. "Oh, David, David, *David*."

25

"I hope I didn't wake you. I wouldn't have troubled you but I thought you'd want me to."

Ambassador Granville's voice over the telephone was more solicitous than David expected it to be. He looked at his watch as he replied. It was three minutes of ten in the morning.

"Oh? . . . No, sir. I was just getting up. Sorry I overslept."

There was a note on the telephone table. It was from Jean.

"Your friend was in contact with us."

"Friend?" David unfolded the note. *My Darling—You fell into such a beautiful sleep it would have broken my heart to disturb you. Called a taxi. See you in the morning. At the Bastille. Your ex-regimented phoenix.* David smiled, remembering her smile.

" . . . the details, I'm sure, aren't warranted." Granville had said something and he hadn't been listening.

"I'm sorry, Mr. Ambassador. This must be a poor connection: your voice fades in and out." All telephones beyond the Atlantic, north, middle and south, were temperamental instruments. An unassailable fact.

"Or something else, I'm afraid," said Granville with irritation, obviously referring to the possibility of a telephone tap. "When you get in, please come to see me."

"Yes, sir. I'll be there directly."

He picked up Jean's note and read it again.

She had said last night that he was complicating her life. But there were no commitments; she'd said that, too.

What the hell was a commitment? He didn't want to speculate He didn't want to think about the awful discovery – the instant, splendid comfort they both recognized. It wasn't the time for it. . . .

Yet to deny it would be to reject an extraordinary reality. He was trained to deal with reality.

He didn't want to think about it.

His "friend" had been in contact with the embassy.

Walter Kendall.

That was another reality. It couldn't wait.

He crushed out his cigarette angrily, watching his fingers stab the butt into the metal ashtray.

Why was he angry?

He didn't care to speculate on that, either. He had a job to do. He

604

hoped he had the commitment for it.

"Jean said you barely made it through dinner. You needed a good night's sleep; I must say you look better." The ambassador had come from around his desk to greet him as he entered the large, ornate office. David was a little bewildered. The old diplomat was actually being solicitous, displaying a concern that belied his unconcealed disapproval of two days ago. Or was it his use of the name Jean instead of the forbidding Mrs. Cameron.

"She was very kind. I couldn't have found a decent restaurant without her."

"I daresay. . . . I won't detain you, you'd better get cracking with this Kendall."

"You said he's been in contact . . ."

"Starting last night; early this morning to be accurate. He's at the Alvear and apparently quite agitated, according to the switchboard. At two thirty this morning he was shouting, demanding to know where you were. Naturally, we don't give out that information."

"I'm grateful. As you said, I needed the sleep; Kendall would have prevented it. Do you have his telephone number? Or shall I get it from the book?"

"No, right here." Granville walked to his desk and picked up a sheet of notepaper. David followed and took it from the ambassador's outstretched hand.

"Thank you, sir. I'll get on it." He turned and started for the door, Granville's voice stopping him.

"Spaulding?"

"Yes, sir?"

"I'm sure Mrs. Cameron would like to see you. Assess your recovery, I daresay. Her office is in the south wing. First door from the entrance, on the right. Do you know where that is?"

"I'll find it, sir."

"I'm sure you will. See you later in the day."

David went out the heavy baroque door, closing it behind him. Was it his imagination or was Granville reluctantly giving an approval to his and Jean's sudden . . . alliance? The words were approving, the tone of voice reluctant.

He walked down the connecting corridor toward the south wing and reached her door. Her name was stamped on a brass plate to the left of the doorframe. He had not noticed it yesterday.

Mrs. Andrew Cameron.

So his name had been Andrew. Spaulding hadn't asked his first name; she hadn't volunteered it.

As he looked at the brass plate he found himself experiencing a very strange reaction. He resented Andrew Cameron; resented his life, his death.

The door was open and he entered. Jean's secretary was obviously an

Argentine. A *porteña* The black Spanish hair was pulled back into a bun, her features Latin.

"Mrs. Cameron, please. David Spaulding."

"Please go in. She's expecting you." David approached the door and turned the knob.

She was taken by surprise, he thought. She was at the window looking out at the south lawn, a page of paper in her hand, glasses pushed above her forehead, resting on top of her light brown hair.

Startled, she removed her glasses from their perch and stood immobile. Slowly, as if studying him first, she smiled.

He found himself afraid. More than afraid, for a moment. And then she spoke and the sudden anguish left him, replaced by a deeply felt relief.

"I woke up this morning and reached for you. You weren't there and I thought I might cry."

He walked rapidly to her and they held each other. Neither spoke. The silence, the embrace, the splendid comfort returning.

"Granville acted like a procurer a little while ago," he said finally, holding her by the shoulders, looking at her blue speckled eyes that held such intelligent humor.

"I told you he was lovable. You wouldn't believe me."

"You didn't *tell* me we had dinner, though. Or that I could barely get through it."

"I was hoping you'd slip; give him more to think about."

"I don't understand him. Or you, maybe."

"Henderson has a problem. . . .Me. He's not sure how to handle it – me. He's overprotective because I've led him to believe I wanted that protection. I did; it was easier. But a man who's had three wives and at least twice that many mistresses over the years is no Victorian. . . .And he knows you're not going to be here long. As he would put it: do I sketch a reasonable picture?"

"I daresay," answered David in Granville's Anglicized manner. "That's unkind." Jean laughed. "He probably doesn't approve of you, which makes his unspoken acceptance very difficult for him."

David released her. "I know damned well he doesn't approve . . . Look, I have to make some calls; go out and meet someone. . . ."

"Just someone?"

"A ravishing beauty who'll introduce me to lots of other ravishing beauties. And between the two of us, I can't stand him. But I have to see him. . . .Will you have dinner with me?"

"Yes, I'll have dinner with me. I'd planned to. You didn't have a choice."

"You're right; you're brazen."

"I made that clear. You broke down the regimens; I'm flying up out of my own personal ash heap. . . .The air feels good."

"It was going to happen. . . .I was here." He wasn't sure why he said it but he had to.

Walter Kendall paced the hotel room as though it were a cage. Spaulding sat on the couch watching him, trying to decide which animal Kendall reminded him of; there were several that came to mind, none pets.

"You listen to *me*," Kendall said. "This is no military operation. You *take* orders, you don't give them."

"I'm sorry; I think you're misreading me." David was tempted to answer Kendall's anger in kind, but he decided not to.

"I misread, bullshit! You told Swanson you were in some trouble in New York. That's *your* problem, not *ours*."

"You can't be sure of that."

"Oh yes I can! You tried to sell that to Swanson and he bought it. You could have involved *us!*"

"Now just a minute." Spaulding felt he could object legitimately – within the boundaries he had mentally staked off for Kendall. "I told Swanson that in my opinion the 'trouble' in New York might have been related to Buenos Aires. I didn't say it *was*, I said it might have been."

"That's not possible!"

"How the hell can you be so sure?"

"Because I am." Kendall was not only agitated, thought David, he was impatient. "This is a business proposition. The deal's been made. There's no one trying to stop it. Stop *us*"

"Hostilities don't cease because a deal's been made. If the German command got wind of it they'd blow up Buenos Aires to stop it."

"Yeah . . . well, that's not possible."

"You *know* that?"

"We know it. . . .So don't go confusing that stupid bastard, Swanson. I'll level with you. This is strictly a money-line negotiation. We could have completed it without any help from Washington, but they insisted – Swanson insisted – that they have a man here. O.K., you're him. You can be helpful; you can get the papers out and you speak the languages. But that's *all* you've got to do. Don't call attention to yourself. We don't want anyone upset."

Grudgingly, David began to understand the subtle clarity of Brigadier General Swanson's manipulation. Swanson had maneuvered him into a clean position. The killing of Erich Rhinemann – whether he did it himself or whether he bought the assassin – would be totally unexpected. Swanson wasn't by any means the "stupid bastard" Kendall thought he was. Or that David had considered.

Swanson was nervous. A neophyte. But he was pretty damned good.

"All right. My apologies," said Spaulding, indicating a sincerity he didn't feel. "Perhaps the New York thing was exaggerated. I made enemies in Portugal, I can't deny that. . . .I got out under cover, you know."

"What?"

"There's no way the people in New York could know I left the city."

"You're sure?"

"As sure as you are that no one's trying to stop your negotiations."

"Yeah. . . .O.K. Well, everything's set. I got a schedule."

"You've seen Rhinemann?"

"Yesterday. All day."

"What about Lyons?" asked David.

"Swanson's packing him off at the end of the week. With his nursemaids. Rhinemann figures the designs will be arriving Sunday or Monday."

"In steps or all together?"

"Probably two sets of prints. He's not sure. It doesn't make any difference; they'll be here in full by Tuesday. He guaranteed."

"Then we've moved up. You estimated three weeks." David felt a pain in his stomach. He knew it wasn't related to Walter Kendall or Eugene Lyons or designs for high-altitude gyroscopes. It was Jean Cameron and the simple fact that he'd have only one week with her.

It disturbed him greatly and he speculated – briefly – on the meaning of this disturbance.

And then he knew he could not allow himself the indulgence; the two entities had to remain separate, the worlds separate.

"Rhinemann's got good control," said Kendall, more than a hint of respect showing in his voice. "I'm impressed with his methods. Very precise."

"If you think that, you don't need me." David was buying a few seconds to steer their conversation to another area. His statement was rhetorical.

"We don't, that's what I said. But there's a lot of money involved and since the War Department – one way or another is picking up a large share of the tab, Swanson wants his accounts covered. I don't sweat him on that. It's business."

Spaulding recognized his moment. "Then let's get to the codes. I haven't wasted the three days down here. I've struck up a friendship of sorts with the embassy cryp."

"The what?"

"The head cryptographer. He'll send out the codes to Washington; the payment authorization."

"Oh. . . .Yeah, that." Kendall was squeezing a cigarette, prepared to insert it in his mouth. He was only half-concerned with codes and cryptographers, thought David. They were the wrap-up, the necessary details relegated to others. Or was it an act? wondered Spaulding.

He'd know in a moment or two.

"As you pointed out, it's a great deal of money. So we've decided to use a scrambler with code switches every twelve hours. We'll prepare the cryp schedule tonight and send it out by patrol courier to Washington tomorrow. The master plate will allow for fifteen hours. . . .Naturally, the prime word will be 'Tortugas'."

608

Spaulding watched the disheveled accountant.

There was no reaction whatsoever.

"O.K. . . . Yeah, O.K." Kendall sat down in an easy chair. His mind seemed somewhere else.

"That meets with your approval, doesn't it?"

"Sure. Why not? Play any games you like. All I give a shit about is that Geneva radios the confirmation and you fly out of here."

"Yes, but I thought the reference had to include the . . . code factor."

"What the hell are you talking about?"

"'Tortugas.' Hasn't it got to be 'Tortugas'?"

"Why? What's 'Tortugas'?"

The man wasn't acting. David was sure of that. "Perhaps I misunderstood. I thought 'Tortugas' was part of the authorization code."

"Christ! You and Swanson! All of you. Military geniuses! *Jesus!* If it doesn't sound like Dan Dunn, Secret Agent, it's not the real McCoy, huh? . . . Look. When Lyons tells you everything's in order, just say so. Then drive out to the airport . . . it's a small field called Mendarro . . . and Rhinemann's men will tell you when you can leave. O.K.? You got that?"

"Yes, I've got it," said Spaulding. But he wasn't sure.

Outside, David walked aimlessly down the Buenos Aires streets. He reached the huge park of the Plaza San Martin, with its fountains, its rows of white gravel paths, its calm disorder.

He sat down on a slatted bench and tried to define the elusive pieces of the increasingly complex puzzle.

Walter Kendall hadn't lied, "Tortugas" meant nothing to him.

Yet a man in an elevator in New York City had risked his life to learn about "Tortugas."

Ira Barden in Fairfax had told him there was only a single word opposite his name in the DW transfer in Ed Pace's vaults: "Tortugas."

There was an obvious answer, perhaps. Ed Pace's death prohibited any real knowledge, but the probability was genuine.

Berlin had gotten word of the Peenemünde negotiation – too late to prevent the theft of the designs – and was now committed to stopping the sale. Not only stopping it, but if possible tracing the involvement of everyone concerned. Trapping the entire Rhinemann network.

If this was the explanation – and what other plausible one existed? – Pace's code name, "Tortugas," had been leaked to Berlin by Fairfax infiltration. That there was a serious breach of security at Fairfax was clear; Pace's murder was proof.

His own role could be easily assessed by Berlin, thought David. The man in Lisbon suddenly transferred to Buenos Aires. The expert whose skill was proven in hundreds of espionage transactions, whose own network was the most ruthlessly efficient in southern Europe, did not walk out of his own creation unless his expertise was considered vital someplace else. He'd long ago accepted the fact that Berlin more than suspected him. In a way it was his protection; he'd by no means won every roll of the dice. If the enemy killed him, someone else would take his place. The enemy would have to start all over again. He was a known commodity... accept an existing devil.

Spaulding considered carefully, minutely, what he might do were he the enemy. What steps would he take at this specific juncture?

Barring panic or error, the enemy would not kill him. Not now. Because he could *not* by himself inhibit the delivery of the designs. He could, however, lead his counterparts to the moment and place of delivery.

What is the location of Tortugas!?

The desperate ... hysterical man in the Montgomery elevator had screamed the question, preferring to die rather than reveal those whose orders he followed. The Nazis reveled in such fanaticism. And so did others, for other reasons.

He – Spaulding – would therefore be placed under *äusserste Überwachurg* – foolproof surveillance, three- to four-man teams, twenty-four hours a day. That would account for the recruitment of the extraterritorial personnel on the Berlin payroll. Agents who operated outside the borders of Germany, *had* operated – for profit – for years. The languages and dialects would vary; deep-cover operatives who could move with impunity in neutral capitals because they had no Gestapo or Gehlen or Nachrichtendienst histories.

The Balkans and the Middle East countries had such personnel for hire. They were expensive; they were among the best. Their only morality was to the pound sterling and the American dollar.

Along with this round-the-clock surveillance, Berlin would take extra-ordinary measures to prevent him from developing his own network in Buenos Aires. That would mean infiltrating the American embassy. Berlin would not overlook that possibility. A great deal of money would be offered.

Who at the embassy could be bought?

To attempt corrupting an individual too highly placed could backfire; give him, Spaulding, dangerous information. . . .Some one not too far up on the roster; someone who could gain access to doors and locks and desk-drawer vaults. And codes. . . .A middle-level attaché. A man who'd probably never make it to the Court of St. James's anyway; who'd settle for another kind of security. Negotiable at a very high price.

Someone at the embassy would be Spaulding's enemy.

Finally, Berlin would order him killed. Along with numerous others, of course. Killed at the moment of delivery; killed after the *äusserste Überwachung* had extracted everything it could.

David got up from the slatted green bench and stretched, observing the beauty that was the Plaza San Martin park. He wandered beyond the path onto the grass, to the edge of a pond whose dark waters reflected the surround-ing trees like a black mirror. Two white swans paddled by in alabaster obliviousness. A little girl was kneeling by a rock on the tiny embankment, separating the petals from a yellow flower.

He was satisfied that he had adequately analyzed the immediate options of his counterparts. Options and probable courses of action. His gut feeling was positive – not in the sense of being enthusiastic, merely not negative.

He had now to evolve his own counterstrategy. He had to bring into play the lessons he had learned over the years in Lisbon. But there was so little time allowed him. And because of this fact, he understood that a misstep could be fatal here.

Nonchalantly but with no feelings of nonchalance – he looked around at the scores of strollers on the paths. on the grass; the rowers and the passengers in the small boats on the small dark lake. Which of them were the enemy?

Who were the ones watching him, trying to think what he was thinking?

He would have to find them – one or two of them anyway – before the next few days were over.

That was the genesis of his counterstrategy.

Isolate and break.

David lit a cigarette and walked over the miniature bridge. He was primed. The hunter and the hunted were now one. There was the slightest straining throughout his entire body; the hands, the arms, the legs: there was a muscular tension, an awareness. He recognized it. He was back in the north country.

And he was good in that jungle. He was the best there was. It was here that he built his architectural monuments, his massive structures of concrete and steel. In his mind.

It was all he had sometimes.

26

He looked at his watch. It was five thirty; Jean had said she'd be at his apartment around six. He had walked for nearly two hours and now found himself at the corner of Viamonte, several blocks from his apartment. He crossed the street and walked to a news-stand under a storefront awning, where he bought a paper.

He glanced at the front pages, amused to see that the war news what there was of it – was relegated to the bottom, surrounded by accounts of the Grupo de Oficiales' latest benefits to Argentina. He noted that the name of a particular colonel, one Juan Perón, was mentioned in three separate subheadlines.

He folded the paper under his arm and, because he realized he had been absently musing, looked once again at his watch.

It was not a deliberate move on David's part. That is to say, he did not calculate the abruptness of his turn: he simply turned because the angle of the sun caused a reflection on his wristwatch and he unconsciously shifted his body to the right, his left hand extended, covered by his own shadow.

But his attention was instantly diverted from his watch. Out of the corner of his eye he could discern a sudden, sharp break in the sidewalk's human traffic. Thirty feet away across, the street two men had swiftly turned around, colliding with oncoming pedestrians, apologizing, stepping into the flow on the curbside.

The man on the left had not been quick enough; or he was too careless – too inexperienced, perhaps – to angle his shoulders, or hunch them imperceptibly so as to melt into the crowd.

He stood out and David recognized him.

He was one of the men from the roof of the Córdoba apartment. His companion David couldn't be sure of, but he *was* sure of that man. There was even the hint of a limp in his gait; David remembered the battering he'd given him.

He was being followed, then, and that was good.

His point of departure wasn't as remote as he'd thought.

He walked another ten yards, into a fairly large group approaching the corner of Córdoba. He sidestepped his way between arms and legs and packages, and entered a small jewelry store whose wares were gaudy, inexpensive. Inside, several office girls were trying to select a gift for a departing secretary. Spaulding smiled at the annoyed proprietor, indicating that he could wait, he was in no hurry. The proprietor made a gesture of helplessness.

Spaulding stood by the front window, his body concealed from outside by the frame of the door.

Before a minute was up he saw the two men again. "They were still across the street; David had to follow their progress through the intermittent gaps in the crowd. The two men were talking heatedly, the second man annoyed with his limping companion. Both were trying to glance above the heads of the surrounding bodies, raising themselves up on their toes, looking foolish, amateur."

David figured they would turn right at the corner and walk east on Córdoba, toward his apartment. They did so and, as the owner of the jewelry store protested, Spaulding walked swiftly out into the crowds and ran across the Avenida Callao, dodging cars and angry drivers. He had to reach the other side, staying out of the sightlines of the two men. He could not use the crosswalks or the curbs. It would be too easy, too logical, for the men to look backward as men did when trying to spot someone they had lost in surveillance.

David knew his objective now. He had to separate the men and take the one with a limp. Take him and force answers.

If they had any experience, he considered, they would reach his apartment and divide, one man cautiously going inside to listen through the door, ascertaining the subject's presence, the other remaining outside, far enough from the entrance to be unobserved. And common sense would dictate that the man unknown to David would be the one to enter the apartment.

Spaulding removed his jacket and held up the newspaper – not full but folded; not obviously but casually, as if he were uncertain of the meaning of some awkwardly phrased headline – and walked with the crowds to the north side of Córdoba. He turned right and maintained a steady, unbroken pace east, remaining as far left on the sidewalk as possible.

His apartment was less than a block and a half away now. He could see the two men; intermittently they *did* look back, but on their own side of the street.

Amateurs. If he taught surveillance, they'd fail his course.

The men drew nearer to the apartment, their concentration on the entrance. David knew it was his moment to move. The only moment of risk, really; the few split seconds when one or the other might turn and see him across the street, only yards away. But it was a necessary gamble. He had to get beyond the apartment entrance. That was the essence of his trap.

Several lengths ahead was a middle-aged *porteña* housewife carrying groceries, hurrying, obviously anxious to get home. Spaulding came alongside and without breaking stride, keeping in step with her, he started asking directions in his best, most elegant Castilian, stating among other points that he knew this was the right street and he was late. His head was tilted from the curb.

If anyone watched them, the housewife and the shirtsleeved man with a jacket under one arm and a newspaper under the other looked like two friends hastening to a mutual destination.

Twenty yards beyond the entrance on the other side, Spaulding left the smiling *porteña* and ducked into a canopied doorway. He pressed himself into the wall and looked back across the street. The two men stood by the curb and, as he expected, they separated. The unknown man went into his apartment house; the man with the limp looked up and down the sidewalk, checked oncoming vehicles, and started across Córdoba to the north side. David's side.

Spaulding knew it would be a matter of seconds before the limping figure passed him. Logic, again; common sense. The man would continue east – he would not reverse direction – over traversed ground. He would station himself at a vantage point from which he could observe those approaching the apartment from the west. David's approach.

The man did not see him until David touched him, grabbed his left arm around the elbow, forced the arm into a horizontal position, and clamped the man's hand downward so that the slightest force on David's part caused an excruciating pain in the man's bent wrist.

"Just keep walking or I'll snap your hand off," said David in English, pushing the man to the right of the sidewalk to avoid the few pedestrians walking west on Córdoba.

The man's face grimaced in pain; David's accelerated walk caused him to partially stumble – his limp emphasized – and brought further agony to the wrist.

"You're breaking my arm. You're *breaking* it!" said the anguished man, hurrying his steps to relieve the pressure.

"Keep up with me or I will," David spoke calmly, even politely. They reached the corner of the Avenida Paraná and Spaulding swung left, propelling the man with him. There was a wide, recessed doorway of an old office building – the type that had few offices remaining within it. David spun the man around, keeping the arm locked, and slammed him into the wooden wall at the point farthest inside. He released the arm; the man grabbed for his strained wrist. Spaulding took the moment to flip open the man's jacket, forcing the arms downward, and removed a revolver strapped in a large holster above the man's left hip.

It was a Lüger. Issued less than a year ago.

David clamped it inside his belt and pushed a lateral forearm against the man's throat, crashing his head into the wood as he searched the pockets of the jacket. Inside he found a large rectangular European billfold. He slapped it open, removed his forearm from the man's throat, and shoved his left shoulder into the man's chest, pinning him unmercifully against the wall. With both hands, David removed identification papers.

A German driver's license; an Autobahn vehicle pass; rationing cards countersigned by Oberführers, allowing the owner to utilize them throughout the Reich – a privilege granted to upper-level government personnel and above.

And then he found it.

An identity pass with a photograph affixed; for the ministries of Information, Armaments, Air and Supply.

Gestapo.

"You're about the most inept recruit Himmler's turned out," said David, meaning the judgment profoundly, putting the bill-fold in his back pocket. "You must have relatives. . . .*Was ist 'Tortugas'?*" Spaulding whispered harshly, suddenly. He removed his shoulder from the man's chest and thrust two extended knuckles into the Nazi's breastbone with such impact that the German coughed, the sharp blow nearly paralyzing him. "*Wer ist Altmüller? Was wissen Sie über Marshall?*" David repeatedly hammered the man's ribs with his knuckles, sending shock waves of pain throughout the Gestapo agent's rib cage. "*Sprechen Sie! Sofort!*"

"*Nein ! Ich weiss nichts!*" the man answered between gasps. "*Nein!*"

Spaulding heard it again. The dialect. Nowhere near *Berliner*; not even a mountainized *Bavarian*. Something else.

What was it?

"*Noch 'mal!* Again! *Sprechen Sie!*"

And then the man did something quite out of the ordinary. In his pain, his fear, he stopped speaking German. He spoke in English. "I have not the information you want! I follow orders. . . .That is all!"

David shifted his stand to the left, covering the Nazi from the intermittent looks they both received from the passersby on the sidewalk. The doorway was deep, however, in shadows; no one stopped. The two men could have been acquaintances, one or both perhaps a little drunk.

Spaulding clenched his right fist, his left elbow against the wall, his left hand poised to clamp over the German's mouth. He leaned against the slatted wood and brought his fist crashing into the man's stomach with such force that the agent lurched forward, held only by David's hand, now gripping him by the hairline.

"I can keep this up until I rupture everything inside you. And when I'm finished I'll throw you in a taxi and drop you off at the German embassy with a note attached. You'll get it from both sides then, won't you? . . . Now, tell me what I want to know!" David brought his two bent knuckles up into the man's throat, jabbing twice.

"Stop. . . .*Mein Gott!* Stop!"

"Why don't you yell? You can scream your head off, you know. . . .Of course, then I'll have to put you to sleep and let your own people find you. Without your credentials, naturally. . . .Go on! Yell!" David knuckled the man once more in the throat. "Now, you start telling me. What's 'Tortugas?' Who's Altmüller? Now did you get a cryp named Marshall?"

"I swear to God! I know nothing!"

David punched him again. The man collapsed; Spaulding pulled him up against the wall, leaning against him, hiding him, really. The Gestapo agent opened his lids, his eyes swimming uncontrollably.

"You've got five seconds. Then I'll rip your throat out."

"No! . . . Please! Altmüller. . . .Armaments. . . .Peenemünde . . ."

"What about Peenemünde?"

"The tooling . . . 'Tortugas'."

"What does that *mean!?*" David showed the man his two bent fingers. The recollection of pain terrified the German. "What is 'Tortugas'?"

Suddenly the German's eyes flickered, trying to focus. Spaulding saw that the man was looking above his shoulder. It wasn't a ruse, the Nazi was too far gone for strategies.

And then David felt the presence behind him. It was an unmistakeable feeling that had been developed over the recent years; it was never false.

He turned.

Coming into the dark shadows from the harsh Argentine sunlight was the second part of the surveillance team, the man who'd entered his apartment building. He was Spaulding's size, a large man and heavily muscular.

The light and the onrushing figure caused David to wince. He released the German, prepared to throw himself onto the opposite wall.

He couldn't!

The Gestapo agent in a last surge of strength – held onto his arms!

Held his arms, threw his hands around David's chest and hung his full weight on him!

Spaulding lashed out with his foot at the man attacking, swung his elbows back, slamming the German back into the wood.

It was too late and David knew it.

He saw the huge hand – the long fingers spread – rushing into his face. It was as if a ghoulish film was being played before his eyes in slow motion. He felt the fingers clamp into his skin and realized that his head was being shoved with great strength into the wall.

The sensations of diving, crashing, spinning accompanied the shock of pain above his neck.

He shook his head; the first thing that struck him was the stench. It was all around him, sickening.

He was lying in the recessed doorway, curled up against the wall in a fetal position. He was wet, drenched around his face and shirt and in the crotch area of his trousers.

It was cheap whisky. Very cheap and very profuse.

His shirt had been ripped, collar to waist; one shoe was off, the sock removed. His belt was undone, his fly partially unzipped.

He was the perfect picture of a derelict.

He rose to a sitting position and remedied as best be could his appearance. He looked at his watch.

Or where his watch had been; it was gone.

His wallet, too. And money. And whatever else had been in his pockets.

He stood up. The sun was down, early night had begun; there were not so many people on the Avenida Paraná now.

He wondered what time it was. It couldn't be much more than an hour later, he supposed.

He wondered if Jean were still waiting for him.

She removed his clothes, pressed the back of his head with ice and insisted that he take a long, hot shower.

When he emerged from the bathroom, she fixed him a drink, then sat down next to him on the small couch.

"Henderson will insist on your moving into the embassy; you know that, don't you?"

"I can't."

"Well, you can't go on being beaten up every day. And don't tell me they were *thieves*. *You* wouldn't swallow that when Henderson and Bobby *both* tried to tell you that about the men on the roof!"

"This was different. For God's *sake*, Jean, I was robbed of everything on me!" David spoke sternly. It was important to him that she believe him now. And it was entirely possible that he'd find it necessary to avoid her from now on. That might be important, too. And terribly painful.

"People don't rob people and then douse them with whisky!"

"They do if they want to create sufficient time to get out of the area. It's not a new tactic. By the time a mark gets finished explaining to the police that he's a sober citizen, the hustlers are twenty miles away."

"I don't believe you, I don't even think you expect me to." She sat up and looked at him.

"I do expect you to because it's the truth. A man doesn't throw away his wallet, his money, his watch . . . in order to impress a girl with the validity of a lie. Come *on*, Jean! I'm very thirsty and my head still hurts."

She shrugged, obviously realizing it was futile to argue.

"You're just about out of Scotch, I'm afraid. I'll go buy a bottle for you. There's a liquor store on the corner of Talcahuano. It's not far. . . ."

"No," he said interrupting, recalling the man with huge hands who'd entered his building. "I will. Lend me some money."

"We'll both go," she responded.

"Please? . . . Would you mind waiting? I may get a phone call; I'd like the person to know I'll be right back."

"Who?"

"A man named Kendall."

Out on the street, he asked the first man he saw where the nearest pay phone could be found. It was several blocks away, on Rodriguez Peña, in a newspaper store.

David ran as fast as he could.

The hotel page found Kendall in the dining room. When he got on the phone he spoke while chewing. Spaulding pictured the man, the doodled obscenities, the animal-like breathing. He controlled himself. Walter Kendall was sick.

"Lyons is coming in in three days," Kendall told him. "With his nurses. I got him a place in this San Telmo district. A quiet apartment, quiet street. I wired Swanson the address. He'll give it to the keepers and they'll get him set up. They'll be in touch with you."

"I thought I was to get him settled."

"I figured you'd complicate things," interrupted Kendall. "No piss lost. They'll call you. Or I will. I'll be here for a while."

"I'm glad. . . .Because so's the Gestapo."

"*What?*"

"I said so's the Gestapo. You figured a little inaccurately: Kendall. Someone *is* trying to stop you. It doesn't surprise me."

"You're out of your fucking mind!"

"I'm not."

"What happened?"

So David told him, and for the first time in his brief association with the accountant, he detected fear.

"There was a break in Rhinemann's network. It doesn't mean the designs won't get here. It does mean we have obstacles – if Rhinemann's as good as you say. As I read it, Berlin found out the designs were stolen. They know they're filtering down or across or however Rhinemann's routing them out of Europe. The High Command got wind of the transactions. The Reichsführers aren't going to broadcast, they're going to try and intercept. With as little noise as possible. But you can bet your ass there's been a slew of executions in Peenemünde."

"It's crazy. . . ." Kendall could hardly be heard. And then he mumbled something; David could not understand the words.

"What did you say?"

"The address in this Telmo. For Lyons. It's three rooms. Back entrance." Kendall still kept his voice low, almost indistinct.

The man was close to panic, thought Spaulding. "I can barely hear you, Kendall. . . .Now, calm down! I think it's time I introduced myself to Rhinemann, don't you?"

"The Telmo address. It's Fifteen Terraza Verde . . . it's quiet."

"Who's the contact for Rhinemann?"

"The what?"

"Rhinemann's contact."

"I don't know. . . ."

"For Christ's sake, Kendall, you held a five-hour conference with him!"

"I'll be in touch. . . ."

David heard the click. He was stunned. Kendall had hung up on him. He considered calling again but in Kendall's state of anxiety it might only make matters worse.

Goddamned amateurs! What the hell did they expect? Albert Speer himself to get in touch with Washington and lend the army air corps a few designs because he heard they had problems?

Jesus!

618

David walked angrily out of the telephone booth and the store and into the street.

Where the goddamned hell was he? Oh, yes, the Scotch. The store was back at Talcahuano, Jean said. Four blocks west. He looked at his watch and, of course, there was no watch.

Goddamn.

"I'm sorry I took so long. I got confused. I walked the wrong way for a couple of blocks." David put the package of Scotch and soda water on the sink. Jean was sitting on the sofa; disturbed about something, he thought. "Did I get the call?"

"Not the one you expected," said Jean softly. "Someone else. He said he'd phone you tomorrow."

"Oh? Did he leave a name?"

"Yes, he did." When she answered, David heard the questioning fear in her voice. "It was Heinrich Stoltz."

"Stoltz? Don't know him."

"You should. He's an undersecretary at the German embassy. . . .David, what are you doing?"

27

"Sorry, *señor*. Mister Kendall checked out last night. At ten thirty, according to the card."

"Did he leave any other address or telephone number here in Buenos Aires?"

"No, *señor*. I believe he was going back to the United States. There was a Pan American flight at midnight."

"Thank you." David put down the telephone and reached for his cigarettes. It was incredible! Kendall had shot out at the first moment of difficulty. Why?

The telephone rang, startling David.

"Hello?"

"Herr Spaulding?"

"Yes."

"Heinrich Stoltz. I called last night but you were out."

"Yes, I know . . . I understand you're with the German embassy. I hope I don't have to tell you that I find your contacting me unorthodox. And not a little distasteful."

"Oh, come, Herr Spaulding. The man from *Lisbon?* He finds unorthodoxy?" Stoltz laughed quietly but not insultingly.

"I am an embassy attaché specializing in economics. Nothing more. If you know anything about me, surely you know that. . . .Now, I'm late. . . ."

"Please," interrupted Stoltz. "I call from a public telephone. Surely *that* tells *you* something."

It did, of course.

"I don't talk on telephones."

"Yours is clean, I checked thoroughly."

"If you want to meet, give me a time and an address. . . .Somewhere in the downtown area. With people around; no outside locations."

"There's a restaurant, Casa Langosta del Mar, several blocks north of the Parque Lezama. It's out of the way, not outside. There are back rooms. Curtains, no doors; no means of isolation. Only seclusion."

"Time?"

"Half past twelve."

"Do you smoke?" asked David sharply.

"Yes."

"Carry a pack of American cigarettes from the moment you get out of the car. In your left hand; the foil off one end of the top, two cigarettes removed."

"It's quite unnecessary. I know who you are. I'll recognize you."

"That's not my concern. I don't know you." David hung up the phone abruptly. As in all such rendezvous, he would arrive at the location early, through a delivery entrance if possible, and position himself as best he could to observe his contact's arrival. The cigarettes were nothing more than a psychological device: the contact was thrown off balance with the realization that he was an identified mark. A target. A marked contact was reluctant to bring trouble. And if trouble was his intent, he wouldn't show up.

Jean Cameron walked down the corridor toward the metal staircase that led to the cellars.

To the "Caves."

The "Caves" – a name given without affection by Foreign Service officers the world over – were those underground rooms housing file cabinets containing dossiers on just about everybody who had the slightest contact with an embassy, known and unknown, friend and adversary. They included exhaustive checks and counterchecks on all embassy personnel; service background, State Department evaluations, progress reports. Nothing was left out if it was obtainable.

Two signatures were required to gain entrance into the "Caves." The ambassador's and that of the senior attaché seeking information.

It was a regulation that was occasionally bypassed in the interests of haste and emergency. The marine officer of the guard generally could be convinced that an established attaché *had* to have immediate background material; the marine would list both the names of the embassy man and his subject on the check sheet, then stand in attendance while the file was removed. If there were repercussions, they were the attaché's responsibility.

There never were. Violations of this sort guaranteed a post in Uganda. The check sheet was sealed daily and sent only to the ambassador.

Jean rarely took advantage of her relationship to Henderson Granville in embassy matters. In truth, the occasion rarely arose, and when it did, the matter was always insignificant.

It was not insignificant now. And she intended to use fully her status as *family*, as well as a respected member of the staff. Granville had left for lunch; he would not return for several hours. She had made up her mind to tell the marine guard that her "father-in-law, the ambassador" had asked her to make a discreet inquiry regarding a new transfer.

Spaulding, David.

If Henderson wished to call her down for it, she would tell him the truth. She found herself very, *very* involved with the enigmatic Mr. Spaulding, and if Henderson did not realize it, he was a damn fool.

The marine officer of the guard was a young lieutenant from the FMF base south of La Boca. The personnel from FMF were sped in civilian clothes through the city to their posts at the embassy; the treaty that permitted the small, limited base did not condone uniformed men outside either territory. These restrictions tended to make the young officers sensitive to the functionary, faceless roles they were forced to play. So it was understandable that when the ambassador's daughter-in-law called him by name and spoke confidentially of a discreet matter, the marine complied without question.

Jean stared at David's file. It was frightening. It was not like any file she had ever seen. There was no dossier, no State Department records, no reports, no evaluations, no listing of post assignments.

There was only a single page.

It gave his description by sex, height, weight, coloring and visible markings. Beneath this cursory data, separated by a three-line space, was the following:

War Dept. Transfer. Clandestine Operations. Finance. Tortugas.

And nothing more.

"Finding what you need, Mrs. Cameron?" asked the marine lieutenant by the steel-grilled gate.

"Yes. . . .Thank you." Jean slipped David's thin folder back into place in the cabinet, smiled at the marine, and left.

She reached the staircase and walked slowly up the steps. She accepted the fact that David was involved with an undercover assignment accepted it while hating it; loathing the secrecy, the obvious danger. But in a conscious way she had prepared herself, expecting the worst and finding it. She was not at all sure she could handle the knowledge, but she was willing to try. If she could not handle it she'd take what moments of selfish pleasure she could and kiss David Spaulding good-bye. She had made up her mind to that . . . unconsciously, really. She could not allow herself more pain.

And there was something else. It was only a dim shadow in a half-lit room but it kept falling across her eyes. It was the word.

"Tortugas."

She had seen it before. Recently. Only days ago.

It had caught her attention because she'd thought of the Dry Tortugas . . . and the few times she and Andrew had sailed there from the Keys.

Where was it? Yes . . . Yes she remembered.

It had been in a very mechanical paragraph within the context of an area surveillance report on Henderson Granville's desk. She had read it rather absently one morning . . . only a few days ago. But she hadn't read it closely. Area surveillance reports were comprised of short, choppy informational sentences devoid of rhythm and color. Written by unimaginative men concerned only with what they could describe briefly, with data.

It had been down at La Boca.

Something about the captain of a trawler . . . and cargo. Cargo that had a lading destination of Tortugas. A violation of coastal limits; said destination rescinded, called an obvious error by the trawler's captain.

Yet the lading papers had said Tortugas.

And David Spaulding's classified operation – *clandestine* operation – was coded "Tortugas."

And Heinrich Stoltz of the German embassy had called David.

And Jean Cameron was suddenly afraid.

Spaulding was convinced that Stoltz was alone. He signaled the German to follow him to the back of the restaurant, to the curtained cubicle David had arranged for with the waiter a half hour ago.

Stoltz entered carrying the pack of cigarettes in his left hand. Spaulding circled the round table and sat facing the curtain.

"Have a seat," said David indicating the chair opposite him. Stoltz smiled, realizing that his back would be to the entrance.

"The man from Lisbon is a cautious man." The German pulled out the chair and sat down, placing the cigarettes on the table. "I can assure you I'm not armed."

"Good. I am."

"You are *too* cautious. The colonels look askance at belligerents carrying weapons in their neutral city. Your embassy should have told you."

"I understand they also arrest Americans quicker than they do you fellows."

Stoltz shrugged. "Why not? After all, we trained them. You only buy their beef."

"There'll be no lunch, incidentally I paid the waiter for the table."

"I'm sorry. The langosta . . . the lobster here is excellent. Perhaps a drink?"

"No drinks. Just talk."

Stoltz spoke, his voice flat. "I bring a welcome to Buenos Aires. From Erich Rhinemann."

David stared at the man. "You?"

"Yes. I'm your contact."

"That's interesting."

"That's the way of Erich Rhinemann. He pays for allegiances."

"I'll want proof."

"By all means. From Rhinemann himself. . . .Acceptable?"

Spaulding nodded. "When? Where?"

"That's what I'm here to discuss. Rhinemann is as cautious as the man from Lisbon."

"I was attached to the diplomatic corps in Portugal. Don't try to make anything more of it than that."

"Unfortunately, I have to speak the truth. Herr Rhinemann is most upset that the men in Washington saw fit to send you as the liaison. Your presence in Buenos Aires could attract attention."

David reached for the cigarettes Stoltz had placed on the table. He lit one. . . .The German was right, of course; Rhinemann was right. The one liability in his having been chosen was the enemy's probable knowledge of his Lisbon operations. Ed Pace. he was sure, had considered that aspect, discarding it in favor of the overriding assets. Regardless, it was not a subject to discuss with Heinrich Stoltz. The German attaché was still an unproven factor.

"I have no idea what you're referring to. I'm in Buenos Aires to transmit preliminary recommendations from New York and London banking circles relative to postwar reconstruction negotiations. You see, we *do* believe we'll win. Rhinemann can't be overlooked in such projected discussions."

"The man from Lisbon is most professional."

"I wish you'd stop repeating that nonsense. . . ."

"And convincing," interrupted Stoltz. "The cover is one of your better ones. It has more stature than a cowardly American socialite. . . .Even Herr Kendall agrees with that."

David paused before replying. Stoltz was circling in, about to deliver his proof. "Describe Kendall," he said quietly.

"In short words?"

"It doesn't matter."

Stoltz laughed under his breath. "I'd prefer as few as possible. He's a most unattractive biped. He must be an extraordinary man with figures; there's no other earthly reason to stay in the same room with him."

"Have you stayed in the same room with him?"

"For hours, unfortunately. With Rhinemann. . . .Now. May we talk?"

"Go ahead."

"Your man Lyons will be here the day after tomorrow. We can accomplish everything very quickly. The designs will be delivered in one package, not two as Kendall believes."

"Does he believe that?"

"It's what he was told."

"Why?"

"Because until late last evening Herr Rhinemann thought it was so. I myself did not know of the change until this morning."

"Then why did you call me last night?"

"Instructions from Walter Kendall."

"Please explain that."

"Is it necessary? One has nothing to do with the other. Herr Kendall telephoned *me*. Apparently he had just spoken with you. He said he was called back to Washington suddenly; that I was to contact you immediately so there's no break in communications. He was most adamant."

"Did Kendall say why he was returning to the States?"

"No. And I saw no reason to inquire. His work here is finished. He's of no concern to us. You are the man with the codes, not him."

David crushed out his cigarette, staring at the tablecloth. "What's your rank at the embassy?"

Stoltz smiled. "Third . . . fourth in command would be a modest appraisal. My loyalty, however, is to the Rhinemann interests. Surely that's apparent."

"I'll know when I talk to Rhinemann, won't I?" David looked up at the German. "Why are the Gestapo here in Buenos Aires?"

"They're not. . . .Well, there's one man; no more than a clerk really. As all Gestapo he thinks of himself as the personal spokesman for the Reich and overburdens the couriers – who, incidentally, cooperate with us. He is, as you *Amerikaner* say, a jackass. There is no one else."

"Are you sure?"

"Of course. I would be the first to know; before the ambassador, I assure you. This game is quite unnecessary, Herr Spaulding."

"You'd better set up that meeting with Rhinemann . . . *that's* necessary."

"Yes. Certainly. . . .Which brings us back to Herr Rhinemann's concerns. Why is the man from Lisbon in Buenos Aires?"

"I'm afraid he has to be. You said it. I'm cautious. I'm experienced. And I have the codes."

"But why *you?* To remove you from Lisbon is costly. I speak both as an enemy and as an objective neutral, allied with Rhinemann. Is there some side issue of which we're not aware?"

"If there is, I'm not aware of it, either," answered Spaulding, neutralizing Stoltz's inquisitorial look with one of his own. "Since we're talking plain, I want to get those designs okayed, send the codes for your goddamned money and get the hell out of here. Since a large share of that financing will come from the government Washington obviously thinks I'm the best man to see we're not cheated."

Both men remained silent for several moments. Stoltz spoke.

"I believe you. You Americans always worry about being cheated, don't you?"

"Let's talk about Rhinemann. I want the meeting immediately. I won't be satisfied that Kendall's arrangements are solid until I hear it from him. And I won't organize a code schedule with Washington until I'm satisfied."

"There's no schedule?"

"There won't be any until I see Rhinemann."

Stoltz breathed deeply. "You are what they say, a thorough man. You'll see Rhinemann. . . .It will have to be after dark, two transfers of vehicles, his residence. He can't take the chance of anyone seeing you together. . . .Do these precautions disturb you?"

"Not a bit. Without the codes there's no money transferred in Switzerland. I think Herr Rhinemann will be most hospitable."

"Yes, I'm sure . . . Very well. Our business is concluded. You'll be contacted this evening. Will you be at home?"

"If not, I'll leave word at the embassy switchboard."

"*Dann auf Wiedersehen, mein Herr.*" Stoltz got out of the chair and gave a diplomatic nod of his head. "*Heute Abend.*"

"*Heute Abend,*" replied Spaulding as the German parted the curtain and walked out of the cubicle. David saw that Stoltz had left his cigarettes on the table; a minor gift or a minor insult. He removed one and found himself squeezing the tip as he remembered Kendall doing – incessantly, with every cigarette the accountant prepared to smoke. David broke the paper around the tobacco and dropped it in the ashtray. Anything reminding him of Kendall was distasteful now. He couldn't think about Kendall and his sudden, fear-induced departure.

He had something else to think about.

Heinrich Stoltz, "third, fourth in command" at the German embassy, was not so highly placed as he believed. The Nazi had not been lying – he *did not* know the Gestapo was in Buenos Aires. And if he didn't know, that meant someone wasn't telling him.

It was ironic, thought David, that he and Erich Rhinemann would be working together after all. Before be killed Rhinemann, of course.

Heinrich Stoltz sat down at his desk and picked up the telephone. He spoke in his impeccable academic German.

"Get me Herr Rhinemann in Luján."

He replaced the phone, leaned back in his chair and smiled. Several moments later his buzzer hummed.

"Herr Rhinemann? . . . Heinrich Stoltz. . . . Yes, yes, everything went smoothly. Kendall spoke the truth. This Spaulding knows nothing about Koening or the diamonds; his only concerns are the designs. His only threat – that of withholding funds. He plays unimpressive games but we need the codes. The American fleet patrols could be ordered to seal off the harbor; the trawler will have to get out. . . . Can you imagine? All this Spaulding is interested in is not being cheated!"

28

At first he thought he was mistaken. . . .No, that wasn't quite right, he considered; that wasn't his first thought. He didn't have a first *thought*, he had only a *reaction*.

He was stunned.

Leslie Hawkwood!

He saw her from his taxi window talking with a man at the south end of the fountain in the Plaza de Mayo. The cab was slowly making its way through the traffic around the huge square; he ordered the driver to pull over and stop.

David paid the driver and got out. He was now directly opposite Leslie and the man; he could see the blurred figures through the spray of the fountain.

The man handed Leslie an envelope and bowed a European bow. He turned and went to the curb, his hand held up for a taxi. One stopped and the man got in; the cab entered the flow of traffic and Leslie went to the crosswalk, waiting for the pedestrian signal.

David made his way cautiously around the fountain and dashed to the curb just as the crosswalk light flashed.

He dodged the anxious vehicles, arousing horns and angry shouts, angling his path to the left in case she turned around at the commotion. She was at least fifty yards ahead of him; she couldn't spot him, he was sure of that.

On the boulevard, Leslie headed west toward Avenida 9 de Julio. David closed the gap between them but kept himself obscured by the crowds. She stopped briefly at several store windows, twice obviously trying to make up her mind whether to enter or not.

So like Leslie; she had always hated to give up the acquisition of something new.

She kept walking, however. Once she looked at her wristwatch; she turned north on Julio and checked the numbers of two storefront addresses, apparently to determine the directional sequence.

Leslie Hawkwood had never been to Buenos Aires.

She continued north at a leisurely pace, taking in the extraordinary color and size of the boulevard. She reached the corner of Corrientes, in the middle of the theater district, and wandered past the billboards, looking at the photographs of the performers.

Spaulding realized that the American embassy was less than two blocks away – between the Avenidas Supacha and Esmeralda. There was no point in wasting time.

She saw him before he spoke. Her eyes widened, her jaw fell, her whole body trembled visibly. The blood drained from her suntanned face.

"You have two alternatives, Leslie," said Spaulding as he came within a foot of her, looking down at her terrified face. "The embassy is right up there; it's United States territory. You'll be arrested as a citizen interfering with national security, if not espionage. Or you can come with me. . . .And answer questions. Which will it be?"

The taxi took them to the airport, where Spaulding rented a car with the papers identifying him as "Donald Scanlan, mining surveyor." They were the sort of identifications he carried when making contact with such men as Heinrich Stoltz.

He had held Leslie by the arm with sufficient pressure to warn her not to attempt running; she was his prisoner and he was deadly serious about the fact. She said nothing at all during the ride to the airport, she simply stared out tile window, avoiding his eyes.

Her only words at the rental counter were, "Where are we going?"

His reply was succinct: "Out of Buenos Aires."

He followed the river road north toward the outskirts, into the hills above the city. A few miles into the Sante Fé province, the Rio Luján curved westward, and he descended the steep inclines onto the highway paralleling the water's edge. It was the territory of the Argentine rich. Yachts were moored or cruising slowly; sailboats of all classes were lazily catching the upriver winds, tacking harmoniously among the tiny green islands which sprung out of the water like lush gardens. Private roads veered off the highway – now subtly curving west, away from the water. Enormous villas dotted the banks; nothing was without visual effect.

He saw a road to his left that was the start of a hill. He swung up into it, and after a mile there was a break in the bordering forest and a sign in front of a flat, graveled area.

Vigia Tigre.

A lookout. A courtesy for tourists.

He drove the car to the front of the parking ground and pulled to a stop, next to the railing. It was a weekday; there were no other automobiles.

Leslie had said nothing throughout the hour's ride. She had smoked cigarettes, her hands trembling, her eyes refusing to make contact with his. And through experience, David knew the benefits of silence under such conditions.

The girl was close to breaking.

"All right. Now come the questions." Spaulding turned in the seat and faced her. "And please believe me, I won't hesitate to run you into military arrest if you refuse."

She swung her head around and stared at him angrily – yet still in fear. "Why didn't you do that an hour ago?"

"Two reasons," he answered simply. "Once the embassy is involved, I'd be locked into a chain of command; the decisions wouldn't be mine. I'm too curious to lose that control. . . .And second, old friend, I think you're in way the hell over your head. What is it, Leslie? What *are* you into?"

She put the cigarette to her lips and inhaled as though her life depended on the smoke. She closed her eyes briefly and spoke barely above a whisper. "I can't tell you. Don't force me to."

He sighed. "I don't think you understand. I'm an Intelligence officer assigned to Clandestine Operations – I'm not telling you anything you don't know. You made it possible for my hotel room to be searched; you lied; you went into hiding; for all I know, you were responsible for several assaults which nearly cost me my life. Now, you turn up in Buenos Aires, four thousand miles away from that Park Avenue apartment. You followed me four thousand miles! . . . *Why?*"

"I can't *tell* you! I haven't been *told* what I can tell you!"

"You haven't been . . . *Christ!* With what I can piece together – and testify to – you could spend twenty years in prison!"

"I'd like to get out of the car. May I?" she said softly, snuffing out her cigarette in the ashtray.

"Sure. Go ahead." David opened his door and rapidly came around the automobile. Leslie walked to the railing, the waters of the Rio Luján far below in the distance.

"It's very beautiful here, isn't it?"

"Yes. . . .Did you try to have me killed?"

"Oh, *God!*" She whirled on him, spitting out the words. "I tried to save your *life!* I'm here because I don't *want* you killed!"

It took David a few moments to recover from the girl's statement. Her hair had fallen carelessly around her face, her eyes blinking back tears, her lips trembling.

"I think you'd better explain that," he said in a quiet monotone.

She turned away from him and looked down at the river, the villas, the boats. "It's like the Riviera, isn't it?"

"*Stop it*, Leslie!"

"Why? It's part of it." She put her hands on the railing. "It used to be all there was. Nothing else mattered. *Where* next; *who* next? *What* a lovely party! . . . You were part of it."

"Not really. You're wrong if you thought that. Just as you're wrong now. . . .I won't be put off."

"I'm not putting you off." She gripped the railing harder; it was a physical gesture telegraphing her indecision with her words. "I'm trying to tell you something."

"That you followed me because you wanted to save my *life?*" He asked the question with incredulity. "You were filled with dramatics in New York, too, if I recall. You waited, how long was it? Five, six, eight years to get me on the boathouse floor again. You're a bitch."

"And *you're insignificant!*" She flung the words at him in heat. And then she subsided, controlling herself. "I don't mean you . . . *you*. Just compared to everything else. We're all insignificant in that sense."

"So the lady has a cause."

Leslie stared at him and spoke softly. "One she believes in very deeply."

"Then you should have no reservations explaining it to me."

"I *will*. I promise you. But I can't *now*. . . .Trust me,"

"Certainly," said David casually. And then he suddenly whipped out his hand, grabbing her purse, which hung from her shoulder by a leather strap. She started to resist; he looked at her. She stopped and breathed deeply.

He opened the purse and took out the envelope she had been given at the fountain in the Plaza de Mayo. As he did so, his eyes caught sight of a bulge at the bottom of the bag, covered by a silk scarf. He held the envelope between his fingers and reached down. He separated the scarf from the object and pulled out a small Remington revolver. Without saying anything, he checked the chamber and the safety and put the weapon in his jacket pocket.

"I've learned to use it," said Leslie tentatively.

"Good for you," replied Spaulding, opening the envelope.

"At least you'll see how efficient we are," she said turning, looking down at the river.

There was no letterhead, no origin of writer or organization. The heading on the top of the paper read:

Spaulding. David. Lt. Col. Military Intelligence.
U.S. Army. Classification 4.0. Fairfax.

Beneath were five complicated paragraphs detailing every move he had made since he was picked up on Saturday afternoon entering the embassy. David was pleased to see that "Donald Scanlan" was not mentioned; he'd gotten through the airport and customs undetected.

Everything else was listed: his apartment, his telephone, his office at the embassy, the incident on the Córdoba roof, the lunch with Jean Cameron at La Boca, the meeting with Kendall at the hotel, the assault on the Avenida Paraná, his telephone call in the store on Rodriguez Peña.

Everything.

Even the "lunch" with Heinrich Stoltz at the Langosta del Mar, on the border of Lezuma. The meeting with Stoltz was estimated to last "a minimum of one hour."

It was the explanation for her leisurely pace on the Avenida de Mayo. But David had cut the meeting short; there'd been no lunch. He wondered if he had been picked up after he'd left the restaurant. He had not been concerned. His thoughts had been on Heinrich Stoltz and the presence of a Gestapo Stoltz knew nothing about.

"Your people are *very* thorough. Now, who are they?"

"Men . . . and women who have a calling. A purpose. A *great* calling."

"That's not what I asked you. . . ."

There was the sound of an automobile coming up the hill below the parking area. Spaulding reached inside his jacket for his pistol. The car came into view and proceeded upward, past them. The people in the car were laughing. David turned his attention back to Leslie.

"I asked you to trust me," said the girl. "I was on my way to an address on that street, the boulevard called Julio. I was to be there at one thirty. They'll wonder where I am."

"You're not going to answer me, are you?"

"I'll answer you in one way. I'm here to convince you to get out of Buenos Aires."

"Why?"

"Whatever it is you're doing – and I don't *know* what it is, they haven't told me – it can't happen. We can't let it happen. It's wrong."

"Since you don't know what it is, how can you say it's wrong?"

"Because I've been told. That's enough!"

"*Ein Volk, ein Reich, ein Führer*, said David quietly. "Get in the car!"

"No. You've got to listen to me! Get out of Buenos Aires! Tell your generals it can't be done!"

"Get in the car!"

There was the sound of another automobile, this time coming from the opposite direction, from above. David put his hand once more under his jacket, but then removed it casually. It was the same vehicle with the laughing tourists that had passed by moments ago. They were still laughing, still gesturing; probably drunk with luncheon wine.

"You can't take me to the embassy! You *can't!*"

"If you don't get in the car, you'll just wake up there! Go on."

There was the screeching of tires on the gravel. The descending automobile had turned abruptly – at the last second – and swung sharply into the parking area and come to a stop.

David looked up and swore to himself, his hand immobile inside his jacket.

Two high-powered rifles protruded from the open windows of the car. They were aimed at him.

The heads of the three men inside were covered with silk stockings, the faces flattened, grotesque beyond the translucent masks. The rifles were held by one man next to the driver and by another in the back.

The man in the rear opened the door, his rifle held steady. He gave his command in a calm voice in English.

"Get in the car, Mrs. Hawkwood. . . .And you, colonel. Remove your weapon by the handle – with two fingers."

David did so.

"Walk to the railing," commanded the man in the back seat, "and drop it over the side, into the woods."

David complied. The man got out of the car to let Leslie climb in. He then returned to his seat and closed the door.

There was the gunning of the powerful engine and the sound once more of spinning tires over the loose gravel. The car lurched forward out of the parking area and sped off down the hill.

David stood by the railing. He would go over it and find his pistol. There was no point in trying to follow the automobile with Leslie Hawkwood and three men in stocking masks. His rented car was no match for a Duesenberg.

29

The restaurant had been selected by Jean. It was out of the way in the north section of the city, beyond Palermo Park, a place for assignation. Telephone jacks were in the wall by the booths; waiters could be seen bringing phones to and from the secluded tables.

He was mildly surprised that Jean would know such a restaurant. Or would choose it for them.

"Where did you go this afternoon?" she asked, seeing him looking out over the dim room from their booth.

"A couple of conferences. Very dull. Bankers have a penchant for prolonging any meeting way beyond its finish. The Strand or Wall Street, makes no difference." He smiled at her.

"Yes. . . . Well, perhaps, they're always looking for ways to extract every last dollar."

"No 'perhaps.' That's it. . . . This is quite a place, by the way. Reminds me of Lisbon."

"Rome," she said. "It's more like Rome. Way out. Via Appia. Did you know that the Italians comprise over thirty per cent of the population in Buenos Aires?"

"I knew it was considerable."

"The Italian hand. . . . That's supposed to mean evil."

"Or clever. Not necessarily evil. The 'fine Italian hand' is usually envied."

"Bobby brought me here one night. . . . I think he brings lots of girls here."

"It's . . . discreet."

"I think he was worried that Henderson might find out he had dishonorable designs. And so he brought me here."

"Which confirms his designs."

"Yes. . . . It's for lovers. But we weren't."

"I'm glad you chose it for us. It gives me a nice feeling of security."

"Oh, no! Don't look for that. No one's in the market for that this year. No. . . . Security's out of the question. And commitments. Those, too. No commitments for sale." She took a cigarette from his open pack; he lit it for her. Over the flame he saw her eyes staring at him. Caught, she glanced downward, at nothing.

"What's the matter?"

"Nothing. . . . Nothing at all." She smiled, but only the outlines were there; not the ingenuousness, not the humor. "Did you talk to that man Stoltz?"

"Good Lord, is that what's bothering you? . . . I'm sorry, I suppose I should have said something. Stoltz was selling fleet information; I'm in no position to buy. I told him to get in touch with Naval Intelligence. I made a report to the base commander at FMF this morning. If they want to use him, they will."

"Strange he should call you."

"That's what I thought. Apparently German surveillance picked me up the other day and the financial data was on their sheet. That was enough for Stoltz."

"He's a defector?"

"Or selling bad stuff. It's FMF's problem, not mine."

"You're very glib." She drank her coffee unsteadily.

"What's that supposed to mean?"

"Nothing. . . . Just that you're quick. Quick and facile. You must be very good at your work."

"And you're in a godawful mood. Does an excess of gin bring it on?"

"Oh, you think I'm drunk?"

"You're not sober. Not that it matters." He grinned. "You're hardly an alcoholic."

"Thanks for the vote of confidence. But don't speculate. That implies some kind of permanence. We must avoid that, mustn't we?"

"Must we? It seems to be a point with you tonight. It wasn't a problem I was considering."

"You just brushed it aside, I assume. I'm sure you have other, more pressing matters." In replacing her cup, Jean spilled coffee on the tablecloth. She was obviously annoyed with herself. "I'm doing it badly," she said after a moment of silence.

"You're doing it badly," be agreed.

"I'm frightened."

"Of what?"

"You're not here in Buenos Aires to talk to bankers, are you? It's much more than that. You won't tell me, I know. And in a few weeks, you'll be gone . . . if you're alive."

"You're letting your imagination take over." He took her hand; she crushed out her cigarette and put her other hand over his. She gripped him tightly.

"All right. Let's say you're right." She spoke quietly now; he had to strain to hear her. "I'm making everything up. I'm crazy and I drank too much. Indulge me. Play the game for a minute."

"If you want me to . . . O.K."

"It's hypothetical. My David isn't a State Department syndromer, you see. He's an agent. We've had a few here; I've met them. The colonels call them *provocarios*. . . . So, my David is an agent and being an agent is called . . . high-risk something or other because the rules are different. That is, the rules don't have any meaning. . . . There aren't any rules for these people . . . like my hypothetical David. Do you follow?"

"I follow," he replied simply. "I'm not sure what the object is or how a person scores."

"We'll get to that." She drank the last of her coffee, holding the cup firmly – too firmly; her fingers shook. "The point is, such a man as my . . . mythical David could be killed or crippled or have his face shot off. That's a horrible thought, isn't it?"

"Yes. I imagine that possibility has occurred to several hundred thousand men by now. It's horrible."

"But they're different. They have armies and uniforms and certain rules. Even in airplanes . . . their chances are better. And I say this with a certain expertise."

He looked at her intently. "Stop."

"Oh, not yet. Now, I'm going to tell you how you can score a goal. Why does my hypothetical David do what he does? . . . No, don't answer yet." She stopped and smiled weakly. "But you weren't about to answer, were you? It doesn't matter; there's a second part to the question. You get extra points for considering it."

"What's the second part?" He thought that Jean was recapitulating an argument she had memorized. Her next words proved it.

"You see, I've thought about it over and over again . . . for this make-believe game . . . this make-believe agent. He's in a very unique position; he works alone . . . or at least with very, *very* few people. He's in a strange country and he's alone . . . Do you understand the second part now?"

David watched her. She had made some abstract connection in her mind without verbalizing it. "No, I don't."

"If David is working alone and in a strange country and has to send codes to Washington . . . Henderson told me that. that means the people he's working for have to believe what he tells them. He can tell them anything he wants to. . . . So now we come back to the question. Knowing all this, why does the mythical David do what he does? He can't really believe that he'll influence the outcome of the whole war. He's only one among millions and millions."

"And . . . if I'm following you . . . this make-believe man can send word to his superiors that he's having difficulties. . . ."

"He has to stay on in Buenos Aires. For a long time," she interrupted, holding his hand fiercely.

'And if they say no, he can always hide out in the pampas.

"Don't make fun of me!" she said intensely.

"I'm not. I won't pretend that I can give you logical answers, but I don't think the man you're talking about has such a clear field. Tight reins are kept on such men, I believe. Other men could be sent into the area . . . would be sent, I'm sure. Your strategy is only a short-term gain; the penalties are long and damned stiff."

She withdrew her hands slowly, looking away from him. "It's a gamble that might be worth it, though. I love you very much. I don't want you hurt and I know there are people trying to hurt you." She stopped and turned her eyes back to him. "They're trying to kill you, aren't they? . . . One among so many millions . . . and I keep saying to myself, 'Not him. Oh, God, not him.' Don't you see? ... Do we need them? Are those people whoever they are – so important? To us? Haven't you done enough?"

He returned her stare and found himself understanding the profundity of her question. It wasn't a pleasant realization. ... He *had* done enough. His whole life had been turned around until the alien was an every-day occurrence.

For what?

The amateurs? Alan Swanson? Walter Kendall?

A dead Ed Pace. A corrupt Fairfax.

One among so many millions.

"Señor Spaulding?" The words shocked him momentarily because they were so completely unexpected. A tuxedoed maitre d' was standing by the edge of the booth, his voice low.

"Yes?"

"There's a telephone call for you."

David looked at the discreet man. "Can't you bring the telephone to the table?"

"Our sincere apologies. The instrument plug at this booth is not functioning."

A lie, of course, Spaulding knew.

"Very well." David got out of the booth. He turned to Jean. "I'll be right back. Have some more coffee."

"Suppose I wanted a drink?"

"Order it." He started to walk away.

"David?" She called out enough to be heard; not loudly.

"Yes?" He turned back; she was staring at him again.

" 'Tortugas' isn't worth it," she said quietly.

It was as if he'd been hit a furious blow in the stomach. Acid formed in his throat, his breath stopped, his eyes pained him as be looked down at her.

"I'll be right back."

"Heinrich Stoltz here," the voice said.

"I've been expecting your call. I assume the switchboard gave you the number."

"It was not necessary to telephone. The arrangements have been made. In twenty minutes a green Packard automobile will be outside the restaurant. A man will have his left arm out the window, holding an open pack of German cigarettes this time. I thought you would appreciate the symbolic repetition."

"I'm touched. But you may have to alter the time and the car."

"There can be no changes. Herr Rhinemann is adamant."

"So am I. Something's come up."

"Sorry. Twenty minutes. A green Packard automobile."

The connection was severed.

Well, that was Stoltz's problem, thought David. There was only one thought in mind. To get back to Jean.

He made his way out of the dimly lit corner and sidled awkwardly past the bar patrons whose stools were blocking the aisle. He was in a hurry; the human and inanimate obstructions were frustrating, annoying. He reached the arch into the dining area and walked rapidly through the tables to the rear booth.

Jean Cameron was gone. There was a note on the table.

It was on the back of a cocktail napkin, the words written in the heavy wax of an eyebrow pencil. Written hastily, almost illegibly:

> David. I'm sure you have things to do –
> places to go – and I'm a bore tonight

Nothing else. As if she'd just stopped.

He crumpled the napkin in his pocket and raced back across the dining room to the front entrance. The maitre d' stood by the door.

"*Señor?* Is there a problem?"

"The lady at the booth. Where did she go?!"

"Mrs. Cameron?"

Christ! thought David, looking at the calm *porteño*. What was happening? The reservation was in *his* name. Jean had indicated that she'd been to the restaurant only once before.

"Yes! Mrs. Cameron! Goddamn you, where is she!?"

"She left a few minutes ago. She took the first taxi at the curb."

"You *listen* to me. . . ."

"*Señor*," interrupted the obsequious Argentine, "there is a gentleman waiting for you outside. He will take care of your bill. He has an account with us."

Spaulding looked out the large windowpanes in the heavy front door. Through the glass he could see a man standing on the sidewalk. He was dressed in a white Palm Beach suit.

David pushed the door open and approached him.

"You want to see me?"

"I'm merely waiting for you, Herr Spaulding. To escort you. The car should be here in fifteen minutes."

30

The green Packard sedan came to a stop across the street, directly in front of the restaurant. The driver's arm appeared through the open window, an indistinguishable pack of cigarettes in his hand. The man in the white Palm Beach suit gestured politely for Spaulding to accompany him.

As he drew nearer, David could see that the driver was a large man in a black knit, short-sleeved shirt that both revealed and accentuated his muscular arms. There was a stubble of beard, thick eyebrows; he looked like a mean-tempered longshoreman, the rough image intended, Spaulding was sure. The man walking beside him opened the car door and David climbed in.

No one spoke. The car headed south back toward the center of Buenos Aires; then northeast into the Aeroparque district. David was mildly surprised to realize that the driver had entered the wide highway paralleling the river. The same road he had taken that afternoon with Leslie Hawkwood. He wondered whether the route was chosen deliberately, if they expected him to make some remark about the coincidence.

He sat back, giving no indication that he recognized anything.

The Packard accelerated on the wide river road which now swung to the left, following the water into the hills of the northwest. The car did not, however, go up any of the offshoot roads as David had done hours ago. Instead the driver maintained a steady, high speed. A reflecting highway sign was caught momentarily in the glare of the headlights: *Tigre 12 kil.*

The traffic was mild; cars rushed past intermittently from the opposite direction; several were overtaken by the Packard. The driver checked his rear- and side-view mirrors constantly.

In the middle of a long bend in the road, the Packard slowed down. The driver nodded his head to the man in the white Palm Beach suit beside David.

"We will exchange cars now, Herr Spaulding," said the man, reaching into his jacket, withdrawing a gun.

Ahead of them was a single building, an outskirts restaurant or an inn with a circular drive that curved in front of an entrance and veered off into a large parking area on the side. Spotlights lit the entrance and the lawn in front.

The driver swung in; the man beside Spaulding tapped him.

"Get out here, please. Go directly inside."

David opened the door. He was surprised to see a uniformed doorman remain by the entrance, making no move toward the Packard. Instead, he crossed rapidly in front of the entrance and started walking on the graveled drive in the direction of the side parking lot. Spaulding opened the front door and stepped into the carpeted foyer of the restaurant; the man in the white suit was at his heels, his gun now in his pocket.

Instead of proceeding toward the entrance of the dining area, the man held David by the arm – politely – and knocked on what appeared to be the door of a small office in the foyer. The door opened and the two of them walked inside.

It was a tiny office but that fact made no impression on Spaulding. What fascinated him were the two men inside. One was dressed in a white Palm Beach suit; the other – and David instantly, involuntarily, had to smile – was in the identical clothes he himself was wearing. A light blue, striped cord jacket and dark trousers. The second man was his own height, the same general build, the same general coloring.

David had no time to observe further. The light in the small office – a desk lamp – was snapped off by the newly appeared white suit. The German who had accompanied Spaulding walked to the single window that looked out on the circular drive. He spoke softly.

"*Schnell. Beeilen Sie sich . . . Danke.*"

The two men quickly walked to the door and let themselves out. The German by the window was silhouetted in the filtered light of the front entrance. He beckoned David.

"*Kommen Sie her.*"

He went to the window and stood beside the man. Outside, their two counterparts were on the driveway, talking and gesturing as if in an argument – a mild disagreement, not violent. Both smoked cigarettes, their faces more often covered by their hands than not. Their backs were to the highway beyond.

Then an automobile came from the right, from the direction of the parking lot, and the two men got inside. The car moved slowly to the left, to the entrance of the highway. It paused for several seconds, waiting for an opportune moment in the thinned-out night traffic. Suddenly it lurched forward, crossed to the right of the highway and sped off south, toward the city.

David wasn't sure why the elaborate ploy was considered necessary, he was about to ask the man beside him. Before he spoke, however, he noticed the smile on the man's face, inches from his in the window. Spaulding looked out.

About fifty yards away, off the side of the river road, headlights were snapped on. A vehicle, facing north, made a fast U-turn on the wide highway and headed south in a sudden burst of speed.

The German grinned. "*Amerikanische . . . Kinder.*"

David stepped back. The man crossed to the desk and turned on the lamp.

"That was an interesting exercise," said Spaulding.

The man looked up. "Simply a – what are your words, *eine Vorsichtsmassnahme-a . . .*"

"A precaution," said David.

"*Ja.* That's right, you speak German. . . . Come. Herr Rhinemann must not be kept waiting longer than the . . . *precautions* require."

Even in daylight, Spaulding realized, the dirt road would be difficult to find. As it was, with no street lamps and only the misty illumination of the moon, it seemed as though the Packard had swung off the hard pavement into a black wall of towering overgrowth. Instead, there was the unmistakable sound of dirt beneath the wheels as the car plunged forward, the driver secure in his knowledge of the numerous turns and straightaways. A half mile into the forest the dirt road suddenly widened and the surface became smooth and hard again.

There was an enormous parking area. Four stone gateposts – wide, medieval in appearance – were spaced equidistant from one another at the far end of the blacktopped field. Above each stone post was a massive floodlamp, the spills intersecting, throwing light over the entire area and into the woods beyond. Between the huge posts was a thick-grilled iron fence, in the center of which was a webbed steel gate, obviously operated electrically.

Men dressed in dark shirts and trousers – quasi-military in cut – stood around, several with dogs on leashes.

Dobermans. Massive, straining at their leather straps, barking viciously.

Commands could be heard from the handlers and the dogs subsided.

The man in the white Palm Beach suit opened the door and got out. He walked to the main gatepost, where a guard appeared at the fence from inside the compound. The two men talked briefly; David could see that beyond the guard stood a dark concrete or stucco enclosure, perhaps twenty feet in length, in which there were small windows with light showing through.

The guard returned to the miniature house; the man in the white suit came back to the Packard.

"We will wait a few minutes," he said, climbing into the rear seat.

"I thought we were in a hurry."

"To be here; to let Herr Rhinemann know we have arrived. Not necessarily to be admitted."

"Accommodating fellow," said David.

"Herr Rhinemann can be what he likes."

Ten minutes later the steel-webbed gate swung slowly open and the driver started the engine. The Packard cruised by the gatehouse and the guards; the Dobermans began their rapacious barking once again, only to be silenced by their masters. The road wound uphill, ending in another huge parking area in front of an enormous white mansion with wide marble steps leading to the largest pair of oak doors David had ever seen. Here, too, floodlights covered the whole area. Unlike the outside premises, there was a fountain in the middle of the courtyard, the reflection of the lights bouncing off the spray of the water.

It was as if some extravagant plantation house from the antebellum South had been dismantled stone by stone, board by board, marble block by marble block, and rebuilt deep within an Argentine forest.

An extraordinary sight, and not a little frightening in its massive architectural concept. The construction engineer in David was provoked and stunned at the same time. The materials-logistics must have been staggering; the methods of leveling and transport incredible.

The cost unbelievable.

The German got out of the car and walked around to David's door. He opened it.

"We'll leave you now. It's been a pleasant trip. Go to the door; you'll he admitted. *Auf Wiedersehen.*"

David got out and stood on the hard surface before the marble steps. The green Packard started off down the winding descent.

Spaulding stood alone for nearly a minute. If he was being watched – and the thought crossed his mind – the observer might think he was an astonished caller overwhelmed by the magnificence in front of him. That judgment would have been partially accurate; his remaining concentration, however, was on the mansion's more mundane specifics: the windows, the roof, the grounds on both visible sides.

Ingress and egress were matters to be considered constantly; the unexpected was never to be projected as too unlikely.

He walked up the steps and approached the immense, thick wooden doors. There was no knocker, no bell; he hadn't thought there would be.

He turned and looked down at the floodlit area. Not a person in sight; neither guards nor servants. No one.

Quiet. Even the sounds of the forest seemed subdued. Only the splash of the fountain interrupted the stillness.

Which meant, of course, that there were eyes unseen and whispers unheard, directing their attention on him.

The door opened. Heinrich Stoltz stood in the frame.

"Welcome to Habichtsnest, Herr Spaulding. The Hawk's Lair; appropriately – if theatrically – named, is it not?"

David stepped inside. The foyer, as might be expected, was enormous; a marble staircase rose beyond a chandelier of several thousand crystal cones. The walls were covered with gold cloth; Renaissance paintings were hung beneath silver portrait lamps.

"It's not like any bird's nest I've ever seen."

"True. However, Habichtsnest, I think, loses something in your translation. Come with me, please. Herr Rhinemann is outside on the river balcony. It's a pleasant evening."

They walked underneath the grotesque yet beautiful chandelier, past the marble staircase to an archway at the end of the great hall. It led out to an enormous terrace that stretched the length of the building. There were white wrought-iron tables topped with spotless glass, chairs of varying sizes with brightly colored cushions. A series of large double doors could be seen on both sides of the arch; they presumably led to diverse sections of the huge house.

Bordering the terrace was a stone balustrade, waist high, with statuary and plants on the railing. Beyond the balcony, in the distance, were the waters of the Río Luján. At the left end of the terrace was a small platform, blocked by a gate. Enormously thick wires could be seen above. It was a dock for a cable car, the wires evidently extending down to the river.

David absorbed the splendor, expecting his first view of Rhinemann. There was no one; he walked to the railing and saw that beneath the balcony was another terrace perhaps twenty feet below. A large swimming pool – complete with racing lines in the tile – was illuminated by floodlights under the blue green water. Additional metal tables with sun umbrellas and deck chairs were dotted about the pool and the terrace. And surrounding it all was a manicured lawn that in the various reflections of light looked like the thickest, fullest putting green David had ever seen. Somewhat incongruously, there were the silhouettes of poles and wickets; a croquet course had been imposed on the smooth surface.

"I hope you'll come out one day and enjoy our simple pleasures, Colonel Spaulding."

David was startled by the strange, quiet voice. He turned. The figure of a man stood in shadows alongside the arch of the great hall.

Erich Rhinemann had been watching him, of course.

Rhinemann emerged from the darkened area. He was a moderately tall man with greying straight hair combed rigidly back – partless. He was somewhat stocky for his size – "powerful" would be the descriptive word, but his stomach girth might deny the term. His hands were large, beefy, yet somehow delicate, dwarfing the wineglass held between his fingers.

He came into a sufficient spill of light for David to see his face clearly. Spaulding wasn't sure why, but the face startled him. It was a broad face; a wide forehead above a wide expanse of lip beneath a rather wide, flat nose. He was deeply tanned, his eyebrows nearly white from the sun. And then David realized why he was startled.

Erich Rhinemann was an aging man. The deeply tanned skin was a cover for the myriad lines the years had given him; his eyes were narrow, surrounded by swollen folds of age; the faultlessly tailored sports jacket and trousers were cut for a much, much younger man.

Rhinemann was fighting a battle his wealth could not win for him.

"*Habichtsnest ist prächtig. Unglaublich,*" said David politely but without commensurate enthusiasm.

"You are kind," replied Rhinemann, extending his hand. "And also courteous; but there is no reason not to speak English. . . . Come, sit down. May I offer you a drink?" The financier led the way to the nearest table.

"Thank you, no," said David, sitting across from Rhinemann. "I have urgent business in Buenos Aires. A fact I tried to make clear to Stoltz before he hung up."

Rhinemann looked over at an unperturbed Stoltz, who was leaning against the stone balustrade. "Was that necessary? Herr Spaulding is not to be so treated."

"I'm afraid it *was* necessary, *mein Herr*. For our American friend's own benefit. It was reported to us that he was followed; we were prepared for such an occurrence."

"If I was followed, you were doing the following."

"*After* the fact, colonel; I don't deny it. Before, we had no *reason*."

Rhinemann's narrow eyes pivoted to Spaulding, "This is disturbing. Who would have you followed?"

"May we talk privately?" David said, glancing at Heinrich Stoltz.

The financier smiled. "There's nothing in our arrangements that excludes the *Botschaftssekretär*. He is among my most valued associates in South America. Nothing should be withheld."

"I submit that you won't know unless we speak alone."

"Our American colonel is perhaps embarrassed," interrupted Stoltz, his voice laced with invective. "The man from Lisbon is not considered competent by his own government. He's placed under American surveillance."

David lit a cigarette; he did not reply to the German attaché. Rhinemann spoke, gesturing with his large, delicate hands.

"If this is so, there is no cause for exclusion. And obviously, there can be no other explanation."

"We're buying," said David with quiet emphasis. "You're selling. . . . Stolen property."

Stoltz was about to speak but Rhinemann held up his hand.

"What you are implying is not possible. Our arrangements were made in complete secrecy; they have been totally successful. And Herr Stoltz is a confidant of the High Command. More so than the ambassador."

"I don't like repeating myself." David spoke angrily. "Especially when I'm paying."

"Leave us, Heinrich," said Rhinemann, his eyes on Spaulding.

Stoltz bowed stiffly and walked rapidly, furiously, through the arch into the great hall.

"Thank you." David shifted his position in the chair and looked up at several small balconies on the second and third stories of the house. He wondered how many men were near the windows; watching, prepared to jump if he made a false move.

"We're alone as requested," said the German expatriot, hardly concealing his irritation. "What is it?"

"Stoltz is marked," said Spaulding. He paused to see what kind of reaction the financier would register at such news. As he might have expected, there was none. David continued, thinking perhaps that Rhinemann did not entirely understand. "He's not being given straight information at the embassy. He may do better at ours."

"Preposterous." Rhinemann remained immobile, his narrow eyelids half squinting, staring at David. "On what do you base such an opinion?"

"The Gestapo. Stoltz claims there's no active Gestapo in Buenos Aires. He's wrong. It's here. It's active. It's determined to stop you. Stop us."

Erich Rhinemann's composure cracked – if only infinitesimally. There was the slightest, tiny vibration within the rolls of flesh beneath his eyes," and his stare – if possible, thought David – was harder than before.

"Please clarify."

"I want questions answered first."

"*You want questions* . . . ?" Rhinemann's voice rose, his hand gripped the table; the veins were pronounced at his greying temples. He paused and continued as before. "Forgive me. I'm not used to conditions."

"I'm sure you're not. On the other hand, I'm not used to dealing with a contact like Stoltz who's blind to his own vulnerability. That kind of person annoys me . . . and worries me."

"These questions. What are they?"

"I assume the designs have been gotten out?"

"They have."

"En route?"

"They arrive tonight."

"You're early. Our man won't be here until the day after tomorrow."

"Now it is you who have been given erroneous information, Herr Colonel. The American scientist, Lyons, will be here tomorrow."

David was silent for several moments. He'd used such a ploy on too many others in the past to show surprise.

"He's expected in San Telmo the day *after* tomorrow," David said. "The change is insignificant but that's what Kendall told me."

"Before he boarded the Pan American Clipper. We spoke subsequently."

"Apparently he spoke to a lot of people. Is there a point to the change?"

"Schedules may be slowed or accelerated as the necessities dictate. . . ."

"Or altered to throw someone off balance," interrupted David.

"Such is not the case here. There would be no reason. As you phrased it – most succinctly – we're selling, you're buying."

"And, of course, there's no reason why the Gestapo's in Buenos Aires. . . ."

"May we *return* to that subject, please?" interjected Rhinemann.

"In a moment," answered Spaulding, aware that the German's temper was again stretched. "I need eighteen hours to get my codes to Washington. They have to go by courier, under chemical seal."

"Stoltz told me. You were foolish. The codes should have been sent."

"*Eine Vorsichtsmassnahme, mein Herr,*" said David. "Put plainly, I don't know who's been bought at our embassy but I'm damned sure someone has. Codes have ways of getting sold. The authentic ones will be radioed only when Lyons verifies the designs."

"Then you must move quickly. You fly out your codes in the morning; I will bring the first set of prints to San Telmo tomorrow night. . . . *Eine Vorsichtsmassnahme.* You get the remaining set when you have assured us

644

Washington is prepared to make payment in Switzerland ... as a result of receiving your established code. You won't leave Argentina until I have word from Berne. There is a small airfield called Mendarro. Near here. My men control it. Your plane will be there."

"Agreed." David crushed out his cigarette. "Tomorrow evening, the first set of prints. The remaining within twenty-four hours. ... Now we have a schedule. That's all I was interested in."

"*Gut!* And now we will return to this Gestapo business." Rhinemann leaned forward in his chair, the veins in his temples once more causing blue rivulets in his sun-drenched skin. "You said you would clarify!"

Spaulding did.

When he was finished, Erich Rhinemann was breathing deeply, steadily. Within the rolls of flesh, his narrow eyes were furious but controlled.

"Thank you. I'm sure there is an explanation. We'll proceed on schedule. ... Now, it has been a long and complicated evening. You will be driven back to Córdoba. Good night."

"Altmüller!" Rhinemann roared. "An *idiot! A fool!*"

"I don't understand," Stoltz said.

"Altmüller. ..." Rhinemann's voice subsided but the violence remained. He turned to the balcony, addressing the vast darkness and the river below. "In his insane attempts to *disassociate* the High Command from Buenos Aires ... to *absolve* his precious ministry, he's *caught* by his own *Gestapo!*"

"There is no *Gestapo* in Buenos Aires, Herr Rhinemann," said Stoltz firmly. "The man from Lisbon lies."

Rhinemann turned and looked at the diplomat. His speech was ice. "I know when a man is lying, Herr Stoltz. This Lisbon told the truth; he'd have no reason to do otherwise. ... So if Altmüller was *not* caught, he's betrayed me. He's sent in the Gestapo, he has no intention of going through with the exchange. He'll take the diamonds and destroy the designs. The Jew-haters have led me into a trap."

"I, myself, am the sole coordinator with Franz Altmüller." Stoltz spoke in his most persuasive tones, nurtured for decades in the Foreign Corps. "You, Herr Rhinemann, arranged for that. You have no cause to question me. The men at the warehouse in Ocho Calle have nearly finished. The Koening diamonds will he authenticated within a day or two; the courier will deliver the designs before the night is over. Everything is as we planned. The exchange will be made."

Rhinemann turned away again. He put his thick yet delicate hands on the railing and looked into the distance. "There is one way to be sure," he said quietly. "Radio Berlin. I want Altmüller in Buenos Aires. There will be no exchange otherwise."

31

The German in the white Palm Beach suit had changed into the paramilitary dress worn by the Rhinemann guards. The driver was not the same one as before. He was Argentine.

The automobile was different, too. It was a Bentley six-seater complete with mahogany dashboard, grey felt upholstery, and window curtains. It was a vehicle suited to the upper-level British diplomatic service, but not so high as to be ambassadorial; just eminently respectable. Another Rhinemann touch, David assumed.

The driver swung the car out onto the dark river highway from the darker confines of the hidden dirt road. He pressed the accelerator to the floor and the Bentley surged. The German beside Spaulding offered him a cigarette; David declined with a shake of his head.

"You say you wish to be driven to the American embassy, *señor?*" said the driver, turning his head slightly, not taking his eyes off the onrushing road. "I'm afraid I cannot do so. Señor Rhinemann's orders were to bring you to the apartment house on Córdoba. Forgive me."

"We may not deviate from instructions," added the German.

"Hope you never do. We win the wars that way."

"The insult is misdirected. I'm completely indifferent."

"I forgot. Habichtsnest is neutral." David ended the conversation by shifting in the seat, crossing his legs and staring in silence out the window. His only thought was to get to the embassy and to Jean. She had used the word "Tortugas."

Again the elusive "Tortugas"!

How could she know? Was it conceivable she was part of it?

"Tortugas' isn't worth it. Jean had said those words. She had pleaded.

Leslie Hawkwood had pleaded, too. Leslie had traveled four thousand miles to plead in defiance. Fanatically so.

Get out of Buenos Aires, David!

Was there a connection?

Oh, Christ! he thought. *Was there really a connection?*

"Señors!"

The driver spoke harshly, jolting David's thoughts. The German instantly – instinctively – whipped around in his seat and looked out the rear window. His question was two words.

"How long?"

"Too long for doubt. Have you watched?"

"No."

"I passed three automobiles. Without pattern. Then I slowed down, into the far right lane. He's with us. Moving up."

"We're in the Hill Two district, yes?" asked the German.

"*Sí.* . . . He's coming up rapidly. It's a powerful car; he'll take us on the highway."

"Head up into the Colinas Rojas! Take the next road on the right! Any one!" commanded Rhinemann's lieutenant, taking his pistol from inside his jacket as he spoke.

The Bentley skidded into a sudden turn, swerving diagonally to the right, throwing David and the German into the left section of the back seat. The Argentine gunned the engine, starting up a hill, slamming the gears into first position, reaching maximum speed in seconds. There was a slight leveling off, a connecting, flatter surface before a second hill, and the driver used it to race the motor in a higher gear for speed. The car pitched forward in a burst of acceleration, as if it were a huge bullet.

The second hill was steeper but the initial speed helped. They raced upward; the driver knew his machine, thought David.

"There are the lights!" yelled the German. "They follow!"

"There are flat stretches . . . I think," said the driver, concentrating on the road. "Beyond this section of hills. There are many side roads; we'll try to hide in one. Perhaps they'll pass."

"No," The German was still peering out the rear window. He checked the magazine of his pistol by touch; satisfied, he locked it in place. He then turned from the window and reached under the seat. The Bentley was pitching and vibrating on the uphill, back country road, and the German swore as he worked his hand furiously behind his legs.

Spaulding could hear the snap of metal latches. The German slipped the pistol into his belt and reached down with his free hand. He pulled up a thick-barreled automatic rifle that David recognized as the newest, most powerful front-line weapon the Third Reich had developed. The curved magazine, rapidly inserted by the German, held over forty rounds of .30 caliber ammunition.

Rhinemann's lieutenant spoke. "Reach your flat stretches. Let them close in."

David bolted up; he held onto the leather strap across the rear of the front seat and braced his left hand against the window frame. He spoke to the German harshly.

"Don't use that! You don't know who they are."

The man with the gun glanced briefly at Spaulding, dismissing him with a look. "I know my responsibilities." He reached over to the right of the rear window where there was a small metal ring imbedded in the felt. He inserted his forefinger, pulled it up, and yanked it toward him, revealing an open-air slot about ten inches wide, perhaps four inches high.

David looked at the left of the window. There was another ring, another opening.

Rhinemann's car was prepared for emergencies. Clean shots could be fired at any automobile pursuing it; the sightlines were clear and there was a minimum of awkwardness at high speeds over difficult terrain.

"Suppose it's American surveillance covering *me?*" David shouted as the German knelt on the seat, about to insert the rifle into the opening.

"It's not."

"You don't *know* that!"

"*Señors!*" shouted the driver. "We go down the hill; it's very long, a wide bend. I remember it! Below there are high-grass fields. Flat. . . . Roads. Hold *on!*"

The Bentley suddenly dipped as if it had sped off the edge of a precipice. There was an immediate, sustained thrust of speed so abrupt that the German with the rifle was thrown back, his body suspended for a fraction of a second in midair. He crashed into the front seat support, his weapon held up to break the fall.

David did not – could not – hesitate. He grabbed the rifle, gripping his fingers around the trigger housing, twisting the stock inward and jerking it out of the German's hands. Rhinemann's lieutenant was stunned by Spaulding's action. He reached into his belt for his pistol.

The Bentley was now crashing down the steep incline at an extraordinary speed. The wide bend referred to by the Argentine was reached; the car entered a long, careening pattern that seemed to be sustaining an engineering improbability: propelled by the wheels of a single side, the other off the surface of the ground.

David and the German braced themselves with their backs against opposite sides, their legs taut, their feet dug into the felt carpet.

"Give me that *rifle!*" The German held his pistol on David's chest. David had the rifle stock under his arm, his finger on the trigger, the barrel of the monster weapon leveled at the German's stomach.

"You fire, I fire," he shouted back. "I might come out of it. You won't. You'll be all over the car!"

Spaulding saw that the driver had panicked. The action in the back seat, coupled with the problems of the hill, the speed and the curves created a crisis he was not capable of handling.

"*Señors! Madre de Jesus! . . .* You'll *kill* us!"

The Bentley briefly struck the rocky shoulder of the road; the jolt was staggering. The driver swung back toward the center line. The German spoke.

"You behave stupidly. Those men are after you, not us!"

"I can't be sure of that. I don't kill people on speculation."

"You'll kill us, then? For what purpose?"

"I don't want anyone killed. . . . Now, put down that gun! We both know the odds."

The German hesitated.

There was another jolt; the Bentley had struck a large rock or a fallen limb.

It was enough to convince Rhinemann's lieutenant. He placed the pistol on the seat.

The two adversaries braced themselves; David's eyes on the German's hand, the German's on the rifle.

"*Madre de Dios!*" The Argentine's shout conveyed relief not further panic. Gradually the Bentley was slowing down.

David glanced through the windshield. They were coming out of the hill's curve; in the distance were flat blankets of fields, miniature pampas reflecting the dull moonlight. He reached over and took the German's pistol from the seat. It was an unexpected move; Rhinemann's lieutenant was annoyed with himself.

"Get your breath," said Spaulding to the driver "Have a cigarette. And get me back to town."

"Colonel!" barked the German. "You may hold the weapons, but there's a car back there! If you won't follow my advice, at least let us get off the road!"

"I haven't the time to waste. I didn't tell him to slow down, just to relax."

The driver entered a level stretch of road and reaccelerated the Bentley. While doing so he took David's advice and lit a cigarette. The car was steady again.

"Sit back," ordered Spaulding, placing himself diagonally in the right corner, one knee on the floor – the rifle held casually, not carelessly.

The Argentine spoke in a frightened monotone. "There are the headlights again. They approach faster than I can drive this car. . . . What would you have me do?"

David considered the options. "Give them a chance to respond. . . . Is there enough moon to see the road? With your lights off?"

"For a while. Not long. I can't remember. . . ."

"Flick them on and off! Twice. . . . Now!"

The driver did as he was instructed. The effect was strange: the sudden darkness, the abrupt illumination – while the Bentley whipped past the tall grass on both sides of the road.

David watched the pursuing vehicle's lights through the rear window. There was no response to the signals. He wondered whether they'd been clear, whether they conveyed his message of accommodation.

"Flick them again," he commanded the driver. "Hold a couple of beats . . . seconds. Now!"

The clicks were beard from the dashboard; the lights remained off for three, four seconds. The clicks again; the darkness again.

And then it happened.

There was a burst of gunfire from the automobile in pursuit. The glass of the rear window was shattered; flying, imbedding itself into skin and upholstery. David could feel blood trickling down his cheek; the German screamed in pain, grasping his bleeding left hand.

The Bentley swerved; the driver swung the steering wheel back and forth, zigzagging the car in the road's path.

"There is your *reply!*" roared Rhinemann's lieutenant, his hand bloodied, his eyes a mixture of fury and panic.

Quickly, David handed the rifle to the German. "Use it!"

The German slipped the barrel into the opening; Spaulding sprung up into the seat and reached for the metal ring on the left side of the window, pulled it back and brought the pistol up.

There was another burst from the car behind. It was the volley of a submachine gun, scattershot, heavy caliber; spraying the rear of the Bentley. Bulges appeared throughout the felt top and sides, several bullets shattered the front windshield.

The German began firing the automatic; David aimed as best he could — the swerving, twisting Bentley kept pushing the pursuing car out of sight-lines. Still he pulled the trigger, hoping only to spray the oncoming tires.

The roars from the German's weapon were thunderous; repeated crescendos of deafening *booms*, the shock waves of each discharge filling the small, elegant enclosure.

David could see the explosion the instant it happened. The hood of the onrushing automobile was suddenly a mass of smoke and steam.

But still the machine-gun volleys came *out* of the enveloping vapor.

"*Eeaagh!*" the driver screamed. David looked and saw blood flowing out of the man's head; the neck was half shot off. The Argentine's hands sprung back from the wheel.

Spaulding leaped forward, trying to reach the wheel, but he couldn't. The Bentley careened off the road, side-slipping into the tall grass.

The German took his automatic weapon from the opening. He smashed the side window with the barrel of the rifle and slammed in a second magazine as the Bentley came to a sharp, jolting stop in the grass.

The pursuing car — a cloud of smoke and spits of fire was parallel now on the road. It braked twice, lurched once and locked into position, immobile.

Shots poured from the silhouetted vehicle. The German kicked the Bentley's door open and jumped out into the tall grass. David crouched against the left door, fingers searching for the handle, pushing his weight into the panel so that upon touch, the door would fly open and he could thrust himself into cover.

Suddenly the air was filled with the overpowering thunder of the automatic rifle held steady in a full-firing discharge.

Screams pierced the night; David sprung the door open, and as he leaped out he could see Rhinemann's lieutenant rising in the grass. *Rising* and *walking* through the shots, his finger depressing the automatic's trigger, his whole body shaking, staggering under the impact of the bullets entering his flesh.

He fell.

As he did so a second explosion came from the car on the road.

The gas tank burst from under the trunk, sending fire and metal into the air.

David sprang around the tail of the Bentley, his pistol steady.

The firing stopped. The roar of the flames, the hissing of steam was all there was.

He looked past the Bentley's trunk to the carnage on the road. Then he recognized the automobile. It was the Duesenberg that had come for Leslie Hawkwood that afternoon.

Two dead bodies could be seen in the rear, rapidly being enveloped by fire. The driver was arched over the seat, his arms limp, his neck immobile, his eyes wide in death.

There was a fourth man, splayed out on the ground by the open right door.

The hand moved! Then the head!

He was alive!

Spaulding raced to the flaming Duesenberg and pulled the half-conscious man away from the wreckage.

He had seen too many men die to mistake the rapid ebbing of life. There was no point in trying to stem death; only to use it.

David crouched by the man. "Who are you? Why did you want to kill me?"

The man's eyes – swimming in their sockets – focused on David. A single headlight flickered from the smoke of the exploded Duesenberg; it was dying, too.

"Who *are* you? Tell me who you are!"

The man would not – or could not – speak. Instead, his lips moved, but not a whisper.

Spaulding bent down further.

The man died trying to spit in David's face. The phlegm and blood intermingled down the man's chin as his head went limp.

In the light of the spreading flames, Spaulding pulled the man's jacket open.

No identification.

Nor in the trousers.

He ripped at the lining in the coat, tore the shirt to the waist.

Then he stopped. Stunned, curious.

There were marks on the dead man's stomach. Wounds but not from bullets. David had seen those marks before.

He could not help himself. He lifted the man by the neck and yanked the coat off the left shoulder, tearing the shirt at the seams to expose the arm.

They were there. Deep in the skin. Never to be erased.

The tattooed numbers of a death camp.

Ein Volk, ein Reich, ein Führer.

The dead man was a Jew.

32

It was nearly five o'clock when Spaulding reached his apartment on Córdoba. He had taken the time to remove what obvious identification he could from the dead Argentine driver and Rhinemann's lieutenant. He found tools in the trunk and unfastened the Bentley's license plates; moved the dials of the dashboard clock forward, then smashed it. If nothing else, these details might slow police procedures — at least a few hours — giving him valuable time before facing Rhinemann.

Rhinemann would demand that confrontation.

And there was too much to learn, to piece together.

He had walked for nearly an hour back over the two hills — the Colinas Rojas — to the river highway. He had removed the fragments of window glass from his face, grateful they were few, the cuts minor. He had carried the awesome automatic rifle far from the scene of death, removed the chamber loading clip and smashed the trigger housing until the weapon was inoperable. Then he threw it into the woods.

A milk truck from the Tigre district picked him up; he told the driver an outrageous story of alcohol and sex — he'd been expertly rolled and had no one to blame but himself.

The driver admired the foreigner's spirit, his acceptance of risk and loss. The ride was made in laughter.

He knew it was pointless, even frivolous, to attempt sleep. There was too much to do. Instead he showered and made a large pot of coffee.

It was time. Daylight came up from the Atlantic. His head was clear; it was time to call Jean.

He told the astonished marine night operator on the embassy switchboard that Mrs. Cameron expected the call; actually he was late, he'd overslept. Mrs. Cameron had made plans for deep-sea fishing; they were due at La Boca at six.

"Hello? . . . Hello." Jean's voice was at first dazed, then surprised.

"It's David. I haven't time to apologize. I've got to see you right away."

"David? Oh, God! . . ."

"I'll meet you in your office in twenty minutes."

"*Please.* . . ."

"There's no *time!* Twenty minutes. Please, be there. . . . I need you, Jean. I need *you!*"

The OD lieutenant at the embassy gate was cooperative, if disagreeable. He consented to let the inside switchboard ring Mrs. Cameron's office; if she came out and personally vouched for him, the marine would let him pass.

Jean emerged on the front steps. she was vulnerable, lovely. She walked around the driveway path to the gatehouse and saw him. The instant she did so, she stifled a gasp.

He understood.

The styptic pencil could not eradicate the cuts from the half dozen splinters of glass he had removed from his cheeks and forehead. Partially conceal, perhaps; nothing much more than that.

They did not speak as they walked down the corridor. Instead, she held his arm with such force that he shifted to her other side. She had been tugging at the shoulder not yet healed from the Azores crash.

Inside her office she closed the door and rushed into his arms. She was trembling.

"David, I'm *sorry, sorry, sorry.* I was dreadful. I behaved so badly."

He took her shoulders, holding her back very gently. "You were coping with a problem."

"It seems to me I *can't* cope anymore. And I always thought I was so good at it . . . What happened to your face?" She traced her fingers over his cheek. "It's swollen here."

" 'Tortugas.' " He looked into her eyes. " 'Tortugas' happened."

"Oh, God." She whispered the words and buried her head in his chest. "I'm too disjointed; I can't say what I want to say. Don't. Please, don't . . . let anything more happen."

"Then you'll have to help me."

She pulled back. "*Me?* How can I?"

"Answer my questions . . . I'll know if you're lying."

"*Lying.* . . . Don't joke. *I* haven't lied to *you.*"

He believed her . . . which didn't make his purpose any easier. Or clearer. "Where did you learn the name 'Tortugas'?"

She removed her arms from around his neck; he released her. She took several steps away from him but she was not retreating.

"I'm not proud of what I did; I've never done it before." She turned and faced him.

"I went down to the 'Caves'. . . without authorization . . . and read your file. I'm sure it's the briefest dossier in the history of the diplomatic corps."

"What did it say?"

She told him.

"So you see, my mythical David of last evening had a distinct basis in reality."

Spaulding walked to the window overlooking the west lawn of the embassy. The early sun was up, the grass flickered with dew; it brought to mind the manicured lawn seen in the night floodlights below Rhinemann's terrace. And that memory reminded him of the codes. He turned. "I have to talk to Ballard."

"Is that all you're going to say?"

"The not-so-mythical David has work to do. That doesn't change."

"I can't change it, you mean."

He walked back to her. "No, you can't. . . . I wish to God you could; I wish *I* could. I can't convince myself – to paraphrase a certain girl – that what I'm doing will make that much difference . . . but I react out of habit, I guess. Maybe ego; maybe it's as simple as that."

"I said you were good, didn't I?"

"Yes. And I am. . . . Do you know *what* I am?"

"An intelligence officer. An agent. A man who works with other men; in whispers and at night and with a great deal of money and lies. That's the way I think, you see."

"Not that. That's new . . . What I *really am*. . . . I'm a construction engineer. I build buildings and bridges and dams and highways. I once built an extension for a zoo in Mexico; the best open-air enclosure for primates you ever saw. Unfortunately, we spent so much money the Zoological Society couldn't afford monkeys, but the space is there."

She laughed softly. "You're funny."

"I liked working on the bridges best. To cross a natural obstacle without marring it, without destroying its own purpose. . . ."

"I never thought of engineers as romantics."

"*Construction* engineers are. At least, the best ones. . . . But that's all long ago. When this mess is over I'll go back, of course, but I'm not a fool. I know the disadvantages I'll be faced with. . . . It's not the same as a lawyer putting down his books only to pick them up again; the law doesn't change that much. Or a stockbroker; the market solutions *can't* change."

"I'm not sure what you're driving at. . . ."

"Technology. It's the only real, civilized benefit war produces. In construction it's been revolutionary. In three years whole new techniques have been developed . . . I've been out of it. My postwar references won't be the best."

"Good Lord, you're sorry for yourself."

"Christ, *yes!* In one way. . . . More to the point, I'm angry. Nobody held a gun to my head; I walked into this . . . this job for all the wrong reasons and without any foresight. . . . That's why I have to be good at it."

"What about us? Are we an 'us'?"

"I love you," he said simply. "I know that."

"After only a week? That's what I keep asking myself. We're not children."

"We're not children," he replied. "Children don't have access to State Department dossiers." He smiled, then grew serious. "I need your help."

She glanced at him sharply. "What is it?"

"What do you know about Erich Rhinemann?"

"He's a despicable man."

"He's a Jew."

"Then he's a despicable Jew. Race and religion notwithstanding, immaterial."

"Why is he despicable?"

"Because he uses people. Indiscriminately. Maliciously. He uses his money to corrupt whatever and whomever he can. He buys influence from the junta; that gets him land, government concessions, shipping rights. He forced a number of mining companies out of the Patagonia Basin; he took over a dozen or so oil fields at Comodoro Rivadavia. . . ."

"What are his politics?"

Jean thought for a second; she leaned back in the chair, looking for an instant at the window, then over to Spaulding. "Himself," she answered.

"I've heard he's openly pro-Axis."

"Only because he believed England would fall and terms would be made. He still owns a power base in Germany, I'm told."

"But he's a Jew."

"Temporary handicap. I don't think he's an elder at the synagogue. The Jewish community in Buenos Aires has no use for him."

David stood up. "Maybe that's it."

"What?"

"Rhinemann turned his back on the tribe, openly supports the creators of Auschwitz. Maybe they want him killed. Take out his guards first, then go after him."

"If by 'they' you mean the Jews here, I'd have to say no. The Argentine *judíos* tread lightly. The colonels' legions are awfully close to a goose step; Rhinemann has influence. Of course, nothing stops a fanatic or two. . . ."

"No. . . . They may be fanatics, but not one or two. They're organized; they've got backing – considerable amounts, I think."

"And they're after Rhinemann? The Jewish community would panic. Frankly, we'd be the first they'd come to."

David stopped his pacing. The words came back to him again; *there'll be no negotiations with Altmüller.* A darkened doorway on New York's Fifty-second Street.

"Have you ever heard the name Altmüller?"

"No. There's a plain Müller at the German embassy, I think, but that's like Smith or Jones. No Altmüller."

"What about Hawkwood? A woman named Leslie Jenner Hawkwood?"

"No, again. But if these people are intelligence oriented, there'd be no reason for me to."

"They're Intelligence but I didn't think they were undercover. At least not this Altmüller."

"What does that mean?"

"His name has been used in a context that assumes recognition. But I can't find him."

"Do you want to check the 'Caves'?" she asked.

"Yes. I'll do it directly with Granville. When do they open?"

"Eight thirty. Henderson's in his office by quarter to nine." She saw David hold up his wrist, forgetting he had no watch. She looked at her office clock.

"A little over two hours. Remind me to buy you a watch."

"Thanks. . . . Ballard. I have to see him. How is he in the early morning? At this hour?"

"I trust that question's rhetorical. . . . He's used to being roused up for code problems. Shall I call him?"

"Please. Can you make coffee here?"

"There's a hotplate out there." Jean indicated the door to the anteroom. "Behind my secretary's chair. Sink's in the closet. . . .Never mind. I'll do it. Let me get Bobby first."

"I make a fine pot of coffee. You call, I'll cook. You look like such an executive, I'd hate to interfere."

He was emptying the grounds from the pot when he heard it. It was a footstep. A single footstep outside in the corridor. A footstep that should have been muffled but wasn't. A second step would ordinarily follow but didn't.

Spaulding put the pot on the desk, reached down and removed both his shoes without a sound. He crossed to the closed door and stood by the frame.

There it was again. Steps. Quiet; unnatural.

David opened his jacket, checking his weapon, and put his left hand on the knob. He turned it silently, then quickly opened the door and stepped out.

Fifteen feet away a man walking down the corridor spun around at the noise. The look on his face was one Spaulding had seen many times.

Fright.

"Oh, hello there, you must be the new man. We haven't met. . . .The name's Ellis. Bill Ellis. . . . I have a beastly conference at seven." The attaché was not convincing.

"Several of us were going fishing but the weather reports are uncertain. Care to come with us?"

"I'd love to except l have this damned ungodly hour meeting."

"Yes. That's what you said. How about coffee?"

"Thanks, old man. I really should bone up on some paperwork."

"O.K. Sorry."

"Yes, so am I. . . . Well, see you later." The man named Ellis smiled awkwardly, gestured a wave more awkwardly – which David returned – and continued on his way.

Spaulding went back into Jean's office and closed the door. She was standing by the secretary's desk.

"Who in heaven's name were you talking to at this hour?"

"He said his name was Ellis. He said he had a meeting with someone at seven o'clock. . . . He doesn't."

"What?"

"He was lying. What's Ellis's department?"

"Import-export clearances."

"That's handy. . . . What about Ballard?"

"He's on his way. He says you're a mean man. . . . What's 'handy' about Ellis?"

Spaulding went to the coffee pot on the desk, picked it up and started for the closet. Jean interrupted his movement, taking the pot from him. "What's Ellis's rating?" he asked.

"Excellent. Strictly the syndrome; he wants the Court of St. James's. You haven't answered me. What's 'handy'?"

"He's been bought. He's a funnel. It could be serious or just penny-ante waterfront stuff."

"Oh?" Jean, perplexed, opened the closet door where there was a washbasin. Suddenly, she stopped. She turned to Spaulding. "David. What does 'Tortugas' mean?"

"Oh, Christ, stop kidding."

"Which means you can't tell me."

"Which means I don't *know*. I wish to heaven I *did*."

"It's a code word, isn't it? That's what it says in your file."

"It's a code I've never been told about and I'm the one responsible!"

"Here, fill this; rinse it out first." Jean handed him the coffee pot and walked rapidly into her office, to the desk. David followed and stood in the doorway.

"What are you doing?"

"Attachés, even undersecretaries, if they have very early appointments, list them with the gate."

"Ellis?"

Jean nodded and spoke into the telephone; her conversation was brief. She replaced the instrument and looked over at Spaulding. "The first gate pass is listed for nine. Ellis has no meeting at seven."

"I'm not surprised. Why are you?"

"I wanted to make sure. . . . You said you didn't know what 'Tortugas' meant. I might be able to tell you."

David, stunned, took several steps into the office. "*What?*"

"There was a surveillance report from La Boca – that's Ellis's district. His department must have cleared it up, given it a clean bill. It was dropped."

"What was dropped? What are you talking about?"

"A trawler in La Boca. It had cargo with a destination lading that violated coastal patrols . . . they called it an error. The destination was Tortugas."

The outer office door suddenly opened and Bobby Ballard walked in.

'*Jesus!*' he said. "The Munchkins go to work early in this wonderful world of Oz!"

33

The code schedules with Ballard took less than a half hour. David was amazed at the cryptographer's facile imagination. He developed – on the spot – a geometrical progression of numbers and corresponding letters that would take the best cryps Spaulding knew a week to break.

At maximum, all David needed was ninety-six hours.

Bobby placed Washington's copy in an official courier's envelope, sealed it chemically, placed it in a triple-locked pouch and called the FMF base for an officer – captain's rank or above – to get to the embassy within the hour. The codes would be on a coastal pursuit aircraft by nine; at Andrews Field by late afternoon; delivered to General Alan Swanson's office in the War Department by armored courier van shortly thereafter.

The confirmation message was simple; Spaulding had given Ballard two words: *Cable Tortugas.*

When the code was received in Washington, Swanson would know that Eugene Lyons had authenticated the guidance designs. He could then radio the bank in Switzerland and payment would be made to Rhinemann's accounts. By using the name "Tortugas," David hoped that someone, somewhere, would understand his state of mind. His anger at being left with the full responsibility without all of the facts.

Spaulding was beginning to think that Erich Rhinemann was demanding more than he was entitled to. A possibility that would do him little good.

Rhinemann was to be killed.

And the outlines of a plan were coming into focus that would bring about that necessary death. The act itself might be the simplest part of his assignment.

There was no point in *not* telling Jean and Bobby Ballard about the guidance designs. Kendall had flown out of Buenos Aires – without explanation; David knew he might need assistance at a moment when there was no time to brief those helping him. His cover was superfluous now. He described minutely Rhinemann's schedule, the function of Eugene Lyons and Heinrich Stoltz's surfacing as a contact.

Ballard was astonished at Stoltz's inclusion. "*Stoltz!* That's a little bit of lightning. . . .I mean, he's a *believer.* Not the Hitler fire "n' brimstone – he dismisses that, I'm told. But *Germany.* The Versailles motive, the reparations – bled giant, export or die – the whole thing. I figured him for the real Junker item. . . ."

David did not pay much attention.

The logistics of the morning were clear in Spaulding's mind and at eight forty-five he began.

His meeting with Henderson Granville was short and cordial. The ambassador was content not to know David's true purpose in Buenos Aires, as long as there was no diplomatic conflict. Spaulding assured him that to the best of his knowledge there was none; certainly less of a possibility if the ambassador remained outside the hard core of the assignment. Granville agreed. On the basis of David's direct request, he had the "Caves" checked for files on Franz Altmüller and Leslie Jenner Hawkwood.

Nothing.

Spaulding went from Granville's office back to Jean's. She had received the incoming passengers manifest from Aeroparque. Eugene Lyons was listed on clipper flight 101, arriving at two in the afternoon. His profession was given as "physicist'; the reason for entry, "industrial conferences."

David was annoyed with Walter Kendall. Or, he thought, should his annoyance be with the bewildered amateur, Brigadier General Alan Swanson? The least they could have done was term Lyons a "scientist'; "physicist' was stupid. A physicist in Buenos Aires was an own invitation to surveillance – even *Allied* surveillance.

He walked back to his own isolated, tiny office. To think.

He decided to meet Lyons himself. Walter Kendall had told him that Lyons's male nurses would settle the mute, sad man in San Telmo. Recalling the two men in question, David had premonitions of disaster. It wasn't beyond Johnny and Hal – those were the names, weren't they? – to deliver Lyons to the steps of the German embassy, thinking it was another hospital.

He would meet Pan Am Clipper 101. And proceed to take the three men on a complicated route to San Telmo.

Once he'd settled Lyons, David estimated that he would have about two, possibly three, hours before Rhinemann – or Stoltz – would make contact. Unless Rhinemann was hunting him now, in panic over the killings in the Colinas Rojas. If so, Spaulding had "built his shelter." His irrefutable alibi. . . . He hadn't been there. He'd been dropped off at Córdoba by two in the morning.

Who could dispute him?

So, he would have two or three hours in mid-afternoon.

La Boca.

Discreetly, Jean had checked naval surveillance at FMF. The discretion came with her utterly routine, bored telephone call to the chief of operations. She had a "loose end' to tie up for a "dead file'; there was no significance, only a bureaucratic matter – someone was always looking for a good rating on the basis of closing out. Would the lieutenant mind filling in? . . . The trawler erroneously listed for Tortugas was moored by a warehouse complex in Ocho Calle. The error was checked and confirmed by the embassy attaché, Mr. William Ellis, Import-Export Clearance Division.

Ocho Calle.

David would spend an hour or so looking around. It could be a waste of time. What connection would a fishing trawler have with his assignment? There was none that he could see. But there *was* the name "Tortugas"; there *was* an attaché named Ellis who crept silently outside closed doors and lied about nonexistent conferences in the early morning.

Ocho Calle was worth looking into.

Afterward, he would stay by his telephone at Córdoba.

"Are you going to take me to lunch?" asked Jean, walking into his office. "Don't look at your watch; you haven't got one."

Spaulding's hand was in midair, his wrist turned. "I didn't realize it was so late."

"It's not. It's only eleven, but you haven't eaten – probably didn't sleep, either – and you said you were going to the airport shortly after one."

"I was right; you're a corporate executive. Your sense of organization is frightening."

"Nowhere near yours. We'll stop at a jewelry store first. I've already called. You have a present."

"I like presents. Let's go." Spaulding got out of his chair as the telephone rang. He looked down at it. "Do you know that's the first time that thing has made a sound?"

"It's probably for me. I told my secretary I was here. . . . I don't think I really *had* to tell her."

"Hello?" said David into the phone.

"Spaulding?"

David recognized the polished German of Heinrich Stoltz. His tension carried over the wire. "Isn't it a little foolish to call me here?"

"I have no choice. Our mutual friend is in a state of extreme anxiety. Everything is jeopardized."

"What are you talking about?"

"This is no time for foolishness! The situation is grave."

"It's no time for games, either. What the hell are you talking about?"

"Last night! This morning. What happened?"

"What happened where?"

"Stop *it!* You *were there!*"

"Where?"

Stoltz paused; David could hear his breath. The German was in panic, desperately trying to control himself. "The men were killed. We must know what happened!"

"Killed? . . . You're *crazy.* How?"

"I *warn you.* . . ."

"Now you cut it out! I'm *buying.* And don't forget it. . . . I don't want to be mixed up in any organization problems. Those men dropped me off around one thirty. Incidentally, they met your other boys, the ones covering my apartment. And also incidentally, I don't like this round-the-clock surveillance!"

Stoltz was blanked – as David expected he would be. "The others? . . . What others?"

"Get off it! You know perfectly well." Spaulding let the inference hang.

"This is all most disturbing. . . ." Stoltz tried to compose himself.

"I'm sorry," said David noncommittally.

Exasperated, Stoltz interrupted. "I'll call you back."

"Not here. I'll be out most of the afternoon. . . . As a matter of fact," added Spaulding quickly, pleasantly, "I'll be in one of those sailboats our mutual friend looks down upon so majestically. I'm joining some diplomatic friends almost as rich as he is. Call me after five at Córdoba."

David hung up instantly, hearing the beginning of Stoltz's protest. Jean was watching him, fascinated.

"You did that very well," she said.

"I've had more practice than him."

"Stoltz?"

"Yes. Let's go into your office."

"I thought we were going to lunch."

"We are. Couple of things first. . . . There's a rear exit, isn't there?"

"Several. Back gate."

"I want to use an embassy vehicle. Any trouble?"

"No, of course not."

"Your secretary. Could you spare her for a long lunch?"

"You're sweet. I had the insane idea you were taking me."

"I am. Could she put her hair up and wear a floppy hat?"

"Any woman can."

"Good. Get that yellow coat you wore last night. And point out any man around here relatively my size. One that your secretary might enjoy that long lunch with. Preferably wearing dark trousers. He'll have my jacket."

"What are you *doing?*"

"Our friends are good at playing jokes on other people. Let's see how they take it when one's played on them."

Spaulding watched from the third-floor window, concealed by the full-length drapes. He held the binoculars to his eyes. Below, on the front steps, Jean's secretary – in a wide-brimmed hat and Jean's yellow coat – walked rapidly down to the curb of the driveway. Following her was one of Ballard's assistants, a tall man in dark trousers and David's jacket. Both wore sunglasses. Ballard's man paused momentarily on the top step, looking at an unfolded road map. His face was covered by the awkward mass of paper. He descended the stairs and together he and the girl climbed into the embassy limousine – an upper-level vehicle with curtains.

Spaulding scanned the Avenida Corrientes in front of the gates. As the limousine was passed through, a Mercedes coupe parked on the south side of the street pulled away from the curb and followed it. And then a second automobile on the north side made a cautious U-turn and took up its position several vehicles behind the Mercedes.

Satisfied, David put down the binoculars and went out of the room. In the corridor he turned left and walked swiftly past doors and around staircases toward the rear of the building, until he came to a room that corresponded to his observation post in front. Bobby Ballard sat in an armchair by the window; he turned around at the sound of David's footsteps, binoculars in his hands.

"Anything?" Spaulding asked.

"Two," answered the cryp. "Parked facing opposite directions. They just drove away."

"Same up front. They're in radio contact."

"Thorough, aren't they?"

"Not as much as they think," Spaulding said.

Ballard's sports coat was loose around the midsection and short in the sleeves, but it showed off David's new wristwatch. Jean was pleased about that. It was a very fine chronometer.

The restaurant was small, a virtual hole-in-the-wall on a side street near San Martin. The front door was open; a short awning protected the few outside tables from the sun. Their table, however, was inside. Spaulding sat facing the entrance, able to see clearly the passersby on the sidewalk.

But he was not watching them now. He was looking at Jean. And what he saw in her face caused him to say the words without thinking.

"It's going to be over soon. I'm getting out."

She took his hand, searching his eyes. She did not reply for several moments. It was as if she wanted his words suspended, isolated, thought about. "That's a remarkable thing to say. I'm not sure what it means."

"It means I want to spend years and years with you. The rest of my life. . . . I don't know any other way to put it."

Jean closed her eyes briefly, for the duration of a single breath of silence. "I think you've put it . . . very beautifully."

How could he tell her? How could he explain? He had to try. It was so damned important. "Less than a month ago," he began softly, "something happened in a field. At night, in Spain. By a campfire. . . . *To me*. The circumstances aren't important, but what happened to me was . . . the most frightening thing I could imagine. And it had nothing to do with the calculated risks in my work; nothing to do with being afraid – and I was always afraid, you can bet your life on that. . . . But I suddenly found I had no *feeling*. No feeling at all. I was given a report that should have shaken me up – made me weep, or made me angry, *goddamned angry*. But I didn't feel anything. I was numb. I accepted the news and criticized the man for withholding it. I told him not to make that mistake again. . . . That I did not act rashly under any conditions. . . . You see, he *rightfully* thought that I would." David stopped and put his hand over Jean's. "What I'm trying to tell you is that you've given me back something

I thought I'd lost. I don't ever want to take the chance of losing it again."

"You'll make me cry," she said quietly, her eyes moist, her lips trembling to a smile. "Don't you know girls cry when things like that are said to them? . . . I'll have to teach you so much . . . Oh, Lord," she whispered. "Please, *please* . . . years."

David leaned over the small table; their lips touched and as they held lightly together, he removed his hand from hers and gently ran his fingers over the side of her face.

The tears were there.

He felt them, too. They would not come for him, but he *felt* them.

"I'm going back with you, of course," she said.

Her words brought back the reality . . . the other reality, the lesser one. "Not *with* me. But soon. I'm going to need a couple of weeks to settle things. . . . And you'll have to transfer your work down here."

She looked at him questioningly but did not ask a question. "There are . . . special arrangements for you to take back the blueprints or designs or whatever they are."

"Yes."

"When?"

"If everything goes as we expect, in a day or two. At the most, three."

"Then why do you need a couple of weeks?"

He hesitated before answering. And then he realized he wanted to tell her the truth. It was part of the beginning for him. The truth. "There's a breach of security in a place called Fairfax. . . ."

"Fairfax," she interrupted. "That was in your file."

"It's an intelligence center in Virginia. Very classified. A man was killed there. He was a friend of mine. I purposely withheld information that might stop the leaks and, more important, find out who killed him."

"For heaven's sake, why?"

"In a way, I was forced to. The men in Fairfax weren't cleared for the information I had; the one man who was, is ineffectual . . . especially in something like this. He's not Intelligence oriented; he's a requisition general. He buys things."

"Like gyroscopic designs?"

"Yes. When I get back I'll force him to clear the data." David paused and then spoke as much to himself as to Jean. "Actually, I don't give a damn whether he does or not. I've got a long accumulated leave coming to me. I'll use a week or two of it in Fairfax. There's a German agent walking around in that compound with a four-zero rating. He killed a very good man."

"That frightens me."

"It shouldn't." David smiled, answering her with the truth. "I have no intention of risking those years we talked about. If I have to, I'll operate from a maximum security cell. . . . Don't worry."

She nodded. "I won't. I believe you. . . . I'll join you in, say, three weeks.

I owe that to Henderson; there *will* be a lot of adjustments for him. Also, I'll have something done about Ellis."

"Don't touch him. We don't *know* anything yet. If we find out he's on an outside payroll he can be valuable right where he is. Reverse conduits are jewels. When we uncover one we make sure he's the healthiest man – or woman – around."

"What kind of a world do you live in?" Jean asked the question with concern, not humor.

"One that you'll help me leave. . . . After Fairfax, I'm finished."

Eugene Lyons edged into the back seat of the taxi between Spaulding and the male nurse named Hal. The other attendant, Johnny, sat in front with the driver. David gave his instructions in Spanish; the driver started out the long, smooth roadway of the Aeroparque.

David looked at Lyons; it wasn't easy to do so. The proximity of the sad, emaciated face emphasized the realization that what he saw was self-inflicted. Lyons's eyes were not responding; he was exhausted from the flight, suspicious of the new surroundings, annoyed by David's aggressive efficiency at hurrying them all out of the terminal.

"It's good to see you again," David told him.

Lyons blinked; Spaulding wasn't sure whether it was a greeting or not.

"We didn't expect you," said Johnny from the front seat. "We expected to get the professor set ourselves."

"We've got it all written down," added Hal, leaning forward on Lyons's right, taking a number of index cards out of his pocket. "Look. The address. Your telephone number. And the embassy's. And a wallet full of Argentine money."

Hal pronounced Argentine, "Argentyne." David wondered how he could be given a course in hypodermic injection; who would read the labels? On the other hand, his partner Johnny – less talkative, more knowing somehow – was obviously the leader of the two.

"Well, these things are usually fouled up. Communications break down all the time. . . . Did you have a good flight down, doctor?"

"It wasn't bad," answered Hal. "But bumpy as a son of a bitch over Cuba."

"Those were probably heavy air masses coming up from the island," said David, watching Lyons out of the corner of his eye. The physicist responded now; a slight glance at Spaulding. And there was humor in the look.

"Yeah," replied Hal knowingly, "that's what the stewardess said."

Lyons smiled a thin smile.

David was about to capitalize on the small breakthrough when he saw a disturbing sight in the driver's rear-view mirror – instinctively he'd been glancing at the glass.

It was the narrow grill of an automobile he'd previously spotted, though with no alarm. He had seen it twice: on the long curb in the taxi line-up and again on the turnout of the front park. Now it was there again, and David slowly shifted his position and looked out the taxi's rear window. Lyons seemed to sense that Spaulding was concerned; he moved to accommodate him.

The car was a 1937 La Salle, black, with rusted chrome on the grillwork and around the headlights. It remained fifty to sixty yards behind, but the driver a blond-haired man – refused to let other vehicles come between them. He would accelerate each time his position was threatened. The blond-haired man, it appeared, was either inexperienced or careless. If he *was* following them.

David spoke to the taxi driver in urgent but quiet Spanish. He offered the man five dollars over the meter if he would reverse his direction and head away from San Telmo for the next several minutes. The *porteño* was less of an amateur than the driver of the La Salle; he understood immediately, with one look in his mirror. He nodded silently to Spaulding, made a sudden, awkwardly dangerous U-turn, and sped west. He kept the taxi on a fast zigzag course, weaving in and around the traffic, then turned abruptly to his right and accelerated the car south along the ocean drive. The sight of the water reminded David of Ocho Calle.

He wanted very much to deposit Eugene Lyons in San Telmo and get back to Ocho Calle.

The La Salle was no longer a problem.

"Christ!" said Hal. "What the hell was that?" And then he answered his own question. "We were being followed, right?"

"We weren't sure," said David.

Lyons was watching him, his look inexpressive. Johnny spoke from the front seat.

"Does that mean we can expect problems? You had this guy tooling pretty hard. Mr. Kendall didn't mention anything about trouble. . . . Just our job." Johnny did not turn around as he spoke.

"Would it bother you if there were?"

Johnny turned to face Spaulding; he was a very serious fellow, thought David. "It depends," said the male nurse. "Our job is to watch out for the professor. Take care of him. If any trouble interfered with that, I don't think I'd like it."

"I see. What would you do?"

"Get him the hell out of here," answered Johnny simply.

"Dr. Lyons has a job to do in Buenos Aires. Kendall must have told you that."

Johnny's eyes leveled with Spaulding's. "I'll tell you straight, mister. That dirty pig can go screw. I never took so much shit from anyone in my life."

"Why don't you quit?"

"We don't work for Kendall," said Johnny, as if the thought was repulsive. "We're paid by the Research Center of Meridian Aircraft. That son of a bitch isn't even from Meridian. He's a lousy bookkeeper."

"You understand, Mr. Spaulding," said Hal, retreating from his partner's aggressiveness. "We have to do what's best for the professor. That's what the Research Center hires us for."

"I understand. I'm in constant touch with Meridian Research. The last thing anyone would wish is to harm Dr. Lyons. I can assure you of that." David lied convincingly. He couldn't give assurance because he himself was far from sure. His only course with Johnny and Hal was to turn this newfound liability into an asset. The key would be Meridian's Research Center and his fictional relationship to it; and a common repugnance for Kendall.

The taxi slowed down, turning a corner into a quiet San Telmo street. The driver pulled up to a narrow, three-storied, white stucco house with a sloping, rust-tiled roof. It was 15 Terraza Verde. The first floor was leased to Eugene Lyons and his "assistants."

"Here we are." said Spaulding, opening the door.

Lyons climbed out after David. He stood on the sidewalk and looked up at the quaint, colorful little house on the peaceful street. The trees by the curb were sculptured. Everything had a scrubbed look; there was an Old World serenity about the area. David had the feeling that Lyons had suddenly found something he'd been looking for.

And then he thought he saw what it was. Eugene Lyons was looking up at a lovely resting place. A final resting place. A grave.

34

There wasn't the time David thought there would be. He had told Stoltz to call him after five at Córdoba; it was nearly four now.

The first boats were coming into the piers, whistles blowing, men throwing and catching heavy ropes, nets everywhere, hanging out for the late drying rays of the sun.

Ocho Calle was in the Dársena Norte, east of the Retiro freight yards in a relatively secluded section of La Boca. Railroad tracks, long out of use, were implanted in the streets along the row of warehouses. Ocho Calle was not a prime storage or loading area. Its access to the sea channels wasn't as cumbersome as the inner units of the La Plata, but the facilities were outmoded. It was as if the management couldn't decide whether to sell its fair waterfront real estate or put it into good operating order. The indecision resulted in virtual abandonment.

Spaulding was in shirtsleeves; he had left Ballard's tan jacket at Terraza Verde. Over his shoulder was a large used net he had bought at an outdoor stall. The damn thing was rancid from rotting hemp and dead fish but it served its purpose. He could cover his face at will and move easily, comfortably among his surroundings – at one with them. David thought that should he ever – God forbid! – instruct recruits at Fairfax, he'd stress the factor of comfort. Psychological comfort. One could feel it immediately; just as swiftly as one felt the discomfort of artificiality.

He followed the sidewalk until it was no more. The final block of Ocho Calle was lined on the far side by a few old buildings and fenced-off abandoned lots once used for outside storage, now overgrown with tall weeds. On the water side were two huge warehouses connected to each other by a framed open area. The midships of a trawler could be seen moored between the two buildings. The next pier was across a stretch of water at least a quarter of a mile away. The Ocho Calle warehouses were secluded indeed.

David stopped. The block was like a miniature peninsula; there were few people on it. No side streets, no buildings beyond the row of houses on his left, only what appeared to he other lots behind the houses and further pilings that were sunk into the earth, holding back the water of a small channel.

The last stretch of Ocho Calle *was* a peninsula. The warehouses were not only secluded, they were isolated.

David swung the net off his right shoulder and hoisted it over his left. Two seamen walked out of a building; on the second floor a woman opened a window and shouted down, berating her husband about the projected hour of his return. An old man with dark Indian features sat in a wooden chair on a small, dilapidated stoop in front of a filthy bait store. Inside, through the glass stained with salt and dirt, other old men could be seen drinking from wine bottles. In the last house, a lone whore leaned out a first-floor window, saw David and opened her blouse, displaying a large, sagging breast. She squeezed it several times and pointed the nipple at Spaulding.

Ocho Calle was the end of a particular section of the earth.

He walked up to the old Indian, greeted him casually, and went into the bait store. The stench was overpowering, a combination of urine and rot. There were three men inside, more drunk than sober, nearer seventy than sixty.

The man behind the planked boards which served as a counter seemed startled to see a customer, not really sure what to do. Spaulding took a bill from his pocket – to the astonishment of all three surrounding him – and spoke in Spanish.

"Do you have squid?"

"No. . . .No, no squid. Very little supplies today," answered the owner, his eyes on the bill.

"What have you got?"

"Worms. Dog meat, some cat. Cat is very good."

"Give me a small container."

The man stumbled backward, picked up pieces of intestine and wrapped them in a dirty newspaper. He put it on the plank next to the money. "I have no change, *señor* . . ."

"That's all right," replied Spaulding. "The money's for you. And keep the bait."

The man grinned, bewildered. "*Señor?* . . ."

"You keep the money. Understand? . . . Tell me. Who works over there?" David pointed at the barely translucent front window. "In those big dock houses?"

"Hardly anybody. . . .A few men come and go . . . now and then. A fishing boat . . . now and then."

"Have you been inside?"

"Oh, yes. Three, four years ago, I work inside. Big business, three, four . . . five years ago. We all work." The other two old men nodded, chattering old men's chatter.

"Not now?"

"No, no. . . .All closed down. Finished. Nobody goes inside now. The owner is a very bad man. Watchmen break heads."

"Watchmen?"

"Oh, yes. With guns. Many guns. Very bad."

"Do automobiles come here?"

"Oh, yes. Now and then. . . .One or two. . . .They don't give us work."

"Thank you. You keep the money. Thank you, again." David crossed to the filthy storefront window, rubbed a small section of the glass and looked out at the block-long stretch of warehouse. It appeared deserted except for the men on the pier. And then he looked closer at those men.

At first he wasn't sure; the glass – though rubbed – still had layers of film on the outside pane; it wasn't clear and the men were moving about, in and out of the small transparent area.

Then he was sure. And suddenly very angry.

The men in the distance on the pier were wearing the same paramilitary clothes the guards at Rhinemann's gate had worn.

They were Rhinemann's men.

The telephone rang at precisely five thirty. The caller was not Stoltz, and because it wasn't, David refused to accept the instructions given him. He hung up and waited less than two minutes for the phone to ring again.

"You are most obstinate," said Erich Rhinemann. "It is we who should be cautious, not you."

"That's a pointless statement. I have no intention of following the directions of someone I don't know. I don't expect airtight controls but that's too loose."

Rhinemann paused. Then he spoke harshly. "What happened last night?"

"I told Stoltz exactly what happened to *me*. I don't know anything else."

"I don't believe you." Rhinemann's voice was tense, sharp, his anger very close to the surface.

"I'm sorry," said David. "But that doesn't really concern me."

"Neither of those men could have left Córdoba! Impossible!"

"They left; take my word for it. . . .Look, I told Stoltz I don't want to get mixed up in your problems. . . ."

"How do you know you're not . . . mixed up?"

It was, of course, the logical question and Spaulding realized that. "Because I'm here in my apartment, talking to you. According to Stoltz, the others are dead; that's a condition I intend to avoid. I'm merely purchasing some papers from you. Let's concentrate on that."

"We'll talk further on this subject," said Rhinemann.

"Not now. We have business to transact."

Again the German Jew paused. "Do as the man told you. Go to the Casa Rosada on the Plaza de Mayo. South gate. If you take a taxi, get off at the Julio and walk."

"Your men will pick me up when I leave the apartment, I assume."

"Discreetly. To see if you're followed."

"Then I'll walk from here. It'll be easier."

"Very intelligent. A car will be waiting for you at the Rosada. The same automobile that brought you here last evening."

"Will you be there?" asked David.

"Of course not. But we'll meet shortly."

"I take the designs straight to Telmo?"

"If everything is clear, you may."

"I'll leave in five minutes. Will your men be ready?"

"They are ready now," answered Rhinemann. He hung up.

David strapped the Beretta to his chest and put on his jacket. He went into the bathroom, grabbed a towel from the rack and rubbed his shoes, removing the Aeroparque and La Boca dirt from the leather. He combed his hair and patted talcum powder over the scratches on his face.

He couldn't help but notice the dark crescents under his eyes. He needed sleep badly, but there was no time. For his own sake – survival, really – he knew he had to take the time.

He wondered when it would be.

He returned to the telephone. He had two calls to make before he left.

The first was to Jean. To ask her to stay in the embassy; he might have reason to call her. At any rate, he would talk to her when he returned. He said he would be with Eugene Lyons at Terraza Verde. And that he loved her.

The second call was to Henderson Granville.

"I told you I wouldn't involve the embassy or yourself in my work here, sir. If that's changed it's only because a man on your staff closed a naval surveillance file improperly. I'm afraid it directly affects me."

"How do you mean 'improperly'? That's a serious implication. If not a chargeable offense."

"Yes, sir. And for that reason it's imperative we raise no alarm, keep everything very quiet. It's an Intelligence matter."

"Who is this man?" asked Granville icily.

"An attaché named Ellis. William Ellis – please don't take *any* action, sir." Spaulding spoke rapidly, emphatically. "He may have been duped; he may *not* have been. Either way we can't have him alerted."

"Very well. I follow you. . . . Then why have you told me . . . if you want no action taken?"

"Not against Ellis, sir. We *do* need a clarification on the surveillance." David described the warehouses on Ocho Calle and the trawler moored between the two buildings.

Granville interrupted quietly. "I remember the report. Naval surveillance. It was a lading destination . . . let me think."

"Tortugas," supplied Spaulding.

"Yes, that was it. Coastal violations. An error, of course. No fishing boat would attempt such a trip. The actual destination was *Torugos*, a small port in northern Uruguay, I think."

David thought for a second. Jean hadn't mentioned the switch – or similarity – of names. "That may be, sir, but it would be advantageous to know the cargo."

"It was listed. Farm machinery, I believe."

"We don't think so," said Spaulding.

"Well, we have no right to inspect cargo. . . ."

"Mr. Ambassador?" David cut off the old gentleman. "Is there anyone in the junta we can trust, *completely* trust?"

Granville's reply was hesitant, cautious; Spaulding understood. "One. Two, perhaps."

"I won't ask you their names, sir. I *will* ask you to request their help. With priority security measures. Those warehouses are guarded . . . by Erich Rhinemann's men."

"*Rhinemann?*" The ambassador's distaste carried over the telephone. That was an asset, thought David.

"We have reason to believe he's aborting a negotiation or tying contraband into it. Smuggling, sir. We have to know what that cargo is." It was all David could think to say. A generalization without actual foundation. But if men were willing to kill and be killed for "Tortugas," perhaps that was foundation enough. If Fairfax could list the name on his transfer orders without telling him – that was *more* than enough.

"I'll do what I can, Spaulding. I can't promise anything, of course."

"Yes, sir. I realize. And thank you."

The Avenida de Mayo was jammed with traffic, the Plaza worse. At the end of the square the pinkish stone of Casa Rosada reflected the orange flood of the setting sun. Befitting a capital controlled by soldiers, thought David.

He crossed the Plaza, stopping at the fountain, recalling yesterday and Leslie Jenner Hawkwood. Where was she now? In Buenos Aires; but where? And more important, why?

The answer might lie in the name "Tortugas" and a trawler in Ocho Calle.

He circled the fountain twice, then reversed his steps once, testing himself testing Erich Rhinemann. Where were the men watching him? Or were they women?

Were they in cars or taxis or small trucks? Circling as he was circling?

He spotted one. It wasn't hard to do. The man had seated himself on the edge of the fountain's pool, the tail of his jacket in the water. He'd sat down too quickly, trying to be inconspicuous.

David started across the pedestrian walk – the same pedestrian walk he'd used following Leslie Hawkwood – and at the first traffic island waited for a change of light. Instead of crossing, however, he walked back to the fountain. He stepped up his pace and sat down at the pool's edge and watched the crosswalk.

The man with the wet jacket emerged with the next contingent of pedestrians and looked anxiously around. Finally he saw Spaulding.

David waved.

The man turned and raced back across the street.

Spaulding ran after him, just making the light. The man did not look back; he seemed hell-bent to reach a contact, thought David; to have someone take over, perhaps. The man turned left at the Casa Rosada and Spaulding followed, keeping himself out of sight.

The man reached a corner and to David's surprise he slowed down, then stopped and entered a telephone booth.

It was a curiously amateurish thing to do, mused Spaulding. And it told him something about Erich Rhinemann's personnel: they weren't as good as they thought they were.

There was a long blasting of a horn that seemed louder than the normally jarring sounds of the Mayo's traffic. The single horn triggered other horns and in a few seconds a cacophony of strident honking filled the streets. David looked over. It was nothing; an irritated motorist had momentarily reached the end of his patience. Everything returned to normal chaos with the starting up of the automobiles at the crosswalk.

And then there was a scream. A woman's scream. And another; and still another.

A crowd gathered around the telephone booth.

David pushed his way through, yanking arms, pulling shoulders, shoving. He reached the edge of the booth and looked inside.

The man with the wet jacket was slumped awkwardly to the floor of the tiny glass enclosure, his legs buckled under him, his arms stretched above, one hand still gripping the telephone receiver so that the wire was taut. His head was sprung back from his neck. Blood was streaming down the back of his skull. Spaulding looked up at the walls of the booth. On the street side were three distinct holes surrounded by cracked glass.

He heard the piercing sounds of police whistles and pushed his way back through the crowd. He reached the iron fence that surrounded the Casa Rosada, turned right and started rapidly around the building to the south side.

To the south gate.

The Packard was parked in front of the entrance, its motor running. A man about his size approached him as David started for the automobile.

"Colonel Spaulding?"

"Yes?"

"If you'll hurry, please?" The man opened the back door and David climbed in quickly.

Heinrich Stoltz greeted him. "You've had a long walk. Sit. The ride will be relaxing."

"Not now." David pointed to the panels below the front dashboard. "Can you reach Rhinemann on that thing? Right away?"

"We're in constant contact. Why?"

"Get him. Your man was just killed."

"Our man?"

"The one following me. He was shot in a telephone booth."

"He wasn't our man, colonel. And *we* shot him," said Stoltz calmly.

"*What?*"

672

"The man was known to us. He was a hired killer out of Rio de Janeiro. You were his target."

Stoltz's explanation was succinct. They'd picked up the killer within moments after David left his apartment house. He was a Corsican, deported out of Marseilles before the war; a gun for the Unio Corso who had murdered one prefect too many under orders from the *contrabandistes* of southern France.

"We couldn't take a chance with the American who possesses the codes. A silencer in heavy traffic you'll agree is adequate."

"I don't think he was trying to kill me," said Spaulding. "I think you moved too soon."

"Then he was waiting for you to meet with *us*. Forgive me, but we couldn't permit that. You agree?"

"No. I could have taken him." David sat back and brought his hand to his forehead, tired and annoyed. "I was *going* to take him. Now we both lose."

Stoltz looked at David. He spoke cautiously; a question. "The same? You wonder also."

"Don't you? . . . You still think the Gestapo's not in Buenos Aires?"

"*Impossible!*" Stoltz whispered the words intensely through his teeth.

"That's what our mutual friend said about your men last night. . . .I don't know a goddamned thing about that, but I understand they're dead. So what's impossible?"

"The Gestapo *can't* be involved. We've learned that at the highest levels."

"Rhinemann's Jewish, isn't he?" David watched Stoltz as he asked the unexpected question.

The German turned and looked at Spaulding. There was a hint of embarrassment in his expression. "He practices no religion; his mother was Jewish. . . .Frankly, it's not pertinent. The racial theories of Rosenberg and Hitler are not shared unequivocally; far too much emphasis has been placed upon them. . . .It is – was – primarily an economic question. Distribution of banking controls, decentralization of financial hierarchies. . . .An unpleasant topic."

David was about to reply to the diplomat's evasions when he stopped himself. . . .Why did Stoltz find it necessary even to attempt a rationalization? To offer a weak explanation he himself knew was devoid of logic?

Heinrich Stoltz's loyalty was supposedly to Rhinemann, not the Third Reich.

Spaulding looked away and said nothing. He was, frankly, confused, but it was no time to betray that confusion. Stoltz continued.

"It's a curious question. Why did you bring it up?"

"A rumor . . . I heard it at the embassy." And that was the truth, thought David. "I gathered that the Jewish community in Buenos Aires was hostile to Rhinemann."

"Mere speculation. The Jews here are like Jews elsewhere. They keep to themselves, have little to do with those outside. Perhaps the ghetto is less definable, but it's there. They have no argument with Rhinemann; there's no contact, really."

"Cross off one speculation," said Spaulding.

"There's another," said Stoltz. "Your own countrymen."

David turned slowly back to the German. "This is a good game. How did you arrive at that?"

"The purchase of the designs is being made by one aircraft corporation. There are five, six major companies in competition for your unending government contracts. Whoever possesses the gyroscope designs will have a powerful – I might even say irresistible – lever. All other guidance systems will be obsolete."

"Are you serious?"

"Most assuredly. We have discussed the situation at length . . . in depth. We are nearly convinced that this is the logical answer. Stoltz looked away from David and stared to the front. "There's no other. Those trying to stop us are American."

35

The green Packard made crisscross patterns over the Buenos Aires streets. The route was programmed aimlessness, and Spaulding recognized it for what it was: an extremely thorough surveillance check. Intermittently, the driver would pick up the microphone from beneath the dashboard and recite a prearranged series of numbers. The crackling response over the single speaker would repeat the numbers and the Packard would make yet another – seemingly aimless – turn.

Several times David spotted the corresponding vehicles making the visual checks. Rhinemann had a minimum of five automobiles involved. After three-quarters of an hour, it was certain beyond doubt that the trip to San Telmo was clean.

The driver spoke to Stoltz.

"We are clear. The others will take up their positions."

"Proceed," said Stoltz.

They swung northwest; the Packard accelerated toward San Telmo. David knew that at least three other cars were behind them; perhaps two in front. Rhinemann had set up his own transport column, and that meant the gyroscopic designs were in one of the automobiles.

"Have you got the merchandise?" he asked Stoltz.

"Part of it," replied the attache, leaning forward, pressing a section of the felt backing in front of him. A latch sprung; Stoltz reached down and pulled out a tray from beneath the seat. Inside the concealed drawer was a thin metal box not unlike the containers used in libraries to protect rare manuscripts from possible loss by fire. The German picked it up, held it in his lap and pushed the drawer back with his foot. "We'll be there in a few minutes," he said.

The Packard pulled up to the curb in front of the white stucco house in San Telmo. Spaulding reached for the door handle but Stoltz touched his arm and shook his head. David withdrew his hand; he understood.

About fifty yards ahead, one of the checkpoint automobiles had parked and two men got out. One carried a thin metal container, the other an oblong leather case – a radio. They walked back toward the Packard.

David didn't have to look out the rear window to know what was happening behind him, but to confirm his thoughts he did so. Another automobile had parked. Two additional men were coming up the sidewalk; one, of course, carrying a container, the second, a leather-encased radio.

The four men met by the door of the Packard. Stoltz nodded to Spaulding; he got out of the car and walked around the vehicle, joining Rhinemann's contingent. He was about to start up the short path to the front entrance when Stoltz spoke through the automobile window.

"Please wait. Our men are not yet in position. They'll tell us."

Static could be heard over the radio beneath the Packard's dashboard. There followed a recitation of numbers; the driver picked up his microphone and repeated them.

Heinrich Stoltz nodded and got out of the car. David started toward the door.

Inside, two of Rhinemann's men remained in the hallway; two walked through the apartment to the kitchen and a rear door that opened onto a small, terraced back yard. Stoltz accompanied David into the living room where Eugene Lyons was seated at a large dining table. The table was cleared except for two note pads with a half dozen pencils.

The male nurses, Johnny and Hal, accepted Spaulding's terse commands. They stood at opposite ends of the room in front of a couch, in shirtsleeves, their pistols strapped in shoulder bolsters emphasized by the white cloth of their shirts.

Stoltz bad relieved one man of his metal case and told David to take the other. Together, Stoltz and Spaulding placed the three containers on the large table, and Stoltz unlocked them. Lyons made no effort to greet his visitors – his intruders – and only the most perfunctory salutation came from Stoltz. It was apparent that Kendall had described the scientist's afflictions; the German diplomat conducted himself accordingly.

Stoltz spoke from across the table to the seated Lyons. "From your left, the designs are in order of sequence. We have prepared bilingual keys attached to each of the schematics, and wherever processes are described, they have been translated verbatim, utilizing English counterpart formulae or internationally recognized symbols, and often both. . . .Not far from here, and easily contacted by our automobile radio, is an aeronautical physicist from Peenemünde. He is available for consultation at your request. . . .Finally, you understand that no photographs may be taken."

Eugene Lyons picked up a pencil and wrote on a pad. He tore off the page and handed it to Spaulding. It read:

How long do I have? Are these complete?

David handed the note to Stoltz, who replied.

"As long as you need, *Herr Doktor*. . . .There is one last container. It will be brought to you later."

"Within twenty-four hours," interrupted Spaulding. "I insist on that."

"When we receive confirmation that the codes have arrived in Washington."

"That message is undoubtedly at the embassy now. David looked at his watch. "I'm sure it is."

"If you say it, I believe it," said Stoltz. "It would be pointless to lie. You won't leave Argentina until *we* have received word from . . . Switzerland."

Spaulding couldn't define why but there was something questioning about the German's statement; a questioning that didn't belong with such a pronouncement. David began to think that Stoltz was far more nervous than he wanted anyone to realize. "I'll confirm the codes when we leave. . . .By the way, I also insist the designs remain here. Just as Doctor Lyons has checked them."

"We anticipated your . . . request. You Americans are so mistrustful. Two of our men will also remain. Others will be outside."

"That's a waste of manpower. What good is three-fourths of the merchandise?"

"Three-fourths better than you have," answered the German.

The next two and a half hours were marked by the scratches of Lyons's pencil; the incessant static of the radios from the hallway and the kitchen, over which came the incessant, irritating recitation of numbers; the pacing of Heinrich Stoltz – his eyes constantly riveting on the pages of notes taken by an exhausted Lyons, making sure the scientist did not try to pocket or hide them; the yawns of the male nurse, Hal; the silent, hostile stares of his partner, Johnny.

At ten thirty-five, Lyons rose from the chair. He placed the pile of notes to his left and wrote on a pad, tearing off the page and handing it to Spaulding.

So far – authentic. I have no questions.

David handed the note to an anxious Stoltz.

"Good," said the German. "Now, colonel, please explain to the doctor's companions that it will be necessary for us to relieve them of their weapons. They will be returned, of course."

David spoke to Johnny. "It's all right. Put them on the table."

"It's all right by who-says?" said Johnny, leaning against the wall, making no move to comply.

"I do," answered Spaulding. "Nothing will happen."

"These fuckers are Nazis! You want to put us in blindfolds, too?"

"They're German. Not Nazis."

"Horseshit!" Johnny pushed himself off the wall and stood erect. "I don't like the way they talk."

"Listen to me." David approached him. "A great many people have risked their lives to bring this thing off. For different reasons. You may not like them any more than I do, but we can't louse it up now. Please, do as I ask you."

Johnny stared angrily at Spaulding. "I hope to Christ you know what you're doing. . . ." He and his partner put down their guns.

"Thank you, gentlemen," said Stoltz, walking into the hallway. He spoke quietly in German to the two guards. The man with the radio walked rapidly through the sitting room into the kitchen; the other picked up the two weapons, placing one in his belt, the second in his jacket pocket. He then returned to the hallway without speaking.

Spaulding went to the table, joined by Stoltz. Lyons had replaced the designs in the manila envelopes; there were three. "I'd hate to think of the money our mutual friend is getting for these," said David.

"You wouldn't pay it if they weren't worth it."

"I suppose not. . . .No reason not to put them in one case. Along with the notes." Spaulding looked over at Lyons, who stood immobile at the end of the table. "Is that all right, doctor?"

Lyons nodded, his sad eyes half closed, his pallor accentuated.

"As you wish," said Stoltz. Picking up the envelopes and the notes, he put then, in the first container, locked it, closed the other two and placed them on top of the first, as if he were performing a religious exercise in front of an altar.

Spaulding took several steps toward the two men by the window. "You've had a rough day. Doctor Lyons, too. Turn in and let your guests walk guard duty; I think they're on overtime."

Hal grinned. Johnny did not.

"Good evening, doctor. It's been a privilege meeting such a distinguished man of science." Across the room, Stoltz spoke in diplomatic tones, bowing a slight diplomatic bow.

The guard with the radio emerged from the kitchen and nodded to the German attaché. They left the room together. Spaulding smiled at Lyons; the scientist turned without acknowledging and walked into his bedroom to the right of the kitchen door.

Outside on the sidewalk, Stoltz held the car door for David. "A very strange man, your Doctor Lyons," he said as Spaulding got into the Packard.

"He may be, but he's one of the best in his field. . . .Ask your driver to stop at a pay phone. I'll check the embassy's radio room. You'll get your confirmation."

"Excellent idea. . . .Then, perhaps, you'll join me for dinner?"

David looked at the attaché who sat so confidently, so half- mockingly, beside him. Stoltz's nervousness had disappeared. "No, Herr Botschaftssekretär. I have another engagement."

"With the lovely Mrs. Cameron, no doubt. I defer."

Spaulding did not reply. Instead, he looked out the window in silence.

The Terraza Verde was peaceful. The streetlamps cast a soft glow on the quiet, darkened sidewalks; the sculptured trees in front of the picturesque Mediterranean houses were silhouetted against pastel-colored brick and stone. In windows beyond flower boxes, the yellow lamps of living rooms and bedrooms shone invitingly. A man in a business suit, a newspaper under his arm, walked up the steps to a door, taking a key from his pocket; a young couple were laughing quietly, leaning against a low wrought-iron fence. A little girl with a light brown cocker spaniel on a leash was skipping along the sidewalk, the dog jumping happily out of step.

Terraza Verde was a lovely place to live.

And David thought briefly of another block he'd seen that day. With old men who smelled of rot and urine; with a toothless whore who leaned on a filthy sill. With cat intestines and dirt-filmed windows. And with two huge warehouses that provided no work, and a trawler at anchor, recently destined for Tortugas.

The Packard turned the corner into another street. There were a few more lights, less sculptured trees, but the street was very much like Terraza Verde. It reminded David of those offshoot streets in Lisbon that approached the rich *caminos*; dotted with expensive shops, convenient for wealthy inhabitants a few hundred yards away.

There were shops here, too; with windows subtly lit, wares tastefully displayed.

Another block; the Packard slowed down at the intersecting street and then started across. More shops, less trees, more dogs – these often walked by maids. A group of teenagers were crowded around an Italian sportscar.

And then David saw the overcoat. It was just an overcoat at first; a light grey overcoat in a doorway.

A grey overcoat. A recessed doorway.

The man was tall and thin. A tall, thin man in a light grey overcoat. In a doorway!

My God! thought David. *The man on Fifty-second Street!*

The man was turned sideways, looking down into a dimly lit store window. Spaulding could not see them but he could picture the dark, hollow eyes; could hear the bastardized English out of somewhere in the Balkans; sense the desperation in the man's eyes:

There are to be no negotiations with Franz Altmüller ... Heed the lesson of Fairfax!

He had to get out of the Packard. Quickly!

He had to go back to Terraza Verde. Without Stoltz. He *had* to!

"There's a café in the next block," said Spaulding, pointing to an orange canopy with lights underneath, stretching across the sidewalk. "Stop there. I'll call the embassy."

"You seem anxious, colonel. It can wait. I believe you."

Spaulding turned to the German. "You want me to spell it out? O.K., I'll do that. . . .I don't like you, Stoltz. And I don't like Rhinemann; I don't like men who yell and bark orders and have me followed. . . .I'm buying from you, but I don't have to associate with you. I don't have to have dinner or ride in your automobile once our business for the day is over. Do I make myself clear?"

"You're clear. Though somewhat uncivilized. And ungrateful, if you don't mind my saying so. We saved your life earlier this evening."

"That's your opinion. Not mine. Just let me off, I'll telephone and come out with your confirmation. . . .As you said, there's no point in my lying. You go on your way, I'll grab a taxi."

Stoltz instructed the driver to pull up at the orange canopy. "Do as you please. And should your plans include Doctor Lyons, be advised we have men stationed about the area. Their orders are harsh. Those designs will stay where they are."

"I'm not paying for three-quarters of the merchandise regardless of what there is back home. And I have no intention of walking into that phalanx of robots."

The Packard drew up to the canopy. Spaulding opened the door quickly, slamming it angrily behind him. He walked swiftly into the lighted entrance and asked for the telephone.

"The ambassador has been trying to reach you for the past half-hour or so," said the night operator. "He says it's urgent. I'm to give you a telephone number." The operator drawled out the digits.

"Thank you," David said. "Now connect me with Mr. Ballard in Communications, please."

"O'Leary's Saloon," came the uninterested voice of Bobby Ballard over the wire.

"You're a funny man. I'll laugh next Tuesday."

"The 'switch' said it was you. You know Granville's trying to find you."

"I heard. Where's Jean?"

"In her room; pining away just like you ordered."

"Did you get word from D.C.?"

"All wrapped. Came in a couple of hours ago; your codes are cleared. How's the erector set?"

"The instructions — three-quarters of them — are in the box. But there are too many playmates."

"Terraza Verde?"

"Around there."

"Shall I send out a few FMF playground attendants?"

"I think I'd feel better," said Spaulding. "Tell them to cruise. Nothing else. I'll spot them and yell if I need them."

"It'll take a half-hour from the base."

"Thanks. No parades, please, Bobby."

"They'll be so quiet no one'll know but us Munchkins. Take care of yourself."

Spaulding held down the receiver with his finger, tempted to lift it, insert another coin and call Granville. . . .There wasn't time. He left the booth and walked out the restaurant door to the Packard. Stoltz was at the window; David saw that a trace of his previous nervousness had returned.

"You've got your confirmation. Deliver the rest of the goods and enjoy your money . . . I don't know where you come from, Stoltz, but I'll find out and have it bombed off the map. I'll tell the Eighth Air Force to name the raid after you."

Stoltz seemed relieved at David's surliness — as David thought he might be. "The man from Lisbon is complicated. I suppose that's proper for a complicated assignment. . . .We'll call you by noon. Stoltz turned to the driver. "*Los, abfahren, machen Sie schnell!*"

The green Packard roared off down the street. Spaulding waited under the canopy to see if it made any turns; should it do so, he would return to the café and wait.

It did not; it maintained a straight course. David watched until the taillights were infinitesimal red dots. Then he turned and walked as fast as he could without calling attention to himself toward Terraza Verde.

He reached the short block in which he'd seen the man in the light grey overcoat and stopped. His concerns made him want to rush on; his instincts forced him to wait, to look, to move cautiously.

The man was not on the block now; he was nowhere to be seen. David reversed his direction and walked to the end of the sidewalk. He turned left and raced down the street to the next corner, turning left again, now slowing down, walking casually. He wished to God he knew the area better, knew the buildings behind Lyons's white stucco house. Others did; others were positioned in dark recesses he knew nothing about.

Rhinemann's guards. The man in the light grey overcoat; how many more were with him?

He approached the intersection of Terraza Verde and crossed the road diagonally, away from the white stucco house. He stayed out of the spill of the lamps as best he could and continued down the pavement to the street behind the row of houses on Terraza Verde. It was, of course, a block lined with other houses; quaint, picturesque, quiet. Spaulding looked up at the vertical sign: *Terraza Amarilla*.

San Telmo fed upon itself.

He remained at the far end of the corner under a sculptured tree and looked toward the section of the adjacent street where he judged the rear of Lyons's house to be. He could barely make out the sloping tiled roof, but enough to pinpoint the building behind it – about 150 yards away.

He also saw Rhinemann's automobile, one of those he'd spotted during the long, security-conscious drive from the Casa Rosada. It was parked opposite a light-bricked Italian townhouse with large gates on both sides. David assumed those gates opened to stone paths leading to a wall or a fence separating Lyons's back terrace from the rear entrance of the townhouse. It had to be something like that; Rhinemann's guards were posted so that anyone emerging from those gates was equally in their sightlines.

And then Spaulding remembered the crackling static of the radios from the hallway and the kitchen and the incessant repetition of the German numbers. Those who carried the radios had weapons. He reached beneath his jacket to his holster and took out the Beretta. He knew the clip was filled; he unlatched the safety, shoved the weapon into his belt and started across the street toward the automobile.

Before he reached the opposite corner, he heard a car drive up behind him. He had no time to run, no moment to make a decision – good or bad. His hand went to his belt; he tried to assume a posture of indifference.

He heard the voice and was stunned.

"Get in, you goddamned *fool!*"

Leslie Hawkwood was behind the wheel of a small Renault coupe. She had reached over and unlatched the door. David caught it, his attention split between his shock and his concern that Rhinemann's guard – or guards – a hundred yards away might hear the noise. There were fewer than a dozen pedestrians within the two-block area. Rhinemann's men *had* to have been alerted.

He jumped into the Renault and with his left hand he grabbed Leslie's right leg above the knee, his grip a restraining vise, pressing on the nerve lines. He spoke softly but with unmistakable intensity.

"You back this car up as quietly as you can, and turn left down that street."

"Let *go!* Let . . ."

"Do as I say or I'll break your kneecap off!"

The Renault was short; there was no need to use the reverse gear. Leslie spun the wheel and the car veered into a sharp turn.

"Slowly!" commanded Spaulding, his eyes on Rhinemann's car. He could see a head turn – two heads. And then they were out of sight.

David took his hand off the girl's leg; she pulled it up and doubled her shoulders down in agony. Spaulding grabbed the wheel and forced the gears into neutral. The car came to a stop halfway down the block, at the curb.

"You bastard! You broke my leg!" Leslie's eyes were filled with tears of pain, not sorrow. She was close to fury but she did not shout. And that told David something about Leslie he had not known before.

"I'll break more than a leg if you don't start telling me what you're doing here! How many others are there? I saw one; how many more?"

She snapped her head up, her long hair whipping back, ha eyes defiant. "Did you think we couldn't find him?"

"Who?"

"Your *scientist*. This Lyons! We found him!"

"Leslie, for Christ's sake, what are you *doing?*"

"Stopping you!"

"*Me?*"

"You. Altmüller, Rhinemann. Koening! And those pigs in Washington. . . . Peenemünde! It's all over. They won't trust you anymore. Tortugas' is finished!"

The faceless name – Altmüller again. Tortugas. . . .Koening? Words, names . . . meaning and no meaning. The tunnels had no light.

There was no *time!*

Spaulding reached over and pulled the girl toward him. He clutched the hair above her forehead, yanking it taut, and with his other hand he circled his fingers high up under her throat, just below the jawbone. He applied pressure in swift, harsh spurts, each worse than the last.

So much, so alien.

"You want to play this game, you play it out! Now tell me! What's *happening? Now?*"

She tried to squirm, lashing out her arms, kicking at him; but each time

682

she moved he ripped his fingers into her throat. Her eyes widened until the sockets were round. He spoke again.

"Say it, Leslie! I'll have to kill you if you don't. I don't have a choice! Not now. . . .For Christ's sake, don't *force* me!"

She slumped; her body went limp but not unconscious. Her head moved up and down; she sobbed deep-throated moans. He released her and gently held her face. She opened her eyes.

"Don't touch me! Oh, *God*, don't touch me!" She could barely whisper, much less scream. "Inside. . . .We're going inside. Kill the scientists; kill Rhinemann's men. . . ."

Before she finished, Spaulding clenched his fist and hammered a short, hard blow into the side of her chin. She slumped, unconscious.

He'd heard enough. There *was* no time.

He stretched her out in the small front seat, removing the ignition keys as he did so. He looked for her purse; she had none. He opened the door, closed it firmly and looked up and down the street. There were two couples halfway down the block; a car was parking at the corner; a window was opened on the second floor of a building across the way, music coming from within.

Except for these – nothing. San Telmo was at peace.

Spaulding ran to within yards of Terraza Amarilla. He stopped and edged his way along an iron fence that bordered the corner, swearing at the spill of the streetlamp. He looked through the black grillwork at Rhinemann's car less than a hundred yards away. He tried to focus on the front seat, on the two heads he'd seen moving minutes ago. There was no movement now, no glow of cigarettes, no shifting of shoulders.

Nothing.

Yet there was a break in the silhouette of the left window frame; an obstruction that filled the lower section of the glass.

David rounded the sharp angle of the iron fence and walked slowly toward the automobile, his hand clamped on the Beretta, his finger steady over the trigger. *Seventy yards, sixty, forty-five.*

The obstruction did not move.

Thirty-five, thirty . . . he pulled the pistol from his belt, prepared to fire.

Nothing.

He saw it clearly now. The obstruction was a head, sprung back into the glass – not resting, but wrenched, twisted from the neck; immobile.

Dead.

He raced across the street to the rear of the car and crouched, his Beretta level with his shoulders. There was no noise, no rustling from within.

The block was deserted now. The only sounds were the muffled, blurred hums from a hundred lighted windows. A latch could be heard far down the street; a small dog barked; the wail of an infant was discernible in the distance.

David rose and looked through the automobile's rear window.

He saw the figure of a second man sprawled over the felt top of the front seat. The light of the streetlamps illuminated the upper part of the man's back and shoulders. The whole area was a mass of blood and slashed cloth.

Spaulding slipped around the side of the car to the front right door. The window was open, the sight within sickening. The man behind the wheel had been shot through the side of his head, his companion knifed repeatedly.

The oblong, leather-cased radio was smashed, lying on the floor beneath the dashboard.

It had to have happened within the past five or six minutes, thought David. Leslie Hawkwood had rushed down the street in the Renault to intercept him – at the precise moment men with silenced pistols and long-bladed knives were heading for Rhinemann's guards.

The killings complete, the men with knives and pistols must have raced across the street into the gates towards Lyons's house. Raced without thought of cover or camouflage, knowing the radios were in constant contact with those inside 15 Terraza Verde.

Spaulding opened the car door, rolled up the window, and pulled the lifeless form off the top of the seat. He closed the door; the bodies were visible, but less so than before. It was no moment for alarms in the street if they could be avoided.

He looked over at the gates across the way on each side of the townhouse. The left one was slightly ajar.

He ran over to it and eased himself through the opening, touching nothing, his gun thrust laterally at his side, aiming forward. Beyond the gate was a cement passageway that stretched the length of the building to some sort of miniature patio bordered by a high brick wall.

He walked silently, rapidly to the end of the open alley; the patio was a combination of slate paths, plots of grass and small flower gardens. Alabaster statuary shone in the moonlight; vines crawled up the brick wall.

He judged the height of the wall: seven feet, perhaps, seven and a half. Thickness: eight, ten inches – standard. Construction: new, within several years, strong. It was the construction with which he was most concerned. In 1942 he took a nine-foot wall in San Sebastián that collapsed under him. A month later it was amusing; at the time it nearly killed him.

He replaced the Beretta in his shoulder holster, locking the safety, shoving in the weapon securely. He bent down and rubbed his hands in the dry dirt at the edge of the cement, absorbing whatever sweat was on them. He stood up and raced towards the brick wall.

Spaulding leaped. Once on top of the wall, he held – silent, prone; his hands gripping the sides, his body motionless – a part of the stone. He remained immobile, his face towards Lyons's terrace, and waited several seconds. The back door to Lyons's flat was closed – no lights were on in the kitchen; the shades were drawn over the windows throughout the floor. No sounds from within.

He slid down from the wall, removed his gun and ran to the side of the kitchen door, pressing his back against the white stucco. To his astonishment he saw that the door was *not* closed; and then he saw why. At the base, barely visible in the darkness of the room beyond, was a section of a hand. It had gripped the bottom of the doorframe and been smashed into the saddle; the fingers were the fingers of a dead man.

Spaulding reached over and pressed the door. An inch. Two inches. Wood against dead weight; his elbow ached from the pressure.

Three, four, five inches. A foot.

Indistinguishable voices could be heard now; faint, male, excited.

He stepped swiftly in front of the door and pushed violently – as quietly as possible – against the fallen body that acted as a huge, soft, dead weight against the frame. He stepped over the corpse of Rhinemann's guard, noting that the oblong radio had been torn from its leather case, smashed on the floor. He closed the door silently.

The voices came from the sitting room. He edged his way against the wall, the Beretta poised, unlatched, ready to fire.

An open pantry against the opposite side of the room caught his eye. The single window, made of mass-produced stained glass, was high in the west wall, creating eerie shafts of colored light from the moon. Below, on the floor, was Rhinemann's second guard. The method of death he could not tell; the body was arched backward – probably a bullet from a small-caliber pistol had killed him. A pistol with a silencer attached. It would be very quiet. David felt the perspiration rolling down his forehead and over his neck.

How many were there? They'd immobilized a garrison.

He had no commitment matching those odds.

Yet he had a strange commitment to Lyons. He had commitment enough for him at the moment. He dared not think beyond that instant.

And he was good; he could – should – never forget that. He was the best there was.

If it was important to anyone.

So much, so alien.

He pressed his cheek against the molding of the arch and what he saw sickened him. The revulsion, perhaps, was increased by the surroundings: a well-appointed flat with chairs and couches and tables meant for civilized people involved with civilized pursuits.

Not death.

The two male nurses – the hostile Johnny, the affable, dense Hal – were sprawled across the floor, their arms linked, their heads inches from each other. Their combined blood had formed a pool on the parquet surface. Johnny's eyes were wide, angry—dead; Hal's face composed, questioning, at rest.

Behind them were Rhinemann's two other guards, their bodies on the couch like slaughtered cattle.

I hope you know what you're doing!

Johnny's words vibrated painfully – in screams – in David's brain.

There were three other men in the room – standing, alive, in the same grotesque stocking masks that had been worn by those in the Duesenberg who had cut short the few moments he'd had alone with Leslie Hawkwood high in the hills of Luján.

The Duesenberg that had exploded in fire in the hills of Colinas Rojas.

The men were standing – none held weapons – over the spent figure of Eugene Lyons – seated gracefully, without fear, at the table. The look in the scientist's eyes told the truth, as Spaulding saw it: he welcomed death.

"You see what's around you!" The man in the light grey overcoat spoke to him. "We will not hesitate further! You're dead! . . . Give us the designs!"

Jesus Christ! thought David. Lyons had hidden the plans!

"There's no point in carrying on, please believe me," continued the man in the overcoat, the man with the hollow crescents under his eyes Spaulding remembered so well. "You may be spared, but only if you tell us! *Now!*"

Lyons did not move; he looked up at the man in the overcoat without shifting his head, his eyes calm. They touched David's.

"Write it!" said the man in the light grey overcoat.

It was the moment to move.

David spun around the molding, his pistol leveled.

"Don't reach for guns! *You!*" he yelled at the man nearest him. "Turn around!"

In shock, without thinking, the man obeyed. Spaulding took two steps forward and brought the barrel of the Beretta crashing down into the man's skull. He collapsed instantly.

David shouted at the man next to the interrogator in the grey overcoat. "Pick up that chair! *Now!*" He gestured with his pistol to a straight-backed chair several feet from the table. "*Now,* I said!"

The man reached over and did as he was told; he was immobilized. Spaulding continued. "You drop it and I'll kill you . . . Doctor Lyons. Take their weapons. You'll find pistols and knives. Quickly, please."

It all happened so fast. David knew his only hope of avoiding gunfire was in the swiftness of the action, the rapid immobilization of one or two men, an instant reversal of the odds.

Lyons got out of the chair and went first to the man in the light grey overcoat. It was apparent that the scientist had observed where the man had put his pistol. He took it out of the overcoat pocket. He went to the man holding the chair and removed an identical gun, then searched the man and took a large knife from his jacket and a second, short revolver from a shoulder holster. He placed the weapons on the far side of the table and walked to the unconscious third man. He rolled him over and removed two guns and a switchblade knife.

"Take off your coats. *Now!*" Spaulding commanded both men. He took the chair from the one next to him and pushed him toward his companion. The men began removing their coats when Spaulding suddenly spoke, before either had completed their actions. "Stop right there! Hold it! . . . Doctor, please bring over two chairs and place them behind them."

Lyons did so.

"Sit down," said Spaulding to his captives.

They sat, coats half off their shoulders. David approached them and yanked the garments further – down to the elbows.

The two men in the grotesque stocking masks were seated now, their arms locked by their own clothes.

Standing in front of them, Spaulding reached down and ripped the silk masks off their faces. He moved back and leaned against the dining table, his pistol in his hand.

"All right," he said. "I estimate we've got about fifteen minutes before all hell breaks loose around here. . . .I have a few questions. You're going to give me the answers."

36

Spaulding listened in disbelief. The enormity of the charge was so far-reaching it was – in a very real sense – beyond his comprehension.

The man with the hollow eyes was Asher Feld, commander of the Provisional Wing of the Haganah operating within the United States. He did the talking.

"The operation . . . the exchange of the guidance designs for the industrial diamonds . . . was first given the name 'Tortugas' by the Americans – one American, to be exact. He had decided that the transfer should be made in the Dry Tortugas, but it was patently rejected by Berlin. It was, however, kept as a code name by this man. The misleading association dovetailed with his own panic at being involved. It came – for him and for Fairfax – to mean the activities of the man from Lisbon."

"When the War Department clearances were issued to the Koening company's New York offices – an Allied requisite – this man coded the clearance as "Tortugas." If anyone checked, "Tortugas' was a Fairfax operation. It would not be questioned.

"The concept of the negotiation was first created by the Nachrichtendienst. I'm sure you've heard of the Nachrichtendienst, colonel. . . ."

David did not reply. He could not speak. Feld continued.

"We of the Haganah learned of it in Geneva. We had word of an unusual meeting between an American named Kendall — a financial analyst for a major aircraft company – and a very despised German businessman, a homosexual, who was sent to Switzerland by a leading administrator in the Ministry of Armaments, Unterstaatssekretär Franz Altmüller. . . .The Haganah is everywhere, colonel, including the outer offices of the ministry and in the Luftwaffe. . . ."

David continued to stare at the Jew, so matter of fact in his extraordinary . . . unbelieveable . . . narrative.

"I think you'll agree that such a meeting was unusual. It was not difficult to maneuver these two messengers into a situation that gave us a wire recording. It was in an out-of-the-way restaurant and they were amateurs."

"We then knew the basics. The materials and the general location. But not the specific point of transfer. And that was the all-important factor. Buenos Aires is enormous, its harbour more so – stretching for miles. Where in this vast area of land and mountains and water was the transfer to take place?"

"Then, of course, came word from Fairfax. The man in Lisbon was being recalled. A most unusual action. But then how well thought out. The finest network specialist in Europe, fluent German and Spanish, an expert in blue-print designs. How logical. Don't you agree!"

David started to speak, but stopped. Things were being said that triggered flashes of lightning in his mind. And unbelievable cracks of thunder . . . as unbelievable as the words he was hearing. He could only nod his head. Numbly.

Feld watched him closely. Then spoke.

"In New York I explained to you, albeit briefly, the sabotage at the airfield in Terceira. Zealots. The fact that the man in Lisbon could turn and be a part of the exchange was too much for the hot-tempered Spanish Jews. No one was more relieved than we of the Provisional Wing when you escaped. We assumed your stopover in New York was for the purposes of refining the logistics in Buenos Aires. We proceeded on that assumption."

"Then quite abruptly there was no more time. Reports out of Johannesburg – unforgivably delayed – said that the diamonds had arrived in Buenos Aires. We took the necessary violent measures, including an attempt to kill you. Prevented, I presume, by Rhinemann's men." Asher Feld stopped. Then added wearily, "The rest you know."

No! The rest he did not know! Nor any other part!

Insanity!

Madness!

Everything was nothing! Nothing was everything!

The years! The lives! . . . The terrible nightmares of fear . . . the killing! Oh, my God, the killing!

For what! . . . Oh, my God! For what?!

"You're *lying!*" David crashed his hand down on the table. The steel of the pistol cracked against the wood with such force the vibration filled the room. "You're *lying!*" he cried; he did not shout. "I'm in Buenos Aires to buy gyroscopic designs! To have them authenticated! Confirmed by code so that son of a bitch gets paid in Switzerland! That's *all. Nothing else! Nothing else at all! Not this!*"

"Yes. . . ." Asher Feld spoke softly. "It is this."

David whirled around at nothing. He stretched his neck: the crashing thunder in his head would not stop, the blinding flashes of light in front of his eyes were causing a terrible pain. He saw the bodies on the floor, the blood . . . the corpses on the sofa, the blood.

Tableau of death.

Death.

His whole shadow world had been ripped out of orbit. A thousand gambles . . . pains, manipulations, death. And more death . . . all faded into a meaningless void. The betrayal – if it was a betrayal – was so immense . . . hundreds of thousands had been sacrificed for absolutely nothing.

He had to stop. He had to think. To concentrate.

He looked at the painfully gaunt Eugene Lyons, his face a sheet of white.

The man's dying, thought Spaulding.

Death.

He had to concentrate.

Oh, Christ! He had to *think*. Start *somewhere. Think.*

Concentrate.

Or he would go out of his mind.

He turned to Feld. The Jew's eyes were compassionate. They might have been something else, but they were not. They were compassionate.

And yet, they were the eyes of a man who killed in calm deliberation.

As he, the man in Lisbon, had killed.

Execution.

For what?

There were questions. *Concentrate on the questions. Listen.* Find error. *Find error* — if error was needed in this world it was *now!*

"I don't believe you," said David, trying as he had never tried in his life to be convincing.

"I think you do," replied Feld quietly. "The girl, Leslie Hawkwood, told us you didn't know. A judgment we found difficult to accept. . . .I accept it now."

David had to think for a moment. He did not, at first, recognize the name. *Leslie Hawk wood*. And then, of course, he did instantly. Painfully. "How is she involved with you?" he asked numbly.

"Herold Goldsmith is her uncle. By marriage, of course, she's not Jewish."

"Goldsmith? The name . . . doesn't mean anything to me." . . . *Concentrate!* He had to concentrate and speak rationally.

"It does to thousands of Jews. He's the man behind the Baruch and Lehman negotiations. He's done more to get our people out of the camps than any man in America. . . .He refused to have anything to do with us until the civilized, compassionate men in Washington, London and the Vatican turned their backs on him. Then he came to us . . . in fury. He created a hurricane, his niece was swept up in it. She's overly dramatic, perhaps, but committed, effective. She moves in circles barred to the Jew."

"Why?' . . . *Listen!* For God's sake, *listen. Be rational. Concentrate!*

Asher Feld paused for a moment, his dark, hollow eyes clouded with quiet hatred. "She met dozens . . . hundreds, perhaps, of those Herold Goldsmith got out. She saw the photographs, heard the stories. It was enough. She was ready."

The calm was beginning to return to David. Leslie was the springboard he needed to come back from the madness. There were questions. . . .

"I can't reject the premise that Rhinemann bought the designs. . . ."

"Oh, come!" interrupted Feld. "You were the man in Lisbon. How often did your own agents — your best men — find Peenemünde invulnerable? Has not the German underground itself given up penetration?"

"No one ever gives up. On either side. The German underground is *part of* this!" *That was the error,* thought David.

"If that were so," said Feld, gesturing his head toward the dead Germans

690

on the couch, "then those men were members of the underground. You know the Haganah, Lisbon. We don't kill such men."

Spaulding stared at the quiet-spoken Jew and knew he told the truth.

"The other evening," said Spaulding quickly, "on Paraná. I was followed, beaten up . . . but I saw the IDs. They were Gestapo!"

"They were Haganah." replied Feld. "The Gestapo is our best cover. If they had been Gestapo that would presume knowledge of your function. . . .Would they have let you live?"

Spaulding started to object. The Gestapo would not risk killing in a neutral country; not with identification on their persons. Then he realized the absurdity of his logic. Buenos Aires was not Lisbon. Of course, they would kill him. And then he recalled the words of Heinrich Stoltz.

We've checked at the highest levels . . . not the Gestapo. . . . impossible. . . .

And the strangely inappropriate apologia: *the racial theories of Rosenberg and Hitler are not shared . . . primarily an economic . . .*

A defense of the indefensible offered by a man whose loyalty was purportedly *not* to the Third Reich but to *Erich Rhinemann*. A Jew.

Finally, Bobby Ballard:

. . . he's a believer . . . the real Junker item . . .

"Oh, my God," said David under his breath.

"You have the advantage, colonel. What is your choice? We're prepared to die; I say this in no sense heroically, merely as a fact."

Spaulding stood motionless. He spoke softly, incredulously. "Do you understand the implications? . . ."

"We've understood them," interrupted Feld, "since that day in Geneva your Walter Kendall met with Johann Dietricht."

David reacted as though slapped, "Johann . . . *Dietricht?*"

"The expendable heir of Dietricht Fabriken."

"J.D.," whispered Spaulding, remembering the crumpled yellow pages in Walter Kendall's New York office. The breasts, the testicles, the swastikas . . . the obscene, nervous scribblings of an obscene, nervous man. "Johann Dietricht . . . *J.D.*"

"Altmüller had him killed. In a way that precluded any . . ."

"*Why?*" asked David.

"To remove any connection with the Ministry of Armaments, is our thought; any association with the High Command. Dietricht initiated the negotiations to the point where they could be shifted to Buenos Aires. To Rhinemann. With Dietricht's death the High Command was one more step removed."

The items raced through David's mind: Kendall had fled Buenos Aires in panic; something had gone wrong. The accountant would not allow himself to be trapped, to be killed. And he, David, was to kill – or have killed – Erich Rhinemann. Second to the designs, Rhinemann's death was termed paramount. And with his death, Washington, too, was "one more step removed" from the exchange.

Yet there was Edmund Pace.

Edmund *Pace.*

Never.

"A man was killed," said David, "A Colonel Pace. . . ."

"In Fairfax," completed Asher Feld. "A necessary death. He was being used as you are being used. We deal in pragmatics. . . . Without knowing the consequences — or refusing to admit them to himself — Colonel Pace was engineering 'Tortugas.'."

"You could have *told* him. Not killed him! You could have stopped it! You *bastards!*"

Asher Feld sighed. "I'm afraid you don't understand the hysteria among your industrialists. Or those of the Reich. He would have been eliminated. . . .By removing him ourselves, we neutralized Fairfax. And all its considerable facilities."

There was no point in dwelling on the *necessity* of Pace's death, thought David. Feld, the pragmatist, was right: Fairfax had been removed from 'Tortugas'.

"Then Fairfax doesn't know."

"Our man does. But not enough."

"Who is he? Who's your man in Fairfax?"

Feld gestured to his silent companion. "He doesn't know and I won't tell you. You may kill me but I won't tell you."

Spaulding knew the dark-eyed Jew spoke the truth. "If Pace was used . . . and me. Who's using us?"

"I can't answer that."

"You know this much. You must have . . . thoughts. Tell me."

"Whoever gives you orders, I imagine."

"One man. . . ."

"We know. He's not very good, is he? There are others."

"*Who?* Where does it *stop?* State? The War Department? *The White House? Where*, for Christ's sake!?"

"Such territories have no meaning in these transactions. They vanish."

"*Men don't!* Men don't vanish!"

"Then look for those who dealt with Koening. In South Africa. Kendall's men. They created 'Tortugas'." Asher Feld's voice grew stronger. "That's your affair, Colonel Spaulding. We only wish to stop it. We'll gladly *die* to stop it."

David looked at the thin-faced, sad-faced man. "It means that much? With what you know, what you believe? Is either side worth it?"

"One must have priorities. Even in lessening descent. If Peenemünde is saved . . . put back on schedule . . . the Reich has a bargaining power that is unacceptable to us. Look to Dachau; look to Auschwitz, to Belsen. Unacceptable."

David walked around the table and stood in front of the Jews. He put his Beretta in his shoulder holster and looked at Asher Feld.

"If you've lied to me, I'll kill you. And then I'll go back to Lisbon, into the north country, and wipe out every Haganah fanatic in the hills. Those I don't kill, I'll expose. . . .Put on your coats and get out of here. Take a room at the Alvear under the name of . . . Pace. *E. Pace.* I'll be in touch."

"Our weapons?" asked Feld, pulling his light grey overcoat over his shoulders.

"I'll keep then,. I'm sure you can afford others. . . .And don't wait for us outside. There's an FMF vehicle cruising for me."

"What about 'Tortugas'?" Asher Feld was pleading.

"I said I'll be in touch!" shouted Spaulding. "Now, get out of here! . . . Pick up the Hawkwood girl; she's around the corner in the Renault. Here are the keys." David reached in his pocket and threw the keys to Asher Feld's companion, who caught them effortlessly. "Send her back to California. Tonight, if you can. No later than tomorrow morning. Is that clear?"

"Yes. . . .You *will* be in touch?"

"Get out of here," said Spaulding in exhaustion.

The two Haganah agents rose from their chairs, the younger going to the unconscious third man and lifting him off the floor, onto his shoulders. Asher Feld stood in the front hallway and turned, his gaze resting momentarily on the dead bodies, then over to Spaulding.

"You and I. We must deal in priorities. . . .The man from Lisbon is an extraordinary man." He turned to the door and held it open as his companion carried out the third man. He went outside, closing the door behind him.

David turned to Lyons. "Get the designs."

37

When the assault on 15 Terraza Verde had begun, Eugene Lyons had done a remarkable thing. It was so simple it had a certain cleanliness to it, thought Spaulding. He had taken the metal container with the designs, opened his bedroom window and dropped the case five feet below into the row of tiger lilies that grew along the side of the house. The window shut, he had then run into his bathroom and locked the door.

All things considered – the shock, the panic, his own acknowledged incapacities – he had taken the least expected action: he had kept his head. He had removed the container, not tried to conceal it; he had transferred it to an *accessible* place, and that was not to be anticipated by the fanatic men who dealt in complicated tactics and convoluted deceits.

David followed Lyons out of the house through the kitchen door and around to the side. He took the container from the physicist's trembling hands and helped the near-helpless man over the small fence separating the adjacent property. Together they ran behind the next two houses and cautiously edged their way toward the street. Spaulding kept his left hand extended, gripping Lyons's shoulder, holding him against the wall, prepared to throw him to the ground at the first hint of hostilities.

Yet David was not really expecting hostilities; he was convinced the Haganah had eliminated whatever Rhinemann guards were posted in front, for the obvious reason that Asher Feld had left by the front door. What he did think was possible was a last-extremity attempt by Asher Feld to get the designs. Or the sudden emergence of a Rhinemann vehicle from some near location – a vehicle whose occupants were unable to raise a radio signal from 15 Terraza Verde.

Each possible; neither really expected.

It was too late and too soon.

What David profoundly hoped he would find, however, was a blue-green sedan cruising slowly around the streets. A car with small orange insignias on the bumpers that designated the vehicle as U.S. property. Ballard's "playground attendants"; the men from the FMF base.

It wasn't cruising. It was stationary, on the far side of the street, its parking lights on. Three men inside were smoking cigarettes, the glows illuminating the interior. He turned to Lyons.

"Let's go. Walk slowly, casually. The car's over there."

The driver and the man next to him got out of the automobile the moment Spaulding and Lyons reached the curb. They stood awkwardly by the hood, dressed in civilian clothes. David crossed the street, addressing them.

"Get in that goddamned car and get us out of here! And while you're at it, why don't you paint bull's-eyes all over the vehicle? You wouldn't be any more of a target than you are now!"

"Take it easy, buddy," replied the driver. "We just got here." He opened the rear door as Spaulding helped Lyons inside.

"You were supposed to be cruising, not parked like watchdogs!" David climbed in beside Lyons; the man at the far window squeezed over. The driver got behind the wheel, closed his door and started the engine. The third man remained outside. "Get him in here!" barked Spaulding.

"He'll remain where he is, colonel," said the man in the back seat next to Lyons. "He stays here."

"Who the hell are you?"

"Colonel Daniel Meehan, Fleet Marine Force, Naval Intelligence. And we want to know what the fuck's going on."

The car started up.

"You have no control over this exercise," said David slowly, deliberately. "And I don't have time for bruised egos. Get us to the embassy, please."

"Screw egos! We'd like a little simple clarification! You know what the hell is going on down in our section of town? This side trip to Telmo's just a minor inconvenience! I wouldn't be here except your goddamned name was mentioned by that smart-ass cryp! . . . *Jesus!*"

Spaulding leaned forward on the seat, staring at Meehan. "You'd better tell me what's going on in your section of town. And why my name gets you to Telmo."

The marine returned the look, glancing once – with obvious distaste – at the ashen Lyons. "Why not? Your friend cleared?"

"He is now. No one more so."

"We have three cruisers patrolling the Buenos Aires coastal zone plus a destroyer and a carrier somewhere's out there. . . .Five hours ago we get a blue alert: prepare for a radio-radar blackout, all sea and aircraft to hold to, no movement. Forty-five minutes later there's a scrambler from Fairfax, source four-zero. Intercept one Colonel David Spaulding, also four-zero. He's to make contact pronto."

"With Fairfax?"

"*Only* with Fairfax. . . .So we send a man to your address on Córdoba. He doesn't find you but he *does* find a weird son of a bitch tearing up your place. He tries to take him and gets laid out. . . .He gets back to us a couple of hours later with creases in his head and guess who calls? Right on an open-line telephone!"

"Ballard," answered David quietly. "The embassy cryp."

"The smart-ass! He makes jokes and tells us to play games out at Telmo! Wait for you to decide to show." The marine colonel shook his head in disgust.

"You said the blue alert was preparation for radar silence . . . and radio."

"And all ships and planes immobilized," interrupted Meehan. "What the hell's coming *in* here? The whole goddamned General *Staff? Roosevelt? Churchill? Rin-tin-tin?* And what are *we?* The *enemy!*"

"It's not what's coming in, colonel," said David softly. "It's what's going out. . . .What's the time of activation?"

"It's damn loose. Anytime during the next forty-eight hours. How's that for a tight schedule?"

"Who's my contact in Virginia?"

"Oh. . . .Here." Meehan shifted in his seat, proffering a sealed yellow envelope that was the mark of a scrambled message. David reached across Lyons and took it.

There was the crackling static of a radio from the front seat followed by the single word "Redbird!" out of the speaker. The driver quickly picked up the dashboard microphone.

"Redbird acknowledge," said the marine.

The static continued but the words were clear. "The Spaulding intercept. Pick him up and bring him in. Four-zero orders from Fairfax. No contact with the embassy."

"You heard the man," laughed Meehan. "No embassy tonight, colonel."

David was stunned. He started to object – angrily, furiously; then he stopped. . . .Fairfax. No Nazi, but Haganah. Asher Feld had said it. The Provisional Wing dealt in practicalities. And the most practical objective during the next forty-eight hours was to immobilize the man with the codes. Washington would not activate a radio–radar blackout without them; and an enemy submarine surfacing to rendezvous with a trawler would be picked up on the screens and blown out of the water. The Koening diamonds – the Peenemünde tools – would be sent to the bottom of the South Atlantic.

Christ! The *irony,* thought David. Fairfax – *someone at* Fairfax – was doing precisely what *should* be done, motivated by concerns Washington – and the aircraft companies – refused to acknowledge! It – they – had other concerns: three-quarters of them were at Spaulding's feet. High-altitude gyroscopic designs.

David pressed his arm into Lyons's shoulder. The emaciated scientist continued to stare straight ahead but responded to Spaulding's touch with a hesitant nudge of his left elbow.

David shook his head and sighed audibly. He held up the yellow envelope and shrugged, placing it into his jacket pocket.

When his hand emerged it held a gun.

"I'm afraid I can't accept those orders, Colonel Meehan." Spaulding pointed the automatic at the marine's head; Lyons leaned back into the seat.

"What the hell are you doing!?" Meehan jerked forward; David clicked the firing pin of the weapon into hair-release.

"Tell your man to drive where I say. I don't want to kill you, colonel, but I will. It's a matter of priorities."

"You're a goddamned double agent! That's what Fairfax was onto!"

David sighed. "I wish it were that simple."

Lyons's hands trembled as he tightened the knots around Meehan's wrists. The driver was a mile down the dirt road, bound securely, lying in the border of the tall grass. The area was rarely traveled at night. They were in the hills of Colinas Rojas.

Lyons stepped back and nodded to Spaulding.

"Get in the car."

Lyons nodded again and started toward the automobile. Meehan rolled over and looked up at David.

"You're dead, Spaulding. You got a firing squad on your duty sheet. You're stupid, too. Your Nazi friends are going to lose this war!"

"They'd better," answered David. "As to executions, there may be a number of them. Right in Washington. That's what this is all about, colonel. . . .Someone'll find you both tomorrow. If you like, you can start inching your way west. Your driver's a mile or so down the road. . . .I'm sorry."

Spaulding gave Meehan a half-felt shrug of apology and ran to the FMF automobile. Lyons sat in the front seat and when the door light spilled over his face, David saw his eyes. Was it possible that in that look there was an attempt to communicate a sense of gratitude? Or approval? There wasn't time to speculate, so David smiled gently and spoke quietly.

"This has been terrible for you, I know. . . .But I can't think what else to do. I don't know. If you like, I'll get you back to the embassy. You'll be safe there."

David started the car and drove up a steep incline – one of many – in the Colinas Rojas. He would double back on a parallel road and reach the highway within ten or fifteen minutes; he would take Lyons to an outskirts taxi and give the driver instructions to deliver the physicist to the American embassy. It wasn't really what he wanted to do; but what else was there?

Then the words came from beside him. *Words!* Whispered, muffled, barely audible but clear! From the recesses of a tortured throat.

"I . . . stay with . . . you. Together. . . ."

Spaulding had to grip the wheel harshly for fear of losing control. The shock of the pained speech – and it *was* a speech for Eugene Lyons – had nearly caused him to drop his hands. He turned and looked at the scientist. In the flashing shadows he saw Lyons return his stare; the lips were set firmly, the eyes steady. Lyons knew exactly what he was doing; what they both were doing – *had* to do.

"All right," said David, trying to remain calm and precise. "I read you clearly. God knows I need all the help I can get. We both do. It strikes me we've got two powerful enemies. Berlin *and* Washington."

"I don't want any interruptions, Stoltz!" David yelled into the mouthpiece of the telephone in the small booth near Ocho Calle. Lyons was now behind the wheel of the FMF car ten yards away on the street. The motor was running.

The scientist hadn't driven in twelve years but with half-words and gestures he convinced Spaulding he would be capable in an emergency.

"You can't behave this way!" was the panicked reply.

"I'm Pavlov, you're the dog! Now shut up and listen! There's a mess in Terraza Verde, if you don't know it by now. Your men are dead; so are mine. I've got the designs *and* Lyons. . . . Your nonexistent Gestapo are carrying out a number of executions!"

"Impossible!" screamed Stoltz.

"Tell that to the corpses, you incompetent son of a bitch! While you clean up that mess! . . . I want the rest of those designs, Stoltz. Wait for my call!" David slammed down the receiver and bolted out of the booth to the car. It was time for the radio. After that the envelope from Fairfax. Then Ballard at the embassy. One step at a time.

Spaulding opened the door and slid into the seat beside Lyons. The physicist pointed to the dashboard.

"Again . . ." was the single, painful word.

"Good," said Spaulding. "They're anxious. They'll listen hard." David snapped the panel switch and lifted the microphone out of its cradle. He pressed his fingers against the tiny wire speaker with such pressure that the mesh was bent; he covered the instrument with his hand and held it against his jacket as he spoke, moving it in circles so as to further distort the sound.

"Redbird to base . . . Redbird to base."

The static began, the voice angry. "Christ, Redbird! We've been trying to raise you for damn near two hours! That Ballard keeps calling! Where the hell are you!?"

"Redbird. . . . Didn't you get our last transmission?"

"*Transmission?* Shit, man! I can hardly hear this one. Hold on; let me get the CO."

"Forget it! No sweat. You're fading here again. We're on Spaulding. We're following him; he's in a vehicle . . . twenty-seven, *twenty-eight miles north.* . . ." David abruptly stopped talking.

"Redbird! Redbird! . . . Christ, this frequency's puke!. . . . Twenty-eight miles north *where*? . . . I'm not reading you, Redbird! Redbird, acknowledge!"

" . . . bird, acknowledge," said David directly into the microphone. "This radio needs maintenance, pal. Repeat. No problems. *Will return to base in approximately.* . . ."

Spaulding reached down and snapped the switch into the "off" position.

He got out of the car and went back to the telephone booth. One step at a time. No blurring, no overlapping – each action defined, handled with precision.

Now it was the scramble from Fairfax. The deciphered code that would tell him the name of the man who was having him intercepted; the source four-zero, whose priority rating allowed him to send such commands from the transmission core of the intelligence compound.

The agent who walked with impunity in the highest classified alleyways and killed a man named Ed Pace on New Year's Eve.

The Haganah infiltration.

He had been tempted to rip open the yellow envelope the moment the FMF officer had given it to him in San Telmo, but he had resisted the almost irresistible temptation. He knew that he would be stunned no matter who it was — whether known to him or not; and no *matter* who it was he would have a name to fit the revenge he planned for the killer of his friend.

Such thoughts were obstructions. Nothing could hinder their swift but cautious ride to Ocho Calle; nothing could interfere with his thought-out contact with Heinrich Stoltz.

He withdrew the yellow envelope and slid his finger across the flap.

At first, the name meant nothing.

Lieutenant Colonel Ira Barden.

Nothing.

Then he remembered.

New Year's Eve!

Oh, *Christ*, did he remember! The rough-talking hardnose who was second in command at Fairfax. Ed Pace's "best friend" who had mourned his "best friend's' death with army anger; who secretly had arranged for David to be flown to the Virginia base and participate in the wake-investigation; who had used the tragic killing to enter his "best friend's' dossier vaults ... only to find nothing.

The man who insisted a Lisbon cryptographer named Marshall had been killed in the Basque country; who said he would run a check on Franz Altmüller.

Which, of course, he never did.

The man who tried to convince David that it would be in everyone's interest if Spaulding would flex the clearance regulations and explain his War Department assignment.

Which David nearly did. And now wished he had.

Oh, God! Why hadn't Barden *trusted* him? On the other hand, he could not. For to do so would have raised specific, unwanted speculations on Pace's murder.

Ira Barden was no fool. A fanatic, perhaps, but not foolish. He knew the man from Lisbon would kill him if Pace's death was laid at his feet.

Heed the lesson of Fairfax. . . .

Jesus! thought David. We fight each other, kill each other ... we don't know our enemies any longer.

For *what?*

There was now a second reason to call Ballard. A name was not enough; he needed more than just a name. He would confront Asher Feld.

He picked up the telephone's receiver off the hook, held his coin and dialed.

Ballard got on the line, no humor in evidence.

"*Look*, David." Ballard had not used his first name in conversation before.

Ballard was suppressing a lot of anger. "I won't pretend to understand how you people turn your dials, but if you're going to use *my* set, keep me informed!"

"A number of people were killed; I wasn't one of them. That was fortunate but the circumstances prohibited my contacting you. Does that answer your complaint?"

Ballard was silent for several seconds. The silence was not just his reaction to the news, thought David. There was someone with Bobby. When the cryp spoke, he was no longer angry; he was hesitant, afraid.

"You're all right?"

"Yes. Lyons is with me."

"The FMF were too late. . . ." Ballard seemed to regret his statement. "I keep phoning, they keep avoiding. I think their car's lost."

"Not really. I've got it. . . ."

"Oh, Christ!"

"They left one man at Telmo – for observation. There were two others. They're not hurt; they've disqualified."

"What the hell does *that* mean?"

"I haven't got time to explain. . . .There's an intercept order out for me. From Fairfax. The embassy's not supposed to know. It's a setup; I can't let them take me. Not for a while. . . ."

"Hey, we don't mess with Fairfax," said Ballard firmly.

"You can this time. I told Jean. There's a security breach in Fairfax. I'm not it, believe that. . . .I've *got* to have time. Maybe as much as forty-eight hours. I need questions answered. Lyons can help. For God's sake, trust me!"

"I can trust you but I'm no big deal here. . . .Wait a minute. Jean's with me. . . ."

"I thought so," interrupted Spaulding. It had been David's intention to ask Ballard for the help he needed. He suddenly realized that Jean could be far more helpful.

"Talk to her before she scratches the skin off my hand."

"Before you get off, Bobby. . . .Could you run a priority check on someone in Washington? In Fairfax, to be exact?"

"I'd have to have a reason. The subject – an Intelligence subject, *especially* Fairfax – would probably find out."

"I don't give a damn if he does. Say I demanded it. My rating's four-zero; G-2 has that in the records. I'll take the responsibility."

"Who is it?"

"A lieutenant colonel named Ira Barden. Got it?"

"Yes. Ira Barden. Fairfax."

"Right. Now let me talk to . . ."

Jean's words spilled over one another, a mixture of fury and love, desperation and relief.

"Jean," he said when she had finished a half-dozen questions he couldn't

700

possibly answer, "the other night you made a suggestion I refused to take seriously. I'm taking it seriously now. That mythical David of yours needs a place to hide out. It can't be the pampas, but any place nearer will do. . . .Can you help me? Help us? For *God's sake!*"

38

He would call Jean later, before daybreak. He and Lyons had to move in darkness, wherever they were going. Wherever Jean could find them sanctuary.

There would be no codes sent to Washington, no clearance given for the obscene exchange, no radio or radar blackouts that would immobilize the fleet. David understood that; it was the simplest, surest way to abort "Tortugas."

But it was not enough.

There were the men behind "Tortugas." They had to be yanked up from the dark recesses of their filth and exposed to the sunlight. If there was any meaning left, if the years of pain and fear and death made any sense at all, they had to be given to the world in all their obscenity.

The world deserved that. Hundreds of thousands – on both sides – who would carry the scars of war throughout their lives, deserved it.

They had to understand the meaning of *For what*.

David accepted his role; he would face the men of "Tortugas." But he could not face then, with the testimony of a fanatical Jew. The words of Asher Feld, leader of the Haganah's Provisional Wing, were no testimony at all. Fanatics were madmen; the world had seen enough of both, for both were one. And they were dismissed. Or killed. Or both.

David knew he had no choice.

When he faced the men of "Tortugas," it would not be with the words of Asher Feld. Or with deceptive codes and manipulations that were subject to a hundred interpretations.

Deceits. Cover-ups. Removals.

He would face them with what he saw. What he knew, because he had borne witness. He would present them with the irrefutable. And then he would destroy them.

To do this – all this – be had to get aboard the trawler in Ocho Calle. The trawler that would be blown out of the water should it attempt to run the harbor and rendezvous with a German submarine.

That it ultimately would attempt such a run was inevitable. The fanatic mind would demand it. Then there would be no evidence of things seen. Sworn to.

He had to get aboard that trawler now.

He gave his final instructions to Lyons and slid into the warm, oily waters of the Rio de la Plata. Lyons would remain in the car – drive it, if necessary –

702

and, if David did not return, allow ninety minutes to elapse before going to the FMF base and telling the commanding officer that David was being held prisoner aboard the trawler. An American agent held prisoner.

There was logic in the strategy. FMF had priority orders to bring in David; orders from Fairfax. It would be three thirty in the morning. Fairfax called for swift, bold action. Especially at three thirty in the morning in a neutral harbor.

It was the bridge David tried always to create for himself in times of high-risk infiltration. It was the trade-off; his life for a lesser loss. The lessons of the north country.

He did not want it to happen that way. There were too many ways to immobilize him; too many panicked men in Washington and Berlin to let him survive, perhaps. At best there would be compromise. At worst.... The collapse of "Tortugas" was not enough, the indictment was everything.

His pistol was tight against his head, tied with a strip of his shirt, the cloth running through his teeth. He breaststroked toward the hull of the ship, keeping his head out of the water, the firing-pin mechanism of his weapon as dry as possible. The price was mouthfuls of filthy, gasoline-polluted water, made further sickening by the touch of a large conger eel attracted, then repelled, by the moving white flesh.

He reached the hull. Waves slapped gently, unceasingly, against the hard expanse of darkness. He made his way to the stern of the ship, straining his eyes and his ears for evidence of life.

Nothing but the incessant lapping of water.

There was light from the deck but no movement, no shadows, no voices. Just the flat, colorless spill of naked bulbs strung on black wires, swaying in slow motion to the sluggish rhythm of the hull. On the port side of the ship – the dockside – were two lines looped over the aft and midships pilings. Rat disks were placed every ten feet or so; the thick manila hemps were black with grease and oil slick. As he approached, David could see a single guard sitting in a chair by the huge loading doors, which were shut. The chair was tilted back against the warehouse wall; two wire-mesh lamps covered by metal shades were on both sides of the wide doorframe. Spaulding treaded backward to get a clearer view. The guard was dressed in the paramilitary clothes of Habichtsnest. He was reading a book; for some reason that fact struck David as odd.

Suddenly, there were footsteps at the west section of the warehouse dock. They were slow, steady; there was no attempt to muffle the noise.

The guard looked up from his book. Between the pilings David could see a second figure come into view. It was another guard wearing the Rhinemann uniform. He was carrying a leather case, the same radio case carried by the men – dead men – at 15 Terraza Verde.

The guard in the chair smiled and spoke to the standing sentry. The language was German.

"I'll trade places, if you wish," said the man in the chair. "Get off your feet for a while."

"No, thanks," replied the man with the radio. "I'd rather walk. Passes the time quicker."

"Anything new from Luján?"

"No change. Still a great deal of excitement. I can hear snatches of yelling now and then. Everybody's giving orders."

"I wonder what happened in Telmo."

"Bad trouble is all I know. They've blocked us off; they've sent men to the foot of Ocho Calle."

"You heard that?"

"No. I spoke with Geraldo. He and Luis are here. In front of the warehouse; in the street."

"I hope they don't wake up the whores."

The man with the radio laughed. "Even Geraldo can do better than those dogs."

"Don't bet good money on that," replied the guard in the chair.

The guard on foot laughed again and proceeded east on his solitary patrol around the building. The man in the chair returned to his book.

David sidestroked his way back toward the hull of the trawler.

His arms were getting tired; the foul-smelling waters of the harbor assaulted his nostrils. And now he had something else to consider: Eugene Lyons.

Lyons was a quarter of a mile away, diagonally across the water, four curving blocks from the foot of Ocho Calle. If Rhinemann's patrols began cruising the area, they would find the FMF vehicle with Lyons in it. It was a bridge he hadn't considered. He should have considered it.

But he couldn't think about that now.

He reached the starboard midships and held onto the waterline ledge, giving the muscles of his arms and shoulders a chance to throb in relief The trawler was in the medium-craft classification, no more than seventy or eighty feet in length, perhaps a thirty-foot midship beam. By normal standards, and from what David could see as he approached the boat in darkness, the mid and aft cabins below the wheel shack were about fifteen and twenty feet long, respectively, with entrances at both ends and two portholes per cabin on the port and starboard sides. If the Koening diamonds *were* on board, it seemed logical that they'd be in the aft cabin, farthest away from the crew's normal activity. Too, aft cabins had more room and fewer distractions. And if Asher Feld was right, if two or three Peenemünde scientists were microscopically examining the Koening products, they would be under a pressured schedule and require isolation.

David found his breath coming easier. He'd know soon enough whether and where the diamonds were or were not. In moments.

He untied the cloth around his head, treading water as he did so, holding the pistol firmly. The shirt piece drifted away; he held onto the line ledge and looked above. The gunwale was six to seven feet out of the water; he would need both his hands to claw his way up the tiny ridges of the hull.

He spat out what harbor residue was in his mouth and clamped the barrel of the gun between his teeth. The only clothing he wore was his trousers; he plunged his hands beneath the water, rubbing them against the cloth in an effort to remove what estuary slick he could.

He gripped the line ledge once again and with his right hand extended, kicked his body out of the water and reached for the next tiny ridge along the hull. His fingers grasped the half-inch sprit; he pulled himself up, slapping his left hand next to his right, pushing his chest into the rough wood for leverage. His bare feet were near the water's surface, the gunwale no more than three feet above him now.

Slowly he raised his knees until the toes of both feet rested on the waterline ledge. He paused for breath, knowing that his fingers would not last long on the tiny ridge. He tensed the muscles of his stomach and pressed his aching toes against the ledge, pushing himself up as high as possible, whipping out his hands; knowing, again, that if he missed the gunwale he would plunge back into the water. The splash would raise alarms.

The left hand caught; the right slipped off. But it was enough.

He raised himself to the railing, his chest scraping against the rough, weathered hull until spots of blood emerged on his skin. He looped his left arm over the side and removed the pistol from his mouth. He was – as he hoped he would be – at the midpoint between the fore and aft cabins, the expanse of wall concealing him from the guards on the loading dock.

He silently rolled over the gunwale onto the narrow deck and took the necessary crouching steps to the cabin wall. He pressed his back into the wooden slats and slowly stood up. He inched his way toward the first aft porthole; the light from within was partially blocked by a primitive curtain of sorts, pulled back as if parted for the night air. The second porthole farther down had no such obstruction, but it was only feet from the edge of the wall; there was the possibility that a sentry – unseen from the water – might be on stern watch there. He would see whatever there was to see in the first window.

His wet cheek against the rotted rubber surrounding the porthole, he looked inside. The "curtain" was a heavy sheet of black tarpaulin folded back at an angle. Beyond, the light was as he had pictured it: a single bulb suspended from the ceiling by a thick wire – a wire that ran out a port window to a pier outlet. Ship generators were not abused while at dock. There was an odd-shaped, flat piece of metal hanging on the side of the bulb, and at first David was not sure why it was there. And then he understood; the sheet of metal deflected the light of the bulb from the rear of the cabin, where he could make out – beyond the fold of the tarp – two bunk beds. Men were sleeping; the light remained on but they were in relative shadow.

On the far side of the cabin, butted against the wall, was a long table that had the incongruous appearance of a hospital laboratory workbench. It was covered by a taut, white, spotless oilcloth and on the cloth, equidistant from one another, were four powerful microscopes. Beside each instrument was a high-intensity lamp – all the wires leading to a twelve-volt utility battery under the table. On the floor in front of the microscopes were four high-backed stools – four white, spotless stools standing at clinical attention.

That was the effect, thought David. Clinical. This isolated section of the trawler was in counterpoint to the rest of the filthy ship; it was a small, clinical island surrounded by rotted sea waste and rat disks.

And then he saw them. In the corner.

Five steel crates, each with metal strips joined at the top edges and held in place with heavy vault locks. On the front of each crate was the clearly stenciled name: KOENING MINES, LTD.

He'd seen it now. The undeniable, the irrefutable.

Tortugas.

The obscene exchange funneled through Erich Rhinemann.

And he was so close, so near possession. The final indictment.

Within his fear – and he *was* afraid – furious anger and deep temptation converged. They were sufficient to suspend his anxiety, to force him to concentrate only on the objective. To believe – knowing the belief was false – in some mystical invulnerability, granted for only a few precious minutes.

That was enough.

He ducked under the first porthole and approached the second. He stood up and looked in; the door of the cabin was in his direct line of sight. It was a new door, not part of the trawler. It was steel and in the center was a bolt at least an inch thick, jammed into a bracket in the frame.

The Peenemünde scientists were not only clinically isolated, they were in a self-imposed prison.

That bolt, David realized, was his personal Alpine pass – to be crossed without rig.

He crouched and passed under the porthole to the edge of the cabin wall. He remained on his knees and, millimeter by millimetre, the side of his face against the wood, looked around the corner.

The guard was there, of course, standing his harbor watch in the tradition of such sentry duty: on deck, the inner line of defense; bored, irritated with his boredom, relaxed in his inactivity yet annoyed by its pointlessness.

But he was not in the paramilitary clothes of Habichtsnest. He was in a loose-fitting suit that did little to conceal a powerful – military – body. His hair was cut short, Wehrmacht style.

He was leaning against a large fishing-net winch, smoking a thin cigar, blowing the smoke aimlessly into the night air. At his side was an automatic rifle, .30 caliber, the shoulder strap unbuckled, curled on the deck. The rifle had not been touched for quite some time, the strap had a film of moisture on the surface of the leather.

The strap. . . . David took the belt from his trousers. He stood up, inched back towards the porthole, reached underneath the railing and removed one of two gunwale spikes which were clamped against the inner hull for the fish nets. He tapped the railing softly twice; then twice again. He heard the shuffling of the guard's feet. No forward movement, just a change of position.

He tapped again. Twice. Then twice more. The quietly precise tapping – intentional, spaced evenly – was enough to arouse curiosity, insufficient to cause alarm.

He heard the guard's footsteps now. Still relaxed, the forward motion easy, not concerned with danger, only curious. A piece of harbour driftwood, perhaps, slapping against the hull, caught in the push-pull of the current.

The guard rounded the comer; Spaulding's belt whipped around his neck, instantly lashed taut, choking off the cry.

David twisted the leather as the guard sank to his knees, the face darkening perceptibly in the dim spill of light from the porthole, the lips pursed in strangled anguish.

David did not allow his victim to lose consciousness; he had the Alpine pass to cross. Instead, he wedged his pistol into his trousers, reached down to the scabbard on the guard's waist, and took out the carbine bayonet – a favorite knife of combat men, rarely used on the front of any rifle. He held the blade under the guard's eyes and whispered.

"*Español* or *Deutsch?*"

The man stared up in terror. Spaulding twisted the leather tighter; the guard choked a cough and struggled to raise two fingers. David whispered again, the blade pushing against the skin under the right eyeball.

"*Deutsch?*"

The man nodded.

Of course he was German, thought Spaulding. And Nazi. The clothes, the hair. Peenemünde *was* the Third Reich. Its scientists would be guarded by their own. He twisted the blade of the carbine bayonet so that a tiny laceration appeared under the eye. The guard's mouth opened in fright.

"You do exactly what I tell you," whispered David in German into the guard's ear, "or I'll carve out your sight. Understand?"

The man, nearly limp, nodded.

"Get up and call through the porthole. You have an urgent message from . . . Altmüller, Franz Altmüller! They must open the door and sign for it. . . . Do it! Now! And remember, this knife is inches from your eyes."

The guard, in shock, got up. Spaulding pushed the man's face to the open porthole, loosened the belt only slightly, and shifted his position to the side of the man and the window, his left hand holding the leather, his right the knife.

"*Now!*" whispered David, flicking the blade in half circles.

At first the guard's voice was strained, artificial. Spaulding moved in closer; the guard knew he had only seconds to live if he did not perform.

He performed.

There was stirring in the bunk beds within the cabin. Crumbling complaints to begin with, ceasing abruptly at the mention of Altmüller's name.

A small, middle-aged man got out of the left lower bunk and walked sleepily to the steel door. He was in undershorts, nothing else. David propelled the guard around the corner of the wall and reached the door at the sound of the sliding bolt.

He slammed the guard against the steel panel with the twisted belt; the door flung open, David grabbed the knob, preventing it from crashing into the bulkhead. He dropped the knife, yanked out his pistol, and crashed the barrel into the skull of the small scientist.

"*Schweigen!*" he whispered hoarsely. "*Wenn Ihnen iHr Leben Lieb ist!*"

The three men in the bunks – older men, one old man – stumbled out of their beds, trembling and speechless. The guard, choking still, began to focus around him and started to rise. Spaulding took two steps and slashed the pistol diagonally across the man's temple, splaying him out on the deck.

The old man, less afraid than his two companions, stared at David. For reasons Spaulding could not explain to himself, he felt ashamed. Violence was out of place in this antiseptic cabin.

"I have no quarrel with you," he whispered harshly in German. "You follow orders. But don't mistake me, I'll kill you if you make a sound!" He pointed to some papers next to a microscope; they were filled with numbers and columns. "You!" He gestured his pistol at the old man. "Give me those! Quickly!"

The old man trudged haltingly across the cabin to the clinical work area. He lifted the papers off the table and handed them to Spaulding, who stuffed them into his wet trousers pocket.

"Thanks. . . . Now!" He pointed his weapon at the other two. "Opec one of those crates! Do it now!"

"No! . . . No! For God's sake!" said the taller of the middle-aged scientists, his voice low, filled with fear.

David grabbed the old man standing next to him, He clamped his arm around the loose flesh of the old neck and brought his pistol up to the head. He thumbed back the firing pin and spoke calmly. "You will open a crate or I will kill this man. When he's dead, I'll turn my pistol on you. Believe me, I have no alternative."

The shorter man whipped his head around, pleading silently with the taller one. The old man in David's grasp was the leader; Spaulding knew that. An old . . . *alter-Anführer*, always take the German leader.

The taller Peenemünde scientist walked – every step in fear – to the far corner of the clinical workbench, where there was a neat row of keys on the wall. He removed one and hesitantly went to the first steel crate. He bent down and inserted the key in the vault lock holding the metal strip around the edge; the strip snapped apart in the center.

"Open the lid!" commanded Spaulding, his anxiety causing his whisper to become louder; too loud, he realized.

The cover of the steel crate was heavy; the German had to lift it with both hands, the wrinkles around his eyes and mouth betraying the effort required.

708

Once at a ninety-degree angle, chains on both sides became taut; there was a click of a latch and the cover was locked in place.

Inside were dozens of identically matched compartments in what appeared to be sliding trays – something akin to a large complicated fishing-tackle box. Then David understood: the front of the steel case was on hinges; it too could be opened – or lowered, to be exact – allowing the trays to slide out.

In each compartment were two small heavy, paper envelopes, apparently lined with layers of soft tissue. There were dozens of envelopes on the top tray alone.

David released the old man, propelling him back toward the bunk beds. He waved his pistol at the tall German who had opened the crate, ordering him to join the other two. He reached down into the steel crate, picked out a small envelope and brought it to his mouth, tearing the edge with his teeth. He shook it toward the ground; tiny translucent nuggets spattered over the cabin deck.

The Koening diamonds.

He watched the German scientists as he crumpled the envelope. They were staring at the stones on the floor.

Why not? thought David. In that cabin was the solution for Peenemünde. In those crates were the tools to rain death on untold thousands . . . as the gyroscopic designs for which they were traded would make possible further death, further massacre.

He was about to throw away the envelope in disgust and fill his pockets with others when his eyes caught sight of some lettering. He unwrinkled the envelope, his pistol steady on the Germans, and looked down. The single word:

echt

True. Genuine. This envelope, this tray, this steel case had passed inspection.

He reached down and grabbed as many envelopes as his left hand could hold and stuffed them into his trousers pocket.

It was all he needed for the indictment.

It was everything. It was the meaning.

There was one thing more he could do. Of a more immediately practical nature. He crossed to the workbench and went down the line of four microscopes, crashing the barrel of his pistol up into each lens and down into the eyepieces. He looked for a laboratory case, the type which carried optical equipment. There had to be one!

It was on the floor beneath the long table. He kicked it out with his bare foot and reached down to open the hasp.

More slots and trays, only these filled with lenses and small black tubes in which to place them.

He bent down and overturned the case; dozens of circular lenses fell out onto the deck. As fast as he could he grabbed the nearest white stool and brought it down sideways into the piles of glass.

The destruction wasn't total, but the damage was enough, perhaps, for forty-eight hours.

He started to get up, his weapon still on the scientists, his ears and eyes alert.

He heard it! He sensed it! And simultaneously he understood that if he did not spin out of the way he would be dead!

He threw himself on the floor to the right, the hand above and behind him came down, the carbine bayonet slicing the air, aimed for the spot where his neck had been less than a second ago.

He had left the goddamned bayonet on the floor! He had discarded the goddamned *bayonet!* The guard had revived and *taken* the goddamned *bayonet!*

The Nazi's single cry emerged before Spaulding leaped on his kneeling form, smashing his skull into the wood floor with such force that blood spewed out in tiny bursts throughout the head.

But the lone cry was enough.

"Is something wrong?" came a voice from outside, twenty yards away on the loading dock. "Heinrich! Did you call?"

There was no second, no instant, to throw away on hesitation.

David ran to the steel door, pulled it open and raced around the corner of the wall to the concealed section of the gunwale. As he did so, a guard – the sentry on the bow of the trawler – came into view. His rifle was waist high and he fired.

Spaulding fired back. But not before he realized he was hit. The Nazi's bullet had creased the side of his waist; he could feel the blood oozing down into his trousers.

He threw himself over the railing into the water; screams and shouts started from inside the cabin and farther away on the pier.

He thrashed against the dirty Rio slime and tried to keep his head. Where was he? What direction? Where? For Christ's sake, *where?*

The shouts were louder now; searchlights were turned on all over the trawler, crisscrossing the harbor waters. He could hear men screaming into radios as only panicked men can scream. Accusing, helpless.

Suddenly, David realized there were no boats! No boats were coming out of the pier with the searchlights and high-powered rifles that would be his undoing!

No boats!

And he nearly laughed. The operation at Ocho Calle was so totally secretive they had allowed no small craft to put into the deserted area!

He held his side, going under water as often as he could, as fast as he could.

The trawler and the screaming Rhinemann–Altmüller guards were receding in the harbor mist. Spaulding kept bobbing his head up, hoping to God he was going in the right direction.

He was getting terribly tired, but he would not allow himself to grow weak. He *could not* allow that! Not now!

He had the "Tortugas" indictment!

He saw the pilings not far away. Perhaps two, three hundred yards. They *were* the right pilings, the right piers! They . . . it, *had* to be!

He felt the waters around him stir and then he saw the snake-like forms of the conger eels as they lashed blindly against his body. The blood from his wound was attracting them! A horrible mass of slashing giant worms were converging!

He thrashed and kicked and fought down a scream. He pulled at the waters in front of him, his hands in constant contact with the oily snakes of the harbor. His eyes were filled with flashing dots and streaks of yellow and white; his throat was dry in the water, his forehead pounded.

When it seemed at last the scream would come, *had* to come, he felt the hand in his hand. He felt his shoulders being lifted, heard the guttural cries of his own terrified voice – deep, frightened beyond his own endurance. He could look down and see, as his feet kept slipping off the ladder, the circles of swarming eels below.

Eugene Lyons carried him – *carried* him! – to the FMF automobile. He was aware – yet not aware – of the fact that Lyons pushed him gently into the back seat.

And then Lyons climbed in after him, and David understood – yet did not understand – that Lyons was slapping him. Hard. Harder.

Deliberately. Without rhythm but with a great deal of strength.

The slapping would not stop! He couldn't make it stop! He couldn't stop the half-destroyed, throatless Lyons from slapping him.

He could only cry. Weep as a child might weep.

And then suddenly he *could* make him stop. He took his hands from his face and grabbed Lyons's wrists, prepared, if need be, to break them.

He blinked and stared at the physicist.

Lyons smiled in the shadows. He spoke in his tortured whisper.

"I'm sorry. . . . You were . . . in temporary . . . shock. My friend."

39

An elaborate naval first aid kit was stored in the trunk of the FMF vehicle. Lyons filled David's wound with sulfa powder, laid on folded strips of gauze and pinched the skin together with three-inch adhesive. Since the wound was a gash, not a puncture, the bleeding stopped; it would hold until they reached a doctor. Even should the wait be a day or a day and a half, there would be no serious damage.

Lyons drove.

David watched the emaciated man behind the wheel. He was unsure but willing; that was the only way to describe him. Every now and then his foot pressed too hard on the accelerator, and the short bursts of speed frightened him – then annoyed him. Still, after a few minutes, he seemed to take a careful delight in manipulating the car around corners.

David knew he had to accomplish three things: reach Henderson Granville, talk to Jean and drive to that sanctuary he hoped to Christ Jean had found for them. If a doctor could be brought to him, fine. If not, he would sleep; he was beyond the point of functioning clearly without rest.

How often in the north country had he sought out isolated caves in the hills? How many times had he piled branches and limbs in front of small openings so his body and mind could restore the balance of objectivity that might save his life? He had to find such a resting place now.

And tomorrow he would make the final arrangements with Erich Rhinemann.

The final pages of the indictment.

"We have to find a telephone," said David. Lyons nodded as he drove.

David directed the physicist back into the center of Buenos Aires. By his guess they still had time before the FMF base sent out a search. The orange insignias on the bumpers would tend to dissuade the BA police from becoming too curious; the Americans were children of the night.

He remembered the telephone booth on the north side of the Casa Rosada. The telephone booth in which a hired gun from the Unio Corso – sent down from Rio de Janeiro – had taken his last breath.

They reached the Plaza de Mayo in fifteen minutes, taking a circular route, making sure they were not followed. The Plaza was not deserted. It was, as the prewar travel posters proclaimed, a Western Hemisphere Paris. Like Paris, there were dozens of early stragglers, dressed mainly in expensive clothes. Taxis stopped and started; prostitutes made their last attempts to find profitable beds; the streetlights illuminated the huge fountains; lovers dabbled their hands in the pools.

The Plaza de Mayo at three thirty in the morning was not a barren, dead place to be. And David was grateful for that.

Lyons pulled the car up to the telephone booth and Spaulding got out.

"Whatever it is, you've hit the rawest nerve in Buenos Aires." Granville's voice was hard and precise. "I must demand that you return to the embassy. For your own protection as well as the good of our diplomatic relations."

"You'll have to be clearer than that, I'm afraid," replied David.

Granville was.

The "one or two" contacts the ambassador felt he could reach in the Grupo were reduced, of course, to one. That man made inquiries as to the trawler in Ocho Calle and subsequently was taken from his home under guard. That was the information Granville gathered from a hysterical wife.

An hour later the ambassador received word from a GOU liaison that his "friend" had been killed in an automobile accident. The GOU wanted him to have the news. It was most unfortunate.

When Granville tried reaching the wife, an operator cut in explaining that the telephone was disconnected.

"You've involved us, Spaulding! We can't function with Intelligence dead weight around our necks. The situation in Buenos Aires is extremely delicate."

"You *are* involved, sir. A couple of thousand miles away people are shooting at each other."

"Shit!" It was just about the most unexpected expletive David thought he could hear from Granville. "Learn your lines of demarcation! We all have jobs to do within the . . . artificial, if you like, parameters that are set for us! I repeat, sir. Return to the embassy and I'll expedite your immediate return to the United States. Or if you refuse, take yourself to FMF. *That's* beyond my jurisdiction; you will be no part of the embassy!"

My God! thought David. *Artificial parameters. Jurisdictions. Diplomatic niceties.* When men were dying, armies destroyed, cities obliterated! And men in high-ceilinged rooms played games with words and attitudes!

"I can't go to FMF. But I can give you something to think about. Within forty-eight hours all American ships and aircraft in the coastal zones are entering a radio and radar blackout! Everything grounded, immobilized. That's straight military holy writ. And I think you'd better find out why! Because I think I know, and if I'm right, your *diplomatic wreck* is filthier than anything you can imagine! Try a man named Swanson at the War Department. Brigadier Alan Swanson! And tell him I've found 'Tortugas'!"

David slammed down the receiver with such force that chips of Bakelite fell off the side of the telephone. He wanted to run. Open the door of the suffocating booth and race away.

But where to? There was nowhere.

He took several deep breaths and once more dialed the embassy.

Jean's voice was soft, filled with anxiety. But she had found a place!

He and Lyons were to drive due west on Rivadavia to the farthest outskirts of Buenos Aires. At the end of Rivadavia was a road bearing right – it could be spotted by a large statue of the Madonna at its beginning. The road led to the flat grass country, *provinciales* country. Thirty-six miles beyond the Madonna was another road – on the left – this marked by telephone junction wires converging into a transformer box on top of a double-strapped telephone pole. The road led to a ranch belonging to one Alfonzo Quesarro. Señor Quesarro would not be there . . . under the circumstances. Neither would his wife. But a skeleton staff would be on; the remaining staff quarters would be available for Mrs. Cameron's unknown friends.

Jean would obey his orders: she would not leave the embassy.

And she loved him. Terribly.

Dawn came up over the grass country. The breezes were warm; David had to remind himself that it was January. The Argentine summer. A member of the skeleton staff of Estancia Quesarro met them several miles down the road past the telephone junction wires, on the property border, and escorted them to the *ranchería* – a cluster of small one-storey cottages – near but not adjacent to the main buildings. They were led to an adobe hut farthest from the other houses; it was on the edge of a fenced grazing area, fields extending as far as the eye could see. The house was the residence of the *caporal* – the ranch foreman.

David understood as he looked up at the roof, at the single telephone line. Ranch foremen had to be able to use a telephone.

Their escort opened the door and stood in the frame, anxious to leave. He touched David's arm and spoke in a Spanish tempered with pampas Indian.

"The telephones out here are with operators. The service is poor; not like the city. I am to tell you this, *señor*."

But that information was not what the gaucho was telling him. He was telling him to be careful.

"I'll remember," said Spaulding. "Thank you."

The man left quickly and David closed the door. Lyons was standing across the room, in the center of a small monastery arch that led to some sort of sunlit enclosure. The metal case containing the gyroscopic designs was in his right hand; with his left he beckoned David.

Beyond the arch was a cubicle; in the center, underneath an oblong window overlooking the fields, there was a bed.

Spaulding undid the top of his trousers and peeled them off,

He fell with his full weight into the hard mattress and slept.

40

It seemed only seconds ago that he had walked through the small arch into the sunlit cubicle.

He felt the prodding fingers around his wound; he winced as a cold-hot liquid was applied about his waist and the adhesive ripped off.

He opened his eyes fiercely and saw the figure of a man bent over the bed. Lyons was standing beside him. At the edge of the hard mattress was the universal shape of a medical bag. The man bending over him was a doctor. He spoke in unusually clear English.

"You've slept nearly eight hours. That is the best prescription one could give you . . . I'm going to suture this in three places; that should do it. There will be a degree of discomfort, but with the tape, you'll be quite mobile."

"What time is it?" asked David.

Lyons looked at his watch. He whispered, and the words were clear. "Two . . . o'clock."

"Thank you for coming out here," said Spaulding, shifting his weight for the doctor's instruments.

"Wait until I'm back at my office in Palermo." The doctor laughed softly, sardonically. "I'm sure I'm on one of their lists." He inserted a suture, reassuring David with a tight smile. "I left word I was on a maternity call at an outback ranch. . . . There." He tied off the stitch and patted Spaulding's bare skin. "Two more and we're finished."

"Do you think you'll be questioned?"

"No. Not actually. The junta closes its eyes quite often. There's not an abundance of doctors here. . . . And amusingly enough, interrogators invariably seek free medical advice. I think it goes with their mentalities."

"And I think you're covering. I think it *was* dangerous."

The doctor held his hands in place as he looked at David "Jean Cameron is a very special person. If the history of wartime Buenos Aires is written, she'll be prominently mentioned." He returned to the sutures without elaboration. David had the feeling that the doctor did not wish to talk further. He was in a hurry.

Twenty minutes later Spaulding was on his feet, the doctor at the door of the adobe hut. David shook the medical man's hand. "I'm afraid I can't pay you," he said.

"You already have, colonel. I'm a Jew."

Spaulding did not release the doctor's hand. Instead, he held it firmly – not in salutation. "Please explain."

"There's nothing to explain. The Jewish community is filled with rumors of an American officer who pits himself against the pig. . . . Rhinemann the pig."

"That's all?"

"It's enough." The doctor removed his hand from Spaulding's and walked out. David closed the door.

Rhinemann the pig. It was time for Rhinemann.

The teutonic, guttural voice screamed into the telephone. David could picture the blue-black veins protruding on the surface of the bloated, suntanned skin. He could see the narrow eyes bulging with fury.

"*It was you! It was you!*" The accusation was repeated over and over again, as if the repetition might provoke a denial.

"It was me," said David without emphasis.

"You are *dead!* You are a *dead man!*"

David spoke quietly, slowly. With precision. "If I'm dead, no codes are sent to Washington; no radar or radio blackout. The screens will pick up that trawler and the instant a submarine surfaces anywhere near it, it'll be blown out of the water."

Rhinemann was silent. Spaulding heard the German Jew's rhythmic breathing but said nothing. He let Rhinemann's thoughts dwell upon the implication. Finally Rhinemann spoke. With equal precision.

"Then you have something to say to me. Or you would not have telephoned."

"That's right," agreed David. "I have something to say. I assume you're taking a broker's fee. I can't believe you arranged this exchange for nothing."

Rhinemann paused again. He replied cautiously, his breathing heavy, carried over the wire. "No. . . . It is a transaction. Accommodations must be paid for."

"But that payment comes later, doesn't it?" David kept his words calm, dispassionate. "You're in no hurry; you've got everyone where you want them. . . . There won't be any messages radioed out of Switzerland that accounts have been settled. The only message you'll get – or *won't get* – is from a submarine telling you the Koening diamonds have been transferred from the trawler. That's when I fly out of here with the designs. That's the signal." Spaulding laughed a brief, cold, quiet laugh. "It's very pro, Rhinemann. I congratulate you."

The financier's voice was suddenly low, circumspect. "What's your point?"

"It's also very pro . . . I'm the only one who can bring about that message from the U-boat. No one else. I have the codes that turn the lights off; that make the radar screens go dark. . . . But I expect to get paid for it."

"I see . . ." Rhinemann hesitated, his breathing still audible. "It is a presumptuous demand. Your superiors expect the gyroscopic designs. Should you impede their delivery, your punishment, no doubt, will be execution. Not formally arrived at, of course, but the result will be the same. Surely you know that,"

David laughed again, and again the laugh was brief – but now good-natured. "You're way off. *Way off*. There may be executions, but not mine. Until last night I only knew half the story. Now I know it *all*. . . . No, not my execution. On the other hand, you *do* have a problem. I know *that*; four years in Lisbon teaches a man some things."

"What is my problem?"

"If the Koening merchandise in Ocho Calle is not delivered, Altmüller will send an undercover battalion into Buenos Aires. You won't survive it."

The silence again. And in that silence was Rhinemann's acknowledgement that David was right.

"Then we are allies," said Rhinemann. "In one night you've gone far. You took a dangerous risk and leaped many plateaus. I admire such aggressive ambitions. I'm sure arrangements can be made."

"I was sure you'd be sure."

"Shall we discuss figures?"

Again David laughed softly. "Payment from you is like . . . before last night. Only half the story. Make your half generous. In Switzerland. The second half will be paid in the States. A lifetime of *very* generous retainers." David suddenly spoke tersely. "I want names."

"I don't understand. . . ."

"*Think* about it. The men *behind* this operation. The Americans. Those are the names I want. Not an accountant, not a confused brigadier. The others. . . . Without those names there's no deal. No codes."

"The man from Lisbon is remarkably without conscience," said Rhinemann with a touch of respect. "You are . . . as you Americans say . . . quite a rotten fellow."

"I've watched the masters in action. I thought about it . . . Why not?"

Rhinemann obviously had not listened to David's reply. His tone was abruptly suspicious. "If this . . . gain of personal wealth is the conclusion you arrived at, why did you do what you did last night? I must tell you that the damage is not irreparable, but why *did* you?"

"For the simplest of reasons. I hadn't thought about it last night. I hadn't arrived at this conclusion . . . last night." God knew, that was the truth, thought David.

"Yes. I think I understand," said the financier. "A very human reaction . . ."

"I want the rest of these designs," broke in Spaulding. "And you want the codes sent out. To stay on schedule, we have thirty-six hours, give or take two or three. I'll call you at six o'clock. Be ready to move."

David hung up. He took a deep breath and realized he was perspiring . . . and the small concrete house was cool. The breezes from the fields were coming through the windows, billowing the curtains. He looked at Lyons, who sat watching him in a straight-backed wicker chair.

"How'd I do?" he asked.

The physicist swallowed and spoke, and it occurred to Spaulding that either he was getting used to Lyons's strained voice or Lyons's speech was improving.

"Very . . . convincing. Except for the . . . sweat on your face and the expression . . . in your eyes." Lyons smiled; then followed it instantly with a question he took seriously. "Is there a chance . . . for the remaining blueprints?"

David held a match to a cigarette. He inhaled the smoke, looked up at the gently swaying curtains of an open window, then turned to the physicist. "I think we'd better understand one another, doctor. I don't give a goddamn about those designs. Perhaps I should, but I don't. And if the way to get our hands on them is to risk that trawler reaching a U-boat, it's out of the question. As far as I'm concerned we're bringing out three-quarters more than what we've got. And that's too goddamn much. . . . There's only one thing I want: the names . . . I've got the evidence; now I want the names."

"You want revenge," said Lyons softly.

"*Yes! . . . Jesus! Yes, I do!*" David crushed out his barely touched cigarette, crossed to the open window and looked out at the fields. "I'm sorry, I don't mean to yell at you. Or maybe I should. You heard Feld; you saw what I brought back from Ocho Calle, You know the whole putrid . . . obscene thing."

"I know . . . the men who fly those planes . . . are not responsible I know I believe that . . . Germany must lose this war."

"For Christ's *sake!*" roared David, whirling from the window. "You've *seen!* You've got to *understand!*"

"Are you saying . . . there's no difference? I don't believe that. . . . I don't think you believe it."

"I don't know what I believe! . . . No. I *do* know. I know what I object to; because it leaves no *room* for belief. . . . And I know I want those names."

"You should have them. . . . Your questions are great . . . moral ones. I think they will pain you . . . for years." Lyons was finding it difficult to sustain his words now. "I submit only . . . no matter what has happened . . . that Asher Feld was right. This war must *not* be settled . . . it must be won."

Lyons stopped talking and rubbed his throat. David walked to a table where Lyons kept a pitcher of water and poured a glass. He carried it over to the spent physicist and handed it to him. It occurred to David, as he acknowledged the gesture of thanks, that it was strange. . . . Of all men, the emaciated recluse in front of him would profit least from the outcome of the war. Or the shortening of it. Yet Eugene Lyons had been touched by the commitment of Asher Feld. Perhaps, in his pain, Lyons understood the simpler issues that his own anger had distorted.

Asher Feld. The Alvea Hotel.

"Listen to me," said Spaulding. "If there's a chance . . . and there may be, we'll try for the blueprints. There's a trade-off possible; a dangerous one . . . not for us, but for your friend, Asher Feld. We'll see. No promises. The names come first . . . It's a parallel route; until I get the names, Rhinemann has to believe I want the designs as much as he wants the diamonds. . . . We'll see."

The weak, erratic bell of the country telephone spun out its feeble ring. Spaulding picked it up.

"It's Ballard," said the voice anxiously.

"Yes, Bobby?"

"I hope to Christ you're clean, because there's a lot of flak to the contrary. I'm going on the assumption that a reasonable guy doesn't court-martial himself into a long prison term for a few dollars."

"A reasonable assumption. What is it? Did you get the information?"

"First things first. And the first thing is that the Fleet Marine Force wants you dead or alive; the condition is immaterial, and I think they'd prefer you dead."

"They found Meehan and the driver. . . ."

"You bet your ass they did! After they got rolled and stripped to their skivvies by some wandering *vagos*. They're mad as hell! They threw out the bullshit about not alerting the embassy that Fairfax wants you picked up. Fairfax's incidental; *they* want you. Assault, theft, et cetera."

"All right. That's to be expected."

"Expected? Oh, you're a pistol! I don't suppose I have to tell you about Granville. You got him burning up my dials! Washington's preparing a top-level scramble, so I'm chained to my desk till it comes in."

"Then he doesn't know. They're covering," said Spaulding, annoyed.

"The hell he doesn't! The hell they *are!* This radio silence; you walked into a High Command *defection!* An Allied Central project straight from the War Department."

"I'll bet it's from the War Department. I can tell you which office."

"It's true. . . . There's a U-boat bringing in a couple of very important Berliners. You're out of order; it's not your action. Granville will tell you that."

"Horseshit!" yelled David. "Pure horseshit! *Transparent* horseshit! Ask any network agent in Europe. You couldn't get a *Breifmarke* out of *any* German port! No one knows that better than me!"

"Interesting, ontologically speaking. Transparency isn't a quality one associates . . ."

"No jokes! My humor's strained!" And then suddenly David realized he had no cause to yell at the cryp. Ballard's frame of reference was essentially the same as it had been eighteen hours ago – with complications, perhaps, but not of death and survival. Ballard did not know about the carnage at San Telmo or the tools for Peenemünde in Ocho Calle; and a Haganah that reached into the most secret recesses of Military Intelligence. Nor would he be told just now. "I'm sorry. I've got a lot on my mind."

"Sure, sure." Ballard replied as if he were used to other people's tempers. Another trait common to most cryptographers, David reflected. "Jean said you were hurt; fell and cut yourself pretty badly. Did somebody push?"

"It's all right. The doctor was here. . . . Did you get the information? On Ira Barden."

"Yeah. . . . I used straight G-2 in Washington. A dossier Teletype request over your name. This Barden's going to know about it."

"That's O.K. What's it say?"

"The whole damn *thing?*"

"Whatever seems . . . unusual. Fairfax qualifications, probably."

"They don't use the name Fairfax. Just high-priority classification. . . . He's in the Reserves, not regular army. Family company's in importing. Spent a number of years in Europe and the Middle East; speaks five languages. . . ."

"And one of them's Hebrew," interrupted David quietly.

"That's right. How did . . . ? Never mind. He spent two years at the American University in Beirut while his father represented the firm in the Mediterranean areas. The company was very big in Middle East textiles. Barden transferred to Harvard, then transferred again to a small college called Brandeis. . . . I don't know it. He majored in Near East studies, it says here. When he graduated he went into the family business until the war. . . . I guess it was the languages."

"Thanks," said David. "Burn the Teletype, Bobby."

"With pleasure. . . . When are you coming in? You better get here before the FMF finds you. Jean can probably convince old Henderson to cool things off."

"Pretty soon. How's Jean?"

"Huh? Fine. . . . Scared; nervous, I guess. You'll see. She's a strong girl, though."

"Tell her not to worry."

"Tell her yourself."

"She's there with you?"

"No. . . . "Ballard drew out the word, telegraphing a note of concern that had been absent. "No, she's not with me. She's on her way to see you."

"*What?*"

"The nurse. The doctor's nurse. She called about an hour ago. She said you wanted to see Jean." Ballard's voice suddenly became hard and loud. "*What the hell's going on, Spaulding?*"

41

"Surely the man from Lisbon expected countermeasures. I'm amazed he was so derelict." Heinrich Stoltz conveyed his arrogance over the telephone. "Mrs. Cameron was a flank you took for granted, yes? A summons from a loved one is difficult to resist, is it not?"

"Where is she?"

"She is on her way to Luján. She will be a guest at Habichtsnest. An honored guest, I can assure you. Heir Rhinemann will be immensely pleased; I was about to telephone him. I wanted to wait until the interception was made."

"You're out of line!" David said, trying to keep his voice calm. "You're asking for reprisals in every neutral area. Diplomatic hostages in a neutral . . ."

"A guest," interrupted the German with relish. "Hardly a prize; a *step-daughter-in-law*; the husband *deceased*. With no official status. So complicated, these American social rituals."

"You know what I mean! You don't need diagrams!"

"I said she was a *guest!* Of an eminent financier you yourself were sent to contact . . . concerning international economic matters, I believe. A Jew expelled from his own country, that country your enemy. I see no cause for immediate alarm . . . Although, perhaps, you should."

There was no reason to procrastinate. Jean was no part of the bargain, no part of the indictment. To hell with the indictment! To hell with a meaningless commitment! There was no meaning!

Only Jean.

"Call the moves," said David.

"I was sure you'd cooperate. What difference does it make to you? Or to me, really. . . . You and I, we take orders. Leave the philosophy to men of great affairs. We survive."

"That doesn't sound like a true believer. I was told you were a believer." David spoke aimlessly; he needed time, only seconds. To think.

"Strangely enough, I am. In a world that passed, I'm afraid. Only partially in the one that's coming. . . . The remaining designs are at Habichtsnest. You and your aerophysicist will go there at once. I wish to conclude our negotiations this evening."

"Wait a minute!" David's mind raced over conjectures – his counterpart's options. "That's not the cleanest nest I've been in; the inhabitants leave something to be desired."

"So do the guests. . . ."

"Two conditions. One: I see Mrs. Cameron the minute I get there. Two: I don't send the codes – if they're to be sent – until she's back at the embassy. With Lyons."

"We'll discuss these points later. There is one prior condition, however." Stoltz paused. "Should you not be at Habichsnest this afternoon, you will *never* see Mrs. Cameron. As you last saw her. . . . Habichtsnest has so many diversions; the guests enjoy them so. Unfortunately, there have been some frightful accidents in the past. On the river, in the pool . . . on horseback. . . ."

The foreman gave then, a road map and filled the FMF automobile's gas tank with fuel from the ranch pump. Spaulding removed the orange medallions from the bumpers and blurred the numbers of the license plates by chipping away at the paint until the Is looked like 7s, and 3s like 8s. Then he smashed the ornament off the tip of the hood, slapped black paint over the grill and removed all four hubcaps. Finally, he took a sledgehammer and, to the amazement of the silent gaucho, he crashed it into the side door panels, trunk and roof of the car.

When he had finished, the automobile from Fleet Marine Force looked like any number of back-country wrecks.

They drove out the road to the primitive highway by the telephone junction box and turned east toward Buenos Aires. Spaulding pressed the accelerator; the vibrations caused the loose metal to rattle throughout the car. Lyons held the unfolded map on his knees; if it was correct, they could reach the Luján district without traveling the major highways, reducing the chances of discovery by the FMF patrols that were surely out by now.

The goddamned irony of it! thought David. Safety . . . safety for Jean, for him, too, really . . . lay in contact with the same enemy he had fought so viciously for over three years. An enemy made an ally by incredible events . . . treasons taking place in Washington and Berlin.

What had Stoltz said? *Leave the philosophy to men of great affairs.*

Meaning and no meaning at all.

David nearly missed the half-concealed entrance to Habichtsnest. He was approaching it from the opposite direction on the lonely stretch of road he had traveled only once, and at night. What caused him to slow down and look to his left, spotting the break in the woods, were sets of black tire marks on the light surface of the entrance. They had not been there long enough to be erased by the hot sun or succeeding traffic. And Spaulding recalled the words of the guard on the pier in Ocho Calle.

. . . There is a lot of shouting.

David could visualize Rhinemann screaming his orders, causing a column of racing Bentleys and Packards to come screeching out of the hidden road from Habichtsnest on its way to a quiet street in San Telmo.

And no doubt later – in the predawn hours – other automobiles, more sweating, frightened henchmen – racing to the small isolated peninsula that was Ocho Calle.

With a certain professional pride, Spaulding reflected that he had interdicted well.

Both enemies. All enemies.

A vague plan was coming into focus, but only the outlines. So much depended on what faced them at Habichtsnest.

And the soft-spoken words of hatred uttered by Asher Feld.

The guards in their paramilitary uniforms leveled their rifles at the approaching automobile. Others held dogs that were straining at leashes, teeth bared, barking viciously. The man behind the electric gate shouted orders to those in front; four guards ran to the car and yanked the smashed panels open. Spaulding and Lyons got out; they were pushed against the FMF vehicle and searched.

David kept turning his head, looking at the extended fence beyond both sides of the gate. He estimated the height and the tensile strength of the links, the points of electrical contact between the thick-poled sections. The angles of direction,

It was part of his plan.

Jean ran to him from across the terraced balcony. He held her, silently, for several moments. It was a brief span of sanity and he was grateful for it.

Rhinemann stood at the railing twenty feet away, Stoltz at his side. Rhinemann's narrow eyes stared at David from out of the folds of suntanned flesh. The look was one of despised respect, and David knew it.

There was a third man. A tall, blond-haired man in a white Palm Beach suit seated at a glass-topped table. Spaulding did not know him.

"David, *David*. What have I *done?*" Jean would not let him go; he stroked her soft brown hair, replying quietly.

"Saved my life among other things . . ."

"The Third Reich has extraordinarily thorough surveillance, Mrs. Cameron," interrupted Stoltz, smiling. "We keep watch on all Jews. Especially professional men. We knew you were friendly with the doctor in Palermo; and that the colonel was wounded. It was all quite simple."

"Does your surveillance of Jews include the man beside you?" asked Spaulding in a monotone.

Stoltz paled slightly, his glance shifting unobtrusively from Rhinemann to the blond-haired man in the chair. "Herr Rhinemann understands my meaning. I speak pragmatically; of the necessary observation of hostile elements."

"Yes, I remember," said David, releasing Jean, putting his arm around her shoulders. "You were very clear yesterday about the regrettable necessity of certain practicalities. I'm sorry you missed the lecture, Rhinemann. It concerned the concentration of Jewish money. . . . We're here. Let's get on with it."

Rhinemann stepped away from the railing. "We shall. But first, so the . . . circle is complete, I wish to present to you an acquaintance who has flown in from Berlin. By way of neutral passage, of course. I want you to have the opportunity of knowing you deal *directly* with *him*. The exchange is more *genuine* this way,"

Spaulding looked over at the blond-haired man in the white Palm Beach suit. Their eyes locked.

"Franz Altmüller, Ministry of Armaments. Berlin," said David.

"Colonel David Spaulding. Fairfax. Late of Portugal. The man in Lisbon," said Altmüller.

"You are jackals," added Rhinemann, "who fight as traitors fight and dishonor your houses. I say this to you both. For both to hear. . . . Now, as you say, colonel, we shall get on with it."

Stoltz took Lyons below to the manicured lawn by the pool. There, at a large, round table, a Rhinemann guard stood with a metal attaché case in his hand. Lyons sat down, his back to the balcony; the guard lifted the case onto the table.

"Open it," commanded Erich Rhinemann from above.

The guard did so; Lyons took out the plans and spread them on the table. Altmüller spoke. "Remain with him, Stoltz."

Stoltz looked up, bewildered. However, he did not speak. He walked to the edge of the pool and sat in a deck chair, his eyes fixed on Lyons.

Altmüller turned to Jean. "May I have a word with the colonel, please?"

Jean looked at Spaulding. She took her hand from his and walked to the far end of the balcony. Rhinemann remained in the center, staring down at Lyons.

"For both our sakes," said Altmüller, "I think you should tell me what happened in San Telmo."

David watched the German closely. Altmüller was not lying; he was not trying to trap him. *He did not know about the Haganah. About Asher Feld.* It was Spaulding's only chance.

"Gestapo," said David, giving the lie the simplicity of conviction.

"*Impossible!*" Altmüller spat out the word. "You *know* that's impossible! *I* am here!"

"I've dealt with the Gestapo – in various forms – for nearly four years. I know the enemy. . . . Grant me that much credit."

"You're wrong! There's *no possible way!*"

"You've spent too much time in the ministry, not enough in the field. Do you want a professional analysis?"

"What is it?"

David leaned against the railing. "You've been had."

"*What?*"

"Just as I've been had. By those who employ our considerable talents. In Berlin and Washington. There's a remarkable coincidence, too. . . . They both have the same initials. . . . A.S."

Altmüller stared at Spaulding, his blue eyes penetrating, his mouth parted slightly – in disbelief. He spoke the name under his breath.

Albert Speer . . ."

"Alan Swanson," countered David softly.

"It can't *be*," said Altmüller with less conviction than he wished to muster. "He doesn't know. . . ."

"Don't go into the field without some advanced training. You won't last. . . . Why do you think I offered to make a deal with Rhinemann?"

Altmüller was listening but not listening. He took his eyes from Spaulding, seemingly consumed with the pieces of an incredible puzzle. "If what you say is true – and by no means do I agree – the codes would not be sent, the transfer aborted. There would be no radio silence; your fleet cruising, radar and aircraft in operation. Everything lost!"

David folded his arms in front of him. It was the moment when the lie would either be bought or rejected out of hand. He knew it; he felt as he had felt scores of times in the north country when the *lie* was the keystone. "Your side plays rougher than mine. It goes with the New Order. My people won't kill me; they just want to make sure I don't know anything. All they care about are those designs. . . . With you it's different. Your people keep their options open."

David stopped and smiled at Rhinemann, who had turned from his sentry position by the balcony and was looking at them. Altmüller kept his eyes on Spaulding . . . the inexperienced 'runner' being taught, thought David.

"And in your judgment, what are these options?"

"A couple I can think of," replied Spaulding. "Immobilize me, force in another code man at the last minute, substitute faulty blueprints; or get the diamonds out from Ocho Calle some other way than by water – difficult with those crates, but not impossible."

"Then why should I not let these options be exercised? You tempt me."

Spaulding had been glancing up, at nothing. Suddenly he turned and looked at Altmüller. "Don't *ever* go into the field; you won't last a day. Stay at your ministry."

"What does that mean?"

"Any alternate strategy used, you're dead. You're a liability now. You 'dealt' with the enemy. Speer knows it, the Gestapo knows it. Your only chance is to *use* what you know. Just like me. You for your life; me for a great deal of money. Christ knows the aircraft companies will make a pile; I deserve some of it."

Altmüller took two steps to the railing and stood alongside David, looking down at the distant river below. "It's all so pointless."

"Not when you think about it," said Spaulding. "Something for nothing never is in this business."

David, staring straight ahead, could feel Altmüller's eyes abruptly on him. He could sense the new thought coming into focus in Altmüller's mind.

"Your generosity may be your undoing, colonel. . . . We can still have something for nothing. And I, a hero's medal from the Reich. We have you. Mrs. Cameron. The physicist's expendable, I'm sure. . . . You *will* send the codes. You were willing to negotiate for money. Surely you'll negotiate for your lives."

Like Altmüller, David stared straight ahead when he replied. His arms still folded, he was irritatingly relaxed, as he knew he had to be. "Those negotiations have been concluded. If Lyons approves the blueprints, I'll send the codes when he and Mrs. Cameron are back at the embassy. Not before."

"You'll send them when I *order* you to." Altmüller was finding it difficult to keep his voice low. Rhinemann looked over again but made no move to interfere. Spaulding understood. Rhinemann was toying with his jackals.

"Sorry to disappoint you," said David.

"Then extremely unpleasant things will happen. To Mrs. Cameron first."

"Give it up." David sighed. "Play by the original rules. You haven't a chance."

"You talk confidently for a man alone."

Spaulding pushed himself off the railing and turned, facing the German. He spoke barely above a whisper. "You really are a goddamned fool. You wouldn't last an hour in Lisbon. . . . Do you think I drove in here without any backups? Do you think Rhinemann *expected* me to? . . . We men in the field are very cautious, very cowardly; we're not heroic at all. We don't blow up buildings if there's a chance we'll still be inside. We won't destroy an enemy bridge unless there's another way back to our side."

"You *are* alone. There are no bridges left for you!"

David looked at Altmüller as if appraising a bad cut of meat, then glanced at his watch. "Your Stolz was a fool. If I don't make a call within fifteen minutes, there'll be a lot of busy telephones resulting in God knows how many very official automobiles driving out to Luján. I'm a military attaché stationed at the American embassy. I accompanied the ambassador's daughter to Luján. That's enough."

"That's preposterous! This is a neutral city. Rhinemann would . . ."

"*Rhinemann* would open the gates and throw the jackals out," interrupted Spaulding quietly and very calmly. "We're liabilities both of us. 'Tortugas' could blow up in his postwar face. He's not going to allow that. Whatever he thinks of the systems, yours *or* mine, it doesn't matter. Only one thing matters to him: the cause of Erich Rhinemann. . . . I thought you knew that. You picked him,"

Altmüller was breathing steadily, a bit too deeply, thought David. He was imposing a control on himself and he was only barely succeeding.

"You . . . have made arrangements to send the codes? From here?"

The lie was bought. The keystone was now in place.

"The rules are back in force. Radio and radar silence. No air strikes on surfacing submarines. No interception of trawlers . . . under Paraguayan flags entering the coastal zones. We both win. . . .Which do you want, jackal?"

Altmüller turned back to the railing and placed his hands on the marble top. His fingers were rigid against the stone. The tailored folds of his white Palm Beach suit were starchily immobile. He looked down at the river and spoke.

"The rules of 'Tortugas' are reinstated."

"I have a telephone call to make." said David.

"I expected you would," replied Rhinemann, looking contemptuously at Franz Altmüller. "I have no stomach for an embassy kidnapping. It serves no one."

"Don't be too harsh," said Spaulding agreeably. "It got me here in record time."

"Make your call." Rhinemann pointed to a telephone on a table next to the archway. "Your conversation will be amplified, of course."

"Of course," answered David, walking to the phone.

"Radio room . . . ," came the words from the unseen speakers.

"This is Lieutenant Colonel Spaulding, military attaché," said David, interrupting Ballard's words.

There was the slightest pause before Ballard replied.

"Yes, sir, Colonel Spaulding?"

"I issued a directive of inquiry prior to my conference this afternoon. You may void it now."

"Yes, sir. . . . Very good, sir."

"May I speak with the head cryptographer, please? A Mr. Ballard, I believe."

"I'm . . . Ballard, sir."

"Sorry," said David curtly, "I didn't recognize you, Ballard. Be ready to send out the sealed code schedules I prepared for you. The green envelope; open it and familiarize yourself with the progressions. When I give you the word, I want it transmitted immediately. On a black-drape priority."

"What . . . sir?"

"My authorization is black drape, Ballard. It's in the lex, so clear all scrambler channels. You'll get no flak with that priority. I'll call you back."

"Yes, sir . . ."

David hung up, hoping to Christ that Ballard was as good at his job as David thought he was. Or as good at parlour games as Henderson Granville thought he was.

"You're very efficient," said Rhinemann.

"I try to be," said David.

Ballard stared at the telephone. What was Spaulding trying to tell him? Obviously that Jean was all right; that he and Lyons were all right, too. At least for the time being.

Be ready to send out the sealed code schedules I prepared ...

David had not prepared any codes. *He* had. Spaulding had memorized the progressions, that was true, but only as a contingency.

What goddamned *green envelope?*

There was no envelope, red, blue or green!

What the hell was that nonsense ... *black-drape priority?*

What was a black drape? It didn't make sense!

But it *was* a key.

It's in the lex. ...

Lex. ...Lexicon. The Lexicon of Cryptography!

Black drape. ... He recalled something ... something very obscure, way in the past. *Black drape* was a very old term, long obsolete. But it meant something.

Ballard got out of his swivel chair and went to the bookshelf on the other side of the small radio room. He had not looked at *The Lexicon of Cryptography* in years. It was a useless, and, academic tome. ... Obsolete.

It was on the top shelf with the other useless reference books and, like the others, had gathered dust.

He found the term on page 71. It was a single paragraph sandwiched between equally meaningless paragraphs. But it had meaning now.

"The Black Drape, otherwise known as *Schwarzes Tuch*, for it was first employed by the German Imperial Army in 1916, is an entrapment device. It is hazardous for it cannot be repeated in a sector twice. It is a signal to proceed with a code, activating a given set of arrangements with intent to terminate, canceling said arrangements. The termination factor is expressed in minutes, specifically numbered. As a practice, it was abandoned in 1917 for it nullified ..."

Proceed ... with intent to terminate.

Ballard closed the book and returned to his chair in front of the dials.

Lyons kept turning the pages of the designs back and forth as if double-checking his calculations. Rhinemann called down twice from the balcony, inquiring if there were problems. Twice Lyons turned in his chair and shook his head. Stoltz remained in the deck chair by the pool, smoking cigarettes. Altmüller talked briefly with Rhinemann, the conversation obviously unsatisfactory to both. Altmüller returned to the chair by the glass-topped table and leafed through a Buenos Aires newspaper.

David and Jean remained at the far end of the terrace, talking quietly. Every once in a while Spaulding let his voice carry across; if Altmüller listened, he heard references to New York, to architectural firms, to vague postwar plans. Lovers' plans.

But these references were non sequiturs.

"At the Alvea Hotel," said David softly, holding Jean's hand, "there's a man registered under the name of E. Pace. *E. Pace.* His real name is Asher Feld. Identify yourself as the contact from me . . . and a Fairfax agent named Barden. Ira Barden. Nothing else. Tell him I'm calling his . . . priorities. In precisely two hours from . . . the minute you telephone from the embassy. . . . I *mean* the minute, Jean, he'll understand. . . ."

Only once did Jean Cameron gasp, an intake of breath that caused David to glare at her and press her hand. She covered her shock with artificial laughter.

Altmüller looked up from the newspaper. Contempt was in his eyes; beyond the contempt, and also obvious, was his anger.

Lyons got up from the chair and stretched his emaciated frame. He had spent three hours and ten minutes at the table; he turned and looked up at the balcony. At Spaulding.

He nodded.

"Good," said Rhinemann, crossing to Franz Altmüller. "We'll proceed. It will be dark soon; we'll conclude everything by early morning. No more delay! Stoltz! *Kommen Sie her! Bringen Sie die Aktenmappe!*"

Stoltz went to the table and began replacing the pages in the attaché case.

David took Jean's arm and guided her towards Rhinemann and Altmüller. The Nazi spoke.

"The plans comprise four hundred and sixty-odd pages of causal data and progressive equations. No man can retain such information; the absence of any part renders the designs useless. As soon as you contact the cryptographer and relay the codes, Mrs. Cameron and the physicist are free to leave."

"I'm sorry," said Spaulding. "My agreement was to send the codes when they were back at the embassy. That's the way it has to be."

"*Surely,*" interjected Rhinemann angrily, "you don't think I would permit . . ."

"No, I don't," broke in David. "But I'm not sure what you can control outside the gates of Habichtsnest. This way, I know you'll try harder."

42

It was an hour and thirty-one minutes before the telephone rang. Nine fifteen, exactly. The sun had descended behind the Luján hills; the lights along the distant riverbank flickered in the enveloping darkness.

Rhinemann picked up the receiver, listened and nodded to David.

Spaulding got out of his chair and crossed to the financier, taking the receiver. Rhinemann flicked a switch on the wall. The speakers were activated.

"We're here, David." Jean's words were amplified on the terrace.

"Fine," answered Spaulding. "No problems then?"

"Not really. After five miles or so I thought Doctor Lyons was going to be sick. They drove so fast. . . ."

After . . . five. . . .

Asher . . . Feld. . . .

Jean had done it!

"But he's all right now?"

"He's resting. It'll take some time before he feels himself . . ."

Time.

Jean had given Asher Feld the precise time.

"All right. . . ."

"*Genug! Genug!*" said Altmüller, standing by the balcony. "That's enough. You have your proof; they are there. The codes!"

David looked over at the Nazi. It was an unhurried look, not at all accommodating.

"Jean?"

"Yes?"

"You're in the radio room?"

"Yes."

"Let me speak to that Ballard fellow."

"Here he is."

Ballard's voice was impersonal, efficient. "Colonel Spaulding?"

"Ballard, have you cleared all scrambler channels?"

"Yes, sir. Along with your priority. The drape's confirmed, sir."

"Very good. Stand by for my call. It shouldn't be more than a few minutes." David quickly hung up the phone.

"What are you doing?!" yelled Altmüller furiously. "The *codes! Send them!*"

"He's *betraying* us!" screamed Stoltz, jumping up from his chair.

"I think you should explain yourself." Rhinemann spoke softly, his voice conveying the punishment he intended to inflict.

"Just last-minute details," said Spaulding, lighting a cigarette. "Only a few minutes. . . . Shall we talk alone, Rhinemann?"

"That is unnecessary. What is it?" asked the financier. "Your method of departure? It's arranged. You'll be driven to the Mendarro field with the designs. It's less than ten minutes from here. You won't be airborne, however, until we have confirmation of the Koening transfer."

"How long will that be?"

"What difference does it make?"

"Once the blackout starts I have no protection, *that's* the difference."

"*Ach!*" Rhinemann was impatient. "For four hours you'll have the best protection in the world. I have no stomach for offending the men in Washington!"

"You see?" said David to Franz Altmüller. "I told you we were liabilities." He turned back to Rhinemann. "All right. I accept that. You've got too much to lose. Detail number one, crossed off. Now detail number two. My payment from you."

Rhinemann squinted his eyes. "You *are* a man of details. . . . The sum of five hundred thousand American dollars will be transferred to the Banque Louis Quatorze in Zürich. It's a non-negotiable figure and a generous one."

"Extremely. More than I would have asked for. . . .What's my guarantee?"

"Come, colonel. We're not *salesmen*. You know where I live; your abilities are proven. I don't wish the specter of the man from Lisbon on my personal horizon."

"You flatter me."

"The money will be deposited, the proper papers held in Zürich for you. At the bank; normal procedures."

David crushed out his cigarette. "All right, Zürich. . . . Now the last detail. Those generous payments I'm going to receive right at home. . . . The names, please. Write them on a piece of paper."

"Are you so sure I possess these names?"

"It's the only thing I'm really sure of. It's the one opportunity you wouldn't miss."

Rhinemann took a small black leather notebook from his jacket pocket and wrote hastily on a page. He tore it out and handed it to Spaulding.

David read the names:

> *Kendall, Walter*
> *Swanson, A.* U.S. Army
> *Oliver, H.* Meridian Aircraft
> *Craft, J.* Packard

"Thank you," said Spaulding. He put the page in his pocket and reached for the telephone. "Get me the American embassy, please."

Ballard read the sequence of the code progressions David had recited to him.

They were not perfect but they were not far off, either; Spaulding had confused a vowel equation, but the message was clear.

And David's emphasis on the "frequency megacycle of 120 for all subsequent scrambles" was meaningless gibberish. But it, too, was very clear.

120 minutes.

Black Drape.

The original code allowed for thirteen characters:

CABLE TORTUGAS

The code Spaulding had recited, however, had fifteen characters.

Ballard stared at the words.

DESTROY TORTUGAS

In two hours.

David had a final "detail" which none could fault professionally, but all found objectionable. Since there were four hours – more or less – before he'd be driven to the Mendarro airfield, and there were any number of reasons during this period why he might be out of sight of the designs – or Rhinemann might be out of sight of the designs – he insisted that they be placed in a single locked metal case and chained to any permanent structure, the chain held by a new padlock, the keys given to him. Further, he would also hold the keys to the case and thread the hasps. If the designs were tampered with, he'd know it.

"Your precautions are now obsessive," said Rhinemann disagreeably. "I should ignore you. The codes have been sent."

"Then humor me. I'm a Fairfax four-zero. We might work again."

Rhinemann smiled. "That is always the way, is it not? So be it."

Rhinemann sent for a chain and a padlock, which he took a minor delight in showing to David in its original box. The ritual was over in several minutes, the metal case chained to the banister of the stairway in the great hall. The four men settled in the huge living room, to the right of the hall, an enormous archway affording a view of the staircase . . . and the metal briefcase.

The financier became genial host. He offered brandies; only Spaulding accepted at first, then Heinrich Stoltz followed. Altmüller would not drink.

A guard, his paramilitary uniform pressed into starched creases, came through the archway.

"Our operators confirm radio silence, sir. Throughout the entire coastal zone."

"Thank you," said Rhinemann. "Stand by on all frequencies."

The guard nodded. He turned and left the room as quickly as he had entered.

"Your men are efficient," observed David.

"They're paid to be," answered Rhinemann, looking at his watch. "Now, we wait. Everything progresses and we have merely to wait. I'll order a buffet. Canapés are hardly filling . . . and we have the time."

"You're hospitable," said Spaulding, carrying his brandy to a chair next to Altmüller.

"And generous. Don't forget that."

"It would be hard to. . . . I was wondering, however, if I might impose further?" David placed his brandy glass on the side table and gestured at his rumpled, ill-fitting clothes. "These were borrowed from a ranch hand. God knows when they were last washed. Or me . . . I'd appreciate a shower, a shave; perhaps a pair of trousers and a shirt, or a sweater. . . ."

"I'm sure your army personnel can accommodate you," said Altmüller, watching David suspiciously.

"For Christ's sake, Altmüller, I'm not *going* anywhere! Except to a shower. The designs are over there!" Spaulding pointed angrily through the archway to the metal case chained to the banister of the stairway. "If you think I'm leaving without *that*, you're retarded."

The insult infuriated the Nazi; he gripped the arms of his chair controlling himself. Rhinemann laughed and spoke to Altmüller,

"The colonel has had a tiresome few days. His request is minor; and I can assure you he is going nowhere but to the Mendarro airfield. . . . I wish he were. He'd save me a half million dollars."

David responded to Rhinemann's laugh with one of his own. "A man with that kind of money in Zürich should at least *feel* clean." He rose from the chair. "And you're right about the last few days. I'm bushed. And sore all over. If the bed is soft I'll grab a nap." He looked over at Altmüller. "With a battalion of armed guards at the door if it'll ease the little boy's concerns."

Altmüller shot up, his voice harsh and loud. "*Enough!*"

"Oh sit down," said David. "You look foolish."

Rhinemann's guard brought him a pair of trousers, a lightweight turtleneck sweater and a tan suede jacket. David saw that each was expensive and he knew each would fit. Shaving equipment was in the bathroom; if there was anything else he needed, all he had to do was open the door and ask. The man would be outside in the hall. Actually, there would be two men.

David understood.

He told the guard – a *porteño* – that he would sleep for an hour, then shower and shave for his journey. Would the guard be so considerate as to make sure he was awake by eleven o'clock?

The guard would do so.

It was five minutes past ten on David's watch. Jean had phoned at precisely nine fifteen. Asher Feld had exactly two hours from nine fifteen.

David had one hour and five minutes.

Eleven fifteen.

If Asher Feld really believed in his priorities.

The room was large, had a high ceiling and two double-casement windows three stories above the ground, and was in the east wing of the house. That was all Spaulding could tell – or wanted to study – while the lights were on.

He turned them off and went back to the windows. He opened the left casement quietly, peering out from behind the drapes.

The roof was slate; that wasn't good. It had a wide gutter; that was better. The gutter led to a drainpipe about twenty feet away. That was satisfactory.

Directly beneath, on the second floor, were four small balconies that probably led to four bedrooms. The farthest balcony was no more than five feet from the drainpipe. Possibly relevant; probably not.

Below, the lawn like all the grounds at Habichtsnest: manicured, greenish black in the moonlight, full; with white wrought-iron outdoor furniture dotted about, and flagstone walks bordered by rows of flowers. Curving away from the area beneath his windows was a wide, raked path that disappeared into the darkness and the trees. He remembered seeing that path from the far right end of the terrace overlooking the pool; he remembered the intermittent, unraked hoofprints. The path was for horses; it had to lead to stables somewhere beyond the trees.

That *was* relevant; relevancy, at this point, being relative.

And then Spaulding saw the cupped glow of a cigarette behind a latticed arbor thirty-odd feet from the perimeter of the wrought-iron furniture. Rhinemann may have expressed confidence that he, David, would be on his way to Mendarro in a couple of hours, but that confidence was backed up by men on watch.

No surprise; the surprise would have been the absence of such patrols. It was one of the reasons he counted on Asher Feld's priorities.

He let the drapes fall back into place, stepped away from the window and went to the canopied bed. He pulled down the blankets and stripped to his shorts – coarse underdrawers he had found in the adobe hut to replace his own bloodstained ones. He lay down and closed his eyes with no intention of sleeping. Instead, he pictured the high, electrified fence down at the gate of Habichtsnest. As he had seen it while Rhinemann's guards searched him against the battered FMF automobile.

To the right of the huge gate. To the east.

The floodlights had thrown sufficient illumination for him to see the slightly angling curvature of the fence line as it receded into the woods. Not much but definite.

North by northeast.

He visualized once again the balcony above the pool. Beyond the railing at the far right end of the terrace where he had talked quietly with Jean. He concentrated on the area below – in front, to the right.

North by northeast.

He saw it clearly. The grounds to the right of the croquet course and the tables sloped gently downhill until they were met by the tall trees of the surrounding woods. It was into these woods that the bridle path below him now entered. And as the ground descended – ultimately a mile down to the river banks – he remembered the breaks in the patterns of the far-off treetops. Again to the right.

Fields.

If there were horses – and there *were* horses – and stables – and there *had* to be stables – then there were fields. For the animals to graze and race off the frustrations of the wooded, confining bridle paths.

The spaces between the descending trees were carved-out pasture lands, there was no other explanation.

North by northeast.

He shifted his thoughts to the highway two miles south of the marble steps of Habichtsnest, the highway that cut through the outskirts of Luján toward Buenos Aires. He remembered: the road, although high above the river at the Habichtsnest intersection, curved to the *left* and went *downhill* into the Tigre district. He tried to recall precisely the first minutes of the nightmare ride in the Bentley that ended in smoke and fire and death in the Colinas Rojas. The car had swung out of the hidden entrance and for several miles sped east *and* down *and* slightly north. It finally paralleled the shoreline of the river.

North by northeast.

And then he pictured the river below the terraced balcony, dotted with white sails and cabin cruisers. It flowed diagonally away . . . to the right.

North by northeast.

That was his escape.

Down the bridle path into the protective cover of the dark woods and northeast toward the breaks in the trees – the fields. Across the fields, always heading to the right – east, and downhill, north. Back into the sloping forest, following the line of the river, until he found the electrified fence bordering the enormous compound that was Habichtsnest.

Beyond that fence was the highway to Buenos Aires. And the embassy.

And Jean.

David let his body go limp, let the ache of his wound run around in circles on his torn skin. He breathed steadily, deeply. He had to remain calm; that was the hardest part.

He looked at his watch – his gift from Jean. It was nearly eleven o'clock. He got out of the bed and put on the trousers and the sweater. He slipped into his shoes and pulled the laces as tight as he could, until the leather pinched his feet, then reached for the pillow and wrapped the soiled shirt from the outback ranch around it. He replaced the pillow at the top of the bed and pulled the blanket partially over it. He lifted the sheets, bunched them, inserted the ranch hand's trousers and let the blankets fall back in place.

He stood up. In the darkness, and with what light would come from the hallway, the bed looked sufficiently full at least for his immediate purpose.

He crossed to the door and pressed his back into the wall beside it.

His watch read one minute to eleven.

The tapping was loud; the guard was not subtle.

The door opened.

"*Señor? . . . Señor?*"

The door opened further.

"*Señor*, it's time. It's eleven o'clock."

The guard stood in the frame, looking at the bed. "*Eál duerme*," he said casually over his shoulder.

"Señor *Spaulding!*" The guard walked into the darkened room.

The instant the man cleared the door panel, David took a single step and with both hands clasped the guard's neck from behind. He crushed his fingers into the throat and yanked the man diagonally into him.

No cry emerged; the guard's windpipe was choked of all air supply. He went down, limp.

Spaulding closed the door slowly and snapped on the wall switch.

"*Thanks very much*," he said loudly. "Give me a hand, will you please? My stomach hurts like *hell. . . .*"

It was no secret at Habichtsnest that the American had been wounded.

David bent over the collapsed guard. He massaged his throat, pinched his nostrils, put his lips to the man's mouth and blew air into the damaged windpipe.

The guard responded; conscious but not conscious. In semi-shock.

Spaulding removed the man's Lüger from his belt holster and a large hunting knife from a scabbard beside it. He put the blade underneath the man's jaw and drew blood with the sharp point. He whispered. In Spanish.

"Understand me! I want you to laugh! You start laughing *now!* If you don't, this goes home. Right up through your neck! . . . Now. *Laugh!*"

The guard's crazed eyes carried his total lack of comprehension. He seemed to know only that he was dealing with a maniac. A madman who would kill him.

Feebly at first, then with growing volume and panic, the man laughed.

Spaulding laughed with him.

The laughter grew; David kept staring at the guard, gesturing for louder, more enthusiastic merriment. The man – perplexed beyond reason and totally frightened – roared hysterically.

Spaulding heard the click of the doorknob two feet from his ear. He crashed the barrel of the Lüger into the guard's head and stood up as the second man entered.

"*Qué pasa, Antonio? Te re –* '

The Lüger's handle smashed into the Argentine's skull with such force that the guard's expulsion of breath was as loud as his voice as he fell.

David looked at his watch. It was eight minutes past eleven. Seven minutes to go.

If the man named Asher Feld believed the words he spoke with such commitment.

Spaulding removed the second guard's weapons, putting the additional Lüger into his belt. He searched both men's pockets, removing whatever paper currency he could find. And a few coins.

He had no money whatsoever. He might well need money.

He ran into the bathroom and turned on the shower to the hottest position on the dial. He returned to the hallway door and locked it. Then he turned off all lights and went to the left casement window, closing his eyes to adjust to the darkness outside. He opened them and blinked several times, trying to blur out the white spots of anxiety.

It was nine minutes past eleven.

He rubbed his perspiring hands over the expensive turtleneck sweater; he took deep breaths and waited.

The waiting was nearly unendurable.

Because he could not know.

And then he heard it! And he knew.

Two thunderous explosions! So loud, so stunning, so totally without warning that he found himself trembling, his breathing stopped.

There followed bursts of machine-gun fire that ripped through the silent night.

Below him on the ground, men were screaming at one another, racing toward the sounds that were filling the perimeter of the compound with growing ferocity.

David watched the hysteria below. There were five guards beneath his window, all running now out of their concealed stations. He could see the spill of additional floodlights being turned on to his right, in the elegant front courtyard of Habichtsnest. He could hear the roar of powerful automobile engines and the increasing frequency of panicked commands.

He eased himself out of the casement window, holding onto the sill until his feet touched the gutter.

Both Lügers were in his belt, the knife between his teeth. He could not chance a blade next to his body; he could always spit it out if necessary. He sidestepped his way along the slate roof. The drainpipe was only feet away.

The explosions and the gunfire from the gate increased. David marveled — not only at Asher Feld's commitment, but at his logistics. The Haganah leader must have brought a small, well-supplied army into Habichtsnest.

He lowered his body cautiously against the slate roof; he reached out, gripped the gutter on the far side of the drainpipe with his right hand and slowly, carefully crouched sideways, inched his feet into a support position. He pushed against the outside rim of the gutter, testing its strength, and in a quick-springing short jump, he leaped over the side, holding the rim with both hands, his feet against the wall, straddling the drain-pipe.

He began his descent, hand-below-hand on the pipe.

Amid the sounds of the gunfire, he suddenly heard loud crashing above him. There were shouts in both German and Spanish and the unmistakable smashing of wood.

The room he had just left had been broken into.

The extreme north second-floor balcony was parallel with him now. He reached out with his left hand, gripped the edge, whipped his right hand across for support and swung underneath, his body dangling thirty feet above the ground but out of sight.

Men were at the casement windows above. They forced the lead frames open without regard to the handles; the glass smashed; metal screeched against metal.

There was another thunderous explosion from the battleground a quarter of a mile away in the black-topped field cut out of the forest. A far-off weapon caused a detonation in the front courtyard; the spill of floodlight suddenly disappeared. Asher Feld was moving up. The crossfire would be murderous. Suicidal.

The shouts above Spaulding receded from the window, and he kicked his feet out twice to get sufficient swing to lash his hands once more across and around the drainpipe.

He did so, the blade between his teeth making his jaws ache.

He slid to the ground, scraping his hands against the weathered metal, insensitive to the cuts on his palms and fingers.

He removed the knife from his mouth, a Lüger from his belt and raced along the edge of the raked bridle path toward the darkness of the trees. He ran into the pitch-black, tree-lined corridor, skirting the trunks, prepared to plunge between them at the first sound of nearby shots.

They came, four in succession, the bullets thumping with terrible finality into the surrounding tall shafts of wood.

He whipped around a thick trunk and looked toward the house. The man firing was alone, standing by the drainpipe. Then a second guard joined him, racing from the area of the croquet course, a giant Doberman straining at its leash in his hand. The men shouted at one another, each trying to assert command, the dog barking savagely.

As they stood yelling, two bursts of machine-gun fire came from within the front courtyard; two more floodlights exploded.

David saw the men freeze, their concentration shifted to the front. The guard with the dog yanked at the straps, forcing the animal back into the side of the house. The second man crouched, then rose and started sidestepping his way rapidly along the building toward the courtyard, ordering his associate to follow.

And then David saw him. Above. To the right. Through foliage. On the terrace overlooking the lawn and the pool.

Erich Rhinemann had burst through the doors, screaming commands in fury, but not in panic. He was marshaling his forces, implementing his defenses . . . somehow in the pitch of the assault, he was the messianic Caesar ordering his battalions to attack, attack, *attack*. Three men came into view behind him; he roared at them and two of the three raced back into Habichtsn-est. The third man argued; Rhinemann shot him without the slightest hesi-tation. The body collapsed out of David's sight. Then Rhinemann ran to the wall, partially obscured by the railing, but not entirely. He seemed to be yelling into the wall.

Screeching into the wall.

Through the bursts of gunfire, David heard the muted, steady whirring and he realized what Rhinemann was doing.

The cable car from the riverbank was being sent up for him.

While the battle was engaged, this Caesar would escape the fire.

Rhinemann the pig. The ultimate manipulator. Corruptor of all things, honoring nothing.

We may work again....

That is always the way, is it not?

David sprang out of his recessed sanctuary and ran back on the path to the point where the gardens and woods joined the lawn below the balcony. He raced to a white metal table with the wrought-iron legs – the same table at which Lyons had sat, his frail body bent over the blueprints. Rhinemann was nowhere in sight.

He had to be there!

It was suddenly ... inordinately clear to Spaulding that the one meaningful aspect of his having been ripped out of Lisbon and transported half a world away – through the fire and the pain – was the man above him now, concealed on the balcony.

"*Rhinemann!... Rhinemann! I'm here!*"

The immense figure of the financier came rushing to the railing. In his hand was a Sternlicht automatic. Powerful, murderous.

"*You. You are a dead man!*" He began firing; David threw himself to the ground behind the table, overturning it, erecting a shield. Bullets thumped into the earth and ricocheted off the metal. Rhinemann continued screaming. "Your tricks are *suicide*, Lisbon! My men come from everywhere! *Hundreds!* In minutes!... Come, Lisbon! Show yourself. You merely move up your death! You think I would have let *you live? Never!* Show yourself! You're *dead!*"

David understood. The manipulator would not offend the men in Washing-ton, but neither would he allow the man from Lisbon to remain on his *personal horizon*. The designs would have gone to Mendarro. Not the man from Lisbon.

He would have been killed on his way to Mendarro.

It was *so* clear.

David raised his Lüger, he would have only an instant. A diversion, then an instant.

It would be enough....

The lessons of the north country.

He reached down and clawed at the ground, gathering chunks of earth and lawn with his left hand. When he had a large fistful, he lobbed it into the air, to the *left* of the rim of metal. Black dirt and blades of grass floated up, magnified in the dim spills of light and the furious activity growing nearer.

There was a steady burst of fire from the Sternlicht. Spaulding sprang to the *right* of the table and squeezed the trigger of the Lüger five times in rapid succession.

Erich Rhinemann's face exploded in blood. The Sternlicht fell as his hands sprang up in the spasm of death. The immense body snapped backward, then forward; then lurched over the railing.

Rhinemann plummeted down from the balcony.

David heard the screams of the guards above and raced back to the darkness of the bridle path. He ran with all his strength down the twisting black corridor, his shoes sinking intermittently into the soft, raked edges.

The path abruptly curved. To the *left*.

Goddamn it!

And then he heard the whinnies of frightened horses. His nostrils picked up their smells and to his right he saw the one-story structure that housed the series of stalls that was the stables. He could hear the bewildered shouts of a groom somewhere within trying to calm his charges.

For a split second, David toyed with an idea, then rejected it. A horse would be swift, but possibly unmanageable.

He ran to the far end of the stables, turned the corner and stopped for breath, for a moment of orientation. He thought he knew where he was; he tried to picture an aerial view of the compound.

The fields! The fields had to be nearby.

He ran to the opposite end of the one-story structure and saw the pastures beyond. As he had visualized, the ground sloped gently downward – north – but not so much as to make grazing or running difficult. In the distance past the fields, he could see the wooded hills rise in the moonlight. To the right – east.

Between the slope of the fields and the rise of the hills was the line he had to follow. It was the most direct, concealed route to the electrified fence.

North by northeast.

He sped to the high post-and-rail fence that bordered the pasture, slipped through and began racing across the field. The volleys and salvos of gunfire continued behind him – in the distance now, but seemingly no less brutal. He reached a ridge in the field that gave him a line of sight to the river a half mile below. It, too, was bordered by a high post-arid-rail, used to protect the animals from plummeting down the steeper inclines. He could see lights being turned on along the river; the incessant crescendos of death were being carried by the summer winds to the elegant communities below.

He spun in shock. A bullet whined above him. It had been *aimed* at him! He had been spotted!

He threw himself into the pasture grass and scrambled away. There was a slight incline and he let himself roll down it, over and over again until his body hit the hard wood of a post. He had reached the opposite border of the field; beyond, the woods continued.

He heard the fierce howling of the dogs, and knew it was directed at him.

On his knees, he could see the outlines of a huge animal streaking toward him across the grass. His Lüger was poised, level, but he understood that by firing it, he would betray his position. He shifted the weapon to his left hand and pulled the hunting knife out of his belt.

The black monstrosity leaped through the air, honed by the scent into his target of human flesh. Spaulding lashed out his left hand with the Lüger, feeling the impact of the hard, muscular fur of the Doberman on his upper body, watching the ugly head whip sideways, the bared teeth tearing at the loose sweater and into his arm.

He swung his right hand upward, the knife gripped with all the strength he had, into the soft stomach of the animal. Warm blood erupted from the dog's lacerated belly; the swallowed sound of a savage roar burst from the animal's throat as it died.

David grabbed his arm. The Doberman's teeth had ripped into his skin below the shoulder. And the wrenching, rolling, twisting movements of his body had broken at least one of the stitches in his stomach wound.

He held onto the rail of the pasture fence and crawled east.

North by northeast! *Not east*, goddamn it!

In his momentary shock, he suddenly realized there was a perceptible reduction of the distant gunfire. How many minutes had it *not* been there? The explosions seemed to continue but the small-arms fire was subsiding.

Considerably.

There were shouts now; from across the field by the stables. He looked between and over the grass. Men were running with flashlights, the beams darting about in shafting diagonals. David could hear shouted commands.

What he saw made him stop all movement and stare incredulously. The flashlights of the men across the wide pasture were focused on a figure coming out of the stable – on horseback! The spill of a dozen beams picked up the glaring reflection of a white Palm Beach suit.

Franz Altmüller!

Altmüller had chosen the madness he, David, had rejected.

But, of course, their roles were different.

Spaulding knew he was the quarry now. Altmüller, the hunter.

There would be others following, but Altmüller would not, *could* not wait. He kicked at the animal's flanks and burst through the opened gate.

Spaulding understood again. Franz Altmüller was a dead man if David lived. His only means of survival in Berlin was to produce the corpse of the man from Lisbon. The Fairfax agent who had crippled "Tortugas"; the body of the man the patrols and the scientists in Ocho Calle could identify. The man the "Gestapo" had unearthed and provoked.

So much, so alien.

Horse and rider came racing across the field. David stayed prone and felt the hard earth to the east. He could not stand; Altmüller held a powerful, wide-beamed flashlight. If he rolled under the railing, the tall weeds and taller grass beyond might conceal him but just as easily might bend, breaking the pattern.

If . . . might.

He knew he was rationalizing. The tall grass would be best; out of sight. But also out of strategy. And he knew why that bothered him.

He wanted to be the hunter. Not the quarry.

He wanted Altmüller dead.

Franz Altmüller was not an enemy one left alive. Altmüller was every bit as lethal in a tranquil monastery during a time of peace as he was on a battlefield in war. He was the absolute enemy; it was in his eyes. Not related to the cause of Germany, but front deep within the man's arrogance: Altmüller had watched his masterful creation collapse, had seen "Tortugas" destroyed. By another man who had told him he was inferior.

That, Altmüller could not tolerate.

He would be scorned in the aftermath.

Unacceptable!

Altmüller would lie in wait. In Buenos Aires, in New York, in London; no matter where. And his first target would be Jean. In a rifle sight, or a knife in a crowd, or a concealed pistol at night. Altmüller would make him pay. It was in his eyes.

Spaulding hugged the earth as the galloping horse reached the midpoint of the field, plunging forward, directed by the search-light beam from the patrols back at the stables a quarter of a mile away. They were directed at the area where the Doberman was last seen.

Altmüller reined in the animal, slowing it, not stopping it. He scanned the ground in front with his beam, approaching cautiously, a gun in his hand, holding the straps but prepared to fire.

Without warning, there was a sudden, deafening explosion from the stables. The beams of light that had come from the opposite side of the field were no more; men who had started out across the pasture after Altmüller stopped and turned back to the panic that was growing furiously at the bordering fence. Fires had broken out.

Altmüller continued; if he was aware of the alarms behind him he did not show it. He kicked his horse and urged it forward.

The horse halted, snorted; it pranced its front legs awkwardly and backstepped in spite of Altmüller's commands. The Nazi was in frenzy; he screamed at the animal, but the shouts were in vain. The horse had come upon the dead Doberman; the scent of the fresh blood repelled it.

Altmüller saw the dog in the grass. He swung the light first to the left, then to the right, the beam piercing the space above David's head. Altmüller made his decision instinctively – or so it seemed to Spaulding. He whipped the reins of the horse to his right, toward David. He walked the horse; he did not run it.

Then David saw why. Altmüller was following the stains of the Doberman's blood in the grass.

David crawled as fast as he could in front of the spill of Altmüller's slow-moving beam. Once in relative darkness, he turned abruptly to his right and ran close to the ground back toward the *center* of the field. He waited until horse and rider were between him and the bordering post-and-rail, then inched his way toward the Nazi. He was tempted to take a clean shot with the Lüger, but he knew that had to be the last extremity. He had several miles to go over unfamiliar terrain, with a dark forest that others knew better. The loud report of heavy caliber pistol shot would force men out of the pandemonium a quarter of a mile away.

Nevertheless, it might be necessary.

He was within ten feet now, the Lüger in his left hand, his right free . . . A little closer, just a bit closer. Altmüller's flashlight slowed to a near stop. He had approached the point where he, David, had lain in the grass immobile.

Then Spaulding felt the slight breeze from behind and knew – in a terrible instant of recognition – that it was the moment to move.

The horse's head yanked up, the wide eyes bulged. The scent of David's blood-drenched clothing had reached its nostrils.

Spaulding sprang out of the grass, his right hand aimed at Altmüller's wrist. He clasped his fingers over the barrel of the gun – it was a Colt! a U.S. Army issue Colt .45! – and forced his thumb into the trigger housing. Altmüller whipped around in shock, stunned by the totally unexpected attack. He pulled his arms back and lashed out with his feet. The horse reared high on its hind legs; Spaulding held on, forcing Altmüller's hand down, *down*. He yanked with every ounce of strength he had and literally ripped Altmüller off the horse into the grass. He slammed the Nazi's wrist into the ground again and again, until flesh hit rock and the Colt sprang loose. As it did so, he crashed his Lüger into Altmüller's face.

The German fought back. He clawed at Spaulding's eyes with his free left hand, kicked furiously with his knees and feet at David's testicles and legs and rocked violently, his shoulders and head pinned by Spaulding's body. He screamed.

"*You!* You and . . . *Rhinemann! Betrayal!*"

The Nazi saw the blood beneath David's shoulder and tore at the wound, ripping the already torn flesh until Spaulding thought he could not endure the pain.

Altmüller heaved his shoulder up into David's stomach, and yanked at David's bleeding arm, sending him sprawling off to the side. The Nazi leaped up on his feet, then threw himself back down on the grass where the Colt.45 had been pried loose. He worked his hands furiously over the ground.

He found the weapon.

Spaulding pulled the hunting knife from the back of his belt and sprang across the short distance that separated him from Altmüller. The Colt's barrel was coming into level position, the small black opening in front of his eyes.

As the blade entered the flesh, the ear-shattering fire of the heavy revolver exploded at the side of David's face, burning his skin, but missing its mark.

Spaulding tore the knife downward into Altmüller's chest and left it there. The absolute enemy was dead.

David knew there was no instant to lose, or he was lost. There would be other men, other horses . . . many dogs.

He raced to the bordering pasture fence, over it and into the darkness of the woods. He ran blindly, trying desperately to swing partially to his left. North.

North by northeast.

Escape!

He fell over rocks and fallen branches, then at last penetrated deepening foliage, lashing his arms for a path, any kind of path. His left shoulder was numb, both a danger and a blessing.

There was no gunfire in the distance now; only darkness and the hum of the night forest and the wild, rhythmic pounding of his chest. The fighting by the stables had stopped. Rhinemann's men were free to come after him now.

He had lost blood; how much and how severely he could not tell. Except that his eyes were growing tired, as his body was tired. The branches became heavy, coarse tentacles; the inclines, steep mountains. The slopes were enormous ravines that had to be crossed without ropes. His legs buckled and he had to force them taut again.

The fence! There was the fence!

At the bottom of a small hill, between the trees.

He began running, stumbling, clawing at the ground, pushing forward to the base of the hill.

He was there. *It* was there.

The fence.

Yet he could not touch it. But, perhaps . . .

He picked up a dry stick from the ground and lobbed it into the wire.

Sparks and crackling static. To touch the fence meant death.

He looked up at the trees. The sweat from his scalp and forehead stung his eyes, blurring his already blurted vision. There had to be a tree.

A tree. The *right* tree.

He couldn't be sure. The darkness played tricks on the leaves, the limbs. There were shadows in the moonlight where substance should be.

There were no limbs! No limbs hanging over the fence whose touch meant oblivion. Rhinemann had severed – on both sides – whatever growths approached the high, linked steel wires!

He ran as best he could to his left – north. The river was perhaps a mile away. Perhaps.

Perhaps the water.

But the river, if he could reach it down the steep inclines barred to horses, would slow him up, would rob him of the time he needed desperately. And Rhinemann would have patrols on the river banks.

Then he saw it.

Perhaps.

A sheared limb several feet above the taut wires, coming to within a few feet of the fence! It was thick, widening into suddenly greater thickness as it joined the trunk. A laborer had taken the means of least resistance and had angled his chain saw just before the final thickness. He would not be criticized; the limb was too high, too far away, for all practical purposes.

But Spaulding knew it was his last chance. The only one left. And that fact was made indelibly clear to him with the distant sounds of men and dogs. They were coming after him now.

He removed one of the Lügers from his belt and threw it over the fence. One bulging impediment in his belt was enough.

He jumped twice before gripping a gnarled stub; his left arm aching, no longer numb, no longer a blessing. He scraped his legs up the wide trunk until his right hand grasped a higher branch. He struggled against the sharp bolts of pain in his shoulder and stomach and pulled himself up.

The sawed-off limb was just above.

He dug the sides of his shoes into the bark, jabbing them repeatedly to make tiny ridges. He strained his neck, pushing his chin into the calloused wood, and whipped both arms over his head, forcing his left elbow over the limb, pulling maniacally with his right hand. He hugged the amputated limb, peddling his feet against the tree until the momentum allowed him the force to throw his right leg over it. He pressed his arms downward and thrust himself into a sitting position, his back against the trunk.

He had managed it. Part of it.

He took several deep breaths and tried to focus his sweat-filled, stinging eyes. He looked down at the electrified barbed wire on top of the fence. It was less than four feet below him but nearly three feet in front. From the crest of the ground, about eight. If he was going to clear the wire, he had to twist and jack his body into a lateral vault. And should he be able to do that, he was not at all sure his body could take the punishment of the fall.

But he could hear the dogs and the men clearly now. They had entered the woods beyond the fields. He turned his head and saw dim shafts of light piercing the dense foliage.

The other punishment was death.

There was no point in thinking further. Thoughts were out of place now. Only motion counted.

He reached above with both hands, refusing to acknowledge the silent screams from his shoulder, grabbed at the thin branches, pulled up his legs until his feet touched the top of the thick limb and lunged, hurling himself straight out, above the taut wires until he could see their blurted image. At that split-instant, he twisted his body violently to the right and down, jack-knifing his legs under him.

It was a strange, fleeting sensation: disparate feelings of final desperation and, in a very real sense, clinical objectivity. He had done all he could do. There wasn't any more.

He hit the earth, absorbing the shock with his right shoulder, rolling forward, his knees tucked under him – rolling, rolling, not permitting the roll to stop; distributing the impact throughout his body.

He was propelled over a tangle of sharp roots and collided with the base of a tree. He grabbed his stomach; the surge of pain told him the wound was open now. He would have to hold it, clutch it . . . blot it. The cloth of the turtleneck sweater was drenched with sweat and blood – his own and the Doberman's – and torn in shreds from the scores of falls and stumbles.

But he had made it.

Or nearly.

He was out of the compound. He was free from Habichtsnest.

He looked around and saw the second Lüger on the ground in the moonlight. . . . The one in his belt would be enough. If it wasn't, a second wouldn't help him; he let it stay there.

The highway was no more than half a mile away now. He crawled into the underbrush to catch his spent breath, to temporarily restore what little strength he had left. He would need it for the remainder of his journey.

The dogs were louder now; the shouts of the patrols could be heard no more than several hundred yards away. And suddenly the panic returned. What in God's name had he been *thinking* of!? What was he *doing!?*

What *was* he doing?

He was lying in the underbrush assuming – *assuming* he was *free!*

But *was* he?

There were men with guns and savage – viciously savage – animals within the sound of his voice and the sight of his running body.

Then suddenly he heard the words, the commands, shouted – screamed in anticipation. In rage.

"Freilassen! Die Hunde freilassen!"

The dogs were being released! The handlers thought their quarry was cornered! The dogs were unleashed to tear the quarry apart!

He saw the beams of light come over the small hill before he saw the animals. Then the dogs were silhouetted as they streaked over the ridge and down the incline. Five, eight, a dozen racing, monstrous forms stampeding toward the hated object of their nostrils; growing nearer, panicked into wanting, needing the wild conclusion of teeth into flesh.

David was mesmerized – and sickened – by the terrible sight that followed.

The whole area lit up like a flashing diadem; crackling, hissing sounds of electricity filled the air. Dog after dog crashed into the high wire fence. Short fur caught fire; horrible, prolonged, screeching yelps of animal deaths shattered the night.

In alarm or terror or both, shots were fired from the ridge. Men ran in all directions – some to the dogs and the fence, some to the flanks, most away in retreat.

David crawled out of the brush and started running into the forest.

He *was* free!

The prison that was Habichtsnest confined his pursuers . . . but he was free!

He held his stomach and ran into the darkness.

The highway was bordered by sand and loose gravel. He stumbled out of the woods and fell on the sharp, tiny stones. His vision blurred; nothing stayed level; his throat was dry, his mouth rancid with the vomit of fear. He realized that he could not get up. He could not stand.

He saw an automobile far in the distance, to his right. West. It was traveling at high speed; the headlights kept flashing. Off . . . on, off . . . on. On, on, on . . . off, off, off, interspersed.

It was a signal!

But he could not stand! He could not rise!

And then he heard his name. Shouted in unison through open windows, by several voices. In unison! As a chant might be sung!

" . . . Spaulding, Spaulding, Spaulding. . . ."

The car was about to pass him! He could not get up!

He reached into his belt and yanked out the Lüger.

He fired it twice, barely possessing the strength to pull the trigger.

With the second shot . . . all was blackness.

He felt the gentle fingers around his wound, felt the vibrations of the moving automobile.

He opened his eyes.

Asher Feld was looking down at him; his head was in Feld's lap. The Jew smiled.

"Everything will be answered. Let the doctor sew you up. We must patch you together quickly."

David raised his head as Feld held his neck. A second man, a young man, was also in the back seat, bending over his stomach; Spaulding's legs were stretched over the young man's knees. The man held gauze and pincers in his hands.

"There will be only minor pain," he said in that same bastardized British accent David had heard so often. "I think you've had enough of that. You're localized."

"I'm what?"

"Simple Novocain," replied the doctor. "I'll retie the stitches here; your arm is filled with an antibiotic – refined in a Jerusalem laboratory, incidentally." The young man smiled.

"What? Where"

"There isn't time," interrupted Feld quietly, urgently. "We're on our way to Mendarro. The plane is waiting. There'll be no interference."

"You got the designs?"

"Chained to the staircase, Lisbon. We did not expect such accommodation. We thought probably the balcony, perhaps an upper floor. Our invasion was swift, thanks be to God. Rhinemann's troops came swiftly. Not swiftly enough. . . . Good work, that staircase. How did you manage it?"

David smiled through the "minor pain." It was difficult to talk. "Because . . . no one wanted the blueprints out of his sight. Isn't that funny?"

"I'm glad you think so. You'll need that quality."

"*What? . . . Jean?*" Spaulding started to rise from the awkward position. Feld restrained his shoulders, the doctor his midsection.

"No, colonel. There are no concerns for Mrs. Cameron or the physicist. They will, no doubt, be flown out of Buenos Aires in the morning. . . . And the coastal blackout will be terminated within minutes. The radar screens will pick up the trawler . . ."

David held up his hand, stopping the Jew. He took several breaths in order to speak. "Reach FMF. Tell them the rendezvous is scheduled for approximately . . . four hours . . . from the time the trawler left Ocho Calle. Estimate the maximum speed of the trawler . . . semicircle the diameter . . . follow that line."

"Well done," said Asher Feld. "We'll get word to them." The young doctor had finished. He leaned over and spoke pleasantly.

"All things considered, these patches are as good as you'd get at Bethesda. Better than the job someone did on your right shoulder; that was awful. You can sit up. Easy, now."

David had forgotten. The British medic in the Azores – centuries ago – had taken a lot of criticism from his professional brothers. Misdirected; his orders had been to get the American officer out of Lajes Field within the hour.

Spaulding inched his way stiffly into a sitting position, aided gently by the two Haganah men.

"Rhinemann is dead," he said simply. "Rhinemann the pig is gone. There'll be no more negotiations. Tell your people."

"Thank you," said Asher Feld.

They drove in silence for several minutes. The searchlights of the small airfield could be seen now; they were shafting their beams into the night sky.

Feld spoke. "The designs are in the aircraft. Our men are standing guard . . . I'm sorry you have to fly out tonight. It would be simpler if the pilot went alone. But that's not possible."

"It's what I was sent down here for."

"It's a bit more complicated, I'm afraid. You've been through a great deal, you've been wounded severely. By all rights, you should be hospitalized. . . . But that will have to wait."

"Oh?" David understood that Feld had something to say that even this pragmatic Jew found difficult to put into words. "You'd better tell me. . . ."

"You'll have to deal with this in your *own* way, colonel," interrupted Feld. "You see . . . the men in Washington do not expect you on that plane. They've ordered your execution."

43

Brigadier General Alan Swanson, lately of the War Department, had committed suicide. Those who knew him said the pressures of his job, the immense logistics he was called upon to expedite daily, had become too much for this dedicated, patriotic officer. They also served who, far behind the lines, primed the machinery of war with all the selfless energy they possessed.

In Fairfax, Virginia, at the huge, security-conscious compound that held the secrets of Allied Central Intelligence, a lieutenant colonel named Ira Barden disappeared. Simply disappeared; substance one day, vapor the next. With him went a number of highly classified files from the vaults. What bewildered those who knew about them was the information these files contained. In the main they were personal dossiers of ranking Nazis involved with the concentration camps. Not the sort of intelligence data a defector would steal. Ira Barden's own dossier was pulled and placed in the archives. Regrets were sent to his family; Lieutenant Colonel Barden was MOA. Missing while on assignment. Strange, but the family never insisted upon an investigation. Which was their right, after all. . . . Strange.

A cryptographer in Lisbon, a man named Marshall, was found in the hills of the Basque country. He had been wounded in a border skirmish and nursed back to health by partisans. The reports of his death had been greatly exaggerated as intended. German Intelligence was onto him. For the time being, however, he was confined to the embassy and returned to duty. He had sent a personal message to an old friend he thought might be concerned; to Colonel David Spaulding. The message was amusing, in an oddly phrased way. He wanted Spaulding to know there were no hard feelings about the colonel's vacation in South America. The cryp had taken a vacation, too. There were codes that had to be broken – if they could be found. They both should plan better in the future; they should get together on vacations. Good friends should always do that.

There was another cryptographer. In Buenos Aires. One Robert Ballard. The State Department was very high on Ballard these days. The Buenos Aires cryptographer had spotted an enormous error in a scrambler and had taken the personal initiative to not only question it, but to refuse to *authenticate* it. Through a series of grave misunderstandings and faulty intelligence, an order for the on-sight execution of Colonel Spaulding had been issued by the War Department. Code: treason. Defection to the enemy while on assignment. It took a great deal of courage on Ballard's part to refuse to acknowledge so high priority a command. And State was never averse to embarrassing the Department of War.

750

The aerophysicist, Eugene Lyons, Ph.D., was flown back to Pasadena. Things . . . things had happened to Doctor Lyons. He was offered and accepted a lucrative, meaningful contract with Sperry Rand's Pacific laboratories, the finest in the country. He had entered a Los Angeles hospital for throat surgery – prognosis: sixty-forty in his favor, if the will was there. . . . It was. And there was something else about Lyons. On the strength of his contract he had secured a bank loan and was building an oddly shaped, Mediterranean-style house in a peaceful section of the San Fernando Valley.

Mrs. Jean Cameron returned to the Eastern Shore of Maryland for two days. The State Department, at the personal behest of Ambassador Henderson Granville in Buenos Aires, issued a letter of commendation to Mrs. Cameron. Although her status was not official, her presence at the embassy had been most valuable. She had kept open lines of communication with diverse factions within the neutral city; lines of communication often jeopardized by diplomatic necessities. Officials at State decided to present Mrs. Cameron with the letter in a small ceremony, presided over by a prominent undersecretary. State was somewhat surprised to learn that Mrs. Cameron could not be reached at her family home on Maryland's Eastern Shore. She was in Washington. At the Shoreham Hotel. The Shoreham was where Colonel David Spaulding was registered. . . . More than a coincidence, perhaps, but in no way would it interfere with the letter of commendation. Not these days. Not in Washington.

Colonel David Spaulding looked up at the light brown stone and square pillars of the War Department. He pulled at his army overcoat, adjusting the heavy cloth over the sling on his arm underneath. It was the last time he would wear a uniform or enter this building. He started up the steps.

It was curious, he mused. He had been back for nearly three weeks, and every day, every night he had thought about the words he was going to say this afternoon. The fury, the revulsion . . . the waste. Resentments for a lifetime. But life would go on and in some curious way the violent emotions had crested. He felt only a weariness now, an exhaustion that demanded that he get it over with and return to something of value. Somewhere.

With Jean.

He knew the men of "Tortugas" could not be reached with words. Words of conscience had lost meaning for such men. As they had so often lost meaning for him. That, too, was one of their crimes: they had stolen . . . decency. From so many. For so little.

Spaulding left his overcoat in the outer office and walked into the small conference room. They were there, the men of "Tortugas."

Walter Kendall.

Howard Oliver.

Jonathan Craft.

None got up from the table. All were silent. Each stared at him. The looks were mixtures of hate and fear – so often inseparable.

They were prepared to fight, to protest ... to salvage. They had held their *discussions*, they had arrived at *strategies*.

They were so obvious, thought David.

He stood at the end of the table, reached into his pocket and took out a handful of carbonado diamonds. He threw them on the hard surface of the table; the tiny nuggets clattered and rolled.

The men of "Tortugas" remained silent. They shifted their eyes to the stones, then back to Spaulding.

"The Koening transfer," said David. "The tools for Peenemünde. I wanted you to see them."

Howard Oliver exhaled a loud, impatient breath and spoke in practiced condescension. "We have no idea what ..."

"I know," interrupted Spaulding firmly. "You're busy men. So let's dispense with unnecessary conversation; as a matter of fact, there's no reason for you to talk at all. Just listen. I'll be quick. And you'll always know where to reach me."

David put his right hand into his arm sling and pulled out an envelope. It was an ordinary business envelope; sealed, thick. He placed it carefully on the table and continued.

"This is the history of 'Tortugas'. From Geneva to Buenos Aires. From Peenemünde to a place called Ocho Calle. From Pasadena to a street ... Terraza Verde. It's an ugly story. It raises questions I'm not sure should be raised right now. Perhaps, ever. For the sake of so much sanity ... everywhere."

"But that's up to you here at this table. ... There are several copies of this ... this indictment. I won't tell you where and you'll never be able to find out. But they exist. And they'll be released in a way that will result in simultaneous headlines in New York and London and Berlin. Unless you do exactly as I say. ..."

"Don't protest, Mr. Kendall. It's useless. ... This war is won. The killing will go on for a while but we've won it. Peenemünde hasn't been idle; they've scoured the earth. A few thousand rockets will be built, a few thousand killed. Nowhere near what they conceived of. Or needed. And our aircraft will blow up half of Germany; we'll be the victors now. And that's how it should be. What must come after the killing is the healing. And you gentlemen will dedicate the rest of your natural lives to it. You will sever all connections with your companies; you will sell all your holdings above a bare subsistence level – as defined by the national economic guidelines – donating the proceeds to charities – anonymously but with substantiation. And you will offer your considerable talents to a grateful government – in exchange for government salaries."

"For the rest of your lives you will be skilled government clerks. And that is all you'll be."

"You have sixty days to comply with these demands. Incidentally, since you ordered ny execution once, you should know that part of our contract is my well-being. And the well-being of those close to me, of course."

"Lastly, because it occurred to me that you might wish to recruit others under this contract, the indictment makes it clear that you could not have created 'Tortugas' alone. . . . Name who you will. The world is in a sorry state, gentlemen. It needs all the help it can get."

Spaulding reached down for the envelope, picked it up and dropped it on the table. The slap of paper against wood drew all eyes to the spot.

"Consider *everything*," said David.

The men of "Tortugas" stared in silence at the envelope. David turned, walked to the door and let himself out.

February in Washington. The air was chilly, the winds were of winter but the snows would not come.

Lieutenant Colonel David Spaulding dodged the cars as he crossed Wisconsin Avenue to the Shoreham Hotel. He was unaware that his overcoat was open; he was oblivious to the cold.

It was over! He was finished! There would be scars deep scars – but with time. . . .

With Jean. . . .